Sheila O'Flanagan is the author of many bestselling novels, including *If You Were Me*, *Things We Never Say*, *Better Together*, *All For You*, *Stand By Me* and *The Perfect Man*.

Sheila has always loved telling stories, and after working in banking and finance for a number of years, she decided it was time to fulfil a dream and give writing her own book a go. So she sat down, stuck 'Chapter One' at the top of a page, and got started. Sheila is now the author of more than nineteen bestselling titles. She lives in Dublin with her husband.

Sheila O'Flanagan. So much more than stories.

'Romantic and charming, this is a real must-read' *Closer*

'A big, touching book sure to delight O'Flanagan fans' *Daily Mail*

'A spectacular read' *Heat*

'O'Flanagan is insightful, witty and full of fun . . . this is touching, tense and clever writing' *Irish Independent*

'A lovely book that will keep you guessing right up until the end' *Bella*

'Her lightness of touch and gentle characterisations have produced another fine read' *Sunday Express*

Sheila O'Flanagan

Yours, Faithfully

R

headline
review

First published in Great Britain in 2006
by HEADLINE REVIEW
An imprint of HEADLINE PUBLISHING GROUP

First published in paperback in 2007
by HEADLINE REVIEW

This edition published in 2014
by HEADLINE REVIEW

21

Cataloguing in Publication Data is available from the British Library

ISBN 978 0 7553 0760 9

Typeset in Galliard by Palimpsest Book Production Limited,
Falkirk, Stirlingshire

Printed and bound in Great Britain by
Clays Ltd, St Ives plc

Papers used by Headline are from well-managed forests and other
responsible sources.

MIX
Paper from
responsible sources
FSC® C104740

HEADLINE PUBLISHING GROUP
An Hachette UK Company
338 Euston Road
London NW1 3BH

www.headline.co.uk
www.hachette.co.uk

Thanks as always, for their support and encouragement, go to:

Carole Blake, my agent and friend
Marion Donaldson, my (very) patient editor
Team Headline in so many different locations and in many different
guises – all of you have been wonderful, I'm lucky to work with
you
My family, fantastic in every way
All of my friends in Ireland and overseas, and in particular everyone
from Raheny Badminton Club, who never let me forget about
other equally important things (like match practice . . .)
Colm, *un gran abrazo*

Extra special thanks on this occasion to Damian Hogan of An
Garda Síochána who was so very helpful when it came to researching
this book, and to Detective Garda Donna McGowan who gave
up so much of her time to talk me through some of the more
technical aspects of the story. Obviously any procedural mistakes
are very much mine and not theirs!

A very big thank you to all of you who take time to email me
and let me know what you think of my books, and to everyone
I've met at book signings and on my various travels – it's been
a real pleasure to hear from you and to meet you. You can get
in touch and see pictures from various events on my website
www.sheilaoflanagan.com

Chapter 1

Iona Brannock wasn't pregnant.

She supposed she shouldn't be surprised. It had been rather optimistic to assume that her first serious attempt at conceiving a baby would be an unqualified success. It wasn't as though women could simply get pregnant on demand after all. But Iona was an optimistic person. And what did surprise her was the sense of bitter disappointment which now engulfed her and how unexpectedly let down she felt by her own body. She'd been so sure of herself. So sure of both of them.

The thing was, she told herself pensively, all of those other times over the past four years when they'd come together beneath the sheets and cried out in mutual passion had been about themselves and the pleasure that they were giving to each other. Now it was different. Making love this last month had been a unique experience because there had been a new purpose to it, and the thrill of their nights together had intensified as a result. Iona hadn't thought it possible that she could love Frank any more passionately than she already did. Or that their sex life could have been any more fulfilling. But she'd been wrong. Trying to make a baby with him was the most intense and passionate experience of her life.

They'd talked about it first, of course. There'd been a long and involved discussion about the whole idea of bringing another life into the world. Frank had been certain that it was the right thing to do. It was Iona who'd had the serious doubts. She simply wasn't certain that she was mature enough to be responsible for another

1

life. The enormity of the task was terrifying, she whispered, as they lay side by side in the big bed together. And then Frank had kissed her and told her that it was precisely because she was scared that she would be a great mother and that he could think of nothing that would bind them together more closely than having a baby. It would make them a real family, he said. And he wanted to be part of a family with her. There was no need for her to be scared. Besides, wasn't she already great at everything she did? Wasn't she fantastic at her job in the house rental agency, dealing with demented tenants and equally demented landlords? Wouldn't a baby be simple in comparison?

She'd smiled then. Anyhow, he added, he'd be with her every step of the way.

'Promise?' She'd been touched by the sincerity of his words.

'Promise,' he replied.

And so they'd made love with the hope of having a baby and it had been the most wonderful of all their nights together. But now, Iona had to admit, wonderful and all though that night and the other baby-making nights that followed might have been, they were still just more nights of great sex because she wasn't pregnant after all. The sudden pain in the small of her back and the crucifying cramping of her stomach confirmed it.

It seemed daft now that she'd consulted her feng shui book and set up a children area in their house, despite Frank's amused scepticism. But as she'd pointed out, there was no harm in harnessing whatever power there might be around the home (hadn't leaving the toilet lid down worked its magic as a way of stopping money leaking out of the house? He'd landed a major contract the day he'd moved in, which proved it really.) and so she'd placed a few photos of her niece, Charlotte, aged six, and nephew, Gavin, aged four, on the plain oak sideboard at the south end of the living room; then she'd added a home-enhancer crystal bowl on the wall shelf nearby. By the time she'd finished upgrading the energy of the home she'd felt certain that getting pregnant would be an enjoyable formality given all the effort she was making.

2

She debated for a moment or two about whether to phone Frank now and tell him the discouraging news about the baby but she decided against it. It wasn't the sort of conversation she wanted to have with him first thing in the morning and she was pretty sure it wasn't the kind of conversation he wanted at that hour either. But she was glad that he was coming home that night so that they could hold each other tight and reassure each other that maybe the next time they'd be successful.

Iona had never told Frank that it had taken her own mother five years to get pregnant. She didn't tell him of the many despairing visits that Flora Brannock had made to the doctor to find out whether everything was all right and her mother's subsequent slavish adherence to a range of different diets, lifestyle regimes and goodness knows what else to help things along. Because in the end it hadn't mattered – Flora eventually succeeded with Iona's older sister, Lauren; then a couple of years later Iona; and finally Craig. There hadn't been a production problem really just a delay in getting started, as she'd told her daughters when giving them her practical facts-of-life discussion as soon as they'd asked the inevitable 'where did I come from?' question.

Iona twisted the thin gold wedding band on her finger. She wouldn't have the same problems as her mother, she knew she wouldn't. Charlotte and Gavin were Lauren's children and Lauren hadn't experienced any delay in conceiving. So there was no big issue here just because Iona hadn't got pregnant at the first attempt.

But still, she thought, as she broke the seal on a box of Tampax, it would have been nice to have the whole thing sorted. She wasn't good at waiting. She knew that. Flora had always called her the impatient daughter. Lauren was the serene one – nothing ever upset or perturbed her and she seemed to float through life without any stress whatsoever. Iona, on the other hand, was always anxious for things to happen, cut up with frustration when she was told that she was too young or too small or just plain not allowed to do something she desperately wanted. Iona had been the one to make the forbidden climb on to the roof of the garden shed, and the one to rip her leg on the thorns of the rose bush as she'd jumped off it. Iona had been the one, aged six, to try riding a two-wheeled bicycle on her own without any supervision whatsoever, and the one who'd managed to wobble a few yards down the road before crashing into the wall of the Delaneys' house, splitting open her lip, banging her nose and knocking out her two front teeth. As a teenager, she'd been the one who'd stayed out past the accepted coming-home time, sneaking in through the bathroom window for three nights in a row before getting caught because Flora had moved the cactus plant on the windowsill and Iona had sent it clattering on to the tiled floor with her foot. At twenty, she'd been the first to move out of the family home, wanting a place of her own while Lauren was still content to live with their parents.

Craig, the youngest, was simply 'the son'. He was tall and broad with deep soulful eyes which made him look particularly sensitive and meant that the impressionable girls on the estate where they lived fancied him like crazy and hung around outside their house to get a glimpse of him. Iona grinned to herself as she thought of her younger brother, now working as a telephone engineer in China and probably still breaking hearts. Their father had been a new-man sort of bloke long before it became fashionable for men to do the washing-up and show their emotions in public and she had no doubt that David Brannock loved both his daughters dearly and expected great things of them; but when Craig had been born there was a whole thing about 'the son' that hadn't been around for 'the girls'.

Iona didn't care. She knew that her parents loved them all equally. The son-and-heir thing – well, it might be old-fashioned, but a part of her understood it. Even though, as she'd pointed out to her father, she'd kept the family name after her marriage so that everyone still knew her as Iona Brannock. And the agreement with Frank was that their daughters would carry her surname, while their sons would carry his. It would all work out fine, she knew. All she had to do was get round to having the children.

She finished in the bathroom and walked into the tiny bedroom.

This was something that would have to change when all the love-making finally paid off. Right now, she and Frank lived in a two-up two-down artisan house near the old Iveagh Markets building in the Liberties district of Dublin. It was a great house in a great location because it was so convenient for the city centre and meant that if she didn't need the car during the day to drive to rental showings she could walk to work; but it wasn't very big, especially since one of the bedrooms was used as an office. Frank had his own company, DynaLite. He arranged the installation of complex lighting systems in hotels and nightclubs and customised lighting shows for special occasions. It was extremely successful for a venture that operated from their back bedroom and from a serviced office on the south side of the city, although that was because Frank was totally committed to the company, travelling throughout the country every week to meet his clients and sometimes having to stay away for days on end to get a particular project completed on time.

Iona, whose job at the rental agency allowed her to work from home sometimes, also used the bedroom as an office, though not as much as Frank did. It was there that they stored all of their work-related stuff; there where they kept the computer and printer and fax; and there where one or the other of them retired to when they absolutely didn't want to be disturbed. That didn't happen very often. With Frank spending so much time away from home, they liked to be together as much as possible when he returned.

But using the bedroom as an office meant that they essentially lived in a one-bedroomed house. Iona felt a bit guilty about her assertion that they'd have to move once they started a family, since she knew that years ago enormous families were reared in the two-up two-down houses, but times had changed since the 1930s and 40s. And besides, their house had been bought from some lunatic interior designer who had done a fantastic job on it but who had styled everything with a single male occupant in mind. Iona was perfectly certain that the trendy glass staircase and angular units would be a death-trap for a toddler even though they fitted perfectly with her personal Zen ideas.

She smoothed the skirt of her blue hound's-tooth Zara suit over her hips. Last night, when she'd been two days late and begun to allow the hope of pregnancy to grow in her mind despite herself, she'd thought about maternity clothes and wondered where she'd be able to buy stylish clothes that would take her through the nine months. She knew that there were plenty of maternity boutiques around the city because she remembered Lauren enthusing about them when she'd been expecting Gavin. But she couldn't remember the name of a single one. She'd stood in front of the mirror with a pillow stuffed beneath her pale pink T-shirt and contemplated her potential change in figure. It would be radical, she thought, because she was (as her father so often pointed out) a mere slip of a girl – exactly five feet and one inch tall (that inch was very important to her), with short ink-black hair which she sometimes wore in gelled spikes but more often allowed to settle into a gamine crop framing her heart-shaped face. Her eyes were blackberry-blue and her lips, even without lipstick, a pouting rosebud red. Her nose was small and neat, though a tiny bump (a legacy of the crash into the Delaneys' wall) robbed it of any cuteness it might otherwise have had. Iona's looks were exotic rather than beautiful, but then she'd never much cared for beautiful over interesting. Anyway, there was no point in her caring, since Lauren was the one who'd been handed the beauty genes, with her clear, smooth skin, violet eyes and burnished copper hair which fell in soft waves around her perfectly proportioned face. Lauren's nose was perfect too. Iona knew that her sister had obviously been handed the leftover height genes as well, because Lauren was a willowy five-six with an enviable figure which had looked fantastic even when she was pregnant. Iona rather thought that she herself would just look dumpy when it finally happened for her.

It doesn't matter, she told herself now as she shoved her mobile into her bag, checked her appearance in the mirror once more and picked up her house keys. Nothing has changed yet. Everything is still exactly the same.

〜

The rental agency had its offices in Dame Street, close to the imposing (though, thought Iona, incredibly ugly) Central Bank building with its smooth piazza, fountain and bronze sculpture facing on to the street. The office was also near Trinity College, a building which Iona much preferred and where she often went during sunny lunchtimes to eat a sandwich on the grassy lawns. Today, despite the promise of clear blue skies and a warm breeze from the south, there would be no lunching on the lawns of Trinity or anywhere else. Her agenda was full – administration in the office in the morning and then back home to collect her lime-green Volkswagen Beetle so that she could drive to the six different apartments she was showing that afternoon and evening.

Her stomach was cramping again as she sat at her white wood desk and logged on to her computer. She hated this time of the month. She hated the bloated feeling that always engulfed her, the nagging pain in the small of her back and those damn cramps which racked her for the first day or two. She opened her desk drawer and took out a couple of gel capsules. When you're in labour, she reminded herself as she swallowed them down, the pain will be worse. Much, much worse! She shivered a little. She was definitely ready to be pregnant now, but she was scared of the physical aspect as well as everything else. Although she was absolutely and utterly determined to do everything as naturally as possible, she worried that the intensity of the pain might stop her. It was extraordinary, she mused, that with all the evolutionary things that had gone on over the past few millennia, humans hadn't yet come up with a better way of having babies. Hens had it cushy, she thought. An egg was a much better shape for the birth process – no inconvenient arms and legs which might present themselves at the wrong moment.

'Morning, Iona!' Ruth Dawson, who looked after rentals on the north side of the city, greeted her. 'How's it going?' She saw the packet of evening primrose oil and starflower capsules on Iona's desk and grimaced sympathetically.

'I'll be fine,' said Iona, 'though I wish I hadn't agreed to so many viewings this afternoon.'

'Take some Feminax,' suggested Ruth. 'I have—'

'Thanks but no thanks.' Iona smiled at her. 'These work fine for me.' She winced.

The other girl opened a desk drawer and took out an assortment of aspirin, paracetamol and ibuprofen which she spread out on the desk in front of her.

'Sure?'

Iona looked at the display and shook her head again. 'You should have shares in Glaxo,' she said disparagingly. 'I'll give you the name of my yoga guru; much, much better for you than all that.'

Ruth snorted and then picked up her ringing telephone.

'Rental Remedies,' she said. 'Ruth speaking. How can I help you?'

⌒

It was after ten before Iona finally rang Frank. He'd been meeting clients in the south-west of the country all week but he was due back in Dublin later that evening. Iona wanted to check on his timetable. She knew, because they had an on-line calendar which each of them updated every evening, that he'd had a meeting at nine this morning but she reckoned he should be finished by now. Frank never needed much time to make a sale. He was born to it, homing in immediately on the issue that most affected his potential customer and managing to make that customer feel as though he personally cared very deeply about any problem they might have. As he truly did, he told Iona. After all, his customers were the ones who paid the bills! And besides, most of them were very nice people. Iona usually chuckled at that – Frank always saw the good in everyone. He insisted in giving them all the benefit of the doubt. It was one of the things she loved about him.

He answered her call almost immediately and she smiled involuntarily at the sound of his voice. Frank had a very, very sexy voice. It was Pierce Brosnan, Richard Burton and Sean Connery all rolled into one. As, indeed, was Frank himself. Iona had been somewhat stunned at the fact that she'd managed to snare a man who was sexier than Colin Firth in a wet shirt.

'Hi, sweetheart,' he said.

'Morning, lover-boy.'

'How's things?'

'Oh, grand.'

'You're not pregnant.'

'How did you know that?' Iona thought she'd managed to keep her tone sufficiently neutral.

'I have my ways,' said Frank, who was adept at reading her voice. 'Don't worry, darling. It'll happen.'

'I'm not worried,' said Iona. 'I know it will. And we'll have a great time making it happen.'

'That's my girl,' said Frank. 'I do love you, you know.'

'You can say those things 'cos you're in the car on your own,' said Iona.

'And you can't because there are people listening in?'

'Exactly. But I do too.'

'You think they can't guess what we're talking about?'

Iona glanced at the desk opposite her. Ruth's dark head was bent over a printed spreadsheet and she appeared to be absorbed in her work, the tip of her pink tongue sticking out between her teeth while she ticked off numbers on the page in front of her. As Iona watched her in silence, Ruth glanced up and gave her a brief smile.

'Oh, you're right as always!'

Frank laughed. 'I know you girls, that's all.'

'What time will you be home?' asked Iona.

'I'll leave as early as I can but it's still a four-hour drive,' said Frank. 'So it'll be after six before I get in, seven if the traffic is bad. What about you?'

'I'm showing apartments until seven myself,' said Iona apologetically. 'I couldn't manage to schedule it better.'

'Don't worry,' Frank told her. 'Give me a call when you've done the last, and if I'm first home I'll order in some pizza.' He chuckled. 'And no saying that a green-leaf salad would be better for you. You need comfort food tonight, sweetheart.'

'You're a pet, you know that.'

'Of course I do. Weren't you lucky the day you met me?'

'OK, OK, you're pushing me to the limits here.'

'And I was lucky the day I met you,' added Frank.

'Charmer,' she said. But she was smiling as she replaced the receiver.

❧

By two o'clock that afternoon Iona was in her car and heading for the first showing, a very luxurious apartment in the suburban town of Dun Laoghaire. The potential tenant had been seconded to a financial services company in the city from its head office in Barcelona, and Iona had already shown him apartments in the docklands area. But Enrique Martinez wanted somewhere further from his place of work and so she'd decided to wow him with an expensive sea-view apartment in the upmarket suburb. I'd rent it myself if I could afford it, thought Iona, as she took the lift to the top floor. It's absolutely gorgeous. Though it's a single person's apartment despite the space, and I – well, I have to start thinking in terms of semi-detached houses with enclosed back gardens. She opened the door and looked in – the apartment was twice the size of her red-brick house and, thanks to its big windows and careful layout, twice as bright and airy too.

A tap at the door signalled that the client had arrived. As with the previous times she'd met him, he was dressed in a carefully tailored suit and the double cuffs on his shirt were held closed by gold cufflinks. His black hair was sprinkled sparingly with grey, his face was square and he wore small but fashionable glasses on his nose. He wasn't as old as he looked, Iona reckoned. But he was choosy and proving to be a difficult client to satisfy.

Her mobile rang just as she was extolling the virtues of the decked balcony and the impressive sea view over the harbour where small boats bobbed merrily at their moorings in the blue-green water.

'A bit delayed,' Frank told her. 'Sorry, sweetheart. I'm only leaving my last meeting now so I might get caught up in some evening traffic. But with luck I should still be home by seven thirty.'

'It'll probably be eight before I make it,' she said. 'My seven o'clock is on the Shelbourne Road. That's my last, though, so you go ahead and order the pizza. Extra cheese for me, please.'

'You got it. And I'll text you when I get in,' promised Frank. 'Maybe later we'll have another shot at the baby-making?'

'Um . . .'

'Ah. Of course.' Frank's voice softened. 'Would you like me just to rub your shoulders instead?'

'You promise the nicest things.' She giggled. Then a noise made her glance up and she saw her businessman standing in the doorway between the lounge and the master bedroom. 'Gotta go,' she said quickly. 'See you later.' She smiled brightly at her client. 'So, Señor Martinez,' she said. 'What do you think? Have we got it right this time?'

༄

By the time she'd finished the Shelbourne Road viewing at seven thirty, she was tired and frazzled and her cramps were worse than ever. All she wanted to do was to get home and put her feet up on the comfortable leather sofa which took up far too much of their tiny living room, and gorge herself on takeaway pizza with extra cheese. And garlic bread, if Frank thought about it. He could massage her aching feet afterwards, she thought hopefully.

She took her mobile out of her bag and frowned. He hadn't called or sent a text. Which probably meant that he'd set out even later than he'd hoped and was now stuck in Dublin's notorious rush-hour traffic. (The rush hour starting at about four o'clock in the afternoon these days and not really finishing until nearly eight!) She rang his number but was diverted to his voice-mail.

11

'I'm on my way back now,' she said as she got into her car. 'If I get home before you I'll order the pizza. But I hope you do. Get some garlicker too, will you? I want to come home to the heady aroma of takeaway cooking. Oh, and Frank – 'cos I couldn't say it earlier I will now. I love you!'

She ended the call and slid her phone into its stand. Then she started the car and headed for home.

Chapter 2

S ally Harper looked at the test in horrified amazement. She closed her eyes, counted to ten, then opened them and looked at the test again. The pink line was as clear as anything. She was, unbelievably, but beyond a shadow of a doubt, pregnant.

She put the test equipment back into its box and shoved the lot into the waste-bin in the cluttered en suite bathroom. At least Jenna wouldn't see it there and ask awkward questions. Not that Jenna asked her questions at all these days, or even spoke to her on a regular basis if she could help it, but better to be safe than sorry. Christ, she thought as she sat on the edge of the bath, better safe than sorry! Pity I wasn't thinking on those lines a few weeks ago.

She hadn't seriously thought that she was pregnant, though. She'd bought the test more to eliminate it from consideration than anything else. She hadn't wanted to go to Dr Dowling's surgery and go through the whole palaver of an unnecessary test – because how the hell could she be pregnant at this time in her life? She was forty-one years old, for heaven's sake! It was supposed to be hard to get pregnant at forty-one. The home test was meant to be a formality, not a confirmation of something that she'd wanted and wanted for years but which hadn't happened since Jenna's birth.

She felt the sudden heave in her stomach and launched herself at the toilet bowl, retching into it uncontrollably. When the vomiting stopped, she sat, shakily, on the edge of the bath again and wiped her face with a damp cloth. This can't be happening to me, she thought in panic, it really can't. I don't want to be pregnant now. It's not at all convenient. It's not at all what I want for my life. I've gone past all that. And, she gritted her teeth, I've just lost over a stone on that damn South Beach diet. She snorted. What a waste of time that was! All that good carb, bad carb stuff. Being ruthless with herself so that she was having to cook different meals for Frank and Jenna, neither of whom had a spare ounce of fat on them anyway. And for what? So that she'd end up pregnant and looking for maternity clothes again. How fair was that?

What the hell would her husband have to say? As far as he was concerned they'd started and finished their family with Jenna, and although it had been a deep disappointment to them not to have more children (because both had been only children themselves and had wanted a bigger family for Jenna's sake) they'd accepted it in the end. They'd built their entire lives around the fact that their daughter was, and always would be, an only child. They believed that the Harper family was just the three of them. Frank, Sally and Jenna. She didn't know if there was room for someone else now. She certainly couldn't imagine Frank thinking there'd be time for someone else. Their lives were no longer based on nappies and night feeds and brightly coloured plastic toys. They'd moved on from that – even if moving on meant not understanding the teenage girl that their daughter had become!

He'll be gobsmacked, thought Sally, as she fought with another bout of nausea. Utterly gobsmacked. Nearly seventeen years after Jenna had been born, she knew that she was gobsmacked herself.

And what in God's name was Jenna herself going to say? Sally presumed that her currently rebellious and truculent daughter, who'd once thought that the sun, moon and stars shone out of her parents' behinds, would now think it was disgusting that they were having sex at all; but that the act had resulted in Sally getting pregnant at forty-one – well, Jenna's reaction to that just didn't bear thinking about. Everything Sally did was wrong and embarrassing these days. Getting pregnant would probably now move quickly to the top of the list ahead of her old-fashioned hairstyle and Frank's penchant for trying to sing along to Top Ten hits.

Those would definitely be outdone by Jenna's embarrassing mother having embarrassing sex with her embarrassing father and the embarrassing result being plainly obvious for all to see.

Sally's empty stomach heaved again. She didn't remember being this sick before. Maybe it was worse when you were older. She didn't know. As far as she could remember (despite a difficult labour) she'd sailed through her actual pregnancy with Jenna, although maybe the length of time since then had played tricks with her memory. But now . . . there could be all sorts of complications, couldn't there? After all, forty-one was old for a pregnant woman. She knew that. As far as the obstetricians were concerned, she might as well show up with a bus pass and pension book. They'd have to take special care of her, do additional checks on both her and the baby. And then, when the time came, she'd be in a room or a ward with young mothers, hopeful mothers, women who were nothing more than children themselves. Like she'd been, sort of, with Jenna.

And after that – leaving aside the whole pregnancy thing – what about her life? She'd begun to feel she was reclaiming it lately, what with losing the weight and Jenna growing up and being more independent and (despite the silences, shrugs and current practice of dressing in nothing but black) being a fairly responsible sort of daughter even if they had indulged her too much because of her only-child status. In the last few months Sally and Frank had been able to go out together a lot more, trusting (more or less) Jenna to be OK by herself. They'd even taken a weekend break in Galway together, leaving her at home in the company of her best friend, Samantha, with a list of instructions a mile long. Sally had been quite determined not to call to check up on her, but when she'd finally cracked on the Saturday night and phoned the house at ten o'clock, Jenna had told her that she and Sam were watching a video and would Sally and Frank please not worry. (It had been the most sociable conversation she'd had with her daughter in months!) And when they got home the following evening Sally was pleasantly surprised to find that the house hadn't been trashed and that Jenna hadn't held any parties or engaged in any antisocial activities and had, in fact, bought fresh milk and a selection of pastries for when they got home. Her next-door neighbour, Philly, told her the following day that everything had been thankfully normal and that she was lucky to have a daughter like Jenna.

Jenna was a basically good girl, thought Sally, as she washed her face and patted it dry. If dressing in black and monosyllabic communication was as bad as it got, she'd consider herself lucky!

The nausea eased and she dotted tinted moisturiser on to her face. She stared at her reflection in the bathroom mirror. When the new baby reached Jenna's age, she'd be fifty-eight. If she sometimes felt exhausted by her teenage daughter now, what the hell would it be like when she was fifty-eight and dealing with adolescent tantrums? As it was, she couldn't even begin to think what having to go through the whole routine of changing nappies, sterilising bottles and mixing feeds interspersed with minimal sleep all over again would be like. And as for Frank – well, he liked his full eight hours! He'd been utterly useless with Jenna at night. Great during the day – a loving and devoted father who'd taken her on long walks to the park and shamelessly indulged her whenever he thought that Sally wasn't paying attention – but when it came to the night-time stints, Frank had been and would be a write-off.

The new baby would be due in December. Sally didn't want to appear gloomy and negative about the whole thing when the reality was that it was a complete miracle really . . . but December! The month when you got up in the dark and came home from work in the dark; the month with the shortest day in the whole year. Jenna had been a summer baby and that had helped because the days had been long and the nights hadn't been as all-enveloping as winter nights. She'd coped in the summer when she was a mere twenty-four years old, full of energy, and happy and excited about her first child.

She smoothed some more moisturiser on to her face. I don't look forty-one, she told herself hopefully. People could mistake me for a woman in her mid-thirties. Maybe. She pulled at the

16

edges of her face to tighten the skin around her eyes. Damn wrinkle lift cream – a horrendous price and it didn't make the slightest bit of difference! Her eyes, a luminous blue-green, had always been her best feature. They still were, despite the tiny network of wrinkles. Until now Sally had always thought that the fine lines gave her face character. But now she was afraid that they simply gave away her age.

She ran her fingers through her thick mane of hair. Her hair was also a good feature, she reminded herself, despite the fact that Jenna didn't like its length. Mature women didn't let their hair grow past their shoulders, she often told Sally. And then putting it into a plait was naff beyond belief. Sally hadn't plaited it yet this morning and it gleamed in the morning light, strands of auburn and gold naturally highlighting the overall chestnut colour. And hardly any grey! That pleased her. Now that some of her friends were spending an absolute fortune getting their roots done every month, Sally appreciated even more the fact that she'd managed to escape, so far at any rate, that most telltale sign of ageing.

But there was no doubt that she'd be grey at fifty-eight. She stopped twisting her hair around her fingers and let it flop on to her back. She wanted to think that she could be happy about this pregnancy, but she wasn't sure that she could.

She'd be happy if Frank was happy. At least she thought she would. If he turned out to be supportive and understanding, and if he decided that the whole thing was an absolute miracle – well, then she'd be able to see it that way too. But if he (as she had when she'd looked at the thin pink line) saw this baby as an intrusion into the rest of their lives together, she simply didn't know how she'd cope.

Sally exhaled slowly and walked out of the bathroom. This *was* absolutely a miracle, she reminded herself. It really was. How could she be so upset about a miracle?

She slid her white blouse over her shoulders and then pulled on her black pencil skirt. Not that she'd be able to wear the pencil skirt for very much longer. But right now it still fitted. So that

17

looking at herself sideways in the mirror she wouldn't have known that she was pregnant at all. She could even pretend, at least for another few hours, that she wasn't. She tried to block it out of her mind as she began teasing her hair into a plait, but it was impossible.

With her hair finally done, she went into Jenna's room, picking her way through the discarded trousers and tops and shoes, and shook her daughter by the shoulder. Jenna moaned and burrowed deeper beneath the heavy-duty duvet. (She wouldn't allow Sally to change it for a lighter-weight one until later in the summer, even though now, just after Easter, the weather had begun to improve and the nights were getting warmer.)

'Come on, Jen,' said Sally impatiently. 'We haven't got all day.'

'Don't feel well,' muttered Jenna.

'Get up.' Sally's voice was sharper than she'd intended and Jenna poked her face over the duvet.

'We don't have time for messing about,' said Sally. 'I have to talk to a couple of members of staff before school starts.'

'Yeah, well, I don't.' Jenna hated the fact that her mother was the vice-principal at the Holy Spirit School just outside Bray where she herself was a pupil. It was utterly loathsome having a parent on the teaching staff. It made the pupils suspect you and the teachers demand more of you. And the fact that Sally was the vice-principal made things even worse, because Jenna knew the teachers were afraid that she might report back on them if they didn't keep good control of the class. Not that Jenna ever would. It wasn't like she actually cared or anything.

There should be a rule against it, she thought. Of course Sally had asked her about it before she'd taken the job the previous year. The rationale that her mother used was that Jenna only had a couple more years to go and then she'd be off to college so it wouldn't matter. But this opportunity for Sally to leave the school in Sutton where she currently worked (and which was an hour's commute on the Dart) to be so much closer to home, was too good to pass by. She'd asked but she wasn't really asking, just telling, so in the end Jenna hadn't felt any option other than to say that it was all right with her even though her heart sank into her boots at the thought.

'Honestly, Mum, I'm a bit queasy this morning,' she said now as she brushed her dark hair out of her eyes. (She'd inherited Frank's brown eyes instead of Sally's wonderful blue-green ones but her hair was as thick and lustrous as Sally's own.)

'Well, I wasn't feeling the best myself either,' retorted Sally, 'but I'm up and about and I expect you to be out of that bed and downstairs in the next fifteen minutes. Come on, it's Friday. You can sleep late tomorrow.'

Jenna looked at Sally in disgust. That was another thing about her mother. She just didn't believe in illness. Queasiness, nausea, unexpected aches and pains – she had no time for any of it. Jenna didn't think that Sally had ever had a headache in her life. Which meant she had very little sympathy with people who did. When Jenna had been studying for her Junior Cert and had complained of headaches, Sally had simply bought her a better table lamp to use and told her to stop slouching.

She pushed the duvet off the bed and swung her legs reluctantly over the side. At least Dad would be back home today. Sally was always more relaxed when Frank was around, less determined to be in control of things and have everything running like clockwork. Frank made her laugh, allowed her to forget that she had to go to the supermarket or wash the kitchen floor or do the hundreds of mundane, boring, housewifely things that she always wanted to do when he was away on one of his customer service trips.

That was why her parents had a good marriage, thought Jenna, as she stumbled into the bathroom. Frank was light-hearted and easy-going. Sally was a bit of a control freak. But they balanced each other out pretty well. Though, in all honesty, she preferred her father's more relaxed attitude to life. After all, he was a successful businessman. They were comfortably, if not extravagantly, well off. It just went to show that you didn't have to account for every second of every day . . .

'Jen, hurry up!' Her mother's voice, tight and anxious, wafted up the stairs.

'All right, all right!' And what the hell was eating her this morning? thought Jenna irritably as she picked up her hated uniform skirt of bottle-green from the back of the soft grey tub chair in the corner of her room and pulled it up over her hips.

The sooner Dad gets back and brings a bit of laughter into the house again the better, she muttered grimly. I can't bear it when he's away. I really can't.

Chapter 3

Siobhán Farrell was sitting on the end of the bed and thinking about sex. She hadn't had any since her fiancé, Eddie, had headed off on his business trip to Boston five weeks ago. But he'd be home soon and she had plans for an orgy of hedonistic lovemaking to make up for lost time. Bedtime fun with Eddie was one of the most pleasurable things in her life (and it would be a long time, she told herself, before they messed it all up by having kids). She looked at her watch. Right now he was somewhere in the skies on his way back to her. She'd been busy over the past few weeks and sometimes it had suited her that Eddie wasn't around. But she was surprised at how much she'd actually missed him.

She picked up the silver-framed photo of him which she kept on the untidy dressing table. She'd had it done over a year earlier and had brought it with her when she'd moved into his apartment in Blackrock six months ago. Eddie had been amused when she put it on the dressing table, telling her that she hardly needed the photo when she had him, but she'd pointed out that there were many times when she woke up and he wasn't there, and it was nice to see his ugly mug first thing.

It wasn't an ugly mug, of course. Eddie McIntyre was a handsome man with a strong face and a smile which, she once told him, reminded her of Elvis Presley. At which Eddie had snorted and pointed out that he had fair hair and grey eyes and so didn't look anything like The King. Siobhán had grinned at him and said that it was still an Elvis smile and that since her mother had been an Elvis fan and had brought her up to be an Elvis fan too, the least that he could do was accept this as the biggest compliment she could possibly offer him. And Eddie had conceded that it was always nice to get compliments and that he'd have to work on swivelling his hips a bit more. So she told him to stop slacking and get back to the gym, which would surely help his hip-swivelling abilities.

Siobhán and Eddie had met in the gym. The day they'd first spoken she'd been working on the rowing machine, her carrot-red hair pinned up on her head and a thin sheen of perspiration glistening on her face as she attacked the machine, trying to better her time. She'd noticed Eddie around the place before, an attractive man in his T-shirt and shorts without being one of those overmuscled types. She'd seen him pounding the treadmill and lifting weights but she hadn't noticed him standing behind her as she rowed intently, focused only on the job in hand. And then he'd asked her if she wasn't actually trying to propel the damn machine out of the building, a question which had broken her concentration and caused her to slow down for a moment.

She'd looked up at him, a curl of damp hair falling over her forehead and her grey top darkened by sweat, then picked up the pace again.

'You waiting for this machine?' she asked.

'God, no,' he replied. 'You've beaten it into submission already. It wouldn't be fit for someone else tonight.'

She glanced at the timer. Five minutes of her workout left.

'Was there something else you wanted?' She looked at him enquiringly.

'Nothing major,' he told her.

She rowed even more intensely.

'Do you ever stop?' he asked.

'In four minutes thirty seconds,' she replied. 'So if there's something you want to say to me, how about you leave it till then?'

He sat on one of the aerobic steps beside the rowing machine and waited until she'd finished. She picked up her towel and ran it through her crop of curls.

'Well?' she asked.

'Jeez, woman, I'm not sure how good an idea this is now,' he said. 'You're scaring me.'

'Why?'

'Well . . .' He looked despairingly at her. 'I'm trying to hit on you, for heaven's sake. Didn't you guess?'

Siobhán stopped towelling her hair and stared at him.

'Is it a crime?' He laughed uneasily under the steady gaze of her clear blue eyes.

She chuckled. 'Actually, no. That one isn't.'

'Whew.' He smiled in mock-relief. 'So – well – how about it?' He held out his hand. 'Eddie McIntyre.'

'Siobhán Farrell,' she replied cheerfully, completely unaware that she was about to fall in love with him.

The sound of a car horn outside the apartment block brought her attention back to the present. She opened the chest of drawers and rummaged through her underwear, wishing that she hadn't, once again, ruined a perfectly good bra and knickers by throwing them in the wash with Eddie's black socks. Her underwear set had been snow white. Now it had joined the rest of the legion of blue-grey garments. Oh well, she thought, nobody to see it today anyway. She took a plain white blouse from the wardrobe and slid it on and completed her outfit by selecting charcoal-grey trousers and a grey jacket from the mound of clothes piled up on the big armchair in the corner of the room.

Then she picked up her brush and tugged it through her wiry locks, pulling them back from her face and securing them with a soft velvet scrunchie and a couple of barrettes. On her time off she allowed her hair to run riot around her face but she always tied it back at work. She looked at herself in the mirror and narrowed her eyes. Efficient, she thought. In control. The kind of woman who knew how to use her Smith & Wesson .38. Eddie had been taken aback on their first date together when she told him that she was a detective garda. He'd blinked a couple of times and had stared at her with a look which told her that he thought (like her other boyfriends before him) that she was taking the piss. And then (also like other boyfriends before him) when he realised that she wasn't, his expression had changed to one of nervous humour.

'Yes, I could cuff you and make you do whatever I wanted,' she told him, 'but I'm not that kind of girl. And I don't care if you've once jumped a red light or exceeded the speed limit or if you don't separate your recyclable stuff from your normal rubbish.'

'I've never dated a policewoman before,' he said.

'If it's too much for you, you don't have to date me again,' she responded. 'We do say that the only people who should marry cops are bankers, civil servants and other cops.' And then she blushed because she hadn't actually intended to use the M word on their first date.

'I think it's kind of cool,' he said. 'I'm just trying to get used to the idea of telling people that my girlfriend is a detective. Have you ever done a murder?'

'Well, I haven't personally murdered anyone.' Her blue eyes twinkled. 'But from time to time I've thought of stabbing my partner.'

'Investigated one,' he amended.

'Yes.'

The rest of the date was spent with Siobhán telling Eddie what it was like to find a dead body. Not exactly what most people would recommend as a topic for a first date, she thought, as they walked hand-in-hand through the city streets later. But his initial ghoulish interest had actually turned into a more general curiosity and suddenly he was asking her if she'd like to come out with him again and she was saying yes.

He had been the one to persuade her to live with him. She'd tried to explain that she worked crazy hours and that when she was deeply involved in a case she could become dreadfully antisocial and that there were times in her life when basically she wouldn't be interested in what he was doing at all, but he said he didn't mind. He told her that he loved her and that he didn't want to

24

live without her. And he'd asked her to marry him. It was her first marriage proposal. Most of her relationships hadn't even got close. She was surprised at how excited she was about it. And how flattered. He'd asked her. He'd actually said, 'Will you marry me,' just like in the books and the movies. (Not that she actually read many books or watched many movies where the outcome was people getting married. Siobhán liked crime fiction and action thrillers and preferred a shootout to a soppy ending any day.)

She loved him but she wasn't ready to marry him. Not yet. It was hard enough being a female on the force (even if things had improved over the past few years); she wasn't ready to take on the baggage of being a married woman too. Her career was important to her. Besides, Eddie's career was just as important to him and she simply didn't see the need for them to get married yet. Eddie worked in investments. Siobhán had no idea what that really meant, other than the fact that he actually enjoyed listening to business bulletins and read the *Financial Times* every day. He talked about things that went so far over her head as to be completely meaningless, but the flip side of the boring stuff was that he made a great deal more money than most of the guys she'd ever known before (and significantly more than her, despite the fact, as she sometimes told him, that she was the one keeping the streets safe for him and his BMW), and he spent a lot of it on her. He'd brought her to Paris for Valentine's Day – a trip which had caused her to suffer more than her fair share of ribbing in Bray garda station, from where she worked. Eddie travelled a lot for business reasons too – a few weeks before the Boston trip he'd spent a week in New York – but that suited her. She liked being with him. She also liked the times when they were apart. Which was why she was happy to be engaged to him but wasn't quite ready to marry him yet. The wedding was planned for a year from now. Which gave her plenty of time to work on her career before people started treating her like a married woman and asking her when she was going to have kids. That was absolutely not on their agenda.

But now, she thought, as she hurried out of the apartment and jabbed the call button for the lift, she was looking forward to being back together with Eddie again. Being single had its attractions, but being part of a couple was even nicer.

⌒

At their cruising altitude of 37,000 feet, Eddie McIntyre was watching an in-flight movie. At least, the movie was showing on the personal screen in front of him, but he wasn't really taking any interest in it. He was thinking about the five weeks he'd spent away from Siobhán. Businesswise it had been great. New clients, new money, new investments. A resounding success. The firm would be delighted. He'd e-mailed them and spoken to them already, of course, so they knew just how successful it had been. But it was always great to walk into the office as a conquering hero.

He shivered involuntarily. He didn't feel like a conquering hero. Not now. He wiped away the beads of sweat which had suddenly broken out on his forehead. Things seemed great whenever he thought about going into the office. But whenever he thought about seeing Siobhán, a black cloud seemed to envelop him.

He got up and went to the toilet. The harsh light made his face seem pale, even though he'd acquired a decent tan over the last few weeks. But otherwise he didn't look any different. It was weird, thought Eddie, that you could look exactly the same and yet feel completely changed. He couldn't help thinking that Siobhán would know straight away. As though by looking at him she would guess that the fabric of their lives might have been changed for ever. And yet why should she? She might be a detective, he told himself, but she wasn't a bloody clairvoyant.

He splashed water on to his face and made his way back to his seat. The steward walked by and asked him if he'd like something to drink. Eddie ordered a whiskey. He hardly ever drank whiskey, but somehow it seemed the right drink for him now. When the steward returned and handed it to him, Eddie knocked it back in three swift gulps. He didn't really feel any better afterwards, but at least it might help him to get some sleep. And that would stop the torrent of thoughts running through his head.

∽

Frank Harper wasn't thinking about how he looked. He wasn't really thinking about anything very much. Perhaps, if forced to say something about his thoughts, it would be that he liked driving. He always had. He liked the feeling of being cocooned in his car, cut off from everything around him while still being an observer of life as he passed it by. He particularly liked it on a day like today when the sun was shining from a china-blue sky dotted with white puffball clouds, and when the countryside was bursting with spring-green meadows and unfurling leaves on the trees.

In the car, cruising along the highways and byways, he could listen to radio phone-ins or country and western music with no one to criticise his choice or ask to switch over to some damn classical station or to self-important twaddle on Radio 4 (not that reception for Radio 4 was anything much in the car anyway – and once you drove any distance outside Dublin it was impossible to get).

The other thing he liked about being in the car was driving through the different towns on his various journeys, towns with interesting names like Birdhill or Oilgate which resonated with past history; or whose Irish names had been anglicised so that people forgot that Killduff actually meant 'black church' and Kenmare meant 'the head of the sea'.

He liked observing the changes too: the improvement of the roads (in some areas at least); new paint jobs on the rectangular houses that lined the main streets; whole new housing developments springing up in places that had once been considered rural but were now being touted as within commuting distance of the nearest city.

He knew that some people disliked the urbanisation of the countryside and he supposed that at some point he'd dislike it too, but it was a sign of the better times that Ireland had gone through in the second half of the 1990s, a time that had given him the opportunity to move his life on, to make a bit of money and to become a different person.

Frank thought about change a lot when he was driving. Mostly he thought about how easier communication had made the country smaller and people always accessible. Nowhere was really isolated any more. Owning a mobile phone meant that you could be contacted on the side of a mountain or in the middle of a lake even if there was nobody for miles around. Nowhere was safe from the people who wanted to get hold of you. That thought had once scared him. But now it didn't bother him at all.

He glanced down at the three mobile phones in the seat pocket of his car. A red one. A blue one. A yellow one. Honest to God, he muttered under his breath. Three damn phones. Sometimes I wonder if I'm off my head completely. At least the three of them were silent right now and he wasn't expecting them to ring.

He looked at the clock on the dash. After five and the traffic was building up, even in the smaller towns. He frowned. He'd messed it up this week, got everything arse over tit so that his whole schedule had been thrown into disarray. He'd made promises that he wouldn't be able to keep and he still hadn't figured out the best way around them. But he would. He always did no matter how complicated things got. That was why he did so well in business; he would invariably come up with a solution for even the most demanding of clients. He'd manage something today too for himself. Only he hadn't quite decided what yet. But he wouldn't push it. It was all about confidence and not letting yourself get rattled, and Frank never allowed himself to get rattled any more. He'd almost been rattled when the letter had come and he'd looked at it with astonishment and complete surprise, but then he'd managed to deal with that too. He'd copied it, as he always did with important stuff, then put the original away and resolved not to think about it but let a decision simply float into his mind instead of thrashing through all the options. He knew he'd do the right thing in the end. He was confident about that.

He whistled tunelessly and allowed a huge oil tanker to overtake him. Bloody fool, thought Frank. Exceeding the speed limit and passing him on a poor stretch of road. And for what? He'd worked out himself, long since, that belting along didn't make a whole heap of difference to the journey in the end. Maybe got you to your destination five or ten minutes earlier than a steady fifty-five or sixty. But you got there stressed out and tense, whereas if you travelled more slowly and in a more relaxed manner the journey didn't become a battle. Yet most people didn't realise that. Most people were sucked into the whole rushing around sort of thing as he'd once been. He was glad to have left that part of his life behind him.

He flexed his shoulders. There was no doubt that these days his life in many ways was actually busier and more stressful than it used to be. But it was all about compartmentalising things, not letting them get the better of you. Finding ways to unwind and people to unwind with. Developing the sort of lifestyle that allowed you to get the most out of everything. The trouble with so many people in the world, Frank thought as he slowed down to go through the next small town (which had once been nothing more than a pinprick on the map but now boasted a huge shopping centre and discount designer outlet, as well as an irritating set of traffic lights), was that they forgot that they only had one life to live and they forgot to extract every moment of pleasure from it that they could. And, in the end, they ended up missing out on the big things because they spent far too much time fussing over the little things.

It had taken him a while to work that out. But once he had, well, everything had just slotted into place for him and he hadn't looked back.

A sudden bump and a pull at the steering made him swear out loud. A puncture. As if he didn't have enough to deal with today! Frank felt his hard-won stress-free mood rapidly recede as he coasted to a stop on the grassy verge. Not the best place to get a puncture, he thought, as he took the large red warning triangle out of the boot and walked back a hundred metres or so to put it on the road. But then that's the way things go sometimes. He took off his jacket and slung it on to the back seat of the Honda. Then he took the jack out of the boot and began to raise the car.

Actually (and he knew that people would think he was crazy if he admitted this), he didn't normally mind changing a tyre. It didn't happen that often, of course, but when it did it reminded him of the mechanical nature of the car. These days they were so damn comfortable that sometimes he forgot the whole magic of petrol and ignition and axles turning wheels. Getting a puncture brought it all back to basics. And he kind of enjoyed rolling up his shirtsleeves and getting a bit grubby from time to time.

He whistled as he worked, even as his mind wrestled with the timing problem that getting back so late to Dublin would bring. He made his decision, and when he'd finished the work and put all of the equipment back in the boot, he picked up the bright red mobile and pressed the speed-dial.

'It's me,' he said to the voice-mail message. 'I'm sorry. I really am. I'm running much later than I thought. I might end up staying here tonight and get back to Dublin tomorrow. I'm really sorry. Give me a shout later.'

He got into the car and put the phone back in the door pocket. Then he frowned. It was covered in oil. He looked at his hands and grimaced. He hadn't noticed the stain on the edge of his palm. He took a tissue from the box on the passenger seat and wiped it. But he was still grimy. He'd end up getting oil all over the steering wheel at this rate.

He knew that there were a couple of pubs side by side a few miles along the road. He'd drive to them and wash up in one of the men's rooms. Since he'd made the phone call, the last vestiges of pressure had disappeared. He placed two tissues on the steering wheel to protect it as he drove. And now people really will think I'm crazy, he thought in amusement. Maybe that I've got some kind of cleanliness complex, that I'm afraid of germs or something. Howard Hughes, that's me! He grinned to himself as the pubs came into view at the crest of the hill on the turn of the road. The first was undergoing some kind of renovation. Its front was swathed in scaffolding and green tarpaulin which flapped gently in the wind.

He pulled in to the gravelled car park of the second pub (though car park was probably too grand a word for what was just a bit of space in front of the building with three other cars already parked there) and switched off the engine. He slid the blue phone into his jacket pocket and the others into his briefcase, which he took with him. He'd once had his car broken into in a pub car park and he didn't leave things to chance any more. He walked into the pub, narrowing his eyes to adjust to the gloom inside. The publican was behind the bar, polishing pint glasses, while another customer – an elderly farmer with a tweed cap pulled down over his brow – sat at the dark wood counter sipping a pint of Guinness. Two younger men – businessmen, thought Frank, passing trade like himself – sat in a corner with a sheaf of papers in front of them.

'Just a mineral water,' he said as he put his case on the bar.

The barman nodded at the new arrival and took a bottle of Ballygowan from the fridge beneath the bar.

'I'll use your facilities first.' Frank didn't want to get oil all over the glass too. He gestured towards the briefcase. 'This OK here?'

The barman nodded again and Frank walked through the pub to the gents'. He wondered why it was that the toilets in so many Irish pubs were so utterly awful. The blue wall tiles were coated in grease and there was black fungus on the grouting. The single urinal was detaching itself from the wall and was caked with lime-scale. And the sink, the only item that he actually wanted to use, was cracked, the tap dripping incessantly.

Oh well, he thought philosophically as he turned the tap on full. It won't kill me.

He began whistling again.

Chapter 4

Sally was both relieved and annoyed that her husband had called to say that he probably wouldn't be home. She was annoyed because he'd been away all of the previous week and three days of the week before. It seemed to her that over the past few years his work had taken her away more and more often, and the semi-detached nature of their marriage was beginning to irritate her. It hadn't at first – she'd liked the fact that the two of them were independent people who didn't need to be joined at the hip to be happy. She'd enjoyed going on weekend breaks without him and him going away without her too. Their reunions were always passionate and welcome, and last year, for their eighteenth wedding anniversary, she'd bought him a plaque in the shape of a heart inscribed with 'Absence makes the heart grow fonder', which she'd told him to put up in his office.

Of course when they first married his absences had been much shorter. But that had changed in the last few years, mainly because the business had grown so much and he had to be away a lot more frequently. It was something that she was going to have to talk to him about. Especially now that she was pregnant again. That, though, was one of the reasons she was relieved he wasn't coming home tonight. She hadn't quite come to terms with the whole idea herself yet and she wasn't ready to talk to him about it. Only she knew that the moment he walked in the door she would have to blurt it out. She was aching with the need to tell someone and that someone had to be him.

'Jenna!' she called up the stairs. 'Are you ready to eat now?'

'Not hungry,' came the reply.

Sally sighed deeply. Another thing to worry about. Jenna was forever telling her that she wasn't hungry or requesting a simple salad for a meal which she then pushed around her plate and only ate a small portion of. Whenever Sally broached the subject of eating properly, Jenna looked wearily at her and told her that she wasn't anorexic or even bulimic but that she was simply going through a not very hungry phase.

'But darling,' Sally would say in her most coaxing tone, 'you need nutrients. You're a growing girl and you're working hard at school.' (Though the second part of her sentence was only half true, because Jenna's grades had slipped over the past few months. The worst part of being a teacher in the same school was knowing how her daughter's behaviour had changed and having the other teachers discuss it with her in detail.)

It didn't matter how much Sally wheedled, Jenna ate what she wanted when she wanted. And then, just to keep her off balance, Sally thought, she would sometimes tuck into an enormous dinner and smile at her like the Jenna of old and ask for more.

I wish I knew what was going through her mind these days, Sally thought. Everyone thinks that because I teach I should know. But I bloody well don't!

∽

Jenna lay on her single bed and gazed up at the ceiling. A tiny crack snaked its way across it from one side of the room to the other. The crack had been there for as long as she could remember. When she'd been very small and noticed it first, she'd rushed downstairs to tell her parents that the house was falling down. She'd burst into the living room to find Sally buttoning up her blouse and her father looking flustered. It was only years afterwards that she realised that the sound of her four-year-old footsteps clattering down the stairs had alerted her parents to the imminent interruption of their lovemaking. She'd shivered when she thought about it – her mum and dad having sex together. It revolted her.

She didn't know quite why it revolted her when the idea of making love to Gerry Cullinan, a guy she'd met at the local sports centre, was so appealing. Last week, in the shadow of the high wall behind her house, Gerry had kissed her in a way she hadn't ever been kissed before. And as his hands had slid down her back, cupping her buttocks and drawing her ever closer to him, she'd held him fiercely too, wanting to merge her body with his until they were one person. One of Gerry's hands had then moved upwards and under her Nike T-shirt, until it covered her left breast. At that moment Jenna thought she would faint with the pleasure of it.

'I don't have anything,' Gerry had whispered. 'I'm sorry.'

Jenna had been shocked. Both at the fact that he'd thought she was ready to have sex with him and the fact that he was being responsible about it.

'Neither do I,' she'd whispered back as though this was a perfectly normal conversation.

Gerry had pulled away from her then. 'Next time,' he said.

Jenna had fallen in love with him a little more. After all, most of the time adults talked about teenage boys it was to say that they had all the self-control of a lit firework. But here was Gerry Cullinan, not making love to her because he didn't want to get her pregnant. He was the most wonderful bloke she'd ever met. She'd pulled him towards her and kissed him again, and she knew that if he hadn't pulled away, she wouldn't have stopped him.

She was going to go into Dublin and buy condoms. She couldn't buy them here, in Bray, because someone would be bound to find out. The town was big but not big enough to keep really important things secret. Even if she went to the chemist at the far end, where the pharmacist didn't know her or her mother or father, she'd be bound to bump into someone there who did. It was the way of things. But if she went into the city to buy them she'd be OK. She could nip into Boots and throw them into a wire basket along with a new mascara and some lippy and nobody would take a blind bit of notice.

And then, when she met Gerry at the party tomorrow night as they'd arranged, she'd be able to let him know that she was sorted, that she had something and that they didn't have to stop with kisses and his touch on her breast.

Remembering it again brought back all of the pleasurable feelings. She moaned softly to herself and closed her eyes.

～

Sally sat at the huge wooden table and poked at the pork chop on her plate. She wasn't really hungry. She'd only cooked it because she'd taken the chops out of the freezer that morning, thinking that they could have a nice family meal once Frank got home. Whenever Frank was in the house Jenna seemed marginally more prepared to eat with them, as though making an effort for her father's sake. Sally pushed the chop to one side and scooped some savoury rice on to her fork. She lifted it as far as her lips and then replaced it, untasted, on the plate. Maybe it was just as well Jenna had shut herself away in her bedroom. If she'd been watching Sally playing aimlessly with her food she'd have considered it justification for her own lack of appetite these days.

Although Sally had been relieved when he left the message earlier, she now felt miserable at the thought of another night without Frank. She wanted the warmth of his arms around her, the closeness of his lips on hers and the sheer joy of making love to him, regardless of the fact that she was pregnant. She stared unseeingly at her plate. It had been Frank's skill as a kisser that had entranced her when she'd first met him at an all-night party in a run-down flat in Ranelagh twenty years ago. Sally had known the girl who rented the flat; Frank had come with a group of friends. They'd met as they both tried to grab the last can of Heineken from the fridge.

'I think you'll find that's mine,' Frank had told her.

'I brought ten,' Sally informed him. 'I haven't had more than six. So it's definitely mine.'

They'd stared at each other, both aware of an electricity that crackled between them as his brown eyes held her blue-green ones, and then he laughed.

35

'How about payment?' he suggested.

'Excuse me?'

'Well, I let you have the beer in return for payment.'

'And that might be?'

'This.' He leaned forward and kissed her.

It was astonishing, thought Sally now, how much the memory of that kiss still had the power to move her. Of course he'd kissed her hundreds of times since then, and every time had been utterly marvellous, but that first kiss had been so unexpected and so wonderful. Sometimes, when she was mad at him for not coming home or having to work over holidays or travel abroad to meetings and miss important family events . . . well, if she remembered the kiss she couldn't help but forgive him.

Remembering the kiss would make her remember the first time they made love too. A week later, after he'd asked her out and taken her to the cinema (she couldn't for the life of her remember what it was they'd gone to see, as they'd spent the entire two hours in an orgy of kissing), they'd gone back to his flat, small and not very appealing with its underlying smell of damp, and she'd felt her excitement at being with him wane in such uninspiring surroundings. Then he'd kissed her again and begun undoing the buttons on her rather prim blouse, and he'd done it so slowly and erotically (and so unlike the other guys she'd gone out with before who were usually all fingers and thumbs in their haste to get down to business) that she'd almost come there and then simply standing in front of him. They'd made love on the padded quilt of his bed and Sally had fallen head over heels in love with the man who was the most sensitive lover she'd ever had. And was ever likely to have, she thought later. She'd wondered, as she went home afterwards, whether you could make a lifetime commitment on the basis of out-of-this-world sex. She felt, somewhat regretfully, that there was probably more to it than that. And then Frank sent her flowers (the only man in her life ever to have sent her flowers) and she knew that there was more to him than being good in bed.

He was a wonderful husband. Other female friends would often joke (enviously) that he was too good to be true. That nobody could be as understanding of a woman's needs as Frank. And not just her physical needs, her emotional needs too. He remembered birthdays. He remembered significant moments in their lives. He knew when she was bothered by something and knew to leave her to her own devices until she'd sorted herself out. He supported her teaching career, pushing her harder than maybe she would have pushed herself so that she finally got the position of deputy principal (although he told her that she really deserved to be the head). And if the flip side of that was that he had to be away more and more because of his business, well, Sally could put up with that. Most of the time.

It was definitely better that he wasn't here tonight, she told herself, as she got up from the table and scraped her uneaten dinner into the bin. Her thoughts were all over the place. Her feelings were equally haphazard. She needed time to be alone.

But part of her didn't want to be.

～

Iona arrived home at a quarter to eight. The house was in darkness with no sign of Frank. She felt a spurt of anger at the fact that he'd been delayed still further and hadn't bothered to call her. She took her phone from her bag and checked it. No missed calls. No messages. No texts.

She drew the curtains in the tiny living room as she dialled the pizza delivery and placed an order. She asked for their Cajun special with extra cheese on the basis that this was her favourite although not one Frank particularly liked. But she was punishing him for being so late. Childish, she thought, as she hung up. But she didn't care. Besides, the takeaway pizza and garlic bread (even though she was really looking forward to it) was a big concession on her part. Always conscious of eating well, she'd been even more choosy in the last few weeks, wanting to get herself into peak condition for getting pregnant. So she'd been loading up on green-leaf veggies and folic acid and cutting out junk food completely.

She massaged her stomach. The worst of the cramps had eased now but she still felt bloated and uncomfortable. She went up to the bathroom and began to run a bath, decanting a few drops of ylang ylang oil into the warm water. The resulting scent was restful and soothing. She went into the bedroom and took off her work clothes. The pizza place had said it would be forty minutes before they could make the delivery. She'd be out of the bath by then, although surely Frank would be home within five or ten anyway. It wasn't like him to be late and not to let her know. She pushed the sliver of worry to the back of her mind. He'd call. He always did. But she picked up her mobile and rang him anyway. All she got was his voice-mail. She left a message saying that he'd better hurry, that the pizza was on its way, and then she went back to the bathroom.

She slid into the silky softness of the bath and closed her eyes, allowing her breathing to slow down and become steadier. A few minutes later, feeling much calmer, she opened her eyes and began massaging her tired legs with the tips of her fingers. She slid lower into the water, feeling the tensions of the day dissolve away from her and the bloatedness of her stomach finally ease as she drifted between wakefulness and sleep. Frank laughed at her ability to sleep in the bath and she knew that he worried (very slightly) that she might slide beneath the water and drown. She always told him that it was impossible in their shortened bathtub, even for someone of five feet and one inch.

There was a ring at the door. Her eyes snapped open again. Bloody pizza people were early for once, she thought. And Frank still hadn't come home. Well, he could just reheat his half in the microwave and he'd have to lump it that it never tasted the same afterwards!

She wrapped her towelling robe around her and padded down the stairs. Unless it was Frank himself, she thought hopefully, having forgotten his keys or something. As she opened the door she realised that she was being particularly stupid. He wouldn't be able to drive the car without keys. And besides, she'd know in advance if it was Frank. She always believed that she was intuitive

38

like that. There were many times when she'd be thinking about him, her mobile would ring and it would be him. It wasn't just Frank either. When Lauren had come down with a debilitating virus, Iona had phoned her the very day she'd been diagnosed, even though they hadn't spoken in weeks. And the day Craig had received the letter from the engineering contractors about the Chinese job, she'd phoned him too, just knowing that something had happened. Iona put her intuition down to the fact that she was in tune with her body. The knowledge comforted her, made her feel as though there was nothing that could ever happen without her being aware of it first.

The pizza delivery girl stood on the doorstep. The warm, tomato-laden aroma wafting from the huge flat box made Iona's mouth water and she realised that she hadn't eaten since her mixed nut salad at lunchtime. She took the box from the girl and tipped her a euro. She set it down in the kitchen, nipped upstairs to give her hair a brisk rub with a towel, thankful that its shortness meant that it dried quickly, and then came down again to attack the food.

She switched on the TV and realised that they were showing *Erin Brockovich*, which was one of her favourite movies. She hacked a slice from the pizza, curled up on the sofa, and indulged herself while she waited for Frank to come home.

⌒

Long before the movie ended she began to worry again. She tried Frank's mobile once more but her call was still being diverted to his mailbox. She left another message, this time telling him that she was probably worrying unnecessarily but asking him to give her a shout and let her know where he was. She tried not to think of the fact that he might have had an accident – Frank was one of the safest drivers she knew. Maddeningly safe, in fact, she often got impatient with him. But although he wasn't the kind of man to do something stupid on the road, other people were. Some lunatic, maybe overtaking on a bad bend, could have smashed into him. Iona swallowed hard and looked at the congealing half of the pizza she'd left for him. She closed her eyes and visualised him driving along the motorway from Cork to Dublin. She couldn't see any problems. She just couldn't understand why he hadn't called.

The movie was failing to keep her attention. Her eyes darted around the room and came to rest on the wedding photo – apart from the recent additions of the photos of her niece and nephew, it was the only photograph on display in the room. Both she and Frank preferred paintings to photos (and especially disliked photographs of themselves), but they agreed that the wedding photo was the one exception. They were standing on the white sands of a Barbados beach, she in her long white dress, an arrangement of colourful flowers in her dark hair, he in a white tux and red bow tie which she'd told him at the time was a bit over the top but which actually looked great against the stunning blues of the sea and sky behind them. They were laughing and toasting each other with champagne. Iona smiled at the memory. It truly had been the happiest day of her life, and it hadn't mattered to her that none of her family was there because being alone together had made the experience somehow more intensely personal.

Four years ago, she thought, and it truly does only seem like yesterday!

She picked up her mobile and called Frank again. She could feel the worry escalate as she listened to him asking her to leave a message.

'Frank,' she said, and she had to struggle to keep the anxiety out of her voice, 'where the hell are you? Call me. I know it's stupid but I'm worried.'

Somehow saying out loud that she was worried seemed to lessen it somewhat, as though by admitting it she could see for herself how silly it was to be concerned. She pressed the end button and stared at the TV screen. *Erin Brockovich* had finished.

Chapter 5

It was early evening when the call came in to the garda station in Ardallen, just as Garda Tim Shanahan finally finished the crossword in the *Herald*. It had been a quiet day in Ardallen, a country town about an hour's drive from Dublin, but Tim wasn't feeling in the slightest bit guilty about having some down-time – they were all still shattered after the two-day jazz festival that had taken place at the GAA sports park the previous week. It was the minor public order offences that were so time-consuming, he thought. All those people getting drunk and pissing in the streets and having rows with each other. A big case would be a damn sight more exciting, even though they really didn't have the manpower for big cases in Ardallen.

'Ardallen garda station. How can I help?' Tim liked sounding pleasant on the phone even though he knew that many of his colleagues still answered it abruptly, as though its ring had disturbed them from far more important business.

'Jesus, Tim, come quick,' said an excitable voice. 'There's been a massive great landslide at Kavanagh's pub and the side of it is buried under rock.'

'Who's that?' he asked, although he was fairly sure that it was Margaret Hobson, who lived on the hillside opposite the pub.

'For crying out loud, Tim, it's me. Mags. I was going to call 999 but I thought it'd be quicker to call you myself. But you'd better come quick 'cos it's a hell of a mess.'

'Right, Margaret,' he said. 'We're on our way.'

He called for his colleague, Ronan Tierney, to join him. The

41

two of them jumped into the marked car outside the station and sped to Kavanagh's pub. As they drove, Tim called the ambulance service – if things were as bad as Margaret suggested (and he trusted her, she was a sensible woman despite her excitable voice), then they'd need them.

Kavanagh's was a well-known pub in the area, although it amused Tim that it was right next door to the much more upmarket Ardallen House, which was currently undergoing its third remodelling in almost as many years. This one was far more radical than any other, since it was to allow for a nightclub on the premises, a fact which wearied Tim because the location of the pubs, five miles outside the town, already caused problems with customers who drove there and then realised that after a few pints they shouldn't really drive back. Having a pub with a nightclub attached would make things even worse. Years ago it wouldn't have mattered that much, but there was now a zero-tolerance policy in Ardallen regarding drink-driving which had made Tim and the rest of the guards both heroes and villains in equal measure.

'Holy Mother of God.' Tim swung the car to a stop outside the pub and looked at it in stunned amazement. Margaret Hobson hadn't been joking. The entire side of the pub was nothing but a mound of rubble and the place was a complete disaster area.

'Let's get some traffic control going,' Tim told Ronan. 'The ambulances will be here soon and we don't want rubbernecking onlookers in the way. And you'd better call for back-up too.'

He scanned the scene as Ronan got to work. He recognised Noel Kavanagh, the owner of the pub, who was sitting on the single wooden table outside the front of the premises, a red blanket around his shoulders. He was unnaturally pale although that could also have been because he was streaked with dust. An elderly man who Tim knew to be Bennie Harrison was sitting beside him. Margaret Hobson was with them, offering them tea out of an old-fashioned thermos flask. Two other men, both in torn and dusty white shirts spattered with blood, were also being comforted. As he watched, a couple of ambulances arrived and the paramedics got working on the injured men.

'Christ.' Ronan Tierney rejoined him. 'What the hell happened?'

'God only knows,' said Tim. He looked around as the sound of sirens indicated the arrival of the reinforcements. 'Get one of the lads to follow the ambulances, Ronan. See how everyone's doing.' He scratched his head. 'I'll have a word with Noel and see what he has to say before they haul him off. We need to know if anyone is trapped inside.'

'D' you think it was deliberate?' Ronan's voice was a mixture of hope and horror.

'Deliberate?'

'Like a terrorist attack or something.'

Tim looked at his young colleague. 'Ah now, get a grip,' he said. 'I have a feeling that terrorists have bigger targets in mind than Kavanagh's pub.'

'Well, a gangland thing then,' suggested Ronan.

'Jesus Christ, Tierney, what sort of stuff are you reading these days?' demanded Tim.

'Well, I hope there weren't too many people inside,' said Ronan, tacitly accepting that Ardallen probably wasn't a gangland or terrorist target.

'Noel says that some bloke came in just before it happened,' said Margaret Hobson, who'd trotted over to them. 'Besides Bennie and those two other guys he was the only person there. He ordered a sparkling water and went to the gents'. The gents' was at the side there. Where the wall fell down.'

'Jesus.' Now Tim could see exactly what had happened. Somehow, in the renovating of Ardallen House, which was higher on the hill than Kavanagh's, the wall at the side of the pub had collapsed and fallen directly on to the other building, burying half of it. And effectively burying whoever was in the gents' toilet at the time.

'We haven't found him yet,' said a fireman.

'Not local?' said Ronan.

43

'Doesn't sound like it, but you never know,' Tim remarked. 'I'd better talk to Noel.'

As he walked over to the wooden table there was a shout from the paramedics still at the scene. Others hurried over to join them. Then a wheeled stretcher was brought over. Tim watched as a body was lifted out of the rubble and a drip inserted into what seemed to him to be a lifeless arm.

With a blare of klaxons the last ambulance departed, followed by a squad car, and Tim set about taking statements from a still shocked Noel Kavanagh and a considerably more garrulous Bennie Harrison.

Neither of them was particularly helpful. Their statements were very similar. They'd been sitting in the pub, minding their own business, when they'd heard a muffled thud and the next thing they knew they were being buried in rubble and dust. They'd fled out of the main door, terrified of being trapped inside, although the collapse of the wall had mainly confined itself to one side of the building. They didn't know anything about the man who'd ordered the Ballygowan, although Noel thought that he'd spoken with a Dublin accent.

'The two other men,' Tim said to Noel. 'Did you know them?'

He nodded gingerly. 'They meet here once a month or so. I don't know much about them – one of them is a rep from some-where in the north of the country. The other's from Waterford. I can't remember their names.'

'OK, Noel,' said Tim. He turned to Ronan and waved in the direction of the car park. 'Do a check on the cars, find out who they're registered to.'

He poked his head nervously through the entrance to the pub. The place was covered in bricks and dust. He could see a tan briefcase on the counter in front of him and he picked his way cautiously through the rubble to get it.

'What the hell do you think you're doing!'

He whirled around at the voice. A fireman looked at him in anger. 'This building isn't secure.'

Tim grabbed the briefcase and stepped outside again. 'Just checking,' he said.

'Don't be such a goddamn fool,' said the fireman. 'Christ almighty, we don't want another fatality.'

Tim looked at him. 'The guy you pulled out? Is he dead?'

The fireman shrugged. 'I don't give much for his chances, let's put it like that.'

'Bloody hell,' said Tim.

His attention was caught by the sudden arrival of more cars and vans. The media, he thought sourly. All with questions that he couldn't answer yet, all after the human angle to the story as well as looking for someone to blame. He recognised Joely McGuirk, a reporter from the local newspaper, as well as Pat Dolan, a photographer. Tim knew that more media wouldn't be far behind.

'Make sure they stay behind the tape,' he warned Ronan. 'Tell them I'll talk to them in a minute.'

Tim felt as though he was on the set of a movie. Yet the destruction around him was real. The men carried off in ambulances to the nearest hospital were real. The shock of Noel Kavanagh and Bennie Harrison was real. It was just hard to believe it.

He opened the briefcase he'd retrieved from the pub, while Ronan dealt with the media hacks. The papers inside were mainly brochures and A4 notepads with scrawled diagrams and notes. There were also two mobile phones in the case. He picked up the red one and scrolled through the address book. There was one number under 'Home'. It was a Dublin area number, although Tim wasn't immediately sure what part of the city it was from.

'Any luck on tracing the cars?' he asked Ronan.

'They're coming back to me,' he said.

'Find out about this number too,' Tim told him, handing him the mobile.

He picked up the yellow one and began scrolling through that too. As far as he could see the numbers on this were all business ones. One phone for personal calls, one for business calls, he decided. Fair enough.

More and more onlookers arrived at the scene, and finally the television cameras. Tim had been interviewed by RTÉ and Sky News once before, although that was when an international pop star and her fiancé had married in Ardallen Castle on the outskirts of the town. It was meant to have been in complete secrecy but the news had been leaked to just about everyone who wanted to know. Tim had laughed and joked with the reporters then, telling them that there was nothing he could say, feeling a little like a media star himself.

But this was different. He told the reporters that the incident was obviously very serious and distressing and that at this point he had no further information. As soon as he had, he told them, he'd let them know.

'We've got ID on the cars,' said Ronan, 'and the two guys who were taken away. I've spoken to our lads at the hospital. The injured blokes are being kept in overnight for shock but actually they're not that badly hurt. They've called their families themselves.'

'And the other guy?' asked Tim.

Ronan made a face. 'They're stabilising him but they think they'll have to transfer him to Dublin. They don't have facilities for him at the county hospital. Looks like a head injury.'

Tim rubbed the back of his neck. He hated hearing about head injuries. He looked at his colleague, who shrugged helplessly and then answered his phone as it rang.

'The third guy,' he said, 'him with the head injuries – the phone number and the car reg match. Frank Harper, River Valley Estate, Bray. The name also matches the business cards which were in the glove compartment of his car – we managed to open it a few minutes ago.'

Tim nodded. Now he recognised the area phone number. Bray, of course, wasn't strictly in Dublin. It was in Wicklow, about a forty-minute drive from the city.

'There are a couple of photos in the phone's memory,' added Ronan. 'A woman and a girl. Could be family.'

'We'd better get to the house and see what's what,' Tim said.

'At least, we'll get Bray to do it. These are always horrible situations.'

'He's not dead yet,' said Ronan.

'If he's got a serious head injury . . .' Tim didn't bother finishing the sentence.

'Maybe it's not that bad,' said Ronan optimistically as Tim called the station in Bray.

Chapter 6

The sound of the phone ringing broke Siobhán Farrell's concentration. The evening shift at the station was a good time to deal with paperwork without being interrupted every five minutes, and she'd been sitting at her desk reviewing the money-laundering file for the past hour. The case was almost ready to go to the Director of Public Prosecutions and Siobhán wanted to be sure that she'd dotted every I and crossed every T and that it was as complete as it was possible to be. The most frustrating part of police work was seeing a case not followed through because of mistakes which would have it thrown out of court. She'd once had a case dismissed on a technicality – she'd called a company Havisham Holdings instead of Haversham Holdings – and she'd never forgotten it.

'Hello,' she said abruptly, annoyed at the interruption. Tim Shanahan winced. That was the kind of phone-answering he didn't go in for. Women were even worse than the men these days in being abrupt and rude, he thought. He introduced himself and explained about the Ardallen incident.

'How awful.' He could hear the genuine sympathy in the woman's voice and he warmed to her a little. 'And you think that one of the victims is from our district?' Tim read out his name and Siobhán nodded. 'I know the area.'

'We need someone to go and check out the house,' said Tim. 'Break the news.'

'How grim is it?' asked Siobhán.

'It doesn't sound good to me,' he said. 'I asked whether his wife should come here or wait for them to send him to Dublin. They said come here, he won't be stable enough to be moved for a while yet.'

'OK,' said Siobhán. 'I'll go around to the house right away.'

'Thanks,' said Tim. He gave her all the information he could. 'Sorry to land this one on you.'

'It's better than having to tell them that he's dead,' said Siobhán matter-of-factly. 'I've had to do that before and I just hate it. At least this way there's still a bit of hope.'

'He looked fairly beat-up when they took him out of the rubble,' said Tim. 'I don't know whether he'll make it.'

'Hope all the same,' Siobhán said.

She hung up on Tim and waved at the uniformed garda who was walking past her door.

'Cathal, the very man, I need you to come with me,' she told him. 'We might have to break some difficult news.'

Cathal Rothery sighed. He was always chosen when there was bad news to be broken. He had a choirboy face and a very sympathetic manner which put people at their ease. 'Fill me in,' he said as they walked out towards the car.

∽

Iona was extremely worried. He'd said that he'd be home around seven thirty and it was now ten o'clock. Three more frantic messages to his mobile had remained unanswered. She couldn't think of a single explanation for this that didn't involve Frank in some kind of accident, because she couldn't believe that he was deliberately ignoring her calls. They hadn't had a row; when she'd last spoken to him everything had seemed perfectly normal. He'd talked about ordering in the pizza, for heaven's sake!

She looked at the remnants of the Cajun with extra cheese, as well as the half-baguette of garlic bread, now cold and unappetising. She closed the pizza box and brought it into the kitchen.

She'd turned on the news earlier to see if there had been anything about accidents on the road from Cork but there had been nothing. Now she went into the office to check breaking news on the internet, just in case. She sat nervously at her computer screen, the metallic taste of fear in her mouth as she logged on and looked at her Irish news service.

There were a number of accident reports but none on the Cork to Dublin road, which was the route that Frank would have taken. Iona stared at the screen with its myriad pop-up ads and colourful exhortations to buy a new phone or sign up for something free and she felt the worry knot inside her stomach and make her cramps even worse.

Maybe, though, he hadn't had an accident. Maybe he'd been taken ill and had been brought to hospital. Appendicitis, perhaps. Or one of his migraines. That could be it, she supposed, feeling the knot unravel slightly. If he'd started feeling a migraine coming on he might have pulled over to the side of the road to wait until it had eased. But deep down she knew that she was only clutching at straws. Unless something was actually preventing him from calling her, Frank would have phoned by now. He always called when unexpected things cropped up, because in his business they often did and they always delayed him.

She went downstairs again and stacked her used crockery into the dishwasher, trying to keep a lid on her mounting fears. She put the uneaten slices of pizza on a plate and covered them with clingfilm, but she threw the unappetising-looking garlic bread in the bin. Then she went into the living room and looked out of the front window. The street, a narrow cul-de-sac, was practically deserted. Parked cars stood outside their owners' homes but none were being driven along the road. A couple walked hand in hand past the house, not noticing her eyes peeping through the slatted blinds.

There's a perfectly good explanation, she thought as she looked at her watch again. And I'm getting worked up over nothing. Frank is always going on at me about getting into a state about things. It's probably worse because of the time of the month. She rubbed her stomach which, since her bath, had settled into a dull ache. I'm hormonal at the moment. I'm not seeing things straight.

50

She frowned suddenly and ran upstairs again. She flung open the door of the double wardrobe. There were two suits missing, the one Frank had been wearing the day he'd left and a second which he always brought when he travelled in case he needed to change. Six shirts had gone from the top drawer of his dresser, as well as socks and a few ties. Nothing abnormal about that. He hadn't suddenly deserted her, hatched some plot about running off with a fancy woman from Cork!

Iona laughed shortly at her own silliness. Frank would never leave her. He loved her. She loved him. From the first moment she'd met him she'd known he was someone that she could love. She'd sensed it straight away.

Their meeting had been totally accidental. She was having a snatched lunch in a crowded city-centre bar, looking through leasing agreements as she ate her spicy chicken wrap and not taking any notice of the people milling around her. So she hadn't spotted Frank standing near the tiny circular table where she was sitting until he cleared his throat a couple of times and said, 'Excuse me.' She'd been taken aback by his good looks, his strong face, dark wiry hair and warm brown eyes. She could never quite explain it afterwards, how it was that she'd been instantly physically attracted by a man she didn't know, so that almost as soon as she'd looked at him she was wondering what he would be like in bed. She'd felt the colour rush into her normally pale cheeks.

'Anyone sitting here?' he asked. 'Would you mind?' He nodded at the vacant seat beside her.

'No, of course not,' she said, sweeping the leasing agreements into her briefcase.

'I'm sorry for interrupting you.' He put his overflowing ham and cheese baguette and a pint of sparkling water on the table in front of her. 'It's jam-packed in here today, isn't it?'

She nodded.

'Never usually so full,' he said as he hung his jacket on the back of the chair.

'I wouldn't know,' she said. 'I've never been here before.'

'I think it's the current in-place,' he told her. 'Apparently Bono or Daniel O'Donnell or someone comes here a lot.'

She giggled at the idea of the two very different singers and personalities enjoying the same pub.

'Or maybe I'm just making that up.' He grinned at her and his brown eyes twinkled.

Iona hadn't been able to go back to the single leasing agreement which she'd left on the table. She'd talked to Frank right through her lunchtime until she realised, with a squeak of dismay, that she would be late for her appointment.

'Shame,' said Frank. 'I was enjoying our conversation. Never mind, maybe I'll see you again sometime.'

She'd looked at him for a moment and then blurted out, 'Tomorrow night? I'm going to a terribly boring work dinner thing and I'm supposed to have someone to go with, only . . . well . . . I've split up with my boyfriend and I don't have someone I can call on . . . What d'you think?' She'd been horrified the moment the words were out of her mouth. For a start, she'd never asked a bloke on a date before. Secondly, it was probably the world's worst date. And thirdly, she didn't know exactly how old he was but it seemed to her that he was certainly older than her usual boyfriends. What the hell was she doing?

He'd considered it for a moment and she'd felt a wave of mortification swamp her. A complete stranger, she mentally hissed to herself, are you out of your mind! And then he'd said yes, why not, and it had been as though the sun had come out from behind the clouds.

She remembered every detail of the following evening together. He'd been formal and distant with her at the dinner itself but afterwards he told her that he'd make sure she got home safely and, sitting beside him in the taxi, she'd felt hot waves of passion gripping her. She couldn't understand it. He was just a bloke. And he seemed perfectly unaffected by her. She couldn't believe he didn't sense that she was imagining ripping his clothes off and making love to him right there and then on the back seat of the cab!

When they got to her house she asked him, as diffidently as she could, whether he'd like to come in for a coffee. She ignored the muffled guffaw of laughter from the cab driver and prayed that Frank would say yes. He hesitated, but in the end he agreed.

They never got around to the coffee. In fact they'd barely got inside the door when she turned to him and he kissed her and she felt herself grow weak with longing for him. And she'd led him upstairs, into her carefully feng shui-ed bedroom, where he'd made love to her like she'd never been made love to before. She'd known then that she was in love with him. She'd known then that she'd always be in love with him. She'd known then that one day she'd marry him.

Knowing that she'd marry him was one thing; making it happen hadn't been quite so straightforward. After a couple of dates Frank told her that he wasn't the marrying type.

'I didn't think I was either,' she told him one night after they'd made love twice, and the second time had been even more wonderful than the first. 'But it's different with you.' She realised what she'd said and felt a wave of embarrassment rush over her. That sentence had been a virtual proposal, she thought. And if anything could freak out a non-marrying man more than a virtual proposal she didn't know what it might be.

But he'd laughed and said that it felt a bit different with her too, that he'd never felt so totally caught up in someone else's life before.

'Maybe it's because you're a little older than me,' she continued with more confidence (she'd discovered that Frank was exactly ten years older), 'but you seem to know what it is I want, even before I do. You're good with women, Frank. I can't understand how you've escaped unscathed before now!'

He'd chuckled then and said something about the luck of the draw.

Once the subject of marriage had been brought up, Iona found that she kept going back to it. She tried not to; she didn't want to force Frank into anything and besides, getting married hadn't been something that was particularly high on her agenda before then. But she didn't want him to get away. He was perfect husband material.

Getting married in Barbados had been his idea. It would be different and special. And it wouldn't matter, he told her, that being an only child whose parents had died he didn't have any family to share the day with, and that hers didn't like him; they could have an idyllic wedding in an idyllic location.

'My family does like you,' she protested. 'Well, of course my parents haven't met you, but quite honestly Mum and Dad aren't the sort of people who interfere in our lives. They're happy once we're happy.'

'Your sister and her husband aren't very keen.'

'Oh, Lauren!' Iona dismissed her with a shrug. 'She thinks every man should be like Myles, boring old fart that he is. Anyway, she hardly knows you really.'

It didn't bother Iona that she'd been going out with Frank for nearly six months and that he'd only met Lauren twice, her brother Craig once and her parents not at all. He hadn't met Flora and David because they had retired to their tumbledown (but now renovated) finca near Javea, on the east coast of Spain, almost as soon as Craig left college.

And so they'd decided on the Barbadian wedding, which had been every bit as wonderful as Frank had promised her. A few weeks later they'd flown to Spain, where Flora and David had met them, and stayed at the finca for a couple of nights before heading on to spend a few days in Barcelona.

'I like him,' Flora had told her daughter as they sat on the veranda overlooking the orange grove (wearing jumpers because it was February and the evenings were cold). 'I'm delighted you've found someone you want to be with, even if he's a bit old.'

'Mum! He's not that much older than me.'

'More experienced, though.'

'I guess he's lived a bit.'

'You're right.' Flora hugged her. 'And you're happy, that's the main thing.'

Iona hugged her mother back. She liked the fact that personal happiness was at the top of her mother's list. But then it always had been. It was through Flora that Iona had developed her interest in feng shui and yoga and generally trying to keep a good balance between her body and her mind. She knew that she'd never be quite as into it all as her mother, who (Iona thought) could actually be quite dippy about New Age stuff from time to time; but she'd always been glad that Flora counted happiness as more important than money or careers or material goods. When the other girls at school had been worrying about exam results and college and what their parents would say if they didn't get the right number of points for the courses they wanted to do, Iona had felt happy and secure in the knowledge that Flora wouldn't consider it a disaster even if she flunked everything.

But she hadn't. She'd always been quite academic and had had a knack of doing well in exams even when she hadn't studied as much as she might have. A good technique, one of the teachers had once told her, and Iona had agreed. Also, she had a good short-term memory and was brilliant at last-minute revision.

Her academic success, plus the fact that she was good at games, meant that she didn't score quite so highly on the dating front. In fact Iona had only gone out with two boys during her entire time at school and she hadn't actually liked either of them. Even afterwards, when she'd started work and expanded her social life dramatically, she still wasn't very successful with men. She was good with them as work colleagues and good with them over a pint or watching football or rugby in the pub, but not good with them as a girlfriend.

Until she met Frank. And he changed everything.

Now she looked at her watch again. There was something badly wrong and it wasn't just her freaking out over something stupid. She had to face facts. He should be home by now and he hadn't called, either because he didn't want to or because he wasn't able to. And regardless of the reason for his silence, it had to be bad news for her.

She took a deep breath, picked up the phone and dialled her sister's number.

'Hello?'

She grimaced. Her brother-in-law, Myles Leary, had picked it up. Iona was never really sure why it was that she and Myles didn't get on, but the fact was that they'd never hit it off. And Myles didn't like Frank either – she'd heard him once refer to him as a smarmy git.

'Hi, Myles,' she said as lightly as she could. 'Is Lauren around?'

'She's out,' replied Myles. 'It's her line-dancing night tonight.'

'Oh.'

'Will I tell her you called?'

'I – yes – yes . . . well, listen, Myles . . .' She couldn't believe she was going to confide in her brother-in-law, but now that she was talking to someone she felt as though she had to share her worry. 'It's probably nothing, but Frank is late home and I can't contact him. I'm a bit concerned.'

She was sure that she heard a knowing snort at the other end of the line.

'He's probably stopped off somewhere for a quick pint and switched off his phone,' said Myles.

'Maybe that's the sort of thing you do,' retorted Iona, 'but Frank isn't like that.'

'All men are like that given half the chance,' said Myles drily. 'It's not that late, Iona. Don't panic.'

'It's after ten,' she said. 'And he was due home by seven or eight.'

'Where was he?'

She explained about the business trip and about checking the news to see if there had been any accidents on the Cork–Dublin road.

'And there haven't, so there's no need to worry. Look, something probably happened to delay or distract him and for some reason he can't call you. There's no reason to get hysterical over it.'

'I'm not hysterical,' she said. 'Just anxious.'

'I'll talk to Lauren when she gets home,' said Myles. 'Let me know if he shows up before then.'

'OK.' She replaced the receiver feeling, as she always did after talking to Myles, somehow silly and foolish. She didn't care what he thought, though. Frank would have phoned her. He always phoned her. That was the way their lives together worked. And now, because he hadn't, she was scared that for the first time in their relationship it wasn't working. And she didn't want it not to work.

Chapter 7

Sally had almost finished unloading the dishwasher when the doorbell rang. She swore softly under her breath and put the last of the crockery on the kitchen table. She knew it was probably one of Jenna's friends looking for her to come out, but that meant the usual battle about how late Jenna could stay out and where she could go and who she was going to be with. Tonight, still anxious and worried about her unexpected pregnancy, Sally didn't have the energy to argue with her daughter. It wasn't that she was a particularly strict parent. On weekend nights, like tonight, she allowed Jenna to stay out until 12.30 a.m. But she still insisted on knowing who she was with and where she was going, and Jenna often either didn't want to or couldn't give her the information. Jenna's view was that it didn't make any difference as long she was home on time, and she was always home on time – even, she'd add, on weekdays, when a ridiculous 10 p.m. curfew was in place, a time which nobody else had to stick to. Sometimes Sally wavered over the curfew but she never gave in. All the same, it's so hard to get the balance right, she thought despairingly. How the hell do other mothers manage it?

She listened as Jenna thumped down the stairs and opened the door. She waited for a call of 'Going out, back later,' which would signal the start of the great 'Where are you going?' debate, but instead there was a low murmuring of voices and then the kitchen door was pushed open. Jenna walked in, followed by a tall, serious-faced woman dressed in a neat fawn suit, her frizzy red hair clipped back from her head, accompanied by a very young-looking male garda. Sally looked from them to Jenna anxiously. Despite her best efforts, had her daughter got into trouble of some sort to bring the police to her door? God, she thought, Frank will totally freak out if Jenna has got into trouble with the police.

'Hi, Mrs Harper.' The woman smiled at her but Sally could see that it was a professional smile. 'My name is Detective Sergeant Siobhán Farrell. I'm with Bray garda station. This is my colleague, Cathal.'

'Yes?' Sally looked at them, her anxiety level increasing.

'We've had a call from our colleagues in Ardallen,' said Siobhán. 'There's been an incident there where—'

'We don't know anyone in Ardallen,' Sally interrupted her. 'Whatever it's about, I think you have the wrong people.'

'. . . where part of a building collapsed causing some injury,' continued Siobhán evenly. 'At the moment there are no fatalities but we do have a serious injury and we're trying to establish the identity of the person concerned.'

Sally saw a sudden flash of sympathy in the other woman's eyes as she read out a car registration. 'It's registered to a Mr Frank Harper, of this address,' said Siobhán. 'We think it's possible that your husband was injured in the incident. He's in the local hospital closest to Ardallen and we think you should probably go to see him.'

'But . . . but . . .' Sally looked at her in bewilderment. 'Frank is away at the moment. He's in the south-west. Cork and Kerry. He's not coming back until tomorrow. There's no reason for him to be in Ardallen. That's only an hour or so away.'

'Maybe he changed his mind,' said Siobhán. 'The local gardai checked out his mobile phone. Again, it was registered to this address. And the home phone number in the mobile's address book matched this phone number.'

'Mum?' Jenna, who'd been standing beside the kitchen table, suddenly slumped on to a chair.

'Are you all right?' asked Cathal Rothery. 'Would you like a drink of water?'

Without waiting for her to answer, he walked to the sink, took the single glass that was on the drainer, filled it and handed it to her. Jenna sipped it even though she felt sick.

'Are you telling me . . .' Sally was still finding it hard to put her thoughts into words, 'that my husband is hurt? He can't be! He wouldn't have any reason to be in an unstable building. He's a businessman. He installs commercial lighting equipment and displays. Well, he doesn't usually install them himself, he has people to do that. He organises it. He sells the systems. But if he occasionally has to visit a site he always wears a safety helmet. He's very safety-conscious. So he can't be hurt.'

'I don't have the full details,' said Siobhán. 'But it appears that he stopped at a pub and it was while he was there that the building beside it collapsed. He was trapped under the rubble.'

'But . . . but Frank doesn't drink and drive!' cried Sally. 'I've been married to him for eighteen years and he's never once touched alcohol if he was getting behind the wheel of the car. And there's no way he'd stop somewhere like Ardallen for a drink – he'd come home first, definitely. But he wasn't meant to be home tonight. He told me he was staying in Cork!'

'Like Siobhán says, maybe he changed his plans.' Cathal's voice was soft. 'Perhaps he was going to surprise you by being home early. He could have stopped for any number of reasons.'

'Well . . . yes . . . maybe . . . but . . .' Sally's thoughts were whirling around her head but she couldn't seem to get them into any order. 'But he just doesn't *do* that. He's very organised. And he *called* me to say that he wasn't coming home. He only made that decision this afternoon. So he wouldn't have changed his mind.'

'Why don't you ring his phone, Mum?' said Jenna anxiously. 'I bet he'll answer it.'

'My colleagues have his phone,' said Cathal quickly. 'I really think that the best thing for you to do, Mrs Harper, is to get to Ardallen tonight. Is there anyone who can drive you?'

'I . . . I don't know.' Sally gripped the edge of the dishwasher. Her breath was coming quickly and she felt faint.

Cathal pulled out a chair and helped her to sit down.

'A family member, perhaps?' suggested Siobhán. 'A brother or sister close by?'

'Mum doesn't have any brothers or sisters,' said Jenna. 'We're it.'

'Perhaps your dad has someone?'

'No.' Jenna looked at them blankly. 'That's the whole thing. It's just us. Me and Mum and Dad.'

'We can arrange for you to get to the hospital,' said Siobhán quickly. 'Don't worry about it.'

'Maybe Denise could bring me . . .' Sally could hear herself speaking but the words sounded like they were coming from somebody else. She shot an anxious look at Siobhán. 'She works with me. And she's a friend. Only she'd have to come from Sutton and it's a long way away, right across town and . . .' Her head snapped up and she looked straight into Siobhán's blue eyes. 'How bad is it? How urgent? How critical?'

'Well, we think it would be a good idea for you to get to the hospital,' said Siobhán. 'I don't have a lot of information right now, Mrs Harper, but he was quite seriously injured.'

'Might he die?' Jenna's words came out as a gasp.

'It would be best if we went now,' said Cathal. 'I can drive you.' He glanced at Siobhán, who nodded.

'I'll get my jacket,' said Sally blankly.

'Whatever you need,' said Cathal.

The two garda exchanged looks as Jenna and Sally went to get their coats.

'Sometimes I hate this job,' said Siobhán.

Cathal nodded. They waited in silence until Jenna and Sally returned.

'I'm going to swing back past the station to let Siobhán out,' said Cathal as they walked out to the car, 'but then I'll drive you straight there – OK, Mrs Harper?'

Sally nodded. She got into the back seat, Jenna clambering in after her. As the car pulled away from the house she noticed the twitching curtain at Noeleen Sharp's house directly across the road. Neighbourhood Watch had its advantages and disadvantages. Sally knew that there would be talk on the road about her and Jenna getting into a garda car, people speculating on what Noeleen might tell them. Not that it really mattered. What mattered was that Frank was all right.

She felt Jenna's hand slide across the back seat and grasp her own as the blue light on the top of the car began to flash. She squeezed it in return, looking quickly towards her daughter, who was actually facing the other direction, peering out of the window as they sped down the road to the garda station. They stopped briefly to let Siobhán out. She smiled at them and wished them good luck. Then the car sped away again.

They were on the N11 now, hurtling along the road towards Arklow and Ardallen. He would have come this way if he was coming home, thought Sally. But why would he be on his way home tonight when he'd told her that he wouldn't be leaving Cork until the morning? It didn't make sense to her. Frank was always such an organised person, there was no way he'd suddenly change his mind about coming home. And never to surprise her. She wasn't a woman who particularly liked surprises and he knew better than to say one thing and do another. So he couldn't really be the person who'd been caught under the rubble of the collapsed building. He was probably in Cork, just like he was supposed to be, and the whole thing was a terrible mix-up.

The car sped over a dip in the road and her stomach somersaulted. She swallowed quickly, choking back the nausea. She'd felt OK since her bout of morning sickness earlier, but the sudden sinking feeling now reminded her of the unexpected pregnancy, which already seemed a distant, unlikely event. I'm not really pregnant, she thought. And Frank's not really hurt. And this is, really, a big, big mistake.

She squeezed Jenna's hand again as the car turned in to the hospital and stopped directly in front of the main door.

Cathal Rothery killed the engine, got out and opened the door for Sally, who, now that they were here, felt quite unable to get out of the car herself. She took Cathal's extended hand and then turned to help Jenna out. They all went up the steps together.

'Mrs Harper and her daughter,' said Cathal to the receptionist. 'The man who was brought in earlier. Building accident.'

'Oh yes!'

The sudden flash of sympathy in the woman's eyes was unmistakable. Sally moistened her lips with the tip of her tongue. It wasn't Frank. It just wasn't.

The receptionist spoke into a mike and a couple of minutes later a young doctor arrived. He smiled at them but, like Siobhán Farrell's smile earlier, it was professional.

'Your husband is stable,' he told Sally. 'He has a number of injuries – ribs, shoulder and legs as well as cuts and contusions. And he suffered a blow to the head.'

'It's not my husband.' Sally was quite definite. 'Frank's away. It can't be him. He's not injured and there's nothing wrong with him.'

'Shall we go down?' The doctor indicated the corridor.

Sally and Jenna, accompanied by Cathal, followed him. He stopped outside the window of a small room. Mother and daughter looked at the bruised and battered figure in the bed, surrounded by drips and tubes, a nurse sitting beside him.

'Oh, Mum,' said Jenna, and fainted.

Iona had switched off the television and was staring at the blank screen when the phone rang. She jumped on it before seeing the caller ID and her voice was breathless and anxious.

'Hello?'

'It's me.'

'Oh.' The anticipation left her as she recognised her sister's voice.

'Is he home yet?'

'No.'

'Are you still worried?'

'Of course I'm still worried!' snapped Iona. 'It's nearly eleven. He wouldn't do this to me, Lauren, you know he wouldn't. He'd call if something had happened.'

'And you've called him?'

'Give me a break!' Iona could feel her anxiety level rising. 'Yes, I bloody called him. I've called him loads of times but I keep getting his bloody message-minder.'

'Look, if something had happened to him you'd have heard by now,' said Lauren comfortingly. 'That's the thing about life these days. Communication is instant. They'd have found out who you were and called you.'

'Not if he was kidnapped,' said Iona.

'Kidnapped?'

'Well, why not?' she said, articulating her most recent thoughts about the situation. 'He's a successful businessman, more or less. Maybe there's something weird—'

'Get a grip, Iona,' said Lauren. She paused for a moment. 'Is he into anything dodgy? You know, businesswise?'

'No!' cried Iona. 'He isn't. Nothing. He's just an ordinary bloke.'

'So why would anyone kidnap him?'

'I don't know!' But, Iona told herself, Frank being kidnapped made a whole heap more sense to her than Frank leaving her of his own accord.

'Do you want me to come round?' asked Lauren.

Iona wiped at her eyes. There was nothing Lauren could do. But she didn't want to be on her own.

'Yes,' she said eventually.

'OK I'll be there in twenty minutes. But if the fucker comes home, ring me on my mobile. I don't want to arrive just as you two are having the biggest bust-up of your married life.'

'Sure,' said Iona wearily.

'I hope you do have to ring me,' said Lauren gently. 'And I bet there's some perfectly rational explanation.'

'I bet,' said Iona, even though she couldn't think what it could possibly be.

She paced around the tiny living room, willing him to come home, squeezing her eyes tightly closed and visualising his car pulling up in front of the house. But when she finally did hear an engine she knew that it wasn't Frank's car. The sound of the door as it closed wasn't the familiar thunk she was used to either. The doorbell rang.

'Hi,' said Lauren.

'Hello.'

'So, no sign of him?'

Iona shook her head. Lauren walked into the house and took off her short fake-fur jacket, draping it over the back of the black leather sofa.

'Would you like some tea?' asked Iona.

'I'll make it.'

'No,' Iona told her sister. 'I have to do something. You sit down. Maybe by the time I've brewed it up he'll be back.' She walked rapidly into the kitchen.

Where are you? she muttered under her breath. Where in God's name are you, and what the hell are you doing and why are you putting me through this?

When she came back into the living room with the tea she saw that Lauren had switched on the TV but had left the sound mute.

'I was looking for the late news,' said Lauren. 'But I think we missed it.'

'I checked the internet again,' Iona said. 'There was nothing new on it.'

'Have you rung hospitals?'

Iona looked at her unhappily. 'I tried. But they wanted to know when he'd been admitted. I said I didn't know, that I thought he might have been in an accident. They told me to call the police, that they couldn't give out information to me.'

'And did you?'

Iona shook her head. 'I was afraid.'

'Maybe you should.'

'Where should I call?'

'What's your local station?'

Iona shrugged. 'I'm not sure. Kevin Street, I think.'

Lauren picked up the telephone directory and looked up the number. 'Will I?'

Iona took a deep breath. 'I suppose you'd better.'

∽

Kevin Street was a busy station, but Garda Keith Carew answered the phone quickly.

'Missing person?' he said. 'How long has he been missing?'

'Well, just tonight,' said Lauren. 'But he's a really punctual person normally and he's not answering his phone. It's totally out of character for him and so we were wondering if he might have been in an accident.'

'Do you have a car reg?' asked Keith.

'What's the reg?' Lauren turned to Iona, who told her. She repeated it to Keith, who tapped the details into the computer. Rather surprisingly, because the system was cumbersome and overloaded, information flashed up almost immediately. He frowned.

'Would you repeat that?'

Lauren repeated the registration.

'And the missing person's name is?'

'Frank Harper,' said Lauren.

'Am I speaking to Mrs Harper?'

'No,' said Lauren. 'I'm her sister, Lauren Brannock.'

'And her address is?'

Lauren felt herself grow tense as she reeled off Iona's address. She'd expected the guard to dismiss her but he seemed to be taking her seriously. And now she was beginning to feel a knot of worry on her sister's behalf.

Keith continued to check the information he'd received as Lauren held the line. There was a Frank Harper listed as an accident victim, although in this case due to a building collapse. But he'd been identified through his mobile phone and a car registration. The car was registered to an address in Bray. Yet the number was exactly the same.

'I'm going to make some enquiries,' he told Lauren. 'I'll get back to you. You're at the address in the Liberties now?'

'Yes,' she said.

'I'll be back to you as soon as possible,' said Keith.

He hung up and stared at the computer screen for a couple of seconds. Normally he wouldn't have bothered with Lauren's enquiry straight away. Frank Harper hadn't been missing for long enough, and in his experience most blokes who didn't come home on time had simply gone on the piss with their mates and were afraid to call to say where they were in case they got an earful from their wives. They preferred to roll home out of their tree with drink and suffer the consequences then, rather than have their night's drinking ruined by an ear-bashing. But there was something odd about this. He tapped his teeth with his pen for a couple of seconds. Then he picked up the phone.

∽

'Well?' demanded Iona.

'He's checking it out. He's going to get back to us.'

'But there wasn't anything he knew about?'

Lauren shook her head. 'He's making enquiries.'

Iona swallowed hard. 'That sounds terribly official. I don't need it to be official. I just want to know what's happened to him.'

Lauren said nothing.

'Something must have happened. Something terrible. He'd never leave me worrying like this—' Suddenly Iona burst into a fit of crying while Lauren put her arms around her and hugged her as tightly as she could.

∽

At the hospital, Jenna and Sally were drinking the hot, sweet tea provided by the staff after Jenna's faint. A nurse sat in the small room with them.

'Is he going to die?' Jenna looked up at her mother. 'Is Dad going to die?'

Sally glanced at the nurse and looked into her daughter's eyes. 'I don't know,' she said.

'You didn't think it would be him,' said Jenna accusingly. 'You were sure.'

'It shouldn't be him,' Sally said tightly. 'He shouldn't be here.' She picked at the waxed cup of tea. 'He said he was late and he had another meeting and he wouldn't be home till tomorrow. So he shouldn't have been on the Ardallen road.'

'Maybe he finished early after all and decided to come home.' A sob caught in Jenna's throat. 'He didn't want to be away from us and so he rushed back anyway.'

Sally said nothing. She'd thought the same, wondered whether Frank had guessed at her irritation over all the days and nights he spent away from them, wondered whether that had made him decide to come home unexpectedly, wondering if it was all her fault.

The young doctor came back into the room.

'We're moving your husband now, Mrs Harper,' he said. 'An ambulance will take him to Dublin. They'll be better able to look after him at one of the major hospitals.'

Sally nodded. 'Can both of us go with him?'

'I don't know,' said the doctor. 'I'll ask the ambulance crew.'

'Why don't you and Jenna wait in reception, Sally?' suggested the nurse.

Sally nodded again. She wasn't used to doing what people told her all the time. But right now she didn't seem to have any choice.

Chapter 8

Siobhán hadn't exactly forgotten about Sally and Jenna Harper when she went back to Bray but she had immersed herself in work again, completing the money-laundering file and opening another, so that when she answered the phone to Keith Carew from Kevin Street garda station she wasn't thinking about car registrations and building collapses, but about her imminent court appearance with regard to a domestic abuse case. She hated going to court and was always afraid that she would sound uncertain about her evidence simply because she was nervous about speaking in public. So when the phone rang she was going through her notes again in order to get everything exactly right. Now, though, she listened with increasing concern as Keith talked and the court case was instantly pushed to the back of her mind.

'So, let me get this straight,' she said when he'd finished. 'There's a woman on the phone saying that she's Iona Harper's sister and that Iona's husband is missing. And the car reg matches that of the Frank Harper in the Ardallen incident. Only *that* Frank Harper has already been identified by Sally Harper. I know this because I was at Sally Harper's house earlier and one of my guys drove Mrs Harper and her daughter to the hospital.'

'Yeah, well . . .' Kevin sighed. 'This other woman seemed very definite about it.'

'Two Mrs Harpers?' Siobhán sounded sceptical. 'Don't you think that's just plain crazy?'

'Hell, Siobhán, you know that in this job everything's crazy,' said Kevin. 'God knows what the true situation is, but the current bottom line appears to be that we have a seriously injured man and two women who seem to be connected to him. One is definitely his wife. The other . . .'

She sighed. 'Let me call the Ardallen guys.'

'Great,' said Kevin. 'Then let us know what to do.'

Siobhán hung up and then spoke to Tim Shanahan who had, theoretically at least, finished his shift. He whistled when she told him the situation.

'My guys are at the hospital with the Harpers now,' he told her. 'I'll contact them, see what's going on. Then I'll get back to you.'

Siobhán hung up again. So much of police work was waiting for people to come back to you. And so much of it was not really liking what they told you when they did.

Tim called her back within ten minutes.

'We have a problem,' he said. 'The Harpers are on their way to Dublin with Frank. They left without his stuff, though. Including a mobile phone.'

'You've already double-checked his identity from his mobile phone,' said Siobhán.

'A different mobile phone,' said Tim grimly. 'This one was in his pocket and, amazingly, wasn't damaged. When we switched it on, we found it had a different home number, even though it's also registered to Mr Frank Harper. It's the number of the other woman claiming to be Mrs Harper.'

'You've got to be kidding me.'

'Nope,' said Tim. 'We've got one injured man with, apparently, two wives.'

'Holy shit,' said Siobhán.

'He's from Bray,' Tim said. 'It's probably your case.'

'I don't want a mess like this,' protested Siobhán. 'I'm really busy.' Tim said nothing and eventually she groaned softly. 'Oh, all right. I'll go and see the second Mrs Harper. But I can't see this being anything but a flippin' disaster for everyone.'

'Me neither.' Tim's words were heartfelt. And he was very

glad that the issue of the injured man's wives was out of his hands.

⌒

It took Siobhán nearly forty-five minutes to reach Iona's tiny house in the Liberties. She stood outside the door for a moment, gathering her thoughts. This Mrs Harper might just be calling herself by the man's name, she reminded herself, and might not be married at all. Or maybe that was the situation with the first Mrs Harper. After all, they had no idea who was who exactly. But no matter what the tangled relationship might turn out to be, the immediate issue was that the man Iona Harper was living with was still the man who'd been seriously injured in the Ardallen building collapse, and that she was going to have to break the news to her. She sighed deeply and rang the bell.

The door opened. An attractive woman with auburn hair cascading around her shoulders, and dark, soulful eyes answered the door.

'Mrs Harper?' asked Siobhán, wishing that she didn't always feel so inadequate when faced with really beautiful women.

Lauren shook her head. 'That's my sister, Iona. I'm Lauren Brannock. My sister is Iona Brannock but she's married to Frank Harper.'

'I'm Detective Sergeant Siobhán Farrell from Bray garda station,' Siobhán told her. 'I'm here about your sister's call regarding a missing person.'

'I called you,' said Lauren. 'At least, I called Kevin Street. Why the hell have they sent someone all the way from Bray? That seems incredibly inefficient when they're only round the corner! My sister is inside.'

'Can I come in?'

Lauren hesitated. 'Is everything all right?'

'Can I come in?' repeated Siobhán.

Lauren stood back and motioned her into the room. Iona looked up as she entered. Her huge dark eyes were now ringed with red and her normally pale, smooth cheeks were roughened by rubbing with a tissue.

'Mrs Harper?' said Siobhán.

She nodded. 'But I call myself by my own name.' She repeated what Lauren had told her. 'Iona Brannock.'

Siobhán nodded. She wished Cathal Rothery was with her for support. She took a deep breath and began to speak. 'You reported your husband missing earlier,' she said. 'And you feared he might have been in an accident. You gave my colleagues the registration of his car and we've checked it out.'

Iona suddenly felt light-headed. She knew by the tone of the other woman's voice that they'd found something out. And she knew it wasn't good.

'The thing is, Iona,' said Siobhán, 'we had a report of a man injured in a building collapse today.'

Iona nodded. 'Ardallen. It was on the internet. It talked about someone being injured but that absolutely couldn't have been Frank. He had no reason to be in Ardallen. It's not on his route home.'

'Maybe not,' said Siobhán. 'When this man was taken to hospital to be treated he was actually identified by someone else. They identified him as a Mr Frank Harper.'

'It can't be my Frank,' protested Iona. 'He wouldn't even know anyone in Ardallen. That's near Bray, isn't it? We don't have any friends in Bray.'

'Since then, though,' continued Siobhán, 'and because we saw a few anomalies on the system, we've looked at this a little bit more closely. He was identified by his wife, Mrs Sally Harper. The car registration that Mrs Harper agreed was theirs is the same one you gave my colleague tonight. It also seems that Mr Harper had a mobile phone with him that has your number as his home number.'

Iona stared at her uncomprehendingly. 'So what are you telling me?'

'Well, Mrs Harper – Ms Brannock – it looks awfully like you and another woman are both talking about the same man.'

This time it was Lauren who spoke. 'But that doesn't make sense,' she protested. 'Frank and Iona are married. They've been married for the last four years.'

'And from what we found out earlier,' said Siobhán evenly, 'the other woman who calls herself Mrs Harper has been married to him for eighteen years.'

This time it was Iona who fainted.

When she came to, she was lying on the sofa. Lauren was beside her while Siobhán Farrell stood motionless behind them.

'I feel sick,' said Iona.

'Have a sip.' Lauren held a tumbler of water to her sister's lips. Iona sipped it cautiously then began to sit up.

'Don't,' said Lauren. 'Wait for a minute or two. You've had a shock.'

Iona tried to pin down the flurry of thoughts that were chasing around in her head. She tried to focus on the fact that Frank – her Frank, no matter what anyone else was trying to imply – was seriously injured. She should be with him. He'd want her there. She struggled to sit up again.

'I need to get to the hospital,' she told Lauren. Her sister looked uncomfortably at Siobhán, who shrugged helplessly. 'Look, I know you all think there's something weird going on here. So do I. But the point is, I need to see Frank. If he's hurt, I need to be there.'

'The thing is, Iona,' said Siobhán gently, 'the other woman is there at the moment.'

'I don't give a toss whether she's there or not!' snapped Iona. 'She's made some kind of mistake. She's obviously a complete crackpot. I want to go and I want to go now.'

'We can't stop you, of course,' said Siobhán.

'Of course you can't.' Iona got unsteadily to her feet. 'Lauren, you'll drive me, won't you?'

'Sure.'

'We'll have to get in touch with you again, Ms Brannock,' said Siobhán. 'To sort this situation out.'

'I'll sort it out when I get to the hospital.' Iona's voice was getting stronger and grimmer by the second. 'I'll fix this woman, whoever she is. I'm going to get dressed.' She walked out of the room and up the stairs.

Lauren looked uneasily at Siobhán. 'What's the story really?' she asked urgently.

'We're honestly not sure,' Siobhán replied. 'This other woman says she's married to Frank Harper. Your sister says so too. Both of them can't be right. Maybe it's a case of two different men and it's just a horrendous mix-up. It could be one of life's extraordinary coincidences.' But Siobhán's expression indicated that she clearly didn't believe in coincidences.

'None of this makes sense,' Lauren told her. 'Iona and Frank were married in a perfectly legal ceremony. I've seen the video! There was a pastor and witnesses and everything. It was lovely!'

'There's no point in everyone getting into a state until we work out the exact situation,' said Siobhán comfortingly. 'Best thing is to get your sister to the hospital . . . but try and keep her out of the way of the other Mrs Harper.'

'Easier said than done, don't you think?' muttered Lauren as Iona came back into the room.

꩜

Lauren rang Myles as they drove to the hospital, merely telling him that it looked like Frank had been injured in an accident and they were off to see what the story was. Meanwhile Iona sat silently in the car, staring unseeingly out through the windscreen.

The drive seemed to take for ever and at the same time be over in an instant. Iona's heart was hammering in her chest as they walked into the hospital and spoke to the man behind the reception desk.

'Oh yes,' he said as he consulted the screen in front of him. 'Mr Harper is in surgery at the moment. You can wait . . .' He hesitated. 'Actually, I need to speak to the sister in charge of that area.'

'Why?' demanded Iona. 'I need to see him right now.'

'You can't see him immediately,' said the receptionist. 'As I said, he's in surgery.'

'Well, where's that other woman?' asked Iona. 'The one pretending to be me? Seems to me I don't see anyone else hanging round here waiting. Have you let her in to see him? You know she's crazy, don't you? You know you shouldn't let her anywhere near him?'

'Io, please,' said Lauren. 'Let him call whoever's in charge.'

Iona glared at Lauren and then shrugged. But while the receptionist dialled a number, she suddenly ran away from the desk and bounded up a nearby flight of stairs.

'Oh, shit!' Lauren looked after Iona's fleeing figure. 'Io – come back!' She glanced at the receptionist, who looked flabbergasted by the turn of events. 'Shit,' said Lauren again. She took off her high-heeled shoes and ran after her sister. There was no sign of her on the first floor. Then she heard Iona's voice shouting Frank's name over and over.

She chased after the sound even as doors were opened and nurses appeared in the corridors. She ran up and down stairs so that she lost track completely of where she was. Finally she caught up with Iona, who was being restrained by a security guard. She'd found the waiting area. And the other Mrs Harper.

Lauren's first thought was that Sally Harper looked old. Much, much older than Iona, although that might have been because the other woman was unnaturally pale, with dark smudges beneath her eyes. Her chestnut and gold hair was escaping from an ageing plait and her entire body seemed to be collapsing in on itself. A much younger girl stood beside Sally, quite obviously her daughter. She too was deathly white.

'This is the woman who identified Frank!' cried Iona. 'She's obviously completely off her head!'

Sally looked at Iona in total bewilderment.

'I've no idea who you are or what you're talking about,' she said, her voice shaking. 'I'm here because my husband was involved in a major accident and—'

'*Your* husband!' Iona interupted her. '*Your* husband! You stupid, stupid woman, you've got it all wrong – you're talking about *my* husband.'

Sally shook her head.

'Don't you think I wish that I was?' she said tautly. 'Someone's made a terrible mix-up here and I'm sorry that you're in the middle of it, but I know my own husband . . .' Her voice broke, 'even in the state he's in now.'

'You're on the wrong end of the mix-up,' Iona told her. 'I know that because the police came and told me that Frank was involved in an accident and he was brought here and—'

'Frank?' Sally stared at her.

'My husband,' said Iona.

'It's a mix-up with names,' said Sally. 'It has to be. And like I said, I'm sorry that you're here and your husband has been in an accident, but I know it's my Frank because I've seen him.'

Iona clenched and unclenched her fists in frustration.

'You're wrong,' she said. 'I don't know why you're so insistent, but you're wrong.'

'My mum knows my dad,' said Jenna anxiously. 'And so do I. And I don't know why you're here talking rubbish while he . . .' She swallowed frantically. 'You're a horrible, horrible woman to do this.'

Iona glanced swiftly at the teenage girl and took a deep breath before turning back to Sally.

'You think I want to be here?' she demanded. 'I was at home waiting for him but he didn't show up and he's been in an accident and I know, I just know it's him.'

'But you haven't actually seen him yet,' said Jenna tightly. She held on to her mother's arm. 'We have. I don't know who you are, but you've some nerve coming here and upsetting me and my mum when my dad is so sick.'

'I'll tell you who I am,' said Iona heatedly. 'I'm Iona Harper. I'm married to Frank Harper. And I'm here to see him.'

The two women and the young girl stared wordlessly at each other. They were still staring at each other when a doctor arrived and introduced himself as John Carroll.

'I believe there's a certain amount of confusion about Mr Harper's identity,' he said.

'No there isn't,' snapped both Iona and Sally at the same time.

'I'm afraid there is.' Dr Carroll looked at them sternly. 'But screaming and shouting in my hospital won't help matters. You're distressing yourselves and my patients as well as my staff.'

The rage and shock suddenly left Iona's body. She swayed slightly and the doctor took her by the arm.

'Sit down,' he said gently.

Iona sank into a seat and started to shake.

'I can't breathe,' she said suddenly. 'I can't . . . I can't . . .'

A nurse who was standing nearby disappeared for a moment and returned with a white paper bag which she handed to Iona.

'Breathe into this,' she said. 'Take your time. You're fine. You are really.'

Lauren watched anxiously as Iona put the bag over her nose and mouth. Sally and Jenna watched too.

'Attention-seeker,' muttered Jenna.

Sally squeezed her daughter's arm.

'Dad wouldn't have anything to do with someone like her,' whispered Jenna. 'You know how he is about people getting dramatic about things. He hates it.'

'I know,' said Sally. She pulled her coat more tightly around her.

'She's lying,' Jenna said aloud.

'I wish I was.' Iona lifted her head from the paper bag and looked at Sally and Jenna.

'You haven't even seen him yet.' Sally repeated Jenna's words of earlier. 'You've come in here and created a great big fuss and scared me and my daughter, who, I have to remind you, is just a teenager – and you haven't even seen him.'

'Nobody can see him right now,' said the doctor. 'He's in surgery and likely to be there for some time yet.'

'When he comes out . . . can I see him then?' asked Iona.

'Of course,' said the doctor.

Sally felt herself grow tense. She didn't want this other woman sitting in the hospital at the same time as her, waiting for news of Frank. She had no right to be here, intruding on their worry and their grief. And Jenna was right. Frank wouldn't be interested in a drama queen like her. He liked his women to be calm and measured, like her. With a bit of spark in the bedroom, of course. But not this public hysteria, this over-the-top sobbing and breathlessness.

'You don't have to look at me like that,' said Iona.

'Like what?'

'Something the cat dragged in,' Iona told her. 'You have no right to sit there and look down on me.'

'I'm trying not to look at you at all.'

Sally closed her eyes. Despite her certainty that Frank wouldn't be interested in Iona, the fact was that the woman was here. And, thought Sally as she peeped through her lashes, she wasn't an unattractive woman either. Not pretty, of course, but she could see why some men might find her worth the effort. What she couldn't see was the possibility of any relationship between her and Frank. But what if there was? Obviously she couldn't possibly be telling the truth about being married to him, but maybe there was something . . . There couldn't be, though. There just couldn't be. Frank was a faithful man. She knew that.

'I realise this is distressing for everyone.' Hearing Lauren's voice made Sally open her eyes properly again. 'And I do understand how you feel, Mrs Harper—'

'*I'm* Mrs Harper,' said Iona. 'You know that, Lauren.'

Jenna reached out and opened her mother's handbag.

'Yeah, well, what's this then?' she demanded as she produced Sally's driver's licence and handed it to Iona.

She blinked at it a number of times as she read the description of Sally Harper. Then she opened her own bag and took out her licence, which she handed to Sally.

'Iona Brannock is what this says.' Sally refolded it and put it in its plastic cover. 'It means nothing.'

78

'That's my maiden name.'

'Still don't see anything to do with Harper on it.' Jenna sounded triumphant.

'My sister *did* marry a man called Frank Harper,' said Lauren. 'I know you think that she's wrong about the man here tonight, but she's telling you the truth about that.'

'Look,' Sally told her, 'the police came and told me about the accident. I drove to the hospital with them before they transferred Frank here. I recognised my own husband, for heaven's sake.' She turned to Iona. 'I'm really sorry if you've been misled, but I can honestly tell you that the man in surgery is Frank Harper and he's my husband. And you should be relieved because it's my husband who's in there on life support, and wherever the hell yours is he's better off than that! Frank is seriously, seriously injured and I have to stand here and listen to your drivel when I should be giving him my support . . .' Her voice broke and she rubbed her eyes with the back of her hand.

'And I'd give anything for you to be right!' cried Iona. 'But if it's not my Frank, then how come he has a mobile phone with my number on it and how come I gave the police the registration of the car he was driving? And how come I'm here at all?'

'Are you his . . . mistress?' Sally could feel herself growing light-headed again. 'Are you having an affair with him? Is that it?'

'Don't be so bloody silly!' cried Iona. 'D'you really think I'd come haring out here if I was having an affair with him? I'm not. I'm married to him. I married him four years ago in Barbados and it was the happiest day of our lives.'

'This isn't getting us anywhere.'

John Carroll was tired. He really didn't want to have to cope with this scene but he had no alternative. 'I'm told that Mr Harper will be out of surgery in about half an hour or so. At that point I will take you' – he turned to Iona – 'to see him. You won't be able to go into the room but you can see him through a window.'

'Why?' demanded Sally. 'I've already seen him. It's my Frank.'

'Please, Mrs Harper,' said John evenly. 'There's clearly some kind of mix-up here. Don't you think the best thing is to sort it out rather than have everyone getting more and more uptight about things?'

'There's no mix-up except in this woman's head,' said Sally firmly. 'But if it makes you happy, Jenna and I will wait and find out exactly what her problem is. Because she has the problem, not us.'

'No I fucking don't,' snapped Iona.

'Please,' said John. 'Can't you just be calm until we sort everything out? Believe me, the hospital wants things clarified just as much as you do. Can I get you all some tea, perhaps?'

'I'd love a cup of tea,' said Lauren feelingly.

When the tea arrived, laced with sugar, Iona wrapped her hands around one of the waxed cups and sipped the scalding, too-sweet liquid. It burned the roof of her mouth and the tip of her tongue, but she didn't care. She stared unseeingly in front of her as she tried to figure out what the hell was going on. How was it that only this morning the worst thing that could have happened in her life was that she wasn't pregnant? And now, less than twenty-four hours later, everything had been turned upside down. Frank hadn't come home like he'd promised. A man was in surgery, seriously injured, and all the indications pointed to it being her husband, her Frank. She didn't want it to be him, but everything so far made her believe that it was. Everything, of course, except for the fact that she was now sitting in a waiting room with another woman who was also claiming to be his wife.

Iona sipped her tea again and peeped over the top of the cup at Sally and Jenna. Not only was there a woman claiming to be his wife, but there was also the glowering girl who claimed to be his daughter. Iona simply couldn't believe that Frank had a daughter. He'd talked so movingly and lovingly about wanting a child of his own with her that it was difficult to accept that he was a father already. She simply couldn't see how he'd kept that from her. And it had been Frank, not Iona, who'd really wanted the baby. At least he'd been the one to suggest it, even though she'd then come to agree with him that the time was right. He'd talked about his need for a family, but why did he need a family with her if he already had one? Why had he made her feel that what would happen between them would be unique and wonderful when it couldn't be? Right now, Iona couldn't figure whether she was more upset about the daughter than the wife.

She'd never even suspected that there might be another woman in Frank's life. How could there be when he was so busy and when their own lives together had been so full of happiness and togetherness? And what was it about them that kept him with them? The woman was nothing to write home about, with her lank hair and tired eyes. The girl . . . Iona swallowed hard as she looked at the girl. The problem was that, although she was clearly Sally's daughter, she also looked like Frank. Until now Iona had tried to push that thought to the back of her mind, but there couldn't really be any doubt. Admittedly her hair was a dark shade of auburn, while Frank's was dark brown sprinkled with grey. But her brown eyes were Frank's eyes, not just in their colour but in the way they looked out at the world. Almost fearless, but with a hint of hidden depths. Iona had been beguiled by Frank's saturnine good looks and brown eyes. She could see that same attractiveness in Jenna.

But how? she wondered. How could it all be? Why would Frank have married her when he had this family already? Was the marriage unhappy? In which case, why hadn't he divorced Sally? And, even worse, why had he been so keen to start a family with her when Jenna was living proof that he'd been down that road before?

Her head was beginning to spin. She couldn't get a firm grasp of the conflicting thoughts and emotions whirling through her mind. She felt as though she was going crazy.

⌒

It was nearly forty minutes later before the surgeon came to tell them that Frank was now in the recovery room.

'Will he be all right?' Jenna asked anxiously.

'It's hard to say at this point.' Sean McManus kept his voice deliberately neutral. 'He had a lot of injuries and we were concerned about his head—'

'Is he brain-damaged?' asked Sally, rigid with fear.

'Like I said, it's difficult to assess at this point. But we've done everything we possibly can.'

'Brain-damaged.' The words left Iona's mouth in a whisper. 'He can't be. Not Frank.'

Sally and Jenna hugged each other. Lauren put her arm around Iona's shoulders.

'Would you like to come along?' John Carroll turned to Iona, who nodded wordlessly. She stumbled as she stood up and Lauren put her arm around her again.

'I don't want it to be him,' whispered Iona in anguish as they walked along the corridor. 'I want it to be that other woman's husband. I want to be the one who's made the mistake.'

Lauren and the doctors exchanged glances over the top of Iona's head. This is not good, thought Lauren, not good at all.

They stopped in front of a window. Iona moved close and looked through. The figure in the bed was swathed in bandages and surrounded by tubes and wires. But it was undoubtedly Frank. Her Frank. She felt a tear slide slowly down her cheek.

'It's him,' she whispered raggedly. She pressed her hands against the window. 'Oh Frank.'

Lauren looked at Dr Carroll. 'What's the prognosis?' she asked.

'Currently Mr Harper is in a coma,' he replied. 'Until he comes out of it we really have no idea of the extent of the damage.'

'But there is damage?' Lauren asked the question while Iona continued to stare at Frank. 'To his brain? To his head?'

'It may be minor,' replied the doctor, 'but we have no way of knowing at this point.' He shrugged noncommittally. 'There's some swelling to the brain which obviously we need to go down as quickly as possible. Mr Harper may be left with nothing more than a severe headache. But we simply can't be certain.'

Lauren rubbed the bridge of her nose. She looked at Iona, who was crying softly.

'Best thing is to go home,' said Dr Carroll. 'Get some rest. Call us in the morning.'

'What if . . . what if something happens during the night?'

Lauren asked anxiously, at the same time thinking that it was already closer to morning than night.

'Right now Mr Harper is stable and on life support. Of course we'd contact you immediately if anything changes, but that's unlikely at the moment.'

'What about the other woman?'

The doctor looked uncomfortable. 'We'll have to contact her too. It's a most unusual situation.'

'Yes,' said Lauren. 'It is.' She put her arm around Iona's shoulder. 'Come on, sis,' she said. 'Let's go.'

'I can't go.' Iona turned her tear-stained face towards her. 'I can't leave him like this.'

'You need some rest,' said Lauren. 'Come home with me, get some sleep and we'll come back in the morning.'

'What about her?' demanded Iona. 'Is she going home too?'

'We've made the same recommendations,' said the doctor.

'But people stay, don't they?' demanded Iona. 'You give them places to sleep.'

'We don't have anywhere for you to stay,' he told her. 'Either of you. I really do recommend you go home and get some rest. I doubt there's any likelihood of Mr Harper regaining consciousness for at least another twelve hours. So you're not doing yourself any favours by staying here. You need rest, you really do.'

'He's right, Io,' said Lauren. 'We'll come back tomorrow.'

Iona's shoulders sagged. 'All right,' she said dully. 'If that's what you think.'

Lauren sighed with relief. Dr Carroll led them away from Frank's room but in a different direction to that from which they'd come. Before they left the hospital he repeated the promise to contact them if there was any change.

'Make sure she gets some rest.' He handed Lauren a tiny envelope. 'Valium,' he said. 'Try and get her to take it.'

Lauren nodded and ushered Iona along the corridor and out of the hospital. A faint promise of dawn was lightening the eastern sky as they drove out of the grounds.

'It's all a horrible mistake,' said Iona. 'That woman didn't know what she was talking about. Stupid fat cow.'

'I know,' said Lauren comfortingly. 'We'll get it sorted. Don't worry.'

'I can't help worrying.' Iona leaned her head against the passenger window. 'He's my husband and he's in a coma and another woman thinks she's married to him. Of course I can't bloody well help worrying.'

Chapter 9

Sally and Jenna got a taxi from the hospital to Bray. They too had been told that it would be a good idea to go home and get some sleep and that they would be contacted immediately if there was any change in Frank's condition.

Sally hadn't wanted to leave. When John Carroll had come back to her in the waiting area and told her that Iona had identified Frank as being her husband, her first thought had been to rush to the recovery room and shake Frank awake to find out what the hell was going on. She still couldn't believe it was true. And yet as Iona had walked away to see Frank, she'd been overcome with a deep sense of dread that it was true, that Iona wasn't the complete flake that Sally wanted to believe she was.

The doctor had brought more tea even more liberally sugared and she and Jenna had drunk it in silence. Sally was worried about Jenna, who hadn't said a word since John Carroll had confirmed Iona's identification of Frank, but she couldn't think of a single comforting thing to say to her. What was the point in the usual assurances that everything would be all right when clearly everything was all wrong? What could she say to Jenna that would in any way help matters? So she sat and sipped the tea and worried about what the hell she was going to do now.

Jenna, too, found it impossible to focus on the reality of the situation. All she kept thinking about was that Frank was her father and she loved him and he'd always been the one on her side in an argument and that she'd thought she'd known him but that she obviously hadn't known him at all. And she simply couldn't accept that the dark-haired woman (who looked light-years younger than her mother and was so completely different to her in just about every way) and the father that she loved were in some way connected. Not in some way, she kept telling herself. They're supposed to be married. Which means he lives with her too. And sleeps with her. At this point Jenna gagged and suddenly the nurse who'd been hovering around the waiting area was beside her with the same sort of paper bag she'd given Iona earlier and holding it up to her mouth.

Jenna made a conscious effort not to be sick. She didn't want them to think that she was so upset by everything that she would throw up. And she didn't want to worry Sally any more than her mother was worried already.

It was after the gagging incident that both the nurse and John Carroll suggested that Sally and Jenna go home and get some rest.

By the time they were deposited outside their neat semi-detached house, morning had almost arrived. The birds were already singing in the sycamore trees that lined the road and, as they got out of the taxi, Sally could hear the shrill of Steve and Philly McCormack's alarm clock going off next door.

Jenna hadn't spoken on the way back from the hospital. In fact she'd slept for some of the journey back, her head lolling from side to side with the movement of the taxi. Now, in the kitchen, she looked wearily at Sally.

'That woman is wrong,' she said. 'Isn't she?'

'Of course she is,' said Sally as robustly as she could.

'Her driving licence . . . she has nothing to prove that she knows Dad at all. So why is she saying that stuff?' Jenna could feel her voice rise with anxiety. 'She can't really be married to him. She can't! Why would she do this when Dad is . . . is . . .' Suddenly she began to cry, short sobs at first and then an almost uncontrollable spasm of tears.

Sally put her arms around her.

'Sssh,' she whispered softly. 'We'll fix things, Jen. Don't worry.'

'But . . . but how can we fix things?' Jenna raised her tear-streaked face to her mother. 'He looked so awful, Mum. So

86

helpless. And all those monitors and tubes coming out of him . . . and her screaming and shouting and everything.'

'I know, I know.' Sally felt a fraud trying to comfort Jenna when she was so scared herself. 'She's got it all wrong. We both know that. So it's just a question of sorting things out. And as for the tubes and stuff – well, that's what it's like when people are in intensive care. You know that, honey. It looks really scary but the doctors are wonderful and, well, in a few days, please God, he'll be back to himself.'

'But he's hurt his head.'

Sally swallowed hard. 'Yes. But your dad is a really strong person. He'll fight. He'll get better.'

Jenna sniffed.

'Come on,' said Sally. 'Let's get you to bed.'

Jenna nodded wearily. Both of them went upstairs. Sally stayed in her daughter's room until she was satisfied that Jenna had really fallen asleep. Then she went into her own bedroom and sat on the edge of the bed, feeling as though she was in some crazy parallel universe. Suddenly she felt the newly familiar heave in her stomach. She propelled herself off the bed and into the bathroom. The sound of the dawn chorus echoed through the windows as she was sick into the sink.

She put her hand into her pocket and took out the small plastic packet containing the Valium tablets the doctor had given her. Somehow she didn't think pregnant women should take Valium, even though a part of her would have loved to swallow the tablets and drift into oblivion. And she really wanted to take Panadol for her pounding head too. Reluctantly, and despite knowing that she really wasn't supposed to dispose of tablets in this way, she threw the Valium down the toilet and flushed it.

She tiptoed out of her room and across the hallway. Frank's home office was in the tiny spare bedroom. She opened the door gently.

The office was as neat as always. A self-assembly desk, pushed against the wall, was the main item of furniture. A four-shelf book-stand filled with technical manuals and blue plastic ring-binders took up a second wall. Beside that was a chrome stand with a number of wire baskets which contained a variety of lighting equipment.

Sally sat at the desk. Frank's closed laptop computer was neatly placed in the middle of it. She hadn't noticed the fact that he'd left without it, although he didn't always take it with him. She opened it and pressed the power button. While it whirred and clicked into action she opened the drawers in the pedestal beneath the desk. The top drawer contained pens and markers as well as a stapler and sellotape. The second was filled with stationery. The third contained a number of folders. Sally took them out and spread them on the desk in front of her. She thought there might be a clue in the folders, an explanation for what had happened tonight. She wasn't sure what sort of explanation there could be, but she wanted to find one. However, the folders merely contained letters to clients and maintenance contracts for installations he'd done. There was nothing at all that said anything about a girl called Iona who thought that Frank was her husband.

The computer was password-protected. Sally looked at the log-in screen in front of her. She had no idea of Frank's password. She typed in his name and, when it rejected that, tried her own name, followed by Jenna's, then the names of the various pets they'd had over the years: their dog, Dimwit; their rabbit, Connie; Romulus and Remus, the pair of hamsters which Jenna had brought home from school because someone had to look after them during the holidays and which had freaked Frank out. Each time the screen beeped at her and asked her to try again.

She tried a selection of birthdays and anniversaries. But none of those were the password either. She stared at the screen helplessly. Then, tentatively, she typed in the name Iona.

She was more relieved than she'd imagined when it beeped at her again. She wasn't sure how she would have reacted if Iona had been the password. She closed the computer again and leaned her head on the desk. And although she hadn't believed that she could, she fell asleep.

With the help of the Valium (which she'd at first refused to take but which Lauren had later tricked her into swallowing by telling her it was one of her herbal remedies), Iona, too, was asleep. In fact she'd fallen asleep almost as soon as she'd lain down on the double bed in Lauren's guest bedroom. Lauren had stayed with her, sitting on the edge of the bed, until she was certain that her sister really was out for the count. Then she walked as silently as she could into her own room.

Myles turned to her as she got into bed.

'What the hell is going on?' he asked.

Lauren was so tired she found it difficult to talk. She knew, as she related the night's events to Myles, that it all sounded impossibly far-fetched. Listening to her own words made it sound even more outlandish. But it was fact nevertheless.

'Jesus Christ,' murmured Myles when she'd finished. 'I always knew that bloke was bad news.'

There wasn't much Lauren could say. It had been a bone of contention between Iona and herself that Myles had never taken to Frank.

'He was too smarmy by half,' said Myles, as he pulled Lauren closer to him. 'Always smiling, always going on about how much he loved her. Ratbag.'

'Well, we don't know the full story yet.' Lauren yawned. 'Maybe there's a reasonable explanation.'

Myles snorted. 'If you think that, you're even softer in the head than Iona.'

'Oh Myles, I just feel so sorry for her,' whispered Lauren. 'I mean, it's bad enough that your husband is in a coma, but that there's someone else who thinks she has as much right to be there . . . oh, and there's a daughter too.'

'Bloody hell.'

'About sixteen or seventeen.'

'It's a mess, isn't it?'

Lauren nodded. 'And I've no idea how it can be sorted out.'

Siobhán arrived home much earlier than either Iona or Sally, but it was still late by the time she eased into the parking space beneath the apartment block and took the lift up to the fourth floor. It was at times like this she was glad Eddie was away – he was a light sleeper and hated being woken up when she arrived home at all hours. She slipped out of her shoes and walked in her stockinged feet into the kitchen, where she put on the kettle and shook a cappuccino mix into a large mug. It didn't matter that there was caffeine in it. She reckoned she was too tired from the events of the evening even for caffeine to keep her awake. As she waited for the kettle to boil, her eyes scanned the apartment.

She hadn't noticed until now, but in the weeks of Eddie's absence it had become a tip. Not a filthy tip, she told herself as she looked at the piles of magazines and newspapers scattered around the room and the collection of bottles on the worktop which she hadn't bothered to take to the bottle-bank; but a messy, untidy tip. Eddie would freak out at the sight of it. He was a neat and meticulous person and she knew that he only barely tolerated her habit of stepping out of her working clothes when she came home and simply throwing them carelessly over the back of the chair beside the bed. Eddie always hung up his suits and folded his shirts and generally left the place as he found it. (Although, she acknowledged, maybe if she spent vast amounts of money on designer gear like he did instead of simply rummaging through the rails at Top Shop looking for bargains, she'd be a bit more careful about hanging things up too!) As she eyed the burnt-down candles dotted around the apartment (she'd had a pampering evening a couple of weeks ago and had turned the place into a grotto of flickering lights to help with the ambience) and the wine glasses which she'd also not bothered to clear away, Siobhán wondered how on earth Eddie put up with a slut like her instead of finding a domestic goddess instead.

Maybe it was a case of opposites attracting, she thought, as she mixed her cappuccino. All the same, she'd better do a bit of a tidy-up before he got home. No sense in bringing him back to earth with such a resounding thud! She'd do it in the morning, though, before she picked him up from the airport. She didn't have the energy to do it now.

She finished her coffee and then got ready for bed. She slid between the cotton sheets and closed her eyes. But whether it was because of the coffee after all, or whether she was simply too tired, sleep just wouldn't come. She found herself thinking about the Harper case again. It had the potential, Siobhán thought, to become very messy indeed. One marriage of eighteen years, she reflected again. Another apparent marriage of four years. Could it be, she wondered, that Frank Harper had met this younger girl and – instead of acting like most men going through a mid-life crisis and having an affair with her – decided to marry her instead?

When she'd got back to the station she'd looked up the law relating to bigamy. The bottom line was that if Frank Harper had knowingly married Iona Brannock while he was still married to Sally, then he was a bigamist. Since both of the Harper wives seemed to think that they were legally married to Frank, she knew that her job would be to see whether the first marriage was valid, and whether the second ceremony was carried out in an accepted way. And whether anyone at the second ceremony knew about the first marriage – in which case they'd have aided and abetted in the crime.

She knew that she had to check Frank's background too. Maybe he was a serial bigamist. Perhaps Iona and Sally were only two in a whole harem of wives. Though God knew, thought Siobhán, it must be hard enough to carry on a double life, let alone a whole network of lives. But if Frank travelled overseas, for example, there was always the chance that he might have married someone outside the country too. Maybe there had been other weddings in Barbados! Siobhán wondered fleetingly what the likelihood was of her superintendent allowing her to go to the Caribbean to take a few statements. Slim, she thought. But it'd be a nice change from having to interview suspects in the dull rooms of the garda station! Actually Frank was the person she really needed to interview, but of course he was currently in a coma and there was no immediate sign of him coming out of it. So no chance of asking him whether Iona and Sally were the only two Mrs Harpers around.

But what did it matter if the poor bugger died? Siobhán had already wondered about the usefulness of conducting the enquiry if the suspect had little or no life expectancy, and then realised that there would probably be all sorts of legal and financial issues to be sorted out whether Frank Harper died or not. So she had to investigate it. It would be up to the Director of Public Prosecutions to decide whether the matter went any further. Their brief would be to see what harm had been caused, and what public interest would be served by prosecuting him. Her job was to present them with the facts. She had to find out the truth of the matter even if she didn't really want to get involved, and even if it would prove to be painful to the two women concerned.

She shook her head and pummelled the pillow into a more comfortable shape. Why did people do crazy things like this? she wondered. Wasn't life complicated enough without making it even worse? I'm glad I have a nice, uncomplicated relationship, she told herself. One which might one day end in marriage. But thankfully not yet. She put her arm around Eddie's pillow and dragged it towards her. Then she fell instantly asleep.

⁓

The ringing of the phone jolted Sally into immediate wakefulness. She winced as she lifted her head from the desk and reached for the receiver. It was the hospital, to say that Frank's condition was unchanged and that the doctor looking after his case would meet her at midday. She looked blearily at the wall clock. It was nine o'clock.

She went into the bathroom and stood under a lukewarm shower, rotating her neck from side to side under the jets to try to ease the tension in her shoulders. When she came out and went downstairs, she found Jenna sitting at the kitchen table again.

'He's dead, isn't he? That's what they were phoning to tell us.'

'Of course not,' said Sally. 'We're to go in at twelve and they'll talk to us then.'

'What about her?' asked Jenna. 'The madwoman? What's she doing?'

'I've absolutely no idea,' replied Sally. 'And I couldn't care less.'

Jenna's mobile phone beeped and Sally looked at her questioningly.

'It's Gerry,' she said.

'Gerry?'

'You met him, Mum,' said Jenna. 'He's my boyfriend.'

'Oh. Right.' Sally remembered a tall, gangly bloke who'd called around to the house one evening and who'd blushed red as he asked for Jenna. She hadn't realised (always assuming that she was thinking about the right guy!) that he was Jenna's boyfriend. I'm not taking enough interest in her, she told herself. I need to know more about what she's up to.

She watched as Jenna sent a text message to Gerry.

'What are you telling him?'

'That I can't go to the party tonight because my dad's had an accident.'

The phone beeped again. Jenna read the message and her eyes welled up with tears. She pushed her chair back from the table.

'I'm going upstairs,' she said, and left Sally sitting on her own.

⁓

Lauren took the call from the hospital while Iona was still sleeping. They gave her the same information about Frank and suggested that Iona come in at one to discuss the case.

'And what about the other woman?' demanded Lauren.

'Sally Harper is coming in at twelve.' The administrator sighed. 'It's a most unusual situation.'

'Well she'd better be gone before my sister arrives,' Lauren warned them. 'She's very emotional right now.'

'I do understand that,' said the woman at the other end of the phone. 'We are aware of the sensitivities involved.'

'Good,' said Lauren. 'Because I don't think you were last night. Iona felt that you weren't taking her seriously.'

'Believe me,' said the woman at the other end of the line, 'we're taking the entire situation very seriously indeed.'

When she woke Iona – a difficult task, as the Valium had clearly knocked her out completely – her sister's first question was why Sally was going in first.

'I don't know,' said Lauren.

'They're making her out to be more important than me. But she isn't. I'm his wife and I'm entitled to be there first.'

'Io – please.' Lauren looked at her sister despairingly. 'Someone has to be first.'

'But why her? Why not me? Because they think it's more likely she's his wife. Well, they only have her word for that. She can say all she likes about having married Frank but it's just not right.'

'She obviously does know Frank.'

'Maybe she went out with him before. Maybe she did have his baby.' Iona gulped. 'I can accept that even if I don't like it. But who's to say that she's actually married to him? We only have her word for that. And she could easily be a pathological liar.'

'Maybe she thinks the same about you.'

Iona stared at Lauren in a silence which crackled with anger and tension.

'Thanks very much for that!' she said furiously. 'You know I'm not lying. But you're prepared to believe that shit she was coming out with last night. You think that she's married to him even though you were the one who saw me and Frank off at the airport. You've seen our wedding photos!'

'Oh, look, Io . . .' Lauren caught her sister by the hands. 'I don't believe anything. I'm just saying that . . . well . . . for people who don't know . . . maybe they think it's more likely she's his wife.'

'That's just great.' Iona's voice was laden with disgust. 'You're giving her the benefit of the doubt. Why? Just 'cos she's older and looks like a hag? You think that's a more likely person for Frank to marry than me? Come on, Lauren, you know Frank! You know what he's like. D'you seriously think he'd want that dowdy old dear with the narky kid more than me? Honestly?'

'No. No, of course not.'

'Good.' Iona got out of the bed and then caught her breath in a jagged cry. She pressed her fingers to her stomach.

'Are you all right?' asked Lauren anxiously.

'Yeah. I'm fine. It's just . . .' She shrugged. 'D'you have any Tampax?'

Lauren nodded. She went out of the room and returned with a box of Super. 'These OK?'

'Thanks.' Suddenly a tear rolled down Iona's cheek and plopped on to the box.

'Come on, honey.' Lauren put her arm around her sister. 'Everything will be all right.'

'But what if it's not?' Iona turned her tear-filled blackberry eyes towards her. 'What if . . . what if he dies, Lauren?' She swallowed hard. 'We were trying for a baby. We'd finally decided . . . I'd finally decided that I could cope with the whole motherhood thing. And if he dies – then there'll never be a baby.'

Lauren squeezed her sister's shoulders very hard. 'He'll be fine,' she said fiercely. 'You know he will. And you'll have your baby.'

Sally and Jenna parked in the multistorey car park. They walked in silence to the hospital, each wrapped up in her own thoughts. They remained silent even when they were directed up to a waiting room on the ICU floor. The room made an effort to be cheerful, with brightly coloured upholstered chairs arranged around a small table stacked with magazines, and a hot-drinks vending machine in the corner. Sally selected tea for herself and hot chocolate for Jenna. They sat and waited for the doctor to arrive. When he did, it was a different man from the one they'd spoken to the previous evening. He introduced himself as David Bream and then sat down beside them. He told them that Frank was still in a coma although there had been some generalised responses. Which meant that his body was reactive but it was inconsistent and not specific. At this point Frank

95

was still unaware of his surroundings. But, said the doctor, the trauma hadn't been as bad as they'd first feared. They'd managed to reduce the pressure on his brain and to surgically repair damaged blood vessels. There had been a blow to his occipital lobe which would probably impair his vision or perhaps his recognition of visual objects at first. It was hard to tell until he regained consciousness.

'Is he brain-damaged?' Sally had let the jargon flow over her and now asked the question tentatively.

'I can't say,' replied the doctor. 'However, we're hopeful that we will be able to move him off life support soon and with a bit of luck he'll wake up.'

Sally nodded. 'A coma's not really the same as him just being asleep, is it?'

'I'm afraid not. We need him to come out of it, Mrs Harper,' said the doctor.

'Can you guess when that will happen?' asked Jenna.

'Not really.' He smiled gently at her. 'You know, it's not like in the movies when someone opens their eyes and suddenly gets better. Sometimes patients can open and close their eyes but still not respond to their surroundings. It can take a while. The brain is a sensitive organ. But the human body is amazing too.'

'Can we see him?' Sally got up.

They followed David Bream to the window of the ICU room. As far as they could see, nothing had changed from the previous night. Frank was still hooked up to a vast array of instruments and still looked waxy and unlike himself.

'Has she been here yet?' asked Sally.

'I'm sorry?'

'The madwoman from last night? The one who lied about him?'

'Not yet,' said David uncomfortably.

'Whatever she's saying, it's not true.' Sally stared through the window at Frank. 'He's my husband. I love him. And I'll be the one to make him better.'

Iona was shaking as she sat in the waiting room. It was a different room from the previous night, at the far end of the corridor. A row of orange plastic chairs lined the wall. A small TV, mounted on a bracket, was showing Sky News. There were a few ancient magazines on a table in the centre of the room; otherwise it was empty. No other families were waiting for news of loved ones.

David Bream pushed the door open.

'Iona?' He looked uncertainly between the two women in front of him.

'I'm Iona.' Her dark eyes looked intently at him.

'Do you want to come with me?'

As Sally and Jenna had done a little earlier, Iona and Lauren stopped by the glass window. Iona burst into loud sobs as she looked at Frank while Lauren held her tightly.

David went through the same explanations as he'd given Sally and Jenna. As he talked, Iona wiped her eyes.

'Has he made any responses at all?' she asked.

David was surprised at the suddenly more businesslike tone of her voice.

'Some. But he's not aware of his surroundings.'

'How d'you know?' demanded Iona. 'What about all those people you read about who seem to be totally out of it and then they say that they could hear everything that was going on, and they remember people saying things about them. I don't want Frank to hear anything bad said when he's there. I don't want people walking into his room and muttering that he's never going to wake up.'

'Nobody will do that,' said David.

'I want to spend time with him and talk to him and let him know that people love him,' said Iona.

'Her favourite TV programme is *ER*,' said Lauren apologetically.

'Don't be so facile,' snapped Iona. 'I've had time to think about this, and I know I've been crying and upset and everything but it doesn't mean I'm completely hopeless. I want to stay with him 24/7 if I have to.'

'Well, Iona, that's all really positive,' said David Bream. 'Of course there are other people who want to visit him too . . .'

'Who?' demanded Iona. 'He has no family. His parents are dead. He doesn't have brothers and sisters.'

'Indeed. But as you know—'

'If you're talking about that other woman, she has no right to be here.'

David exchanged uncomfortable looks with Lauren.

'I've thought about that too,' said Iona relentlessly. 'If he was, at some point, married to her it makes no difference. For the last four years he's been married to me. So I'm the most important person in his life. If that woman wants to see him, she has to ask me first.'

'I'm really not so sure that—'

'I'm sorry, but that's the way it is,' said Iona.

'And I'm sorry, but we're going to have to work something out,' said David firmly.

Iona looked angrily at him. 'Don't you understand?' she cried. 'Other patients have people with them all the time, helping them. Because of this . . . this . . . nonsense . . . Frank doesn't have anyone. He needs me.'

'He needs support,' agreed David. 'He doesn't need dissent.'

'So what did she say to you?' asked Iona. 'That she wanted to be here all the time too?'

'To be honest with you,' said David, 'I'm not sure either of you being around will be very helpful at this point. If Mr Harper is aware of what's going on, he could be extremely anxious. We want to keep him calm.'

'So what are you saying? That I can't be here?' Iona's voice was filled with fury. 'I'm telling you, I'm his wife, and you're trying to keep me away from him. You've no right to do that.'

'I'm saying that you and Mrs Harper—'

'Can't you get it into your thick skulls that *I'm* Mrs Harper!' cried Iona.

'You and the other Mrs Harper,' amended David. 'Well, neither of you should be here if it upsets him.'

'You can't seriously think that he's better off on his own?'

'I don't know enough about the situation,' said David. 'But I think you need to discuss it with her and come to an arrangement.'

'You've got to be kidding me.'

'I said the same to her.'

'And what did she say?'

'More or less the same as you. But really and truly, until you come to some kind of arrangement you're doing more harm than good.'

'How dare you?' hissed Iona. 'How dare you imply that I'm doing harm to Frank by being here?'

David Bream sighed deeply. He'd been in situations where there were family feuds before, where sisters or brothers who hadn't spoken to each other for years suddenly turned up at a parent's bedside and then fought over who should care for them. And he'd been in situations where a patient's lover had shown up, wanting to see him or her after the family (including wife or husband) had left. But he'd never had two women both claiming to be married to a man turn up in ICU before. And he really didn't feel equipped to handle it.

'Is she still here?' asked Iona.

David nodded. 'She travelled from Bray. It's a long way.'

Iona exhaled slowly. 'I'll be back at six o'clock this evening. Make sure she's gone by then.'

She pressed her face against the glass once more.

'I love you, Frank,' she whispered. 'I really do. I won't let you down. And we will have our baby.'

Chapter 10

Siobhán made a determined effort to tidy up the apartment the following morning. She gathered up all the papers and magazines and put them into the big box which they kept in the store cupboard for paper recycling. She put all the bottles (she hadn't realised she'd lashed into quite so many bottles of wine over the last few weeks on her own!) into their other recycling box. She gathered up the empty pizza cartons and Chinese takeaway bags from the previous few weeks and tied them up in a black refuse sack, thinking that as well as having drunk too much wine she'd certainly eaten far too much takeaway food. But, she told herself hopefully, the wine would help with the fat content of the food. So maybe her diet had been perfectly balanced after all!

When she'd finished tidying stuff away, she rushed around the apartment with a duster and a tin of Mr Sheen, shook out the cushions, and finally gave the rugs a quick going-over with the Hoover. When she'd finished, she eyed her handiwork critically. There was still a pile of ironing heaped up on the bed in the spare room waiting for attention. Ironing was something she often didn't mind doing because it helped her to think, but she'd been too busy over the last few weeks to bother with it. Oh well, she thought, out of sight and all that sort of thing. Overall, the apartment was a lot tidier. Although certainly not as tidy as when Eddie was around. It was a bit disconcerting to suddenly realise that he was the one who kept the whole domestic side of their lives running smoothly.

It's not my fault, she told herself as she stood in front of the mirror and massaged tinted moisturiser into her naturally pale cheeks. I don't do domesticity. It was never really an option for me. She thought briefly of her upbringing as a middle child among five brothers who had all inherited the usual male genes of complete aversion to housework. Her mother had fought a losing battle against the tide of male paraphernalia around the house and had eventually told Siobhán that it was what was deep down, not appearances, that counted. Siobhán agreed with her mother, but she also realised that sometimes appearances did count. And she certainly didn't want Eddie coming home to an apartment which looked as though it had been part of a stakeout operation.

In fact, she thought, a proper girlfriend would have made the place warm and welcoming and romantic so that he'd realise just how much he'd missed her. God, but she was useless with the soppy stuff. She stood indecisively in front of the mirror. She should do something, she thought, to mark his return. Most women would do something, surely?

She slicked some lipstick on to her lips and grabbed her jacket from the back of the bedroom door, vowing that she'd hang it up properly when they got home. Then she rushed out of the apartment and across the road to the convenience store where she bought three bunches of flowers and a couple of scented candles (she was really overdoing the whole candle thing these days, she thought, but what the hell!). Then she nipped into the adjoining off-licence and bought a bottle of champagne. She raced back to the apartment, shoved the flowers into their beautiful Louise Kennedy vases (a gift to Eddie from a grateful client), placed the candles in the bedroom and put the champagne in the fridge.

Now I'm a proper thoughtful girlfriend, she told herself as she hurried down the stairs and into the car.

～

Frank Harper could hear the nurse in the ICU unit talking. He knew that she was a real person and that he wasn't living some sort of dream, but what he didn't know was exactly where he was and why he was here. And he couldn't quite pin down what she was saying either. He knew that, in some way, he was the object of her concern, because her voice was gentle whenever she was near him. He just didn't know why she was worried about him. He felt perfectly all right. Tired, of course. And not quite ready to open his eyes yet because really that would take far too much effort. In a lot of ways he was very content with how things were.

Marion. That was her name. He remembered now. Marion was looking after him, which was kind of ironic of course because he was the one who was supposed to be looking after Marion. She was his girlfriend, after all. But obviously something had happened and now he was in bed and Marion was concerned about him.

Had he drunk too much at the party? Was he suffering from alcoholic poisoning? She'd said that to him last night. Drink any more of those vodka shots and you'll end up with liver failure. But she'd laughed. She hadn't really meant it. And he'd told her that he was drinking them because . . . because . . . The thought was somewhere just out of reach and he struggled to capture it. Yes. He remembered now. He was drinking because it was her going-away party. She was leaving him. Abandoning him for America with her Morrison visa and her hopes of a new life with brighter prospects. He hadn't wanted her to go. He'd told her he loved her. She'd laughed at him then and retorted that she knew perfectly well that it was all about sex and nothing really to do with love. Hadn't Johnny Doherty told her that both himself and Frank pursued nurses because they had a reputation for being up for anything?

Frank had responded with shock in his voice. He'd said that he loved her for herself and not just for sex, even though sex with her was wonderful. He couldn't bear the thought of her abandoning him.

Only now she was here. She hadn't gone. Frank was finding it difficult to concentrate. If she was in the room with him now, she couldn't have boarded the Aer Lingus flight to New York departing this morning, 12 April 1986.

He needed to wake up. It was easy to lie here with his eyes

closed and think about Marion and how his life might turn out now that she was still here, but it would be better to snap out of his drunken stupor and get back into things again. Only he didn't really feel like it. His head hurt. His body hurt too. Better leave it for a while.

Terri Cooper, the nurse in charge of the ICU unit, heard her patient sigh. She looked at him. His eyes were open but they were staring blankly at the ceiling. As she watched, he closed them again.

He was still in a coma.

⤳

The traffic in Dublin was, as always, appalling. Siobhán sat in her car and fumed, wishing that she could stick her blue light on the roof. But she was driving her own car, and besides, even in a police car she wouldn't be allowed to use the light to clear a route from Blackrock to the airport just so's she could be on time to meet her fiancé from the plane. Pity, she thought. It'd be a nice perk to the job. Despite the delays, however, she arrived five minutes before Eddie emerged into the arrivals hall.

She squealed with delight at seeing him and rushed towards him, flinging her arms around him and hugging him tightly to her. He hugged her too, so tightly that she couldn't even move.

'OK, OK,' she said eventually. 'You'd better let me come up for air.' She wriggled out of his hold and then kissed him on the lips. He moved away from her and she looked at him in astonishment.

'Sorry,' he said. 'I'm . . . you know . . . in public.'

Her eyes opened wide. Kissing in public had never been an issue before. At least, she didn't think so. They didn't do it very much, Eddie was a very private person, but still . . . She clamped down on the feeling of hurt which she felt.

'But it's wonderful to see you,' he told her, and she didn't doubt the sincerity in his voice. He put his arms around her and hugged her close to him again. 'I really, really missed you.'

Her hurt feelings evaporated and she leaned her head against his shoulder.

'I missed you too,' she said.

He yawned widely. 'I'm so sorry. Jet lag. I know I should sleep on the plane but I can't.'

'Never mind,' she told him as they walked back to the car park and retrieved the car. 'You can sleep for hours when we get home. I'm going to drop in to the station early this evening. I have loads to do.'

'New case?'

She told him about the potential bigamy situation. 'I need to do some background checks,' she said. 'Find out about this Harper bloke. For all we know he could have dozens of women stashed away.'

'You think so?' he asked as she edged out of the parking space.

She made a face. 'Hard to know. Depends on his motive, I guess.' She chuckled. 'Most guys I know struggle with one wife, let alone two.'

Eddie nodded, then opened the glove compartment and slid a CD into the deck.

'You don't mind if I chill for a while?'

Siobhán shook her head as the voice of Aretha Franklin filled the car.

Eddie fell asleep fifteen minutes into the journey and she had to wake him when they eventually arrived back at the apartment building. He yawned widely, then got out of the car and took his case from the boot.

'You're lucky you came home at the weekend,' said Siobhán as they made their way to their apartment. 'At least you don't have to be alert for the morning.'

'I have to go through some of my paperwork,' he told her. 'Get everything in order for next week.'

'No problem.'

She unlocked the apartment door and he followed her inside. He dumped his case in the bedroom, then walked back out into the living room again. He looked around critically before picking up a used tea-light which Siobhán had overlooked in the great clean-up.

'I thought the place would be trashed,' he told her.

'Why?'

'I didn't think you'd manage to keep it so tidy. And I'm impressed by the flowers.'

She grinned. 'OK, I have to admit it wasn't like this all the time. But I did my best.'

'I think we should get professional cleaners in,' said Eddie.

'It's not that bad!'

'On a regular basis,' he told her. 'So that you don't have to bother with it.'

'It's impossible to get a reasonably priced cleaner,' she told him. 'And really this place isn't that big. I'll make more of an effort next time.' She opened the fridge and took out the bottle of champagne. 'Come on, honey. I do feel that the domestic goddess scenario means that I should be a goddess in the bedroom too.' She opened the bedroom door again. 'Grab some glasses for the bubbly and see what you've been missing the last five weeks!'

By the time Eddie followed her inside, she was already pulling off her jeans and sliding into bed. He undressed more slowly, as always hanging his clothes carefully in the wardrobe before getting in beside her. She put her arms around him and pulled him towards her.

'I've so, so missed you,' she whispered. 'I didn't realise how much you mattered to me until you'd gone.'

He put his arms around her too and held her close. She slid her hand down his side and between his legs.

'You know what,' he mumbled into her flame-red hair, 'I'm just totally knackered right now. I can't think straight. And my body is wrecked.'

She moved away from him and looked at him in puzzlement.

'You don't want to?'

'Of course I want to,' he responded. 'I'm just really, really tired.'

'Oh. Well, come on, let's have the champagne anyway.'

He looked at her apologetically. 'I appreciate it, I really do. But maybe later? Right now would you mind awfully if I went to sleep?'

'No. No, that's fine.' Her voice was hesitant. 'I thought . . . but you're right. You've been awake all night.'

'Stay with me,' he said. 'I like to know you're close to me.'

'Sure.'

They lay side by side for a few minutes and then Eddie's breathing became slower and steadier. Siobhán raised herself on to one elbow and looked at him. He was sound asleep. She eased herself out of the bed and took the bottle of champagne back to the fridge, then made herself a cup of tea instead.

∾

It was mid-afternoon when Siobhán pulled up outside the neat semi-detached house in Bray. She got out of her unmarked car, noticing in the daylight that the front lawn was neatly trimmed and the flowerbeds carefully tended. The windows sparkled and the paintwork on the hall door had recently been redone.

She got out of her car and walked up the cobbled driveway.

A middle-aged woman answered the door. She raised her eyebrows in silent query, but Siobhán simply gave her name and said that she was here to see Sally.

'Sally's resting. I don't think she needs to see anyone right now.'

Siobhán walked past the woman and into the living room. Sally was sitting on the long settee, her legs drawn up under her. Her face was pale, with blue-black shadows under her eyes.

'I told her you were resting . . .' Sally's neighbour, who had called in to see her and taken it on herself to fuss over her, had followed Siobhán into the room.

'It's OK,' said Sally. 'This is the garda who told me about Frank's accident.'

'And I'd like to talk to Mrs Harper on her own for a while,' said Siobhán firmly. 'So if you could leave us to ourselves . . .'

The neighbour reluctantly picked up her bag from a chair. 'Well, you know where to find me if you need me.' She nodded to both women and let herself out of the house.

'How are you?' Siobhán asked gently.

Sally hesitated before answering. 'I don't know,' she replied eventually. 'I was at the hospital this morning. Frank is still in a coma. That other woman was there.'

'How's your daughter?'

'She's gone out,' said Sally. 'I think that's a good thing. Her boyfriend called around for her and I told them to go for a walk.' Sally nibbled at her thumbnail. 'Why are you here?' she asked.

'Well, Sally, we need to investigate the whole situation between you and Iona and Frank.'

'There is no situation,' said Sally. 'I'm his wife. Everyone knows that.'

'Do you have a marriage certificate?' asked Siobhán. 'And Frank's birth certificate too, perhaps?'

'Of course I do.' Sally uncurled her legs and got up from the settee. She went out of the room. While she was alone, Siobhán walked around it. It was a big L-shaped room with an olive-green settee and armchairs at one end and a walnut dining table and chairs in the short end of the L. The furniture was old-fashioned, darker than Siobhán herself preferred, but of a good quality. There were framed prints on the walls and one portrait photograph of Frank, Sally and Jenna. Siobhán guessed that Jenna had been around ten or twelve when the photo had been taken – her wide beaming smile revealed train-track braces on her teeth. There were two other photographs in the room, both in silver frames. One was of Jenna as a baby, a wide smile on her chubby face; the other was of Frank and Sally on their wedding day. It was an outdoor photograph taken in a garden setting, with spectacular views over Dublin Bay.

'The Deerpark Hotel in Howth,' said Sally as she came back into the room.

Siobhán replaced the photograph on the sideboard.

'It was a beautiful day,' continued Sally. 'Cloudless blue sky and very warm. I was too hot in my dress really.'

Siobhán looked at the photograph again. Sally's dress was very traditional, with a square neck and puffed sleeves. Her hair had been teased into a myriad of curls on the top of her head and her veil was secured by a glittering tiara.

'It looks naff now,' said Sally, 'but it was the height of fashion then.'

Siobhán grinned at her. 'I know what you mean. You think you're getting something timeless but years later you wonder what in God's name you were thinking. That's a nice dress, though.'

'Are you married?' asked Sally.

Siobhán said nothing. Instead she walked back towards Sally and held her hand out to take the certificates from her. She had no intention of discussing her personal life with Sally Harper.

'I brought you our wedding album to look at too,' said Sally. 'Not that there were a lot of people there; Frank and I are both only children.'

'Best man and bridesmaid?' asked Siobhán as she looked at the glossy photos.

'A friend of Frank's,' said Sally. 'Johnny Doherty. He's living in the States now. Or maybe Canada, I'm not sure which. And the bridesmaid is a girl I was in college with. Denise. We're still good friends – work together, actually. She lives on the other side of the city, though.'

'How many people were there?' Siobhán continued to look at the photographs. She stopped turning the pages and looked at one of them more closely. 'Parents, of course.'

'Mine,' said Sally. 'And Frank's dad. His mum left them when he was a kid.'

Siobhán continued to look at the photograph.

'They're all dead now,' said Sally starkly, which made Siobhán look up at her. 'Well, you can see that my folks were getting on a bit. My mum was . . . old . . .' She stumbled on the words and Siobhán put an arm around her.

'Sit down,' she said. 'D'you want me to get you a drink of something?'

'No.' Sally shook her head. 'No, it's fine. What I was going to say was that my mum was quite old when she had me. She was forty-five. She'd lost three other children.'

'Oh.'

'I mean, it's not old, of course,' said Sally. 'But old for a baby.'

108

She struggled to keep herself under control and kept her hand on her own stomach while Siobhán watched her carefully.

'Anyway, she'd never been in the best of health, so it wasn't unexpected. My dad died two years after her, of a broken heart I always thought.'

'I'm sorry.'

Sally moistened her lips with her tongue. 'It was a long time ago now,' she said more easily. 'And it wasn't as though it was entirely unexpected.'

'And what about Frank's father?'

'Oh, rude health for years,' said Sally. 'Then had a heart attack and died sitting in front of the telly.'

'Is the family from Dublin?' asked Siobhán.

'Oh, gosh, no. Frank was born and raised in Sligo,' replied Sally. 'He's still a country man at heart. He used to stay with his dad once a month until Mr Harper's heart attack.' She shrugged. 'I went a few times too, but to be honest with you, I wasn't interested in driving for a couple of hours to a dark old house that needed repairing. I never really got on with the old man and I don't think he liked me very much either. I know it sounds crazy, but Frank's dad really wanted him to marry a Sligo girl and settle back there. I think he was afraid that I'd be flighty, like his own wife.

'He tried to trace her, I think, but gave up on it. All we know is that she headed to London when Frank was two or three. He doesn't talk about it much any more. I don't know whether she's still alive and neither does Frank. She was from Dublin too, and so as far as old Mr H. was concerned we're a bunch of Jezebels! I don't blame her for heading off, though – he was a grumpy old man and not very nice, to be honest with you. I don't think he actually liked women very much. Frank himself did go out with a Sligo girl for a while but she went off to the States or something.' Sally looked at Siobhán ruefully. 'You know how it was, everyone headed out of Ireland twenty-odd years ago!

'I didn't want to live in Sligo after Frank and I got married but Mr Harper took it as a bit of a slight. Said that I thought I was too good for them. Complete nonsense. As far as I was concerned, Sligo in the 1980s – probably the whole north-west in the 1980s – was a dump.' She laughed faintly. 'I always feel terrible when I say that. As though he can hear me. But the thing was, I had a good teaching job in Dublin and I didn't want to move anywhere else. In the end, though, Mr Harper left the house to Frank. He renovated it and he rents it out. He goes up to Sligo once a month to check things out. The current tenants are a local family with a child, so I know that there isn't something awful going on there.'

'And how would you say your relationship with Frank is?' asked Siobhán.

A tear slid down Sally's cheek. 'Good,' she said eventually. 'We have a good relationship.'

'No trial separations or anything like that?'

Sally looked at her angrily, her eyes still bright with tears. 'I've just said we have a good relationship,' she snapped. 'Of course not.'

'And yet there's a girl who claims to be married to him,' said Siobhán gently. 'Why would she say that, d'you think?'

Sally grabbed a tissue from the box on the coffee table in front of the settee. 'I've no idea. She's obviously deranged.'

'What I thought was that perhaps she's in some kind of relationship with him,' suggested Siobhán, 'and likes to say that they're married. Is it possible, do you think, that there is something between them only you didn't know about it?'

Sally rolled the tissue into a ball and said nothing. She stared at the blank TV screen in the corner of the room. Siobhán watched her silently.

'What does any of it matter?' asked Sally eventually. 'Frank can only be married to one person and that's me.'

Siobhán remained silent.

'There was a period,' said Sally edgily, 'when things weren't great between us. About five years ago.' She pulled at the tissue, shredding it between her fingers and finally dropping it into the wastepaper basket beside her. 'The company where he worked was bought out. Frank was offered a job with the new crowd, a good job, but he didn't want it. He said he didn't like their ethos. I told him I didn't care about their ethos; the point was they were actually offering him an increase in salary. But Frank just wasn't interested. He said he wanted to go out on his own.'

Sally pulled another tissue from the box and blew her nose.

'I was really worried about it. He didn't have a lot of money to back it up so I couldn't see how we were going to cope. He said we'd manage by increasing the rent on the Sligo house, selling the one we were living in and moving out here. We were near the city, you see, where prices had gone through the roof, whereas it was much cheaper here. But I didn't really want to move. I was working on the north side of town, in Sutton, so it was much further away. Frank said that I could get the train across every day and it'd be much quicker than driving even though it was further.'

She threw the second tissue into the wastepaper bin too.

'I suppose I'm a terrible stick-in-the-mud sort of person. I hate being in debt. I hate not knowing where the money is coming from. I thought Frank felt the same way but he didn't really. He was so excited about the new business and he didn't seem to mind working all the hours God sent. I suppose that during that time, what with moving here and him working and all that sort of stuff . . . well . . . there could have been a point where he . . .'

She broke off and sighed. 'But I don't see where he would've got the time, to be honest. He really was working like crazy. And, you know, in the end we resolved it all. He loves me and I always knew that.'

Siobhán nodded. 'How is he?'

'No change,' said Sally. 'We're going in to see him later.' She sniffed. 'It's all so unreal. He's in a coma. He might never wake up. And instead of being able to concentrate on him and what I can do for him and how he is and all that sort of stuff . . . all I'm thinking of is why on earth that girl thinks that . . . It's not possible, you know. Absolutely not. There was never a chance of Frank and me getting a divorce. Never. We went through a rough patch but so does everyone and it was never so bad that we even for a second contemplated divorce.'

111

'I'll be visiting her,' said Siobhán. 'I'll keep you in touch with whatever's going on.'

Sally's smile was weak. 'Thanks.'

'Can I ask you something else?'

'Go ahead.'

'Well, what about Christmas and holidays?'

'Christmas is a busy time for him,' said Sally defensively. 'He sometimes has to stay over if a hotel's doing a spectacular display. He gets well paid for it, though. To be honest, I've never really minded. Once your children are grown up the whole thing sort of loses its appeal . . .' Her voice trailed off and she rested her hand on her stomach while she stared unseeingly at the far wall of the room.

'Are you all right, Sally?' asked Siobhán after a moment or two.

Sally blinked. 'Yes. Yes. Sure.'

'I'll be getting on then,' said Siobhán. 'As soon as I have any more information I'll contact you. In the mean time, are you sure you don't want me to ask your neighbour to call in again?'

'God, no,' said Sally with feeling. 'I want to be on my own for a while.'

'OK.' Siobhán got up. 'Look after yourself.'

'I will,' said Sally as she let her out.

Chapter 11

It took Siobhán a little longer than she'd expected to drive the thirty kilometres from Bray to Dublin and she was afraid that Iona would already have left the house. She'd earlier called Lauren, who'd said that Iona had gone home to change before going to the hospital that evening. Siobhán hadn't wanted to insist on Iona waiting for her, but she did want to talk to her.

The green VW was still parked outside. Siobhán drew up behind it and got out of her car. The area where Iona lived was very different to Sally's. The houses here were much older and smaller and faced directly on to the street. Previously the home of working-class families struggling to make ends meet, the Liberties of Dublin had become a sought-after district for young urban professionals. Siobhán liked the higgledy-piggledy streets and the wildly different colours of the houses, though she supposed that for modern families it might all be a little too cramped.

She rang the bell to Iona's house and heard the muffled sounds of her coming down the stairs.

'Hi,' she said when Iona opened the door. 'How are you?'

Iona shrugged. Siobhán saw that, like Sally, she was very pale. In her case the dark shadows under her eyes seemed even more pronounced. But there was a defiant gleam in her dark eyes.

'What d'you want?' she asked curtly. 'I'm getting ready to go out.'

'I know that,' said Siobhán. 'I'll only take up a few minutes of your time.'

Iona looked at her disbelievingly.

113

'We do need to clarify a few things,' said Siobhán. 'The sooner we sort it all out the better.'

'There's nothing to sort out.' But Iona opened the door wider and allowed Siobhán into the house.

'I know that's what you think,' said Siobhán, 'yet obviously there's a situation here, Iona. And it's in everyone's interest to resolve it.'

'You believe her, don't you?' Iona's glance in Siobhán's direction was contemptuous. 'Mrs Suburban Lifestyle Dream. You think she's really his wife.'

'I don't think anything,' answered Siobhán calmly. 'I just want to know the truth.'

'Oh, quit talking like a TV cop,' snapped Iona. 'You don't care what the truth is. You just need to close a file that you shouldn't have opened in the first place. It's none of your damn business.'

'Unfortunately it is my business at the moment,' said Siobhán. 'And you're right, I want to resolve it and move on.'

'I don't believe in the state poking its nose into people's private lives,' said Iona rudely. 'You should be out catching real criminals, not getting involved in a personal matter.'

Siobhán sighed. She couldn't begin to count the number of times that members of the public had told her to go off and catch real criminals. But police work was more than that. At least that was how she looked at it. Maybe, she thought, she was just a fool.

'What I was wondering,' she said as she sat down on one of Iona's cream leather armchairs, 'was whether you had a marriage certificate.'

'Of course I do,' said Iona. 'I'm not unhinged. I didn't make the whole thing up, you know. Frank and I are legally married.' She stomped out of the room and up the stairs.

As she had in Sally's house, Siobhán took the opportunity to look around the room. Not that there was much to see. Unlike the warmth of the house in Bray, with its jumble of photos and ornaments, Iona's home was much more modern and minimalist. Siobhán recognised the feng shui bowl on the sideboard, but she was surprised to see two framed photographs of children there

114

too. She wouldn't have thought of Iona as the maternal type. The only other photograph was one of Frank and Iona on their wedding day in Barbados.

'Here.' Iona came downstairs again and thrust the piece of paper into Siobhán's hand. 'Marriage certificate. Barbados. Iona Brannock and Frank Harper.'

Siobhán studied the certificate. 'And who were these witnesses?' she asked.

'Oh, just a couple we met while we were there,' said Iona. 'They were both from England. We didn't keep in touch, though. I think they run a nursing home in Yorkshire. Nice couple, but you know how it is on holiday. You meet people and they're friends for a fortnight but that's it.'

'Any of your family there?' asked Siobhán casually. She thought the department would probably send her to Yorkshire if she needed. Not as glamorous as Barbados, though!

Iona shook her head. 'It's not like it was spur of the moment or anything, but we just wanted to do it on our own. Besides, Lauren had only given birth to Gavin a few weeks earlier so she wasn't really interested in travelling. My folks are retired and they live in Spain.'

Siobhán sighed. Sometimes she hated her job. No matter what, there always came a time when she had to tell people things they didn't want to hear. And those people in turn always hated her for it.

'I was with Sally earlier,' she said. 'She has a marriage certificate too.'

Iona's eyes darkened even further. 'It's all nonsense,' she said.

'I don't see how it can be.' Siobhán kept her voice soft and even. 'It seems possible to me that Frank and Sally did get married.'

'Well they must be divorced.' This time Iona's eyes glittered with tears. 'I'm telling you, he loves me. We have a good life together. How could he possibly be married to someone else?' She blinked a few times and looked angrily at Siobhán. 'I mean, you're suggesting that he's living some sort of double life. That's just not realistic! I'd know about it if he was.'

'Did he ever stay away for long periods?' asked Siobhán. 'Or have to head off unexpectedly for a while?'

Iona said nothing.

'I know it seems impossible,' continued Siobhán, 'but we have to eliminate the impossible to work out what the exact situation is.'

'Why do you care?' burst out Iona. 'What does it matter?'

'Well, there are a whole heap of things that matter,' Siobhán told her. 'In terms of your rights and entitlements as a married woman. In terms of why – if he married you when he was married to Sally – well, why he did it, what he hoped to gain by it—'

'He had nothing to gain!' Iona cried. 'It's not like I'm rolling in money or anything.' She covered her face with her hands.

Siobhán watched her, wishing once again that she hadn't got involved in this case but had stuck with the money-laundering instead. Meanwhile she hoped fervently that there weren't any more Mrs Harpers waiting to emerge from the woodwork. A sudden image flashed across her mind of a dozen more Sallys and Ionas claiming to be the one and only Mrs Frank Harper.

'We were trying for a baby,' whispered Iona finally. 'He wanted a baby. More than me at first. And so we were trying for one.' The tears trickled through her fingers and rolled across her wrists and down her arms. 'Why would he want a baby if he already had a daughter?'

'Oh, Iona, I don't know.' Siobhán got up from the armchair and sat on the sofa beside Iona. She put her arm around her shoulders and hugged her tightly.

'He has to stay away a lot.' Iona spoke through her hands. 'He has a business of his own. He works from the house and from an office in Stillorgan. It's one of those serviced offices, you know, a lot of people use them. But the work means he has to travel a lot, and so . . . yes, there are times when he's not here.'

'What about . . . what about holiday times, like Christmas or New Year?' asked Siobhán.

'Our first Christmas we went to Salzburg,' said Iona dreamily. 'It was absolutely wonderful. It snowed and everything was totally

Christmas-cardy. We went skating at an ice-rink wearing turn-of-the-century clothes. Frank's a good skater but I kept falling over. I was covered in bruises! And last year we went to Tenerife. It was so cold and gloomy here, if you remember, and I really wanted some sun. Frank doesn't particularly like the sun. He likes being outdoors but he prefers a bit of cloud, even though he tans quite easily. But he agreed to Tenerife for me. We had Christmas lunch by the pool and then the hotel did a big dinner . . .' Her voice trailed off and she sniffed again.

'And the other Christmases?' asked Siobhán.

'Well, it's his work, you see,' said Iona. 'Light shows and that sort of thing. He has to be away sometimes because he might be looking after a particular display . . . Christmas and New Year are busy times.'

'And the summer?'

Iona shrugged. 'We never take two-week holidays; usually just a week at the beginning and a week at the end as well as lots of long weekends. Frank doesn't like being away from the office for more than that. We were planning to go to Italy in May and maybe Prague in September.'

'Did he ever stay away from you for more than a week at a time?'

'Of course,' said Iona. 'There's the annual industry conference – that's nearly a fortnight. And other events from time to time too.'

'And where is the annual conference held?'

'It depends,' replied Iona. 'Last year it was in Malta.'

She rubbed her eyes and looked at Siobhán.

'Are you trying to tell me that he wasn't at a conference? That he was with her instead?' Her voice rose. 'Is that it?'

'Look, Iona, I know this is really stressful for you. You love Frank and he's badly injured and in hospital, so everything else is just a distraction to you. But the point is . . . well, it does seem very likely that he was still married to Sally when he married you.'

'But why!' wailed Iona. She got up and stood in front of the feng shui bowl. 'Why would he do that? He didn't have to get involved with me. Nobody forced him . . .' Her voice trailed away again as she thought of the number of times she'd mentioned marriage to Frank. How, in the end, she was the one who'd practically proposed to him. But she hadn't made him say yes! If he hadn't been able to marry her, then why on earth had he done it?

Iona looked at the wedding photograph again. It just wasn't possible, she told herself for the hundredth time. How could he have taken her to Barbados and married her knowing Sally and Jenna were at home? And how could he have told her, only the other day, that he was looking forward to the time when their baby arrived and they'd be a real family. He wanted so much to be part of a family.

'I don't know why,' said Siobhán in answer to Iona's question. 'I really don't. To be honest, it's not something that I've ever encountered before. We have had cases of bigamy, but they were nearly all related to immigration issues. I've never come across a situation where a man has apparently married two women just for the hell of it.'

'It wasn't just for the hell of it!' cried Iona. 'It was because he loved me.'

Siobhán said nothing. Iona sat down on the sofa again and rested her head on her knees.

'I've got nothing.' Eventually Iona raised her dark eyes towards Siobhán. 'If this is true . . . if he married me . . . and he wasn't entitled to marry me . . . then I've got nothing.'

Siobhán stayed silent.

'I mean – if she's his official wife, then she's the one they'll talk to about his treatment,' continued Iona miserably. 'They won't want to know me. She'll be the one to take all the decisions. And that's not fair!'

'Maybe you'll be able to come to some kind of agreement,' suggested Siobhán.

'Agreement! You're joking!' Iona looked at her angrily. 'You saw how she reacted. She thinks – if anything – I might be his bit on the side. But I'm not. It was never like that. I'm the one who

118

brings him to the dentist because he's so scared of needles and stuff. I'm the one who found a decent physio for the shoulder injury he got lugging boxes around the place. I help him with updating his business records. What kind of input does she have into all that? Nothing as far as I can see. But everyone will take her side because she's the legal wife. If she was all that great, then why did he come to me?'

'I can't answer those questions for you,' said Siobhán. 'You'll have to deal with it yourself. I guess what I have to find out is if there was any particular reason he decided to go through with this marriage.'

'I told you. He loves me.'

'As I said, what would he hope to get out of it? I'm sorry I have to ask you this, Iona. I really am. But – is your family well off? Would you expect to come into an inheritance?'

Iona stared at Siobhán in disbelief. She was quite unable to speak.

'A lot of times it does all come down to money,' said Siobhán apologetically.

'I already told you I'm not rich!' cried Iona eventually. 'I – for heaven's sake, look at where we live! Sure it's my house – I bought it before I met Frank. It's cute and convenient but it's hardly the home of a millionaire! As for an inheritance – that's a joke. My parents are totally unmaterialistic. They live in a small farmhouse in Spain and they're practically self-sufficient. Dad has a pension and they have some olive groves which bring in a little money, but it's certainly not a vast business empire.'

She got up from the sofa and went into the kitchen, reappearing a few moments later with a bottle of green-gold oil.

'This is from the finca,' she said, holding it out to Siobhán. 'They sell it in the local market and sometimes to tourists.'

'Is the finca worth much?' Siobhán unscrewed the top and sniffed at the oil. It was rich and aromatic, with a slight hint of lemon.

'No it bloody isn't,' said Iona. 'Well, I suppose property prices have gone up a bit, but it's nothing spectacular.'

'Do they have a house here?' asked Siobhán.

Iona nodded. 'In Templeogue. It's a very, very ordinary 1970s house which is currently rented out. The rent isn't anything spectacular but it's a steady income. Mum and Dad decided not to sell it because they wanted to have something to fall back on. Not that they'd come home, of course, just that they could sell it for extra funds. But the rental seems to be enough to keep them happy.' She looked at Siobhán curiously. 'Why does this matter?'

Siobhán said nothing.

'You don't think . . . you don't think that Frank was planning to kill me or something, do you?' Iona's voice was laden with bewildered scorn. 'I mean, this is real life, not some stupid made-for-TV play.'

'We have to think of everything, no matter how silly it may seem,' said Siobhán.

'Yeah, well, if Frank was thinking of knocking me over the head and making off with anything, he should've done it a couple of years ago,' said Iona. 'When I met him first he was struggling with financing for his company. But he managed to put it all in place. And he didn't need the off-chance that I'd pop my clogs and leave him a third share in a suburban house to keep him going. You're just being ludicrous.'

Siobhán shrugged. 'I still have to ask.'

'Have you asked her?' demanded Iona. 'Have you asked her why he married her and then decided to marry someone else? Have you?'

'I've spoken to Sally, yes,' said Siobhán.

'And I suppose she's full of it now.' Iona bit her lip to keep it from trembling. 'I suppose she thinks that everything's fine and that she's the one in charge.'

'Everything isn't fine, of course it isn't,' said Siobhán. 'Regardless of the legal situation, you've had a relationship with Frank and you think of yourself as his wife. That can't be easy for her either, you know.'

'I don't give a shit about her,' snapped Iona, 'and she doesn't give a shit about me.'

'But you both love Frank.'

Iona sighed. The fire had suddenly gone out of her eyes.

'I don't know,' she said softly. 'I love someone. But if Frank isn't the person I thought . . . then how can he be the man I love?'

Chapter 12

Frank was incredibly tired. His arms and legs were too heavy to lift and he simply didn't have the energy to make the effort. He felt bad about this because he knew that he should at least try. But he didn't want to. He knew, too, that . . . that . . . He struggled to remember her name and at last it came to him. Sally! Sally Campion. Sally would be furious with him. She hated it when he got himself into this kind of state, too drunk to move. It didn't happen very often these days, of course, but it did happen. And then her blue-green eyes would harden and her lips would thin and she would leave him to his misery, also leaving him in no doubt that he would have to spend time earning back her forgiveness.

He didn't mind that really. He loved Sally. As he lay there he thought about how much he loved her and how good she was for him. He remembered meeting her at a party and having some make-believe quarrel over a can of beer, and he remembered kissing her.

It had been a bit obvious, kissing her like that, but she hadn't objected. And it had been a surprisingly good kiss. He'd kissed a lot of women since Marion but none of them had kissed him back in the same way as Sally. And afterwards she'd smiled at him so that he couldn't help but imagine her naked, her copper tresses falling tantalisingly across her porcelain-skinned body. He'd seen lots of women naked after Marion too. But this woman was different. He didn't know why. But he did know that he wanted to sleep with her and he didn't want to let her go.

Remembering made his head hurt. When he'd been going out with Marion she used to look after him if he'd gone on a bender. She'd been sympathetic. She'd put something cool on his forehead and make him drink a concoction that she said all the nurses swore by. It didn't always make him feel better but at least it was something.

Sally wasn't like that. Sally was impatient with illness and didn't like it when he got drunk. And because of that, and because he loved her, he didn't drink so much any more. Hardly ever, actually. Which was why he was surprised to realise he had such a hangover now. Where had he been to get so wasted? Had he been out with Sally? But surely he wouldn't have gone out with her and got drunk. When he went out with Sally they did cultural things. They went to concerts – not gigs in the park type of concerts, real grown-up concerts in theatres where the men wore suits and the women dressed up; they went to the theatre, they went to art galleries. And he liked doing these things with her. Of course he also liked it when they went to the latest action movie or for a basket of chicken and chips in their favourite pub. But Sally added something to his life. An extra dimension. And he liked it.

He liked her. He loved her. And he didn't want her to be angry with him. The thing to do, he thought, as he tried to ignore the pounding in his head, the thing to do was to marry her. Because he wouldn't find anyone better. Marion had been his first love. And maybe he should have tried to hang on to Marion, because they'd been good together. Actually, yes, he should have tried to hang on to Marion, because they'd been more than good together. They'd been fantastic. Sally was good in bed, but not as good as Marion. None of them had been as good as her.

He sighed. Marion wasn't coming back, though. She'd sent him a letter telling him about her great job in the States and how she'd never come back to boring old Ireland. She didn't even say that she missed him. He should have made her miss him, should have treated her better so that she wouldn't leave him.

But Sally would actually be better for him because she didn't

123

indulge him like Marion. And she was good in bed too – not as intuitive as Marion had been, but good all the same. Nurses and teachers, of course. Everyone knew they were good in the sack!

He'd let the nurse go. He needed to hang on to the teacher. He *would* hang on to her. As soon as he felt half-human again he was going to bring her out for the most expensive meal he could possibly afford and he was going to ask her to marry him.

⌒

Jenna looked at her watch and then slid out of Gerry Cullinan's arms.

'I have to get home,' she told him. 'We're going to the hospital again in half an hour.'

'And will that other woman be there?' Gerry was stunned by the idea of Jenna's father having another wife. He'd listened in amazed silence as she'd blurted out the story of Iona arriving at the hospital, claiming to be married to Frank. He'd been as sympathetic as possible, even though there was a part of him that was quite taken with the idea of a bloke having an unknown extra wife, a small part of him that was saying, 'Fair play to you, Frank.' Because he knew that the idea of a second woman and the reality were two different things.

'I don't know whether she'll be there or not.' Jenna's voice was taut in response to his question. 'She's a nutter, you know. Real dramatic. Stomping her feet and being rude to everyone. But she's not married to my dad. I know she's not.'

Gerry looked at Jenna sympathetically. 'I know it's shit for you,' he said. 'If there's anything I can do to help . . .'

'Thanks.' Jenna rested her head on his shoulder for a couple of seconds and then lifted it again. 'But right now I don't think there's anything anyone can do. Unless you happen to own a helicopter? It's such a long way to the hospital.'

'Can't they move him closer to Bray?' asked Gerry.

'I don't think so.' Jenna sighed. 'Maybe when he comes out of intensive care. I hate it there.' She shuddered. 'All screens and tubes and equipment. He looks like some kind of robot. And I hate the hospital smell too. It makes me feel sick.'

'It probably won't be for long,' said Gerry comfortingly.

'From what the doctors are saying, it could be for ever.' Jenna choked back a sob. 'Nobody seems to know when he might come out of it. And you hear about it, don't you? People who've been in comas for years and who just don't wake up.'

'He'll not be in a coma for years,' said Gerry.

'How d'you know?' demanded Jenna. 'If they don't know, you don't know.'

He said nothing as she walked down the road ahead of him, her back ramrod straight, anger crackling around her. Eventually he called her name and she stopped. She turned to him as he caught up with her and he could see that her eyes were bright with tears.

'I'm sorry,' he said. 'I was trying to be helpful. But I suppose it isn't helpful when you're right and I don't have a clue.' He put his arm around her again and pulled her close to him. She looked up at him.

'It's OK,' she said. 'I guess I'm just . . . well, a bit strung out.'

'Understandable.' His cheek was close to hers.

'You've been great,' she said softly.

'I care about you,' he told her.

'Thanks.'

She was the one who kissed him. They moved into the shadow of the large sycamore tree at the corner of the road. Jenna slid her hands under Gerry's black leather jacket and hugged him close to her. She loved him. She really did. He was so great about everything, so understanding . . . Abruptly she pulled out of his arms again.

'I really have to go,' she said reluctantly. 'I don't want to be late.'

'I know.'

'But I don't want to go.'

'I know.'

'I love you,' she said.

'My parents are away next weekend.'

She looked into his eyes. 'Call me.'

'Of course,' he said.

They walked the rest of the way to her house in silence.

'Hope everything's OK,' he told her.

'Yeah. I hope so too.'

She put her key into the door and unlocked it. She knew that she was later than she'd promised and that her mother would probably be annoyed with her, but she didn't care.

'I'm home,' she called as she walked into the living room.

There was no sign of Sally. Jenna felt a spasm of fear and her heart began to race as she looked around the empty room. Then she heard the flush of the toilet upstairs and the sound of running water in the sink.

'I'm sorry I'm late,' she said as she climbed the stairs and poked her head around her mother's bedroom door. She stopped. Sally looked dreadful. Her long hair was damp and her face was pale. 'Are you all right?'

'Upset stomach,' said Sally.

Jenna felt the spasm of fear again. 'There's nothing wrong with you, is there?' Her voice was suddenly childlike.

'Of course not,' said Sally. She ran her fingers through her hair. 'Obviously I'm upset and worried about your dad, and that probably has something to do with it.'

'You can't get sick too,' said Jenna anxiously.

'I won't,' Sally assured her. The colour was already coming back into her cheeks. 'I'm fine, pet, honestly.'

Jenna looked at her uncertainly.

'Really I am,' said Sally. 'And you're not too late because Denise got stuck in traffic so she won't be here for another few minutes. I'm just going to change into something a bit more suitable for going out. How about you?'

'I'm all right,' said Jenna.

'Fine. Well, I'll see you downstairs.'

'Are we going to have to do this every day?' asked Jenna.

'What?'

'Go to the hospital all the time? What about school? What about your job?'

'We'll work something out,' said Sally. 'It'll be different when we get the car back, which should be any day now.'

'But you can't spend all day, every day in the hospital.' Jenna looked worried. 'Neither can I.'

'I'll take some time off,' said Sally. 'You can too.'

'I'll miss out on stuff,' said Jenna anxiously. 'I'll fall behind.'

'I can help you,' said Sally.

'Not with Irish,' said Jenna. 'You're hopeless at Irish.'

'Look, honey, please don't worry. We'll sort it out. Anyway, there's plenty of evening visiting hours so we can go after school.'

'I won't have time to do my homework.'

'You don't have to come every day,' said Sally. 'Dad'll understand.'

'Yeah. Seems to me it's us that have to do a lot of understanding,' said Jenna. 'I mean, Dad . . . well . . . you know. That woman.' Jenna swallowed hard. 'How could he, Mum? How could he?'

'That's something we have to sort out too,' agreed Sally. 'But there's no point in us getting into a state about it now, is there?'

'Well it's all wrong!'

'I know.'

'She's there and what – what if they have a kid too?'

Sally looked at Jenna in shock. She'd never even considered it.

'I don't think that's likely,' she said eventually.

'Yeah, well, Dad having another wife stashed away wasn't exactly likely either, was it?'

'Jen, please.' Sally sighed. 'I know it's difficult, but we can't keep going on and on about it.'

'We can't ignore it either. We can't pretend that he hasn't lied to us. That he isn't a complete bastard and that I hate him.' Jenna looked accusingly at her mother, then walked out of the room.

Sally sat on the bed and pressed her fingers to her temples. Her head was pounding and she desperately wanted some paracetamol. It was the headache that was making her feel ill, she told herself, although she knew that part of her nausea was due to Jenna's question about whether Frank and Iona had a child. Another thing to worry about. And the gardai were involved too. Since Siobhán Farrell's visit Sally hadn't been able to rid her mind of the fact that her relationship was now part of some kind of police investigation! Siobhán had been polite and sympathetic but Sally had felt humiliated having to show her a marriage certificate and photographs of her wedding. And she couldn't help wondering about that other woman too. Sally knew that Siobhán was going to see Iona as well. Would she have a marriage certificate and wedding photos to show her? And if so, how had it all happened?

Sally desperately wanted to stop thinking about it. She wanted to concentrate on Frank's accident, not on Frank's other wife. Mistress. Whatever. She kept telling herself that she was Frank's legal wife, but that wasn't much comfort when Iona had identified him as her husband too. So who would be in charge of his treatment? What if everything went terribly wrong for Frank and there was a question of turning off life support? What if this woman wanted to kill him but she didn't? Sally knew that she would never switch off Frank's life support. She felt herself grow hot at the idea. And tonight. She'd phoned the hospital about coming tonight and John Carroll had told her that Iona wasn't going to be there in the evening, but how could he be sure about that? As far as Sally could see, the woman was demented enough to show up whenever she liked. And the thing was . . . she pressed her fingers to her temples again . . . the thing was that if she really believed that she was married to Frank, then why shouldn't she?

But how could she believe it now? After all, Siobhán would have told her that Sally was Frank's lawful wife, so Iona would know that her position was completely untenable. In which case she should be staying at home. Sally felt the pressure in her head build up again as her anger at Frank grew. How could he have done this? How could he have betrayed her like this? She'd felt herself grow hot and cold with embarrassment as Siobhán Farrell had quizzed her about her marriage, asking her about the likelihood of Frank having somebody else. She'd never, not for one second, imagined that there'd been another woman. Even during that bad time when things had been so strained between them, she'd believed that Frank still loved her. She'd never supposed that the nights he spent away were nights spent with another woman and not, as he'd told her, dealing with his subcontractors or having client meetings at far-flung places in the country.

And the other woman! That was what was so awful about it. If there'd been someone on the side, or occasional lapses, well, maybe she could have dealt with it. But his relationship with Iona was obviously different. He must at least have thought he was in love with her to have gone through a marriage ceremony with her! What in God's name had he been thinking at the time? And what in God's name did it mean now, both for Sally's past and for her future?

'Denise is here!' Jenna's voice wafted up the stairs and galvanised Sally into action. She changed into a pair of stretchy jeans and a freshly ironed T-shirt, then pulled on a lightweight jumper over it. Although the temperature outside was cold, she knew that the hospital was uncomfortably warm.

Denise and Jenna were in the kitchen. When she saw her friend, Sally felt like crying all over again. She'd known Denise for years; they'd trained together and worked together and they'd only ever had one argument. That had been about Frank. Denise had never really liked him, even though she'd eventually admitted to Sally that she'd been wrong. Only maybe she hadn't after all.

Denise hugged her and Sally kept her head on the other woman's shoulder. She hadn't told Denise the whole story, although she knew she would have to tell her at some point, so Denise didn't yet know about Iona Brannock. All she knew was that Frank had been critically injured.

'Come on, come on,' she murmured comfortingly to Sally. 'Everything will be fine. Frank's a hard nut. He'll get over this.'

Maybe he will, Sally thought as she got her emotions under control again; but will I?

⌒

The apartment was empty when Siobhán finally got home. There was a note from Eddie to say that he'd gone for a walk to clear his head and that he'd be home shortly. But there was no time on the note and so Siobhán had no idea how long he'd been gone. She made a face at the empty room. She'd hoped that he'd have been rested by now and that they might have indulged in the champagne and sex which they hadn't got round to earlier. She picked up the phone and dialled his mobile number but was diverted to his mail-box.

'I'm home,' she said. 'And waiting for you!' She stood indecisively in the living room for a moment and then decided that she would continue with her earlier flurry of domesticity. She made herself a cup of coffee first and then set up the ironing board (almost, as always, losing the tips of her fingers as she opened it out) and plugged in the iron. Then she gathered up the mound of clothes that needed ironing.

Even though she did find it restful, she was also aware of the fact that she was fairly hopeless at ironing, managing to put razor-sharp creases into things that shouldn't have creases in them at all. Actually Eddie often brought his shirts in to work because there was a pick-up and return laundry service there, but of course there was no such thing in Bray garda station, and even if there was, Siobhán couldn't justify the expense to herself. That was the thing about living with Eddie. He could afford so much more than her. Like earlier, when he'd talked about the cleaning service. She never thought of herself as the kind of person who could afford cleaners. Still, it was a nice thought! But the money issue rankled a little. Siobhán wanted to be an equal partner in their relationship, but financially she never would be. And she found that difficult to accept. She'd read before that money was one of the biggest problems that people had in their marriages and she could see why. Money was one of life's biggest problems, full stop. The pursuit of money was why most crimes were committed after all.

Thinking of crimes made her thoughts turn to the potential bigamy case again. If money was the motivation for most crimes, then money was probably the motivation behind this one too. And yet . . . having talked to both Sally and Iona, Siobhán wasn't so sure.

Frank's relationship with Iona had obviously commenced while he was going through a difficult patch in his marriage to Sally. The two women were like chalk and cheese – intriguing in itself, because experience told Siobhán that people usually formed subsequent relationships with people who were very similar to those in previous ones. Maybe Frank had wanted something very different to the cosy domestic set-up he seemed to have with Sally. But then why would he actually set up a second home with Iona? And heavens above, she thought as she accidentally ironed a crease across the back of her favourite white blouse, how on earth had he managed to keep his two lives separate for so long? At least if he'd been simply having an affair with Iona he would have been at home at Christmas or other holiday times. And yet he'd seemed to work it all very well. His job gave him a perfect excuse to be away, even over the holidays, and neither Sally nor Iona seemed to be too worried about his absences. She would've thought that they'd be suspicious of him not being there, but of course why would they? After all, she herself had been at work last Christmas – although Eddie had been really annoyed about it, complaining that he'd be stuck in the apartment on his own for the whole day, which surely wasn't the spirit of the season, was it?

Her next step would be to investigate Frank Harper's background. She'd go to Sligo and do a bit of digging there, check out the house (Christ, she hoped there wouldn't be a third Harper wife holed up there) and find out a little more about the Harper family. She'd also check to ensure that Sally and Frank hadn't actually divorced despite Sally's firm statement that it wasn't ever on the cards. Sally and Jenna seemed genuine enough, but heaven only knew what was really going on. Siobhán was prepared to believe anything about anybody. Once you joined the police, your views of human nature changed for ever.

She'd just finished the ironing when Eddie walked in the door.

She smiled at him and told him that he could fold up the finger-snapping ironing board while she put away the clothes.

'I brought back some chicken wings and dips from the deli down the road,' Eddie told her. 'Thought you might fancy something to eat.'

'Only you.' She grinned at him. 'But that can wait, I guess. You're actually quite right, I'm starving. I didn't have any lunch, just a coffee and a KitKat when I got home.'

'I'll get some plates,' said Eddie.

Five minutes later they were sharing the chicken wings in front of the TV.

'So tell me about Boston,' said Siobhán as she nibbled at a wing. 'Was it good fun?'

'Hardly fun,' Eddie told her. 'I was working.'

'Yeah, yeah.' She grinned at him.

'No, truly,' he said. 'It was all about securitising debt so that—'

'Zzzz.' Siobhán yawned exaggeratedly. 'Don't know. Don't need to know.'

'Revel in your ignorance,' said Eddie.

'I will,' she said. 'Actually I nearly got there myself a few years ago.'

'Did you?'

'Well, sort of. It was a drugs thing. The gang had an operation near here but they were getting stuff from the States. But those lucky bastards in the drugs squad went instead.'

'Poor you.'

'Ah well. Next time maybe. Or there's always the Caribbean.'

'Huh?'

'The bigamy case? Remember? The second wedding was in Barbados. I could so go for an investigative trip there.' She took another wing. 'But the furthest I'm really likely to get is Sligo, which is where the bloke is from.'

'Brave man,' said Eddie. 'Two wives.'

'Ah, but neither of them as hot stuff as me.' Siobhán snuggled up to him. 'Hope you had a good sleep earlier, because you're going to have things done to you tonight that you've never had done to you before.' She slid her palm beneath his shirt.

He caught her wrist with his hand. 'Not now.'

She looked at him. 'I wasn't going to do it now. But . . . I thought . . . Is something wrong?'

'I'm sorry,' he said. 'It's long flights. They just . . . they take it out of me.'

'But you've been asleep for hours.'

'I know. I know. Later. I'll be fine later.'

'OK.' She kissed him on the cheek. But she was frowning as she got up and cleared the debris from the chicken wings away.

Chapter 13

Iona didn't know what to do next. The thinking part of her brain told her that she needed to get some legal advice on her situation (as well as some information about Frank's business – she was worried about his clients and what might happen to them), yet all she could really think about was that Frank was still critically injured and that somehow she wasn't the most important person in his life or the only person who had an interest in his recovery. And since the hospital – having spoken to Siobhán Farrell – had accepted that Sally was Frank's lawful wife, they'd made it clear to her that Sally was the one who had to be consulted about his treatment.

The accident would have been bad enough by itself, but now it was as though a whole chunk of her existence had been suddenly ripped away and there was nothing she could do to replace it. Everything she'd believed about herself and about Frank had been based on a web of lies and deceit. She was angrier than she'd ever been in her life; but it was impossible to maintain the level of fury that she felt while at the same time worrying herself sick about the fact that he was still in a coma.

After her meeting (or interview, as she supposed Siobhán Farrell would call it) with the detective, she'd simply curled up on the sofa and cried. Lauren had called around later to see how she was and Iona was completely incapable of talking to her. Lauren had begged her to take another Valium but Iona had refused and had then had a complete fit of hysterics when she realised that Lauren had given her one the night before. Her older sister had suggested that she spend the night at her house again, but she'd refused to do that too. She wanted to stay in her own place with her own things around her where people couldn't fool her into taking prescription drugs against her will. Anyway, it was bad enough that everything else had been taken away from her without uprooting herself and spending another night at Myles and Lauren's. Besides, the kids would be up and about and she knew she wouldn't be able to cope with them right now.

She was aware that Lauren was worried about her but she couldn't help that. She promised her sister that she wouldn't do anything stupid like overdosing on valerian or slashing her wrists (Lauren had an occasional tendency to imagine the worst), but the fact that she said these things at all seemed to worry her sister all the more. In the end Lauren had insisted in staying the night at Iona's, sleeping on the sofa because of the fact that the spare bedroom had been given over to office space.

Now, at six o'clock on Sunday morning, Iona had woken properly from her fragmented sleep. She pulled a heavy Aran jumper over her blue cotton pyjamas and stuck her feet into her enormous green fluffy slippers before making her way into the office. She was looking for anything that would give her a clue as to why Frank had done what he'd done.

If he'd done what he'd done. Deep down she wanted to believe that it was still all some terrible, terrible mistake.

She didn't find anything in the office. In fact, she thought, as she looked through the files, there was remarkably little information even about Frank's business. And nothing on the desktop computer. She knew that he mainly used a laptop for business, which she assumed he'd taken with him, but she'd always thought that he kept a few files and folders on the desktop too. Yet when she went in to look at them she found that they were simply template letters or links to folders on the laptop, with nothing in them.

What would happen with his business? she wondered again. Who would deal with his clients? Where was his business phone? Maybe people were already calling, looking for him. He often got calls at the weekends even though he rarely did installation and maintenance work himself. He contracted all that out. But Iona suddenly realised that she didn't have a clue who any of those people were. With Frank now lying in hospital, the business which he'd so carefully built up could go down the tubes. He wouldn't want that to happen. She knew he wouldn't. But how could she stop it? Maybe his solicitor could do something – always provided he knew about the business. She sighed. She would find out who Frank's legal people were and contact them first thing in the morning. That, at least, would be something worthwhile to do.

Meantime she opened her internet browser and typed the word 'bigamy' into it. There was nothing especially helpful there; most of the sites seemed to deal with marriages of convenience that turned out to be bigamous. As far as the cyber-community was concerned, people didn't get married over and over again just for the fun of it. Of course they didn't. What normal person did?

Swallowing hard, she typed 'coma' into the search engine. *A profound state of unconsciousness,* she read, *where a person is alive but unable to move or to respond to his environment.* The scariest thing, she thought, as she clicked her way through the pages, was that people knew so little about it all. Most comas rarely lasted longer than a month but there was nothing definite about it. And, of course, people could lose their thinking functions and be in a vegetative state for years.

Her hands were shaking. She couldn't begin to think of Frank being in a coma for years. She leaned her head against the screen and began to cry again. And she didn't know whether she was crying with worry or self-pity or anger.

'Are you all right?' Lauren's voice at the doorway made her sit up straight again. She grabbed a tissue from the box on her desk and wiped her eyes.

'I suppose I will be,' she said. 'But right now – not really.' She swallowed hard. 'It's just that nothing about us was true!' she choked. 'He lied to me every single day about every single thing. I mean – a wife! A daughter! A whole other life and I hadn't a clue! How stupid could I be?'

'Look, honey, nobody could possibly imagine that their husband

136

had a second wife,' said Lauren. 'Maybe that they're having an affair or that they're having problems at work or something, but how on earth could you have guessed?'

'The thing is, I feel like it should all be a mistake,' cried Iona. 'I trusted him completely.' This time she wiped her eyes on the extra-long sleeve of the Aran jumper. 'I could've understood if he'd been married before and didn't tell me. I'd have been hurt but I could have dealt with it. Sometimes it's hard to tell people things. But that he was still married! And living with her at the same time as living with me! I can't believe it. Everyone will look at me and think that I'm the world's biggest eejit and they'll be dead right.'

'No they won't,' comforted Lauren. 'They'll think that he's a slick bastard.'

'But he isn't!' wailed Iona. 'That's the whole point. He was lovely to me. Always.'

Lauren rubbed her sister's shoulders.

'I know Myles hates him,' mumbled Iona. 'I suppose he's basking in the knowledge that everything he ever thought about him has turned out to be right.'

'No he's not,' said Lauren. 'He's horrified, of course. Maybe he did think that Frank was a bit too good to be true. But he never wanted you to be hurt.'

'What am I going to tell Mum and Dad?' continued Iona. 'They loved him. At least . . .' She hesitated. 'I know Mum said that the important thing was that he made me happy. I can't help wondering whether she suspected.'

'Of course she didn't!' Lauren paused in her shoulder massage.

'Well, not suspected,' admitted Iona. 'How could she? But she did comment on him being a bit older and . . . well, maybe she didn't really like him that much after all. Only you know Mum, she wouldn't have said anything.'

'I called her,' admitted Lauren.

Iona pulled away from her sister. 'Why did you do that?' she cried. 'It wasn't up to you.'

'Io, honey, she was going to have to find out sooner or later,' said Lauren. 'But I told her to leave it a bit before contacting you; give you time to get to grips with everything.'

Iona clenched her jaw and shook her head in despair. 'You see, that's just what I hate. People talking about me. Feeling sorry for me. Wondering when they should phone me.' She swallowed hard. 'How could I have been such a bloody fool? Being married already is obviously why he insisted on having the wedding in Barbados. I thought he was being romantic but he manipulated me. I'm a moron.'

'It's not your fault,' said Lauren. 'How were you to know?'

'I should've guessed.' Iona turned around on the swivel chair and faced her sister. 'You know, I felt like a total idiot in front of that policewoman. I could see that she thought I was a complete simpleton. She asked me what happened about Christmas and holidays and of course I said what Frank had told me – that sometimes he had to stay over at venues because they might need his expertise. And that we didn't go for long holidays. And that he did sometimes go to conferences without me. And all the time she was making notes and I bet they were saying how gullible I was to believe a word he told me.'

'But we do believe people when they tell us things,' said Lauren. 'Why should you have doubted him?'

'Why? Maybe because normal people don't spend Christmas in a hotel away from their families claiming that they have to stage-manage a lighting spectacular. Maybe normal people bring their wives to conferences and stuff – in fact he probably did bring his damn wife to the conferences; it just wasn't me.' Iona rubbed the back of her neck. 'D'you have any headache tablets? I feel as though my head is going to explode.'

'Sure,' said Lauren, thinking that Iona must be feeling really awful to ask for paracetamol. 'In my bag. Come on downstairs and you can have them.'

Iona hit the sleep button on the computer. She hated taking paracetamol or ibuprofen. But right now she needed something stronger than what nature had to offer.

⤔

138

Sally still felt embarrassed walking into the hospital. She couldn't help feeling that all the doctors and nurses knew exactly who she was and what had happened, even though she told herself over and over again that they had better things to talk about than the woman whose husband had married someone else and never said a thing. There was no point in her pretending otherwise as far as Frank's second marriage was concerned. Iona's reaction had been heartfelt. And Siobhán Farrell had contacted her again to tell her about Iona's Caribbean wedding and the marriage certificate that didn't really count.

Sally didn't know how she would have reacted if she'd found out about this when Frank was fit and healthy. She would have definitely been equally shocked. She told herself that she'd probably have thrown him out of the house, although that was a difficult thing to be sure about given that she was pregnant with his child.

She touched her stomach unconsciously. Frank didn't deserve a second child. Not with her. Not with anyone. He wasn't a fit person to be a father and it didn't matter how wonderful and loving he'd been towards her, or even how good he'd been with Jenna, he was a deceiving bastard and he didn't have the right to be with either of them.

And yet, as she sat alone in the room with him, listening to the sounds of the machines gently hissing and whirring, and the rhythmic beat of the heart monitor, she knew that she couldn't simply abandon him. Besides, if she did that, maybe Iona would take over.

Sally rubbed the back of her neck. She didn't want Iona taking over even though she was finding it hard to forgive Frank herself. Though the younger woman mightn't want to have anything to do with him either, now that she'd discovered that she too had been duped. She hadn't turned up at the hospital again and Siobhán had said that as far as she could see, Iona had accepted the fact that her marriage wasn't legal.

Poor girl. Bad enough as she felt herself, Sally thought it would be even worse to discover that she hadn't been married at all. So although she hated Iona for taking Frank away from her, she also felt sorry for the younger woman because her life with him had been based on a lie.

She studied the man in the bed. Already Frank was beginning to look like a different person, his handsome face pale and expressionless, the tubes and machines almost a part of him. Despite his still attractive features, Sally couldn't see in him the person who'd almost literally swept her off her feet, who'd charmed her in an instant, who'd helped her discover that her body was an almost unlimited playground of desire. Frank looked old in the bed. Dependent. He'd never been dependent on her before. He'd always been the one to take charge of things. She hated seeing him like this and she knew he'd hate to think of her sitting with him, watching and waiting.

What would happen if he didn't come out of the coma? Everyone in the hospital was trying to be positive, despite their concerns. Sally wanted to be positive too. She couldn't believe that he wouldn't open his eyes in a day or two and look around and ask where the hell he was and what the hell he was doing here.

Would he expect to see her? Or would he think that Iona was the one who should be beside him? She swallowed hard. How would she feel if he opened his eyes and asked for Iona?

'Hi, Mrs Harper.' The nurse who'd been there on the first night was on duty again. Sally glanced at her name tag to remind herself of who she was.

'I just need to do a few bits and pieces for him,' Terri Cooper said. 'You can stay if you want, or wait outside.'

Sally got up. She needed a break anyway. She walked down the corridor and got herself a coffee from the dispenser. Jenna hadn't come with her on this visit. She'd asked, in a worried tone, whether it would be all right not to come because the hospital gave her the creeps. Sally had nodded in agreement. She didn't want Jenna to feel that her whole life had to revolve around hospital visits. Besides, the place gave her the creeps too.

'Finished now.' Terri smiled brightly at Sally, who finished the tepid coffee and crumpled the plastic cup in her hand.

'Will he get better?' Sally knew that the nurse wouldn't be able to give her an answer, but she couldn't help asking anyway.

'You'd be surprised at how many people get better,' said Terri. 'Though I have to be honest with you and say that it takes time for them to get back to normal. It's a huge trauma.'

Sally nodded.

'We're all keeping our fingers crossed for him,' Terri said. 'He's a very attractive man, isn't he?'

'He's more attractive when he's awake,' said Sally wryly.

Terri grinned. 'But you can see it in him all the same.'

'Seems more than me did.'

Terri looked at her cautiously. She'd been trying to be cheerful with the sad-faced woman, but of course in this case saying that her husband was attractive might have been like waving the proverbial red rag at a bull.

'It's an awkward situation,' agreed Terri.

'This morning the doctor told me to talk to him,' Sally said. 'And so I read him the papers. But what if it's not me he needs to hear? What if it's her?'

Terri shrugged uncomfortably. 'I'd say any familiar voice would be a help,' she said.

'Maybe I should just get my daughter to do it,' said Sally. 'At least we know that he loves her.' Her eyes opened wide. 'Is there another one?'

'Pardon?'

'Child? Does that woman have a child? She didn't say and I didn't ask, but . . .'

'I don't know,' said Terri.

'Oh fuck him!' cried Sally suddenly, startling Terri. 'Fuck him, fuck him, fuck him!' She threw the crumpled coffee cup across the corridor. 'How could he do this to me and to Jenna? How could he do it to Iona either? I thought I loved him but he's nothing but a bastard!'

'You don't really mean that, Sally,' said Terri gently. 'You're overwrought.'

'I'm not,' snapped Sally. 'I'm just – I'm just . . .' The fight went out of her and she swayed on her feet. Terri put her arm around her and guided her to a chair.

'Sit down,' she said. 'It's been a huge strain on you and anyone would be upset.'

'A strain for everyone except Frank,' she said bitterly. 'He's lying there with everyone fussing around him but we're left to cope with the mess. I don't know what to do about his work – I've never had anything to do with it. I'm not sure what I'm supposed to do myself about my own job. I don't know what to do about Jenna and school . . . He's left us with all these problems and I just can't bloody cope!'

'Sit there and I'll get you something,' said Terri. 'Isn't there anyone with you today?'

'I got a taxi,' said Sally. 'We should get our car back tomorrow. That's another thing to worry about. I have to deal with everything. All he has to do is lie there!'

Terri gestured to Susan Carpenter, another nurse, who was walking down the corridor, and whispered into her ear. Susan returned a few moments later with a small pill and a cup of water.

'Come on, Sally,' said Terri. 'You'll feel better after this.'

'I can't take those tablets.'

'Of course you can,' said Terri. 'It'll help you to relax, and you need to relax right now.'

'You don't understand.' Sally looked at both of the nurses and closed her eyes in despair. When she opened them again they were both watching her anxiously. 'I can't take the damn tablets because on the day he was in the accident I discovered I was pregnant.' Her laugh was short and croaky. 'As if I didn't have enough to be dealing with, huh?'

Terri and Susan exchanged shocked glances. Then Susan walked away with the water and the pill and Terri put her arm around Sally's shoulders again.

Chapter 14

Iona wasn't sure how to go about finding Frank's lawyer, but in the end it was Myles who said he'd check it out for her. Lauren had told him of Iona's concerns about Frank's company and Myles said that he would use his legal and accountancy contacts to find out what he could. Iona wanted to thank him but she was finding it difficult to talk to Myles, who she was sure would only say that he'd told her so and that Frank was the complete shit he'd always thought him to be.

'Myles isn't like that,' said Lauren, when Iona finally admitted this to her sister. 'I don't understand why you've always been so horrible to him.'

Iona heard the sudden break in her sister's voice and she looked at her in surprise. 'I'm not horrible to him,' she said.

'You are,' said Lauren. 'Even before you met Frank. You always went on and on about Myles being a boring accountant.'

Iona flushed. What Lauren had said was true. She did think accountants were boring.

'I'm sorry,' she said. 'I didn't mean that he was boring. Only that it was a boring profession.'

'You know, you've a bit of a cheek thinking that when Frank works in lighting and you work in a damn letting agency,' said Lauren.

Iona looked contrite. 'I know. Though I always wanted to do something more exciting than house-letting,' she said.

'Well maybe Myles wanted to do something more exciting than accounting,' said Lauren. 'Only he's got a wife and family to provide for and it's a damn good job.'

'Just as well I wasn't planning on Frank providing for me,' said Iona shakily. 'Just as well I wasn't pregnant after all.'

'Oh, hell, Io . . .' Lauren looked at her sympathetically. 'I'm sorry.'

'I don't know where to go from here,' said Iona. 'I'm not married to him. I really don't have any say in what's going on. I want to go to the hospital but . . .'

'Maybe you can come to some arrangement with Sally.'

'I don't want to come to an arrangement with her,' said Iona fiercely. 'As though she can give me permission to go and see the man I've been sleeping with for the last four years. As though she's somehow in control.'

'She *is* in control, it seems,' said Lauren. 'You have to decide what you're going to do. Did you talk to your solicitor this morning?'

Iona nodded. 'He said they could try to prosecute me if they thought I was part of some crazy plan,' she said. 'Not that I even thought of that, which is just as well or I . . .' She shook her head tiredly. 'He's going to contact Frank's solicitor, once we find out who he is. He wants to try to establish some rights based on the fact that I thought I was married. To be honest, though, I don't see the point. I know the situation. I can't be part of it all, Lauren. Not while she's the real wife and I'm nothing. I'm not going in to see him again.'

'But you need to think about this a bit more,' said Lauren. 'After all, what if he dies?'

'I don't want to think about him dying,' said Iona.

'But you're entitled to something, surely?'

'Like what?'

'Well . . .' She shrugged. 'There's the house in Sligo, isn't there? And if his company was profitable you should have a slice of that. After all, you supported him with it, didn't you?'

'I helped out from time to time,' said Iona. 'That was just doing letters and stuff for him.'

'All the same . . .'

'I can't!' Iona thumped her fist on the table. 'Lauren, if he dies

144

there's just me. But for them – well, it's Sally and her daughter. They're entitled to more.' She exhaled sharply. 'I don't want to think about him dying. I want to think about him getting better.'

'And that'll create even more problems.'

'Maybe,' said Iona. 'But I'd rather them than anything else.'

❧

Later that day Siobhán phoned both Sally and Iona and asked them to make witness statements about their relationship with Frank. At first neither of them was very happy about the idea, but, each concerned about what the other might say, they finally agreed. Siobhán told them that it was an easy process and that she'd call out to their houses if that was what they wanted. But somewhat to her surprise they both said they'd come into the station instead. She'd been taken aback when they'd both suggested Thursday and in the interests of peace and sanity had asked if Sally could come a day earlier.

So on Wednesday afternoon Sally found herself sitting in the bright reception area of Bray garda station while she waited for Siobhán Farrell to take her to an interview room. Even though they'd lived in Bray for the past five years Sally had never been in the station before, although she'd often driven by it on her way to the town centre. It was big and modern and as unlike her preconception of a garda station as it was possible to be. She thought, as she gazed at the pastel-painted walls and watched the young garda behind the reception desk deal with a telephone query, that it was relatively welcoming and certainly not as threatening as she'd expected. But she was overcome by a sense of unreality at the idea that she, Sally Harper, was here as a witness to a crime and that that crime was that her husband had married someone else. If she'd ever had to come up with a reason for visiting a garda station, that wouldn't have even appeared on the list. She sat on the wooden seat and stared at the blue sky through the angular glass roof while she tried to slow down the rapid beating of her heart. She was nervous about the interview and uncertain what Siobhán would want to know.

When the detective walked into the reception area to greet her, Sally couldn't help feeling that the other woman was much more serious and formal than she'd been previously, even though she smiled warmly at Sally and thanked her for coming.

'D'you want to follow me?' she asked.

Sally grabbed her bag and walked after the detective, who showed her into a small interview room and told her to take a seat. Sally noticed that there was a video camera over the door of the room which was pointed in her direction. She swallowed nervously as she tugged on the arms of the black leather chair to bring it nearer to the table. It didn't budge. She pulled it again.

'It's heavy,' said Siobhán. 'We normally have suspects in here and we don't want them to be able to lift up the chair and throw it at us.'

Sally swallowed nervously again at the thought of the other people who might have sat in that chair, and Siobhán smiled reassuringly at her.

'You're not a suspect in anything, Sally,' she said. 'You're just here to help us sort things out.'

Sally's eyes flickered towards the camera.

'We're not recording anything either,' Siobhán told her. 'Don't worry.' She stood up and popped a button on the video console. 'There you go, there's nothing in there.'

'OK.' Sally swallowed hard.

'D'you want me to get you a drink?' asked Siobhán. 'Water? Or tea, maybe?'

Sally shook her head. Now that she was here, she just wanted to get on with it.

'Right-o,' said Siobhán. 'Let's get started.'

She went over much of the ground she'd already covered, although she asked the questions in a different way. Sally found it a surreal experience as she gave her answers honestly but with an increasing feeling that the detective must surely take her for a complete fool. All the same, she was utterly unable to take in the fact that as far as the legal system was concerned, Frank was actually a criminal. A lying, philandering shit maybe, she'd thought

146

that morning as she sat on the edge of the toilet following her regular bout of morning sickness, but not a criminal. Here, though, in the station, everything seemed much more serious than it had done before.

She wiped a bead of sweat from her forehead and then looked anxiously at Siobhán. What if the detective thought she was sweating because she was involved somehow in a scam of Frank's? What if she thought it was some elaborate hoax that the two of them had perpetrated.

'Are you going to charge him?' she asked.

Siobhán looked at her noncommittally. 'It's not up to me. It's the Director of Public Prosecutions who decides, and to tell you the truth, Sally, I've no idea what he'll think. I guess it depends on whether he believes the public interest would be served in charging him.'

'And would it?'

'It depends on how things eventually pan out,' said Siobhán. 'I mean, what did Frank stand to gain by marrying Iona?'

'Great sex?' Sally looked at Siobhán wryly.

The other girl blanched. 'I'm sorry?'

'I've no bloody idea what he had to gain,' said Sally. 'But Frank wasn't . . . isn't good at sex outside a relationship. He told me before that he didn't like one-night stands. Of course this is different, I know, but . . .' She chewed the inside of her lip. 'Frank is good at sex.'

Siobhán tried to hide her unease. She didn't want to hear about the Harpers' sex life – especially not how good it might have been. But Sally was suddenly talking about how she and Frank had met and how there was an instant attraction between them; how, in fact, they'd hardly been able to keep their hands off each other. And that there was something more to it than that – Frank was a vibrant person who made a woman feel good about herself. Sally knew that she blossomed in his company because her self-confidence grew when she was with him. So maybe it was the same with Iona. She looked at Siobhán questioningly.

'That's the thing.' Siobhán had regained her composure. 'Mostly

147

there's a more tangible benefit than, well, just sex. There's plenty of that available without having to get married! Usually in these cases people are trying to gain nationality. Or sometimes it's financial. But I can't see a financial reason here.'

'Maybe she's incredibly rich,' suggested Sally morosely. 'Maybe there were money problems I didn't know about. Maybe he felt that by marrying her . . .' Her voice trailed off. She didn't like where her thoughts were taking her.

'It doesn't really seem like it,' said Siobhán. 'Although obviously we're checking out that angle.' She looked apologetically at Sally. 'We're also looking into Frank's company, to see if there were money problems. And – I know this is hard for you, Sally, I really do – but under the circumstances, I'd like to take Frank's fingerprints.'

Sally's expression was shocked. 'Why?'

'I need to check to see if he's been in trouble before,' said Siobhán.

'For crying out loud!' Sally looked at her in exasperation. 'He's an ordinary bloke. Of course he hasn't been in any trouble. Except maybe a few unpaid parking fines. Or perhaps you got him on camera breaking the speed limit or something. Only he doesn't. He's a careful driver. He's a law-abiding man.'

'I do understand that,' said Siobhán. 'But it would help in the investigation.'

Sally sighed deeply. She liked Siobhán, who, she thought, had been kind and understanding and very non-judgemental about the situation. But she wished that the other woman wouldn't talk about Frank as though he was a criminal. He wasn't. He was her husband.

'If you really need to do this, then go ahead,' she said tiredly. 'But you know, Siobhán, I truly loved him. I know, I absolutely know, that he wasn't involved in anything dodgy and you're wasting your time if you think that. His solicitor has been in touch about the company. Frank has critical illness cover, which kicks in for me. Frank's accountant is contacting the clients and arranging for them to be looked after. I gave him Frank's mobile. There's absolutely nothing dodgy going on. And you probably think that I'm crazy saying this, but I do know my husband. He's an honest man. Obviously I don't understand why he did all this. How the hell can I? But I understand some of it.'

'Jeez, Sally, nobody understands everything to do with men,' said Siobhán with feeling. 'If we did we'd all be a lot bloody happier.'

Sally raised an eyebrow. Siobhán's words had been heartfelt.

'Are you married?' She repeated the question which Siobhán hadn't answered when she'd been at Sally's house.

Siobhán shook her head.

'Anyone special?'

She thought of Eddie. He was special.

'I'm engaged,' she told Sally.

'Do you live with him?' asked Sally.

Siobhán considered before answering. By talking about her own life, even a little, she hoped she might reassure Sally that she wasn't her enemy. She nodded.

'I never lived with Frank before we got married,' said Sally. 'I slept with him, of course, but in those days people didn't live together much. There wasn't plenty of it around without having to get married. In fact getting married was probably the only way to have a regular sex life!'

Siobhán looked at her sympathetically.

'Will you have a family some day? Or are you one of those really dedicated career women? Are you looking to be the chief superintendent or something?'

'Oh, I'll never make chief super,' said Siobhán. 'I'm probably very lucky to be where I am at all.'

'Rubbish. I bet you're great at your job.' Sally glanced around the spartan room. 'Is it horribly male-dominated?'

'It's not as bad as it used to be,' admitted Siobhán. 'And of course crime has changed too over the past few years. There's more technological stuff going on. And domestic crimes . . . well, I know it's a cliché, but women are often good in those situations.'

149

'I suppose me and Iona are a domestic crime,' said Sally.

Siobhán smiled at her. 'I'm not really sure how we'll categorise this.'

'I don't want them to prosecute him,' said Sally urgently. 'I know he's done an awful thing and I hate him for it, but . . .'

'I just prepare the file,' said Siobhán. She shifted in her seat. 'And with him being so ill, it's difficult to say . . . How is he doing now?'

Sally sighed deeply. 'Still in a coma,' she said. 'The longer he stays that way the more worrying it gets. I've taken this week off work so that I can spend as much time as possible at the hospital with him, but I can't stay out indefinitely.'

'And your daughter?'

'Jenna went back to school today. It wasn't doing her any good being at home, moping around. At least this way she's kept busy.'

'You're being really brave about everything,' said Siobhán.

'Not really,' Sally said. 'I cry a lot.'

'I don't blame you,' said Siobhán. She closed her files. 'Come on,' she said. 'Why don't we go for a coffee?'

Sally looked at her uncertainly. 'Coffee? Are you allowed to go and have coffee with the wife of a criminal?'

'You'd be surprised at the kind of people I sometimes have coffee with.' Siobhán grinned and Sally couldn't help smiling too.

Although there was a kitchen and coffee area in the station, Siobhán thought it would be better to take Sally outside. It was about half a mile to the town centre. Siobhán decided to drive. She could justify spending some time in having coffee with Sally, she thought, but not in strolling to and from the town, even though the day was warm and sunny and a gentle walk would have been very pleasant. She parked in the Herbert Street car park, then led the way to a small bright café where she ordered a frothy cappuccino for herself and a skinny latte for Sally. They sat in a window seat and looked out at the bustling street.

'What other sort of crimes do you investigate?' asked Sally as she tipped brown sugar into her coffee.

'All sorts.' Siobhán talked about the petty crimes that made up so much of the daily workload of the station, as well as some of the more difficult cases, while Sally half listened and half watched the people walking by.

She liked Siobhán. She felt as though it were somehow disloyal to Frank to like the person who wanted to brand him a criminal, but she couldn't help it. Siobhán was an easy person to talk to, and because at the moment she was one of the few people to know about Frank's other wife, Sally felt more comfortable with her than anyone else. She hadn't told anyone – still not even Denise – about Iona. She simply couldn't. Everyone was being so kind and thoughtful and worrying so much about him, she didn't have the heart to tell them that he was a two-timing git. And the worst of it all was that she still hadn't really accepted that he was a two-timing git herself. Every time she thought about his marriage to Iona, it seemed unreal to her.

She realised that Siobhán had finally stopped talking about the Bray garda station caseload and was staring absent-mindedly into her coffee mug.

'Siobhán?' Sally looked at her enquiringly. 'Is everything OK?'

'Sure, sure,' she said quickly. 'It's fine.' She looked at her watch. 'Listen, I'm sorry but I have to get back. I have a meeting in a few minutes.'

'Of course.' Sally nodded. 'I didn't mean to keep you out for so long.'

'That's OK,' said Siobhán. 'I enjoyed it.'

'So did I.' Sally surprised herself by her comment. How could she have enjoyed sitting talking to the policewoman? But she had. 'When are you going to take Frank's fingerprints?' she asked as she gathered up her things.

'I'm not sure,' said Siobhán. 'Depends on when I get time.'

'Yeah, well it's not as though he's going anywhere,' said Sally wryly.

'I do hope he comes out of the coma soon,' said Siobhán.

'D'you know what? I'm not so sure about that any more.'

Sally pushed back her chair and walked out on to the street.

⤸

Iona had been dreading her visit to the police station. It was years since she'd been to Bray. Even though the seaside town wasn't really that far away, she didn't know anyone in the locality and never had any reason to go there. As a child, though, she'd often come with her family during the summer and, as she drove into the town now, fragmented memories of walking along the seashore resurfaced in her mind.

She parked in the visitors' area of the station, getting the last available space, and hurried into the building. The garda in charge looked at her with interest as she asked to see Detective Siobhán Farrell. Iona felt herself blush as she spoke. She supposed that everyone in the police station knew about the situation, and now that she thought about it, they were probably all thinking what a fool she was. But the garda didn't make any comment about her foolishness and merely told her to sit down and wait while he contacted Detective Farrell.

Iona perched on a wooden seat and rubbed the back of her neck. The headache that had started on the day of Frank's accident still hadn't gone. Sometimes it was more noticeable than others, but it continued to pound away at the back of her head and she didn't know when it might ever lift.

Five minutes later Siobhán walked into the waiting area and asked Iona to follow her. She led her to the room where the previous day she'd sat and taken Sally's statement, and now went through exactly the same procedure with Iona, although she soon realised that the younger woman was much more businesslike about the whole thing than Sally had been. Iona seemed to have recovered more quickly, even though Siobhán could see that she had huge dark circles under her eyes.

'Obviously I don't know whether the DPP will actually prosecute this case,' Siobhán told her, pre-empting the question that Sally had already asked. 'Given Frank's current health it seems unlikely. On the other hand, it is a criminal offence.'

Iona nodded wordlessly.

'I'm really sorry,' Siobhán told her. 'I know this must be difficult for you.'

'Oh for heaven's sake!' Iona looked at her despairingly. 'It's more than bloody difficult. It's impossible!'

'Unfortunately—'

'I didn't mean that literally,' Iona interrupted. 'Of course it's possible in the sense that he obviously did it! It's just . . . it's just an impossible situation to be in.'

'I understand that too,' said Siobhán.

'Yeah, well, I can't see that there are many people who could,' retorted Iona. 'I'm sure your experience of the wives of criminals is that they might be shocked that their husbands have raided a bank or something. Not that their husbands turn out not to be husbands at all.'

Siobhán grimaced.

'You know what the problem is?' said Iona. 'I can't tell anyone what's happened. That's the problem.'

'What d'you mean?'

'I'm off work right now and I've told them I have a bug, that I'll be back soon. I can't tell them that Frank's been in an accident because they'll want to send him flowers, and what's the point in that? And I don't know how to tell them that he's not and never was my husband! They'll think I'm barmy. Tell you the truth, *I* think I'm barmy! I didn't even guess.'

'I'm sure they'll understand,' said Siobhán.

'Oh, get a grip, woman.' Iona looked impatient. 'Of course they won't.'

'Well, I'm sure they'll sympathise,' amended Siobhán.

'I don't want sympathy,' said Iona fiercely. 'I want certainty. I want to know when he'll get better and I want to know why he did it, but nobody can answer either of those questions for me and it's driving me crazy.'

Siobhán nodded. 'I do understand, honestly. Come on, let's get a coffee. I know a good place in Bray.'

～

The café was crowded but they got the last remaining table.

'I don't know what I'm supposed to do,' said Iona as she added

153

sugar to her latte (Siobhán had been slightly taken aback that Iona ordered the same coffee as Sally). 'I mean – if we had been married and I found out about someone else I could divorce him. But as it stands . . . well, as it stands it's just like he's suddenly out of my life. I can't go to the hospital and I don't have any say in his treatment.'

'Really?'

'I suppose I could insist,' said Iona. 'My solicitor wants me to try. But honestly, Siobhán, what's the point? He was married to Sally for eighteen years! I've only known him for five.' She took a sip of the coffee. 'And besides, they have a daughter to consider. How would she feel to see me there?'

Siobhán looked at her sympathetically. 'I can see that it's hard.'

'Part of me wants to be there and part of me doesn't ever want to see him again,' said Iona. She massaged the back of her neck. The headache had started to pound more ferociously again.

'You know, I'm sure Sally would come to some arrangement with you,' said Siobhán.

'You're joking!' Iona snorted. 'We nearly came to blows at the hospital, you know. I can't remember exactly what we said to each other but I'm pretty sure none of it was pleasant.'

'Tempers have cooled a little since then,' Siobhán told her. 'And Sally is as gutted about everything as you. Don't forget he was cheating on her too. So she's angry about that.'

Iona shrugged. 'I guess so.'

'I might be wrong,' said Siobhán, 'but it can't do any harm to call her and see if you can work something out.'

'I'm not sure if I want to,' admitted Iona. 'There's a part of me that feels he can just rot away in hospital for all I care.'

'It's up to you.'

'I'll think about it,' said Iona. She stared into space for a moment. 'You know, ever since we talked before, I keep asking myself over and over again what he had to gain by marrying me.'

Siobhán looked at her with interest. 'I wonder about that myself.'

'He could have told me that he was married and that his home life was shit and . . . well . . . I probably would've believed him. Maybe I would have been one of those really good mistresses who provide sex and a haven for the poor stressed-out married man.' She shrugged.

Siobhán said nothing.

'But then I wondered whether it was simply that he wanted me for himself.'

Siobhán raised an eyebrow.

'He's very possessive. And we were great in bed together. Maybe he didn't want to think of me with anyone else.'

Siobhán gulped. Her efforts to be warm and sympathetic to the two women were rewarding her with far too much insight into their sex lives!

'There's just something about him.' Iona sighed. 'He's good with women.'

'So it seems.' Siobhán couldn't keep the wryness out of her voice.

'Look, I know you probably think that Sally and I are both bonkers,' snapped Iona, 'but you've got to understand what it was like. Frank – well, he's special. I might be mad at him – more than mad at him now, I guess – but I can't . . . I can't really hate him. I want to, but I don't. He gave me such a great time . . .' Her voice trailed off. She finished her coffee and looked ruefully at Siobhán. 'I suppose I'd better get going. I'm sorry if I've ranted on a bit.'

'That's OK,' said Siobhán. 'It helps to talk.'

'I'm sure you've better things to do than listen to me,' said Iona.

'There's always something to do,' said Siobhán. 'But if you need to talk to me about it any time, you're more than welcome to call.'

'I asked him to marry me,' said Iona abruptly. 'I practically forced him into it. It wasn't his idea.'

Siobhán didn't say that all the best con-men make you think you're deciding something for yourself. She just nodded in acknowledgement of Iona's words.

155

'Thanks for the coffee.' Iona smiled and Siobhán suddenly saw what might have attracted Frank to her. Her dark eyes were lighter now, and held a hint of mischief. And even though her face was still pale, the smile changed her look completely.

Iona offered her hand and Siobhán shook it.

'I suppose you'll be in touch?' Iona added. 'If there's any news?'

Siobhán nodded. 'Of course. In the meantime, look after yourself,' she said.

'Yeah. I will.' Iona smiled shortly at her and walked out into the street.

Chapter 15

As she walked back towards the car park, Siobhán wondered just how delusional both Sally and Iona were about Frank and his relationship with them. He couldn't love both of them equally. And surely he couldn't be that good in bed with both of them too. Didn't he ever feel too tired? Or call out the wrong name by mistake? How could he possibly switch from one to the other like that?

Was there the faintest chance, though, that by having two women, and apparently loving two women, it was actually making things better for them all? Because both Sally and Iona seemed to have had happy and fulfilling lives with Frank up to now. And, of course, they both agreed he was great in bed.

She sighed deeply. What wouldn't she give for a great-in-bed moment herself right now. Not that she actually wanted to share Eddie with someone to make that happen, but at least the Harper women were confident about that part of their relationship. Whereas she and Eddie . . . She sighed again. Something had gone horribly wrong in the bedroom between them.

She hadn't realised it until the day after he'd come back from Boston. Obviously she'd been hurt that he hadn't wanted to make mad passionate love to her the day he'd arrived home, but she did understand that he was probably exhausted. But the following day she'd expected that they'd pop the champagne and light the candles and get down and dirty. Well, get down to it anyway – they'd never been madly adventurous in bed together but they'd always enjoyed themselves in a relatively staid kind of way.

Occasionally Siobhán had taken the initiative and made things just a little more exciting – like when she'd handcuffed Eddie to the bed (but he hadn't really liked being totally under her control so it hadn't been quite as much fun as she'd expected) – but usually they were quite happy to make conventional love in the dark and beneath the sheets.

Only that hadn't happened. Neither on Sunday nor the following day – not at all since he'd come home. She'd tried to kiss him and cuddle him but each time he'd turned away from her and told her that he really just wasn't in the mood. And when, last night, she'd asked him straight out what the hell was going on, he'd responded by saying that they didn't have to be screwing each other senseless every single night and that he was under a huge amount of pressure at work and was there even the faintest chance that she'd let him get some sleep?

Siobhán had been shocked by the tone in his voice. She'd asked him whether there was anything the matter, whether she'd said or done something to upset him. And he'd rolled on to his back and said that the biggest problem any bloke could have with a woman was that she wanted to analyse every single thing in their lives together, and no, she hadn't said or done anything but could she just, for once, stop interrogating him like a suspect in the fucking cells.

She blinked away a tear as she remembered the harshness of his voice and the way that he'd rolled away from her. And she wondered what the hell had happened in Boston, because everything had been fine until he'd left. Had he met someone else there? Was he afraid to tell her? But Eddie had never been afraid to tell her things before. They'd always been upfront and honest in their relationship. They'd shared their likes and dislikes. They got on well together.

So what the hell was going on?

Maybe he'd simply gone off her. She wasn't sure what to do if he'd simply gone off her. She didn't want to lose him. She hadn't realised, until he'd gone away, just how much she really loved him.

Siobhán crossed the road and turned towards the car park.

But her attention was caught by the window display of the shop nearby. The store had opened recently, she knew; she remembered there had been a takeaway sandwich store on the site. Now it was a lingerie boutique and the display was of ethereal wisps of pastel chiffon and lace floating on a background of soft white feathers.

Would that make a difference? she wondered. If she wore sultry lingerie for Eddie instead of her slightly greying M&S knickers and sturdy bra, would he want to make love to her again? She didn't always wear sensible underwear, of course, but on work days it was usually her plain white or black cotton Lycra mixes with her equally plain support bra. Siobhán had (as Eddie had told her on one of their early dates) a fine chest which needed decent support. So that was what she gave it. But she never bothered to change when she got home, even though, perhaps, her day-time bras weren't exactly knee-tremblers.

Is it me? she wondered. Have I just become so caught up in the whole work thing that I've forgotten how to be feminine? It isn't, after all, as though I have to wear frumpy underwear to be a good cop. But maybe wearing frumpy underwear is making me a terrible girlfriend.

She hesitated for another moment or two and then pushed open the door of the shop. A bell pinged with a genteel chime and a woman of around Siobhán's own age emerged from the back of the shop. She smiled helpfully at her and Siobhán felt herself flush. 'Just looking,' she said hastily and knocked against a display of thongs, sending them scattering to the floor. She felt her face flame red. 'Sorry.'

'No problem,' said the sales assistant as she began scooping them up again. 'I'm afraid we're a bit tight for space here.' She began to replace the wispy thongs on the rack. 'Are you looking for anything in particular?'

Siobhán stared at the insubstantial piece of lace in the woman's hand. Surely she was looking for more than that, despite wanting something sexy. She needed more than a wisp to cover her generous bum, after all. She cleared her throat.

'I'm not sure,' she said. 'Something . . . well . . . nice, I suppose.'

'We've lots of nice things!' The assistant smiled at her. 'And some naughty things too.'

'How naughty?' Siobhán felt herself flush again even while she told herself that she was a policewoman, for heaven's sake, and nothing could be too naughty for her to think about.

'Well, we have crotchless panties and peephole bras,' said the shop assistant. 'Very tasteful, though. All of our goods are tasteful and of very high quality.'

Would crotchless knickers turn Eddie on? Siobhán's teeth worried her bottom lip.

'Or, of course, we have a superb collection of basques and French knickers too,' continued the saleswoman. 'You'd look great in a basque,' she added. 'You have the chest for it.'

'You mean I'm big and bulky?' suggested Siobhán.

'Not at all!' The assistant looked horrified. 'You're voluptuous. You should enhance that look.'

Siobhán snorted. 'I can't afford to look voluptuous – even if I was – during the day.'

'Everyone can and should look their best at all times,' said the sales assistant firmly. 'But of course, if you're looking for something more in the playwear line . . .'

'No,' said Siobhán hastily. 'I just want something . . . something nice.'

'Have you tried a basque at all?'

Siobhán shook her head.

'I promise you, you'll love it. And you'll look fantastic!' The woman moved across the tiny shop to another rail. 'Look at these. Absolutely exquisite.' She picked up a black and cream lace basque and held it up for Siobhán to inspect. 'Chantilly lace. Very popular and not too expensive at all.'

Siobhán looked at it. Like much of the rest of the stock, it seemed to her almost impossibly delicate.

'Of course, if you want something more . . . more substantial . . .' the sales assistant was watching her closely, 'you could try

160

this one. She picked up a confection in red lace. 'It's La Perla so it's one of our more expensive items but worth every cent. Feel the quality of that! And,' she added, 'it really emphasises the cleavage. Which is perfect for you! You're a 36C, right?'

Siobhán nodded but looked undecidedly at the basque.

'And if you do go down the more playful route . . .' the woman grinned at her and opened a drawer, 'there's always good old Agent Provocateur.'

Siobhán's eyes narrowed as she saw the assistant take out what appeared to be a selection of PVC strings.

'They call it a playsuit,' she told Siobhán as she handed her a brochure. 'And you put these little pasties on your boobs.'

'You've got to be kidding me.' Siobhán looked at the picture of the model wearing nothing but the PVC strings and two tassels hanging from her nipples. 'People buy this stuff? Here? In Bray?'

'Of course they do,' said the assistant. 'After all, everyone can do with adding a bit of spice to their sex lives, don't you think? And what man could resist you in this?'

Eddie, probably, thought Siobhán glumly. She gazed at the selection of goods on the counter in front of her to which the sales assistant added another couple of basques, one of which was straight out of a porn fantasy.

'It depends on the man, of course,' added the assistant helpfully. 'Some of them like the kind of dominatrix approach. But others prefer you to look a bit more helpless.'

And which would Eddie prefer? wondered Siobhán. Did he want to dominate her? Or did he want her to appear in need of rescuing? He hadn't liked the handcuffs, so she supposed he wouldn't be too enamoured of black leather and whips. Yet she couldn't see herself looking sweet and virginal in black and cream lace.

'I also have a lovely Moschino,' the assistant continued. 'Just in. Dark lace with a little silver detail. Fabulous. Matching thong, or, if you prefer, little boxers. Looks less like a *Playboy* centrefold and a bit more assertive.'

Siobhán looked at the Moschino basque. The assistant was right.

If any of this frothy stuff could be described as being her, this was the most likely candidate. It was sexy without being submissive; seductive without being trashy.

'How much?' she asked and nearly fainted when the saleswoman told her. But, she thought, it was an investment in her future. If she was to save her relationship, then maybe this was the way forward. She took out her credit card and handed it over before she changed her mind.

'Are you taking the thong or the boxers?' asked the assistant.

She couldn't do the thong, she really couldn't. She wanted to attract Eddie again, not repel him.

'The boxers,' she said.

'You can try on the basque,' said the assistant. 'You might want to be sure that it fits. Though I'm pretty certain it'll be great on you.'

Siobhán shook her head. She didn't want this woman poking her head into the changing room, watching her wobble over the top of the silk and lace garment. She'd try it on at home and hope to hell that she hadn't blown half her salary on a wasted piece of lingerie. Because if it didn't fit, there was no way she'd have the nerve to come back with it.

She watched as the assistant lovingly wrapped her purchases in swathes of tissue paper and then put them in a discreet box.

'We also have toys,' she added, 'if you're interested in anything else for fun.'

Siobhán really wasn't sure how Eddie would feel about sex toys. They were a perfectly normal and acceptable part of people's lives these days, but they'd never been part of hers and Eddie's. So if she brought something home . . . She shook her head. 'Not right now,' she said.

The sales assistant smiled. 'No bother. Enjoy these. It'll all look fabulous on you.'

'I'll do my best,' muttered Siobhán.

She made one more stop on the way back to the car park, and that was in the little home accessories shop, where she bought a selection of scented candles and aromatic oils. Not exactly sex toys, but the ambience might help. Eddie wouldn't know what had hit him, she thought as she handed over her credit card yet again. He'd be overcome by her sensuality, and if that didn't kick-start their sex life again, she simply didn't know what would.

⤴

When she got back to the station she took out the Golden Pages and looked up house cleaning agencies. She called the one with the biggest ad and organised for them to come twice a month to clean the apartment, feeling confident that Eddie would approve. After all, she told herself as she replaced the receiver, if she was going to turn into some kind of sex goddess she couldn't be expected to spend hours cleaning and scrubbing. She had to be in the mood. Actually, she was getting quite excited about the thought of turning herself into a sex goddess for Eddie that evening. Maybe she was spending too much time trying to be tough in her job and not half enough time being a bit more feeble at home.

She turned her attention to the folders on her desk and tried to stop thinking sexy thoughts. There were a couple of files from the DPP which she had to look through, as well as a report to write on the money-laundering enquiry. And, of course, she had to finish her work on the Frank Harper case too. The fact that the man was in a coma didn't make him any less of a bastard, thought Siobhán. And those women were really nice. She'd liked both of them, even though her initial reaction had been to think that it was poor Sally who'd been hard done by. She couldn't help remembering the night they'd told Sally about the accident and how shocked she'd been. So her sympathies had somewhat naturally lain with her. But then, having met Iona, she'd found herself feeling sorry for her too. Iona seemed tougher than Sally, but Siobhán wasn't sure that was truly the case. She wondered, quite suddenly, how Iona would have coped with a man who didn't have sex with her. She rather thought that she would just have walked out. After all, she'd simply stopped going to see Frank at the hospital, which proved that she could made tough decisions. She probably wouldn't give Eddie a second chance either.

Siobhán frowned. It wasn't a case of second chances. It was a case of working through something that had become a problem even though she didn't know why.

'Hey, Siobhán!' Larry Masterson, her usual partner, walked into the room and sat down at his desk. 'Looking forward to tomorrow?'

She looked at him in surprise and then groaned. She'd been so caught up with Iona and Sally and her own problems with Eddie that she'd forgotten about her upcoming court appearance. She supposed that the good thing about everything that was going on in her life was that she hadn't had time to be nervous about it. She tapped her pen against her teeth and shook her head in determination. She had work to do to prepare for tomorrow. But tonight she'd deal with Eddie.

⁓

She was home ahead of him that evening, which she'd expected, as he was meeting a client for drinks after work. Although she didn't quite turn into a cleaning tornado, she did tidy the apartment a little more, this time concentrating on the bedroom, where she hung up the piles of clothes that she'd left on the armchair in the corner of the room; then she ruthlessly dumped a variety of half-empty and little-used jars of face creams in the bin. She hated throwing things out unless they were finished, but, she muttered, if she hadn't used them for more than a month, she wasn't going to miss them now! She filled the washing machine with laundry from the laundry basket, although she decided not to switch it on. It wouldn't do for their moment of passion to be interrupted by the asthmatic rattle of the machine as it settled into the spin cycle.

She placed the scented candles in small glass bowls which she arranged carefully around both the living room and the bedroom. Then she went into the tiny bathroom and had a shower, lathering herself with the Chanel shower soap which she'd bought in the airport on last year's holiday to Spain but hardly ever used because it had been so bloody expensive. But she knew that she smelled good when she patted herself dry and she asked herself why on earth she didn't use the damn soap regardless of how much it had cost, since it wasn't doing a lot of good simply sitting on the bathroom shelf.

Then she went back into the bedroom and slid her new purchases out of their box.

The sales assistant had been right. The black and silver basque made her look extremely voluptuous. Rather like a Tudor girl, thought Siobhán, as she looked at her pale breasts pushed into two round globes over the cups of the basque. She was glad she'd elected to get the little boxer shorts, though. The thong would have simply made her look like a trussed chicken.

She pulled her hair back into a ponytail and then pinned it to the top of her head. In all the romantic fiction she'd read as an impressionable teenager (well, the two historical romances she'd ploughed through before she'd turned to police procedurals instead), the heroines had allowed the hero to unpin their hair from the top of their heads. It was, apparently, very sensual to have your tresses fall down across your face, and she was going to work her sensuality to its utmost tonight.

She looked at her watch. It was nearly nine and Eddie had said he'd be home before then. She hoped that he wouldn't choose this evening to be late or to drink so much that all her efforts would be in vain. She put on her dressing gown (that would have to be changed too, if sexy nights together became a regular feature – it was positively tatty) and sat on the edge of the bed with a book.

It was nearly half past when she heard the sound of his key in the lock. She pulled off the dressing gown and lay back on the bed, striking a pose which she hoped was provocative, playful yet vulnerable.

The door opened and Eddie walked in. The colour drained from his face as he saw her.

'Jesus Christ, woman,' he said eventually. 'What the hell d'you think you're doing?'

165

'Waiting for you,' replied Siobhán in what she hoped was a sultry voice. 'I know you've had a long, hard day. But I wanted to give you a long, hard night too.'

'Are you all right?' he asked. 'You haven't been raiding the station's supply of illegal substances, have you?'

'Of course not.' Siobhán abandoned her provocative pose and sat upright. 'I just thought this would be . . . that you'd find it . . . attractive. That's all.'

Eddie stared at her.

'Why on earth would you think that?' he demanded. 'Have I ever expressed an interest in having you dress up like a slut?'

'I am *not* dressed like a slut!' she cried. 'This is perfectly acceptable underwear. Loads of women wear it.'

'Loads of women who aren't you!' retorted Eddie.

'Great.' She swung her legs over the side of the bed. 'That's just great. I suppose it's those loads of women you're interested in. Not me. I don't know what I've become to you, Eddie McIntyre, but a girlfriend isn't one of them. There isn't anything I can do that's right any more, or anything I can give you that you want. Well, fine! Most normal men would love their girlfriends to greet them after a business trip with champagne and sex. You wanted to go to sleep instead. Most normal men would think it was great that their girlfriend was prepared to buy the world's most uncomfortable underwear just to look good for them. You don't. So there's only one conclusion, isn't there? There's someone else. Who is she? Have you met someone else? How about that girl in your office – what's her name, Carol McClelland? The one you told me looked like a waif who needed protecting? Is that it? That what you prefer?'

'For heaven's sake, Siobhán, of course not!'

'Oh really? Why of course not? You're a hotshot business bloke. You probably like them helpless. I bet you if Carol danced around in front of you in a basque and knickers you'd be gagging for it!'

'No I bloody wouldn't!' cried Eddie.

'No? So you're not interested in me and you're not interested in her? What the hell is it then, Eddie? Are you interested in blokes?'

'Don't be so fucking ridiculous.'

'It's not me being ridiculous!' Siobhán's voice rose higher. 'I just want normal, that's all. I want a boyfriend who comes home after five weeks away and makes love to me. I don't think there's anything fucking ridiculous about that.'

'I can't talk about this right now,' said Eddie tightly. 'I just can't.'

'When?' demanded Siobhán. 'Why should we pretend that everything is all right when it so obviously isn't?'

'I don't want to pretend everything is all right. I just . . . I just . . .'

'Just what?'

'I can't talk about it,' repeated Eddie. 'I'll – I've got to go out.' He turned away and strode through the apartment.

'Don't you dare!' cried Siobhán, running after him. 'Don't you dare walk out on me.'

But he'd already opened the apartment door.

'For God's sake, Eddie.' She went out after him. 'If we don't talk about this now, we never will.'

He hesitated, and then hurried along the corridor towards the stairs.

'Eddie!' Siobhán moved after him and then whirled around as the apartment door clunked shut behind her. And she realised that she was standing in the corridor in a basque and knickers. Without a key.

She wasn't going to cry. That was the first thing. If any of her neighbours opened their doors she didn't want them to see her sobbing in her basque. All she had to do was stay calm. She'd been trained in calmness in difficult situations. The police were supposed to be good at that.

Chapter 16

Iona leapt out of the chair when the phone rang. She'd been sitting staring at the TV and drinking wine, not taking in anything of the history programme that was showing. The picture was just a blur in front of her, the narration a meaningless jumble of words. She yanked the receiver off the stand and said, 'Yes,' in a breathless voice.

'Iona, sweetheart, it's me.'

Her heart plummeted. It wasn't that she didn't want to talk to her mother, but she couldn't bear having to explain it all to her. And God knows what Lauren had already said, what slant she'd put on things.

'Darling, are you all right?'

'Of course I'm all right,' she said quickly. 'I'm fine.'

'You can't possibly be fine,' said Flora. 'Who in their right mind could be fine after what you've gone through?'

'Oh, I'm sure there's worse.' Although right then Iona couldn't think of what.

'Someone really close to you is critically ill,' said Flora. 'That's one of the worst things that could happen.'

'No, Mum.' Iona choked on the words. 'What's worse is that he wasn't close to me at all.'

'Of course he was,' said Flora firmly. 'You loved him and he loved you.'

'Don't be stupid,' said Iona. 'He used me, that's all.'

'He loved you – I could see it when you were here,' said Flora.

'But you thought there was something odd about him.'

'No. I thought he was very . . . self-contained,' said Flora.

168

'Which is understandable now. But I never thought he didn't love you.'

'He wasn't entitled to love me!' cried Iona. 'He was supposed to be in love with Sally.'

Flora said nothing.

'I hope he dies,' said Iona.

'Do you?'

She swallowed the lump in her throat.

'He deserves to die. He doesn't deserve to end up a vegetable.'

'Maybe neither of those things will happen.'

'I dunno.' Iona wiped her eyes.

'Do you want to come here for a few days?' asked Flora. 'Get away from it all?'

'I can't,' said Iona. 'I can't be away if . . . right now, I can't.'

'I understand,' said Flora. 'You know you're welcome to come. You only have to call me.'

'I know.'

'I want to be there with you,' said Flora. 'I want to put my arms around you and hug you and tell you everything will be all right.'

'I don't think everything will be all right,' said Iona. 'But I can pretend that you're hugging me.'

'Will I come over now?' asked Flora. 'Lauren warned me against phoning you too soon and absolutely forbade me to come haring home, but—'

'No,' said Iona. 'I'm better on my own right now. Maybe later.'

'Sure?'

'Certain.'

'OK,' said Flora. 'Look after yourself, honey. Dad sends his love. Take lots of echinacea.'

'I was actually thinking of alcohol,' said Iona as she refilled her glass.

Flora chuckled. 'That's my girl.'

Iona hung up and went back to staring at the TV screen.

169

Siobhán stood indecisively in her basque and boxers and shivered. Brilliant, she thought. Just bloody brilliant. She thought about running after Eddie and demanding that he at least let her back into the apartment, but she knew that by now he'd be in the communal hall area, and running down there in her underwear really wasn't an option. There were times when she complained that the apartment block was soulless and that you never really met anybody, but she knew that today would, of course, be the day that everyone would suddenly congregate in the damned hall and see her in her basque and boxers.

A door opened and she stood stock still. Then she groaned. Of all of the people she'd choose to walk out of their apartment right now, Carl O'Connor would have been bottom of her list.

'Good grief!' He looked at her in complete astonishment and then his face broke into a wide grin. 'Well if that's the new uniform for the Garda Siochana all I can say is that criminals will be simply queuing up to be arrested.'

'Oh, give it a rest, O'Connor,' she said shortly.

'Well, honey, you've got to admit that it's a new approach from the force,' he said. 'Are you undercover? Though cover isn't exactly the right word, is it?'

Siobhán said nothing. Carl O'Connor was a journalist. Her least favourite kind of journalist too. He wrote a scathing gossipy column in a Sunday tabloid called 'Carl's Corner' and an equally scathing column in an evening paper under the banner 'Carl Cares'. In it he supposedly exposed the injustices perpetrated on the ordinary people of the country – drivers caught for barely exceeding the speed limit, people arrested for drunk and disorderly offences when, according to Carl, they were just being high-spirited – failures on the part of the state and the system where decent law-abiding citizens were concerned. Siobhán didn't disagree that sometimes the system was unfair. But it irritated her that Carl only ever showed things from one point of view.

'So do tell me,' he continued. 'What's the ploy? Is someone in our apartment block running a brothel?'

She looked at him edgily.

'I got locked out of my apartment,' she said. 'My . . . Eddie had to go out in a hurry and . . . and I . . . needed to go after him for something but I missed him and the door closed behind me.'

Carl regarded her thoughtfully with his deep blue eyes and Siobhán felt herself blush.

'You know,' he said, 'if I was living with you and you were gadding about in that little outfit, I wouldn't care who tried to get me out of my home urgently, I'd tell them to sod off. Your boyfriend . . . your fiancé . . . is clearly a man of little taste.'

'Don't be stupid,' said Siobhán wearily.

'But seriously.' This time Carl's eyes twinkled at her. 'I didn't realise you had such hidden depths. Or such charming assets.'

'Look, I'm freezing my butt off out here,' Siobhán told him. 'Is there any chance I could use your phone so that I can ring him and get him to come back?'

'Of course you can,' said Carl. 'I was just about to bring my rubbish to the bin. I'll do that while you phone Mr Plod.'

'Eddie isn't a policeman, as well you know,' said Siobhán.

'True. But he's part of the Plod family, isn't he, thanks to you.' Carl grinned at her. 'I'd have thought you'd be pleased to see a kind of reverse discrimination in play.'

Siobhán made a face at him and then shivered. Suddenly Carl's voice softened.

'Ah, look, I'm sorry for teasing you,' he said. 'Come on in before you do actually freeze to death. And call your fiancé.'

'Thanks,' she said, surprised by the unexpected gentleness in his voice. She walked into his apartment and stood uncertainly in the middle of the room.

'Hang on a second,' said Carl. He disappeared into the bedroom and then emerged with a heavy blue T-shirt in his hand. 'You might want to put this on,' he said. 'It's a warmer option and it'll stop me running after you too!'

She pulled the T-shirt over her head and immediately felt a little better, although she knew that her figure was still stunningly buxom beneath it thanks to the uplifting powers of the basque.

Carl handed her his phone and she dialled Eddie's number. She grimaced as she got his message-minder.

'It's me,' she said urgently. 'I'm locked out of the apartment. Can you come home as quickly as possible? I'm at Carl's place.' She ended the call and looked apologetically at her neighbour. 'I'm sure he'll be back soon,' she said.

'Hey, you can stay here as long as you like,' said Carl easily. 'I wasn't doing anything much. As I said, I was only going out to put my rubbish in the bin.'

'What?' Her smile was a little wobbly. 'No lurking among the trash to find out the dirt on the inhabitants of our little community? No trawling the nightclubs for celebrities off their heads with drink?'

'You have a very low opinion of me, don't you?'

She shrugged. 'I just don't think that what you do is very helpful,' she said. 'Who really needs to know that some two-bit singer is having an affair? And what's the point in slagging off the police all the time, saying that we're crap at our jobs, just because the justice system means that we have to pick our way through a damn minefield to get a conviction.'

'Everyone has their rights,' Carl reminded her.

'Oh, please.' She looked at him in disgust. 'You're the one who does the sob story on the victims. And then you do a different sob story on the criminal – you know, my sordid life of crime but it's because my parents wouldn't buy me a PlayStation when I was six.'

He laughed. 'People want to read it,' he said.

'And then . . .' her voice rose in indignation, 'you journalists give them all nicknames like the Safecracker or something so that they think they're some kind of celebrity themselves and they then need to live up to it.'

'You're exaggerating,' he said mildly. 'Anyway, what about corruption in the police force, or gardai failing in basic procedural actions so that the trials collapse?'

'Everyone makes mistakes,' she said. 'We do a million things right but do one tiny thing wrong and some shifty barrister is getting a criminal off on a technicality. Plus there'll always be corruption. It's there in everything. I bet there are corrupt journos too. Except you guys can slag off everyone else and not have to take it yourselves.' She rubbed her forehead and looked at him tiredly. 'Look, I don't want to argue about this with you. I don't want to talk about work or anything. I just want to go home.'

'I'm sure Mr Pl . . . Eddie, isn't it? I'm sure Eddie will come rushing back when he gets your message. In the mean time, let's call a truce on dissing each other's jobs. How about a cup of coffee?'

She nodded. She was dying for a coffee. Although, she thought as she accepted the steaming mug from him a few minutes later, what she really needed was a major blast of alcohol to wipe out the memory of a horrible day.

〜

Sally wouldn't have minded a drink herself. She was fed up with the lukewarm, watery coffee that the hospital vending machine dispensed. She'd tried all the choices on offer by now – black, white, cappuccino, espresso, tea and hot chocolate – and they all tasted exactly the same to her. She only drank them for something to do. Sitting around the hospital was mind-numbingly boring. It was amazing how quickly she was getting into a routine of driving to Dublin and waiting for Frank to wake up. She knew all the nurses on the floor now and most of the doctors. They all smiled at her when she came in but pretty much left her to her own devices, which meant that she sat beside Frank and talked to him about inconsequential rubbish or read pieces out of the paper. She was doing the kind of thing that she'd read about in books or seen people do in movies, and it seemed totally unreal to her that this was actually happening in real life. She kept expecting Frank to wake up and laugh at her for reading the editorials in the *Irish Times* out loud to him, or to snap to attention when she told him that Jenna and her boyfriend were practically inseparable these days.

Which was why Jenna hadn't come to the hospital this evening. Gerry had asked her to go to the movies with him. Following their earlier conversation about how to deal with hospital visits, Sally had suggested that Jenna come to see Frank every second day, and her daughter had agreed with alacrity. The only worrying factor, as far as Sally could see, was that Jenna was spending more and more time with that boyfriend of hers and Sally wished she knew a little bit more about him. It wasn't that she didn't trust her daughter (at least, she more or less trusted her), but she'd have preferred it if Jenna was hanging out with her girlfriends rather than a new boyfriend right now.

She folded the newspaper and looked at Frank. It seemed to her that he was becoming less and less like the man she knew with every passing day. His face was thinner, his whole body appeared weaker in the bed. Of course she wasn't used to seeing him in bed at all – at least, not lying in bed asleep. He was always first up in the mornings, always full of get up and go. That was the thing that had always attracted her to him. The fact that he crackled with vitality. The fact that he loved life so much. The fact that just seeing him every day made her feel good about herself. The sleeping man in front of her was almost a stranger. They told her to talk to him and tell him things about their daily lives, remind him of things that had happened in the past, but she found it really difficult to do that when nothing got a reaction. So it was easier to read the newspaper editorials or talk about the traffic. It was harder to talk about the things that really mattered. But maybe the fact that she hadn't was part of the problem. She bit her lip as she studied Frank's expressionless face and then took a deep breath.

'We need to talk,' she said.

He didn't move.

'I know that's silly,' she continued. 'I mean, you can't talk, can you? Or maybe you won't talk. I don't know which.'

He still didn't move.

'But the thing is, there's a lot for us to talk about.' She moistened her lips. Should she start by freaking out about Iona? Or by giving him the news about the baby? Which was more likely to get a reaction?

'I didn't tell you this before,' she said quickly, 'because I wanted you to be properly awake when I did. The thing is, I don't know *when* you'll be properly awake again. It could be weeks. And it wouldn't be fair to spring it on you then, not that I actually could, I suppose. So . . . so I have to tell you now.' She swallowed hard. From the moment she'd discovered it herself, she'd wondered how she'd tell him. She hadn't expected it would be like this. She took a deep breath again. 'You're hardly going to believe it, darling, because it's so unexpected – the thing is, we're going to have a baby.'

From the moment she'd discovered it, she'd imagined his reaction. He lay impassively in the bed.

'I suppose it's a shock to you,' she continued. 'It sure was a shock to me after all this time. I hope you're happy about it, though. It's going to be a big change for us all.'

It was amazing, she thought, how still a living person could be. That was what was so difficult to accept. That Frank, who was always on the go, could remain so immobile.

'I haven't told Jen yet,' she said. 'The only people who know are the nurses here. I don't know what they'll say at school when I tell them. I'm going back next week. Well, Frank, I have to. I can't spend all of my time here, can I? I mean, we've got to go on living and . . . I'm not abandoning you, you know. I hope you realise that. But . . .'

She swallowed hard as he continued to lie there, oblivious to everything she said. Somehow she'd expected a reaction to the news of her pregnancy. She didn't know what sort of reaction, but she'd thought that he might move, give some kind of a sign that he'd heard her. She really couldn't believe that nothing was getting through to him. She threaded her fingers through his and squeezed gently.

'You know, it's really hard,' she told him. 'I'm pregnant and you're lying here and I just don't know when you're going to wake up. And when you do . . .' She faltered. 'When you do, there's such a mess to deal with.'

She took a deep breath. He deserved to know everything. She'd been too nice until now, talking to him in her most soothing tone of voice, reading him chunks of the paper, telling him that she loved him. She'd been treating him like a sick person, only he wasn't really sick, just out of it. She was fed up with being nice.

'Look – not that I particularly want to worry you,' she said as she disentangled her fingers, 'especially given the new state of affairs in our family; but there's a policewoman preparing a file about you. You might be prosecuted, you know. For . . . for . . .' She stopped. She hadn't brought up the subject of his second wife before. She'd only talked about herself and Jenna and how worried they were about him. She hadn't even mentioned the fact that Iona had called to the hospital and gone absolutely nuts. 'Well, Frank, for getting married to someone else,' she continued. 'I mean, it was a pretty bizarre sort of thing to do. And I have to tell you that me and Jen were very hurt by it. Not just hurt, furious. I'm furious with you. Jen is devastated. And both of us hate you for what you've done.'

His eyes opened. She stood up abruptly and the plastic chair scraped against the floor.

'Frank?' She reached towards the buzzer to summon the duty nurse. 'Frank?'

He stared straight ahead.

'Can you hear me?' she asked breathlessly as she kept her finger on the buzzer. 'Frank, do you understand what I've just told you?'

Terri Cooper hurried into the room. 'Everything OK?' she asked.

'He opened his eyes.' Sally's own eyes didn't leave Frank's face. 'He must be awake. He opened his eyes.'

'We told you about this, Sally, remember?' said the nurse gently. 'Sometimes this happens. It doesn't mean that the patient is alert. It's a motor function.'

'But I was talking and he just . . . it . . .' Sally was on the verge of tears. 'I said something and I know he heard me. I know he did.'

'Maybe so,' said Terri as she looked at the monitors beside Frank's bed. 'But he's still not conscious, Sally. I'm sorry.'

Sally said nothing, but walked out of the room. Her body was trembling. She'd felt sure that somehow she'd connected with Frank. She'd sensed something in him when she'd spoken about his marriage to Iona, something that hadn't been there for anything else, not even when she told him about the baby. But he'd heard her when she spoke of Iona, she knew he had. It was guilt over the whole thing that had got to him and that was why he'd opened his eyes!

'Here.' Terri stood beside her and handed her a cup of the disgusting coffee. Or tea. 'Drink this.'

'I don't want it.' She shuddered. 'I've been drinking it all evening and it's horrible.'

'I have to agree with you there,' said Terri. She looked at Sally. 'What were you talking to him about when he opened his eyes?' she asked. 'The baby?'

'No,' said Sally. 'The other woman.'

Terri's silence was sympathetic.

'I talked to him about the baby too,' said Sally tightly. 'But it meant nothing to him. It was only when I mentioned her that . . . that . . .'

'I really don't think his eyes opening had anything to do with it,' said Terri.

'But you don't actually know, do you?' demanded Sally.

'No,' said Terri. 'Though like I said to you, Sally, it's a motor function.'

'Yeah, well the motor function happened when I mentioned his damn bit on the side.'

Terri remained diplomatically silent.

'I know. I know. She's not really a bit on the side, is she?'

'I think you're all in a really difficult situation,' said Terri gently.

Sally said nothing, but swallowed hard over and over.

'Maybe you should go home,' suggested Terri. 'Get some rest.'

'Do you think she should be here?' asked Sally. 'Do you think it would help him to hear her voice?'

Terri shrugged.

'Maybe she doesn't even want to be here,' said Sally. 'After all, she didn't put up much of a fight once she realised that her marriage was a sham. She didn't even try.'

'Different people have different ways of reacting to things,' said Terri.

'Do you think I'm wrong?' asked Sally. 'To want to have things the way they were?'

'But what exactly is the way they were?' asked Terri.

'Me and Jen and Frank,' said Sally angrily. 'A family.'

Terri said nothing.

'Do the doctors think it would help if she came back?' asked Sally eventually.

'They haven't said anything to me.'

'If he reacted to her name, maybe hearing her voice would bring him out of it.'

'He did hear her voice on the first night,' Terri reminded her.

'Yes, but it was all a bit mad then, wasn't it?' Sally nibbled at the tip of her finger. 'Maybe it would be different now.'

'Maybe,' said Terri.

Sally stared back in through the window of the room. Frank's eyes were still open and he stared unseeingly in front of him.

'If it helps, maybe she should come in. Although she might not want to. She might be as furious with him as I am.'

'You still love him, though,' said Terri. 'You still want him to get better.'

'And if he does, what then?' Sally frowned. 'There's still the whole crazy situation to deal with.' She closed her eyes and swayed gently on her feet.

Terri took her by the arm and made her sit down.

'You need to look after yourself,' she told her. 'It won't help anyone if you become ill.'

'I know,' said Sally. Her eyes flickered towards Frank's room again. 'Sometimes I wish I was him,' she told the nurse. 'Out of it completely.'

Frank loved Sally. He hadn't expected to fall in love with her, because he'd found getting over Marion really difficult. He still thought of Marion occasionally, off in the States, meeting new men and sharing her gorgeous body with them. Whenever he thought of her he grew angry with himself for not having tried harder to keep her. She would have been a good wife and a good mother and they could have been a good family together. And then he wondered why he would think that when he knew that Marion was actually just good at socialising and great at sex.

Sally was good for him. She was more practical, more down-to-earth than Marion had ever been. She was a steadying influence. She encouraged him but she also pointed out the down side of some of the things he wanted to do. She was the kind of person that any man could love because she was clever and sweet and he couldn't help falling for her. He loved her sparkling eyes and her river of thick copper hair. He loved the way she put her head to one side and stuck the tip of her tongue out of the corner of her mouth when she was thinking hard about something. He loved her intelligence. He told her that she was wasted in teaching, that she should be out there doing something for herself. But then he loved the way she said that she got more out of seeing a young girl understand something that she'd never understood before than anything else. Sally Campion was a good person and Frank Harper wanted her to be part of his life for ever.

But now she was talking to him and he could hear her voice but he couldn't make out her words. And suddenly he knew that she was telling him that she was thinking of moving to England, where there were more jobs and where the salaries were higher.

'Why on earth would you want to go there?' he demanded. 'Sure isn't their education system a mess? Aren't we always reading about overcrowded schools and wayward pupils?'

'Get over yourself, Frank,' she replied in amusement. 'Some schools are crap; some are great. Just like here. Just like anywhere. There's a friend of mine working near London and she says that there are vacancies in her school for teachers of maths and English. The great thing about being a maths teacher is that there are always vacancies!

It's a nice school in a good area and the pay is a damn sight better than here.'

'But what's wrong with here?' Frank asked her. 'Why would you want to go away?'

'I have to think about my life and what I want from it,' she told him. 'I feel it's time for a change.'

He stared at her. He couldn't believe that another girlfriend was leaving him to work abroad. He knew that lots of people were leaving Ireland, where the prospects for work were pretty grim, but Sally had a good job and there was no need for her to leave. Marion had had a good job too, of course, but she'd gone all the same. Why did they always have to leave? What was it about women? What was it about him?

'Don't go,' he said abruptly. 'I'll miss you.'

She laughed. 'I'll miss you too. But it's a great opportunity.'

'Marry me,' he said quickly. 'I love you, Sally. I don't want to lose you. Marry me and stay.'

'I don't know, Frank,' she said. 'I don't know whether you're the marrying kind.'

He stared at her. 'I'm absolutely the marrying kind,' he told her. 'And I've met the woman I want to marry. I love you, Sally. I always will. I want us to be together and I want us to have a family together.'

'You do?'

'Yes. Lots of kids. Dozens of them.'

She laughed. 'Then it's definitely not me you want.'

'Don't you want children?' He looked at her. 'I thought you liked kids.'

'Of course I do,' she said. 'And I certainly want more than one. I didn't like being an only child, Frank. I want a family too. But cut me a bit of slack – dozens!'

He grinned at her. 'A round dozen then.'

'Get back in your cave, you Neanderthal!'

'Half a dozen?'

'Frank, I'm not a pea pod. I won't be able to pop them out like that.'

He laughed. 'Three?'

'How about four?' she suggested.

'Four it is.' He put his arms around her and pulled her close to him. 'I love you,' he said again.

'I love you too,' she whispered. 'I always will.'

❧

Terri Cooper changed the drip which was feeding Frank Harper. He was a devastatingly handsome man, she thought, even in his current state, even with his eyes closed and his face expressionless. She wondered what his chances were. And, if he pulled through, which of the two women would look after him.

'There you go, Mr Harper.' Terri always chatted to her patients, even the ones who could talk back. 'That should help to keep you going. Let me know if there's anything else you need.'

Frank said nothing. Terri smiled at him and left him on his own again.

❧

Iona was still curled up on the sofa, her knees drawn up underneath her chin, but now she was listening to the gentle music of her well-being CD as it wafted around her. She was trying to be very chilled out and relaxed because the bottle of wine had made her sleepy and she wanted to stay that way.

She looked around the room. After her marriage to Frank she'd had to rearrange things somewhat to take account of the fact that there were now two of them using the space. Previously, and in accordance with her feng shui book, she'd used bright colours in the room to keep the energy moving. But Frank had brought enough energy for both of them and she'd toned things down a little, replacing some of the primary-coloured cushions with more muted tones. She'd kept her cheerful prints on the wall, though, and her ornaments grouped in pairs so that the energy would remain positive, but she'd still worried that she was slowing it down.

It's all nonsense really, she muttered as she looked at the pictures of Gavin and Charlotte in the children area. Nothing actually slowed Frank down in the end except a damn freak accident, and I'm never going to have a child of my own. She blinked back the tears that threatened to fall as she contemplated the carved wooden bird which she'd bought on the day she'd first moved into the house. The idea of the bird had been to make the energy of the house soar. Right now, her energy levels were somewhere around zero.

That was why she was being so passive about everything, she thought miserably. Letting things happen around her, not doing anything about the situation even though Myles had found out the name of Frank's solicitor and told her to contact him. But she hadn't done that. She hadn't been able to.

The reality was that she'd been so shocked by what Siobhán Farrell had told her that she'd simply walked away from Frank and from her marriage to him. OK, it might not have been a valid marriage, but he'd still loved her enough to want to marry her, hadn't he? And he'd lived with her and talked about having a family with her. Flora had said that he loved her and Iona trusted her mother's judgement when it came to people. She was also grateful that Flora hadn't got at her for being stupid enough not to realise that Frank had a whole other life. It was the feeling of stupidity that really upset her, she thought. Well, that and the feeling of worry and every other damn feeling . . .

She sighed. Maybe there really was nothing left between him and the boring middle-aged woman who'd somehow managed to be the one everyone deferred to. Maybe he'd wanted to leave Sally only he didn't know how. Maybe his plan had been to divorce her anyway. Maybe she should fight to keep her relationship with Frank in everyone's minds instead of simply backing off. She was just as entitled as anyone to have a say in his treatment. Maybe not legally. But surely morally.

The phone rang and she picked it up immediately, her heart thumping again.

'Is that Iona?' The voice at the other end was nervous.

'Yes.'

'This is Sally. Sally Harper.'

Iona felt her grip on the receiver tighten so much she thought she was going to shatter it.

'I think we need to talk,' said Sally. 'I'd like to meet with you. As soon as possible.'

Chapter 17

Each time Carl O'Connor's phone rang Siobhán hoped it was Eddie to say that he was on his way back home. And each time she was disappointed. Actually the journalist's phone never seemed to stop ringing; Carl walked around the apartment with the handset jammed against his ear for most of the evening as he carried on conversations with a wide variety of people, peppering every second sentence with comments like 'You can't be serious!' and 'She did what?' so that Siobhán desperately wanted to know who he was talking about, even though she totally disapproved of his career. But she studiously avoided catching his eye even when his final conversation ended with him asking, 'And how d'you think the duck felt about it?' which had her both gagging for further information and not at all sure that she really wanted to know what was going on.

'You'll never guess who that was about,' said Carl as he finally took the phone away from his ear and grinned at her.

'Probably not,' she said drily.

'Don't you want to know?'

'Not really.'

'Oh, come on, Mizz Plod. You're an investigator. Surely your instincts are all fired up?'

'As you so pointedly tell me often enough, my job is to catch criminals, not listen to salacious gossip,' she told him tartly. 'I think you have a nerve being even the tiniest bit critical of my job when you spend your life fishing in the bottom of life's murky pond.'

He laughed. 'You're priceless,' he told her. 'Do they teach you to talk like that in cop school? Or are you totally strait-laced?'

'I'm only saying what loads of people believe,' she snapped.

'Everyone has to earn a living,' said Carl mildly. 'OK, I'm hardly going to win Pulitzer prizes, but I'm not actually a criminal myself.'

If only Eddie would come home, thought Siobhán miserably. She didn't want to be here. She felt the tears prickle at the back of her eyes again. How could he do this to her? She'd made such an effort tonight. She really had. How many other men would walk away from a woman dressed as she'd dressed that evening? How many men would feel nothing at the sight of her? Even Carl, horrible journalist though he was, had appreciated her appearance.

'Are you all right?' There was concern in his voice as he sat down in the deep armchair opposite her.

She blinked a couple of times and looked up at him. 'Yes, I'm fine,' she said wearily. 'I'd just rather be at home.'

'I'm sure he'll be back soon,' he said. 'In the meantime, would you like another tea or coffee?'

She shook her head.

'A drink?' he suggested. 'A short? A beer? A glass of wine?'

A drink would be nice, she thought, but she really didn't want to sit here sharing glasses of wine with Carl O'Connor. Anyway, she needed to keep a clear head. She didn't want to drop her guard in front of a journalist. She glanced down at her shapely figure beneath his T-shirt. Maybe it was a bit late to worry about that!

'I'm opening a bottle of Sangre de Toro myself,' he told her. 'Nod if you want some.'

'Some wine would be lovely,' she admitted finally.

Siobhán had always loved the sound of a cork popping from a wine bottle and the comforting glug-glug of the ruby-red liquid into the glass. He handed one to her and she tasted it.

'Very nice,' she said.

'Brought it back from Spain,' he told her. 'A third of the price of here.' His blue eyes twinkled at her. 'I suppose you'll arrest me if I tell you that I brought home loads!'

'That's Customs and Excise,' she told him. 'You can bring home casks of it for all I care.'

'Look, I know you hate and despise me, but you're sitting in my living room wearing my T-shirt,' said Carl. 'I think the least you can do is be nice to me.'

'I don't actually hate and despise you, but – but how can I be nice to you when I know that you're cracking up with amusement at the situation and I'll probably end up as the anonymous prostitute policewoman in one of your articles?' She looked at him miserably.

'That won't happen,' he promised her. 'You know, Mizz P., the people who appear in my columns want to appear in them. It's important to them. The celebs, the party-goers – they measure their lives in column inches.'

'Well all I can say is that they're sad individuals if that's what they think is important in life,' she said.

He shrugged. 'Anyway, I won't be writing about you if that's all that's worrying you.'

She smiled ruefully at him. 'It'd be a good story, though.'

He grinned. 'And I'd love to put you on the front page in that get-up. But I won't.'

She shuddered at the thought. 'Eddie would have a fit.'

'Hmm.' He grinned some more. 'Then we could have a fight over you and—'

'And I could arrest you,' she finished.

Carl looked at her curiously. 'Would you really be able to restrain me and handcuff me and frogmarch me to your car?'

'Of course.'

'I love that in a woman,' he said with mock wistfulness. 'Authority.'

'You probably don't really,' Siobhán told him. She sighed as she thought of how Eddie had also seemed to like the fact that she could throw him over her shoulder in a judo move, but how nowadays he wouldn't let her get near enough to put her arm round his shoulder.

She drained her glass and sat back in the chair. She still wished Eddie would come home. But at least she didn't feel quite so uncomfortable with Carl now. She nodded as he refilled her glass. Sod it, she thought. It didn't matter how many glasses she drank. She still wouldn't let her guard down in front of him.

～

She'd actually nodded off when there was a firm rap at the door which startled her into wakefulness. Carl was already out of the chair and peering through the peephole.

'It's Mr Plod,' he told her. 'Come to rescue you at last.'

Siobhán blinked a couple of times and yawned widely. 'You said you wouldn't call him that.'

'Sorry,' said Carl as he opened the door.

Eddie strode into the room. His six-foot-two frame towered over Carl and the difference in their physiques was unmistakable. Carl's slightly pudgy stomach looked positively fat beside Eddie's lean, muscular body.

'Jesus Christ,' Eddie said as he took in Siobhán in Carl's blue T-shirt, her boobs still defined by the basque she was wearing underneath. 'What the hell is going on here?'

'I told you,' said Siobhán. 'I came out of the apartment and the door closed behind me.'

'You never said that you came out of the apartment dressed like that!'

'Actually she didn't,' remarked Carl. 'She came out wearing an enticing little lingerie number which, I have to tell you, makes the most of her undeniable charms.'

'What the fuck . . .' Eddie looked from Siobhán to Carl.

'I was wearing my underwear,' said Siobhán.

Eddie stared at her. 'You mean you . . .'

'I told you,' she said. 'I came after you. I was still wearing my underwear.'

'Have you no sense?' he demanded.

'Obviously not,' she said. 'But fortunately Carl was kind enough

187

to let me stay in his apartment. Just as well, because you weren't answering your phone.' She glared at him in a way that told him that she knew he'd decided to ignore her request to come home quickly.

'Well, let's get back now,' said Eddie. 'Carl, thanks for putting up with her.'

'Hey, no question of putting up with her,' said Carl. 'We had fun. Though she refused to throw me over her shoulder and arrest me.'

'I'm so glad to hear that.' Eddie's tone was glacial.

Siobhán smiled tightly at Carl and thanked him for the wine and the company. She told him that she'd wash the T-shirt and return it the next day. Then she followed Eddie back to their apartment. As soon as they were inside, he turned to her.

'What in God's name made you run out of the apartment dressed like a tart?' he demanded angrily. 'I told you I was going out.'

'Yeah, you did. I did my best to do something for you, something for our relationship, and all you can do is storm out!'

'I never asked you to dress up like a whore for our relationship.'

'I did not dress up like a whore,' she yelled as she pulled the T-shirt over her head and stood in front of him in the basque and boxers again. 'This isn't cheap or nasty stuff. This is silk and lace and it was bloody expensive and I bought it because I thought that by wearing it there might be a rat's chance in hell that you'd look at me as the woman you love and not some stranger who's sharing your house.'

Eddie said nothing.

'I've done my best to figure out what's gone wrong between us,' cried Siobhán. 'I've asked myself over and over what it is that I could do. Whether I haven't been around enough. Or loving enough. Or . . . or . . . anything really! I know I'm not the housewifely type, but I didn't think that was what you wanted. But I cleaned the place today and I've arranged to have someone come once a fortnight to keep it clean . . . I don't know what else I can do. I don't know what you want from me.'

188

'I don't want anything from you,' said Eddie.

'Brilliant!' Siobhán felt the sting of tears in her eyes. 'You don't want me. But you're prepared to keep living with me instead of having the decency to tell me that you don't love me any more and that it's over between us.'

'It's not like that,' said Eddie. 'I didn't say that I didn't want you. I didn't say our relationship was over. I just said I didn't want anything from you.'

'Don't be so fucking pedantic,' snapped Siobhán. 'People who love each other want things from each other. People who love each other talk to each other. People who love each other make love to each other. You can't want me and not want the rest too.'

Eddie stood in front of her, clenching and unclenching his jaw.

'If it's over, it's over,' said Siobhán. 'You made me feel cheap and awful tonight. You're making me feel cheap and awful now, standing here like this, in these things. I don't know what you want but I can't live like this any more.'

'Siobhán, please.' Eddie swallowed hard. 'Don't . . . don't . . .'

'Don't what?' She looked at him pleadingly. 'What the hell is it, Eddie? What's gone wrong?'

'I know we have to talk about it.' He moistened his lips with the tip of his tongue. 'I guess I've been avoiding it. And I *will* talk about it with you. But not tonight.'

'Why the hell not tonight?' she demanded. 'When will there ever be a better night?'

'Because I just can't talk about it now. I'm stressed out and I'm really tired. And I have an early start in the morning. I'm due in for a breakfast meeting and it's after midnight now and if we start talking—'

'So your job is more important than us?' said Siobhán tartly.

'Look, how many times have we come home from things early because you've had to be in work early?' asked Eddie.

Siobhán said nothing.

'That's your police mode, isn't it?' He snorted. 'Staying quiet in the hope that the suspect says something incriminating.'

'For heaven's sake, Eddie. You're my fiancé! Not a suspect in a crime.'

'Yeah, but you're treating me like one.'

'Because you're acting so out of character!' she cried. 'We're supposed to love each other. But all you've done since you've come home is push me away and I can't take it any more. If it's something I've done, then for God's sake just tell me!'

'It's nothing you've done,' he said tersely.

'What then?' She looked at him in frustration. And then warily. 'Is it something you've done?'

'You just can't leave it alone, can you? Of course it's something I've done.'

'There's nothing you could do that should make you act like this.'

'Oh, don't be naïve.' He looked at her with a mixture of anger and despair. 'I slept with someone else. It was a big mistake. OK? Satisfied?'

She stared at him wordlessly.

'So, yes, this is something we have to discuss,' he said. 'But I can't do it now, Siobhán. I need to get my head together about it. And I do have this big meeting in the morning.'

'Yes, but . . .' Her tone was shocked.

'At the weekend. We'll talk at the weekend.'

'I—'

'Please. I know you're upset now. I'm upset. I don't talk well when I'm upset. Leave it till Saturday and we'll have the big discussion and you can . . . you can . . . well . . . whatever.'

'Oh, Eddie.'

'Don't say anything else.' His voice held more despair than anger now. 'I know I've done something terrible. You're right to be mad at me. But we have to talk about it properly. And we can't do that now.'

They looked at each other in silence for a moment and then Eddie walked into the bathroom and closed the door behind him.

Chapter 18

The city streets were thronged with people lured out of their homes by an unexpectedly warm Saturday morning and now strolling around town chatting happily as they popped in and out of Dublin's boutiques and department stores.

Iona strode along Dame Street, the sun warm on her back as she made her way to the small café where she had arranged to meet Sally Harper. Iona was incapable of walking slowly, even though she'd left the house far too early for her twelve-thirty appointment with the other woman. She snorted as the phrase came into her mind. Sally wasn't the other woman. *She* was the other woman. That was how everyone else would see it, wasn't it? That was how Siobhán Farrell, the kindly detective garda, saw it. That was how Lauren and Myles saw it. That was the reality of her situation.

Iona didn't know why Sally wanted to meet her. She couldn't see what there was to talk about. But Sally had been insistent, and in the end Iona had been too intrigued to turn down the invitation. Besides, she wanted to know what was going on with Frank. How he was. What sort of treatment he was having. What they thought might happen to him.

She bumped into a hand-holding couple as she spun around the corner into Trinity Street. She apologised briefly, but the young girl and her boyfriend didn't even react. They were caught up in each other and barely noticed her. Me and Frank were like that, thought Iona sadly. When we were out together nobody else mattered. And then she wondered how strictly true that was, because it suddenly occurred to her that she and Frank had rarely come into town together and that all of their socialising seemed to have been on the north side of the city, despite the fact that they could stroll into Grafton Street in about fifteen minutes.

Had he been trying to keep her out of sight, afraid that his other friends, the people who knew him and Sally, would spot them together? She realised, too, that she and Frank had rarely socialised with any of his friends. It hadn't really cost her a thought until now, but the truth of the matter was that when they went out in a group, it was always with people she knew, never with friends of his. Frank had always told her that most of his close friends were still in Sligo, where he'd originally come from, and that he wouldn't dream of dragging her along to the occasional business dinner he went to as part of his work. They'd existed for the past few years in a tight-knit bubble of their own making, and Iona couldn't help asking herself how it was that she hadn't really noticed the limitations of their social circle before. But then Frank had always wanted to be alone with her when he came back from his business trips, and she liked being alone with him too. Only it wasn't normal, was it? She couldn't believe that it hadn't bothered her before now.

She continued to walk briskly towards Wicklow Street while her thoughts spun around in her head, making her feel dizzy. She was glad to arrive at the café even if she was ten minutes early. She ordered a skinny latte and took a copy of the *Irish Times* from the stand on the wall. Then she sank gratefully into one of the soft leather sofas beside a low table. She turned to the letters page of the newspaper first and then blinked back the tears which suddenly threatened to fall. Turning to the letters page first was one of Frank's habits which she'd adopted. She squeezed her eyes closed and tried hard not to cry.

❧

It took Sally longer than she'd thought to drive from the hospital into the city centre. And then she'd got lost coming along the quays because she hadn't been able to turn left where she'd anticipated. Of course she hadn't driven around this part of the city in years and so she was completely unfamiliar with the latest one-way system. She wasted nearly twenty minutes looping around the congested streets before managing to find a car park, and then had to drive to the very top of it to find a space. It occurred to her that the city had grown out of all recognition in the few short years that she'd been living in Bray. She'd hated moving away from Dublin at the time, but now she felt overwhelmed by the sheer volume of traffic and numbers of people clogging up the streets.

She manoeuvred the car carefully into what seemed to be the last available space, cautiously checking for unexpected pillars to pop up and scrape it. Parking wasn't Sally's strong point – actually she didn't really like driving very much – but the few days without the car had been a nightmare. Siobhán Farrell had arranged for it to be brought back from Ardallen and at first, Sally had wondered whether Iona would try to claim it for herself. But she hadn't tried to claim ownership of anything. The weird thing about Iona was that after those first terrible hours she'd simply stepped back from the whole situation as though it had nothing to do with her.

Well, thought Sally as she got out of the Honda and locked the doors, she'd soon get a handle on Iona's thought processes about the whole thing. If the girl had waited for her. She looked at her watch and frowned in agitation. She'd intended to be early but she was nearly half an hour late. And she couldn't be sure that Iona was the sort of woman who would hang around for her. In fact she rather thought she'd be the opposite.

She hurried out of the multistorey and along the street, perspiring slightly under her wool cardigan, which had been perfect earlier in the morning but was now too warm for the early May sunshine. She arrived at the café and pushed open the door.

⌒

Iona had been thinking of leaving. She'd finished her coffee and the paper and for the last five minutes had been working herself up into a rage over the fact that she hadn't really wanted to meet Sally Harper but she'd come all the same and now the damn woman hadn't shown up. And she'd wondered whether it hadn't been some evil ploy of Sally's to . . . to . . . Well, she hadn't been able to figure out the context of Sally's evil plot, but she felt sure that there was something. But just as she'd folded the paper and was gathering her things together, the door opened and the other woman walked in.

Iona's first thought was that Sally had lost an incredible amount of weight. It wasn't that she'd spent ages sizing her up when they'd met at the hospital, but she'd gained the impression that Sally was a slightly overweight middle-aged woman with a dull dress sense. The woman walking through the café towards her was taller than Iona remembered, and certainly thinner, at least facially. It was hard to tell about the rest of her as she was wearing a loose black skirt and a chunky jade-green wraparound cardigan. The jade green would probably have brought out the colour in her eyes and hair except for the fact that her eyes were lost in the pallor of her face and her hair was pulled back into the same tired-looking plait she'd worn the first time Iona had seen her.

Iona was glad that she'd taken the time that morning to wash and gel her own ink-black hair and that she'd made an effort with her tinted moisturiser, eyeliner and lippy. She'd worn her large silver Celtic-knot earrings and matching chain and had dressed in faded jeans teamed with a shocking-pink top which emphasised her blackberry eyes and lightly tanned skin.

I am the younger woman, she thought, as Sally walked towards her. I'm prettier. I have more sense of style. I'm the fun person in the relationship. She's pathetic.

'Hello,' said Sally as she arrived at the table. 'I'm sorry I'm late. The traffic was terrible and I took a wrong turn. It's ages since I was in town. I was afraid you'd be gone.'

'I was thinking about it,' said Iona.

'I would've called,' Sally told her. 'Only I didn't have a mobile number for you.'

194

And you're not likely to ever get it, thought Iona darkly. 'Would you like a coffee?' she asked.

'Um, yes. Sure.' Sally looked around the café.

'It's OK,' said Iona. 'You have to order at the counter. I'll get it for you. What do you want?'

'Skinny latte,' said Sally.

'Anything else?' Iona was startled that Sally drank the same coffee as her.

She shook her head. 'I'm not hungry.'

Iona ordered two skinny lattes and a blueberry and apple muffin. She wasn't hungry either but she decided that if Sally wasn't going to eat, she was.

'Thank you,' said Sally as Iona placed the coffee in front of her.

The two women sat on opposite sides of the low table and looked at each other.

'How is he?' asked Iona eventually.

'Still unconscious.'

'Is there any improvement at all?'

Sally sighed. 'I guess not. Sometimes I think he hears me, and then other times . . . nothing.'

Iona peeled the waxy paper from the muffin and said nothing because she didn't trust herself to speak. The image of Frank as she'd last seen him in the hospital had rushed into her mind and it was all she could do to stop herself crying out in pain at the thought of him.

'The longer it goes on, the more worrying it becomes,' said Sally.

Iona was surprised that Sally was talking in such a matter-of-fact kind of way. She'd thought her hopeless and befuddled before, and she still seemed slightly dippy and unfocused, yet she was suddenly dealing with the situation in a very down-to-earth manner.

'There's brain activity,' continued Sally, 'he's not brain-dead or anything, but he just won't wake up. And the problem is that if he doesn't wake up and he loses his higher brain functions then he could be like that for ever. Until he gets some kind of infection and dies from it.' At these words she choked slightly and Iona looked up from the muffin. She could see that Sally's eyes were clouded with tears.

'And have they any suggestions for waking him up?' Iona knew that her own voice was harsh, but it was the only way she could keep from crying herself.

'Not really.' Sally cleared her throat and then took a sip of coffee. 'I've done all the stuff they suggested. I've read him bits of the paper. I've talked to him about work. About Jenna. About the house. But nothing.'

'What bits of the paper?' asked Iona.

'Well, the editorial.' Sally looked surprised at the question. 'And Weather Eye. He loves Weather Eye.'

'What about the letters?' asked Iona. 'Do you read him the letters?'

Sally said nothing. Iona watched her intently.

'Of course I read him the letters,' said Sally eventually. 'He loves the letters.'

'I think he prefers them to Weather Eye,' said Iona.

Sally shook her head. 'Weather Eye first,' she said. 'Then the letters.'

'I don't think so.' Iona frowned. 'Letters first, then Weather Eye.'

The two women looked at each other warily.

'Well, not that it matters,' said Iona eventually. 'You're reading him the papers.'

'And the radio is on beside him,' continued Sally. 'He likes classical music.'

'I know,' said Iona. 'And Enya.'

'And Pavarotti.'

'And Madonna.'

'And Frank Sinatra.'

'He doesn't!' Iona looked surprised. 'Sinatra?'

'Yes.' Sally nodded. 'He has a greatest hits collection.'

'I've never seen it.'

'Maybe he doesn't do Sinatra with you. But at parties he sings "Mack the Knife".'

Iona was shocked. 'He's never sung "Mack the Knife" when he's been with me.'

Sally shrugged.

'You're making that up,' said Iona accusingly.

'Don't be stupid,' said Sally. 'Why would I make it up?'

'What's his favourite colour?' Iona's voice was abrupt.

'He doesn't have one.'

'Wrong. It's red. That's why he does so many shows with red lights. His favourite computer game?'

'He doesn't play computer games,' said Sally. 'He doesn't have time.'

'Wingnuts,' Iona told her defiantly. 'And he's brilliant at it.'

'I've never even heard of Wingnuts,' said Sally sharply.

'He plays it all the time,' Iona said. 'It's loaded on the laptop.'

Sally snorted. 'Computer games are irrelevant,' she said. 'What about his favourite food?'

'Spaghetti carbonara,' Iona responded almost before Sally had finished asking the question.

'Roast pork with apricot and coconut sauce.'

'Oh, come on!' Iona looked at her sceptically. 'Frank hardly ever eats roast dinners.'

'Not with you, obviously,' retorted Sally. 'But I'm a good cook.'

Iona looked at her angrily. 'I can cook. I just don't do traditional meat-and-two-veg things.'

'Nor do I,' said Sally. 'I liven them up with nice sauces. And I make the veg interesting.'

Iona felt the rage simmer within her. She bit into her muffin furiously. 'His favourite book,' she said through a mouthful of crumbs. 'What's his favourite book?'

'*Goldfinger* by Ian Fleming,' said Sally at once. 'I always felt it was a silly choice but he really loves it for some insane reason.'

Iona closed her eyes. She could see the copy of the book on the bookshelf in the bedroom. She'd bought it for him shortly after he'd moved in. They'd been talking about books, and he'd told her he'd read it as a teenager and had got into the whole Bond thing way before he'd ever seen a movie. And that it was a brilliant book but that he hadn't seen it in a bookshop in years. So she'd gone looking for it and found it. He'd laughed with delight when she'd given it to him, telling him he couldn't really have looked very hard. But if it was his favourite book he probably had a copy in his other house too and her gift was meaningless. She took a tissue from her bag and blew her nose.

'Oh, look, I didn't ask to meet with you so that we could score points over him!' cried Sally, seeing Iona's very real distress. 'I – well, I wanted to ask you to visit him.'

'Huh?' Iona looked at her in astonishment.

'Like I said, I've tried everything,' Sally told her despairingly. 'Jenna's tried everything too. We've talked and talked until there's nothing left to talk about. I thought that maybe the reason he's not responding is because . . . because he actually needs to hear your voice.'

Iona replaced the half-eaten muffin on the plate and pushed it to one side.

'He heard my voice,' she said. 'On the first night.'

'Yes, but he was totally traumatised that night,' said Sally. 'I thought that maybe now . . . it'd be different.'

Iona twisted her earring around in her ear while she tried to compose herself again.

'And what then?' she asked. 'What if I talk to him and he wakes up?'

Sally shrugged. 'I don't know. But we have to try, don't we?'

'Do we?'

'You don't have to if you don't want to,' said Sally. 'But it's for his sake.'

'Oh, don't be fucking stupid,' snapped Iona. 'It's killing me not being able to see him, not being able to comfort him. I want to talk to him. I love him.'

Sally flinched. 'But you didn't come back to the hospital.'

'Why the hell would I, with you and your kid getting so possessive about it all?' demanded Iona. 'I didn't know what to do. I was giving it some time. But I'm going crazy.'

'So you'll talk to him now?'

'Of course I will,' she said.

'Thanks,' said Sally. 'Thanks very much.'

They sat in silence. Iona finished her muffin and sipped her coffee, although she noticed that Sally wasn't drinking hers.

'Is it all right?' she asked abruptly.

'What?'

'Your coffee,' said Iona. 'You're not drinking it.'

'I'm not very thirsty.' Sally didn't think it was a good time to tell Iona that the last few coffees she'd drunk, including the one with Siobhán Farrell, had left her feeling queasy. She was sure it was something to do with her pregnancy but she wasn't going to talk to the younger woman about that. And then she remembered the question she had to ask.

'Have you and Frank any children?'

Iona felt as though she'd been kicked in the stomach.

'Why?'

'I just . . . wondered,' said Sally.

'No, we haven't.' Iona tried to sound dismissive, as though it didn't matter to her.

'Probably just as well given the circumstances,' said Sally.

'How the fuck do you know what's good or bad for me?' demanded Iona angrily.

Sally flinched at her words. 'I only meant . . . with him sick and everything . . .' she didn't want to continue the conversation. She wished she hadn't started it. She was afraid that Iona would somehow guess about her own pregnancy and she simply wasn't prepared to talk to her about it.

There was an awkward silence which Iona eventually broke.

'Were you at the hospital today?'

Sally nodded.

'So when do you want me to go?'

'Whenever you like,' said Sally.

'How about tonight?'

Sally swallowed. 'I was going to come in with Jenna tonight. I'm not sure whether . . .'

'Tomorrow then,' said Iona. 'I'll go in tomorrow morning.'

'OK.' Sally looked at her uneasily. 'But I want to be there too.'

'Why?' demanded Iona. 'You asked me to go and see him. Why do you need to be there? What about our privacy?'

'What if he wakes up?' asked Sally simply. 'I want to be there.'

'Why?' This time Iona looked at her wryly. 'You want to rush in and hit me over the head so that he doesn't get to see me?'

'Don't be silly.' Sally rubbed the side of her nose. 'I just – well, if he wakes up I want to be there.'

'And then what?' asked Iona.

'Then . . . then I don't know,' admitted Sally.

'We have to have some kind of plan,' said Iona. 'I mean, what if he wakes up but he's lost his memory? What then?'

'Depends on which bit of it he loses, I suppose.' Sally smiled faintly. 'If he forgets about being married to me then you're in pole position. If he forgets about supposedly marrying you—'

'It wasn't supposedly,' said Iona heatedly. 'It was real.'

Sally shrugged.

'It was fucking real,' said Iona fiercely. 'It might not have been legal but it was real. I have the photos.' Her voice cracked and she was horrified to find her eyes fill with tears.

'Oh God, I'm sorry.' Sally looked at her contritely. 'I didn't mean to upset you.'

'What did you think meeting me would do?' Iona sniffed. 'I was always going to get upset no matter what the hell you wanted.'

'Yes. I should've thought of that.' Sally exhaled slowly. 'I suppose I wasn't thinking about you. Only Frank.'

'Yeah, well, I guess I'm thinking about Frank too,' said Iona. She blew her nose again. 'This is all so weird. It's not what happens to normal people. I feel like I'm in some awful reality TV show, expecting them to jump out any minute and tell me it's some kind of joke.'

'I feel a bit like that myself,' admitted Sally. 'Though joke is probably the wrong word.'

'Well, you know what I mean.'

Sally nodded.

They sat in silence again.

'There is another issue,' said Iona.

'Yes?'

'His business.' She told Sally that Myles had found out the name of Frank's solicitor and accountant and that he'd been in touch with them on her behalf. They'd told him that the directors of the company were Frank Harper and Sally Campion. She said that she'd seen S. Campion on the letter heading before but that Frank had never told her who it was and she'd assumed that it was a business colleague or accountant or someone like that.

'Yes. I'm a director,' agreed Sally.

'So what's happening about the business?'

Sally looked at Iona wryly. 'Richard Moran, the accountant, has contacted Frank's clients and contractors. There are fewer clients than I thought, although they're more profitable than I thought too. He didn't need to be away half as much.'

'That figures.'

'Anyway, Pete Maguire, one of the contractors, is looking through the schedules of maintenance and all that sort of stuff. A lot of it is booked in well in advance and there's no big problem there. So it can run itself with a bit of input from Richard for a couple of months. I don't know what happens after that.'

'Are you telling me that he didn't need to be away at all?' asked Iona.

'No.' Sally shook her head. 'There was a lot of client visiting to do but half of it was just because he liked it. And half the time both of us thought he was with clients . . . well, he wasn't.'

'You know, part of me feels he can stay in a damn coma,' said Iona angrily.

'I know how you feel.'

The two women shared a sudden complicit glance.

'But he needs someone to care for him,' said Sally eventually. Iona nodded.

'So is it OK if I come tomorrow morning too?' Sally asked.

'Yeah. Sure.' Iona reached for her bag and flinched as Sally caught her by the hand. The other woman looked at her third finger where Iona wore a half-hoop of rubies in place of a traditional wedding ring.

201

'I don't like diamonds,' she told Sally. 'And I always thought that a gold wedding ring was a bit . . . possessive.'

'I can't believe he did this,' Sally said tightly. 'I really can't.' She swallowed hard as she looked at the glow of the rubies under the café lights. 'It's a lovely ring.'

'Are you thinking that it should have been the electricity bill or something?' asked Iona.

'No.' Sally shook her head. 'I'm thinking that it's really classy.' She extended her own hand and showed Iona the narrow band with three tiny diamonds which was her engagement ring. 'We didn't have a lot of money at the time,' she said. 'He always talked about buying me one to replace it but I didn't want him to.'

'Of course not,' said Iona. 'Why would he think you'd want another one?'

'More expensive. Better. He always told me I deserved it.'

The two women fell silent again. Then Iona stood up.

'I'll see you tomorrow,' she said.

Sally stayed sitting down. She nodded. 'Tomorrow.'

She watched Iona stride out of the café and on to the sun-drenched street outside, then got up from her seat and ordered a tea, which she took back to the table. She sipped it cautiously. It didn't have the same heaving effect on her stomach as the coffee. She'd been afraid that she'd chuck up the coffee in front of Iona, and that would have been a complete disaster. She didn't want to give the younger girl any more ammunition. She could tell that Iona had despised her by the way she'd looked appraisingly at her before she'd sat down. Iona's dark eyes had flickered with a degree of superiority as she'd looked Sally up and down and Sally knew that her judgement had been made. She guessed that it had been unfavourable. She imagined Iona's thoughts – that she, Sally, was old and dowdy. That her clothes had been unsuitable for the warmth of the day. That she was, relative to Iona's dark, exotic looks, plain and middle-aged. But she didn't normally look like that. People generally thought she looked good for her age. Not, perhaps, as stunning as she could be (and there was always the dreaded struggle with her weight), but then she didn't have time to look stunning, did she? She had a job and a family and she was always running around trying to keep all the balls in the air because the smooth operation of the home depended on her. It had to – Frank was away too often for it to depend on him.

Away with Iona!

Despite the fact that she was drinking tea and not coffee, Sally barely managed to stop herself from throwing up at the thought. She got up abruptly and walked out of the café, catching sight of herself in the plate-glass window as she pushed open the door. She frowned and walked slowly down Exchequer Street. When she came to a shop with a mirror in the window she looked at her reflection again.

She looked wretched. Really, really wretched. If she went into the hospital in the morning looking like this, and if Frank came out of his coma and saw her standing there beside Iona – well, the first thing he'd do would be make comparisons. And she'd lose out big-time, because Iona was gorgeous. Sally hadn't realised how attractive she was before, but those smouldering eyes and that dark elfin hair were extremely eye-catching. Maybe, she thought, maybe Frank would see both of them and pretend that he didn't know who Sally was because he'd want to be with Iona.

Only he couldn't really do that. In the whole mess she had to remember that she was actually his wife. Not Iona.

She turned in to Grafton Street. She didn't know why she was walking this way, away from the car park, but she wasn't ready to get into the car and drive home yet. She strolled up the pedestrian street, noticing the mime-artists and the musicians, the hair-braiders and the flower-sellers, all of whom were getting on with their lives not knowing that she, Sally Harper, was going through hell.

She stopped in front of a hairdressing salon. The door opened and a woman walked out, her hair expertly cut and styled. The scent of shampoo and hairspray wafted on to the street. Sally stood indecisively for a moment and then pushed the door open and walked inside.

Chapter 19

At eight o'clock on Saturday morning the phone rang with an urgent call for Siobhán to attend a possible crime scene. An elderly woman had been found dead in her home and the circumstances were described as being suspicious. She could see a mixture of accusation and relief in Eddie's eyes as she spoke on the phone – he was peeved at her for having to go out so early but relieved that he didn't have to talk about his infidelity yet.

'I'll be back as soon as I can,' she told him as she dressed hastily. 'And then we're talking.'

He shrugged and rolled over in the big bed which they had continued to share despite the fact that Siobhán was sleeping on the very edge of it and, since his confession earlier in the week, hadn't made the slightest attempt to come near him.

She tried not to think about Eddie and what was going to happen to their relationship as she drove to the small detached house where the elderly woman had died. A neighbour had called and, not getting any reply, had eventually phoned the police. When they'd entered the house they'd found the woman, Claudia Hill, lying at the bottom of the stairs with an open hardback book nearby. Siobhán could see, from the condition of the body, that she'd been dead for a couple of days.

The first time she'd seen a dead body she'd wanted to throw up. She'd never really got used to it. But she could cope with it.

The local garda on the scene introduced her to the neighbour who'd alerted the police. From her she learned that Claudia was a lovely woman but a bit scatty.

'In what way was she scatty?' asked Siobhán, wondering whether the woman had been absent-minded enough to leave her door unlocked so that someone could have come in and attacked her.

'Ah, you know. She'd forget to eat and things like that. She used to spend all her time reading books. There's millions of them in that house. She'd walk around with her head stuck in a novel and you wouldn't get a word out of her until it was finished.'

Theresa, the neighbour, confirmed that Claudia had been in good health and wouldn't have dreamed of leaving her door unlocked.

Siobhán nodded and left Theresa with another female garda. She wandered around the house, noting the overflowing bookshelves and the general air of untidiness; the sparsely stocked kitchen cupboards, the few generic tablets in the bathroom cabinet and the sterilising lotion for false teeth on the sink. Claudia's bedroom was like an antiques shop with its big bed covered in pillows, maroon satin quilt and assortment of delicate glass bottles in a variety of colours on the dressing table. The room was airless, although a hint of lavender overlaid the slightly musty smell. Siobhán opened the window to allow some fresh air in.

As she contemplated the room around her there was a sudden thud near the window she'd opened. An enormous black cat with jade-green eyes regarded her balefully. He stalked across the room and then jumped on to the bed and began kneading one of the pillows.

I might have guessed, she thought. Elderly woman, lives alone, reads books and has a cat. Dies and nobody notices. She's who we're all afraid of becoming. Maybe she's the reason I didn't just walk out on Eddie straight away. I know I should. He slept with someone else. He doesn't love me, and I don't know if I still love him, but I don't want to just walk away. She exhaled slowly and went down the stairs.

The doctor told her that Claudia had fallen down the stairs, broken her neck and died instantly. He couldn't tell whether she'd been pushed, although, as he said cheerfully, it seemed a bit unlikely.

As far as he could see the poor old dear had just tripped and fallen. Though deciding that was Siobhán's job, wasn't it?

Siobhán nodded. She supposed the coroner would come to the same conclusion. Accidental death. But you had to be certain, had to follow the procedures.

Normally she was able to put cases like this out of her mind fairly quickly. But as she drove back to her apartment later, she kept thinking about Claudia Hill. Although the pathologist had said she'd died instantly, Siobhán couldn't help wondering what would have happened if she'd simply broken a leg in the fall. Would she have been able to call for help? Or would she have died anyway simply because nobody visited the house every day?

I don't want to be on my own, she thought, I want to have someone who matters to me in my life.

The low hum of the TV greeted her as she put her key in the door and she realised that she'd been holding her breath, afraid that he'd gone out despite his promise to her when she'd rung to say that she was on the way home.

'Do you want something to eat?' he asked.

She shook her head. 'I'm not hungry.'

'Horrible scene?' His voice was sympathetic but edgy.

'Could've been worse.' She flopped down on to the sofa. 'Old woman falls downstairs and dies. Nobody notices.'

'It wouldn't happen to you,' said Eddie. 'You're too smart to fall down the stairs. And everyone would notice if you weren't around.'

Siobhán laughed shortly. 'Who knows? The future might be . . . well . . . who knows?'

Eddie said nothing and the silence between them began to grow. Siobhán felt more and more uncomfortable.

'So?' she said eventually. 'Tell me about it. Who is she?'

Eddie looked at her in a hunted kind of way. As though he was afraid of her. No need to be, she thought. I can't throw you into the cells for sleeping with another woman.

'Nobody important,' he said.

Siobhán frowned. 'Then why did you sleep with her?'

'Because I could.'

'Great,' she said.

'That's not strictly true,' he told her. 'I'm being flippant, I suppose.'

'Do you love her?'

'Oh, come on, Siobhán. Don't be stupid. Of course I don't love her. If I loved her why the hell would I have come home?'

Loads of reasons, thought Siobhán. She could have dumped you. You could have wanted to have two women on the go. Just like Frank Harper. Except for the great sex.

'How often?'

'Just once.'

'Lambay Rules?' she asked.

He shrugged. She knew that there was a general decree in Eddie's firm – anything goes when you're overseas; you just forget about it once you return home and catch your first sight of Lambay Island as your plane descends into Dublin airport.

'I didn't mean to do it,' he said.

He sounded like a child who'd broken a window. She said nothing.

'It was a big night out,' he continued. 'Peter Murtagh arranged everything. We went to a superb restaurant and a club and then afterwards back to his apartment.'

Siobhán clenched her jaw. Peter Murtagh was a high-rolling businessman who was a client of Eddie's firm. Sometimes the newspapers called him an entrepreneur. Other times a mogul. Other times, in the less flattering pieces, a Svengali. They made a big play about his palatial home in the exclusive Dalkey enclave in Dublin, and of his other homes in Spain, Cape Town and Boston. Of his fleet of expensive cars. Of his jet-set LA lifestyle and his incredible wealth. Whenever he was photographed, it was with a huge cigar in one hand and a glass of whiskey in the other. And there was usually a gorgeous girl draping an arm around him too.

'There were a lot of us,' continued Eddie. 'Mostly blokes. When we got back to Peter's place he made a few phone calls. Next thing I know the place is crawling with stunning girls. Absolutely gorgeous. And they were all over us.'

'You mean he ordered them?' Siobhán frowned and Eddie sighed.

'I knew you'd react like this,' he said. 'You're thinking that they're prostitutes and wondering does he do that sort of thing here so that you can arrest him.'

'No I'm not.'

'Yeah, right.' Eddie didn't believe her.

'Look, I don't care about Peter Murtagh and his girlfriends,' snapped Siobhán. 'Especially his overseas girlfriends. Although I do happen to know that he sails close to the wind age-wise with some of them and that one day it'll all come crashing down for him. All I care about is that you slept with one of them and obviously it was the best night of your life because you haven't slept with me since. So what's the deal, Eddie? Was she so wonderful that you can't get it up for me any more? Is that it? Do you want me to move out only you haven't got the bottle to ask me? Or – despite what you've said – are you actually in love with her?'

'Stop it!' he cried. 'It's not like that at all.'

'Then what *is* it like, Eddie? Tell me. I'm obviously not such a great detective after all, because I sure as hell can't work it out for myself.'

'You're right,' he said. 'They were prostitutes.'

Siobhán crumpled into the seat.

'Look, I know what you're thinking!' cried Eddie. 'You're thinking that I'm a complete bastard who can't keep his dick in his trousers for a few weeks just because I'm out of your sight. You're feeling betrayed and let down and you hate me.'

'Something like that.' Siobhán's voice cracked.

'And you're right,' he told her. 'I was a fool, Siobhán. A complete and utter fool. I can't believe that I got suckered in by the whole thing. But it was – well, it was like a movie set or something. Loads of girls, loads of drink . . .' He hesitated. 'Soft drugs. Coke, you know.'

'Christ, Eddie.'

'It was wild and crazy and . . . and I just felt wild and crazy too. I'm not normally. You know that. I know that. I'm a bit anal and stodgy and I know that you sometimes get frustrated with me because I don't like change and I don't do wild things in bed with you—'

'So you thought you'd do wild things in bed with someone else instead?' Siobhán stared at him. 'And I'm supposed to be happy about that?'

'Of course not,' said Eddie. 'It was . . . I'm just trying to explain what happened. Everyone was there. The buzz was fantastic. And the girls—'

'I'm not sure I want to hear about the girls,' said Siobhán.

'The girls were beautiful,' said Eddie simply.

She closed her eyes and compared herself to beautiful girls. There was no contest, of course. There couldn't be.

'Look, Siobhán, I didn't mean to let you down,' said Eddie. 'But—'

'What I don't understand,' she said quietly as she wiped away the tear that had escaped from the corner of her eye, 'is why you're bothering to tell me all this. Lambay Rules, after all. You could've just pretended it never happened. You could have made love to me the day you came home and I'd never have guessed because I trusted you completely.'

'I know,' he said.

'So why?'

He looked at her pleadingly. She stared back uncomprehending. And then he spoke again.

'I might have contracted a disease,' he told her.

For a moment the words didn't penetrate her mind. Then she understood what he was saying.

'A sexually transmitted disease?' she said, aghast.

'Peter called me afterwards. The girls weren't from his usual supplier. Some of them might not have been . . . entirely—'

'Oh, Jesus, Eddie!' Siobhán felt sick.

'That's why I haven't slept with you,' he said. 'I couldn't take the risk of . . . of . . .'

'What disease?' she asked.

'Well, any of them, I guess,' he replied shakily. 'But I've gone for an HIV test.'

Siobhán had met many people who had been infected by HIV. It wasn't necessarily a death sentence. At least, not in the way it had once been. But she couldn't accept the possibility that Eddie, her Eddie, had contracted it.

'When will you get the results?' she asked.

He shrugged. 'Next week, I hope.'

'What do you want me to say?' Her voice was laden with despair.

'Look, I know it was a terrible, awful, insane thing to do,' cried Eddie. 'Believe me when I tell you that I really and truly wish I hadn't done it.'

'Why?' she asked.

'Why what?'

'Why do you wish you hadn't done it?'

'Because it was a crazy moment,' he told her. 'Because I've put everything in jeopardy. Because I've totally messed up our lives. Because I could die.'

'Not because you're supposed to be in love with me?' asked Siobhán. 'Not because we were supposed to be getting married? Or that by doing this you've betrayed me?'

'Of course I wish I hadn't betrayed you,' said Eddie. 'I hate that damned word, by the way. It condemns without understanding. But I wasn't thinking like that at the time. I wasn't thinking at all. And I know you find that hard to believe with your good-and-evil, black-and-white view of the world, but sometimes normal people do get caught up in things they didn't mean to do.'

'Eddie, what you're describing isn't something that normal people do whether they mean to or not.'

'I suppose for Peter Murtagh that kind of sex, drugs and rock and roll kind of party is perfectly normal,' said Eddie. 'And while I was there it did seem normal. I mean, I know it wasn't really but it seemed like it. Everyone was doing everything.'

'Did you take the drugs too?' she demanded.

'Some coke.'

210

'Hell, Eddie!'

'Yeah, I know. Garda fiancé in sex and coke drugs bust,' he said grimly.

'That's not what I . . .' She sighed despairingly. 'What I'm thinking is that if you felt it was OK to do drugs and prostitutes – whether it was because you were somehow getting carried away in the moment or not – well, if you felt OK about it all, then you and I . . . I thought we were good together but obviously there's something missing and I . . .' She broke off. She'd cry if she tried to carry on, and she didn't want to cry.

'I promise you that I love you,' said Eddie. 'I know it doesn't seem like it because I know that women and men think differently about things. I know that you think I've been a total and utter shit and that there's no way I should have gone back to Murtagh's apartment in the first place. But it was the opportunity to be a different kind of person for a while. To mix with the kind of people who I don't normally mix with. To live a different sort of life even if it was only for a couple of hours.'

'I'm all for trying out different things, but you've been really stupid,' cried Siobhán. 'And this different life – was it worth it?'

'Of course it wasn't.' He swallowed. 'I've felt terrible ever since. I've been a complete fool and I could be seriously ill and . . . and I know I've been a nightmare to you and that everything I've done is shitty and awful, but I don't want to die.' Eddie started to cry.

Siobhán looked at him in silence. She felt as though she should be comforting him, but right now she wanted someone to comfort her.

'I love you, Siobhán.' He raised his eyes to her. 'I always have. I know that it was an awful thing to do but it was a mistake! It really was. It's hard to stand back from something when everyone else is doing it.'

'You had sex with a woman who isn't me,' said Siobhán. 'You asked me to marry you but you still had sex with someone else. You didn't do it because you loved her or anything. You did it because you felt like it. And you took drugs. Nobody made you do those things.'

'I've said I know it was wrong,' he told her. 'But we can't all live a blameless life, not breaking any rules ever. Even if the gardai would like it, we don't live in a police state yet.'

'So it's my fault?' Siobhán felt herself bubble with anger. 'You sleep with some tramp and it's my fault?'

'No! I didn't mean that. I just mean . . .' He looked at her despairingly. 'I shouldn't have done it. I know that.'

'Does anyone else know about it?' she asked after another silence. 'Your friends? People at work?'

'Are you mad?' he asked. 'Of course not. You're the only person who knows.'

She couldn't think of anything else to say. She stared unseeingly across the room, watching the wisp of voile curtain move gently in the breeze from the open balcony window. She wanted to feel sorry for Eddie, but she was too angry with him for that. She was afraid for him, and for her too. Part of her didn't believe that he could possibly have HIV. Part of her was afraid that he'd been very unlucky and that he did. And most of her was very angry that he'd gone away and behaved like an idiot and betrayed her with a woman who meant nothing to him.

She got up.

'Where are you going?' His voice was anxious.

'Out. I'm going for a run,' she replied.

'Don't leave me.'

'I'm not leaving you,' she said sharply. 'I'm going for a run, that's all. I need to clear my head.'

'I'll do anything to make it up to you,' said Eddie. 'Anything.'

But right then she couldn't actually think of anything she wanted him to do.

∽

She ran out of the apartment block and up Temple Hill, following the road along towards Monkstown. She liked running around here, even though it was a residential area. A sheen of sweat covered her body, and her red ponytail bobbed. Normally she didn't think about anything when she ran. But now she was thinking about the bombshell that Eddie had dropped.

Tears began to spill down Siobhán's cheeks. She couldn't believe that this had happened to her. To them. She'd loved him so much but she'd always felt that he was too good for her, too attractive. That was part of the reason she hadn't married him yet. She'd been afraid that in the end someone else would take him away. She just hadn't imagined it would be like this.

❧

It was over an hour later when she arrived back at the apartment building. She stood in the hallway and pressed the button for the lift. Quite suddenly she didn't have the energy to make it up the stairs.

The doors slid open and Carl O'Connor stepped out.

'Hi, Mizz Plod,' he said. 'How's things?'

'Fine,' she said tightly.

He frowned, suddenly noticing her tear-streaked cheeks.

'Hey – something the matter? You don't seem fine.'

'Nothing's the matter,' she told him shortly. 'I'm tired.'

'Hope everything went OK for you the other night,' he said. 'Hope that outfit you were wearing worked its charms in the end.'

'Oh, fuck off, O'Connor,' she said as she got into the lift and stabbed the button with her finger. 'Go and annoy someone else for a change.'

She leaned her head against the mirrored glass of the lift as it moved slowly upwards and brought her back to her own floor.

Chapter 20

Iona walked along the corridors of the hospital. It was busier than it had been the last time she'd been there, and she had to pick her way through the throngs of chattering visitors to reach Frank's unit. Her mouth was dry and she knew that her voice was unsteady as she told the nurse in charge who she was and who she wanted to see. She tried to sound more commanding as she said that the visit had been cleared by Frank's doctor.

Terri Cooper nodded at her. John Carroll had informed her earlier that morning that Iona would be coming in to see Frank. He'd said that Sally and Iona had reached an agreement about it. Terri was pleased that Sally had felt able to agree to Iona's visit, but she hoped that it wouldn't degenerate into some kind of cat-fight between the two women again. She trusted Sally to be calm and measured but, having seen Iona's behaviour that first night, she wasn't so certain that the younger woman would be able to keep her temperament in check. She hoped that Iona was aware that Sally had already been in the hospital for the best part of an hour, reading the newspapers to an unresponsive Frank.

Iona followed Terri to Frank's room, where Sally looked up from the *Irish Independent.* Iona's eyes widened in surprise at her appearance. Sally's long, thick hair had been cut into a shorter, softer style which framed her face and made her seem at least five years younger. She was wearing make-up too, which brought out the light in her blue-green eyes and defined the shape of her wide mouth. She'd replaced her cardigan with a navy-blue long-sleeved

214

T-shirt worn over a pair of loose-fitting jeans. She was totally transformed from the woman Iona had met for coffee.

Iona smoothed her own ink-black hair and sighed with relief that she'd chosen style over comfort that morning herself. She was wearing a black cotton dress which clung to every contour of her slight frame, emphasising the fact that she didn't have a spare ounce of fat on her body. She'd also elected to wear spiky-heeled sandals which showed off the shape of her smooth legs – although the uncomfortable footwear was already giving her blisters on both feet.

'Good morning,' she said to Sally. 'I like your hair.'

'Thanks.' Sally shrugged. 'It's easier to keep this way.'

Iona nodded. My arse, she thought, as she pulled up a chair and sat beside the bed. You've had it cut because you know that beside me you were a total frump and you were afraid of what would happen when Frank wakes up and sees both of us together.

'I've been reading him the papers.' Sally was unable to keep the hint of despair out of her voice. 'No reaction, though.'

Iona got up from the chair and leaned over Frank's immobile body.

'It's me,' she whispered softly. 'I'm here. I've come to be with you.'

It was unbelievably disconcerting to talk to someone who didn't react at all. Somehow she'd thought that it would be like speaking to him while he was sleeping, but it wasn't like that. He was in a completely different place to the rest of them. She knew that he hadn't heard her.

'He doesn't react,' said Sally brutally. 'At least, not usually. He did once. He opened his eyes. But according to the nurse, that happens sometimes. It didn't mean anything.'

'Was he just, you know, staring into space, or did he look around?'

'Pretty much just staring into space. His eyes were open but he wasn't seeing anything.'

Iona suddenly felt dizzy. She hated sickness, and all at once she felt overwhelmed by the sense of her own mortality, the hum of the monitors and the sight of the drip on its stand. She steadied herself by holding on to the bed.

'Are you all right?' asked Sally.

'Of course.' Iona plopped back on to the chair. 'Are you going to leave us alone now?'

Sally said nothing.

'After all, you've had time alone. I need time alone too.'

'Sure. I understand.' Sally got up. 'I'll come back in a while.'

'I'll let you know if he wakes up,' said Iona. 'Don't worry.'

It was different without Sally. She leaned her head on the counterpane, holding Frank's hand in hers, squeezing it from time to time and hoping that he would squeeze it in return. But he didn't. She whispered things to him – how worried she'd been about him, how she felt about what had happened, how devastated she was at the thought that she wasn't really his wife.

'But I feel as though I'm your real wife,' she said softly. 'You chose me after her. You love me. I know you do. And I know that you want to get better to be with me because you want me to have your baby. Our baby. I know that, Frank, and that's why I know you're going to wake up.'

She lifted her head. It was impossible to believe that he hadn't heard her or felt the depth of her love for him. Even though, she thought suddenly, she should hate him. As she had, on and off, ever since the accident.

She sat in silence for a few minutes and then took the book that she'd brought with her out of her bag. She opened it at the beginning and began to read.

⁓

Sally walked out of the hospital and into the crowded grounds. She'd never had much to do with hospitals before – her only stay in one herself had been when she was giving birth to Jenna; and Frank had never darkened the doors of one before now either. She'd had to rush into Casualty once, when Jenna had fallen off the back wall and broken her ankle, but Sally didn't consider broken limbs to be real illnesses. They were accidents that happened but they weren't organic problems. She didn't mind broken bones or cuts and bruises. She didn't faint at the sight of blood. But she hated the idea of something going on inside someone's body that no one understood – the idea of tiny cellular creatures dividing and multiplying and creating havoc for the person whose body they had invaded. Or in Frank's case, what bothered her was the thought that the whole structure of his body had changed, that the cells were doing the wrong things simply because they'd been shaken up by the accident, but because of that Frank might die.

She caught sight of herself suddenly, reflected in a car window. She saw her shorter hair and her specially chosen clothes and she wondered why she had bothered. Jenna had been shocked at the haircut.

'You've never worn it that short before,' she'd told Sally accusingly. 'Why have you done this now?'

Sally had tried to explain that it seemed the right thing to do, that her long hair had always been difficult to keep tidy and that plaiting it every day had been a real chore. But Jenna had chosen to ignore Sally's efforts at explanation.

'Is it because of her?' she'd demanded aggressively. 'Is it because she has short hair?'

Sally had also tried to explain that it wasn't a matter of short hair or long hair, that it was about not letting yourself go. But Jenna was having none of it.

'You've always worn it long,' she said accusingly. 'I don't see why you've cut it now. Besides, you look shit.'

Sally had wondered about that. About whether the new style really suited her. It had looked great in the salon but now, at home, she worried that she'd been conned into something that wasn't really her after all. And yet, as she looked at herself in the mirror, she couldn't help but think that the style was much better than the one she'd had before. That she looked more confident and controlled with shorter hair. And that she needed to look like that.

She sat down on one of the wooden benches in the garden of the hospital and wondered what Iona was talking to Frank about. What could she say that Sally hadn't already said a thousand times? Was there anything she could offer that would be different to what Sally had already tried? Part of her knew there wasn't. Part of her was afraid there was. All of her worried about the outcome.

Because what if Frank did wake up and decide that Iona was the one he wanted for his wife? Where did that leave her? Looking for a divorce, she supposed. Right now she could see that it had its attractions. Frank was a shit and he deserved to be divorced. But it was hard to accept that she should be the one to divorce him.

∽

Time had looped back on itself. Frank could feel it. He was sitting in the attic and rummaging through the big cardboard box with *Tayto* written across the side and he knew that he was fifteen years old. Except . . . except somehow he was sure that he had done this before. It was more than a sense of déjà vu. He couldn't explain it. He was watching himself but he was also participating in the action. It was a weird experience.

Maybe it was because of the beer he'd drunk the previous night at the GAA disco. Far too much beer, he knew. He'd been sick on the way home but was kind of glad that he'd thrown up outside the house rather than inside. His father, Derek, who liked a drink himself, nevertheless strongly disapproved of Frank even touching a drop. But then, thought Frank, as he pulled at the contents of the box, Derek strongly disapproved of everything. Frank had investigated the box because he'd hoped – for all of half a second – that it was a supply of crisps for the coming Christmas, but he soon realised that it was packed with stuff that his father hadn't got around to throwing out. Frank knew that he should've had more sense than to think that Derek Harper gave a toss for Christmas. His dad made Scrooge seem positively benevolent by comparison. When Frank was five years old Derek had sat him down and told him that the whole Santa lark was a complete load of nonsense and that anyone with a bit of wit could see that it was impossible for a fat man to get down all the chimneys of the world in one night.

Frank's lower lip had trembled as he looked at his father. 'What about magic?' he asked.

Derek snorted. 'No such thing,' he said. 'If there was, your mother would be back here.'

Frank took out a manilla folder. It was stuffed with receipts and invoices and newspaper clippings about the building of a new school in the area. Derek had worked as the school gardener ever since it had been built. Frank didn't know what his father had done before that. A blue sheet of paper fluttered out of the folder and he picked it up. The sender's address, in the top right-hand corner, was Mount Street, Dublin, and it was dated 1958.

Dear Derek,
I really don't know what to say. I'm honoured that you would want me to be your wife, but you know how I feel about marriage. It's an outdated institution. I love you too and I'd be happy to live with you here (despite how scandalised everyone would be!) but I won't marry anyone. I beg of you to read Simone de Beauvoir to understand how I feel about being a woman. I don't dislike or despise men as so many feminists seem to, but I don't want to be the chattel of one either. And so I can't marry you but I will live with you.
Love always,
Christine

A small photograph was attached to the letter. Frank stared at it. It was a photograph of his mother. He'd never seen a photograph of his mother before. Derek didn't have a camera and had told him that taking photographs was a waste of time and effort anyway. The only photograph in the house was one of Frank himself as a baby, propped up on a white blanket, staring out at the camera, his eyes big and enquiring.

His mother was stunningly beautiful. She had dark hair,

laughing eyes and an upturned nose. Her skin appeared flawless. She wasn't wearing any make-up in the photograph (Frank recalled others of that time where the women all seemed to wear very dark lipstick), but her features were well defined without it. And he could see his own likeness in the shape of her mouth and her high forehead.

Frank dropped down from the attic and walked out into the garden, where Derek was pulling weeds from the flowerbeds. He thrust the letter in front of him. Derek's face darkened as he read it.

'I suppose I'd better tell you,' he said, 'now that you're practically grown. She was crazy, that's what. I thought she was a bit flighty but that in the end she'd be sensible. But she never was.'

'All the same . . .' began Frank.

'You deserve to know the truth,' Derek told him sharply. 'I suppose I protected you when you were younger. Had to really, this town being the gossipy place that it is. But she isn't dead.'

Frank stared at his father. He could almost feel the blood drain from his face.

'No. I had to say that for your sake. Couldn't let you know it. Would have hurt you. But she didn't die. She bolted.'

'You told me . . . you said that she'd been sick . . .' Frank couldn't take his eyes off the set face of his father. 'You lied to me.'

'Not a lie,' said Derek. 'Saving you from the truth.'

'But everyone else knows!' cried Frank. 'I know they know. It makes sense now. The way the old biddies in the shops look at me sometimes. I thought it was because my mother had died. But that's not it at all.'

Derek shrugged.

'For crying out loud, Dad!' Frank looked at him in anger and disbelief. 'All these years. What the hell were you thinking?' He scratched the back of his head. 'Did she look for me? Did she want to know anything about me?'

'No,' said Derek shortly. 'Never once. She didn't care about you and me. I should have done it differently with her. Made her care. Made her get married like she should have done. I should have made her realise how important family is, got her pregnant again, got a brother or a sister for you.'

'You never got married? You and Ma? Never got married?'

'What does it look like, boy? You have her letter. You can see what she says.'

'Yes, but – I thought she changed her mind.'

'That woman! No chance.'

'If she was so different from you, if she didn't want to be married or to have a family, then why did you want to marry her at all?' asked Frank.

'Look at her,' said Derek. 'Lovely girl. And a sensible person when she wasn't going on and on about being oppressed. Women's movement.' He sniffed. 'Feminism. Her bloody Simone de bloody Beauvoir. Complete bollocks.'

Frank stared at his father in utter astonishment. Derek never swore in front of him.

'Oh, she was a part-time feminist all right,' said Derek. 'But it was a passing thing. When I took her back here, she was happy enough to pretend. She was pregnant, you see, and despite everything she couldn't quite bring herself to correct people when they called her Mrs Harper. She said she was doing it for your sake. I thought she just needed a bit of time and then we could get married properly. Nip over to London and do it, I thought.'

'What went wrong?'

Derek sighed and rested his chin on the handle of the garden spade.

'We disagreed. I wanted more kids. She didn't. I told her that if she was married to me she'd have them, and she said maybe it was just as well she wasn't. She said she was trapped enough the way things were. Strangled, was what she told me. Suffocated. A load of nonsense. She said she never meant to have a baby. I told her that it was what she was put on this earth for when it came down to it. That all her poncey ideas were well and good when she was a single woman but she was a mother now and that changed everything.' Derek snorted. 'She said she was still a single woman. I told her that if she walked out on me she'd be an

221

unmarried mother with a crying kid and that she could sing for her supper then because no man would ever look at her.'

Frank blinked. 'Did you have to be so cruel?'

'It wasn't cruelty,' said Derek. 'It was love. I needed to bring her to her senses.'

'But you didn't,' said Frank. 'Because she left us.'

'Stupid, stupid woman,' said Derek. 'She didn't know when she had it good. She didn't love you. Couldn't have. No woman leaves her child. Not with only a bloke to bring him up. Selfish bitch is what she was. I couldn't believe she left you.'

He took the photograph from Frank and studied it for a moment. Then he tore it into little pieces and threw them on the pile of weeds.

'Well shot of her in the end,' said Derek. 'Well shot of her.'

His father stomped back to the house. Frank waited until he was inside and then retrieved the pieces of the torn photograph. He liked the idea of his mother being an unconventional person, but there was a hollow feeling in the pit of his stomach whenever he thought of her simply abandoning him. She hadn't loved him enough. She'd walked out and it had been easy for her because she hadn't married his dad. And his dad had been horrified at her leaving him behind. If she hadn't done that, Derek might have been able to find someone else. But not with a toddler.

Frank clenched his jaw. Neither of his parents had really wanted him when it came down to it. It'd be different when it was his turn. He'd be a good father to his kids and a good husband to his wife.

Unless, of course, he didn't bother with all that marrying nonsense and just became a spy instead. He blinked a couple of times. He'd never thought about being a spy before.

∽

Iona stopped reading as the door opened. She'd reached the third chapter of *Goldfinger*, the chapter where James Bond first sees Auric Goldfinger. Frank had told her, when the film was on TV

222

and they were watching it together, that the description of Goldfinger was so exact that it was amazing they'd managed to get an actor to fit the role so well. Gert Frobe, he lectured, was fantastic, even if the shorts he wore at the beginning of the movie were somewhat more decent than the 'yellow bikini slip' described in the book.

Sally tensed as she realised what Iona was reading aloud. She was angry with herself for not having thought of the book before now. But her anger disappeared as she realised that it hadn't made any difference. Frank was still immobile in the bed.

'No change?' she said as she walked across the room.

Iona shook her head. 'I suppose I was stupid to think that I'd make a difference,' she told Sally. She closed the book. 'I guess I came here believing that he'd wake up. Because it was me, not you. I was stupid. I'm sorry.'

'No need to be sorry,' said Sally wryly. 'I suppose I was in two minds about the whole thing. I want him to wake up. But I didn't really want you to be the one to wake him.'

Iona nodded in understanding. 'Can I ask you something?'

'Yes?'

'You said that people were looking after his business.'

'Yes.'

'Do you depend on it?' asked Iona. 'The company? For money?'

'We're lucky,' Sally told her. 'The mortgage isn't crippling and we've never been big spenders. I work, of course. I'm a teacher. But I don't know where we go from here with the business. I don't really care, to be honest with you. But I told Richard, that's the accountant, to keep me informed.'

'I accessed his company e-mails last night,' said Iona. 'There are a number of things outstanding. And his calendar is online too. I just forgot about it all.'

'How did you do that when you don't have the computer?' asked Sally.

'We . . . I have one at home. I knew his password.'

'Oh. What?'

'Goldfinger,' she said simply.

223

The door to Frank's room opened and the two women looked up in surprise.

Siobhán Farrell was equally surprised. She'd more or less expected to see Sally at the hospital but she hadn't expected to see Iona. And even less had she anticipated seeing both of the Harper wives standing side by side at Frank's bed. She frowned slightly as she tried to work out the implications of what she was seeing.

'Hello, Sally. Iona,' she said.

'Siobhán.' Iona was the one who reacted first. 'What are you doing here?'

'I needed to drop in to see him,' said Siobhán. 'So here I am.'

'On a Sunday morning?' Sally looked sceptical. 'You haven't come to . . .?' She broke off and looked accusingly at Siobhán.

'It was convenient for me today,' said Siobhán. She obviously wasn't going to tell Iona and Sally that she couldn't stay in the apartment with Eddie, that she'd needed to get out and had decided to come and fingerprint Frank Harper instead.

'Iona was reading to him,' said Sally. '*Goldfinger*. His favourite book.'

Siobhán nodded and walked further into the room. She looked at Frank as he lay in the bed, noting the angry bruise over his eye and the dark row of stitches on his partially shaved head. But even with the facial injuries, and even with his expressionless features, she could see that Frank Harper was an attractive man.

'No change then?' she asked.

'No,' said Iona and Sally simultaneously.

'There was some increased brain activity last night,' said Sally. 'But it didn't mean anything in the end.'

'You never told me that.' Iona looked at her accusingly.

'Because it didn't mean anything,' said Sally.

'It might. How do you know?'

'Because that's what the doctor said this morning.'

'That's a load of shit,' said Iona. 'You can't tell me that increased brain activity in a coma patient doesn't mean anything!'

'Well, nothing useful,' suggested Sally. 'I mean, it's hopeful that his brain is still working, I suppose.'

Siobhán looked from one to the other. 'Are you visiting him together from now on?' she asked.

'No,' said Iona. 'But we'll both visit him. I suppose.' She looked at Sally for confirmation.

'We could set up a roster,' said Sally. 'You one day, me the next. It would make it a lot easier.'

Iona nodded slowly. 'Thank you.'

'Do you want to come in tomorrow or will I?' asked Sally.

'We're starting from tomorrow?'

'When d'you want to start?' asked Sally. 'It seems to me if we're doing this we should begin straight away. No?'

'Well, sure, yes,' agreed Iona hastily. 'I'll come tomorrow.'

'The roster will be for the evenings,' said Sally. 'If either of us has time to come in during the day, that's up to us.'

'OK.'

'I'm glad you two have worked that out,' said Siobhán.

'I might have been a bit . . . hysterical . . . the first day,' said Iona. 'But that was shock. I can be reasonable too.'

'When did you arrange today?' asked Siobhán.

'We met for coffee,' said Sally.

'Very civilised,' said Siobhán.

'No point in not being,' said Iona. 'Who knows how long Frank might be like this?'

'Indeed.' Siobhán's eyes flickered over his body.

'I suppose I'd better get going,' said Sally into the silence that had developed between the three women. 'I've been here since early this morning and I've got to get back to Jenna.'

'Doesn't she visit?' asked Siobhán.

'She hates it,' explained Sally. 'She hates the hospital smell and she hates seeing her dad like this.'

Siobhán nodded in understanding.

'I'll go too,' said Iona. 'I've read him loads of the book and I've talked to him and . . . well . . . I guess there's not much more I can do.'

'Did you drive?' asked Sally.

Iona nodded.

'I'll walk with you to the car park.'

'OK.' Iona turned to Siobhán. 'Coming?'

Siobhán shook her head. 'I need to see a nurse or doctor on the ward,' she said. 'Just to get more info on when Frank was admitted.'

'You know that already,' said Iona. 'Walk with us.'

Siobhán glanced from Frank to Iona and Sally and shrugged. 'OK.'

She followed them out of the door. She'd walk to the car park with them, then she'd come back. She had her fingerprint kit in her bag. And, having seen Sally and Iona together, she was beginning to reassess the relationship between the two women. Everything had seemed perfectly straightforward, and she was sure that it still was. But making certain was important too.

Chapter 21

I ona needed to go back to work. She couldn't stay in the house all day, worrying about Frank and frantically trawling her mind for memories which would show her what a fool she had been to believe him when he'd used the words 'forsaking all others' on their wedding day. She needed to be in a place where she couldn't think about it all the time and blame herself for making the issue of being married so important even while telling herself that it wasn't her fault. Frank could have admitted that he was married already when she first broached the subject. He could have dumped her without saying anything at all. Nobody had forced him to lie and cheat and pretend. That had been his own choice. The thoughts whirled around and around in her head like a washing machine on a fast spin cycle, and she knew that the only way she'd get peace of mind was to go back to Rental Remedies and lose herself in something else.

Ruth Dawson smiled at her as she walked into the office and asked her how she was feeling. Although the message she'd left at the office had said that she was off sick, Iona had somehow imagined that her colleague would guess, by some kind of mental osmosis, that the real reason for her absence was entirely different. But Ruth was sitting back in her chair and telling Iona that everyone seemed to be getting crazy virus infections and that echinacea wasn't all that it was cracked up to be, was it, because otherwise Iona wouldn't have succumbed, would she?

'I've got to talk to Garret,' said Iona blankly, ignoring Ruth's puzzled stare as she walked towards their boss's office.

The founder of Rental Remedies smiled at Iona as she sat down in front of him. She was one of his favourite employees, clever and sparky and totally dependable. Her absence through illness had been the first time in two years that she'd taken time off sick from work.

'Feeling better?' he asked casually, and then listened in stunned amazement as Iona told him everything that had happened over the past week. She hadn't been sure what she was going to tell people – had briefly thought about not saying anything about Sally and Jenna at all, just that Frank had been in an accident and she'd been too shocked to tell them about it before – but she simply wasn't able to lie. So she held nothing back, and Garret's jaw dropped lower and lower as she recounted the tale.

'I don't know what to say to you,' he said as she finished. 'I can't believe he would do a thing like that. And the police are involved?'

'They have to be,' explained Iona. 'It's a criminal offence.'

'Jesus wept.' Garret stared at her. 'I'm sorry, Iona. I really am.'

'Yeah, well, so am I.' She gave him a half-hearted smile. 'I'm in a bit of a quandary at the moment. He's still in hospital and we really don't know whether he'll recover or not.'

'Have they given you any kind of time frame?' asked Garret.

'They can't.' Iona shrugged. 'Really, though, from what they say, he needs to come out of it soon.' She swallowed hard. 'The doctor says that there is brain activity but right now he's simply not responding to anything. But that doesn't mean he doesn't know what's going on around him. It's really difficult to tell. Unfortunately, the longer he goes without reacting, the worse it is.'

'I can see that.' Garret nodded. 'You do hear about people coming out of comas, though.'

'Yes, you do. And in the movies they just kind of wake up and everyone clusters around and it's all happy families. But the reality is different. He might be brain-damaged. He might have memory loss. He might not even know who we are. He might be physically impaired. He might have to learn how to do simple things again. Or he might be all right.' She shrugged helplessly. 'We don't know.'

'And this other woman. How are you coping with her?'

Iona sighed. 'We're working things out between us,' she said. 'At the moment it's a kind of one day at a time scenario.'

'I'm sorry,' repeated Garret. 'It must be difficult for you.'

'It was a nightmare.' Iona straightened up in the seat. 'But I'm ready to work again now. I can't sit at home and wait for him to wake up. I need to do things.'

Garret nodded. 'Well, if you need time out, just let me know.'

'Thanks,' said Iona. 'I appreciate that.'

'No problem.'

Garret's eyes followed her as she walked out of his office and then he rubbed his forehead. He never would have imagined that Frank, whom he'd met a couple of times, would have been the sort of guy to have such an involved personal life. Marrying two women! On the one hand Garret couldn't help admiring the fact that he had managed to juggle his life in secret for so long. On the other . . . Well, Garret was married himself. He loved Emily dearly. But one wife was more than enough!

Ruth looked up again as Iona sat down behind her desk. She frowned. But before she had the chance to say anything, Iona launched into a repetition of what she'd told Garret. Ruth was equally shocked and asked exactly the same questions. Iona answered her patiently. Although she hated having to say it all over again, she was finding talking about it to other people a little therapeutic. As though by admitting to what had happened she was lessening the horror of it all.

'He'll come out of it and he'll be fine,' said Ruth finally. 'Frank is such a positive person, he's bound to recover.'

'Yes.' Iona nodded. 'And when he comes out of it, I'll fucking kill him.'

'Iona!' Ruth looked shocked.

'Sorry,' said Iona. 'But I feel a bit like that about it. It's very tiring. I want him to get better and then I want to hit him over the head again.' Her smile wobbled. 'I'm completely schizophrenic about it all, to be perfectly honest with you. However, it's not going to happen in the next couple of hours, so you'd better tell me – anything need doing?'

'Um, sure.' Ruth was still in shock from Iona's news as she looked at her computer. 'We got the final contract to manage that block in Monkstown last week,' she told her. 'Everyone was really pleased about that. Carmela is working on it but there'll be a number of rentals, so I thought you'd probably want to talk to her about it. The tenant in Craighill Manor keeps ringing up with new complaints . . .'

Iona listened as Ruth continued with the list of things that needed her attention. It was nice to have other problems to worry about instead of how Frank was and how things would develop and what the hell she was going to do with her life; but it was hard to concentrate on them. She felt as though she should be doing nothing other than sitting at Frank's bedside and reading him more chapters of *Goldfinger*. She was sure the novel would eventually reach him. Absolutely certain. And she still wanted to be the person beside him when he woke up.

'. . . you could drop out with them?' Ruth looked at her enquiringly and Iona dragged her attention back to her colleague.

'I'm sorry,' she said. 'What was that?'

'Enrique Martinez,' said Ruth. 'He's signed the contract for Apartment 7 in the Waterside Building, but he went back to Spain for the weekend. He sent an e-mail asking if we could get the keys to him today and go through the apartment again with him. D'you want to do that? I could do it but my schedule is a bit crowded.'

'No, it's OK, I will.' Iona nodded. It would be nice, she thought, to get out of the office for a while. She didn't want to see Ruth's sympathetic face all bloody day.

～

Sally had decided to take another week off work. She simply wasn't able to concentrate on anything long enough to give any kind of coherent lesson to the students, and she knew that her mental state was too fragile to keep a class of thirty adolescent females under control anyway. The previous night she'd phoned Denise to tell her that she simply couldn't come back yet, although, she said, she'd absolutely definitely be back the week after.

'Sally, honey, you'll need more than another week!' exclaimed Denise, who, when she'd eventually heard about Iona, had been apoplectic with rage on her friend's behalf. 'I'll talk to the head about it. She'll understand.'

'I'll ring her myself,' said Sally tiredly. 'I can't let you do it for me.'

'Don't be daft,' retorted Denise firmly. 'I'll do it, you phone her later. Is there anything else I can do for you at the moment?'

Sally had told her that there was nothing anyone could do. Except wait. And worry.

In addition to worrying about Frank, of course, she was equally worried about Jenna, who had retreated into a world of silence about it all. Every time Sally asked her daughter if she was OK, Jenna snapped that she was fine, she wasn't the one who was in a coma and she wasn't the one who was probably going to die. When Sally protested that the fact that Frank was in a coma didn't mean he was going to die, Jenna had responded with a sheaf of information she'd downloaded from the net which gave a variety of prognoses in relation to comas.

'If he doesn't die he could still be a vegetable,' she said shortly. 'He might as well be dead.'

'We have to be positive,' said Sally.

'Yeah.' Jenna tossed back her hair disdainfully. 'If he's a veggie then that other woman can have him!'

'Jenna!'

'Well, why should we have to put up with it?' demanded Jenna. 'I hate him. I wanted to die myself when I saw him in the hospital

231

and I felt so awful for him. And then we find out about her! She's welcome to him.'

'He's your dad,' said Sally gently. 'You don't mean it.'

'I absolutely do.' Jenna got up and stalked out of the room while Sally pressed her fingers to her throbbing temples and wondered how long she could live like this.

She was surprised when Jenna said that she wanted to go to school the next day. She told her that she could stay home if she wanted, but Jenna replied that there was nothing to do at home, and that she wanted to be with her friends. She added that she wasn't going to ruin her life by missing out on her schooling just because of him and that she needed to study. Sally had acquiesced, even though she worried about Jenna's pinched face and tired eyes, and had watched her daughter anxiously as she walked down the road to school, her long uniform skirt flapping in the breeze.

Now, alone in the house, she went up to Jenna's room and switched on her daughter's computer. She opened up the web browser and looked at the history of searches which Jenna had done on comas. There was a great deal of information and lots of different coma stories, but all of it came down to the same thing. Nobody knew. Nobody could be sure. Nobody could predict what might happen.

But Sally had to know. She had to get their lives into some kind of order. It wasn't as though time could stand still while Frank was in the hospital. And it wasn't as though sooner or later Jenna wasn't going to find out about the baby too. If she'd thought it would be difficult to talk to Jenna about the baby before, Sally felt it would be a million times harder now.

'Why?' she muttered as she leaned her head against the screen. 'Why me? Why us? Why now?'

⌣

Frank wanted Sally to have a good time. They were in town, in a swanky restaurant on St Stephen's Green where the prices were astronomical and where the wines were the sort you didn't find on the supermarket shelves. But this was a major celebration. They were going to have a baby. Every time he said the word, he looked at Sally as though she was a fragile piece of glass which needed the gentlest of care, even though she looked stronger and fitter than ever.

'I'll look after you,' he said sincerely. And he knew that he would. Because she was giving him everything he'd ever wanted. The family that they'd promised each other. They'd discussed it, of course, after she'd accepted his marriage proposal but before they'd actually got married. She'd been quite specific about it, telling him that they should both know what they wanted from each other, and although he'd been taken aback by her practical way of looking at it, he'd agreed that before they signed up to a lifelong commitment they should set out a few ground rules.

The main rule was that both of them wanted children. And although they'd compromised on four, it didn't really matter in the end whether they had four or fourteen or whether this was their only child. They would be a family. A strong unit, there for each other. And this baby was the start of that.

Frank was looking forward to being a father. He wanted to be a good dad. He wanted his kids to look up to him but not to fear him. He wanted them to think that he knew about lots of things but that he wasn't always right. He wanted them to love him, although he was pretty sure that children never loved their parents as much as parents loved their children. In most cases anyway. His had surely been an exception.

She was sitting back in her chair, looking around the restaurant. He wanted to lean forward and kiss her on the lips but somehow his body couldn't quite manage it. Probably because I'm a bit overwhelmed at being here, he said to himself. Probably because I never thought I'd be sitting in a swanky restaurant. So instead of kissing her, he just smiled.

〜

Siobhán Farrell was waiting for information on the fingerprints she'd taken from Frank Harper as he lay in his hospital bed. Her sudden suspicion that there was some kind of collusion between the two Harper wives had dissipated and she was inclined to go back to her first thoughts, that the whole thing was simply a case of a devious, if apparently loving, man deceiving both of them. But she still had a process to go through and she still intended to go through with it. She was also running background checks on Frank both in Ireland and the UK, but so far nothing had come back, which reinforced her belief that this was a domestic disaster.

She could see how it had happened, though. At least, she could see why both of the women had been attracted to Frank Harper, because she'd been attracted to him herself. It was hard to believe that this had been the case when he'd been lying there, motionless in the bed, but even in his comatose state he radiated a certain presence. She could imagine that he was an active man, a man of energy, someone it would be hard not to find attractive. And he was probably good in bed. No, definitely good in bed. Both Iona and Sally had said so.

Had he ever worried about giving either of them a sexually transmitted disease? She supposed not. It shouldn't matter, should it, if the sex was only happening in their little triangle, if Frank wasn't going outside it for additional excitement and gratification. Unlike Eddie. She clenched her teeth as she thought about his terrible betrayal.

Was it fair to feel so angry with him? One mistake, that was all it was. Frank Harper had consistently deceived both women in his life, but Eddie's mistake had been a stupid, drunken one. So the circumstances were utterly different. And Eddie, at least, had had the decency not to sleep with her when he realised he could be exposing her to a disease. Which was a point in his favour, surely? Nonetheless, he could have come clean a lot sooner, instead of simply pushing her away every night and making her feel unwanted and unloved. If he really and truly thought he had AIDS then he'd been right not to come near her. But she couldn't believe that he honestly thought that. Siobhán believed that Eddie had been unable to make love to her out of guilt. She was glad if that was the case. She didn't like to think of him having even a moment of pleasure when he was causing her so much pain. He'd apologised to her over and over again, begging her not to walk out on him, repeating how much he loved her and how he still wanted to marry her and how it had all been a terrible, terrible mistake. The people she arrested usually said that to her too. And they still got convicted in the end.

⟿

Iona had arranged to meet Enrique Martinez at the entrance to the apartment block. They both arrived at the same time and she greeted him warmly, amazing herself that she could smile at a client when inside she felt an emotional wreck.

She unlocked the apartment and then handed the keys to Enrique, telling him that it was all his.

'We go around to check everything together first?' he said, and she nodded. She followed him as he identified everything on the inventory, ticking it off with a beautiful silver fountain pen. He was going through the kitchen equipment when her phone rang.

'Hello,' she said.

'Iona!' Flora's voice was crystal clear. 'I called the house and there was no answer. Are you all right?'

Iona groaned inwardly. She didn't want to talk to her mother right now, but Flora was asking whether she was all right and fussing as Iona knew she would, shocked when she heard that Iona was at work and telling her she needed time to grieve.

'For heaven's sake, he's not dead yet,' snapped Iona. She winced as she saw her client glance in her direction. 'Look, Mum, I appreciate your calling, but I'm busy right now. I'll call you later.' She closed her mobile and shoved it back into her bag.

'Problems?' Enrique looked at her sympathetically.

'Not at all,' she said briskly. 'My apologies. Now, is everything in order? Is there anything else that you need?'

It was good to do ordinary things, she thought, as she eventually left the apartment block. Ordinary things made her feel as though she was living an ordinary life after all. And that was all she really wanted to do.

Chapter 22

It was four weeks since the accident.

Sally had insisted that Jenna come to the hospital with her that evening because she felt that it was more important for both of them to be around tonight than ever. In her mind, and especially because of what the doctors had told her, she'd set four weeks as the target for Frank to recover. Until then she was prepared to allow his brain to stay switched off from reality, thinking that maybe he needed time to heal himself. But four weeks was her mental cut-off time, the date for things to return to normal.

She didn't say to Jenna that she had a feeling Frank would wake up tonight. She didn't want to raise her daughter's hopes in the same way as she was raising her own. But he had to come out of it now, he just had to. The doctors said that there was no swelling on his brain, and that he was recovering from his other injuries too. So with all of that more promising physical improvement, surely he could let himself wake up. Sally had likened Frank's current state to the way she felt in the mornings these days – knowing that she had to get up and out of bed but trying desperately (and out of character for her) to snatch a few more minutes of sleep before the reality of how things were washed over her again.

They walked through the hospital corridors to Frank's room. By now they recognised many of the nurses, and most of them knew them too. Despite the fact that they seemed perpetually busy and always hurrying somewhere, the nurses always had time to say hello and ask them how they were doing. Sally appreciated their concern. She no longer felt as though they were laughing at her behind her back or whispering about her at their coffee breaks. And, she thought, as she pushed open the door and went into the now familiar room, so what if they were? Maybe she would find the situation one to whisper about too if other people had been involved.

'Oh!' Jenna grasped at her hand. 'His eyes are open.'

'But he still can't see us,' said Sally. 'This has happened before, Jen.'

'Not when I've been here.'

'No,' admitted Sally. 'And it freaked me out the first time it happened.'

'Did it?' Jenna was still holding her hand. 'I can't imagine you getting freaked out.'

'You'd better believe it.' Sally squeezed her daughter's fingers and then pulled out a chair. 'Hi, Frank. You scare us when you open your eyes like that.'

He closed them. Sally and Jenna looked at each other.

'Frank?' said Sally. 'You want to open those eyes again for us?'

But nothing happened.

'Dad?' said Jenna. 'Please open your eyes.'

They stayed closed.

'Oh well.' Sally tried to keep the bitter disappointment out of her voice. 'Maybe he'll open them again later. Do you want to talk to him first or will I?'

'I will,' said Jenna. 'I'm going to have a girl-to-father conversation, so actually you can butt out if you don't mind.'

Sally smiled. OK,' she said. 'I'll be back in ten minutes.'

'Fine,' said Jenna.

Once Sally had left the room, Jenna pressed play on the portable CD player she'd brought with her so that he could hear the sounds of Westlife singing Frank Sinatra (she felt it would be just too much for her to have to listen to a recording of Sinatra himself). Then she leaned her elbows on her father's bed.

'I hate you,' she said conversationally over 'Mack the Knife'. 'You betrayed us. We loved you and you lied to us. You always said that we were the most important people in the world to you, but you don't believe that, do you? 'Cos if you did you wouldn't have done what you've done.

'But it probably doesn't matter. Mum thinks you're going to get better and – well – I want you to, but it's not looking very promising. She won't read the stuff I downloaded and she only listens to the good stuff the doctors say. They're muttering about psychological reasons why you won't wake up. Well, it's not really so surprising, is it? You lied to me and to Mum and to . . . to her, that woman as well, and if you wake up now – well, I wouldn't want to be in your shoes! So I guess that's why you're staying in bed. Because you can't face us. Because you're such a shit.'

She sat back and looked at him. His expression hadn't changed. His eyes were still closed. 'So what I want to know, Dad, are all men shits? I'm asking you because I have a boyfriend and his name is Gerry and I love him. I'm not just pretending I love him. I really do. He's the nicest bloke you ever knew and he's been really great to me, especially over all this crap. When I'm feeling bad about everything he tells me that it's not my fault and there's nothing I can do and that I have my own life to lead. That's pretty cool, don't you think? So that's why I'm reacting to this by telling you that you're a shit. But I still love you.'

Her voice cracked slightly. 'I mean, Dad, I remember all the stuff we did together and I know that you loved me then. So what did I do to make you not love me? Or what did Mum do? I always thought it was us three; that's what you told me all the time. So how come there had to be someone else? Anyway, I guess it's all changed now. It's us three and her. And Gerry makes another person because, Dad, right now I love Gerry more than you. Well, it's different of course. I love him like a boyfriend.'

She sat back in the chair and observed her father for a moment. It was hard to imagine that the feelings he and her mother had for each other could ever have been like the feelings she now had for Gerry Cullinan. But she supposed they must have been once.

'I've slept with him, Dad.'

She scrutinised his face for any sign that he'd heard her, but there was nothing.

239

'I've slept with him more than once. We used condoms, so you don't have to worry about being a grandfather just yet. I wasn't crazy about the first time. It was OK but I was too conscious of everything going on around me, which I guess you shouldn't be. But the second time was great. Really great. I loved it. So I couldn't wait to sleep with him again. He makes me . . . fizz.'

She got up and poured herself a drink from the water jug beside the bed. She wondered why on earth there was a water jug there when Frank clearly wasn't able to use it – when he didn't even know it existed.

'I couldn't help wondering if you and the other woman fizz,' she said as she sat down again. 'I mean, I have to tell you that it's disgusting. For you and for her. You're my dad, for heaven's sake. But if there was something about her that made you feel like I feel about Gerry, then I understand. But I can't forgive you for it. You know that, don't you?'

The door opened and Sally walked in again.

'No change,' said Jenna.

'So I see.' Sally pulled out a chair and sat down beside the bed.

'I'm going for some air,' said Jenna. 'It's far too hot in here.'

'Stay a bit longer,' said Sally. 'Let's be with him together for a while. He needs his family around him now.'

Jenna looked longingly at the door. But she didn't get up from the chair.

∼

The office block was relatively new, but squashed between two older, more elegant buildings. Frank liked the newness but he couldn't help feeling that glass and chrome were out of place beside the Edwardian structures either side of it. He walked into the lobby, which was very modern – red leather and chrome chairs and glass coffee tables strewn with copies of a glossy women's magazine – and stood in front of the elderly security guard, who ignored him for a full minute before looking up.

'I'm here to see Christine Harris,' said Frank.

'Fill out a slip.' The security guard had no interest in him.

Frank did as he was told. The man looked at the slip and picked up a phone.

'Got an appointment?' he asked Frank as a voice at the other end spoke to him.

'Not as such,' said Frank.

'Miss Harris is busy,' said the security guard.

'Tell her I need to talk to her,' said Frank. 'Not seeing me isn't an option.'

The security guard raised an eyebrow and spoke into the receiver again.

'She'll be down in ten minutes,' he told Frank. 'You can sit over there.'

Frank lowered his long limbs into one of the red leather chairs, thinking that it was incredibly uncomfortable. He felt as though it were going to tip over at any minute. He picked up a magazine and flicked through it.

In his teens he'd read a lot of women's magazines. Ones like *Woman* and *Woman's Own* and *Woman's Weekly*. His main interest was in the problem pages, where he was astonished to read of so many women who were unhappy, mostly with their husbands or boyfriends or their sex lives. Frank mainly read the magazines for information on the kind of sex they were having. It wasn't a conversation he felt he could have with his father, and most of his mates in Sligo were equally ignorant of the workings of the female body. Frank had kept his collection of magazines with their advice from Anna Raeburn and Irma Kurtz on the top shelf of his wardrobe. He felt sure that if Derek found them his worry would be that Frank was a poofter, wanting to know about make-up and clothes; not that he was a seventeen-year-old virgin wanting to get it right the first time.

The doors to the lift opposite him opened and a woman, wearing a lilac suit with a nipped skirt and short jacket, walked out. She was tall, her height accentuated by the incredibly high-heeled shoes she wore. Her chestnut hair was scooped into a chignon which emphasised her oval face and slender neck. She looked straight at him from her dark eyes as she crossed the lobby and held out her hand.

'Frank,' she said.

'Mam.'

She raised an eyebrow. 'Christine,' she told him.

'Still Mam,' he said.

'Do you want to go for a coffee?' she asked. 'There's a place around the corner. But I have to be back in forty minutes. I have a meeting.'

He followed her out of the building and along the Old Marylebone Road. The sun shafted between the buildings, reflecting shades of russet from her sleek hair and highlighting her flawless skin. She pushed open the door of a small coffee shop where the aroma of roasting beans was all-pervading.

'Turkish,' she told him. 'The best in London.'

They sat down at a small Formica table. The voice of Michael Bolton filtered through from the radio behind the counter. The proprietor came to take their order, which for Frank was a black coffee and a sticky pastry. Christine just ordered coffee. They sat in silence until their drinks arrived, and then she shook a cigarette from the packet she'd taken from her bag, lit it, inhaled sharply and exhaled slowly so that the blue-grey smoke furled in the air between them.

'Why did you leave me?' asked Frank.

'I'm not the maternal type.'

'Why did you have a baby in that case?'

'I didn't mean to.'

'Why did you live with my father?'

'I thought I loved him. I thought he was a different sort of person. I was wrong.'

'Was it me?' asked Frank. 'Would you have stayed with him if it hadn't been for me?'

She took another deep drag from the cigarette. 'I doubt that very much,' she said.

'Why couldn't you have had the life you wanted living with him?' demanded Frank.

'Be realistic,' she said sharply. 'Sligo? In the sixties?'

Frank shrugged. 'You can't change things by running away,' he said.

Her dark eyes hardened. 'I didn't run away.'

'What else d'you call it?'

She ground out the cigarette in the glass ashtray. 'Your father was the wrong person for me. I don't know why I fell for him in the first place. But he seemed different then. When we got back to Sligo it all changed.'

'And you pretended,' Frank said. 'Pretended to be married to him even though you weren't. Selling out a bit, weren't you?'

'I did that for you,' she said. 'I might not have planned you but I didn't want them calling you a bastard. And they would have.'

'They probably knew anyway,' he told her. 'People find things out.'

'I'm sorry if I messed up your life,' she said. 'I never meant to.'

'That's real easy to say, isn't it?' He looked at her. 'People do it all the time. "I didn't mean to do something awful so you should forgive me." Just because you didn't mean it doesn't make it any less crap.'

She said nothing.

'Did you ever love me?' he asked.

'Of course,' she said sharply. 'That's why I left you. Because if I'd stayed I'd have hated you.'

'Easy way out,' he said.

'It's the truth.'

'You never tried to get in touch,' he told her. 'Not when I was younger and not when I was more grown-up. I had to track you down. And that was bloody difficult.'

'I didn't see any point in getting in touch.'

'Don't you give a toss?' His voice rose. 'I'm your son. Your flesh and blood. I'm family. But you're talking to me as though I was a stranger.'

'You are,' she said. 'I don't know you.'

243

'You're my mother!'

'That's a matter of biology,' she told him. 'Nothing else.'

'You're a hard-hearted cow,' he said.

She pushed the coffee cup away. 'I'm sorry you think that. I'm not. I do think about you from time to time, but the bottom line is that I would have been a shit mother if I'd stayed. I do actually realise that from your point of view I'm a shit mother anyway. I'm sorry about that. I really am. I got out of your life, which was better for you and better for me and that's the end of it. I wish you every success in the future. I hope you get everything you want out of life. But I'm sorry, I can't be the person you want me to be because that's just not how I am.'

'Are you married?' he asked.

She laughed. 'No.'

'Live with anyone?'

'No.'

'Have any other kids?'

'Absolutely not.'

'Are you lonely?'

She smiled. 'Why do people always seem to think that anyone who lives on their own must be lonely? I've achieved a lot of things. I edit a forward-looking magazine. I have lots of friends and a social life which I enjoy. I occasionally sleep with men but I don't want to be tied to any one of them. I'm happy to be on my own and I'm not lonely.' She crossed one elegant leg over the other. 'I'm happy, Frank. I'm doing what I want to do.'

'You're nothing like me, are you?' said Frank.

'Probably not,' she agreed. 'You're more like Derek. Wanting people to love you. Thinking that everything will turn out for the best. Looking for warm and fuzzy when life is cold and hard.'

'It doesn't have to be cold and hard,' he said.

'I like it like that,' she told him.

'I'm married,' he told her. 'I tried to find out about you before the wedding but I couldn't.'

She pursed her lips. 'Why? Did you want to invite me?'

'Would you have come?'

'Would it have made any difference?'

'Don't you have any feelings at all? What's the matter with you?'

'Nothing,' she said. 'I believe in a different way of life. And that whole maternal thing – well, I'm sorry. You were a cute baby. But it did nothing for me.'

'Bloody hell. Thanks a bunch.'

'I'm sorry. You asked.'

He looked at her, real puzzlement in his eyes. 'How can we be so different? We're biologically the same.'

'I was naïve and silly when I met Derek. But I was right about what I believed. The interlude with him was the biggest mistake in my life.'

'And me? You think I'm a mistake?'

'You were my mistake,' she agreed. 'It doesn't mean I don't care about you at all. I do. I want you to be happy with your life. But not the way you want me to.'

'So you don't want to keep in touch or anything? Even cards at Christmas, that sort of thing?'

'I really don't see the point, do you?'

'I think I hate you.'

'I'm sorry,' she said. 'I just don't do family.'

He stood up. 'Well I do. I'm glad I met you. But you don't have to worry. I won't be in touch again.'

'That's fine by me,' she told him. 'I'm glad that you've found some nice girl who loves you and who's letting you live your suburban dream.'

'Don't patronise me,' said Frank.

She nodded. 'That *was* patronising. I didn't mean it to be.'

'Dad was gutted when you left.'

'Derek always knew how I felt,' she told him. 'I warned him and warned him, but he wanted the warm and fuzzy stuff too. I'm not like that. I wanted what I have now.' She sighed. 'I can't keep apologising to you for the sort of person I am. Your father kind of bowled me over and made me think that perhaps I didn't want what I have as much as I thought. But I sure didn't want what I had with him. It's my fault for not sticking to my principles.'

'I don't think we'll meet again,' said Frank. 'But it was . . . worthwhile.'

'I'm glad,' she told him. 'I want you to be happy.'

'I guess that's all everyone wants in the end,' he said as they walked out of the coffee shop and back on to the street. He'd been going to tell her about the love of his life. About her grand-daughter, Jenna. That was why he'd come. To tell her about his wonderful daughter. But she wouldn't have understood. And he didn't see the point any more.

⌒

Iona knew that it was the four-week deadline too. Since she'd been visiting the hospital regularly she'd talked to the doctors and nurses, and she'd bought books about coma and recovery as well as psychology, since she too wondered whether Frank was just too damn scared to wake up. Like Sally she'd set a four-week time scale for his return to consciousness. She couldn't let herself believe that he wouldn't wake up at all. Each evening she'd called to the hospital and seen him lying there motionless she'd wanted to shake him and shout at him and tell him to move his butt – just as she did every weekend when he was home with her. But of course she couldn't do any of these things. She just sat and read her way through more James Bond novels instead.

She closed her eyes and thought about him. Maybe calling in to the hospital and sitting beside him wasn't the answer. Maybe what she needed to do was to try and communicate with him on an unconscious level; the same level that he was on now.

But he was too far away to communicate with. She needed to be closer. She needed to be there. She got up from the sofa and grabbed her bag. It wasn't her turn tonight. But that didn't matter. She let herself out of the house and got into her car, gunning it down the road and on to the busy main street. She was thinking about him all the time, thinking of how important it was that he knew that she still loved him.

Frank, she told him. Listen to me. Think about me too. Think

246

about the good stuff. Think about how much we meant to each other.

She parked the car on the upper storey of the car park and clattered down the stairs and towards the main hospital building.

'You've got to get better,' she whispered under her breath. 'You've got to wake up, Frank. It's time. It really is.'

⌒

Frank didn't know why he was somewhere hot. Sun holidays really weren't his thing. He liked travelling around Ireland or Scotland, where the grass was green and the sky could be either the clearest of blues or an unrelenting gun-metal grey. He liked the soft colours of peat and heather and gorse, not the garish pinks and purples of bougainvillea. He'd always choose chestnut trees over palms. And he preferred frothy white-topped waves to the gentle turquoise millpond of . . . wherever he was. He couldn't exactly remember where he was. Nor could he remember why he was wearing a suit. It was far too hot to be wearing a suit – he should be in a pair of shorts and a loose-fitting T-shirt.

Frank looked around him. He was standing in a pergola, looking back towards the beach. He realised now that the pergola was on a tiny outcrop, a miniature island off a bigger landmass. He wondered how he'd got here. There were other people with him too. Two men he'd never seen in his life before. One was around the same age as him and his face was scorched red from the sun. The other man was mahogany brown. He too was wearing a suit.

Suddenly Frank heard the rhythmic cough of an outboard motor and saw a small boat chugging out from the nearby jetty. In the back of the boat was the tiny figure of a girl in white. Frank's eyes narrowed. He knew her, of course. And in fact now he remembered that he was marrying her. Here in . . . well, he still couldn't exactly remember where he was, but he did remember that they were getting married.

He struggled to put that thought into context. There was something wrong about this. He remembered getting married

247

before. To . . . to . . . It had gone from him. It had been at the edge of his mind and he'd seen an image of her face, but it had suddenly slid from his memory. Right now it seemed to him that there were lots of things that had suddenly slipped away from him, names and faces and a whole heap of other stuff that was there somewhere but just out of reach. His head hurt with the effort of thinking about it.

The boat drew up at the island outcrop and the girl jumped lithely on to the soft sand. She held the skirt of her white mid-length dress clear of the water, revealing white flip-flops decorated with brightly coloured shells. She looked up to where he was waiting for her and waved. He waved back. She was beaming with happiness and excitement and he suddenly felt excited too. The other faces, the other people that were lurking in his mind didn't matter right now. The important thing was that this was the girl he was going to marry and he knew that she was beautiful and that he loved her and that they were going to be a family together.

She stood beside him and smiled. The pastor began to speak. Frank was finding it difficult to understand his singsong accent. He wished the man would speak more distinctly because then he'd be able to catch the name of the girl he was marrying. It was, he knew, particularly awful to forget the name of your bride-to-be, but right now it was stuck in the corner of his mind and he simply couldn't remember it. But he knew that he was doing the right thing in marrying her. She was understanding, he knew that. She wanted to be with him, he knew that too. She cared about him.

A warm envelope of contentment sealed itself around him. But something else nagged at him and worried at the edges of his thoughts. He didn't know exactly what it was, since it seemed there was nothing in the world that should worry him now that he was in this wonderful place with this wonderful girl.

He'd never seen eyes like hers before. So dark you could lose yourself in them as they drew you to her. And her mouth was wide, with round, kissable lips. The sun had lent a golden sheen to her skin and the white flower tucked behind her ear emphasised the raven blackness of her hair.

They were going to have a great life together, thought Frank contentedly. If only he could just remember exactly who she was.

∽

Iona was almost running along the corridor. She skittered to a stop outside Frank's room and pushed open the door. Both Sally and Jenna turned to look at her.

'You!' cried Jenna. 'What the hell are you doing here?'

'Iona?' Sally stood up and looked at her in puzzlement. 'Why are you here? It's our night tonight.'

'I know.' Now that she was in the room, Iona was feeling guilty. She looked at Frank and then at Sally and Jenna. 'I know. I'm sorry. But I had a feeling. I just had to come.'

'What sort of feeling?' demanded Jenna. 'Why did you come here?'

'I thought – I thought he was trying to communicate with me.'

'Oh, please.' Jenna looked at her in disgust. 'I never heard such crap in all my life. He's not trying to communicate with anyone. We've been here nearly an hour and all that's happened is that he's closed his eyes.'

'Were they open?'

'Yes. But they've been open before.'

'What were you talking to him about?' asked Iona.

'Mind your own damn business.' Jenna flushed.

'Jenna Harper!' Sally looked at her daughter in annoyance. 'There's no need to be rude.'

'Would you listen to yourself!' cried Jenna. 'This is the woman who tried to break up our family and you're telling me not to be rude to her? C'mon, Mum. Get a life.'

At her words they all looked at Frank, who continued to lie unresponsively in the bed.

'Look, I'm sorry. I never come when I'm not supposed to,' said Iona. 'But it's four weeks and I just thought . . .'

'I know,' said Sally flatly. 'So did I.'

'Just thought what?' asked Jenna.

'He needs to wake up now,' said Sally. 'You know that.'

'Yeah, but it's not like clockwork, is it?' said Jenna scathingly. 'I mean, he doesn't know it's four weeks, does he?'

'Of course not,' said Iona. 'Not consciously. But maybe his body knows.'

'You're such a sap,' said Jenna.

'Please,' said Sally again.

'Why am I the one who's being got at here?' demanded Jenna. 'I'm entitled to be here. She isn't.'

'Look, Jen, we've discussed all this before,' said Sally. 'And I'm really not going through it all again. I'm tired and I'm . . .' She broke off.

'You're what?' asked Jenna. 'You're delusional if you ask me. We come here all the time, talking to him and playing music to him and reading to him, and it *isn't making any difference*. And I'll tell you why. Because he doesn't care!'

'He cares.' Sally's face was contorted with pain. 'He cares for all of us.'

'In some sad-fuck menagerie!' said Jenna.

'Jenna!' Sally gritted her teeth. The atmosphere was upsetting her. And making her feel ill.

'It's always me, isn't it!'

'No.'

'Yes. Jenna this, Jenna that. As though I'm a kid. Well I'm not, you know. I'm a lot more mature and responsible than you think. And at least I'm not shacked up with a bigamist!'

'Oh God.' Sally swayed. Iona reacted first. She grasped the other woman's elbow and eased her on to a chair. 'Are you all right?' she asked anxiously. 'You're very pale.'

'I'm OK.'

'Mum, what's the matter?' Jenna felt terrible. She'd been so annoyed with her mother, and with Iona, but now she could see that Sally was really upset.

The door to the room opened and Susan Carpenter walked in.

'What the hell is going on here?' she demanded. She saw Sally's pale face and her voice softened. 'Are you OK, Sally?'

250

'I just feel a bit sick.'

'You need to relax for a minute,' said Susan. 'Come outside and stretch on the settee.'

'I'll be fine,' said Sally.

'Just for a couple of minutes,' said Susan. 'Clearly whatever's been going on in here hasn't been exactly peaceful, and that certainly isn't good for Frank. As well as which, really and truly, Sally, you need to take care of the baby, if not yourself.'

'Baby?' said Iona and Jenna in unison.

Susan looked at them in puzzlement, and then at Sally.

'I didn't . . .'

'Oh, shit,' said Susan.

'What baby?' asked Iona tautly.

'My baby.' Sally started to cry. 'Mine and Frank's. I'm sorry, Jen. I should've told you before now. I'm pregnant.'

∽

It was as though time stood still. Iona heard Sally's words but they seemed to float in the air towards her, so that although she knew what the other woman was saying, she hadn't really grasped it. Jenna stared at her mother in silent disbelief. Susan Carpenter kept her arm around Sally's shoulders. And Sally didn't move.

In the bed, unseen by anyone, Frank's eyes opened and closed again.

'I don't believe you!' It was Jenna who spoke first, and her tone was horrified.

'It's true,' said Sally. 'I'm pregnant.'

'Since when?'

'I found out the day of the accident,' said Sally.

Iona couldn't speak. She felt numb inside.

'So you and Dad . . . you were . . . A baby!' The horror still hadn't left Jenna's voice. 'After all these years! Mum, that's disgusting. *You're* disgusting.' She looked over at her father in the bed. 'He's disgusting. God, Mum, he was sleeping with you and making you pregnant and pretending to be married to her – I can't believe what sort of family I'm part of. I always thought we were nice and normal and we're not, we're fucking freaks!' She pushed past Iona and rushed out into the corridor. 'Total freaks!' she yelled through the glass window before striding away.

Sally struggled to her feet, but Susan restrained her.

'I've got to—'

'You've got to stay sitting down for a minute,' Susan said firmly. 'Jenna will be fine. She's just upset.'

'I'm going to get a drink of water.' Iona didn't know how she'd managed to speak because her brain didn't seem to be functioning properly. She wasn't even sure whether the words she'd formed in her mind were the words that actually came out of her mouth. She stumbled out of the room and then pushed open the door of the ladies' toilets. She leaned her head against the wall and tried to control the rising waves of nausea building up inside her. But eventually she couldn't help herself and she threw up into the nearest toilet.

'Are you all right?' It was Susan Carpenter again, standing behind her holding a wad of tissues.

'I'm . . . fine.'

'Come on,' said Susan. 'I'll get you some water.'

'I need to sit down.'

'I know. Come with me and you can go somewhere private.'

Iona felt tears blister her eyes. She couldn't cope with someone being nice to her. She followed Susan to a small room where the nurse sat her down on a padded chair and handed her a waxed cup filled with water.

'Sip it,' she said.

Iona swallowed the water cautiously. She felt its coldness as it flowed down her gut.

'I can't believe it,' she whispered. 'She's pregnant.' She looked up at Susan Carpenter and her eyes filled with tears again. 'We were trying for a baby,' she said shakily. 'To make our family complete. I didn't know about this baby. I didn't know about Jenna. I didn't know about Sally. And I'm not pregnant.'

'Don't upset yourself about it now,' said Susan gently.

'It's kind of hard not to be upset.' Iona wanted to appear strong in front of the nurse, but she had a horrible feeling that she was going to dissolve into little pieces. How can it be? she asked herself in anguish. The accident was bad enough. Finding out about Sally and Jenna was worse. But this . . . As far as Iona was concerned, this was the ultimate betrayal. She'd gone to so much trouble to eat properly and set up the home for a baby and do all the right things, and she wasn't pregnant. But Sally was. And to judge by the huge age gap that would exist between Jenna and the new baby, not to mention the way Sally had kept the whole thing secret, well, it seemed to Iona that this hadn't been planned. And how fair was that? Sally, who probably didn't want another baby, was pregnant. Iona, who desperately wanted her first child, wasn't. And who knew what was going to happen to Frank?

Chapter 23

Ten minutes later Iona felt able to walk out of the tiny room where Susan had left her. Her legs were still shaky and she knew that her hands were trembling, but at least she didn't feel as though she was going to faint any more. Some of her despair had been replaced once again by rage at Frank and at the dual life he was leading. Some of it was still there, lining her heart, a mere moment away from bubbling up to the surface again.

She hadn't expected that Sally would still be there, but she was, sitting on one of the chairs outside Frank's room, her face pale and her hair damp around her face. The new short look had grown out a little and needed to be redone to keep the style. Right now, Sally looked wretched again. Iona suddenly thought that she had picked a really terrible time to get pregnant.

Sally glanced up at her, her eyes dull.

'I'm sorry,' said Iona.

'For what?'

'Coming. I shouldn't have. It wasn't my night. And a day wasn't going to make much difference one way or the other.'

'No,' agreed Sally.

'It was just that . . . I was thinking about him, you see. And the month being up. And I couldn't help feeling . . .'

'I know,' said Sally. 'I was so sure about tonight too.'

They sat beside each other in silence for a moment.

'But instead of Frank coming out of the coma, I discover that you and he are having a baby.'

254

'You would have found out sooner or later.'

Iona clenched and unclenched her fists. 'It's one more shock I didn't need,' she said.

'We didn't plan it.'

'I guess not.'

'We'd wanted more children but unfortunately it didn't work out that way,' said Sally. 'Frank always wanted a bigger family. Family mattered to him so much. This was . . . a bolt out of the blue.'

'How d'you think he'll feel about it?' asked Iona.

'I suppose that depends,' said Sally wryly, 'on whether he wakes up while I'm still pregnant or not.'

Iona couldn't stop the tears spilling down her cheek.

'What's the matter?' asked Sally.

'It's not important.'

'What?' repeated Sally. She stared at Iona for a moment and then gasped. 'Don't tell me you're pregnant too.'

'No,' said Iona. 'I'm not.' She pinched the bridge of her nose. 'But I wanted to be.'

'Oh.' Sally looked at her blankly.

'We'd talked about it,' said Iona rapidly as she wiped the tears away. 'We were . . . Frank wanted children. More than me at first, but then I wanted them too. I – I set up a feng shui corner of the room to help me get pregnant. It didn't work for me. But – well – it looks like it worked for Frank.'

'Oh my God.' Sally gasped. 'You can't believe that had anything to do with it.'

Iona sniffed. 'Not seriously. Not . . . you know. But still. You're pregnant, and I'm not. And Frank was making love to both of us.'

'I can't deal with this,' said Sally. 'I'm sorry. I could hardly deal with the idea of being pregnant anyway.' She pushed her hands through her hair despairingly. 'I won't accept it's because of some crazy hippy-dippy lifestyle thing Frank was doing with you.'

'Feng shui isn't hippy-dippy,' said Iona. 'It's about harmony.'

'Yeah, well, that worked, didn't it?' Sally laughed wryly. 'Things have been very harmonious around us all lately, haven't they?'

Iona's smile was ironic. 'You have a point.'

'How was he going to deal with it?' demanded Sally. 'Two families? Surely it was hard enough for him without having another child with you?'

'He'd have dealt with it the same way he deals with everything,' said Iona. 'Don't worry. Be happy. You know Frank.'

'Yes. I know Frank.'

They shared a look of understanding.

'But do we really know him at all?' asked Iona. 'Was he really happy? With two of us? It surely must have been stressful.'

Sally nodded.

'So why'd he do it?'

'Maybe it was because of the family thing.' Sally sighed. 'Maybe he wanted more than I was giving him.'

'But you *are* a family!' cried Iona. 'You, Frank and Jenna. What more did he want?'

'Honestly . . . kids,' said Sally. 'We had Jen fairly quickly but I didn't have a very good experience at the birth – it ended up being an emergency Caesarean and scared me rigid. I told Frank I didn't want to get pregnant again for a while and he understood that. The only problem was that once I felt able to think about it again I just didn't get pregnant.'

'Did you try anything? IVF?'

'Well . . .' Sally looked uncomfortable. 'The thing was that, yes, I did want a baby. But I wasn't prepared to go through the whole IVF procedure. Which made me think that maybe I just didn't want one enough.'

'Hey, I can understand how you felt! I wonder about it myself, sometimes, all that messing around with your hormones and everything.'

'It has a reasonable success rate,' said Sally, 'but it was just something I wasn't prepared to do. Frank was OK about it all, though. He always said that whatever we did we did as a couple and as a family. I thought he totally understood.'

'Sally, he wasn't with me simply to have another baby even though we'd decided to try for one,' said Iona.

'Just as well you're not pregnant, I guess,' said Sally. 'Bad enough that one of us is.'

'And what does your doctor say about it this time?' asked Iona.

'Oh, that I'm an old mother and that there are certain things I have to be specially careful about because of that. And because of the problems with Jenna. And that I should be eating well and living a healthy lifestyle and have no stress.'

Iona looked sympathetically at her. 'Like that's actually happening.'

'I know.' Sally sighed. 'I should be looking after this baby more, and I'm not because I'm caught up about Jenna and Frank and you—'

'There's no need to be caught up about me,' said Iona. 'I don't matter.'

'Of course you do,' said Sally. 'He damn well married you!'

They sat in silence. Iona couldn't believe she was actually talking to Sally and feeling sorry for her when she'd just delivered such shattering news; yet in a way it was comforting to talk to someone else who knew Frank and cared about him.

'What do you think is really going to happen to him?' she asked eventually.

Sally shrugged wearily.

'Stupid question.' Iona shook her head. 'This whole thing is making me feel more and more stupid by the day.'

Sally nodded, then got up and said that she was going to phone Jenna so that they could go home. Iona stayed where she was, watching the other woman walk down the corridor to make the call. She continued to observe her as she walked back again. How hadn't she realised before now that Sally was pregnant? It was obvious in the way she carried herself. I'm a fool, thought Iona. A complete and utter fool.

'She's not picking up,' said Sally. 'She hates me, of course.'

'Why?'

'She thinks it's my fault that Frank and you . . . well, you know.'

Iona shrugged.

'Do you?' asked Sally. 'Do you think it's because of me?'

'I honestly don't know,' said Iona after a pause in which she struggled not to lash out and say that of course it was Sally's fault, that there was obviously some issue going on about the whole baby thing and that somehow Frank hadn't found what he was looking for in his wife because otherwise why the hell had he started a second relationship? Because the thing was, of course, that Frank might have started a second relationship, but he sure as hell hadn't finished with his first.

'It's got to be him,' she continued. 'Much as I love . . . loved . . . well, it's got to be his fault. After all, he's the bigamist. Not you or me.'

Sally smiled faintly. 'It sounds so – so dramatic. Not like it really is.'

'I know.' Iona nodded. 'How is it that when you're living in a weird situation you don't think it's weird at all; but if you read about someone else's weird situation you think they should all be carted off to the nearest funny farm?'

'I keep thinking that if we were a plot line in *Coronation Street* it'd be written out as being too implausible,' said Sally.

'Well, obviously,' Iona told her. 'They all live within a few hundred yards of each other on that soap. Frank was very careful to keep us a good distance apart.'

The two of them sat in silence again as they contemplated Frank's adept handling of his two wives. Eventually Sally looked at her watch and then checked her phone again.

'I'll go and look for her,' she told Iona. 'She's probably in a snit somewhere having decided to give me the cold shoulder.'

'D'you mind if I stay here a bit longer?' asked Iona.

Sally shook her head. She got up and walked out of the unit. Iona went back in to Frank's room. Jenna's portable CD was on its second run-through of *Allow Us To Be Frank*. She remembered Sally saying that Frank had sung 'Mack the Knife' at parties, but of course she'd never gone to a party with Frank.

How could she not have known? Why hadn't she guessed that

there was, at the very least, someone else? Was she impossibly naïve? Or was Frank just a very, very good con-man?

She switched off the CD and took her book out of her bag. She'd moved on to *Moonraker* since finishing *Goldfinger*. Frank had said that he liked all of the Ian Fleming books but she didn't know his main preferences after *Goldfinger*. She'd expected the book to be different from the film (after all, they were written in the 1950s and 60s, so no chance of space-age technology then), but she was surprised to see that there was actually no relationship between novel and movie at all. Other than the title and the name of the main character.

'Hugo Drax,' she said out loud. 'He cheats at cards. And Frank Harper cheats at wives.'

Her gaze flickered to Frank and she stifled a gasp. His eyes were open again.

'Can you hear me?' she demanded. 'Can you understand what I'm saying?' She grasped his hand. 'Squeeze if you can hear me.'

She couldn't feel any response from him. But she was certain that he could hear something. That he knew she was there.

'Oh, come on!' she cried. 'You're with us somewhere, Frank. I know you are.'

She squeezed his hand, but it remained limp within her hold.

'Fuck you!' she yelled, picking up the paperback and hurling it across the room so that it clattered into an empty plastic container and knocked it to the floor. 'Make a fucking effort.'

'Iona?' It was Susan Carpenter again. 'I think maybe you should go home for the evening.'

Iona dropped Frank's hand on to the bedspread and turned towards the nurse.

'I'm sorry,' she said. 'I just thought there was something . . . I'm sorry.'

'No need to be,' said Susan. She picked up the book and handed it back to Iona.

'Do you think he's afraid?' asked Iona.

'Afraid?'

'Of what will happen to him? Everyone is saying that now. Saying that's why he's still in the coma.'

'I don't know,' said Susan. 'The mind is a very fragile thing.'

'So maybe that's it, and maybe he will wake up but he'll be . . . he won't be himself?' Iona's voice was agonised.

'Don't torture yourself about it,' said Susan. 'His physical injuries have definitely improved. There are certainly issues about his relationships. But you can deal with those.'

Iona put *Moonraker* back into her bag. 'Has Sally gone?' she asked.

'I presume so,' Susan told her. 'I haven't seen her in a while.'

Iona nodded. 'Well, OK. See you.'

'See you,' said Susan. 'And don't worry, if there's any change, we'll call you straight away.'

'Thanks,' said Iona as she walked out of the door.

Susan watched her leave and then moved towards her patient. She straightened the bed covers and checked the monitors. No change as far as she could see. She knew how hard it was to believe that those open eyes weren't seeing anything. But, she thought as she closed the door behind her, if she was in his situation, she'd be having a long think about waking up and embroiling herself with two spouses again.

⁓

Iona walked towards the car park, past the cluster of people smoking outside the hospital entrance and past the group of taxis waiting to pick up fares. She frowned as she saw the auburn hair of Sally Harper in the queue for taxis. She'd presumed Sally drove herself to the hospital every day. And then she realised that Sally wasn't trying to hail a taxi, she was talking to the cab drivers and looking at the passengers.

'Hey, Sally, everything OK?' she asked.

Sally turned hunted eyes towards her. 'Not really.'

'What's up?'

'I don't know where Jenna is.' There was a note of desperation in her voice. 'I've called her and texted her but she's not responding.'

'Maybe she's just gone home,' suggested Iona.

'Maybe. But it's not easy from here. She'd have to get to the nearest Dart station, and that's quite a distance away. I don't know what the buses are like on this side of town. I thought maybe she'd taken a taxi to the Dart.'

'You're asking them if they picked her up?'

Sally nodded. 'I know it's daft to be worried about her. She's seventeen. She's not a baby. But . . . she's upset about everything and . . .'

Iona nodded too. 'Maybe she got a taxi all the way to Bray?'

'I doubt it,' said Sally. 'She probably wouldn't have enough for the fare.'

'If she got a taxi to the Dart as soon as she left the hospital, would she be home by now?' asked Iona.

'Perhaps. If she was lucky with the timing,' said Sally.

'Why don't you try your landline?' suggested Iona.

'I did, although I don't really think she could be home yet. If she is, she's not answering,' said Sally ruefully. 'To be honest with you, our relationship wasn't great before all this started. Initially Frank's accident drew us together. Finding out about you drove us apart. But we'd started to get a bit of a thing going in coming to the hospital and it was improving. The news about the baby . . . well, that sure hasn't helped.'

Iona nodded. 'I think you're wasting your time hanging round a taxi rank in the hope that you'll either see her or find the bloke who drove her somewhere,' she said. 'You should get home yourself and wait for her.'

'I know.' Sally looked at her ruefully. 'Thing is . . . thing is . . . right now, I don't think I can drive.'

Iona stared at her.

'I'm a crap driver at the best of times,' Sally told her. 'This isn't the best of times.' She sighed. 'I'm still shaking. I feel dizzy. My head is buzzing. Bad enough for Jen to have one parent in hospital, without me smacking the car into a lamp-post or something and ending up here too.'

'I'll drive you,' said Iona abruptly.

'That's stupid,' said Sally. 'My car is here. I'll still have to come back and fetch it later.'

'Let later worry abut itself,' said Iona. 'Come on, I'll drive you home.'

Sally stood indecisively beside her. 'I can get a taxi. You don't need to drive me. It's miles out of your way.'

'I'll drive and you can keep a look out for Jenna,' said Iona. 'I'll go towards the Dart station in case she tried walking that way.'

'OK,' said Sally eventually.

She followed Iona to the car park and waited while the other girl paid for her ticket. They went up to the third floor and Iona pointed to the bright green Beetle.

'Actually, it's not the easiest car in the world to drive,' she told Sally as she got behind the wheel. 'But it's cute and I like it.' She started the engine. 'Frank always said I'd be better off with a sporty little number, but that's just not me somehow.'

She eased her way out of the car park and into the flow of traffic. She stayed silent as Sally anxiously scanned the streets for any sign of her daughter and continued to drive in silence as they went through the city and out towards Bray. She switched on the radio, which was tuned to Lyric FM. The sounds of Pachelbel's Canon in D Major filled the car. By the time they reached Bray, the station had moved on to Holst's Planet Suite and the music had become fiercer.

'Turn here,' said Sally as they approached the housing estate where she lived.

Iona indicated and eventually drew up in front of the neat semi-detached house.

'Come in,' said Sally.

Iona shook her head. 'If Jenna is there I really don't think me coming in would help matters.'

'She's not,' said Sally. 'The house is in darkness.'

'Maybe she's sitting in the dark.' Iona looked at her wryly. 'I do that a lot these days.'

'If she's here you can leave right away,' said Sally. 'Please. I don't want to go in on my own.'

Iona nodded and got out of the car. She felt sorry for Sally, but she couldn't help thinking that the other woman was a bit feeble. Why had Frank, such an outgoing man, married such a wishy-washy woman? she wondered. Was that why he'd hooked up with her instead? Was he fed up with Sally's helpless ways? She noticed, as Siobhán Farrell had done, the neatness of the garden and the carefully maintained front of the house. Obviously Sally, in the depths of her despair about Frank and in the throes of her pregnancy, had still found time to cut the grass and clean the windows. Iona grimaced at the thought of her own once pristine house in the Liberties, where feng shui had been replaced by items left in any old place and which hadn't seen a duster or a vacuum cleaner in over a month.

It felt strange to be inside Sally's house, knowing that it was Frank's house too. Her eyes swivelled tentatively around as she took in the more classical décor, the heavier furniture and the richer colours. How could he like this and like her house too? she wondered. Was he truly a split personality? How could the Frank who'd bought the Joan Miró print with her be the same Frank who'd hung that ornate gilt mirror on the wall? The two styles were completely different.

The kitchen was different too; this was warm and homely against her own clinical granite and steel – though, of course, if her kitchen had been the size of Sally's, maybe she would have done it in a warmer style herself. She could see how a kitchen could be the heart of a home when it wasn't a small utilitarian space tacked on as a virtual afterthought and whose main item of equipment was a microwave.

'Tea or coffee?' asked Sally as she filled the bright yellow kettle.

'Tea,' said Iona. 'Preferably camomile if you happen to have it by any chance. Or green. But any tea is fine really.' She shrugged apologetically. 'Sorry. I shouldn't be so picky.'

Sally nodded and took a packet of camomile tea off the shelf. Neither of them spoke as they waited for the kettle to boil. When it did, Sally poured water into the two blue mugs which she'd taken from the cupboard.

She offered one to Iona and then sat at the table beside her.

'She has to be home by ten every evening,' said Sally. 'She hates it but she knows she has to stick by it otherwise she can't stay out later other times.'

'Fair enough,' said Iona.

'She hates me,' said Sally. 'She hated me before all this and she hates me twice as much now.'

'Of course she doesn't,' said Iona.

'She does.' Sally looked idly into her mug. 'She thinks I'm an old bat. I embarrass her.'

'Why?'

Sally explained about being a teacher at Jenna's school, which she knew Jenna didn't really like. She told Iona that when they did good parent, bad parent, she was always the bad parent. She made the rules, she said. Frank got to break them.

'It's always the way, isn't it?' said Iona. 'Mothers come off worst no matter what. But I bet she doesn't really hate you. She's seventeen. It's all a growing-up kind of thing.'

'I know, I know,' said Sally. 'It's just that it's exhausting being seen as the imbecile all the time.'

Iona laughed, and to her own surprise, Sally smiled too.

'I guess it's not that bad,' she admitted. 'I know it's only a phase. But she's such a lovely girl really, and for the past six months it's all been about wearing nothing but black, and that terrible pale make-up which does nothing for her, and sighing every time I open my mouth. And the fact that I've seen loads of girls at school turn into perfectly adequate adults even when they've been sheer horrors makes no difference when it's your own daughter.'

'I suppose not,' agreed Iona. Her eyes flickered around the room. 'You have a lovely house.'

Sally looked at her warily. 'It's OK. We've been here a long time.'

'I'll level with you,' said Iona. 'Part of the reason I offered to drive you was so that I could get to see where you live.'

'Oh.'

'But then when I got here I didn't want to come in. I didn't want to see Frank's other life.'

'You wouldn't get to see much of it in the kitchen anyway,' said Sally. 'He's not really into cooking.'

Iona nibbled her lip.

'Or does he when he's with you?' asked Sally.

'Sometimes,' said Iona. 'We don't have such a great kitchen, of course, and my efforts are usually with the microwave. I cook healthy stuff, I'm just not very good at it.'

'So what does Frank cook?'

Iona shrugged. 'Pasta mainly. He makes good sauces.'

'Of course,' said Sally. 'You thought his favourite food was spaghetti carbonara.'

'It is,' said Iona. 'When he's with me, anyhow.'

'How the hell can he be two such different people?' demanded Sally in a spurt of anger. 'Roast pork with me. Spaghetti carbonara with you. I'm betting your house is completely different to mine too. It's beyond freaky.'

'You're right about my house,' said Iona. 'All of it would fit into your kitchen.'

'Oh.'

They sat in silence again. Eventually Sally looked at the clock. It was just after ten.

'She'll be back soon,' said Iona.

Sally took out her phone and called Jenna's number. Iona could hear the recording of the younger girl's voice telling callers to leave a message.

'She's doing it deliberately,' said Sally.

'Maybe not.'

'She's punishing me,' said Sally. 'For the baby. For being disgusting. You heard her.'

265

'She didn't mean it.'

'I think she did.' Sally sighed and rubbed her stomach gently. 'Poor baby. Everybody hates it.'

'No.' Iona looked at her in shock.

'Not hates,' amended Sally. 'Just – it's the wrong time. It really is. To tell you the truth, when I realised I was late, I just thought that maybe I was pre-menopausal.'

The clock ticked around to ten thirty.

'She *is* doing it deliberately,' said Sally. 'Look, you go home. I'm OK now.'

'Are you sure you don't want me to wait till she comes in?' Iona had detected a slight note of anxiety in Sally's voice.

'Why? So you can see me box her around the ears and report me for child abuse?'

Iona smiled slightly and Sally shrugged. 'Perhaps you could stay a little longer. If you don't mind?'

'I don't mind.'

'But I don't want to talk any more,' said Sally. 'I can't. Is that all right?'

'Perfectly fine,' said Iona. 'I'll read the paper.'

'OK.'

They both sat at the kitchen table. Iona read her way through the *Irish Times*, while Sally leafed through a teaching magazine. Every so often one or the other of them would glance up at the clock, but neither of them said anything.

At eleven o'clock, Sally phoned Jenna again. Calls were still being diverted to Jenna's mailbox.

At a quarter past eleven Sally dialled another number.

'We're away at the moment.' Iona could hear a woman's voice. 'Leave a message and we'll get back to you.'

Sally disconnected and tried a third number.

'This is Sam,' Iona heard. 'I'm in Barcelona for the weekend with my folks. Text me.'

'Her best friend,' said Sally. 'I was hoping Jenna would be with her. But they're all away.' Worry lines creased her face. 'I'm not sure where else she might be.'

'Does she have a boyfriend?' asked Iona.

Sally nodded. 'Gerry. But I don't know him. He's fairly recent.' She frowned. 'I have the phone numbers of quite a few of her friends, but not his.'

'Perhaps you should call them,' suggested Iona. 'See if any of them has his number.'

Sally nodded again and began dialling.

Chapter 24

By midnight Sally was really concerned about Jenna and Iona was having to try very hard to keep her calm.

'You know that she's doing it to worry you,' she told Sally. 'And she's succeeded. That's what you can tell her.'

'Right.' Sally dialled Jenna's number again and left a message saying that she was demented with anxiety and that she understood how Jenna felt about everything but could she please come home so that they could sort everything out. 'But what if something's happened?' she said to Iona. 'What if she isn't doing this to worry me at all but has grabbed a lift from some stranger and he's taken her somewhere . . .'

'Oh Sally, you're totally overreacting.'

'I know, I know,' wailed Sally. 'But it's past midnight and she simply doesn't stay out this late. She really doesn't.'

Iona recognised the anxiety in Sally. She'd felt it herself the night that Frank hadn't come home. But she was certain that nothing had happened to Jenna, that the teenager had simply decided to stay out as an act of defiance.

'She's had a hard evening,' she told Sally. 'Cut her a little slack.'

'I would if I knew where she was or if she'd answer her phone. I can't take this, Iona. What if something terrible has happened to her? What if—'

'Come on, Sally,' said Iona. 'In your heart you know that she's perfectly fine and she's just staying out late.'

'In my head I know what she's up to. In my heart . . .' Sally's voice trailed off and she looked at the wall clock again.

'Maybe you should call the police,' said Iona eventually. 'I'm sure there's absolutely nothing wrong and she's probably with one of her friends – or most likely the boyfriend. The fact that none of them have his number is irrelevant. Maybe they just won't give it to you. You know what teenage girls are like. But it'd put your mind at rest if you called the cops.'

'They won't react to this straight away,' said Sally. 'They'll want her to be missing for longer.'

'They reacted pretty damn quick to Frank's disappearance,' said Iona.

'Only because there was something weird going on.'

'Sally, are you always this negative?' demanded Iona. 'Because if you are, I can see how you drive her nuts. No matter what I suggest, you have a reason not to do it. I'm trying to be helpful but you don't want to be helped.'

'All right, all right.' Sally picked up the phone. 'I didn't want a big deal made out of it, that's all. I know what they'll say – that she's upset about her dad. And they'll ask if there was a row, which there was, and they won't take me seriously.'

'Why don't you call the detective woman?' suggested Iona. 'She'll take you seriously.'

Sally looked at her contemplatively. 'That's a good idea.'

'That's me,' said Iona. 'Full of good ideas.'

❧

Siobhán had almost finished her shift. She'd just returned to her desk having brought two young men, arrested on suspicion of drug-dealing, down to the cells. She hated going down to the cells, which were the one part of the station which made her feel grubby about her work. Like every prison cell she'd ever seen on TV or in the movies, they were empty, soulless places. But what the TV and movies couldn't bring to the viewer was the smell of the people locked inside them – fear and bodily scents – overlaid with that of the strong disinfectant that was used every day.

She yawned as she picked up the phone. She was tired. It had been a long day. She was looking forward to going home.

'Hello,' she said.

'Is that Siobhán Farrell?'

Siobhán recognised the voice, although she couldn't place it straight away.

'This is Sally Harper.'

Siobhán listened as Sally related the events of the evening and sighed when she heard that Jenna had run off. She hated missing children reports, even if the children were really young adults and even if they'd apparently gone missing of their own accord.

'Tell me about the boyfriend,' she said. 'He sounds the most likely candidate for your daughter to be with.'

Sally felt like a worse than useless mother as she gave what little information she could about Gerry. She wasn't even sure of his surname, although she knew that Jenna had told her.

'Does Jenna have a diary or anything?' asked Siobhán. 'It's very possible that his name would be in it.'

'Oh God.' Sally sighed. 'I never thought of that. I'm hopeless. Totally hopeless.'

'No you're not, Sally,' said Siobhán gently. 'Why don't you go and have a rummage around in Jenna's room, and in the mean time I'll make sure that the guys are alerted to look out for her.'

'Right.'

'Phone me back,' said Siobhán.

'Will do,' said Sally.

'I've got to check her room,' said Sally.

Iona frowned. 'I never thought of that.'

'I should have,' said Sally.

They both went to Jenna's room. Walking inside gave Iona the feeling of suddenly moving backwards in time to her own teens. Her room had been a bomb-site like Jenna's, with posters of INXS plastered all over the walls. Jenna's tastes were surprisingly rap-orientated for someone who was going through a semi-goth phase, though Iona had no idea who the blinged-up star of the enormous poster at the foot of her bed was.

270

'Don't ask me,' said Sally. 'I can't keep up with them all. I ask her things like why they can't spell their names properly and she goes crazy.'

Iona laughed. 'What did you say you taught?'

'Maths and English.'

'I wish I'd been good at maths,' she said regretfully. 'I never listened. If I didn't understand it straight away I could never be bothered to try to work it out.'

'You're like most of my pupils.' Sally picked up a Filofax from beneath a mound of books and papers on the desk in the corner of the room and began to look through it. 'Nobody can be bothered to put in the time.' She grimaced as she looked at empty pages where she'd have expected to see names and addresses. 'The trouble, of course, is that nobody writes anything on paper any more. Certainly not Jenna's age group. Phone numbers are just stored on the phones.'

'Oh, that's the same for everyone,' said Iona. 'I'm as bad. I don't even know Frank's number off by heart.'

Sally reeled off a number and Iona frowned. 'That doesn't sound – oh yeah, I forgot. Different phones.'

'He was a shit about things, wasn't he?' Sally was looking more intently at the Filofax. The to-do pages were filled with notes in Jenna's spiky handwriting: meet gang; revise French; read poems; go to library; remember I am smart. She swallowed hard at the last note. Of course her daughter was smart. Of course she was.

'I'm kinda getting used to that idea,' said Iona.

'Here it is!' Sally's grip tightened on the Filofax. 'Gerry,' she looked up, 'and then a little heart, so it must be him. And it's a mobile number.'

She dialled it immediately. This time the message – to leave a message – was in a young man's voice.

'If that's Gerry who's a friend of my daughter, Jenna, can you tell her she'd better get home right now,' said Sally sharply. 'Or else she'll be in even more trouble. I'm worried about her and I'm calling the police.'

She hung up and looked at Iona. 'What d'you think?'

271

'It'd sure as hell scare me,' said Iona. 'Now why don't you ring Siobhán and give her the number? Maybe she can track it down for you.'

~

The fact that Gerry Cullinan's phone was on his parents' monthly bill made it easy to find out his address. Siobhán offered to go and see if Jenna was there and to bring her home if she was. Sally was uncertain whether it was a good idea but in the end she agreed. For starters, she didn't have her car and she didn't want Iona to have to drive her to the other side of town. Iona said that it was a small town and that she really didn't mind, but that maybe being picked up by Siobhán would jolt Jenna out of her petulance, whereas being picked up by Iona and Sally would only annoy her even more.

'I can't believe that all this stuff is happening to me,' said Sally as they waited for word from Siobhán. 'This is not my life. My life is uncomplicated. I'm just an ordinary person. I'm supposed to be married with a kid and the only trauma is that she's a teenager and therefore can't stand me. My life should be boring! I shouldn't have a hot-line to a detective at the police station!'

'My life is ordinary too,' said Iona. 'I have a reasonably good job and a city-centre house and I shouldn't have hot-lines to police stations either. I feel like I've stepped into someone else's life by mistake.' She sighed. 'Maybe I should go before Siobhán gets back here with Jenna.'

'She said she'll call if Jenna's there,' said Sally. 'Please just wait until we find out if she is.'

'Sure, if that's what you want.'

Sally smiled faintly at her. 'And in my life I didn't think I'd ever be asking my husband's wife to wait until the police called to say that my daughter was safe.'

'In my life I didn't know that my husband had a wife.'

The phone rang and both of them jumped.

'She's here,' Siobhán told Sally. 'I'm bringing her home now.'

'Oh, thank you.' Sally felt relief flood over her and tears spill down her cheeks. 'Thank you, thank you, thank you.'

'I gather she's found her,' said Iona as Sally replaced the receiver.

Sally nodded. Iona handed her a tissue. Sally blew her nose.

'I'll head off,' said Iona. 'But give me a call, let me know how things go.'

Sally nodded again.

'Take care,' said Iona as she let herself out of the house.

'Thank you again,' Sally called after her as Iona walked down the path.

⤳

Jenna face was sullen as she got out of the car. Sally was relieved to see that Siobhán hadn't turned up in a marked car with its blue lights and reflective stripes, giving the neighbours still more to gossip over. She knew that there was already plenty of talk about Frank and the fact that all wasn't entirely well with the marriage, though nobody knew the full story yet. Still, there was enough for them to gossip about.

'It's not that late,' said Jenna as she stomped through the front door. 'And I really don't see why you had to freak out and involve the police in all this. I'm sick of the sight of that woman.'

Siobhán said nothing as Jenna pushed past her and ran up the stairs, slamming her bedroom door behind her.

'Thanks,' said Sally.

'They were watching a DVD,' said Siobhán. 'His parents were out but were due back pretty soon.'

'I'm not naïve,' said Sally. 'I know I must seem like the world's stupidest person to you, but actually I'm not. I'm the vice-principal of a girls' school and I know what they're like.'

Siobhán smiled sympathetically at her. 'She's obviously going through a hard time.'

'Oh, look, I know!' cried Sally. 'We all are. And I suppose I've been so caught up with Frank that I haven't had time to really worry about Jen. Even though I do worry about her. But then she's been a worry for the last few months, so . . .' She let her breath out with a sigh. 'I've no idea where my priorities should be right now.'

'Well, I guess Frank is safely tucked up in a hospital bed,' said Siobhán.

Sally laughed shortly. 'I guess so.' She ran her fingers through her hair. 'I need to get to grips with things again. I used to be organised and in control. I'm not any more.'

'What made you cut your hair?' asked Siobhán suddenly.

'My hair?' Sally was surprised at the question. 'I – I'm not sure.'

'It suits you like that.'

'Needs to be cut again,' said Sally. 'I'd forgotten that I kept it long because it grows like wildfire.'

Siobhán yawned involuntarily.

'You should get home,' said Sally. 'Get some sleep. I'm sorry if I caused you hassle.'

'All part of the job,' said Siobhán. She made a wry face. 'And at least this has turned out OK.'

'Yes.' Sally nodded. 'Thanks.'

'Good night,' said Siobhán, and walked back to her car.

✺

Siobhán was exhausted. What she would really have liked to do was go home and soak in a luxurious bath, only lying in a bath would give her more time to think and she didn't want to think right now.

Eddie didn't have AIDS. Not that she'd ever really believed that he'd turn out to be HIV positive, but the last few weeks had been traumatic. His doctor had contacted them to say that there had been some contamination of the blood in Eddie's test and that it would have to be done again. And Siobhán hadn't felt able to walk out on him while he was so tense about everything. She wanted to – but she couldn't. Then yesterday Eddie had received the all-clear and she'd seen the darkness lift from his eyes and the weight suddenly disappear from his shoulders, and he'd put his

274

arms around her and thanked her for standing by him. He'd told her that he truly loved her and that he was inexpressibly sorry for what had happened and that she needn't have another second's doubt in her life about him because there was no way he was ever going to put what they had at risk again. And then, for the second time in their lives, he'd asked her to marry him.

She hadn't known what to say. She'd looked at him wordlessly and then he'd brought his lips down very gently on hers and he'd kissed her. And although she'd desperately wanted not to kiss him back, she wasn't able to prevent herself responding to something she'd been missing for so long. But when he'd tried to undo the buttons on her cream blouse she'd found it impossible to block the image of him and the Peter Murtagh orgy out of her mind. She told herself that orgy probably wasn't the right word for what had gone on, but it captured the essence of it all the same and she couldn't bring herself to make love to a man who hadn't given her a thought while he'd had sex with a woman whose name he'd never even know.

Eddie had accused her of trying to punish him, and she'd said that punishment was far from her mind but that she wasn't ready to make love to him. That she needed time to think about it.

Now she wondered whether she'd ever want to make love to Eddie again. Or to anyone else, for that matter. Somehow she felt entirely unsexual these days and she didn't really care. The thing was, she mused, as she drove along the Dublin road, she understood how it had happened. But understanding it didn't make it any less hurtful or make her feel any better.

She slowed down at the warning triangle placed ahead of the stopped car. She could see that the driver was a woman. She pulled in to the side of the road.

'Need a hand?' she asked.

Iona looked up in surprise at the voice.

'You looked familiar even in the dark,' said Siobhán. 'You're having an eventful night, aren't you?'

'Far too eventful.' Iona used her foot to unsuccessfully try to loosen the nut on the wheel. 'And it's pretty ironic that I've got a bloody puncture, since you guys seem to think that it was a puncture that caused Frank to call into that pub last month and start this whole mess in the first place.'

Siobhán had given both Iona and Sally the information that the emergency spare wheel on the Honda had replaced one of the rear wheels, and that it seemed, based on how little wear there was on the tyre, that Frank had called into the pub almost directly after changing it. Probably to wash his hands, Siobhán had said, because there'd been a couple of oil-stained tissues in the car. So it was just his bad luck to be in the wrong place at the wrong time. When Sally had got the car back, she'd looked at the replacement wheel and then kicked it in impotent rage.

'Can I help?' asked Siobhán again.

Iona nodded. 'I can't seem to turn the damn screw. It's years since I've had to change a tyre and I'm not sure I was much good at it then.'

Siobhán picked up the wrench and pushed hard on it. The screw loosened.

'Impressive,' said Iona.

Siobhán laughed. 'That's us garda girls. Muscles to burn.' She did the same to the other screws and then helped Iona to jack up the car and change the tyre.

'How're Sally and Jenna?' asked Iona as she rolled the spare wheel round from the boot.

'I don't know,' said Siobhán. 'Jenna didn't say much in the car and I basically left them to it.'

'Crap situation for Sally,' said Iona. 'I'm sure that Jenna is a lovely girl, but she's obviously totally ticked off with her mother about the way things are right now. I think she sort of blames Sally for me and Frank, and now she's disgusted about the baby . . .' Iona's voice faltered.

'Baby? What baby?' asked Siobhán.

Iona told her about Sally's pregnancy.

'What a mess.' Siobhán manoeuvred the new tyre into place. 'So that's why Jenna ran off.'

Iona nodded. 'Jenna called her mother disgusting.' She smiled faintly. 'I suppose it's hard for a teenager to think of their parents having sex without feeling disgusted.'

'I suppose,' Siobhán agreed. 'And how do you feel about it?'

Iona sighed heavily. 'I'm gutted,' she admitted. 'We were hoping to have a baby ourselves.' She handed Siobhán one of the silver screws.

'Oh.'

'Why are men so much trouble?' Iona rubbed her nose, streaking it with dirt from the tyre.

'God, I wish I knew.' Siobhán's words were so heartfelt that Iona looked at her in surprise.

'Are you married?' She frowned. 'Did you say you were?'

Siobhán shook her head. 'I'm . . . I was going to . . . I'm living with someone.'

'You don't sound so sure.'

'I guess right now I'm not.'

'Does he hate the fact that you're a cop?' asked Iona curiously. 'I can imagine some guys might.'

'It's not really to do with me,' Siobhán told her. 'Not entirely. It's more to do with him.' She leaned against the car. 'I'm pretty much trying to decide whether to leave him or not. And I don't know what to do.'

'Yeuch.' Iona looked at her sympathetically. 'I guess I thought of you as a kind of invincible person because you're a garda and because you seem to be so in charge of things. I didn't think you'd be in a man trouble kind of place.'

'Yeah, well, I'm completely in a man trouble kind of place and I can't help feeling that being in charge of my own life might be a good thing.'

'Fancy a coffee?' Iona pointed at the twenty-four-hour newsagent which offered coffee to go. 'I need something to wake me up a bit and, well, why don't you sit in the car with me for a while and tell me about it?'

'I don't need to talk about it,' said Siobhán.

'Y'see, that's what I felt about Frank. But when I started talking to you, it helped,' said Iona. 'OK, you don't have to talk about it, but let me grab you a coffee anyway, as thanks for helping with the tyre.'

'Fair enough.' Siobhán thought she could do with a shot of caffeine. 'If they do double espresso, that's the one for me.'

～

'You scared the living daylights out of me.' Sally looked furiously at Jenna. 'And I don't care whether you were upset or not, you should've answered the phone. At least then I'd have known you were all right.'

'Get off my case, would you?' Jenna rolled over on her bed and ignored her mother.

'Please, Jen. Can't we just talk about this. Like grown-ups?'

'Oh yeah, it's treating me like a grown-up sending the police after me! Have you any idea how humiliating that was? I'll be lucky if Gerry ever speaks to me again. And someone will be bound to tell his parents.'

'How will they even know?' asked Sally. 'It wasn't as though a posse of cops drew up outside with their sirens blazing. It was just Siobhán in an ordinary car.'

'Just Siobhán was bad enough,' said Jenna mutinously. 'And she must think that our whole family is psycho. We're probably under observation right now!'

'Don't be infantile,' said Sally. 'We have rules in this household and you broke them and you worried me and that's what happened as a result.'

'Oh yeah? And Dad breaks them and what happens? We spend our fucking lives in hospital reading to him and playing music to him and he doesn't even know.'

'Jenna!'

'It's true.' She buried her face in the pillow. 'You're being nice to him and you're trying to make me be nice to him, but it's only because he's in a coma. If he wasn't you'd have thrown him out as soon as you found out about Iona.'

'And is that what you want?' asked Sally.

278

Jenna said nothing.

'I can't and I won't abandon your father. Even Iona doesn't want to abandon him. What happens when he gets better may well be a different story.'

'And if he doesn't?' Jenna turned a tear-streaked face to her mother. 'You're going to have a baby! At your age. With no dad. So what'll happen is that I'll be looking after it 'cos you'll have to be at work and it'll mess up everything and I might have wanted a brother or sister when I was small but not now. And I just *hate* the way everything has happened.'

Sally leaned down and gathered her daughter into her arms.

'No matter what's happened, the important thing is that I love you,' she told her as she stroked her dark hair. 'I love you more than anything. And however we resolve things, you have to remember that you're a very important member of this family. With or without your dad. With or without a new baby.'

'Yeah, right.' Jenna let her head rest on her mother's arm. None of Sally's so-called comfort was really making her feel any better inside. She didn't want to be here. She wanted to be with Gerry, who really understood her.

Chapter 25

Siobhán stood on the balcony of the apartment and looked across the harbour at Dun Laoghaire. The sun skimmed over the gently rolling waves, reflecting golden light from the water and causing her to shade her eyes from the glare. She turned back into the apartment and walked across the polished floor of the living room again and through to the galley kitchen with its spotless tiles and granite worktop. She noticed that the microwave was expensive stainless steel, boasting an integrated grill and convection oven. Everything I could possibly want, she thought wryly, to heat up the ready meals for one from the supermarket up the road.

She looked at the woman who was sitting in one of the comfortable armchairs waiting for her decision.

'It's a short rental?' she asked again.

Iona nodded. 'Three months, four max. The owner is in Chile. Personally I wouldn't bother renting out a place for such a short time, but I suppose he feels it's worth it to have some extra cash in the bank.'

'What if I want it for longer than that?' asked Siobhán.

'Well, I know that he's meant to be back by the end of the summer,' said Iona. 'But we've plenty of apartments on the books so I could get you something else if that's what you decide.' She looked sympathetically at Siobhán. 'Hopefully things will work out and it won't matter.'

Siobhán swallowed the lump in her throat. 'Hopefully,' she said. She shivered in the cool breeze that wafted through the open patio window. 'But I don't know what working out really means.'

⁓

That was what she said to Eddie the following evening when she told him of her decision to move out for a while. She needed some time on her own to think things over.

'I don't know what else I can do to make you see how sorry I am,' he said as he looked at her miserably. 'I've gone through hell over all this. I've apologised a million times. I'm clean and I'm healthy. And Siobhán, I love you, which is the most important thing. You can't tell me that it's all over between us.'

'I never said it was over,' Siobhán told him shakily. 'I said that I needed some time and some space to myself and that's what I'm getting.'

'But you expect me to wait for you?' demanded Eddie.

'That's rather up to you,' she said. 'I can't be with you right now. I'm still furious with you. Making me feel that there was something wrong with me because you wouldn't sleep with me. Eddie, it's been a horrible time.'

'It's been a horrible time for me too,' he said.

'You brought it on yourself,' she told him sharply. 'It's not my fault.'

'You just want to punish me,' he said. 'Make me feel bad about it.'

'Moving out isn't about punishing you,' said Siobhán. 'It's about me. I need to think about what I want from our relationship, Eddie, and I can't do that here right now.'

'And how long will this think-fest take?' asked Eddie curtly.

'I don't know,' said Siobhán. 'But if I move out for a couple of months it'll give us both time to think things over.'

'A couple of months!' he exclaimed. 'Do you really expect me to sit around and wait for that long?'

'Are you trying to give me some kind of ultimatum?' she demanded. 'You were the one who broke the trust, Eddie. Not me. Now you seem to be saying that if I take a bit of time out to get over it all, you might not be there for me afterwards. If that's how you want it . . .' Her voice wavered and she turned away so that he couldn't see the tears forming in her eyes.

He got up from the chair and put his arm around her shoulders. 'I don't want to break up with you,' he said. 'I just don't want you to go.'

'I didn't want you to sleep with that . . . woman,' mumbled Siobhán. 'But you did it anyway.'

'Is it always going to be thrown in my face?' he asked.

'That's why I need to be on my own for a while.' She blinked hard and looked up at him. 'So that I don't keep throwing it in your face. So that I can come to terms with it at my own pace.'

He released his hold on her. 'Why don't you believe me when I say it was a one-off mistake?'

'I *do* believe you,' she said sincerely, 'but that's not the point. The point is that I need some time to remember why I loved you and to trust you again.'

'I still don't see why you have to move out,' he said.

'We're just going round and round in circles,' Siobhán told him. 'I thought we had something good going between us. I still love you, Eddie. But I can't just forgive and forget. If I'm on my own for a while it might help.'

'All right,' said Eddie resignedly. 'If that's what it takes.'

She tugged at a stray wisp of her hair. She didn't really want to go at all. But she knew that she had to, even if it was only for a short time. The whole thing had sapped her confidence in herself and she needed to get it back. But she wouldn't if she didn't leave.

'I'll go and pack,' she said.

He looked at her in complete astonishment. 'Now? You're going now?'

She nodded. 'It's better to get it over and done with right away.'

'You mean you've already sorted out a place to go?'

She nodded again.

'Sometimes you can be very hard-hearted,' he said. 'It's no wonder you're good at your job.'

~

Siobhán knew that she wouldn't have gone through with it so quickly if it hadn't been for Iona. Sitting in the car at the side of the road a couple of nights previously, her hands wrapped around the takeaway cup of coffee that Iona had brought back from the newsagent, she'd given the other woman a diluted version of events, simply saying that Eddie had slept with another woman and that she was having a hard time trusting him. And that she couldn't help thinking that she needed to be away from him for a while. Iona had listened intently and then told her that she knew of a lovely apartment overlooking the harbour in Dun Laoghaire which was available for a short let at a very competitive rate. If Siobhán was interested in it, Iona could set things up so that she could move in straight away.

Siobhán hadn't known what to say. Moving out had been a vague thought, an idea which she'd felt might be a good one but which she hadn't entirely taken seriously. Suddenly having the option to carry it out had flustered her and she'd told Iona that she'd have to think about it, that she wasn't sure exactly what she wanted to do. And Iona had nodded and handed her a business card, telling her to contact her if she wanted to take it any further. Siobhán had suddenly seen Iona as a professional person rather than (as she'd previously always viewed her) the victim of a crime, no matter how unusual that crime was. The following day, hardly believing what she was doing, she'd called Iona's number and made an appointment to see the flat in Dun Laoghaire and had made the decision to take it.

Now, as she wheeled her suitcase out of the apartment, she still couldn't quite believe that her life had taken this unexpected turn.

'Hi, Mizz P. Off for a jaunt at the taxpayer's expense?' Carl O'Connor was walking up the corridor.

'No,' she said shortly.

283

'Holiday?' he asked.

She said nothing.

'You OK?' He looked at her quizzically.

'Fine,' she said. She stepped into the lift.

'Sure?' He sounded concerned. 'Everything going all right?'

She wished he'd stop being nice to her. The one constant in her changing world was that Carl O'Connor wasn't really supposed to be nice to her. She was glad when the doors slid closed and hid him from view.

～

She'd arranged to meet Iona at the apartment as she hadn't yet got the keys. The other woman was there ahead of her, sitting in her green VW and listening to a CD, the window open. The music wafted on the air to Siobhán as she walked across the car park.

'Wouldn't have pegged you for a Sinatra fan,' she said as she arrived at the car.

Iona, who hadn't seen her, switched off the CD player in a hurry. 'Not really my kind of stuff,' she said. 'I was just . . . It doesn't matter.' She got out of the car. 'Here are the keys. You have to sign for them. Do you want me to go in with you and check that everything's OK?'

'If you like,' said Siobhán.

'Come on, so.' Iona led the way.

The apartment seemed smaller than before. Siobhán looked around at it again, not quite able to take in the fact that she was actually going to live here away from Eddie. She twisted her engagement ring around on her finger. She'd wondered whether she should take it off and, while she'd been packing, had slid it from her finger. But she'd felt naked without it and had put it on again, telling herself that she was still engaged to Eddie and that she wasn't ready to break it off with him. The weird thing was that she'd wanted to stay then. She'd been telling herself that she was lucky all this had happened before they got married when she could simply leave and it wouldn't matter. But it was hard to walk out when they'd created a shared past. It wasn't easy to be strong.

'Hey, it'll work out,' said Iona as she spotted the anxious look on Siobhán's face. 'You're right, Siobhán. You need to be by yourself for a while.'

'You think?'

'Absolutely,' she said. 'Anyway, I brought this along to help.' She opened the huge duffel bag which was slung over her shoulder and took out a bottle of champagne.

'Champagne is supposed to be a celebratory drink,' she pointed out.

'Yes. We're celebrating the start of you getting your life back on track,' said Iona. 'Hopefully the end result will be exactly what you want and what you deserve – whatever that is.'

Siobhán smiled slightly and took the bottle. What the hell, she thought. I could do with a drink. She began to twist off the foil.

'Don't open it now!' cried Iona.

'If I don't open it now, when will I open it?' demanded Siobhán. 'No point in me sitting here tonight on my own drinking a bottle of champagne. That's pathetic.'

'I guess so,' admitted Iona.

'So, come on, have some.'

Iona looked at her watch. It was nearly five o'clock and she didn't have any more appointments. And although she had some paperwork to do in the office, she reckoned it could wait.

'There are glasses in the cupboard,' she said. 'I'll get some.'

'Excellent,' said Siobhán as she popped the cork. 'Let's celebrate.'

⁓

Sally didn't feel like celebrating anything. She was sitting in front of the TV, her fingers beneath the elasticated waist of her navy loungers, which had suddenly become too tight. They'd always been comfortable before. Now they weren't. Since the morning sickness had abated a little over the last couple of weeks, she had been able to push the thoughts of her pregnancy to the back of her mind. But now she couldn't. She was getting bigger.

She got up and went to her bedroom. There was another pair of loungers in the wardrobe, an ancient green pair that she knew would be more forgiving. She took off the navy ones and put them on the shelf and pulled on the green ones instead. Instantly she felt better. She wandered down into the kitchen and opened the freezer. There was a tub of Ben & Jerry's Cherry Garcia on the middle shelf. Frank was the Ben & Jerry's fan in the house. She didn't eat much ice cream herself, although that was because she was generally on some kind of diet and almost all of them forbade ice cream of any description.

She took the tub out of the freezer and wiped the smear of frost from the lid. She closed the freezer door, took off the lid, then peeled away the plastic. The ice cream was rock hard. Even stabbing it with a spoon wasn't making much difference. If Frank had been here, of course, it would never have lasted this long and become extra-frozen. She put the tub into the microwave and gave it a few seconds on the defrost setting.

When Jenna arrived home from her art class a few minutes later, Sally was scraping the last of the ice cream from the tub. Her daughter looked at her in amazement.

'You ate Dad's ice cream?'

'It's our ice cream,' said Sally.

'You don't even like cherries,' said Jenna.

'I do now.' Sally rubbed the back of her hand across her mouth.

'I don't believe this.'

'What?'

Jenna dumped her bag on the table. 'You've eaten a whole tub of ice cream that you buy for Dad and that you don't like.'

'I'm pregnant,' said Sally. 'I get cravings.'

Jenna stared at her. 'You can't have got a craving for ice cream.'

'I can,' said Sally. 'I did.'

'I don't know what to say to you.' Jenna sat down opposite her.

'You haven't said very much for the last few days,' said Sally. 'No need for you to start talking to me now.'

286

'I don't want you to be pregnant,' said Jenna.

'I know.'

'You're too old to be pregnant.'

'Well, apparently not,' said Sally mildly.

'You'll be a laughing stock.'

'I don't see why.' Sally pushed the empty tub away from her. 'I'm sure there are other mothers having babies in their forties. It's just that the gap between you and this one will be big. That's what the problem is.'

'That and the fact that its father may not come home ever again.'

'That too,' agreed Sally.

'Why?' asked Jenna. 'Why now?'

'I didn't choose to get pregnant,' said Sally. 'It wasn't as though we were trying.'

'You should have told me,' Jenna said. 'I hated finding out in the hospital like that. It was awful.'

'I know,' said Sally. 'But I was having difficulty coming to terms with it myself.'

'I don't care,' said Jenna. 'You still should have told me.' She got up from the table. 'Have you made anything for dinner?'

Sally shook her head. 'But there's cold meat and cheese in the fridge. And plenty of fresh fruit. Or you could do pasta for yourself if you like. I did the shopping over the internet.'

Jenna stared at her. 'Why didn't you just go to the supermarket?'

'I didn't feel like it,' said Sally.

'I hate this!' cried Jenna. 'Everything's different and I hate it!' She picked up her bag again. 'I'm going to my room.'

'Sardines,' said Sally suddenly.

'What?'

'That's what I got a craving for when I was pregnant with you.'

Jenna looked at her sceptically. 'People don't get cravings for sardines.'

'Why wouldn't they?' asked Sally. 'Anyway, I ate them every day for about six months.'

287

'You never told me about that before,' said Jenna.

Sally shrugged. 'You never asked.'

'I'm going to my room,' repeated Jenna. 'I've homework to do.'

She stomped out of the kitchen, her bag banging against the table and knocking the empty ice cream tub to the floor.

⌒

'Maybe I should get a test done,' said Sally.

Sally! Of course. That was his wife's name. He remembered again now. The other incident, the wedding under the sun, that must have been a dream. Vivid, though. Very real. He dragged his mind back to what she was saying. A test. About . . . Yes! About the babies. They still only had one child. Their lovely daughter.

'The doctors said everything was fine.' He wanted to be reassuring.

'Doctors! What do they know really?' Sally pulled at her long auburn hair. 'They don't know why I had such trouble with Jenna and they don't know why I had the miscarriage and they sure as hell won't have any idea why I haven't got pregnant since. All they'll say – like they said before – is that I'm a normal healthy woman and so I should get pregnant again.'

'Do you want to get pregnant again?' asked Frank.

She stared at him. 'How can you possibly ask that?'

'It was hard for you, with Jenna. All that last-minute emergency stuff. Maybe it's traumatised you. Maybe there's something stopping you.'

'For heaven's sake, Frank – I got pregnant again, didn't I? OK, it didn't work out, but nothing stopped me.'

He said nothing.

'Are you thinking that it's the miscarriage on top of the Caesarean that's the problem?'

'I don't know!' he cried. 'I just wondered.'

'D'you think I'm on birth control unknown to myself?' she demanded. 'That I'm secretly stuffing myself with the pill?'

'Of course not,' he told her. 'But I do know you're agitated about it and that probably doesn't help.'

'We can't all be as laid-back as you,' she retorted.

He caught her by the arm. 'I'm sorry,' he said. 'I didn't mean to imply that . . . that your state of mind had anything to do with it. I really didn't. I was trying to be helpful.'

She looked at him. His dark eyes held hers and suddenly she could feel the familiar spark of chemistry between them.

'Tonight we'll just do it for pleasure,' Frank told her. 'You, me and a tub of Ben and Jerry's. No baby talk. Just us, the way it should be.' He slid his hand beneath her filmy top.

'Frank!' she giggled.

'Think about me licking it off you.'

'It'll be cold,' she protested.

'I'll make you so hot that it'll bubble,' he promised.

She kissed him.

He kissed her.

He loved the taste of her, with or without the ice cream.

Chapter 26

The days grew warmer and the nights grew shorter. There was no change in Frank's condition. Sally and Iona continued to take turns visiting the hospital and didn't meet each other there again. Sally went back to work. Iona took on more work herself.

Iona didn't know whether it was because of work or because of Frank that she was having so much trouble sleeping. It seemed to her that she was always thinking of either one or the other, her concerns about tenants and rental agreements alternating with concerns about Frank. Her life had become one long set of worries – about things she could control, which wasn't too bad; about things she couldn't, which was harder. And as she tossed and turned for the fifth night in a row, she wished that she could be transported somewhere where she didn't have to worry about anything ever again.

She pushed the duvet away from her and sat up. The green glow from the alarm clock beside the bed (not that she needed an alarm to get her up these days) showed that it was four in the morning. She got out of bed and peeked through the slatted blinds.

Faint wisps of light were already sneaking over the horizon. It would be another glorious day. Another day where she sat at her desk in Rental Remedies by day and sat at Frank's bedside by night. It wasn't fair, she thought angrily, that she had to put her whole life on hold for him. It really wasn't. They'd planned to travel together during the summer this year. Short breaks. Of course, she thought bitterly now, they had to be short breaks. When they'd discussed it she'd thought the idea of lots of city breaks would be great fun. Frank had suggested that if she was pregnant she mightn't want to go away for longer periods. And she'd agreed with him. Fool that she was, she muttered now. He'd manipulated her into thinking that they were a good idea because they were the only holidays he was able to take without Sally getting suspicious. How stupid could she have been!

She walked out of the bedroom and into the office. She hadn't worked from home very much lately, not liking to be there on her own. Which was silly, she thought, given that she'd lived there quite happily by herself before Frank had come into her life. She'd changed everything for him. But it didn't really look as though he'd changed anything for her.

She switched on the computer and waited as it whirred into life. The only thing she'd done on it lately was – like Jenna – look up information on comas. She sat down in front of it and opened her web browser. This time she typed in the word holiday. It was a stupid thing to type in, of course. There were far too many hits for it to be of the slightest use. So she looked up cheap flights instead. And then she followed the link that led her to a Dublin–New York flight leaving that morning for a ridiculously low fare. It got into New York at lunchtime, US time. That would be fun, she thought. A quick hop to NYC for a bit of shopping. She'd never been to New York before. She'd always wanted to go but had never quite got around to it.

Still, she could hardly just up and go, could she? Not when she was supposed to be visiting him every second day, reading to him, talking to him, trying to bring him out of the damn coma.

She leaned her chin in her hands. It would be nice, though. Nice to be away from everything and everybody. Nice not to feel as though she was being held to Frank and Sally and Jenna by some kind of spider's web. Nice to have fun. It seemed like forever since she'd had fun. It was impossible. She couldn't do it.

It was a very cheap flight, though. And she could get a return one almost as cheaply. It wouldn't do any harm to see if it was actually available. A couple of days in New York. It was a kind of laid-back thing to do. The sort of thing that a young, free and single girl might do. But she wasn't young, free and single. Was she?

~

Lauren went to the airport that morning to pick up Flora. She hadn't told Iona that their mother was coming for a visit because she knew that her sister would freak out over it. Iona was adamant that she didn't need her mother fussing over her, but Flora was equally adamant that the time had come for her to see Iona for herself and try to talk to her about her future.

Flora knew that it was difficult. She knew that Iona loved Frank. She'd liked him herself when he'd come to visit them in Javea, even though she'd found him difficult to get to know. But he had undoubtedly been charming, and as far as Flora could see, he was utterly besotted with Iona. He'd treated her well, with an almost old-fashioned courtesy, and Flora had been happy for her because Iona wasn't the sort of girl who lost her heart easily.

And now . . . Flora grimaced. Now it was all an unbelievable mess.

She waved as she spotted Lauren's tall frame standing at the meeting point, waiting for her. Lauren smiled in return and hugged her mother. They made their way to the car park.

'I'm going to invite her to dinner tonight,' said Lauren in response to Flora's question about Iona. 'I won't tell her you're here, though. You know how stubborn she can be. If she thinks it's all a plot to check up on her and see how she is, she's just as likely not to come.'

Flora nodded. 'D'you think she's sticking by him out of stubbornness?'

'I'm not sure about that.' Lauren inserted her ticket into the machine and drove out of the car park. 'If she'd found out about Sally and Jenna before now she probably would have put him into a coma herself! But because he's so sick she can't let herself be angry with him.'

Flora sighed.

'And now she's in this situation where she and Sally alternate nights at the hospital,' said Lauren. 'You know how much Io hates hospitals! But she goes in because . . . oh, I don't know! Because she wants him to choose her when he wakes up maybe.'

'It's not right,' said Flora.

'I know,' responded Lauren, 'but I really don't know what we can do about it.'

❧

Iona slept on the plane. She'd never slept on a plane before because she found it far too uncomfortable, but as she settled into her seat and they began to taxi towards the runway, she was lulled by the engines into a trance-like state which ended up with her nodding off and not waking up even when the steward made an announcement about the in-flight service.

She did wake up when they brought around the food. She ate the meal, watched the movie and then fell asleep again so that by the time they arrived at JFK she was, unlike many of her fellow passengers, completely refreshed and even the security checks didn't bother her.

She caught a cab outside the airport and asked the driver to drop her at the Le Parker Meridien on West 57th. When she got out she tipped him generously though she wished she'd asked for some lower-denomination bills at the airport bureau de change. But what the hell, she thought, as she wheeled her small case behind her through the huge lobby. It's only money. I saved a bundle on the flight and I paid off my Visa bill last month so I've plenty of credit. She still didn't quite believe that she'd gone ahead and booked it so impulsively. But she was glad that she had. The alternative would have been to spend the day in Rental Remedies listening to tenants complaining about broken washing machines or stuck doors or other equally irritating problems.

It suddenly occurred to her that she'd forgotten to call Ruth and say that she wasn't coming in that day. She'd meant to phone from Dublin airport but it had been frantically busy with long queues and in all of the fuss it had gone completely out of her head. Oh well, she thought, Garret had told her to take time off if she needed it. She wasn't going to bother ringing them now.

Her room was high enough up for her to have a view of Central Park. She smiled to herself as she looked over it and laughed at the idea that a few hours ago she'd been feeling bleak and dull in Dublin and now she was in the city that never sleeps. And she wasn't tired!

She peeled off her travelling clothes and then hopped under the shower. Despite her lack of tiredness she knew that a shower would perk her up even more. Afterwards she dressed in a light top and cotton skirt, slid her feet into her most comfortable sandals and walked out on to the street and towards 5th Avenue.

It was like everything she'd ever imagined. The noise, the heat, the crowds, the whole bustling, teeming momentum of it all. Yellow cabs clogged the streets and every so often an impatient driver would lower his window and shout at another driver just like in the movies. Iona giggled as she walked past enormous condos with awnings covering the pavement (sidewalk, she told herself, sidewalk) to the kerb, where liveried doormen opened the doors for women with more money than style as they went out for a day doing whatever it was that rich New York women do.

It was a world away from Rental Remedies and the intensive care unit in Dublin. In fact, right now, she could almost believe that none of it had ever happened, that she'd never met Frank Harper and married him, that she really was young, free and single in the best city in the world.

She went into Saks and emerged some time later with one bag and a bruised credit card. Then she went into Bloomingdale's and came out with half a dozen bags and a credit card that was almost up to its limit. It was true, she told herself as she swung the bags in her hands, shopping helped. It might be shallow and it might be vacuous and the prices you paid for stuff might be totally outrageous (thought not as outrageous here as in Dublin, she added), but it made you feel good and forget things and that was exactly what she wanted to do today.

They were doing makeovers in Macy's. She sat down and allowed the Benefit consultant to colour her cheeks, lips and eyes and turn her from dull into dazzling in twenty minutes. When she looked in the mirror she recognised herself as the Iona of old and she puckered up her tinted lips to blow herself a kiss. The consultant smiled at her – and smiled even more widely when Iona bought every product she'd used – and then told her to have a nice day.

'I sure will,' Iona replied as she walked out on to the street again.

She was getting tired now, though. She needed to sit down and have something to eat. But she wasn't going to waste her gorgeous makeover and her fabulous new clothes on some fast-food outlet. She caught a cab back to the hotel, changed once again but this time into the stunning Donna Ricco rose-print strapless dress and Joey O sandals that she'd picked up in Macy's (it hadn't just been make-up, and she'd had to move on to her second credit card) and walked back out into the New York streets.

She bought a copy of *Vanity Fair* at a kiosk and then strolled towards Central Park again before heading down Broadway. She stopped outside Gabriel's restaurant. She knew, from what she'd heard, that most restaurants in New York required bookings and that famous restaurants had waiting lists. It would probably be impossible to get a table for one in a restaurant which had, she'd discovered, hosted an Oscar-night dinner and where people like Tom Cruise and Cameron Diaz fetched up from time to time. But there was no harm in asking.

Benny Arvizo, the waiter, looked up as the door opened. He saw a petite girl with dark hair, dark eyes and knockout lips, wearing a figure-hugging dress and high heels.

'Can I help you?'

'Table for one?' She looked at him hopefully. 'I'm starving.'

Benny Arvizo couldn't resist her smile. He showed her to a

table, brought her a bottle of mineral water as she requested and left her to look at the menu.

So, thought Iona, I'm here in New York, in a great restaurant, about to have a meal on my own. And it's a damn sight better than being in Dublin picking at a green-leaf salad and not even wanting that. So although it sounded gorgeous, she didn't order the salad at Gabriel's but chose grilled mushrooms instead, followed by a tuna steak. She also ordered a bottle of Dolcetto d'Alba, ignoring the flash of surprise in Benny's eyes at the possibility of her drinking an entire bottle of red herself. Americans, she felt, had a very puritan attitude towards alcohol. But she hadn't enjoyed alcohol in ages. The times that she'd drunk red wine at home had been miserable times. This was different.

The restaurant buzzed and bustled with life. Iona was a little disappointed that she hadn't spotted any celebrities, but she supposed that it was unlikely Hollywood's latest heart-throb would be in town just because she was. And it didn't really matter. The place was great just the way it was.

⤳

Lauren, Myles and Flora sat in the living room and looked at each other anxiously. Lauren had first phoned Iona's mobile while her plane was halfway across the Atlantic. She'd left a message about dinner and asked Iona to call her back. When her sister hadn't responded a few hours later she'd phoned again. And got her voice-mail again. That hadn't worried her particularly, because during the working day Iona could be out and about with clients and unable to return calls. But when six o'clock passed and she still hadn't received a call from her sister, Lauren became more concerned.

She didn't know exactly what she was concerned about. After all, Iona was a grown woman and didn't have to come hopping just because Lauren wanted it. Plus, Lauren hadn't said anything about Flora's visit, so Iona wouldn't have realised that the dinner invitation really mattered that much. All the same, Lauren would have expected her to call back even if she couldn't come; she knew that it might be Iona's evening at the hospital. But not responding at all, that was unusual.

Eventually Lauren phoned the hospital to see if Iona was there. Susan Carpenter, who was on duty, said that she wasn't but that Sally Harper was. Did Lauren want to talk to Sally?

Not especially, had been Lauren's first reaction, but then she decided to ask the other woman whether she'd spoken to Iona that day.

'No,' said Sally. 'We don't talk that much. Sometimes we leave each other notes when we've visited Frank. You know, to say that there was no change or that he looked a little better . . . Why?'

Lauren explained that they were anxious to get in touch with Iona.

'Maybe she's just gone out for the night,' said Sally. 'After all, she's an attractive girl. Perhaps she wanted to go socialising.' Inside Sally was kind of hoping that that was the case. It put some distance between her and Frank.

'You're probably right.' Lauren sighed. She hated making plans and having them messed up. But it was her own fault. She should've told Iona that Flora was here.

She hung up and phoned Iona again. This time she left the message that Flora had come to see her. And that they wanted her to call them.

⌒

In the end Iona didn't drink the entire bottle of red. After two glasses she was feeling pleasantly relaxed. She didn't want to tip her laid-back feeling into a degree of drunkenness which she knew might happen if she had another glass. She was tired now and, despite the food, she knew that more alcohol would lessen her co-ordination and dull her senses.

She ordered coffee and the bill and sat back in her chair, the magazine open in front of her.

The restaurant was busier now, but not full. There were tables of women laughing and joking with each other, obviously on some kind of celebratory girls' night out. There were tables of men, businessmen, having serious conversations occasionally punctuated by false laughter. There were mixed tables, some business, some social. And there were couples who were out together, looking lovingly over the starched tablecloths at each other, happy to be together.

Would we have come here? she wondered. Would Frank and I have sat at a table together and kissed like that couple in the corner? Or would we have just gone to the burger joint down the road?

Benny came with her coffee and told her that the bill had been taken care of. She frowned and looked at him enquiringly.

'The gentleman over there.' He nodded towards a table where six men and three women were sitting. She'd put them down on her list as a business group. The man indicated by Benny saw her puzzled look and raised his wine glass in her direction. Iona frowned again.

'Why?' she asked Benny.

'I don't know, ma'am,' he said. 'But the gentleman asked me to take care of it.'

Iona continued to look over at the table. The man had been distracted by something one of his companions had said and wasn't looking in her direction any more. She knocked back the coffee and got up, her chair scraping the floor as she pushed it out of the way. Then she walked over to the table.

'Excuse me,' she said, looking directly at the guy who had paid for her dinner. 'Can I have a word?'

'Certainly.' He got up from the table and smiled at her.

He was in his mid-thirties, she reckoned, well groomed, wearing an expensive suit, although his shirt collar was open. Dark hair, grey eyes, smooth-shaven.

'What's with paying for my dinner?' she asked.

'I wanted to.'

'Why?'

'I got a great deal of pleasure out of looking at you this evening,' he told her. 'You're gorgeous.'

'Well, it was very kind of you, but I'm going to go and pay for my own dinner myself.' She turned away.

He caught her by the arm and she froze. He let go of her immediately.

'I'm sorry,' he said. 'I didn't mean to offend you.'

'How else do you expect me to be when someone says they've paid for my dinner because I look gorgeous?'

'Flattered?' he asked hopefully.

'No,' she said. 'Offended.'

'That's what's so hard with women,' the man complained. 'I'd be flattered.'

'Actually,' she told him, 'you wouldn't. You'd feel like a hooker.'

'I don't think you're a hooker!' He looked horrified. 'Hookers don't read *Vanity Fair* in Gabriel's.'

'You have experience with them, then?' she asked.

'No!'

'Maybe if I was a high-class hooker I *would* read *Vanity Fair* in Gabriel's,' she told him. 'You're making all kinds of assumptions.'

'I'm sorry,' he said again. His eyes flickered back to the table, where his dinner companions were glancing covertly at him.

'What did you expect to get out of it?' she asked.

'To tell you the truth, I'm not sure,' he admitted. 'Maybe drinks together, an evening together . . . I don't know.'

'You're with people already,' she pointed out.

'Business colleagues,' he said. 'We concluded a good deal today. Minor celebration.'

She nodded.

'I didn't realise you were from out of town. I should have, though. You look different. Irish?'

She nodded again.

'Come on, then, Irish,' he said. 'Have a drink with me.'

It could be a dangerous situation, she thought. She still wasn't convinced about the concept of someone she didn't know paying for her dinner and asking her out for a drink. But maybe it would be fun. And fun was what she was here to have.

'All right,' she said abruptly. 'Take me somewhere nice.'

❦

'Should we be worried?'

At midnight and with still no response from Iona, Lauren didn't know what to do.

'It's been a hard time for her lately,' said Myles. 'Maybe she just wants to be on her own. She might have got your message but not wanted to call you.'

'For heaven's sake!' Lauren was suddenly angry. 'She knows what it's like when someone doesn't call. She was hysterical over Frank when he didn't come home and she was right. What if something has happened to her?'

'She's OK,' said Flora gently. 'I'd know if she wasn't.'

'Mum, I don't want to knock your spiritual side, but you wouldn't,' said Lauren.

'Trust me,' said Flora.

'Till the morning,' Lauren said.

❦

He brought her to a club on Columbus. The lighting was muted and the music eclectic. They sat in blue suede chairs either side of a black marble table and he bought her a Cosmopolitan. His name was Brandon and he worked in property development. He was interesting to talk to and fun to be with and Iona didn't once think about Frank while she laughed and joked with him about movies they'd both seen or fun things to do in New York or Dublin (he'd never been), and in the moments that they were silent she didn't feel awkward but simply relaxed. It might, she conceded, have had something to do with the second Cosmopolitan. (She was allowing herself two cocktails. She knew that they had nudged her into the silliness she hadn't wanted earlier, but she didn't care. After all, she didn't have to get up in the morning.) But she was too tired for a third. And so she asked Brandon to bring her back to the hotel, slipping her new sandals off her feet as they went outside because they were too high and too new to walk in any more.

He kissed her at the junction of West 57th and Columbus. She kissed him back. She could feel the warmth of his hands through her rose-print dress and the strength of his body as he held her close to him.

God, but it was good to be in someone's arms again. Good to be with someone who didn't know anything about her or Frank or Sally. Because she and Brandon hadn't talked about themselves. Not in any detail. She'd just said that she was over for a break and he'd told her about working for the property company and that had been it. She supposed, as he kissed her, that he was simply looking for someone for the night. Obviously nobody in his group of work colleagues did it for him. But she, Iona, in her summer dress and high heels, had. And he was doing it for her too. Strong and healthy and very alpha-male. She liked it. She liked him. She felt good again.

⌒

Flora lay awake in the guest room bed. She was thinking about Iona and hoping that she'd been right when she told Lauren that she was all right. She was sure that she'd know if she wasn't. But how could she be certain?

⌒

'I'm sorry.' Iona looked at him. 'I can't do this with you.'

Brandon nodded very slowly. 'I understand that. You want to check me out, healthwise. I should do the same with you. But I can tell you that I get tested every year and that my last test was two months ago and that I'm perfectly fine. Also, I insist on using protection.'

301

'It's nothing to do with that,' said Iona. 'I . . . well, I know it's a cliché, but I'm not in that kind of place right now.'

'I always think that some scriptwriter came up with that line and people have copied it ever since because they think it sounds deep,' said Brandon. 'But it's complete bullshit really.'

Iona smiled at him. 'OK. I can't sleep with you because I'm mentally fucked up and it would be a really bad idea.'

'I'm not sure about that,' said Brandon. 'It seems like a really good idea to me right now.'

'Are you going to make an issue of it?' she asked.

'God, of course not!' He looked horrified. 'I want to sleep with you. I know it'd be great.'

'Maybe,' said Iona. 'But I just can't do it.'

Maybe if he'd made an issue of it she wouldn't have kissed him good night. But he didn't and she did and she really, really didn't want to sleep alone.

❧

The following morning, with still no response from Iona's mobile phone, Lauren rang Rental Remedies. Ruth told her that Iona hadn't been in the previous day, which was very unlike her, but that given the stress she'd been under, none of them were all that surprised. All the same, said Ruth, it was bloody inconvenient. They were very busy.

Lauren and Flora decided to go to Iona's house. With no answer to the bell, Lauren let herself in with her spare key. They called out Iona's name and then went through the house, noticing that the wedding picture of Frank and Iona was now on the locker beside the king-size bed, and noticing too that the bed hadn't been made.

'So,' said Lauren tartly to her mother, 'do you still think she's OK?'

'Yes,' said Flora, but she sounded less convinced than previously.

Lauren walked out of the bedroom and into the office. She saw

302

that Iona's computer was still on, although in sleep mode. She jiggled the mouse to start it up again.

The screensaver was another wedding picture – this time Iona and Frank toasting each other on the pale sands of the Caribbean island. Lauren looked at the files on the desktop, realising from the names that most of them were to do with Rental Remedies or Frank's company. She felt bad about looking at Iona's computer, as though she was rummaging around in her sister's desk, but she'd hoped that maybe there'd be something there to give her a clue. She opened the web browser and looked at the history details. She shivered as she noted the coma websites, and then focused on the last site that Iona had visited. The session had been timed out, but it was clear to Lauren that Iona had been looking at flights. The only question was to where.

'Maybe to Spain,' said Flora when Lauren told her about it. 'Perhaps she's at the finca. That'd be just typical, wouldn't it!'

'You'd know by now if she was there,' said Lauren. 'Dad would have called. Or she would.'

Flora and Lauren agreed that Iona could have gone anywhere. And that there was no way to find out where.

'Maybe . . .' Lauren's voice trailed off as she gazed at the screen again. 'Maybe there is.'

'How?'

'Well, Io told me that the garda who came asking questions about Frank also had to go looking for his daughter when she disappeared. Perhaps she can help us.'

'The daughter disappeared!' Flora was astonished. 'When? Where did she go?'

'She didn't really disappear,' said Lauren. 'She just stayed out late. But Sally was really worried and the detective managed to find her. Maybe she can do the same for Iona.'

'She's hardly going to go wherever Iona is and bring her home,' said Flora.

'No, but she might be able to find out if she did take a flight somewhere,' said Lauren.

'Possibly, I suppose.'

'I'll ring her,' said Lauren. 'Anyway, she has a kind of obligation towards Iona. Io found her an apartment to rent. So maybe she'll play ball with us.'

'Iona rented her an apartment?' Flora was even more astonished. 'How – oh, never mind. Give her a call and let's see what she says.'

~

Iona decided to devote her day to culture. She'd done the shopping and now she wanted to see the landmark sites. Given her limited time, she opted for an all-day tour package which whistle-stopped its way around the city and then dropped her back at Central Park, where she sat down at Strawberry Fields and thought about the random nature of the things that happened to people. Then she went back to her hotel, took a swim in the pool and went to bed.

~

'She's in New York.' Siobhán Farrell, feeling as though she'd become a private detective for the Harper and Brannock families, reported back to Lauren at around the same time as Iona was swimming in the pool.

'For God's sake! Why didn't she say anything?'

'I've no idea,' said Siobhán. 'I'm wondering if it has anything to do with the marriage. Whether she's found out something else.'

'Oh, no,' said Lauren. 'It couldn't have. She couldn't have.'

'I'm inclined to agree,' said Siobhán. 'Anyway, she's booked to come home tomorrow. Arriving back at midday.'

'We'll be there,' said Lauren grimly. 'She'll have some explaining to do.'

'Maybe.' Siobhán spoke warily. 'But, you know, I think she's had a really hard time of it. Both of them have. I suppose all wives might wonder at some point about their husbands having an affair.

304

I'm not sure that too many of them discover that they've never been married at all.'

'I don't care,' said Lauren. 'She's scared us all rigid.'

'Sure,' said Siobhán. 'Well, I hope you work it out.'

'Thanks,' said Lauren. 'We will.'

⤙

Iona found it harder to sleep on the return flight. All of the thoughts about Frank and Sally and Jenna which she'd managed to put completely out of her head for the last forty-eight hours now came tumbling back. She knew that the break had been worth it. But it had only been a break. Real life was still waiting for her when she got back.

⤙

It was Flora who spotted her walking through the arrivals doors, wearing the Donna Karan jeans and top that she'd bought in Bloomingdale's. Flora scanned her daughter from top to toe, instantly taking in the fact that she'd lost weight since she'd last seen her. That bastard Harper, she thought furiously. What has he done to her!

Iona thought she was hallucinating when she saw her sister and her mother. She stopped in her tracks and stared at them unbelievingly.

'What the hell d'you think you were doing?' demanded Flora when Iona asked why they were there. 'We were worried sick about you.'

'Why?' asked Iona.

'I called and called,' said Lauren. 'You didn't return any of my messages.'

'I was in New York,' said Iona. 'My mobile isn't triband. It doesn't work there.'

'You shouldn't have disappeared without a word,' said Flora.

'It was only a couple of days,' protested Iona. 'I often don't speak to either of you for weeks on end. Get a grip, for heaven's sake!'

'We were worried,' repeated Lauren. 'We thought . . . we thought . . .'

'What?' asked Iona.

'Well, I'm not sure,' said Lauren. 'But with all this stuff about Frank and everything and you being so upset . . . we didn't know what to think.'

'Look, I'm sorry if I scared you,' said Iona. 'But I needed to be on my own for a while.'

'And did it help?' asked Flora.

Iona thought about her shopping expedition and her tour of the city and her night on the town. She thought about Brandon, who'd bought her dinner and kissed her, who had made her feel like she was part of the human race again, even if only for a few hours.

'Yes,' she said. 'It did.'

Chapter 27

The following morning Iona apologised to Ruth and Garret for disappearing without notice and promised that she'd work extra hard to make up for it.

'Ah, don't worry about it,' said Ruth. 'You're entitled to a bit of down time, Io.'

'Not really,' Iona told her. 'I don't want people feeling sorry for me. My mother came haring over from Spain to check up on me too and I hate thinking that everyone is watching me and making excuses for me.'

'OK, so.' Ruth grinned. 'No more Mizz Nice Gal from me. Any chance you could show apartment six in Waterside this afternoon? It's on my agenda but I'm up to my neck because you pissed off without saying—'

'All right, all right.' Iona made a face at her. 'I'll show it. Everyone's interested in that block, aren't they?'

'Near to the lovely coastal town of Dun Laoghaire,' intoned Ruth. 'Spectacular views over the bay. Walking distance of the Dart and—'

'I know the marketing spin.' Iona grinned.

'Good,' said Ruth. 'At the same time you can drop the keys to his mailbox in to Mr Martinez.'

'He already has keys to his mailbox,' said Iona. 'He got them when he took the apartment.'

'Yes, and he managed to post them into it by mistake,' said Ruth.

'Dirty eejit. How did he do that?'

Ruth shrugged. 'Dunno.'

'So do you want me to show the other apartment later tonight instead?' asked Iona. 'To be sure he's in?'

'Nope,' replied Ruth. 'He's working from home today so he said that if someone was around they'd be able to get him.'

'OK.' Iona didn't mind the idea of heading out to Dun Laoghaire again that afternoon. She liked the chi-chi town when the sun was shining. And on a day like this she could see why the apartments were renting out so easily too, making her job a lot easier. It was actually good to be back at work, and after her unplanned break, she felt less stressed out by it.

❧

Iona pulled in to the car park and met her clients – a couple who were looking for something within an easy commute of the city. She showed them around the apartment and was pleased when they said they'd take it. When they'd gone she walked back into the lobby of the block with the intention of checking that the keys which Ruth had given her actually opened Mr Martinez's mailbox. It's the little things, she said to herself as she held open the door for another resident, that can go horribly wrong and make you look like a fool. She didn't want for him to try out the keys in front of her and discover that they were the wrong ones and think that everyone in Rental Remedies was incompetent.

She stood in front of the bank of mailboxes, looking for the one for apartment 7.

She checked the keys and was relieved to see that they worked. Then her phone beeped with a message and she stood to one side while another resident of the block checked his mail too. Only he wasn't checking his own box. Iona could see that the one he was looking at was, in fact, Siobhán Farrell's, although Siobhán hadn't got around to slipping her name tag on the box yet. He was peering inside, straining to see if there was any mail, while at the same time trying a couple of keys on the lock.

'Excuse me,' she said as she put her phone back in her bag (the message had been from Ruth to remind her about an early-morning meeting the next day). 'Can I help you?' He turned towards her. The first thing she noted about him was that he was very attractive. He had caramel-blond hair and smoke-grey eyes and his face was smooth and chiselled. He wasn't handsome, thought Iona. He was beautiful. Which was different.

'I'm sorry,' he said. 'I seem to have lost my keys.'

'Are you sure you've got the right mailbox?' Even as she spoke the words Iona realised that she was being incredibly stupid in talking to him at all. The beautiful man could be some kind of thief, robbing people's identities or something. Accosting him wasn't a very clever thing to do.

'Right mailbox but wrong keys,' he said easily. 'Don't worry. I must have left them in my office. It's not far away. I can collect them.' He turned away from her and walked out of the building.

Iona could feel her heart thudding in her chest. She'd suddenly felt very vulnerable in the empty lobby with the beautiful man who was lying to her, and she wondered how Siobhán Farrell managed to control her fear when she confronted criminals. But then Siobhán was trained for it. She wasn't.

She pressed the button for the lift and went up to the seventh floor, where she knocked on Mr Martinez's door. Unlike the last time she'd seen him, when he'd been wearing the obligatory suit, he was now dressed casually in a pair of jeans and a loose-fitting T-shirt. His feet were bare and the door to the balcony was open. Working at home obviously meant working to a different rhythm, thought Iona, as she saw the glass of wine on the patio table. For an instant she remembered Brandon Williamson sitting in her room at the Le Parker Meridien, sipping wine, a New York version of Enrique Martinez. A shiver ran along her spine.

'Thank you.' He smiled at her. 'I'm feeling like a complete fool. I don't know what I was thinking.'

'We all do silly things sometimes,' said Iona, pushing the memory of Brandon out of her mind and wondering instead how on earth

309

Enrique Martinez had managed to post his keys into his own mailbox.

'There was a piece of paper sticking out of it.' He read her thoughts. 'And I had the keys in my hand. I tried to pull out the paper and I dropped the keys into the box.'

She smiled. 'Never mind.'

'Do you want to take the other set?' he said. 'In case I do it again?'

She followed him down the stairs to the lobby, where he opened the mailbox and handed her the pair of silver-coloured keys.

'I am not always a stupid tenant,' he told her. 'I am sure you will find that there will be no more problems from me.'

'That's what we're here for, Señor Martinez,' she said. 'To fix problems.'

She glanced towards the entrance door as it opened and smiled as Siobhán Farrell walked in.

'Ah, my neighbour.' Enrique Martinez smiled too. 'We met already.'

'Hi, Enrique,' said Siobhán. 'Are you a client of Iona's too?'

'Yes.' He nodded. 'It is a reunion for the Rental Remedies here, no?'

'I don't usually have meetings in the lobby,' said Iona. Her eyes narrowed. Lauren had explained that it was Siobhán who'd discovered she was in New York. 'But can I have a quick word with you?' She looked apologetically at Enrique Martinez. 'I'm sorry. Do you mind?'

'Not at all,' he said. 'But if you wish to join me for a glass of wine on the balcony later, you are very welcome. Both of you.'

'Thanks,' said Siobhán. 'It's very nice of you, Enrique. But I'm working this evening so I'd better pass on the wine.'

'As you wish.' He nodded at them and began to walk up the stairs.

'Gosh, Siobhán.' Iona's eyes were wide. 'You're only in the place a couple of weeks and you have the hotshot financier drooling over you.'

'He's nice,' said Siobhán. 'I've bumped into him a few times.

The first time he was working on his balcony and a gust of wind blew some papers straight over the divider between us and practically into my lap. I brought them back to him.'

'Quick work,' said Iona. 'Quick work too in finding out that I was in New York and letting everyone know about it.' Her tone was edgy.

'They were worried about you,' said Siobhán gently.

'Yes, but it was my business,' Iona told her. 'You didn't have to give out information to them.'

'Would you rather they worried unnecessarily?'

Iona sighed. 'No. Of course not. It was just . . . I was surprised when they turned up at the airport, that's all. And it jolted me back to reality.'

'You didn't want to come back?'

'Oh, I was happy enough to come home. I was just planning a few more hours to myself.'

'Did it help?' asked Siobhán. 'Running away?'

'I didn't run away,' said Iona sharply. 'It was only a couple of days! I just needed to get away, that's all.'

Siobhán nodded. 'I do understand. And I'm sorry if I messed it up for you.'

'No, you didn't.' Iona smiled wryly. 'Not really. And the truth is that I appreciate you looking after my family when you don't have to. You're a nice person and I've no right to bitch at you.'

'You're not.' Siobhán grinned. 'It's fine. You're going through a tough time.'

'So are you,' said Iona. 'How are things?'

'Not bad. A bit weird being on my own again, but I like the apartment.'

'And, of course, your attractive neighbour!'

Siobhán laughed. 'I'm not interested in him. He's very much not my type.' She looked more seriously at Iona. 'Any change with Frank?'

Iona shook her head. 'No. Not at all. And of course my mother has flown over from Spain on a mission of mercy to see that I'm not slashing my wrists or anything.' She frowned suddenly. 'Do you need to interview her?' she asked. 'I don't know what she can tell you, but as part of your investigation into Frank's potential multiple marriages, which I know you still somehow suspect—'

'I don't need to interview her,' Siobhán interrupted her. 'I've done a lot of investigating, Iona. There doesn't seem to be anyone else.'

Iona swallowed. 'You know, that's a kind of relief. There was a part of me that thought . . . well, he goes to the UK quite a bit. Went to the UK, I mean. I thought maybe . . .' She shivered. 'I'm glad there isn't anyone else.'

'I'm glad too,' said Siobhán. She looked at her watch. 'I'd better go,' she said. 'I'm on a shift later tonight and I need to have a bite to eat and change first.'

'Sure. But before you go . . .' Iona looked at her hesitantly. 'I don't know whether there's an innocent explanation for this or not, but when I arrived today there was a bloke trying to break into your mailbox.'

'What!' Siobhán looked at her in surprise.

'I thought that maybe he was an informer or something,' said Iona. 'I mean, at first I thought he was just breaking in. And then I thought about you being a detective and everything and that you must have informers and stuff and so I thought maybe that was it. Although obviously that doesn't make sense because why would he be snooping around your mailbox? I asked him if I could help, you see, and he implied it was his flat and he'd just forgotten his key.'

'What did he look like?'

Iona described the beautiful man. Siobhán opened her bag and took out a wallet, from which she removed a photograph. 'This him?' she asked.

Iona nodded. 'Who is it?'

'Eddie,' said Siobhán.

'Oh.'

'He must have found out where I was living – maybe trying to guess which apartment was mine by checking out the mailboxes. Eejit!'

312

Iona started to giggle. 'Good job I didn't threaten to report him to the police,' she said.

'Pity you didn't,' said Siobhán. 'I can't imagine how he would've felt if one of the uniformed guys had called around to accuse him of petty theft.'

'He's very attractive,' said Iona after a moment or two.

'Yes,' said Siobhán. 'He is.'

'Do you love him?'

'Hell, I got engaged to him.' Siobhán sighed deeply. 'I must do, mustn't I?'

'He must love you too,' said Iona, 'if he's trying to check your mail.'

'He's an idiot,' said Siobhán, 'and sometimes I think I'm still an idiot for caring about him.'

'Makes two of us idiots, so,' said Iona drily. 'Three if you count Sally.'

⁓

Sally was sitting at a table in the staff room correcting English homework. She was thankful that the summer holidays would begin soon because she was finding it very hard to concentrate. She'd set the girls an essay on the topic 'A Person I Admire' and was wading through pages of praise for a slew of pop stars, interspersed with the occasional essay on the latest hot super-model. She knew that most of the girls in the school were intelligent and hardworking, but she rather wished they admired a greater variety of people than stick-thin celebrities who wore scanty clothes. Although maybe that was because, she thought wryly, she herself was currently madly envious of stick-thin celebrities who could wear scanty clothes. She'd never been stick-thin herself and now, as her pregnancy progressed, she was feeling fatter by the minute. She was scared too, although she didn't really have time to be. Her doctor had been both sympa-thetic and practical and had arranged for her to be seen by a gynaecologist based at the same hospital as Frank, so that at

313

least she didn't have to spend her life shuttling between various medical centres. And then he had given Sally a pep talk about looking after herself, mentally as well as physically and staying positive. It was easy, Sally had thought ruefully, for doctors to talk about staying positive. It was another matter altogether to actually do it.

She'd made an effort, though, by buying herself some new maternity clothes and getting her hair trimmed again before going back to work.

She knew, too, that Jenna had been only partly in favour of her return to the school. Leaving aside the fact that Jenna had never been entirely happy with her position as vice principal anyway, Sally was aware of her daughter's fear that her mother's return would cause people to start taking notice of her again. When Jenna had first returned after the accident, she'd come home tense and irritable because, she told Sally, they were a topic of conversation. The headmistresses, Mrs Lyndon, had said prayers for Frank at morning assembly one morning (although obviously she hadn't mentioned the secret wife!) and everyone kept asking her about the accident.

Sally had told her to be as honest as she wanted, and so Jenna had told the truth, knowing that everyone would find out eventually anyway. The result of that, though, was that girls looked at her curiously, and although her closest friends tried to be understanding, she couldn't help feeling somewhat isolated from them and so didn't hang out with them as much as before. But she agreed with Sally that it was better to be at school and the object of curiosity than to structure all her days around visits to the hospital. Jenna was doing fewer and fewer of these anyway and Sally had no intention of forcing her to visit her father more often. There wasn't any point, especially when she knew that Jenna was still incredibly angry with him. She hoped that her daughter would get over it some day soon, but in the meantime she was prepared to live with it.

As she finished marking an essay her mobile phone rang and she grabbed it from the table in front of her.

'Is it bad news?' She asked the question before the doctor even had time to speak.

'No, Mrs Harper,' he said. 'In some ways it's the contrary. Frank has been displaying some responses to stimulus in a much more positive way than previously. We thought you might like to know that.'

'What kind of responses?' she asked breathlessly. 'Is he talking?'

'Nothing like that yet,' said Dr Carroll. 'But he does seem to be following certain sounds and we're pretty sure that he can understand what people are saying. It's a hopeful sign.'

'Oh.' Sally felt the tears that she'd managed to keep under control all day suddenly spill from her eyes. 'Thank you. Thank you for calling.'

She packed up her things and went out to her car. Jenna rarely came home with her, preferring to hang around with her friends or attend after-hours school activities, but Sally sat in the front seat and phoned her daughter anyway, glad that although the girls weren't allowed to have their phones switched on in class there was no problem in bringing them to school.

'What?' asked Jenna as she answered.

Sally told her of Frank's improvement.

'So what does that mean?' Jenna sounded young and girlish again, instead of abrupt and sullen as she had when she'd answered the phone.

'Well, nothing much at this point, I suppose,' said Sally. 'But it's a good sign and I can't wait to see him tonight.'

'Sure,' said Jenna. 'But you're not supposed to be going to the hospital tonight. It's Iona's turn.'

Sally closed her eyes. 'So it is. I'd forgotten.'

'Maybe if they've rung her too she won't mind if you go.'

'And you?' asked Sally. 'Do you want to come with me?'

Jenna hesitated. Gerry had asked her round to his house that night. His parents, once again, were going to be away. And she hadn't been to bed with him in over a week.

'Tell you what,' said Sally. 'You don't have to come tonight if you've got plans. I'll go and see how things are. You can come tomorrow.'

'No,' said Jenna. 'I'll come.'

'It's great, isn't it?' Sally couldn't keep the hope out of her voice. 'Maybe in a few weeks everything will be back to normal.'

Although, she acknowledged as she started the car and began to drive home, she had no idea what normal was any more.

~

Iona had suggested that Flora and Lauren could both come with her to the hospital that evening after Dr Carroll phoned to tell her about Frank's improved responses.

'How important is this?' she asked him. 'If you think that part of the whole problem is actually his mental state, how much does any of this matter?'

'Well, Iona, we don't know how much is his mental state and how much is purely physical,' said Dr Carroll. 'So it's good to see a positive improvement.'

'If he wakes up now, will there still be real adjustment problems? Will he have lost his memory? Will he know how to do things? Will—'

'There are always problems after trauma,' said Dr Carroll. 'Any sort of trauma, whether it's a head injury or anything else. There's physical trauma and there's mental trauma, and sometimes it's harder to deal with things that have happened to us than to repair the physical damage.'

'I guess you're right about that,' she said.

'But you're doing well too, Iona,' he said.

She laughed shortly. 'If only you knew,' she said.

When she arrived home, the light on her answering machine was blinking. The message was from Sally, asking her if she'd mind if she came along that night because the doctor had told her that Frank was getting better. Iona thought about ringing Sally back and saying that better was entirely relative as far as Frank's condition was concerned, but she didn't. She phoned the other woman and said that she was perfectly welcome to show up, but warned her that Lauren and Flora were going to be there too.

316

'You're lucky,' said Sally. 'You've a good support system behind you.'

'Oh, nonsense,' Iona told her. 'I don't really want them supporting me, asking me questions all the time, telling me what I should be doing with my life. I want to be left alone.'

'I can see your point,' agreed Sally, 'but it's still nice to know that there are people looking out for you.'

'I suppose so,' said Iona shortly. 'Sometimes, though, people meddling in your life is more trouble than it's worth.'

'All the same, it must be nice to have an adult to talk to. Jenna – well, you know what she's like at the moment, and I don't really have anyone else to share it with.'

'Don't you have family or friends?' asked Iona curiously.

Sally explained about her only-child status and the fact that both her parents were dead. 'And I do have a friend, but she lives the other side of the city and I can't keep dumping on her over the phone,' said Sally.

'You can dump on me,' said Iona.

Sally laughed. 'Hardly, if I'm complaining that you exist.'

'I suppose not,' Iona agreed. 'Anyway, I'll see you tonight.'

'Thanks for letting me come,' said Sally.

'Don't be crazy,' said Iona. 'You've more right to be there than me, and you know it.'

⌒

Lauren drove to the hospital, and Iona was happy to be a passenger so that she could let her thoughts wander. She wished that the situation with Frank and his condition wasn't so vague. She hated the uncertainty of it all. But this improvement did make the possibility of his waking up a million times less remote. And the consequences of his waking up a million times closer.

She led the way through the hospital to Frank's room, Flora and Lauren exchanging glances as they followed behind her. When she got to the ICU, Iona said hello to Terri Cooper and to Susan Carpenter, who were both on duty.

317

'An improvement,' Susan said cheerfully. 'You must be pleased.'

Iona nodded. 'Is Sally here yet?' she asked.

'No,' said Susan. 'Is she coming today?'

'Of course,' said Iona. 'She needs to see this for herself.'

'Don't get your hopes up too much,' warned Susan. 'It's not like he's sitting up and watching the telly, you know.'

'I know,' said Iona.

'Did you enjoy your break?' asked Terri. 'You missed a day or two, didn't you?'

Iona looked at her uneasily. 'Did you say anything to Sally about it?'

'Of course not,' said Terri.

'I needed a bit of time,' Iona told her.

'We understand that perfectly,' Terri said.

'But Sally might not. So . . .'

'It's fine, don't worry.' Terri nodded.

Iona walked into the room. Flora, following right behind her, was unable to hold back her gasp of shock at the sight of Frank in the bed, his attractive features flattened out by the lack of expression on a face that was much paler and thinner than she remembered.

'He hasn't been outside in weeks,' Iona said as she sat down. 'You've got to remember that. And of course he's just been lying there too. Hi, Frank,' she added conversationally. 'Mum and Lauren are here too, so mind your manners.'

His head moved slightly and Iona held her breath. He'd never moved at the sound of her voice before. Never.

'And Sally's coming later,' she said. 'So you'll be in deep doo-doo if you actually do arse yourself to wake up.'

'Iona!' Flora sounded shocked. 'You can't talk to him like that.'

'Well how d'you expect me to talk to him?' demanded Iona. 'I've done the sorrowful whispering sort of stuff. I've told him I love him. There's not a lot left.'

The door opened and both Sally and Jenna walked in. Jenna glowered at Iona.

'Hello, Jenna,' she said. 'This is my mother. And my sister.'

318

'I met your sister already.'

'Of course you did. I'd forgotten.' Iona kept her voice steady.

'Hello, Jenna.' Flora got up from her chair. 'I'm really sorry about your dad.'

Jenna swallowed hard.

'It was an awful thing to happen,' said Flora. 'And it's a mess right now. But it will get sorted out, you know.'

'I don't see how,' said Jenna mutinously.

'Things always do work themselves out,' said Flora easily.

'Yeah, right.' Jenna leaned against the wall.

'He moved his head.' Iona looked at Sally. 'Only a little, but he did it.'

'Really?' Sally edged closer to the bed.

'Yeah,' said Iona. 'I told him you were coming and that stopped him in his tracks, though.'

Sally looked surprised and Iona smiled at her. 'Well, if it didn't, it should,' she amended.

Sally smiled faintly too. She leaned over to look at Frank. 'Can you hear me?' she asked.

There was no response from Frank.

'It's me, Sally,' she said. 'Iona told me you moved your head earlier. Can you do it again?'

But there was nothing. Sally's shoulders sagged.

'Hey, I bet it's not like he does it all the time,' said Iona. 'And I wouldn't worry that he's not responding to you right now. After all, his first response was to the doctors, not either of us.'

'That's true,' said Sally.

'So don't feel personally slighted.'

'I wasn't.'

'You were.' Jenna detached herself from her position against the wall and stood beside the bed. 'Hey, Dad, any chance you'd open your eyes for us?'

All of the women watched intently, but Frank remained still. Jenna walked out of the room, saying that she was going to get a drink.

'It's a bit of a battle.' Iona looked up at her mother and sister.

319

'To see which of us he responds to the most. Thing is, he hasn't actually responded to any of us. For a while I thought there was another woman.'

'Iona!' Lauren looked horrified.

'Well, it was always a possibility,' said Iona. 'Another woman who really matters. The one who'll unlock his mind for us.'

'God, I hope not,' said Flora.

'Actually, the police don't think so,' Sally told them. 'Siobhán Farrell says they've done a lot of investigating and so far nothing has turned up. She even went to Sligo to check out the tenants there.'

Iona froze. Siobhán had said she didn't think there was another woman, but she hadn't told her anything at all about going to Sligo.

'It's fine, there's no problem with them,' said Sally hastily. 'I've actually met them, they're locals building their own house. They've moved back there from Dublin.'

'Trouble is, no matter what Siobhán says, it wouldn't really surprise me if someone else turned up,' said Iona.

'Realistically I don't think so,' Sally said. 'I mean, he just didn't have the time, did he?'

They both looked at Frank.

'Hope not,' said Iona as Jenna walked back into the room with a bottle of flavoured water.

'Pity he didn't manage to do something about the tenancy agreement before the accident.' Sally sighed. 'It was originally for a year while the family renting it build their own place. But they've run into planning permission problems and now they're looking for an extension to the lease while they sort things out.'

'That's straightforward enough,' said Iona. 'Who's looking after it for you?'

'Well, Frank did it all, that's the thing. They hadn't been too worried because they'd heard about the accident, but then when Siobhán turned up they got into a flap about the renewal and they phoned me last night. I haven't a clue what I'm supposed to do about it. I was going to ring Frank's accountant today.'

320

'I'll look after it if you like,' offered Iona. 'It's the one thing I know about.'

'Will you?' Sally looked at her hopefully. 'That'd be a relief.'

'Mum!' Jenna exclaimed. 'You can't have her looking at stuff.'

'Why not?' asked Sally.

'I don't mind.' Iona shrugged. 'We don't want everything to fall into a complete mess. Do we?' She addressed her last remark to Frank.

They sat around the bed in silence, nobody able to think of anything to say either to each other or to Frank. Eventually Flora got up.

'Jenna, will you show me where the drinks machine is?' she asked.

Jenna shrugged in agreement.

'Think I'll get something too,' said Lauren.

The three of them walked out of the room, leaving Iona and Sally alone.

'I saw Siobhán Farrell,' said Iona eventually. 'She never said anything about going to Sligo.'

'Why did you see her?' Sally looked anxious.

'Nothing to do with this,' said Iona.

'Really?'

'Yes.' Iona hesitated and then laughed shortly. 'I rented her an apartment.'

'What?' Sally was surprised. 'I thought she was engaged and living with her fiancé.'

'She was.' Iona told Sally about Eddie's unfaithfulness.

'And she felt she had to move out?'

'You know, I get the impression that there was slightly more to it,' said Iona. 'Though I'm not sure what exactly. Anyway, she was very upset. I got her an apartment in Dun Laoghaire.'

'Are men always bastards?' Sally looked at Frank as she spoke.

'I don't think so,' said Iona. 'I sure hope not.'

'She's a nice girl,' said Sally.

'He's a right hunk,' Iona added.

'How d'you know that?'

Iona explained about meeting Eddie at the apartment block.

'That's hopeful,' said Sally. 'At least he cares.'

'Oh, Sally, Frank cared too,' said Iona. 'But he still managed to divide his time between both of us.'

Sally winced.

'I was just thinking,' said Iona idly. 'How about you and me and Siobhán get together?'

'What for?'

'A night out,' said Iona. 'Girl talk. You know.'

'Iona, she's a bloody detective. You can't just chat with a detective. Particularly one who's trying to build a case against our husband.'

Iona giggled.

'What?'

'Our husband?'

Sally smiled too, a wobbly smile. 'You know what I mean,' she said.

'Sure. But we deserve a night off,' said Iona. 'You and me, always coming in here to be with him – and today rushing in because there was some hope . . . we need to do normal things.'

'I'm not much fun these days,' said Sally.

'And I'm not either, mostly,' said Iona. 'But I know I can be. And I don't think it's right for us to sit around being mournful. It's not what Frank would want either. You know that, Sally. And I thought – well, given that Siobhán's going through a break-up, maybe she needs some fun too.'

'Well . . . OK,' said Sally slowly. 'Why not?'

'I'll phone Siobhán and sort it,' said Iona.

The door opened and Jenna, Flora and Lauren returned.

'Any change?' asked Lauren.

Both Sally and Iona shook their heads. And Frank's eyes remained closed.

～

He wondered if he was dead. He wondered this because he kept hearing strange noises and because suddenly he was catapulted into situations which seemed familiar to him only he couldn't remember how. It was very disconcerting, as if he was stepping in and out of a time machine. Maybe that was what happened when you were dead, he thought. Maybe you were sent back over and over again to relive the parts of your life that you'd messed up. Only that would be a complete nonsense, wouldn't it? After all, how would you know you'd messed things up until afterwards? And if you didn't know what was going to happen in the future, how could you stop yourself from doing the same wrong thing once again? He sighed. It was all too complicated for him. He wanted to rest. He wanted to rid himself of the thoughts and people who crowded into his head and then left so abruptly. He wanted to sleep for a month.

But he couldn't. Because he had to deal with the situation he was in now. It was difficult, but he had to do it. He had to tell her that he was sorry, that he'd made a terrible mistake, that he couldn't come to the event with her. Of course he hadn't meant to say yes to her invitation. It had come out of the blue and he'd been surprised by it and he'd just said yes. And now she was looking at him with a mixture of apprehension and pleasure in her eyes.

But why had he agreed to go with her? It wasn't as though he were a free agent. It wasn't as though he could actually start dating the girl. He frowned. What the hell was her name again? She was a pretty little thing, slight and gamine and with a wicked grin. She reminded him a little of Marion, but not at all of Sally.

Sally, he thought suddenly. That was his wife's name. It had been bugging him for a while, but now he remembered again. Sally of the auburn hair and the porcelain skin. Sally wouldn't be very pleased if he started accepting invitations from strange women to go to parties. Sally would be pissed off with him, in fact. Actually, though, wasn't Sally pissed off with him already? Hadn't he heard her say loads of times that she couldn't take much more of this, that she was exhausted, that she needed him to come back and devote time to his family? He wasn't sure exactly what her problem was. Although . . . it was work, wasn't

323

it? He wanted to set up a new company and Sally wasn't happy because he'd suggested selling their house and moving out of the city. She'd wanted him to sell the house in Sligo instead. But he couldn't do that. Sally didn't understand that he couldn't sell the Sligo house because if Christine came back that was where she'd go first. Not that he expected her to come back, or even wanted her to come back, but still . . .

Sally was angry too, because moving house made it more difficult for her to get to work. She'd been incandescent with rage when he'd suggested that maybe it was time for her to give it up for a while, that if she was at home perhaps she'd get pregnant again, which was what they both wanted. She'd said that a big family was what he had wanted – she was happy with one child. And that losing the second baby had been very difficult for her and that she wasn't sure whether she wanted to go through all that again.

It was strange, he thought, how time changed people. How living together changed people. He'd never before understood how Christine could seem like one person to Derek when he knew her first but someone else completely when he'd brought her back to Sligo. Now he was beginning to feel as though the Sally he'd fallen in love with was a different person altogether. And yet, he loved her. He knew he would always love her. She said that she loved him too. But he wanted her to need him.

The thing was, she didn't. She could walk out if she wanted, despite the fact that he'd married her so that she couldn't ever walk out. Only times had changed. It wasn't such a big deal any more. You couldn't force people to stay with you if they didn't want to. And Sally wouldn't walk out by herself, he knew that. Sally wasn't Christine. She'd take Jenna with her and leave him on his own. At the thought of being on his own he began to shiver. He couldn't let that happen. He really couldn't. He still loved her but he was angry with her for making him feel suddenly vulnerable. She told him that she couldn't constantly massage his ego and tell him that things didn't matter when they did. He asked her what sort of things. She talked about his mood swings, his irritation with her, the fact that he didn't take her into account when he was planning things. She thought that maybe he'd outgrown her and outgrown marriage. He hadn't realised she'd felt like that. He told her that she was being silly and that he loved her. But he wasn't entirely sure that she believed him.

He was still feeling bruised and angry when he met . . . the girl. And she was so sweet and so nice that he couldn't help saying yes to her invitation. And so now he was in the ballroom of a hotel in Dublin with a girl he didn't know, listening to a terrible DJ playing songs of the seventies. She was smiling at him, leaning forward so that he could see her pert breasts underneath the filmy silver-grey dress she was wearing. She didn't make him feel bruised or angry. When she looked at him with her blackberry eyes she made him feel wanted and loved. But guilty. Because he shouldn't be here with her. Even though she was grabbing him by the hand and leading him on to the dance floor because the DJ was playing 'Manic Monday' and she said it was one of her favourite songs. And suddenly they were back in her house and the filmy dress was on the floor by the bed and she was smiling at him again and he wanted to be with her and make it good for her because she'd made it good for him. So he pushed the guilty feelings to the back of his mind and he smiled too.

∽

'He's smiling,' said Sally suddenly. She stared at Frank. 'Omigod, he really is.'

The other women stared at him too.

'Hey, Frank!' Iona took him by the hand. 'Can you hear me?'

The smile suddenly left his face and it smoothed into an expressionless mask again. She dropped his hand and it fell on to the covers.

'He was thinking about something,' said Sally.

'Maybe it was you,' suggested Iona. 'Or Jenna.' Her glance

flickered towards the teenage girl, who was looking at Frank with a mixture of hope and despair.

'Probably pizza,' said Jenna abruptly as she stared intently at her father. 'Or ice cream. Food always makes him smile.'

Chapter 28

As soon as she received it in the post, Iona updated the tenancy agreement and returned it to Sally. Then she phoned Siobhán Farrell and asked the detective if she'd like to meet up with them for something to eat.

'Why?' asked Siobhán suspiciously. 'What's happened?'

'Nothing.' Iona told her about visiting Frank and her sudden notion that it would be good for them all to get together. 'We can talk about him if you like,' Iona said. 'If you've any other questions you want to ask us. But to be honest, we just want to go out.'

'You and Sally hate each other,' said Siobhán.

'No we don't.' Iona realised that she must sound crazy to Siobhán now. After all, she'd been white-hot with rage over Sally a few weeks earlier. But there was no point in raging any more. 'We've had to accept each other,' she told Siobhán. 'And . . . well, I kind of like her.'

'Really?' Siobhán was sceptical.

'Yes, really,' said Iona. 'Look, in the whole scheme of things it's Frank who's the bad guy. Not Sally or me. Or Jenna.'

'Well . . .' Siobhán was doubtful about it all. But, she told herself as she tapped her pencil on the pad in front of her, meeting the Harper wives in a social situation might not be a bad idea. As far as she was concerned she'd completed her work on the case, but she never knew what else might turn up. 'What had you got in mind?' she asked.

'Meeting somewhere in Dun Laoghaire,' said Iona promptly.

'It's handy enough for us all. You live there, Sally can get the Dart from Bray and I can get one from Connolly. Everything still OK with the apartment?'

'Great,' said Siobhán. 'It's a nice block.'

'Good. And everything OK with you?'

Siobhán hesitated. 'I'm fine,' she said firmly. 'Just fine.'

'So.' Iona sounded definite. 'How does the weekend suit you?'

'I'm off Friday,' said Siobhán.

'Friday it is. I'll let Sally know. Any suggestions?'

Siobhán suggested a recently opened bar and restaurant near the seafront and Iona agreed.

'Around seven,' she said. 'See you then.'

∽

Siobhán ended the call and put her mobile back in her pocket. She gazed unseeingly at the computer screen in front of her. She really wasn't sure why she'd accepted the invitation to meet up with Sally and Iona. She supposed she could justify it because of the case, although she'd done as much work on it as she could without actually being able to interview Frank Harper himself. There probably wasn't any new information that his wives could give her. Going out with the two main witnesses wasn't exactly professional. Siobhán liked both of them, but she had to keep her wits about her no matter how much she thought the case was closed. She really didn't want to go down in station folklore as the detective who was conned in the bigamy case.

But still . . . she'd done everything possible to check out Frank. His prints had come back negative. Nobody had heard of him in the UK. The tenancy in Sligo had turned out to be OK, and in fact she'd quite enjoyed the drive to the north-west and her meeting with Frank's tenants.

'A lovely man,' Sorcha Sheerin had told her. 'Really gentle and kind. My parents knew the family, of course.'

Siobhán had questioned Sorcha and her husband about the Harpers, although the information she received had tied in with everything she'd already found out about Frank and his family. That Christine and Derek Harper had lived in the area, that they hadn't been married, only nobody had known that at the time. That Christine had left Derek with the child. That Derek had died around sixteen years ago.

Interesting, she thought, that Derek hadn't married Christine. It must have been hard to raise a child on his own back in the sixties and seventies, especially as an unmarried father. That just didn't happen in Ireland back then. She wondered what sort of a father Derek had been.

The sound of the office phone ringing jolted her out of her reverie.

'Siobhán Farrell,' she said.

'Hello, Siobhán,' said Eddie.

She groaned softly. She didn't want to talk to Eddie right now. 'What?' she asked.

'I was just checking on you,' he said. 'To see how you were.'

'I'm fine,' she told him.

'I'm not,' said Eddie.

'What d'you mean?' Her heart skipped a beat. What if the tests had been wrong? What if Eddie had contracted an STD in Boston after all?

'I miss you, is what I mean,' said Eddie.

Her heart slowed down again.

'C'mon, Siobhán. Forgive and forget.'

'I'm not ready yet.'

'Are you still wearing my ring?' asked Eddie.

She glanced down at her left hand. 'Yes.'

'Do you still love me?'

'I'm not going to have this conversation right now,' she said. 'Oh, Eddie, by the way . . .'

'What?'

'Don't prowl around my mailbox any more.'

'Huh?' But she heard the tone of discomfiture in his voice.

'I'm a detective,' she told him. 'I detect. It's my job to know stuff like that.'

'I was just—'

'I don't care what you were doing,' she said. 'Don't do it again.'

Eddie gritted his teeth. 'OK,' he said.

'Eddie?'

'Yes?'

'I don't not love you.'

'Jeez, Siobhán.' His tone was dry. 'That makes me feel a whole heap better all right.'

She put down the receiver and stared at the computer screen again. Then the phone rang for a second time. I hope it's something nice and ordinary like a murder, she thought as she picked it up, I've had enough of family drama for a while.

∽

Sally was in the staff room, on the phone to Richard Moran, Frank's accountant. He'd called to say that they were going to have to make new arrangements about the business. Frank was clearly going to be incapacitated for some time. As a director, Sally was empowered to make decisions on its future.

'Don't you need Frank to sign things?' she asked.

'Not the way it's all put together,' said Richard. 'You can do it.'

'Is it worth anything?' asked Sally. 'Are there buyers?'

'Yes and yes,' said Richard. 'Can you come into the office to talk about it?'

'As soon as the school holidays start,' said Sally. 'I can't take time off during the day at the moment.'

'OK,' said Richard. 'We can more or less keep things going as they are in the short term. But there are a number of new installations that Frank was going to work on. If they're to get done you really have to let someone else take over.'

'Can I appoint someone?' Sally wished she had the faintest clue about business.

'You need someone with skills, Sally,' said Richard. 'It's not like just picking a name out of the phone book.'

'I know that.' She was annoyed at how patronising he suddenly sounded. 'I'll give you a call next week and set something up.'

She slid her phone back into her bag and poured herself a cup of tea, then sat down in one of the less than comfortable armchairs. She wondered whether the head had deliberately bought uncomfortable chairs so that the staff wouldn't be tempted to stay in the staff room for too long. She sipped her tea. She had a free period now which she intended to use to mark up the homework of her third-year class. But first she was going to chill out for a few minutes. She was finding that keeping her concentration for a full lesson period was difficult. Sometimes her mind wandered on to Frank's condition, but more and more it was turning to her own. Her pregnancy was now more obvious. And she was beginning to think more about the implications of having the baby while Frank was still in hospital. She hoped it wouldn't come to that. But even though there'd been the so-called breakthrough when he'd seemed to respond to voices, it hadn't meant all that much in the end. And he hadn't responded to her voice anyway. Bastard!

She drained her tea and picked up an exercise book.

'Am I interrupting?' Marsha Tyndall sat down beside her and Sally stifled an irritated sigh. She put down the book and looked at the geography teacher instead.

'What's up, Marsha?' she asked.

'I just wanted a quick word with you,' said Marsha. 'It's about Jenna.'

Sally's eyes darkened. 'What about her?'

'I've got to tell you that she's being really disruptive in class,' said Marsha. 'I've been cutting her some slack because of all this stuff with . . . with her dad, but honestly, Sally, I've had as much as I can take from her.'

'How disruptive?' asked Sally.

'Not listening. Talking. Making comments.' Marsha shrugged. 'I gave her extra homework but she ignored it. She seems to have fallen out with her friend Sam, too. They were at it hammer and tongs in the cloakroom earlier this week. Now Jenna's hanging around with Aline Keogh and that set and you know what they're like! It's all boys and make-up and a complete lack of interest in their work.'

'Shit,' said Sally.

'Sorry to have to break it to you,' said Marsha sympathetically. 'I'm sure she's just going through a bad patch. You know what they're like.'

'Oh, of course I do,' said Sally. 'And she was already going through a bad patch before her dad's accident. Though at least then she had the decency to do her homework.'

Marsha smiled. 'She's a good girl really and I don't want to see her going down the wrong track.'

'Hopefully she won't,' said Sally. 'I'll have a talk with her. I'm not happy about her taking up with Aline.'

'If she'd been a bit disruptive but still pally with Sam I wouldn't have said anything,' Marsha told her. 'But Aline . . . well, if that girl doesn't get into serious trouble before she leaves school, I'll eat my hat.'

Sally rubbed the back of her neck. 'I know. I just hope she won't drag Jenna down with her. Thanks for telling me.' She picked up the exercise book again, even though she knew that just at that moment she wouldn't be able to get her head around geometry.

❧

It was searingly hot and Frank was very grateful for the air-conditioning in the rented Ford. He glanced at the girl beside him who was gunning it along the motorway towards the costal town of Javea. Her parents lived in Javea and he was going to meet them.

Why, he wondered, why am I going to meet her parents? If this is a business call I don't have my gear with me. And why on earth am I in Spain anyway? He knew that he was in Spain – they'd just passed a road sign pointing them in the direction of Benidorm. He'd gone to Benidorm with a few of his mates one year. It had been a sun, sand and sex holiday, although less sexual adventuring for him than anyone else. He hadn't really liked the concept of the one-night stand and so he'd found one girl and she'd been his holiday romance, even though both of them knew it wasn't going to last.

It wasn't this girl, though. He frowned. He'd married this one. He remembered now. He'd married her very recently on the island. She'd come out to him on a boat. And he hadn't been able to remember her name. He thought it was Sally but he was convinced that Sally was someone else. And yet whenever he said the name in his mind, it seemed right to him. Frank and Sally seemed to go with each other perfectly.

'Nervous?' She glanced towards him, her eyes full of mischief.

'Why would I be nervous?' he asked.

'Meeting the parents,' she said. 'Big deal. Your first time.'

Meeting the parents! Flipping heck, he thought. He didn't want to meet her parents when he couldn't even remember her name. He frowned again. He'd done this already. He knew he had. He'd met her parents before and he was sure that they'd called her Sally too. So maybe, since he was clearly getting something horribly wrong, the best thing to do was just play along with her and say nothing.

'They'll love you,' she told him.

'I hope so.'

'Oh, absolutely. And you'll love the finca. Some day I want to buy it from them and move there myself.' She chuckled. 'Well . . . maybe. Now that we're married you might have different ideas.'

'A finca sounds good.'

'We can grow our own olives. Oranges too.'

He didn't think she was the orange-growing type.

She laughed out loud. 'Oh, Frank, the expression on your face! Don't worry, honey. I'm not about to turn into a dash-for-the-country person. I'm a city girl. If we ever move to Spain I want to live in an apartment in Madrid or Barcelona.'

'Watch out for that . . . lorry!'

She gestured rudely at the driver as the oil tanker overtook her. Then she pressed her foot on the accelerator to catch him up.

'Don't,' he said.

'Why not?'

'No point,' he told her. 'I do a lot of driving now and the best thing is to stay cool on the road. Don't let anyone aggravate you.'

'Is that your philosophy?' She eased off on the speed.

'Absolutely.'

'All right then.'

They drove in silence. She was a good driver, he thought, but too aggressive. She needed to chill out. He wished he felt a little more chilled out himself. He couldn't help feeling as though something terrible was about to happen. That was why he'd got so jumpy when she'd speeded up.

'Our turn,' she said eventually.

She'd said it was a finca, and so he'd imagined a run-down shack set in the middle of arid land and surrounded by a few straggly olive trees. But this house was beautifully renovated and clearly well maintained. The walls were white but the roof was made of blue tiles, which, the girl told him, was typically Valencian. And on the other side of the short driveway he could see clusters of round fruit on the lush olive trees. Behind the house the mountains scraped the blue sky with purple tips.

'Palmyra,' she said as she hopped out of the car. 'Not very original, but who cares.'

The door of the finca opened and a tall woman walked out. He could see the resemblance right away.

'Iona!' she cried. 'How lovely to see you.'

Iona! He remembered now. How could he have forgotten? And yet . . . if she was Iona and he was married to her . . . then why was he so sure that he was married to someone called Sally?

Chapter 29

Siobhán arrived at the bar first. She wanted to see whether Sally and Iona turned up together or whether they came separately, so she got there fifteen minutes early. She sat down at one of the outside tables because the day had been another glorious one and the evening air was balmy. She ordered a glass of wine and watched as people strolled along the promenade, while in the background a cluster of small boats skimmed across the blue-green water of the Irish Sea.

She'd drunk about a quarter of the glass when Sally arrived, looking slightly breathless, her hair mussed by the evening breeze. Siobhán raised her hand in greeting.

'Hello.' Sally sat down beside her. 'Sorry I'm late.'

'Not really,' said Siobhán. 'Five minutes.'

'I hate that Irish thing about always being late,' said Sally. 'I don't like unpunctuality but I missed the train I meant to take. Jenna and I . . . well, it doesn't matter.' She opened her bag, took out a wide-toothed comb and ran it through her hair. 'I'm sorry. This is rude. I should go to a bathroom to do this.'

'You're fine,' said Siobhán. 'Would you like a drink?'

'Water.' Sally unconsciously touched her swelling stomach. 'But make it sparkling.'

Siobhán ordered a water and glanced at her watch. 'Iona really is late,' she said.

'It was her turn to visit Frank,' said Sally. 'She'll have been to the hospital first.'

'Oh.'

Sally's jaw tightened. 'Maybe something happened. Maybe he woke up. Perhaps I should give her a call.'

'I'm pretty sure she'd call you if he woke up,' said Siobhán.

'You think?'

'You don't?'

Sally put her comb back in her bag. 'Of course she'd call,' she said, though there was a hint of doubt in her mind. 'We promised each other.'

'Well then,' said Siobhán. 'She's probably just been delayed.'

'I know.' Sally took a sip of the water which had just been placed in front of her. She sighed. 'It's awful suspecting her all the time. Feeling as though she might have some kind of edge.'

'I rather think that she believes you have the edge.'

Sally laughed shortly. 'I don't think so.'

'Why not? He's married to you, after all.'

'But he met her afterwards,' said Sally wryly.

'It must be very difficult,' said Siobhán.

'It's impossible,' Sally stated. 'But we still have to get on with it. And . . .' she half smiled, 'obviously nothing has happened because here she is.'

Iona waved as she walked rapidly towards them.

'I'm so sorry,' she said as she arrived and pulled back a chair. 'The phone rang just as I was leaving. My mother. Nagging. Nothing important.'

'Sally thought that maybe something had happened with Frank,' said Siobhán, 'and that that had delayed you at the hospital.'

'I didn't go to the hospital.' Iona looked at them from her dark eyes. 'I had to show an apartment at five and I wouldn't have had time to get home and change and come out.'

'So nobody's been in all day!' Sally looked horrified.

'Sally, much as I hate to say this, he probably hasn't noticed,' said Iona.

'I know. But . . . I would have gone,' said Sally.

'And then *you'd* never have got here. Be reasonable.' Iona shrugged and stopped the passing waitress, ordering a Bacardi and Coke. 'Diet Coke,' she amended. 'I don't like the other stuff.'

'Maybe today would have been the day,' said Sally. 'And now neither of us has been there.'

'Sally, if anything had changed they would have called us,' said Iona. 'And I know you have your mobile on all the time. Nobody called. It made no difference the last time I didn't call in either.'

Sally looked at her shrewdly. 'When you were out of touch?'

'How did you know about that?' asked Iona.

'Your sister rang me asking about you.'

'For heaven's sake!' Iona was angry that Lauren hadn't told her about contacting Sally. She hadn't wanted Sally to know about her being away at all.

'I was going to check whether you'd turned up at the hospital. But I didn't. And then, of course, there was all that commotion about him responding to sounds. So it kind of went out of my head.'

'It's not important.'

'Where were you?' asked Sally.

Iona sighed. 'I needed a break,' she said. 'It was all getting to me.'

'Where did you go?'

Iona explained about the New York trip while Sally listened in amazement.

'That's why I'm so surprised about you and Frank,' she told Iona. 'You're different to me. You do impulsive things. I don't. And Frank wasn't very impulsive himself.'

'Hey, Frank couldn't afford to be impulsive,' said Iona. 'Otherwise he'd have made a mistake and the whole thing would've gone pear-shaped.'

Sally nodded thoughtfully. 'I suppose, when you think about it, it was always going to be a chance thing that got him found out.'

'That's the way of it.' Siobhán added her voice to the conversation. 'In criminal cases it's always a small thing that breaks it.'

Sally and Iona looked at her.

'Frank's not a criminal,' said Sally evenly.

337

'I – yes, well, not exactly.' Siobhán wished she'd kept her mouth shut.

The three of them sat in silence.

'Oh, look, don't worry about it,' said Iona. 'We didn't come here to rake over issues about Frank. We're just socialising.'

'Perhaps you should have picked other people to socialise with,' remarked Siobhán. 'After all, we only know each other because of Frank.'

'Yes. I know.' Iona's shoulders sagged. 'I guess this was incredibly stupid.'

'No,' said Sally. 'It's not really. It's easier to be together because we all know about Frank. We should just talk about someone . . . something else instead.'

'OK,' said Iona. 'No Frank talk. Let's discuss . . . I don't know . . . world peace?'

The other women chuckled.

'Well then,' said Iona, 'since world peace isn't on the agenda, have you two any other suggestions?'

'Um, no,' said Sally. 'But you must have something, Siobhán. Any juicy scandals?'

'I don't do scandals,' said Siobhán. 'I investigate crime.'

'Yeah, but there must surely be something scandalous going on,' Iona said hopefully. 'Any cabinet ministers involved in dodgy deals?'

Siobhán laughed. 'I don't know.'

'Jeez.' Iona grinned. 'I didn't realise we lived in such a crime-free state. To read the papers you'd think that there's one committed every second. D'you ever read Carl O'Connor in the evening paper? You'd swear the place was falling down around our ears if you believed him.'

'Don't get me started on O'Connor,' said Siobhán.

'Siobhán!' Sally was intrigued by the vehemence in the detective's voice. 'Why? What has he done?'

'Oh, nothing.' Siobhán wished she hadn't said anything about Carl. 'He lives in the same apartment block as Eddie, that's all. I used to see him regularly and he always had a go at me because he has a thing about the police. And me in particular.'

Sally and Iona stared at her.

'What sort of thing?'

'I don't think he's good with women in authority,' she said quickly.

'Why?' Iona asked.

'It's just the way he is,' said Siobhán. 'And then he tries to cover it up by being nice once or twice . . .'

This time Iona and Sally exchanged glances.

'How is he nice sometimes?' asked Sally.

'What's that got to do with anything?'

'Humour us,' suggested Iona. 'Tell us.'

Siobhán closed her eyes as the humiliation of being locked out of her apartment in her basque and boxers washed over her again. Along with the feeling of despair about her relationship with Eddie and where it had suddenly ended up.

'Hey, Siobhán, are you OK?' Iona sounded anxious.

Siobhán squeezed her eyes tighter, then opened them again.

'Fine,' she said.

'Look, sorry if talking about him actually upsets you,' said Iona. 'I didn't think he mattered to you.'

'He doesn't matter, of course he doesn't,' said Siobhán quickly. 'It was just . . .' She broke off. Iona and Sally felt uncomfortable as they watched her struggle to get control of herself. Neither of them had ever seen Siobhán at a loss for words, but she was clearly distressed now.

'Don't worry,' said Sally. 'We'll talk about something else.'

'No.' Siobhán swallowed hard. 'No. Actually this is something I'd quite like to talk about. I haven't . . . There's no one to talk to.'

'No problem talking to us,' said Iona. 'I mean, we're in no position to pick holes in anyone else's life.'

'You know a bit already,' said Siobhán. 'You found me the apartment.'

'Crikey!' Sally looked at Siobhán, her eyes wide. 'Were you having a bit on the side with the journo and your fiancé found out?'

Siobhán giggled weakly. 'No. I guess you both know that my boyfriend had a bit of a fling.' She looked at Iona who blushed slightly.

Siobhán knew about human nature, thought Iona. She'd guessed she wouldn't have been able to keep it to herself.

'Well,' Siobhán continued, 'it wasn't a fling exactly.' She filled in the details of Eddie's night at Peter Murtaugh's. 'I just didn't even think for a second that he'd do something like that,' she said. 'And I don't know whether he was ever going to tell me.'

Sally frowned. 'But what's this got to do with the journalist?' she asked.

'Ah well . . .' Siobhán filled them in. Iona tried to keep a straight face, but as she pictured the other girl standing in the corridor in her underwear she couldn't help but giggle. Suddenly Sally was giggling too and Siobhán, who'd been close to tears telling them, smiled faintly.

'I know it's not funny,' said Iona. 'I do really. But, well, in your bra and knickers in front of a journalist!'

'If only it had just been a simple bra and knickers combo,' said Siobhán ruefully. 'But it was a really raunchy outfit.'

'Why are men such fools?' demanded Sally. 'What is it about them that makes them be so – so – shitty?'

'I dunno.' Iona sighed. 'I didn't think Frank was shitty.'

'Of course you didn't, neither did I,' said Sally hotly. 'But the bottom line is that he was. And so was Siobhán's bloke. And so's the journalist . . .'

'Actually, I suppose he wasn't in the end,' said Siobhán.

'He made fun of you,' protested Sally.

'Yeah, but I was probably a comic figure,' admitted Siobhán wryly. 'And, well, I hate to admit it, but I guess he was kinda nice to me really. He might have made fun of me, but to be honest it wasn't malicious.'

'Even so.' Sally was still indignant.

'Maybe it's in their nature.' Iona sipped the Bacardi which the waitress had placed in front of her a few minutes earlier. 'I mean, maybe they just can't help themselves. If you read magazines and stuff they're always telling us how men are led by their dicks.'

'Iona!'

'Well, it's true,' she said hotly. 'Frank came after me because . . . sorry to say this, Sally . . . but because we were great in bed.'

'Actually, Frank and I had no problems in that department,' said Sally tightly. 'We got along very well together sexually.' Her eyes narrowed. 'He didn't say anything different, did he? He didn't say that I didn't do it for him any more?'

'Sally, I didn't know you existed. He never mentioned you. And I suppose I just assumed . . .'

'Why should you assume that?' demanded Sally. 'I'm damn well pregnant, aren't I?'

'Yes, but that's just sex. It doesn't have to be good sex,' said Iona.

'Frank and I had great sex!' cried Sally.

Siobhán and Iona shot glances at the nearby tables whose occupants had turned towards them at the sound of Sally's raised voice.

'Great sex,' she repeated more quietly. 'Always.'

Iona made a face. 'I thought it was probably because of the sex,' she said unevenly. 'I know you're pregnant, Sally, but . . . well . . . you're older than me, and I suppose . . .'

'Great,' said Sally bitterly. 'You're thinking that he shagged me once in the past year and only out of sympathy for an old hag and unfortunately knocked me up.'

'God, no. Of course not.' Iona was rattled.

'We had a great sex life, and every time he came home he made love to me, which means that he slept with me directly after sleeping with you.'

'And he slept with me directly after sleeping with you,' said Iona flatly. 'Christ. Maybe we should get ourselves checked out medically too.'

'Not on my account,' snapped Sally. 'I was monogamous in my relationship with him.'

'Yeah, well, so was I!'

341

'I'm glad for you both,' said Siobhán drily. 'I, too, was monogamous but it didn't do me and Eddie any good.'

'Oh, Siobhán, I'm sorry.' Iona looked at her penitently. 'You really do have something to worry about on the health side of things, and we – we're bickering over who was a better lover.'

Siobhán shrugged. 'Actually I don't have anything to worry about,' she said. 'Like I told you, Eddie and I didn't sleep together after he came back. So that's not the issue. What is the issue is whether I should even consider going back to him.'

'Thing is, Siobhán,' said Sally, 'you don't have to forgive and forget. You're only engaged to him, not married to him, so you didn't make any "till death us do part" promises. You can walk away.'

'But I don't want to walk away,' protested Siobhán. 'At least . . . in my head it was "till death us do part" already. And I thought he believed that too. We were planning to get married. It was supposed to be for ever. You can't say that it didn't matter just because we hadn't actually made it up the aisle. And even though I'm angry and feel betrayed and hurt and all that sort of stuff, I can't just forget about it even though most of me says I should.'

'I tried to walk away from the Frank situation,' said Iona. 'I didn't go to the hospital. I sat at home and cried instead.'

Sally looked uneasily at her. 'That wasn't my fault.'

'I know, I know,' said Iona. 'You did your good deed and told me I could come and see Frank after all.'

'If you're going to snipe at me all the time then I don't think there's much point to all of this,' said Sally. 'It was your idea for us to meet up and it was supposed to be a social thing, but all you've done is whinge.'

Iona sighed deeply. 'I know. I'm sorry. It's just – well, you two actually have real relationships. You're married, Sally. Siobhán was – is – engaged. I'm not anything.'

'We're supposed to be talking about other things,' said Sally firmly. 'Rehashing it over and over isn't doing us any good. Siobhán, please come up with something awful and gruesome to cheer us up – like a mad serial killer on the loose in Bray.'

Siobhán smiled faintly. 'There's an ID scam going on at the moment,' she told them. 'A gang is printing up fake driver's licences and using them as ID to get money out of people's accounts. We've had three complaints in the last two weeks.'

'How are they doing it?' asked Sally.

'Looks like they're managing to intercept post, finding out people's account numbers and then withdrawing cash.'

'You'd better watch out, Sally,' said Iona. 'You don't want people robbing your identity.'

'Oh, it's OK, I've had that done.' Sally looked at her ruefully. 'You managed it.'

'I thought you said we were talking about something else?'

'We are. It was a joke.'

'Oh.'

'I think it's the first joke I've made in weeks,' said Sally. 'So even if it was awful, I don't care.'

'Fair enough,' said Iona. 'And moving on to other things completely – that guy walking past our table is a George Clooney lookalike. Oh, and the couple behind him rent a flat in your apartment block too, Siobhán.'

'Do they?' Siobhán squinted. 'I haven't seen them before.'

'Have you seen any more of Enrique?'

'Enrique?' Sally looked bemused.

'Bloke renting the duplex in Siobhán's block. Sexy Spaniard. Invited her for drinks.'

Sally looked at Siobhán and raised an eyebrow.

'I've said hello to him once or twice but he hasn't reissued the invitation,' said Siobhán. 'But, you know, he does talk about you a bit, Iona.'

'Me?' Iona looked incredulous. 'I hardly know him.'

'Well, each time I've said hello he's asked after you.'

'Really?'

'Yes. He said you worked really hard to get him the right place.'

'I work really hard for everyone.' Iona's cheeks were tinged with pink.

'You made an impression on him anyway.' Siobhán grinned at her.

'So, Iona, you're moving on?' Sally's voice was carefully neutral.

'You're not getting away with it that easily,' said Iona, pushing the image of Brandon Williamson to the back of her mind and mentally crossing her fingers, because even if she wasn't lying to Sally, she was being economical with the truth. 'I'm certainly not moving on with Enrique,' she added. 'I suppose it's flattering if he finds me attractive, but that's it.'

'The thing is, you *can* move on,' said Sally. 'I can't.'

'Why?' asked Iona.

'There's the more and more obvious matter of my pregnancy,' said Sally. 'You can't have forgotten.'

Iona said nothing. Of course she hadn't forgotten. But Sally's pregnancy was something she was trying very hard not to think about. In all of this mess it was the fact that Sally was pregnant that upset her the most. But she didn't want Sally to know that.

'At least you have something to look forward to,' said Iona.

'You think I'm looking forward to it!' Sally stared at her in disbelief. 'I'd give anything not to be pregnant, even though before now I wanted and wanted it to happen.'

The air between the women suddenly crackled with tension. Siobhán knew for sure now that there'd been no collusion between them. The edginess of their relationship was proof of that. She watched as Iona gulped back the remainder of her drink.

'I know this is cold comfort to both of you,' she said. 'But Frank did seem to love you both. I've checked out everything to do with him that I could. There's absolutely no evidence of any other women stashed away or anything else out of the ordinary going on.'

'And we're supposed to be relieved about that?' asked Iona.

'I thought you would be, actually,' said Siobhán.

'And I am,' said Sally. 'I kept thinking and thinking that maybe there were more of us. Someone before me.'

Iona looked aghast. 'I never thought about that. I mean, I thought of someone else . . . but not before you, Sally.'

'I did. A lot,' Sally told her. 'In which case I'd have been in the exact same situation as you, only with a rebellious daughter and a baby on the way.'

'Another drink?' Iona drained her glass. 'I need alcohol.'

'Let's go inside and order some food,' suggested Sally. 'You can have more drink if you want.' She looked ruefully at Iona. 'You know, I'd love to get out-of-my-tree drunk just to wipe it all out of my head, but because of the baby I can't.'

'I don't drink much,' said Iona. 'I look after my body. But one night I drank all the wine in the house. And in New York I had Cosmopolitans. It didn't actually help.' She stood up. 'You're right. We should eat.'

They didn't talk about Frank or Eddie over their food. Iona said that she was tired of defining herself by her relationship with Frank. She was a career woman, after all. Admittedly, she felt that she could do more with her career, but she was good at what she did. Enrique had said so after all.

'You did a good job on the tenancy agreement for me,' Sally told her. 'So you are good at what you do. You deserve to think of yourself as a person other than Frank's sort-of wife.' There was no irony in her voice. Anyway, she agreed with Iona. She herself was the vice principal of a girls' school with over four hundred pupils. She was more than just the woman Frank had married.

'I'm good at my job too,' said Siobhán. 'I've broken some important cases and I've put criminals behind bars. It won't wreck my life that Eddie McIntyre behaved like a shit.'

They clinked their glasses and toasted their independent woman-hood. Then Siobhán grimaced and ducked out of sight.

'What the hell are you doing?' asked Iona as the other girl kept her head below the level of the table.

'That bloke,' said Siobhán. 'The one who just walked in with the dark-haired girl. Is he within visual range?'

'D'you mean can I see him?' asked Iona. 'They've gone to the back of the restaurant. They're in a booth.'

'Oh good.' Siobhán sat up again and patted at her hair, which had fallen around her face in a cloud of fiery curls.

'Is that Eddie?' asked Sally. 'Is he out with another woman?'

'God, no,' said Siobhán. 'That was Carl O'Connor. And the woman he was with is Joely . . . McGuirk, I think her name is. She's a journo too. She works for one of the regional papers.'

'Why don't you want him to see you?' asked Iona. 'I mean, you told us about the bra and pants episode, but that's no good reason to hide.'

'I think it's a very good reason actually,' said Siobhán. 'I just don't want to talk to him, that's all. He's so fucking inquisitive. He'd start asking me about Eddie and calling me Mizz Plod, and I don't have the strength for it.'

'I'll keep an eye out for you,' said Sally, who was facing towards the back of the restaurant. 'If he comes back you can dive under the table again.'

Siobhán sighed. 'I guess that doesn't really make me seem like a woman in control of her life, does it?'

Sally and Iona exchanged glances.

'No,' they agreed in unison.

Chapter 30

Carl O'Connor liked Joely McGuirk. They'd been to college together and she was fun and feisty. After they graduated she'd headed off to work in the UK while he'd cut his teeth on the Irish papers. They'd lost touch and he'd been surprised when she contacted him after ten years, telling him that she was back in Ireland, living in the sunny south-east and working for one of the regional papers there. She'd married a Wexford man, she told him, and he'd always wanted to move back.

Carl was surprised at how many of the girls he'd gone to college with had got married and adapted their lives to fit in with their husbands. They'd all seemed totally fierce and independent when he'd known them, and yet somehow they'd ended up married after all. And he couldn't understand why someone like Joely, who'd been doing well in London, had decided to chuck it all in for a regional rag back home.

'It's about compromise,' she told him as he got on his hobby horse again. 'And quality of life.'

'Yeah, but you were going to rock the world, JoJo.'

'You know, I guess we all want to do that. But sometimes you realise that rocking the world isn't everything. Besides, my world is Michael and Robbie.'

'I can't believe you haven't divorced Michael yet,' teased Carl. 'A PR man, of all people!'

'Ah, I stay with him because of Robbie.' Joely returned his banter. 'I couldn't leave him with a four-year-old. He'd never cope. Anyway, what about you, O'Connor – anyone in your life?'

'No one special,' he told her. 'Don't have time in my life for that sort of thing. Besides, who'd put up with me?' He grinned. 'I'm still waiting to rock the world with my big story.'

'I like the column,' said Joely. 'Even if you are a bit OTT sometimes. The cops must hate you.'

He shrugged. 'Some do, some don't.'

'It's different down my way,' said Joely. 'You can't help getting on with them. Though they can be right bastards about keeping schtum. I was trying to do a story about that case in Ardallen where the wall of the Ardallen House buried the pub next door, but our local boy, Tim Shanahan, won't play ball. I know there's something going on there.'

'Like what?' asked Carl.

'Two issues,' said Joely. 'One, of course, is the whole incompetence thing as far as the builders are concerned in not securing the site properly. I've done a lot of work on that and the fact that they didn't follow the proper procedures. There are potentially huge claims against them. The owner of the bar next door is going to sue. The second is human interest. Remember the bloke who was pulled from the wreckage?'

'Only vaguely.'

'He wasn't a local, he'd just called in for a drink,' said Joely. 'Anyway, there's some story going around that he was married twice.'

'I hate to break it to you, but lots of people get married twice,' said Carl. 'Divorce has so much to answer for!'

'Clown!' Joely gave him a dig in the ribs. 'I mean, married twice without having got a divorce.'

'Really?' Carl looked more interested.

'Yes,' said Joely. 'Tim tried to palm me off on some detective in Bray who's supposed to be looking after the case, but the bitch won't return my calls.'

'What detective?'

'Siobhán Farrell,' said Joely. She noticed the look of surprise on Carl's face. 'You know her?'

'You could say that,' said Carl. 'I'll talk to her if you like.'

'You steal my story and I'll break your neck,' she threatened. 'I might not want to rock the world, but I'm sure as hell not going to let you rock it instead.'

'Don't worry,' said Carl. 'It's not really my sort of thing. But I'll try to get some info for you.'

'Thanks.'

'No problem.'

⌐

'They're heading this way again,' hissed Sally.

Siobhán swallowed the last piece of her apple pie and ducked under the table for the second time.

'You're OK,' said Iona after a couple of seconds. 'They've gone.'

'This really isn't good for my digestion,' said Siobhán as she sat upright.

'Actually, I think it's a bit of fun,' Iona told her. 'Obviously this is real detective agency stuff!'

Siobhán made a face at her. 'Let's get the bill,' she said. 'I'm in work tomorrow and I really want to get to bed at a reasonable hour.'

'And I have to get home before Jen,' said Sally.

The others nodded. Sally had already told them that Jenna was behaving as truculently as ever and that she was desperately worried about her. She'd told them of her concerns that Jenna was hanging around with a bad crowd, but that every time she tried to lay down the law Jenna simply said that at least she knew everything there was to know about the people she was with and that Sally wasn't in a position to pass judgement on her. She'd told them that Jenna resented being picked up from Gerry Cullinan's house by Siobhán and that she didn't seem to trust her mother any more. And, she'd said, Jenna was still utterly disgusted by the idea of the baby.

Both Iona and Siobhán had assured her that Jenna would get over it while admitting that they had no idea about *how* she'd get over it. And although Iona had been vehement in her insistence that Jenna seemed a sensible girl at heart, she felt herself freeze up almost as soon as she uttered the words. Jenna was Frank's daughter. A part of him. Something precious that she had wanted from Frank and now would never have. She wished fervently that her roller-coaster of emotions would settle down. But she really hadn't a clue when, or if, that would ever happen.

'Oh, by the way, Iona . . .' Sally said as she put her share of the bill on the saucer which the waitress had placed in front of them. 'I meant to say to you that I'm calling in to see Frank's accountant about the business. He says that I have to do something about it. He thinks he has a buyer for it.'

Iona looked at her warily. 'You want to sell it?'

'I don't know,' said Sally. 'But it's not like Frank can deal with it. If I don't do something it'll fold, won't it? So maybe if there's a buyer, better to sell it.'

'I really don't want to appear picky or anything,' said Iona, 'but I did a bit of work for Frank from time to time. Records and stuff like that. It's a good business. It would be a shame to let it go.'

'Without Frank it's definitely going to go,' said Sally.

Iona nodded. 'Well, look – let me know what your guy says,' she suggested. 'I could . . .' She hesitated. 'My brother-in-law is an accountant. I could ask him to give a second opinion.'

Sally looked at her curiously. 'Don't you trust our guy?'

'I . . .' Iona was uneasy.

'What?'

'It's just that Frank talked about getting rid of him,' she said finally. 'So I'd like someone else to run over the figures first.'

'OK,' said Sally. 'Thanks.' She winced suddenly.

'You all right?' asked Siobhán.

She nodded. 'Heartburn. I used to really suffer with it with Jenna. I'd forgotten. I used to swig back bottles of bloody antacid.'

'You should try papaya juice,' Iona told her. 'Much better for you and it really works.'

'Maybe.' Sally stood up and burped. 'Oh God, sorry.'

Iona giggled and Siobhán smiled at her. And then Siobhán's expression changed to one of dismay.

'Hello, Siobhán.' Carl O'Connor's voice was both surprised and cheerful. 'Fancy seeing you here.' He frowned. 'In fact, strange seeing you here, because I was here earlier and didn't spot you at all.'

'Didn't you?'

'Nope.'

'Not quite such an observant journalist after all,' she said.

'Did you spot me?'

'I know it'll break your heart to hear this,' she said, 'but I don't spend my time looking out for you.'

'It does break my heart,' he said. 'But I'll do my best to live with it.' He glanced at Sally and Iona. 'Going to introduce me?'

'I'm off-duty. I'm with friends,' said Siobhán. The last thing she wanted to do was introduce Carl to women whom she was sure he'd regard as a great potential story. It didn't matter that sometimes she thought he wasn't as bad as his profession might make him out to be. She wanted to protect Sally and Iona.

'Are you out for the night or can I give you a lift home?' he said. He frowned suddenly. 'Not that I've seen you there much lately. Social life on fire, is it?'

Siobhán shrugged noncommittally. 'Thanks for the offer, but we're . . . um . . . we're heading off somewhere else now.'

'Have a great evening,' he told her.

They stood looking at each other for a moment.

'Did you come back for anything in particular?' she asked eventually.

'Huh?'

'You said you were here earlier. You've obviously returned.'

'Oh, yes,' he said. 'I left a notebook at my table.'

'Right,' said Siobhán. 'We won't delay you. Nice to have seen you.' And with Sally and Iona in tow she swept out of the restaurant.

Carl O'Connor retrieved his notebook and watched the three women leave. But it was Siobhán Farrell he was thinking about. Until recently he'd never really thought much about her at all, other than the fact that she was a cop and on principle he was suspicious of the motivation of anyone who joined the police force. But now he felt differently. Ever since she'd been locked out of her apartment he'd seen her in a completely different light. (Well, of course, that was only natural, given the outfit she'd been wearing!) But it wasn't just her body that had made an impression on him. It was everything about her. He'd enjoyed talking to her, listening to the passion in her voice when she talked about victims of crime. She wasn't the heartless bitch he'd imagined. She was actually rather nice. It was a pity that she disliked him so much. He couldn't help thinking that if only the circumstances were different . . . but then how could they be? She was engaged, wasn't she? And she was a cop, no matter what.

He shook his head. He was being stupid. He couldn't afford to have feelings for Siobhán. He *didn't* have feelings for Siobhán. Not beyond lust, anyway. Obviously it was perfectly acceptable to have lustful feelings for her when he knew just how gorgeous she really was. He needed to put her out of his mind. He had better things to do than think about Siobhán Farrell. But then he suddenly wondered why he'd seen so little of her lately. Now that he thought about it, he hadn't noticed her in the apartment block in ages. He'd seen that irritating fiancé of hers, of course, self-obsessed tosser! Carl had spoken to Eddie once or twice but had always found him pompous and overbearing. He'd wanted to punch him when he'd knocked at the apartment door to collect Siobhán that evening she'd been locked out of their own place.

And then he remembered that he'd seen her leave the apartment block with a suitcase. He'd thought at the time that she was just going away for a few days, but maybe he'd been wrong. Had she left Eddie? That'd be no great loss.

He couldn't contact her, though. He wasn't interested in having a relationship with a detective. Not that sort of relationship anyway! But there was always the story that Joely wanted checked out.

He'd promised Joely that he'd try to get information on it. In which case he was obliged to get in touch with Siobhán. For work reasons only, of course.

❧

The house was in darkness when Sally returned. She'd expected it because Jenna had told her that she was going to a party. Sally had asked whether she was meeting Sam there and Jenna had looked at her witheringly and told her that Sam wasn't going to the party, that her friend (and she'd sniggered as she said the word) was too wet to go. Sally had wanted to know what sort of a party it was that Sam wouldn't go, and Jenna had said that Sam just didn't fit in with the crowd any more, that she was no fun. It was an eighteenth birthday party, Jenna said, to be held in one of the bars in town. And Sally had worried about it but hadn't said that Jenna couldn't go, because she didn't think that would help matters. But she'd reminded Jenna that she was too young to drink in bars and she'd also insisted that her daughter keep her mobile switched on and that she was home, as usual for the weekend, at midnight.

She was partly relieved when Jenna had nodded distantly at her. Since Siobhán Farrell had brought her home from Gerry's, Jenna had actually been extremely dependable as far as coming home on time was concerned. So Sally wasn't as worried as she could have been about letting her go to parties. But she *was* worried, ever since her conversation with Marsha, about the kind of people her daughter was socialising with at those parties.

And yet . . . could they be any worse than Frank?

That was what it came down to in the end, wasn't it? That Sally couldn't make any judgements on Jenna's choices because her own had been so spectacularly bad.

She put the kettle on and made herself a cup of tea. It was eleven o'clock. She hoped that Jenna would continue to be dependable.

❧

Iona's house was in darkness too. When she got in she switched on all the lights because she hated the dark. She looked at the children corner in the living room with its photos of Gavin and Charlotte and she thought of Sally Harper and her heartburn and she felt her stomach knot with envy. She didn't want to be envious of Sally. There was so much of Sally's life that she didn't need to be envious about. But Sally was pregnant. And Sally had Jenna. And Iona knew that she could have put up with the idea of having a troublesome teenage daughter in seventeen years' time if only she was pregnant now.

She sat down on the leather sofa and hit the remote so that the TV flickered into life. She changed the channel until it showed Sky Sports. She had no interest in Sky Sports but Frank had loved watching it. Footie, obviously. But golf too. And athletics. Just about anything really. She stared at the screen, not knowing who was playing in the football match that was being shown or what they were playing for. She wished that Frank was with her again. She wondered why she was wishing this when at the same time she was telling herself that she had to move on with her life, but right now she wanted it back the way it had been. And if that meant sharing Frank with Sally . . . A tear trickled down her cheek. She couldn't share Frank with Sally. Not now. Not knowing her. She couldn't ever have things back the way they were. There was no way of turning back time.

⌒

There was a faint glow coming from the bathroom, but that was because Siobhán had accidentally left the light on the bathroom cabinet switched on when she'd done her make-up earlier. She was used to coming home in the dark, either to an empty apartment or to one in which Eddie was already soundly asleep, forcing her to tiptoe around as quietly as possible. Eddie told her that she should be good at tiptoeing around the apartment – what about all those stakeouts she went on when she had to be super-quiet? She'd punch him gently on the arm when he said that and remind him (though he didn't need reminding) that she'd only been on a couple of stakeouts where she'd needed to be quiet and that it wouldn't really matter whether she clattered around the apartment because Eddie, when he was asleep, was always dead to the world.

What was he doing now? she wondered. Was he thinking about her? Was he hoping that she was thinking about him? Was he wondering whether she was going to forgive him and come on home?

She walked out on to the balcony of the apartment and stared across the dark water of the harbour. Maybe he wasn't wondering any such thing, of course. Maybe he was finding comfort with somebody else. She closed her eyes. Was this how it would always be? she asked herself. Wondering. Worrying. Not trusting him.

'Damn you,' she muttered under her breath. 'Damn you, damn you, damn you.'

Chapter 31

The bar was noisy and crowded and Jenna could feel a trickle of perspiration slide down her back as she talked (though shouted was really the word, because the music was blaring from a speaker just above her head) to Jerome Knightly, whose birthday it was. Jenna didn't really know Jerome very well. Neither did Gerry, though they both played rugby for the same club.

'I love your outfit!' Jerome smiled drunkenly at her and she could smell the beer on his breath.

'Thank you,' she said. Her eyes flickered down towards the short black dress which she was wearing with knee-high pink boots. The colour of the boots matched her new underwear, and the lacy pink bra peeked out over the low-cut neckline of the dress. She knew her look was great, but the boots were growing more hot and uncomfortable as the night wore on and she couldn't help thinking that shoes would have been a better, if less fashionable, option.

'Any time you get fed up with Cullinan, give me a shout,' Jerome said as he stumbled in her direction. She put out a hand to steady him and he grinned in thanks. She could see that his eyes were bloodshot and unfocused.

She was feeling a little unfocused herself. Despite her promises to her mother, she'd had a few alcopops and, although she hadn't noticed it at first, she realised that they were making her feel slightly disconnected from everything going on around her. But disconnected in an OK sort of way. Not stupid. Just happy. She could understand why people got drunk. It made you feel as though there was nothing so terrible in the world, she thought fuzzily. It made you feel as though you could cope with things. Even things like your mother being as big as an elephant and your father being a shit.

Jerome Knightly stumbled again and, quite suddenly, puked all over her bright-pink boots.

'Oh, you dickhead!' she screeched. 'My lovely boots.'

Jerome sank to his knees and puked again. There was a flurry around the bar area, and before she knew what was happening, two burly security guards had come over and Jenna, Jerome and a group of party revellers were ejected on to the pavement outside the bar.

'Bastards!' cried Jerome, who had recovered remarkably quickly. 'Fascist bastards!'

Jenna looked around for Gerry, but he hadn't been thrown out of the pub with the rest of them. She couldn't remember exactly where he'd been when Jerome had done his chucking-up act. She wrinkled up her nose at the smell now emanating from her boots.

'You've ruined them, you cretin,' she snapped.

'Ah, come on, love. Don't be like that.' Jerome tried to put his arm around her. 'It'll be OK. You can wash it off.'

'Ugh.' She shuddered.

'Kiss and make up?' he suggested, this time managing to drape his arm across her shoulders.

'You've got to be joking!' she cried. 'Let go of me!'

'Come on,' he said. 'We were having fun earlier. You and me. Birthday boy. Birthday girl.'

'It's not my birthday,' she said hurriedly. 'And you're drunk.'

'It's the weekend. Of course I'm drunk,' he said. 'Everyone's drunk! Hey, y'all, let's go back to Jenna's place.'

'You can't come back to my place,' she said, horrified. 'My mum would have a fit.'

The group laughed.

'Don't think the vice principal would take too kindly to seeing us,' asked Aline Keogh, who'd been thrown out too. 'I get the feeling she doesn't entirely approve of me.'

'You could come back if she wasn't home,' said Jenna hastily. 'But—'

'Teacher's pet,' said Aline.

The group laughed again. Jenna felt her eyes well up with tears.

'Where's your boyfriend?' asked Cindy Ryan, Aline's best friend. 'Dumped you at last, has he?'

Jenna looked around, hoping that Gerry had come out of the bar. But he was nowhere to be seen.

'You think that being Gerry Cullinan's girlfriend gives you a bit of cred?' Cindy asked. 'As if. He's only with you because you're an easy ride.'

Jenna said nothing and the other girls giggled.

'Easy-peasy,' said Aline. 'That's what he said getting into your knickers was.'

Jenna felt her heart sink into her ruined boots. 'Fuck off,' she said.

'It's true,' said Aline. 'I was going out with him before you. But I wouldn't put out for him. That's why he dumped me.'

'That's not true,' said Jenna shakily. 'He loves me.'

The girls cackled with laughter.

'He does.'

'Yeah, right,' said Cindy. 'That's why his hand was up Lorraine Brady's skirt, is it?'

'Shut up, you liar!' cried Jenna.

'Make me.'

'I will.'

'Yeah! Go on then. Teacher's pet!'

Jenna lashed out at the other girl and caught her across the face.

'You cow!' Cindy held her hand to her cheek, which had been grazed by Jenna's birthstone ring. 'You've ruined my face, you bitch!'

'Oh! I thought I'd improved it.'

'Go on, ya' good thing!' The others had crowded around the two girls now and were urging them on.

'Give it to her, Cindy!' called a voice.

Jenna didn't want to hang around. But there was nowhere to go. Cindy lunged at her and grabbed a handful of Jenna's dark hair.

'Let go, you wagon!' Jenna felt the tears sting her eyes.

'Make me.'

'I will fucking make you!' Jenna kicked at her with her vomit-stained boots and, much to her surprise, connected with Cindy just below the knee. The girl gave a howl of pain and sank to the ground.

'You've broken her leg!' cried Aline.

'No I haven't,' retorted Jenna. 'If I'd broken her leg she'd be in a damn sight more pain than she is now.' She was panting slightly and her hair was dishevelled. 'She's a stupid cow and she deserves to have her leg—'

'OK, what's going on here?'

Jenna recognised the authority in the voice and her heart sank again. It sank even further when she looked up and, through her bleary vision, recognised the policeman who'd come to the house with that smug detective the night of her father's accident. Cathal someone-or-other. She groaned. She was getting tired of meeting people from Bray garda station.

'That bitch was trying to kill Cindy,' cried Aline. 'She should be locked up.'

Jenna looked around desperately for a way to escape. Or for Gerry to come and rescue her. Then, horrified, she realised that Gerry was standing watching them, a look of disgust on his face.

'I could take you all down the police station for breaching the peace,' said Cathal. 'It's late and you're creating a nuisance.'

'She's the nuisance,' Cindy snarled. 'And I might charge her for assault. Look what she did to my face!' She pointed to her grazed cheek.

Cathal looked at Cindy and then at Jenna. His eyes narrowed as he recognised her. It had taken him a moment or two to realise who she was, because she looked very different from the girl he'd met before. Tonight, with her face heavily made up, wearing the short dress and the ruined pink boots, she looked at least five years older than the anxious young girl he'd driven to Ardallen a couple of months earlier.

'Does your mother know where you are, young lady?' he asked her.

'Yes,' replied Jenna.

'Does she know what you're up to?'

'I'm not up to anything,' said Jenna sullenly. 'She started it.'

'I did not! I—'

'OK, OK, enough is enough,' said Cathal. 'Let's break this up. It's time you all went home.'

The group began to disperse, Cindy and Aline continuing to mutter about Jenna.

'You live on the other side of town, don't you?' said Cathal.

Jenna nodded.

'Do you want a lift home?'

'Are you joking?' she cried. 'My mother would have a fit if she saw a police car outside the door again.'

'To the end of the road,' said Cathal. 'She doesn't have to see the car.'

'I don't care,' said Jenna. 'I can look after myself. My boyfriend . . .' She turned towards Gerry, who was still watching them silently.

'Jenna – it's not that I don't care for you, because I do,' he said. 'But – you were fighting in the street! I really don't think—'

'Because of what they said!' she cried. 'They said you were only going out with me because I let you sleep with me. And they said that you had your hand up Lorraine's skirt!' She broke off as she saw the expression on Gerry's face. And on the face of Cathal Rothery. 'Oh for God's sake,' she snapped, looking from one to the other. 'You're all the bloody same. He sleeps with me, he has someone else on the side, he's a great guy. I sleep with him and I'm—'

'Jenna, I really think it's better if we don't see each other any more,' said Gerry abruptly. 'If you think for one minute that's the sort of bloke I am, then you don't know me at all. And I don't know you either.'

360

'Yeah, well, that's a good thing.' But her voice cracked as he turned and walked away.

'Sure you don't want that lift home?' asked Cathal Rothery gently.

Jenna swallowed hard. It was three miles to her house and she didn't want to walk it in the boots. But the garda had heard everything. He probably thought she was nothing more than a tramp.

'Someone was sick on me,' she said tiredly. 'I smell.'

'There've been plenty of people in the car who have been a hell of a lot worse,' said Cathal. 'Come on. Hop in.'

His colleague, who'd been standing in support while Cathal dealt with the disturbance, opened the car door. Jenna got inside.

What's happened to me? she asked herself as the car turned in the direction of her house. I used to be an ordinary person. Now I'm in a car with a cop for the third time this year. How the hell has that happened? She closed her eyes as a tear rolled gently down her face.

⤳

Cathal was as good as his word and dropped her at the end of the road.

'You OK?' he asked.

'Fine,' she sniffed.

'Look, I know you don't want to hear it from me,' he said, 'but you're better off out of that crowd. Late-night drinking and brawling . . . I know it's not popular to say that it's cheap and common, but honestly, Jenna, there are better things to do with your life.'

'I know that,' she snapped. 'I don't need a lecture from you.'

'Siobhán told me that you'd been in a bit of bother before,' he said.

'Gossiping bitch,' said Jenna. 'All that happened was that my mother got into a state because I was late home and she rang the police! I'm practically an adult, for heaven's sake, and that's what she does, ring the police! So that interfering detective cow found out where I was and brought me home. Can you imagine how embarrassing that was? It's no wonder Gerry doesn't love me any more.'

'It's been a hard time for you and your mum,' said Cathal. 'She was probably just extra anxious about you.'

'She'd have been better off being anxious about my dad, wouldn't she?'

'No news on him?'

'I used to love him,' said Jenna. 'I thought he loved me too. But it's all bollocks, isn't it? Gerry pretended to love me. Dad pretended to love me.'

'I'm sure your dad does love you,' said Cathal.

'Yeah, right.' Jenna got out of the car. She looked ruefully at Cathal from her mascara-streaked eyes. 'Thanks for the lift.'

'You're welcome,' he said. 'But – I have to tell you this, Jenna – if you're involved in any more bust-ups outside pubs, I won't be just running you home. I'll be taking you down to the station.'

She looked at him warily.

'Public order is a big issue these days,' he said. 'Binge drinking and causing trouble afterwards is something that people are getting fed up with. And we have to deal with it.'

'Yeah, right.'

'Take care of yourself,' he said.

She smiled suddenly, transforming herself from the sullen teenager into someone entirely different. 'I'll do my best.'

'Good night.'

She turned on to her road and walked the few yards to the house. When she got to the front door she unzipped the pink boots and slid them off. The whiff of vomit was disgusting. She knew that no matter how much effort she put into cleaning them, she'd never be able to wear them again. So she dropped them into the dustbin before opening the front door and letting herself into the house.

She tiptoed into the kitchen, walking extra carefully so that she didn't bang into anything that would make a noise and wake up

362

Sally. She filled the kettle with water and switched it on, then took a tea bag from the tin on the worktop and dropped it into the big red mug which had always been her special one. When the kettle boiled she made the tea and leaned against the edge of the kitchen table while she sipped it slowly.

Cathal Rothery might be right about Aline and Cindy and that gang. But until tonight they'd been easier people to be with than Sam and Kelly and her other friends. Aline and Cindy hadn't asked questions about her father or her mother. They didn't care. They knew, of course, that there was some hassle at home, but then Jenna knew that Aline's parents were divorced and that Cindy had a kid of her own. And it wasn't that having divorced parents was any big deal these days, or even that having a kid at seventeen was much of an issue, but at least they had something other than a happily married set of parents in the background. What the hell could Sam or Kelly, both of whom had two loving parents (or at least parents who lived together in the family home!), as well as a selection of siblings, well, what the hell could they know about what she was going through? They were probably gossiping about her at every available opportunity. Laughing that it had all gone so wrong for Jenna Harper, whose mother was the vice principal and who had it all so easy.

And now what was she? Jenna Harper who was in a kind of one-parent family right now and whose mother was going to have a baby even though her dad wasn't around. It was all wrong. It wasn't their lives. It wasn't fair. Jenna wiped another tear away from her eyes and dumped the remainder of her tea in the sink.

Then she climbed the stairs and fell, fully clothed, into bed.

∽

Frank could hear the sound of voices in the distance. At first he thought it was Marion again, but he knew that Marion had gone. And since Marion there'd been Sally, who'd given him the beautiful baby daughter. He could feel his heart constrict with love for his baby daughter who, of course, wasn't a baby any more but a young girl on the threshold of becoming an adult. He enjoyed her company. She was fun to be with and hadn't yet turned coquettish and silly like so many of them did around her age. She would talk to him about cars and motorbikes and blokeish stuff and that made him proud to have her as a daughter. Maybe, then, it was Jenna he could hear? But the voice was more mature than Jenna's. And it was saying something about blood sugar and respiration . . . something that he didn't understand.

He tried to move but he couldn't. He felt as though there was a weight pressing down on his body, holding him in position. He thought about lifting his arm but he couldn't quite make the thoughts and the actions connect. It was a horrible feeling. It frightened him. He could hear rhythmic sounds too. Of monitors. Like in a hospital. Which would make sense, wouldn't it, if someone was talking about respiration? So maybe he was in hospital. That would explain not being able to move. Something had happened and he was in hospital and he couldn't move. Was he paralysed? He felt panicked at the thought. Had he crashed? Fallen? Had he been struck down by a mystery virus?

He tried to think about what he'd been doing before being here. But he couldn't. His mind was like a bowl of porridge, thick and gloopy, and he couldn't seem to fix on anything definite. Well, Sally and Jenna were definite, of course. He remembered saying goodbye to them that morning. Or maybe it had been the previous morning? He couldn't quite remember. Sally had said something about cutting the lawn. He could picture that, all right. The grass suddenly spurting higher because of the spring weather and Sally wanting it to look good.

His head hurt. If something had happened and he was in hospital, then maybe, just for a while, he'd give in to it. Let himself drift. They'd probably given him drugs to make him sleepy, which was why he couldn't remember anything. Maybe if he just let them work he'd feel better when he woke up the next time. He sighed deeply and let himself fall into the darkness again.

Chapter 32

Siobhán sat at her desk and thought about the briefing they'd just been given on the fake ID scam. The feeling was that although the initial withdrawals from people's accounts had happened in Bray, the centre of operations was probably somewhere outside the area. In the last week new complaints had come in from the towns of Killiney and Glenageary, still on the east coast but heading closer to Dublin city itself. She'd interviewed the people concerned in her area, and the banks, and she was confident that even if Bray didn't nab the people responsible they would eventually get caught. It was only a matter of time. But of course that was of little comfort to someone who'd just discovered that a complete stranger had managed to empty his or her current account.

They reckoned there were four people involved, two women and two men. The CCTV in the banks had caught pictures of them, but they'd all been wearing baseball caps pulled low over their eyes so that it was difficult to get a clear view of them. Still, in one case they'd managed to get a glimpse of one of the women, and Siobhán was confident that she'd be sighted again soon enough. This was a case that would break, she knew it.

The phone rang and she reached out to answer it.

'Hello, Mizz Plod.'

She jerked upright in her chair.

'Carl?' She frowned.

'I wanted to ask you something.'

'What?'

'A colleague of mine has been trying to get hold of you, but you've been avoiding her calls.' He chuckled. 'Glad you took mine.'

'I didn't know it was going to be you,' she pointed out. Then her voice mellowed. 'What do you want?'

'Ardallen,' he said. 'Man crushed under falling building. Still in hospital, I believe. Married to two women.'

Siobhán said nothing.

'Is that a no comment?' asked Carl.

'I'm just wondering what you want,' she said.

'It's an interesting story,' said Carl. 'JoJo, my colleague, she'd do a sensitive piece about it.'

'I can't imagine any of your colleagues being sensitive,' said Siobhán drily.

'You have such a low opinion of us.' Carl laughed. 'Come on, Mizz Plod, it's human interest.'

'Not this time, really,' said Siobhán.

Carl was acutely aware of her tone. 'There is something?'

Siobhán chewed the end of her biro.

'C'mon, Mizz P. Why don't you talk to JoJo? She works on one of the local papers around there. There is a lot of talk going on in the town about the whole incident. Maybe the truth is less sensational than anything they might come up with.'

'You know, you're always going on at me about catching real criminals,' she said mildly. 'Why don't you go and get a real story?'

'You're very sensitive about this,' said Carl. 'Is there something more to it? Is he linked to serious crime or something? Was the building collapse not an accident?'

'Crikey, O'Connor, I don't know why you're a journalist and not a fiction writer,' Siobhán told him. 'Your imagination is running at about a thousand per cent there.'

'OK, OK. But if I find something out, or if JoJo does, will you talk then?'

'There's nothing important to find out,' she said. 'I honestly don't think it's a story you want to run with.'

'So, what's new with you?' He knew perfectly well that there was something to the story but that she wasn't going to tell him anything about it, so he changed the subject. 'You were looking well the other night, out with the girls.'

She said nothing.

'Any chance we could meet up and talk about the Ardallen case?'

'You never give up, do you?'

'Nope,' he said cheerfully.

'Well, there's no actual chance,' she said calmly. 'But if there's anything really interesting happening about anything at all, I'll be sure to let you know.'

'Oh really?'

'Yes, really,' she said. 'Now I've got to go and make a few arrests.'

'Have fun,' said Carl and hung up.

Siobhán replaced the receiver and stared into space for a few moments. Then she picked it up and dialled a number.

'This is Eddie McIntyre,' said the voice. 'Leave a message.'

'Call me,' she said, and hung up.

❧

Iona was showing yet another apartment in the Waterside building, this time on the ground floor and without the spectacular views of either Siobhán Farrell's small apartment or Enrique Martinez's much bigger one. But, once again, the prospective tenants liked the complex and told Iona that they were interested in renting there. They were, they said, going to see another apartment first, but unless it was absolutely fantastic they'd be back to her about this one.

She gave them her card and told them to call, reminding them that there was a lot of interest in Waterside and suggesting that the apartment would certainly be gone by the end of the week.

As she unlocked her lime-green Beetle, she saw the last couple who'd rented from her hurrying back into the block. And, following close behind them, Enrique Martinez striding up the pedestrian pathway. He caught sight of her and waved. She waved back.

367

'Everything going all right?' she asked as he veered from the path and came towards her.

'Fine,' he said. 'I like it here. I like being able to see the sea. I'm used to it. In Barcelona my apartment is near the sea. When I worked in London I always felt trapped by the buildings. This is perfect.'

'Good,' she said.

They stood in silence for a moment. Then Iona's stomach rumbled loudly.

'Oh God, excuse me!' She blushed. 'I skipped lunch today.'

'That's not good,' said Enrique sternly.

'I was busy.'

'Why don't you join me for something to eat?' asked Enrique. 'I was just about to have some food.' He grinned. 'At home I eat late, but here it's different.'

Moving on, she thought, like Sally thinks. And Siobhán thinks this bloke is attracted to me. But I'm not ready. Brandon was different. New York was different. This is back home and it just isn't realistic.

'No, no, it's fine, honestly,' she said.

'I have some really nice Serrano ham in the apartment,' he told her. 'But if you're worried about being alone with me . . .' his eyes twinkled, 'well, let's go to the restaurant on the seafront. It's really good.'

'I know,' said Iona. 'I was there very recently. But—' Her stomach rumbled again.

'I can't take no for an answer!' Enrique's voice was firm. 'You are really hungry.'

'Enrique—'

'Oh, come on.' He grinned. 'For the last few weeks all I've done is eat with boring businessmen. And boring businesswomen. I'd like to eat for fun. Also, I want to thank you for finding the right place for me. I know I was a difficult client.'

She was starving. But she couldn't go to a restaurant with Enrique. It just wouldn't be right. He was looking at her enquiringly.

He was a client, though. It was a business thing after all. She knew that she wasn't interested in him, not in any kind of flirty way. How could she be at the moment, when the man she loved (even if he had messed up her life) was still critically ill in hospital? If Frank had been fine and well she would've just told this guy that she was married and that she wasn't available to go to dinner. And if he implied that it was just a casual dinner to say thanks for finding the apartment, well then, because she really was hungry, she might agree and it would all be perfectly above board. That was the problem, she realised. Having a meal with Enrique while Frank couldn't know anything about it seemed somehow sly and underhand. Cheating on him when he wasn't able to do anything. Although hardly as bad as how he'd cheated on her. The thought sneaked into the back of her mind and then she thought of Brandon again. Cheating on Frank in a different time zone. Or not, as it turned out.

She hadn't slept with him in the end. She knew she would have been doing it for all the wrong reasons. He'd been remarkably understanding, even though she knew that he'd been annoyed too. He'd told her that he hoped she'd manage to deal with her issues and that he'd enjoyed her company. And then he'd gone, and despite everything, she had actually slept alone.

'Just a quick bit to eat,' said Enrique easily. 'I have to do some more work this evening anyway so I can't stay out long.'

Having something to eat when she truly was hungry wasn't wrong, she told herself. She was just making it sound wrong because she was still feeling guilty about Brandon and because it seemed wrong to have fun when Frank was ill. Yet she hadn't felt like this about going out with Siobhán and Sally. It was because Enrique was a good-looking bloke. That didn't matter to her, though. Her heart was well hardened against good-looking blokes.

'OK,' she said eventually. 'I suppose – yes, all right. Thanks.'

'Excellent!'

She fell into step beside him and they walked out of the gardens and down towards the seafront.

Because the school holidays had begun, Sally was able to go to the hospital during the afternoon. Rather to her surprise, Jenna had decided to accompany her and was now sitting on the opposite side of the bed, reading one of the Ian Fleming novels which Iona had left at the hospital. She wasn't reading it aloud but to herself, her dark head bent over the book, engrossed in it.

Sally had read the Letters to the Editor and Weather Eye to Frank and now she was skimming through the rest of the paper, also reading to herself. At the same time she was thinking about her meeting with Frank's accountant and his analysis of the business. Basically Richard was saying that they needed to sell it and take what money they could out of it before all of Frank's clients defected somewhere else. Sally supposed that he had a point, but at the same time felt bad about the idea of selling a business into which Frank had poured so much of his time and effort. However, she could see what Richard meant. Unless someone was co-ordinating the maintenance of the installations on a regular basis (and she couldn't expect Richard himself and Pete Maguire, Frank's contractual engineer, to do it for ever), and unless there was someone actively looking for new business, then it would all go wrong. Whatever Frank would have hoped and dreamed for, the company folding because he was incapacitated would not have been on the agenda. He'd prefer her to sell it. She knew he would.

But she was worried about what Iona had said about Richard too. That Frank had been thinking of getting rid of him. As far as Sally knew, Richard had been Frank's accountant ever since he'd set up the company. She'd never heard her husband say a bad word about him. But then, she admitted ruefully to herself, she'd never really listened when he talked about the company. And that was because she'd been so set against the idea in the first place.

Her teeth worried against her lower lip as she thought about it. She remembered Frank's enthusiasm and her own misgivings. She remembered how angry she'd felt about the notion of selling their house and moving further from the city so that Frank could have capital to invest. She remembered accusing him of pursuing a stupid dream when he'd already been offered such a good position in the recently taken-over company. And she remembered that this had been the time when their marriage had run through its really rocky patch so that, in the end, perhaps it wasn't entirely surprising he'd found someone new to confide in. And cheat on her with. She shook her head fiercely. She wasn't going to go down the road of anger again. There wasn't any point right now.

From what Sally could tell, though, Iona knew a lot more about Frank's company. She was more interested in the outcome too. Maybe it was because she worked in the whole area of developing business and clients, whereas Sally was caught up in developing people. She looked at the folder on the locker beside her. She would give it to Iona, she decided, and let her show it to her brother-in-law and see what they had to say about it all. And she'd trust them to give her the right information. She massaged her temples. It seemed extraordinary to her to think that she now trusted Iona more than a professional accountant. But she did.

Her gaze flickered across the room to Jenna, who had closed the Ian Fleming book and was now staring into space.

'Good?' asked Sally.

'Huh?'

'The book.'

Jenna glanced down at the copy of *Dr No*.

'It's OK,' she said. 'Old-fashioned. Not like I thought it would be at all. But it's interesting.'

Sally smiled. This was the most information Jenna had volunteered to her in ages.

'Maybe you'd like to read him something,' she suggested.

'Iona's already read this one to him,' said Jenna.

'Not James Bond,' said Sally. 'Something else altogether.'

'Not really.' Jenna shrugged. 'You're giving him all the newspaper stuff, she's doing the books . . .'

'You can just talk to him,' said Sally.

'I know,' Jenna said. 'But I don't want to.'

'Why not?'

'I've nothing to say to him.'

'Jenna . . . he may not be perfect, but he's your dad.'

'If I was a really horrible person, would you say it didn't matter, I was your daughter?' she asked.

Sally spoke carefully. 'I can't say that I'd tell you nothing mattered. But I'd still love you. Mothers do, with their children. No matter what.'

'Say if – oh, I dunno – if I had an affair with a married man. What would you say then?'

'All these things depend on circumstances,' Sally told her. 'I doubt that I'd be very happy, but I'd listen to your point of view.'

'And if I got pregnant?'

Sally's heart almost stopped. She could see that Jenna's face was slightly flushed and that there was an anxious look in her eyes. Dear God, she thought. Not Jenna. Please. I really don't think I could cope with that right now.

'I still wouldn't be very happy,' she said as neutrally as she could. 'But I would, of course, still love you.'

'How are you feeling?' asked Jenna.

'Me? I'm fine.'

'Because you're getting quite fat now, aren't you?'

'Big,' amended Sally. 'Not fat.'

'Whatever. Is it horrible?'

'It's kind of weird,' Sally said. 'Your body is doing something that you can't control and it's a little bit freaky. But then you feel the baby move and it's magic.'

'Has . . . has this baby started to move?'

Sally nodded.

'Ugh.'

'It's not so bad,' she told Jenna. 'It's actually quite comforting once you get used to it.'

'Did I move?'

'Of course.'

'What did Dad say when you told him you were pregnant with me?' asked Jenna.

'He was delighted,' said Sally immediately. 'He always wanted lots of children. It didn't work out like that, but that's what he wanted.'

'I know. And now, finally, there's going to be another one. Only he might never know about it.'

'He'll know,' said Sally.

'Do you still love him?' asked Jenna.

Sally considered her answer before she spoke. 'Maybe it's the same as how I feel about you,' she said. 'I get angry with you but I don't stop loving you. I don't agree with some things you do but I don't stop loving you. Sometimes I don't even like you! But I don't stop loving you.'

'So you haven't stopped loving Dad?'

'No.'

'Can I be on my own with him for a while now?'

'Sure you can.' Sally picked up her bag and walked out of the room.

Jenna pulled her chair closer to the bed.

'I told you before that I hated you,' she said. 'And I do. But it's like what Mum says. I hate you but then when I see you I still love you. It's wrecking my head.'

She sighed. 'The bloke I told you about. Gerry. He's broken up with me because I got into a fight with some girls outside a pub.' She giggled. 'It was crazy, we were pulling each other's hair and everything. If you can hear what I'm saying I know you'll be freaked out, but I couldn't help myself. It didn't seem real. Gerry wasn't pleased about it so he dumped me. There and then, Dad. On the pavement. In front of the cops. I forgot to tell you that – they turned up because of the fight. It was totally weird. One of them was the guy who told us about you. He drove me home and made me promise to be a good little girl in future.' She leaned her head against the bedspread. 'Thing is, I don't know that I want to be any more. And that's because of you. Everything's because of you. Sam and Kelly kept trying to be nice to me but I hated it. I didn't want them to look at me as though I needed special treatment because my dad hitched up with a younger model. At least if you'd got divorced we could talk about it. People do get divorced. But what you did was so awful that I just can't. So I made friends with the others. Only they're not really my type of person either. I guess I've realised that I don't really like the pub scene, even though getting pissed was sort of fun. But not when it ends up in fighting and people getting sick over boots that cost a fortune. I used to know what I wanted, Dad. But now . . .'

She stopped and looked at him. Despite the fact that he now occasionally moved his head, he was immobile.

'I do love you, Dad,' she said shakily. 'I hate you and I love you and life is so messy . . . I never thought it would be this messy.' She reached out and took his hand. She squeezed his fingers. And then she sat completely still. Because, although his grasp was very weak, she was sure that he'd squeezed her fingers in return.

～

There were two of them, Frank remembered now. Sally and Iona. He loved them both. He loved Sally because she was strong and dependable and the mother of his beautiful daughter, Jenna. He loved Iona because she was strong and independent and because she encouraged him in everything he wanted to do. He wanted to care for both of them, to protect both of them. He wasn't sure how he'd manage to do this. He knew that most women wanted to feel protected even if they were strong and independent.

Everything he did was geared towards protecting the women in his life. Sally and Jenna and Iona too – even though he knew that Sally didn't understand his need for his own company and had been upset with him about the changes in their lives. But the new company would make him a lot more money than simply being employed by the old one, and even though she'd hated the change, Sally had accepted it now. She'd realised that what he was saying made sense. So he was protecting them by setting it up and running a good business and making sure that they were always well provided for.

Iona – well, she always said that she didn't need protecting, but he could see how hard she worked and how much she wanted to get on and how little confidence she really had in herself. She was good at what she did but there was nobody there to praise her and tell her that. Her parents lived in Spain, and although she said she got on fine with them, she didn't keep in constant contact. Her sister was married and seemed to think that until Iona got married too there would always be something missing in her life. Her brother was in China. Frank thought that Iona was lonely. He was more sure than ever about that when she kept turning the conversation around to marriage. He couldn't marry her, of course, because of Sally. But he wanted to, to make her happy. Because if she was happy she wouldn't leave him. He didn't want her to leave him. She'd become an important part of his life. It was difficult to be in love with two people at the same time, but that was the way it was.

His head hurt again. It was all too much for him. He'd wanted things to be simple because it hadn't been simple for Derek, what with Christine bolting like that. He hadn't wanted to cause hassle himself. But it seemed that he was. He was certain that he could hear Iona now, telling him that she loved him and hated him, and he didn't know why anyone would hate him, because he always tried to do his best. For her. For Sally. For Jenna. Jenna loved him and hated him too. It was Jenna saying these things to him now, he recognised her voice. There were too many voices in his head lately, crowding in on top of him, making it difficult to think. He clenched his hand.

'I love you.'

He heard that clearly. It didn't matter who was saying it. If she loved him it didn't matter. He unclenched his hand again.

⌒

Iona realised that she was ravenous when she walked into the restaurant and the aroma of garlic and spices wafted towards her. She was surprised at how hungry she felt. In the weeks since Frank's accident, and except for the night in Gabriel's, food had barely registered in her consciousness. The night that she'd come here with Siobhán and Sally had been enjoyable, but she couldn't even remember what she'd eaten.

The waiter showed them to a booth and handed them menus. Iona opened hers and looked at it intently. She was going to have fish and chips, she thought. Good, solid comfort food, even if fish and chips in restaurants bore no resemblance to the deep-fried cod and greasy chips laced with vinegar and wrapped in brown paper that Frank would sometimes bring home from the chipper down the road. As she thought of Frank, all her doubts about the wisdom of being here with Enrique rushed through her head again and she almost cried out.

'Everything OK?' Enrique looked at her curiously.

'I . . . well . . . I shouldn't actually be here,' she said. 'I have – other things to do this evening. I can't really stay.'

Enrique's brown eyes regarded her thoughtfully. 'You are hungry,' he said. 'There is nothing that you can do properly when your stomach tells you that it needs food. Have something to eat and then you can do whatever you need to do afterwards.'

'Yes, but—'

'I work in this cut-throat industry,' he said dismissively, 'where they used to say that lunch was for wimps. Some people still take that view. But me, I think we should all enjoy our food and that our lives would be much better for it. You do not have to spend a lot of time with me, Iona, but you should still have something to eat.'

'You don't understand,' she said. 'I can't be here with you. I just can't.'

'Why?' he asked calmly. 'Am I going to do something terrible?'

'No – it's that – well, I'm sort of – sort of married.'

'Sort of married?' He frowned. 'What exactly is that, sort of married? It is not something I have heard of before.'

'No. I'm not surprised,' she said ruefully.

'But does being sort of married stop you from eating?' he asked.

'Of course not. It's just—'

'Then, sort-of-married Iona, do not worry about it and have something to eat.'

What was the harm? she asked herself. The idea of walking out when the aroma of food was so intense was deeply disappointing. But if she stayed, it would mean that she was having dinner with a man who wasn't Frank. She mentally shook her head. Of course she'd often had dinner with men who weren't Frank! She'd gone out with Garret a few times, and occasionally with other people in the rental agency business. Having dinner with a man wasn't some kind of declaration of intent. It just meant that you were . . . well, having dinner.

'OK,' she said eventually, closing the menu and putting it down on the table beside her. 'I'll have something to eat.'

'Good,' said Enrique. 'What have you chosen?'

They gave their orders to the waiter who had materialised at the table as soon as they'd closed the menus. Enrique ordered a glass of wine for himself but Iona told him that she had to drive home and was sticking to water. And no Cosmopolitans either, she told herself.

'Do you live far from here?' he asked as he buttered a slice of walnut bread.

She told him about the Liberties and her house and she told him about her parents and the finca in Javea and he nodded and agreed that it was a beautiful place to live. She liked his accent and his slightly gravelly voice. She liked the way he didn't pry but simply allowed the conversation to ramble in a range of directions. But she didn't like the fact that her marital status didn't seem to bother him in the slightest. Is it me? she wondered. Have I become one of those types of women who only see men as potential bedfellows? She laughed internally at herself. She wasn't thinking of Enrique as someone to sleep with. Not really. It was just that he was attractive and it was hard not to wonder about what an attractive person might be like in bed. She'd done that when she was married to Frank too. It didn't mean anything. And, she reminded herself, when she could have done it with no complications, she still hadn't slept with Brandon.

'I am divorced,' said Enrique casually in response to a question she asked him about family life and working overseas. 'My wife didn't like me being away so much and she was right. But I am sorry that it didn't work out. She is a nice woman. She is marrying again. Me, naturally not.'

'Why naturally not?'

'Because when you lose your wife to your job, you must concentrate on your job,' he said.

She nodded.

'And you? Sort-of-married?'

She'd known eventually that he'd ask her about it. But she really didn't know what to say.

'You wear a ring,' he said. 'Not a wedding ring?'

She looked down at her half-hoop of rubies. 'I thought it was,' she said simply. 'It turned out not.'

'And so there is or is not a husband in your life right now?'

'It's – complicated,' she said.

'Ah, yes.' He smiled slightly as he nodded. 'Modern lives, they are always complicated.'

They sat in silence. I wonder is he going to try to ask me out? Iona thought. And if so, what am I going to say? I don't want to have to talk about Frank. I'll say no but it seems rude when he's been so nice . . . but then if he asks me back to his place (even if it's only eight o'clock in the evening) then he won't be expecting nice, he'll be expecting more. Just like Brandon was expecting more. This is why I shouldn't have let Brandon pay and why I shouldn't have said yes to dinner with Enrique. This is why I'm a stupid, stupid person.

'I have to go.' Enrique signalled for the bill and then smiled at her. 'I have a report to write before tomorrow morning and I must start it now to have any hope of finishing it on time.'

'Oh.'

'It was nice to spend some time with you,' he said.

'You too.'

The waiter brought the bill. Enrique picked it up and looked at it.

'Split it,' said Iona quickly.

'But you know I wanted to thank you for the apartment,' he said. 'So I will pay.'

'I'd prefer if we split it.' She didn't want anyone else paying for her meals.

'If that's what you want.'

He took a bank note out of his wallet and placed it on the saucer with the bill. 'The same from you will cover it.'

'Great,' she said. She placed a note on the saucer too.

It was still warm and sunny outside. Enrique extolled the pleasures of long summer evenings as they strolled back to the apartment building together.

'This is me.' She indicated the lime-green Beetle.

'I like your car.' He grinned at her.

'Thank you. And thank you for dinner.'

'Maybe some time we'll meet and I can pay for your dinner,' he said. 'So this time you are just thanking me for making you eat.'

She laughed. 'OK.'

'So, good night, Iona.'

'Good night,' she said.

She was surprised that he hadn't given her the continental kiss on each cheek. But relieved too.

Chapter 33

Siobhán had just returned to her desk following an interview of a suspected burglar when her mobile rang with a distinctive tone.

'Hi, Eddie,' she said.

'You called?'

'I need to see you.'

'Why?'

'I've been thinking things over. It's time to talk.'

'About time,' he said gruffly. 'Tonight?'

'Fine,' she said.

'Call to the apartment?'

She hesitated. Her plan had been to meet Eddie somewhere for a drink and talk to him then. The apartment was a bit too personal. But she was afraid that if she said no, Eddie would think she had a problem with the idea of being alone with him.

'OK,' she said eventually. 'Around seven.'

'Fine,' said Eddie. 'See you then.'

She replaced the receiver. Then she made two calls, one to Sally and one to Iona to tell them about Carl O'Connor and the fact that journalists were digging around at the story. As she'd suspected, both women were horrified. She promised that she'd do everything she could to keep it private and assured them that she certainly wouldn't be giving O'Connor any information and that she was hoping to divert him into something else altogether.

But that, as she'd told them before, he was a complete tosser and she found it hard to trust him.

Then she turned her mind back to burglaries.

~

Iona rang Sally after the call from Siobhán.

'Do you want to talk to a journalist?' she asked.

'Are you nuts?'

Iona laughed. 'It's just that Siobhán said the journo bloke, O'Connor, insists that some people like to have their stories in the paper.'

'I most certainly am not one of those people,' said Sally. 'Are you?'

'Now who's nuts?' asked Iona. 'Of course not. But I wanted to be sure we both felt the same way. Because if one of us felt differently, it would impact on the other and—'

'We're in this together,' said Sally firmly. 'Nobody does or says anything unless the other person agrees.'

'Great,' said Iona. 'That's perfect.'

'I won't ever agree to do a story about My Marriage Hell,' said Sally.

Iona giggled. 'No My Husband Was A Cheating Bastard head-lines, so?'

'No pictures of The Tragic Women Who Were So Terribly Betrayed.'

'No crappy copies of Our Wedding Photos.'

Sally sighed deeply. 'Can you believe it, really? The idea of someone wanting to put it all in the papers?'

'Hey, Sal, you know what tripe goes into the papers these days,' said Iona. 'I'm not surprised. I'm just glad that neither of us wants to do it.'

'Like I said, anything that happens about Frank and his treat-ment, about the company – whatever – we both have to agree.'

'All for one,' said Iona.

'Something like that,' said Sally.

'You're a good friend,' Iona told her.

'You too,' Sally replied. 'You too.'

⌇

At seven o'clock exactly Siobhán arrived at the apartment to see Eddie.

'You have a key.' Eddie's voice came over the intercom when she hit the buzzer.

'Yes, but I wouldn't use it,' she told him. 'It wouldn't be right.'

'Oh, don't be so silly!' But he buzzed the door open for her.

He was standing at the door of the apartment when she got to the fourth floor. He kissed her on the cheek and ushered her inside.

Siobhán stood in the apartment and looked around her in astonishment. It was pristine. Every surface gleamed with a polished sheen. There were fresh flowers in all the vases. No magazines or circulars or unpaid bills littered the work surfaces and there was no mound of ironing piled up in the armchair in the corner of the room.

'Gosh,' she said. 'This is like it was before I moved in.'

'The cleaners came,' he said drily. 'You organised it, if you remember.'

She nodded slowly. 'Yes. I did. But I didn't realise they'd do such an amazing job.'

'It looks good, doesn't it?' He smiled at her. 'Why don't you sit down?'

She perched nervously on the edge of the armchair. The apartment didn't feel like home any more. It was too clean, too tidy and far too glamorous for her now. She wished she'd called into her rented place in Dun Laoghaire to freshen up before coming out, but it hadn't even crossed her mind. Which makes me the bad girlfriend again, she thought disconsolately. Every normal woman would do themselves up for a meeting with their fiancé. Even if they were going through a relationship crisis.

Eddie had disappeared into the kitchen. He returned carrying a bottle of champagne and two glasses.

'And it's not the same stuff as you bought to welcome me home,' he told her. 'This is the real deal.'

'The stuff I got was the real deal,' she said indignantly.

'This is a 1990 Dom Perignon,' he said. 'You can't get it in the local off-licence.'

She said nothing as he eased the cork out of the bottle with a gentle pop and without spilling a drop of champagne. He filled both glasses and then raised his to hers.

'Welcome home,' he said.

'I'm not home yet.' She tried to keep her tone light-hearted. 'I mean, I didn't bring stuff or anything. This is just to talk it through.'

'Sweetheart, we've talked already,' said Eddie. 'And you've had your time to think about it. To me the time for talking and thinking is over.' He put his glass on the table and walked over to the chair where she was sitting. 'I love you,' he said. 'Since the day I met you I've loved you, and I know that you love me too. And I also know that you know how deeply sorry I am about what happened. But it truly was one moment of utter madness. It's not as though I'm ever likely to do it again. I was stupid and crazy and I paid a hard price for it. I could have been seriously ill and I could have lost you for ever.'

He reached under the chair and took out a red velvet box, tied with a gold ribbon and handed it to her. She turned it over in her hand.

'Open it,' he said.

'Eddie—'

'Open it,' he repeated.

She pulled at the ribbon and lifted the lid of the box. The thin necklace of diamonds sparkled in the evening sunlight slanting through the window and exploded into a kaleidoscope of rainbow colours.

'Oh my God,' she breathed. 'It's beautiful.'

'And you deserve it,' he told her. 'I don't know what I can do to make it up to you, but I will. This is just a token to show you how I feel.'

She was mesmerised by the light and the beauty of the diamonds. She closed the box gently.

'Aren't you going to put them on?' he asked.

'We need to finish talking first.'

'We don't need to talk,' he told her.

'Eddie, you've got to understand how difficult all this is for me. I understand it was a one-off. I understand how it could happen. But that doesn't make it any more acceptable. And that's what I'm struggling with.'

'Siobhán, sweetie, you've seen people at their absolute worst,' said Eddie. 'You've arrested them. Some of them are victims of circumstances. Some of them regret what they did. You must be able to see how sincere I am.'

She knew that he was sincere. She could hear it in his voice and see it in his face. His sincerity wasn't the question.

He leaned his face towards her and suddenly he was kissing her and she was kissing him back. And then he slid his arms beneath her and carried her into the bedroom.

It was the first time he'd ever carried her anywhere, and she felt him stumble as he laid her down on the bed. I'm not built for being carried around the place, she thought wryly. I could have put his back out! But he didn't seem to be too worried about his back. As she lay on the bed he undid the buttons of her pale blue blouse. She sighed with relief in the knowledge that the bra she was wearing – while not as gorgeous and sexy as the basque – was nevertheless a pretty balcony style in a shade which matched the blouse. She'd half-known, as she'd dressed that morning, that she was going to see him. Obviously her subconscious mind had told her that wearing the tired grey M&S wasn't the way to go.

He was undoing the belt on his trousers now, and suddenly he was on top of her, covering her face with kisses, moving his lips down her face and neck and resting them in the hollow between her breasts.

'I love you,' he whispered. 'I've always loved you.'

He entered her quickly and she squirmed slightly because she wasn't really ready for him. She'd wanted to be, of course, and as he kissed her she'd tried to think passionate thoughts, but the problem was that all she could think of was that he'd done this with a prostitute in Boston. She tried to push the image to the back of her mind and concentrate instead on the rhythm of his movement. But it was too difficult. And the idea of him doing it with the Boston girl wasn't a turn-on.

'I love you,' he said as he increased the pace. 'You're my girl, Siobhán, and you always will be.'

She squeezed her eyes tighter and tried to recapture the feelings that she'd had the first time they made love. The feeling that she'd found the right person for her. The connection between them. The sudden sense of rightness about being with him.

He cried out and then pulled her closer to him.

'That was fantastic,' he breathed into her ear.

She tried to move into a slightly more comfortable position.

'I've missed you so much.'

She'd missed him too. Even though there were times when she'd enjoyed being on her own, not having to worry about letting him know where she was or what she was doing or having him tell her that her job took up far too much of her time and that she wasn't paid nearly enough for it, she'd missed his nagging at her and his concern for her and the simple comfort of having someone else in her home and in her life.

'You know you have the most amazing body.' They were lying facing each other, still joined together. He ran his fingers along her spine, which he knew she loved.

'So have you.'

'We're good for each other,' he said softly.

'What was it like?' she asked.

'Huh?'

'With the . . . woman in Boston.'

'Oh, come on!' He looked angrily at her. 'I thought we were over all that.'

'You might be over it,' she said. 'I'm not.'

'Look, I was off my head in Boston,' he told her. 'I'd taken coke and stuff and so I can't even remember it properly.'

'Was it good, though?' she asked.

'If you must know – yes, it was,' he said. 'But for God's sake, Siobhán, she was a professional woman! She knew exactly what she was doing.'

'Any new tricks?' asked Siobhán.

He raised an eyebrow as he looked at her. 'Would you try them?'

'I just asked if there was something different she did,' said Siobhán.

'The whole thing was different,' he replied. 'But I didn't love her. It was just – sex.'

'I've got to go to the bathroom.' She slid away from him and walked into the bathroom. It too had undergone the ruthless cleaning courtesy of the agency, although the bottles of bath essence and pearl bath drops which she'd bought months earlier were still on the glass shelf. She leaned her head against the mirror over the sink. What did she want from Eddie? What was she going to say to him when she walked back into the bedroom?

She didn't want to let go of the life she'd expected to have with him – getting married, being even closer, being a real couple. She wanted all that. She really did. And she wanted the lovemaking too. Not the way it had just been, of course, which she hadn't enjoyed because she was still too upset with him to love him the way he wanted, but the way it had been before, when she'd given herself to him completely, trusting him, believing that he was the only person in the whole world for her. It had been perfect before. And she couldn't help wondering whether it could ever be perfect again.

In the course of her work she met people who were the victims of crimes, who demanded justice and wanted everything to be back the way it was before. And she had to tell them that it wasn't always possible. That even if they got justice, things could never be the way they were. She had to accept that for her and Eddie it could never be the way it was before either.

That didn't mean that it couldn't be just as good. But it had to be different.

She walked back into the bedroom and picked up her balcony bra from the floor. She fastened it around her, then picked up the blue blouse and slid her arms into the sleeves.

'Come back to bed,' said Eddie lazily. 'It's been so long . . . I think I'm ready to go again if you're up for it.'

She shook her head. 'I'm not up for it,' she told him. 'You probably realised that I wasn't really up for it the first time.'

'Hey!' He sat up. 'I didn't force—'

'God, no, of course not,' she said quickly. 'What I meant was . . . well, I wanted to but I wasn't really . . . my body and my mind weren't exactly ready for it.'

His eyes narrowed. 'What are you saying?'

'Eddie, I really and truly loved you. I wanted to be with you. I wanted to marry you. But I can't forgive you. I know that maybe I should. I know that you're sorry. It's just that . . .' Her voice trailed off. 'I'm sorry,' she said again as she removed her delicate engagement ring (she'd insisted on something small and neat so that it didn't get in the way) from her finger.

'Don't do this, Siobhán,' said Eddie. 'You're throwing it all away just because of one mistake.'

'I know,' she said as she continued to get dressed. 'I realise that. But it was the wrong mistake, Eddie.'

'It's all so bloody black and white with you, isn't it?' he demanded angrily. 'Crime and punishment. I've committed the crime and now you're punishing me.'

'It's not like that,' she protested.

'Well, how is it then?'

She couldn't answer.

'In that case,' he said, 'don't let me delay you.'

'Oh, Eddie.'

'Tonight you made me feel worse than the girl in Boston ever did,' he said. 'As though I tricked you into having sex with me just now.'

'You didn't trick me,' said Siobhán. 'I tricked myself.'

She took her bag from the armchair in the corner of the room. 'I'll leave my keys on the table. Goodbye, Eddie.'

But he said nothing in reply.

❧

She was in the underground car park, opening the driver's door, when a car pulled into the space beside her.

'Hello, Mizz P.,' said Carl O'Connor.

She wiped her eyes as she turned around but he could still see that she was upset.

'What's the matter?' he asked.

She shook her head wordlessly.

'Has that shithead you live with locked you out of the apartment again?'

'Don't be stupid,' she said.

'I was only looking out for you.'

'Yeah, well, I can look out for myself,' she retorted.

Carl laughed. 'You needed me once.'

She said nothing but got into the car. Carl stopped her from closing the door.

'Are you OK?' he asked. 'Do you want to go for a drink or anything?'

'I might be upset but I'm not stupid,' she said with a hint of spirit.

He looked at her shrewdly. 'If not now, another time perhaps?'

'Christ, you're all the same, aren't you!' she said hotly. 'I've just – I told you I'm upset and you're asking me for a date. Can't any of you damn well tell when a girl has had enough?'

'I never said I was asking you for a date,' he told her mildly. 'You're upset. I'm trying to be friendly, that's all.'

Her look was pure scepticism. 'Yeah, like you ever were before.'

'C'mon,' he said gently. 'I may be a member of the hated journo class, but it doesn't make me a monster.'

'You know, if you were a computer-generated ideal man I wouldn't go for a drink with you,' said Siobhán. 'I'm not doing men any more. I don't have the energy for it. Murder is easier.'

⤙

Iona was in the office the next morning when Sally phoned her to say that she had the accountant's report and, since she planned to be in town that day, would it suit Iona if she dropped it in to the office. Iona told her that she would be there until lunchtime if that suited, and Sally confirmed that she'd be in before twelve thirty.

It was actually midday when she walked into Rental Remedies with the buff folder under her arm. Because the office was open-plan, she immediately saw Iona sitting at her desk, using the tip of her pencil to scratch her head as she peered at the computer screen, a pair of fashionable reading glasses on the tip of her nose.

Sally cleared her throat loudly and Iona looked around. She smiled in greeting at Sally and beckoned her in past the reception desk.

Ruth Dawson looked up as Sally sat on the edge of Iona's desk.

'Sally – Ruth. Ruth – Sally,' said Iona as she put her glasses on the desk.

'Sally?' Ruth's eyes widened in surprise. 'Sally – as in – Sally?'

'Yes.'

'The Sally?'

'OK, I think we've established that this is Sally,' Iona told her colleague.

'Yes. But. Well. Sally. Hi, Sally,' said Ruth finally. 'Nice to meet you.'

'Have I been a topic of conversation?' asked Sally.

'To some extent,' admitted Iona.

'She never said that you were pregnant.' Ruth was staring at Sally's bump.

'Oh. No. I didn't.' Iona shrugged, while Ruth stared at both of them.

Sally blushed.

'Hey, look, Sally – why don't we grab a quick sandwich next door,' said Iona hurriedly. 'Ruth'll keep an eye for half an hour or so, won't you?' She looked demandingly at the other girl.

'Sure,' said Ruth. 'Nothing going on here now anyway.'

'Great.' Iona took her jacket from the back of her chair. 'Let's go.' She ushered Sally out on to the street and then looked at her apologetically.

'I'm sorry,' she said. 'It's just that I've got used to knowing you. I guess that . . . well, I haven't talked about it much to Ruth since I came back to work and of course nobody wants to ask anything. So I suppose they thought that we were still at loggerheads.'

'And we're not.' Sally followed Iona into the small café. 'I can see why that would surprise people actually.'

'To be honest it kind of surprises me too. What d'you fancy?' asked Iona as they nabbed a table and chairs.

'Salad would be perfect. And a coffee.' Sally had regained the ability to drink coffee without feeling nauseous.

Iona went up to the counter and ordered an Italian salad for Sally and a ham and cheese sandwich for herself, plus a couple of lattes.

'How are you feeling?' asked Iona as she brought the order back to the table. 'You're looking great.'

'Thanks,' said Sally. 'I feel good.'

The benefits of pregnancy had kicked in for her in the last week or so and she definitely looked a lot healthier than she'd done for a long time. Her skin was flawless and her hair gleamed under the soft lights of the café. The tired expression had gone from her face and her eyes sparkled.

Iona, who'd looked at herself in the mirror that morning and wondered if she could possibly flit back to New York just to get another makeover and feel like a normal person again, felt a stab of envy at Sally's new radiance.

'You haven't been contacted by the mad journo, have you?' she asked.

The sparkle went out of Sally's eyes.

'No, but if anyone comes around asking questions I'll kill them,' she said.

Iona chuckled. 'Another crime for Siobhán.'

Sally shrugged. 'I hope she manages to do as she said and distract them.'

'I hope so too,' agreed Iona. 'But the one thing you can say for her is that at least she's on our side.'

'Yes. She's a good person,' agreed Sally.

'And how's Jenna?'

'A bit weird, to tell you the truth,' said Sally. 'I didn't call you last night because like so many times nothing actually happened in the end, but she thought that Frank squeezed her hand yesterday afternoon.'

Iona's spoon clattered to the floor and she left it there.

'Yesterday afternoon?' she repeated.

'We went into the hospital in the afternoon because, of course, I'm off work now with the holidays. And Jenna asked to spend a bit of time with Frank on his own. She said that while she was talking to him he squeezed her hand.'

'Omigod, Sally.' Iona stared at her. 'This is huge progress.'

'I know. I know,' said Sally. 'Only the thing is, he didn't do it again. We stayed there until nine in the evening and nothing happened.'

'You could have called me,' said Iona sharply. 'Maybe if I'd come in . . .'

'I thought about it,' admitted Sally. 'But I wasn't really sure if Jenna had imagined it. That's partly what I mean about her being weird right now.'

Iona's jaw was clenched.

'If something had happened I would have called,' Sally assured her. 'Honestly.'

Iona said nothing but eventually relaxed her jaw.

'And Jenna – well, she's been acting so strange and worryingly,' said Sally. 'I thought maybe this was a good opportunity for her to feel loved and wanted by Frank. I know that's selfish of me, but that's what was going through my mind.'

'How is she acting strange?'

Sally explained about Jenna's friendship with the wild set of the school and her continued truculence at home.

'But a few days ago she suddenly started being sweetness and light again and talked about getting a summer job. Then yesterday she was back to being sullen. She's so difficult at the moment, she really is.'

'If something like that happens again you've got to call me,' said Iona. 'I mean, you said that nothing happens without us both agreeing . . .'

Sally nodded. 'I know. I told the hospital to let both of us know if there's any change.'

'Thanks,' said Iona. She opened the folder. 'Anything interesting in this?'

'I don't know,' said Sally. 'That's why I'm giving it to you.'

Iona skimmed through the sheets of paper and pursed her lips. 'I'll talk to Myles about it,' she said. 'I'm not sure, Sally, because I didn't do that much work for him, but I thought there were more clients than this.'

'It's hard to tell,' said Sally.

'You didn't bring the laptop, did you?'

'Sorry. I never thought of that.'

'When you go home, could you e-mail his client files to me?'

'All of his stuff is password-protected,' Sally told her. 'I know you gave me the Goldfinger password for the laptop itself but that won't let me access the files, will it?'

'You don't need to access the files themselves to send me the database,' said Iona. She cleared her throat. 'The password for that is Pussy Galore. I think there's an income and expenditure account on there too. And the password is simply 007.'

'Naturally.' Sally made a face. 'I should've guessed them all.'

'You probably would have if you'd kept at it,' said Iona. 'My password is Moneypenny.'

Sally smiled wryly.

'Don't get all upset because I have a password of my own,' Iona told her. 'You weren't as involved in that part of it as me. But you are now. So . . .'

'I'll check it out,' promised Sally. 'What's your e-mail address?'

Iona gave it to her.

'As soon as I get home I'll send them,' said Sally. 'If I've got a problem I'll phone you.'

'Great.' Iona closed the buff file and took a bite of her sandwich. 'Hopefully everything's fine, but if it isn't we'll know soon.'

'I won't let anything bad happen to the company,' said Sally. 'It's part of him.'

'I know,' said Iona. 'I won't let anything bad happen to it either.'

～

When she got back to the office Ruth was sitting at her desk eating a bagel.

'Am I late?' asked Iona.

'No, I just got hungry and ordered in,' said Ruth. 'How was lunch with the other woman?'

Iona shrugged. 'I don't think of her like that any more,' she said. 'We're kind of in this thing together.'

'Iona, you know that's beyond weird, don't you?'

'Why?'

'She's his first wife. You're . . . well, technically I know you're not, but – but morally you're his second wife. You shouldn't be friends.'

'We're not exactly friends,' said Iona. 'We just . . . well, we've had to get on, I suppose.'

'I couldn't do it,' said Ruth.

'You'd be surprised at what you can do when you put your mind to it,' responded Iona as she tapped the mouse and woke her computer from sleep.

～

It was Iona's turn to see Frank that night. She was excited about the fact that he might have squeezed Jenna's hand the day before and hoping that maybe this would be the night that he finally came back to them. If it was, she'd be at the hospital all evening.

But if not, she thought it might be a good idea to drop out to Lauren and Myles and see if her brother-in-law would look at the accountant's report and the list of clients that Sally had e-mailed her when she got home. She phoned Lauren, who told her that it would be fine to call by and that Myles would look at the files.

Iona took a lot of time and care over her appearance for this visit. She knew that she was on one of the up moments in her cycle of hope with Frank, feeling that he was coming out of the coma, that he loved her, that everything would work out for the best, even while she knew that there could still be months to go before he regained consciousness, and she had no idea whether he loved her and no idea what working out for the best actually meant any more. At the start of the whole thing it had been that Frank would wake up, disown Sally and come home with her. Now . . . now she simply didn't know.

'The worst thing is,' she murmured to him as she sat beside the bed and listened to the beep of the monitors, 'someone's going to be hurt at the end of it all. I mean, me and Sally are hurt already, of course. So are you, although that's physical, not mental. But at the moment we're kind of going through the motions with you. We're in limbo, Frank. We can get up every day and do things, but it's not really getting on with our lives. When you wake up – then we have to decide what's next. And I don't know what she wants to decide. I don't know what I want to decide. And neither of us know what the hell you'll decide, Frank. So it's really, really hard.'

She picked up the copy of the accountant's report. 'I'm meeting Myles about this tonight,' she said. 'I know you never really got on with him, but you know Frank, he's been great. So has Lauren.' Her glance flickered over the report again. 'I think I looked down on them because they were so suburban and ordinary – same way as I kinda looked down on Sally too. But they've all been fantastic really.' She leaned back in the chair and looked at him speculatively. 'I guess there's something else to tell you,' she said. 'I didn't before now because I felt guilty about it.'

Frank still didn't respond.

394

'I nearly slept with a bloke in New York.'

Frank's eyes opened. He stared straight ahead of him.

'I wish you wouldn't do that,' she told him. 'Unless you're going to participate in the conversation. Are you?'

He said nothing.

'I went for a break and I nearly slept with him because I was lonely. But I didn't because I still love you, Frank.'

Frank continued to stare impassively in front of him.

'And then last night I went for dinner with a client. It was a casual sort of thing, nothing more. But I felt really guilty about it because I liked him, and even though I don't fancy him or anything I just thought you should know. I don't want to hide things from you.'

His eyes fluttered closed again.

She looked at him intently for a while, then got up from the seat beside the bed and kissed him gently on the forehead. 'I'll be back the day after tomorrow,' she said. 'Maybe you'll be ready to talk then.'

⌒

Myles and Lauren were sitting in the conservatory at the back of the house when she arrived half an hour later.

'Gorgeous evening,' Myles said.

'Lovely,' Iona agreed. She thrust the folder at him. 'Can you cast your accountant's eye over this, Myles, and tell me what you think?'

He took the folder from her. She'd lost the slightly hectoring tone she normally used when talking to him and he was suddenly interested in what might be going on with the business.

While he looked through the file, Iona and Lauren sat on wicker recliners and watched Charlotte and Gavin race around the garden like mini tornados. Iona felt her heart constrict. It was this kind of domesticity that she'd wanted from Frank, no matter how afraid of it she also felt, and it was the idea that this could never happen for her now that was so difficult to accept. And yet, she realised, she was accepting it. Regardless of what happened with Frank's health, she was certain now that she would never have a baby with him, and although the thought hurt her, it wasn't as numbing as it had been a couple of months earlier.

'I have to tell you something,' said Lauren eventually.

Iona turned towards her and looked at her enquiringly, while Myles peeped over the top of the folder at them.

'Myles and I are going to have another baby.'

Somehow it didn't surprise Iona. Her sister was good with children.

'Congratulations,' she said as evenly as she could. 'When is it due?'

'I'm only three months gone,' said Lauren. 'There's a bit of time yet.'

'I'm glad for you.' Iona was surprised to realise that she actually meant it. She'd thought, as she'd heard Lauren's words, that she'd be jealous, but she wasn't. She was pleased for her sister.

'I know it's not ideal—'

'It's ideal for you,' said Iona.

'I know. But with all this stuff going on with Frank . . .'

'That's my problem and my life,' Iona told her. 'And just because it didn't work out for me, it doesn't mean you should feel rotten about your brilliant news.'

'Thank you,' said Lauren.

Iona got up from her chair and kissed her sister. Then she walked over to Myles and kissed him too.

'Steady on,' he said. 'You've never done that before.'

'I should've,' she told him. 'I was always a bit snotty with you, Myles, and I'd no right to be.'

'Ah, you're grand.' Myles was embarrassed.

'I'm not just being nice to you because you're looking at stuff for me,' added Iona hastily. 'It's because you're a nice bloke and a good husband and you're great with Lauren and the kids.'

'Take it easy,' warned Myles. 'I'll get notions about myself.'

Iona laughed and Lauren, who'd been extremely worried about telling Iona her news, but who knew that she couldn't keep it from her any longer, smiled with relief.

'I need to spend some more time with this,' said Myles after a period of time. 'But it seems to me that your accountant has undervalued the core business. Also, there's a big contract coming up with a leisure and spa complex which could be extremely profitable. I don't know whether any work has been done on it or not, but it's a long-term deal and it would be very good for the company.'

Iona remembered Frank talking about a big one, a great one, that he'd landed.

'I knew it,' she said. 'I knew that there was something not quite right about that bloke. Frank had his doubts too.'

'Seems like he's trying to take the company from you . . . well, I suppose from Sally really, on the cheap.'

'What'll we do?' asked Iona.

'You need to talk to this contractor guy, Pete, and see what's going on. And then talk to the accountant.'

Iona made a face.

'Do you want me to do it?' he asked.

'Would you?'

'Of course.'

'Myles, you're a star!' She beamed at him.

'But someone needs to contact the new client – Belleza del Serene – and see how things are going there too,' warned Myles. 'The installation isn't due to start for a few weeks, so you have time on your side, but it's still important to meet the person in charge and to talk to Pete to see that everything's in place.' He hesitated. 'Do you want me to do that too?'

'Jeez, Myles, that's asking too much,' said Iona.

'I don't mind,' he said. 'The only problem is that the client might want to meet someone from the company itself. Frank ran things on a very personal basis.'

'I'm surprised they haven't been in touch already,' said Iona.

'Maybe they have. Maybe Richard Moran has contacted everyone,' Myles told her.

'And maybe he's trying to get control of everything before Frank wakes up,' said Iona.

Lauren and Myles looked at her sympathetically.

'There was more progress yesterday.' She told them about Frank squeezing Jenna's hand. 'And when I go in I get the impression more and more that he has some idea of what's going on around him. But it's just taking so long.'

'Have you thought any more about what happens when he does wake up?' asked Lauren cautiously.

'No. Not really.'

'How's Sally?'

'Very well,' answered Iona. 'Her pregnancy suddenly seems to be doing her good.' She looked wryly at Lauren. 'You can meet her and share maternity tips.'

Lauren laughed. 'I don't think so.'

'No, really.' Iona's voice was definite. 'You and her have a lot in common. You're both caring sort of people. I'm just a selfish cow.'

'Ah, Io, you're not,' said Lauren.

'I try not to be,' said Iona. 'But sometimes I am. I practically forced Frank to marry me. Or not, as it turned out.'

'Oh, that's a family trait,' said Myles confidently. 'Sure Lauren did it to me too.'

'I did not!' Lauren looked accusingly at her husband and then started to laugh.

And Iona suddenly found herself laughing with her sister and brother-in-law and feeling light-hearted for the first time in months.

Chapter 34

Siobhán went for a run along the seafront. The late evening was an ideal time for running, not too warm but not cold, and with an almost imperceptible southerly breeze behind her. She emptied her mind as she ran, not thinking about the end of her relationship with Eddie or the piles of work on her desk, but simply allowing herself to be taken over by the here and now of running so that by the time she got back to the apartment she was glowing with a sheen of perspiration and physically tired although mentally refreshed.

She pushed open the door to the block and noticed her neighbours – one of the couples to whom Iona had rented an apartment – at the mailboxes. The woman was short and pretty, with a blonde ponytail peeking out from the back of her navy baseball cap. The guy with her was tall and athletic, wearing a matching baseball cap and navy Bermuda shorts. Siobhán smiled briefly at them as she ran up the stairs to her apartment, but the image of them remained in her mind as she let herself in and opened the patio doors to allow the air to circulate. She hopped under the shower and freshened up. Then she dressed in a pair of dark trousers and a white T-shirt, took the lift to the underground car park and drove to the station.

'What are you doing here?' asked her colleague, Joe O'Riordan. 'It's not your shift.'

'I wanted to look at the pix of the bank account scam people,' said Siobhán as she sat at her desk and booted up her computer. 'New info?'

'I'm not sure.' She opened the video pictures and looked at them pensively. Then she glanced up at Joe, who was observing her.

'I think I know where these people are based,' she said.

'Really?'

She studied the pictures again. 'Almost certainly.'

'Excellent! Where?'

'My apartment block,' she told him drily.

Joe's eyes widened. 'You've got to be kidding me.'

'Nope. I moved there a few weeks ago and they took an apartment around the same time. I remember the girl who rented the place out mentioning that she'd made a number of lettings in the block.'

'Are you sure?'

'Absolutely.'

'Well, this will be brownie points for Bray.' He grinned at her and she smiled back.

'We'll organise surveillance, get a handle on what they're doing, when they're there, how things are panning out. And then, hopefully, nab them and the gear in the apartment.'

'Let's go and talk to the Super,' said Joe.

The chief's office door was open. Siobhán looked inside and asked if they could have a chat. He raised an eyebrow at her, sensing from her tone that there was good news brewing, and waved them to the seat in front of him.

'Well?' he asked.

Siobhán gave him a run-down of what she'd told Joe.

'I can get more information about the tenants from the person who did the rental,' she told him. 'She's the person who rented to me too.' She cleared her throat and looked at the Super. 'She's actually one of the wives in the bigamy case.'

'What?' He looked at her in astonishment.

'I know, I know. But renting apartments is her business . . .'

'You've nearly completed the work on that case, haven't you?'

Siobhán nodded. 'Just waiting to see whether the husband wakes up or not,' she said. 'Hardly worth going any further while he's comatose.'

'I hate it when cases overlap,' complained her chief.

'They don't,' she told him. 'Iona Brannock has nothing to do with this other than the rental.'

'Fair enough,' he said. 'OK. Let's work out how we're going to deal with it. And by the way, Siobhán – good work.'

'Thanks,' she said as she tried to hide her smile of satisfaction.

~

After the meeting she contacted Iona and told her about the tenants in apartment number 4.

'Oh no!' Iona groaned. 'Not again.'

'What d'you mean, not again?' asked Siobhán, suddenly concerned. 'Has this happened before?'

'Of course not,' Iona told her. 'But a year or so ago one of my tenants was busted for drugs. The damn drug squad did a stakeout of the apartment then. I'm beginning to feel like an extra on *The Bill* or something.'

Siobhán laughed. 'Don't worry. You don't have to do anything other than give me some information.'

'You'll need a warrant,' said Iona. 'I can't let you just burst into the apartment.'

'I'll get everything in order,' promised Siobhán.

'Right.' Iona sighed as she replaced the phone. Garret would be really pissed off to discover that another one of their apartments was about to be raided by the gardai.

~

Almost as soon as she'd finished speaking to Iona, Siobhán's mobile rang.

'Hi,' said Carl O'Connor. 'Busy?'

'Actually, yes,' she said.

'Anything exciting?'

Siobhán thought about it for a moment. Perhaps if she gave O'Connor a little inside information on the ID scam he'd lose

401

interest in the Ardallen case. She'd promised Iona and Sally that she'd protect them as much as possible, and this might be the best way.

'Maybe,' she said finally.

'How about that drink?' he asked.

'OK.'

'OK?' Carl was surprised. He hadn't expected her to agree so quickly.

'I'll meet you in Blackrock,' she said. 'Not in the town centre, though. The Playwright?'

'Fine.' The bar was big and impersonal despite its thatched roof and traditional theme.

'An hour,' said Siobhán.

'Right,' said Carl.

He was there before her and saw her as she walked through the door, tall and confident, her eyes scanning the crowd for him. He raised his hand in greeting and she sat down on a bar stool beside him.

'Drink?' he asked.

'Sparkling water.'

'I'm having a beer,' he told her. 'Just one. So no need to arrest me on suspicion of drink-driving or anything like that.'

'Fine,' she said. 'I won't.'

'I was only kidding.'

'I know.'

He sighed as the barman poured him a pint of lager and placed a bottle of water in front of Siobhán.

'You're hard work sometimes,' he told her.

'I don't mean to be,' she said.

'Maybe it's the job.'

'I like my job,' she told him. 'But it's not about giving information to crusading journalists.'

'All journalists get information from the cops,' he said.

'I know. I know. But . . .'

'I'm not a heartless bastard, you know,' he told her. 'I do have a sensitive side.'

402

She smiled suddenly. 'I know,' she said. 'You were actually very sensitive when I was locked out of my apartment. And I didn't thank you properly. So – thanks.'

'You're nice when you're not trying to make me feel like a shit.'

'If I've ever made you feel that way, I'm sorry,' she said.

'You're being very understanding tonight,' said Carl. 'It's scary!'

She took a sip of her water.

'I'm going to be completely honest with you,' she said.

Carl laughed. 'That's usually the signal for the big lie.'

'I'm not going to lie to you. What's the point in that?'

She gave him a brief resumé of the facts about Frank, Sally and Iona while he sipped his beer. He didn't take any notes.

'And so,' she concluded, 'those women are trying to get on with things in very difficult circumstances. You, or your friend, writing a story about them is the very last thing they need.'

'Sometimes people like to have their story told,' said Carl. 'We wouldn't print anything unless they wanted it.'

'Oh, come on.' She grimaced. 'You're always printing stuff that nobody wants printed.'

'Not really,' he said. 'Certainly stuff that the gardai don't want printed. But most of the other stuff – people invite us into their homes and tell us.'

'But it's hardly ever what they imagined in the end,' she said. 'Sally and Iona are private people. This is a private tragedy for them. Maybe at some time in the future either one of them might decide that it's newsworthy and decide to spill their guts to you. But couldn't that be their choice, not yours?'

Carl tapped his fingers lightly on the bar counter. 'And instead of this very interesting story, you want me to write – what?'

'You know the fake ID scam going around?'

He nodded.

'We've got a good lead and a good break in the case,' she said. 'I'll give you the inside track on it plus let you know when the whole thing is going down.'

'It's not as exciting as the bigamy,' complained Carl.

'Oh come on!' she said. 'I bet you'll get lots of interviews from people who were ripped off. And I'll make sure you have exclusive info.'

'Siobhán—'

'I know it's not the same as rummaging around in people's lives,' she said fiercely. 'But it's the best I can do. These are nice women, Carl. They don't deserve to have things written about them.'

'You really care about them, don't you?'

'Of course I care!' she cried. 'That's the problem with you guys. You think it's all a job to us. Well, yes, it is a job, but you'd have to be made of ice not to care about some of the things that go on. And it's not just the victims we feel sorry for. I know that some of the people who commit crimes are products of circumstances. I feel sorry for them too. We're not all heartless bastards in uniform, you know.'

'You don't wear a uniform at all,' Carl pointed out.

'Don't be so pedantic!'

'I'm sorry,' said Carl. He looked at her thoughtfully. 'You're a nice person, Siobhán Farrell, despite your hard heart.'

'I don't have a hard heart,' she said.

'I'll talk to JoJo,' he said eventually. 'I'll let her know the set-up regarding the bigamy case. It is human interest, Siobhán. She's justified in going after it.'

'I know. But you have to ask yourself – what possible good can come out of it?'

'Might stop other blokes with the same idea,' he said.

'If there was a bigamy epidemic maybe,' said Siobhán. 'But there isn't.'

'All right, all right,' said Carl. 'I'll do what I— hey, I've just thought, two women, one pregnant. Weren't they the women with you that night I bumped into you in Dun Laoghaire?'

Siobhán nodded.

'Are you sure you're not the one getting too involved here?'

'Absolutely positive,' said Siobhán. 'I'm not naïve, Carl. I checked out both women thoroughly. And the husband. It's as straightforward as anything like this can be. He deceived them. I met them because . . . well, I liked them and they wanted to go out.'

'Gosh, you're actually a real softie,' he teased gently.

'I'm not,' she assured him. 'I . . .' Suddenly she thought of Eddie. He used to call her a softie too, whenever she cried at something on the TV or a particular piece of music.

'How's things with the fiancé?' asked Carl casually.

'Ex-fiancé,' she told him.

'Ah.'

'Better ex-fiancé than ex-husband,' she said.

'Indeed.' He smiled shortly at her. 'You were right to dump him. Anyone who didn't appreciate you in that bas—'

'Shut up, O'Connor,' she said quickly. 'I'd like to forget about that, thank you.'

'I can't forget about it,' he told her.

'You'd better,' she said.

He grinned. 'Another drink?' he asked.

She thought about it for a moment and then shook her head. 'I've things to do,' she told him.

'Another time?'

'Maybe,' she said as she gathered her belongings. 'You never know.'

Chapter 35

Myles arranged a meeting between Frank's accountant and Sally and Iona. He came along too and was glad that he'd done so because he realised very quickly that Richard Moran had been trying to pull the wool over Sally's eyes in relation to the value of the company.

'You haven't considered the deal with the spa and therapy centre, Belleza del Serene, as far as I can see,' Myles pointed out.

'Yes, but that deal was arranged by Frank and contingent on him getting a team together to carry it out,' protested Richard.

'And you were just going to let it fall by the wayside?' asked Myles. 'You weren't going to get anyone to talk to this guy . . .' he looked down at his notes, 'Anthony Brady, at all?'

Richard looked uncomfortable. 'Well of course I've had a conversation—'

'In which case you should have been considering this deal,' said Myles firmly. He stood up. 'I don't think you've been acting in Sally's best interests, and it's my belief that the ladies would be better off not dealing with you any more. I'll contact you to make arrangements.'

'Hey, you can't do that!' cried Richard.

'Yes I can,' said Myles, and ushered Sally and Iona out of the office.

⌒

They went for a coffee in a nearby hotel where both Iona and Sally looked at Myles in admiration.

'You know, I can totally understand what Lauren sees in you now,' said Iona. 'I never knew you accountants could be so macho.'

Myles laughed. 'Don't be such a dope,' he said. 'Now look, we need to organise a meeting with the contractors, particularly Pete Maguire, and see what they have to say about everything. And then, if you agree, Sally, we'll make the necessary changes to the company set-up. I can get my solicitor to look through this for you.'

'You're being really kind,' said Sally as she shifted in the seat to make herself more comfortable. 'You didn't have to do all this for us.'

'I'm certainly not going to let someone like Richard Moran give all accountants a bad name,' said Myles cheerfully. 'Besides, Iona already has a low enough opinion of us.'

'Not now,' she said. 'You truly have been great, Myles.'

'Thanks,' he said. 'This afternoon I'll set up the meeting. You'll be able to come along, Sally?'

She nodded and he looked at his sister-in-law. 'Io?'

'Sally's the director,' she said. 'I don't really have anything to do with the company at all.'

'Oh, but you must come,' Sally insisted. 'It wouldn't be right without you. Besides, we have an agreement.'

'What agreement?' asked Myles.

'That both of us have an equal say in what happens about Frank in hospital and the company,' Iona told him. 'Can you set something up for late afternoon? That way I won't have to juggle my time at work so much.'

'Sure,' he said.

Sally and Iona smiled at each other.

'I like having this to do,' said Sally. 'I mean, I know nothing about business and even less about this business, but . . . well, it's good to be involved.'

'I know,' said Iona. 'And I'll tell you something, Sally, when Frank finally does bother his arse to wake up, he'll be gobsmacked at how wonderfully his company has been run while he was out of it. He certainly won't be able to pretend that it's all really technical and difficult any more.'

∽

The meeting with the contractors went extremely well. Pete Maguire was a hardworking man who was loyal to Frank but who had worked under Richard Moran's instructions. Myles took charge of the meeting and introduced Sally as a co-director and Iona as an interested party.

'I worked with Frank on Belleza del Serene of course,' Pete said. 'I spoke to the other accountant, Richard, about it too. We need to get off our backsides and do something about it.'

'But it can be done?'

'If we start now, of course.'

'Excellent,' said Iona. 'Then let's get going.'

∽

Their next step was meeting Anthony Brady, the managing director of the holding company which operated the spa and therapy complex. Anthony had expressed worries about the contract because he hadn't heard from Frank for so long and had only dealt with Richard Moran, but Sally, Iona and Myles assured him that everything was under control, that the work would be done and certified and that Anthony had absolutely nothing to worry about.

Sally herself was worried that Anthony would dismiss them and say that he wanted to deal with a company whose managing director wasn't lying comatose in a hospital bed, but she knew that Myles added a certain air of gravitas to their meeting, while Iona was incredibly brisk and businesslike (and looked, thought Sally, extremely efficient and composed in her tailored suit and high-heeled shoes).

'A good day's work,' said Myles as they drove back from the complex.

'Fantastic,' agreed Sally. 'Thanks again, Myles.'

'You're welcome,' he said. 'Lauren asked me to ask both of you if you'd like to join us for dinner some evening?'

'I'd love to,' said Sally. 'But I'm trying to be around for Jenna in the evenings. She's in a lot right now and I'm afraid to go out and leave her at home.'

'For heaven's sake, why?' asked Iona. 'I thought everything was OK with her again.'

'Since her dad squeezed her hand she's been up and down,' said Sally. 'And me getting bigger and bigger doesn't seem to be helping either. She appears to have rowed with all of her friends, and the relationship with her boyfriend is over too as far as I can see. She was working for a while in the local Spar but gave that up . . . I'm still not sure where I am with Jenna.'

'Is she going to the hospital with you?' asked Iona.

Sally nodded. 'But of course Frank hasn't squeezed her hand since. It's really disheartening.'

'Why don't you get her to do some work on Frank's files?' asked Myles. 'There's lots of stuff to update based on the info that Richard Moran and Pete Maguire gave us, and there's a whole timetable to be done up for the spa job. Maybe that would interest her?'

'Gosh, Myles, you're hitting all the buttons today,' she said. 'Jenna likes computers. You're right. This could be just the thing for her.'

'Call me a super-god,' said Myles as he turned into Sally's driveway.

Iona giggled. 'OK, now you've lost it completely,' she said as Sally got out of the car and said goodbye.

～

Jenna was lying on her bed, the earphones of her MP3 player tucked into her ears and the music loud enough to be an irritating tinny beat to anyone else in the room. Sally picked her way through the discarded clothes, magazines and shoes to sit on the edge of the bed. Jenna opened her eyes and stared at her mother.

God, she thought, but Sally was like an enormous blimp now. Plenty of her friends' mothers had been pregnant at some stage or another when Jenna was growing up, but she was a hundred per cent certain that none of them had been as huge as Sally at this point in their pregnancy. Her mother couldn't even get away with wearing bigger-sized normal clothes. Every stitch in her wardrobe was maternity wear.

'I was with your dad's accountant today,' said Sally as Jenna removed the earphones and asked her what she wanted. 'We've done a lot of work on keeping his company going.'

'We?'

'Iona and me. Helped by Iona's brother-in-law.'

'You know that you're getting madder by the minute, don't you?' said Jenna. 'At first you hated her, then you put up with her, and now you're positively friendly with her. This is insane.'

'She has expertise that I don't,' said Sally. 'And she's a victim too. So. Listen to me.'

Jenna made a face of exaggerated boredom.

'This is important,' said Sally. 'You know that your dad kept all his records on computer?'

'Where else would you expect him to keep them?' demanded Jenna. 'The back of an envelope?'

'Well, we'd love you to go through them and update them based on the information we have from the accountant,' said Sally as though Jenna hadn't spoken. 'We realised that he was trying to rip us off.'

'Not really?' Jenna sat upright on the bed.

'Yes,' said Sally. She explained about the new contract and the valuation that Richard Moran had put on the business, and the fact that she and Iona were going to make sure that the system was installed for the spa.

'But Mum, you know nothing about it!' cried Jenna.

'No, but the contractor guy does. And Myles is completely up to speed with everything,' said Sally. 'So what we really need, to get a good handle on everything about the company, is to have those records updated. Iona doesn't have time, she's working. I'm

410

hopeless at your dad's stuff – you know how complicated he always made it with all those folders and sub-folders and God knows what. I e-mailed some files to Iona but we need to have the whole thing looked at properly. Myles has already done loads for us. So we thought about you.'

Jenna looked thoughtful.

'If you don't want to, that's fine. It's your choice, of course.' Sally tried to keep her voice as dismissive as she could. She didn't want Jenna to know how much she wanted her to be involved.

'No . . . it's OK.' Jenna swung her legs over the side of the bed. 'I'll do it. You're right. You're useless with the computer.'

'Great,' said Sally, unable to keep the relief out of her voice. 'It's all on the laptop. Oh, you need a password for that. It's—'

'Goldfinger. I know,' said Jenna impatiently.

'I didn't realise you already knew that.' Sally looked at her in surprise.

'Don't be so feeble, Mum.' Jenna grinned at her. 'How else could I have played games on Dad's computer if I didn't know his password?'

~

It took Jenna two days to work her way through Frank's clients and update everything. When she'd finished, she had a neat folder of information about the clients and the company and she also had a few ideas about how they should schedule some of the jobs that needed to be done. She was very, very pleased with herself, especially as she hadn't been distracted by the Wingnuts game on the computer, nor the very addictive tic-tac-toe game that Frank also had.

However, with all her work done, and with Sally asleep in the bedroom next door (she had taken to having afternoon naps between two and four, which Jenna thought was both a blessing and a curse), Jenna devoted her time to blasting planes out of the virtual sky and playing twelve games of tic-tac-toe in a row. Before she shut down the computer she checked all of the files once more to make sure that she hadn't missed anything. There was only one folder that was bothering her. Like everything else it was password-protected, and the password wasn't Goldfinger or James Bond or any of the other Bond-friendly words that she tried. Jenna was worried that there might be information on another project like the spa kept there, and that it could be potential business that might be lost to the company.

She frowned as she looked at the little icon on the desktop. From what she could see, it didn't contain a lot of information, which was both bothering and a relief. All of the other individual folders on the computer were quite large because they held digital photographs of Frank's work, schematics of installations or of products and copies of contracts with individual companies. But this folder contained much less. Frank hadn't named it in the same way as the others either; they had company names and a reference of his own, while this was simply a reference, CH1936, which didn't mean anything to her. It was really bugging her that she hadn't managed to figure it out.

Sam was the person to ask about it. Jenna's former best friend knew everything there was to know about computers, and had been suspended from school once for hacking into student records from her own wireless laptop. But, of course, Jenna and Sam weren't speaking ever since Jenna had started going out with Gerry Cullinan and had hooked up with Aline Keogh and Cindy Ryan. Sam hadn't been bothered that Jenna and Gerry were having sex (although at first, and when they'd still been speaking, she'd lectured Jenna about safe sex and not getting pregnant whatever else she did), but she'd been disgusted when Jenna had dropped her in favour of Aline and Cindy. Jenna didn't blame her. If the shoe had been on the other foot, she would have been pretty pissed off with her friend too. After all, Aline and Cindy were the sort of girls they normally didn't hang around with at all. Disruptive, spending all their time and money on boys and make-up, thinking that it was fun to get wasted every night . . .

Well, they were right and wrong about that. Jenna leaned back in the chair and closed her eyes. Getting wasted had been kind of

412

fun until it had all gone wrong and she'd ended up being driven home in a police car. She felt herself grow hot with embarrassment at the memory. But the thing was, Aline and Cindy weren't judgemental. Sam was. As she herself had been until it was her own family which was being judged.

She hadn't seen Sam since they'd broken up for the school holidays. She knew that her former friend was doing some work experience at a local IT firm in the town centre. Maybe she'd be willing to talk to her.

She sent Sam a text message asking her to call and wondered when, or if, her friend would do as she asked. Two minutes later her mobile chirped.

'Hi, Sam,' she said.

'Hello.' Sam's voice was cautious.

'I'm sorry,' said Jenna.

'For what?'

'Everything. Can you talk?'

'Not now.'

'Would you like to call around tonight? Can you?'

'OK,' said Sam.

'Great.'

And as she ended the call Jenna realised that a weight had been lifted off her shoulders.

❧

He could hear the nurses talking, chatting about something that had happened on the wards that day. He couldn't exactly figure out what they were saying because there was a lot of jargon involved and he wasn't able to concentrate on it. That was the problem. Concentrating. He wasn't sure where he was at any particular moment in time. At first he'd thought that he was in another time and place, as though he'd passed through some strange portal into his past. He'd lived events and yet he'd lived them with the feeling that he'd done it all before. Other times he was with Sally or Iona and it seemed as though those times were just happening. His

413

perception of space and time was all over the place. He wasn't able to pin down exactly what was happening and when.

Yet the constant, the thing that kept coming back to him, was that he was in bed and that there were people around him. He would snap into an experience with people he knew which seemed so vivid and so immediate, and then, quite suddenly, he would be back in this other place where he couldn't seem to move or communicate with anyone and where things seemed to be happening around him but he wasn't able to take part. It was a horrible feeling. The other thing was that he couldn't really remember things properly once he'd snapped back to this reality. And so he seemed always to be trying to fight his way out of a kind of mental soup, only he was never sure about what was real and what wasn't.

He didn't want to think that what was real was that there were two of them. Iona and Sally. Sally and Iona. Both loved by him. Both loving him, he thought. Christ, he'd made such a mess of it all. He'd never intended for it to end up like this. He'd never intended to fall in love with two women. But he had. At different times and for different reasons. And he'd been too weak-willed to let one of them go.

He'd married Iona because he was afraid he'd lose her. And he hadn't divorced Sally because he loved her and didn't want to lose her either. He knew that was ridiculous. But both of them gave him different things in his life. And both of them gave him the sense of family that he craved so much.

After he and Sally had come to the conclusion that there wouldn't be any more children he'd felt cheated. He'd wanted her to consider IVF but she wouldn't, and in the end he'd accepted that. He'd thrown himself into his work instead so that he could provide for the daughter he did have. His lovely, lovely Jenna.

And yet the support came from Iona, whom he'd met so unexpectedly, and not from Sally. Iona, who was so different but so much fun to be with. Who made him feel wanted at a time when Sally wasn't able to make him feel that way.

He'd known it was wrong from the start. There was no excuse. He hated himself for what he'd done. He deserved whatever was happening to him now, whatever punishment was being meted out to him.

He was afraid that he was paralysed. He was sure, now, that when he was walking and talking to people it wasn't really happening no matter how real it seemed at the time. The feeling of not being able to move, of being somehow trapped inside his own body, was a much stronger feeling.

He tried to form words but he seemed to have forgotten how. He thought that there might be lots of things that he'd forgotten only he didn't know what they might be. He felt a wave of panic overwhelm him. He tried to cry out.

∾

Susan Carpenter looked at her patient. Frank's eyes were closed but she knew that she'd heard him make a sound. And his fists were tightly clenched, grasping the sheet that covered him.

'Can you hear me, Frank?' she asked.

He said nothing. But she was sure that his grip had tightened on the sheet.

∾

Sam called around to Jenna's later that evening. Sally was surprised but delighted to see her daughter's friend again, even though both of them disappeared upstairs to Jenna's room almost immediately. The boyfriend was gone, the new girlfriends seemed to be gone too, and Sam was back. Sally wondered whether things were turning the corner for her daughter at last.

∾

'I'm not sure I can crack this,' said Sam as she looked at the laptop files.

'I bet you can,' said Jenna as she watched her friend's fingers fly over the keyboard. 'You're like wired to computer code.'

'Ha-bloody-ha. But of course you've spent the last few months thinking airhead thoughts and having sex so you know nothing about important things like computer codes.' Sam turned to look at her.

'You're right,' said Jenna.

'And you want something done, you come to me.'

'Is it any use to say I was going through a bit of a rough patch?' asked Jenna.

'What happened with Gerry?'

Jenna told her about his dumping of her.

'Bit shitty,' remarked Sam.

'I don't blame him really,' said Jenna. 'I was in a state that night. Aline and Cindy weren't much better. I hate thinking about it.'

'Yeah, but he'd been sleeping with you.'

'You're going to hold that against me for ever.'

'No I'm not,' said Sam. And then she laughed slightly. 'I guess. He's a good-looking bloke, isn't he? Was it good, the sex?'

Jenna shrugged. 'At first, yes. And then it became a bit like something I had to do. I loved him because he was so great about my dad and everything, but in the end I felt like I was sleeping with him to say thanks for being nice to me. But I enjoyed it.'

'I would have been nice to you.' Sam grinned. 'But I wouldn't have made you sleep with me.'

'Eejit.' Jenna threw a small cushion at her friend.

Sam smiled. 'So we're cool again?' she asked.

'Absolutely,' said Jenna. 'I was a bit of a dipstick.'

'Ah, Jen, you were going through a bit of a trauma.'

'I suppose.'

'Look, I'd freak out if my dad did the same as yours. But it's OK. It's not your fault.'

'Thanks.'

'Really.' Sam scrunched up her nose and peered at the computer screen again. 'Why would your dad protect this file differently?'

416

'Dunno.' Jenna shrugged. 'He's into that, though. He's the only person I know who has different pin numbers for all his cards and stuff and can remember them all.'

'If he picked a random number for this . . .' Sam sighed. 'I need some kind of clue.'

'Like what?' asked Jenna.

'Is there anything else he's into besides James Bond?'

Sam continued to stare at the screen.

'Not that I know of,' Jenna told her. 'If he's just used a number we are in trouble, aren't we?'

'I have a programme at home that might crack it,' said Sam. 'I could copy the file and run it there.'

'OK,' said Jenna.

'Your mum won't mind?'

'She's the one who wants to know all about the company,' said Jenna. She looked at Sam, a worried expression on her face. 'You don't think he was involved with some weird stuff, do you? And that's why he's given it special protection?'

'I protect all my files really well,' said Sam. 'This could be anything. Don't worry.'

'The thing is,' said Jenna gloomily, 'when it comes to my dad, these days we seem to do nothing but worry.'

Chapter 36

Siobhán contacted Iona again about the residents of apartment 4. She explained that they were going to mount some surveillance on the apartment and that the plan was to arrest the two people, hopefully surrounded by plenty of evidence of the ID scam. She asked Iona whether it would be possible to get the key to the apartment since that way they wouldn't have to break down the door. Iona had gone through this before with the drugs bust, although the idea of having to do it all again made her wonder whether she had become utterly hopeless at picking tenants. Yet the couple to whom she'd leased the apartment had excellent references. Now she supposed that they, too, had been faked. She called the landlord and explained the situation to him and, horrified and shocked, he agreed to co-operate as fully as possible with the police. So she met up with Siobhán and gave her the key.

'And we'd really like it if you didn't trash the place,' she told her hopefully.

Siobhán grinned. 'You'll hardly even know we were there,' she said, pleased that everything was coming together so well.

On the day of the planned raid, Siobhán rang Carl O'Connor.

'Thanks,' he said. 'But you've got to know, Siobhán, that if you guys make a complete hash of it, I'll have to report it like that.'

'What makes you think we'll make a hash of it?'

'Nothing,' he said. 'I just wanted you to know that I wasn't going to do a puff piece on how great the cops are.'

'Wouldn't dream of you doing that,' she said. 'Wouldn't dream of it.'

As they approached the apartment building, though, her heart was hammering in her chest. She, too, hoped that they wouldn't make a hash of things. Sometimes a case could fail on the silliest of errors. But they had their search warrant, which she had ensured was properly executed, they had the keys, they knew the movements of the people concerned, and intelligence they'd gathered in recent days meant they were pretty certain that there was a supply of blank driver's licences and passports in the apartment. But it could still all go wrong. Things did.

'Ready to go?' Her partner, Larry, raised his eyebrows at her as they stood in the hallway of the block, the uniformed gardai in support.

'As I'll ever be,' she said.

They knocked at the apartment door and the blonde woman answered it. Her eyes widened in recognition as she saw Siobhán and then darkened as she realised that her neighbour was accompanied by the gardai.

And then they were in the apartment and the pile of blank licences was in full view, piled on a coffee table, while the athletic man looked around him in despair and Larry started to read him his rights.

'You bitch!' cried the blonde woman. 'You were spying on us. And we were nice to you. I said hello every time we met.'

'You do not have to say anything . . .' Siobhán intoned the words hoping that this was an arrest which would lead to a conviction.

There was a notebook on the table too, filled with names and addresses, and a bag containing over ten thousand euros.

'Aladdin's cave,' said Larry cheerfully, after the man and woman had been brought outside. 'Good one, Siobhán.'

'Luck, really,' she said, although she was bursting with pride that it had worked out so well. 'If I hadn't been living here I wouldn't have spotted them. But the case would've broken sooner or later.'

'False modesty *so* doesn't become you!' He grinned.

'I know.' She laughed, feeling the tension that had been building up in her over the days of surveillance disappear. 'Super-cop, that's me.'

'And any chance I could have a few words with you?' Carl O'Connor, who'd arrived in time for the arrests, looked enquiringly at her.

'I've got to get back to the station now,' she told him. 'There's paperwork to deal with. It's not all bursting into apartments and arresting everyone in sight, you know.'

Larry looked horrified at her casual way of speaking to the reporter, but Carl grinned.

'How about later?' he suggested. 'I could meet you for a coffee? There'll be two pieces for the paper. The story of the arrest and then the story behind it – you know, following the gang and all that sort of stuff.'

'Happy to help,' said Siobhán.

'You want me to come along too?' asked Larry.

'I don't think so,' Carl told him. 'I'm sure Detective Garda Farrell will be more than enough help all by herself.'

⌒

Iona was thinking about the arrest of her two tenants and wondering whether they'd get bail and return to the apartment (the idea of which was freaking out her landlord) when the phone rang.

'This is Dr Carroll,' said the voice. 'It's another good news update. Frank is showing a much greater awareness of his surroundings now, and we think it would be good for you to come in.'

'And Sally?' she asked. 'Have you called Sally?'

'My colleague is speaking to her now,' said the doctor. 'Of course it's still not what you'd want, Iona. We're not talking about him suddenly waking up, you know. But it's a substantial improvement.'

'I'll be there right away,' Iona said.

She was at the hospital before Sally. Terri Cooper explained that she'd asked Frank to move his hand that morning and that he'd actually done it. She'd asked him a second time and he'd repeated the action. But he hadn't done it a third time.

'Oh, God,' whispered Iona. 'But that's immense.'

'Every case is different, of course,' said Terri. 'But as you both know, the thing about Frank is that there is brain activity. He just doesn't seem to want to come out of the coma.'

'We're not entirely surprised,' said Iona. 'If I were him I mightn't be in too much of a hurry to wake up either.'

She moved closer to the bed. 'Frank,' she said softly. 'It's me. Iona. Can you move your hand? Make a fist?'

She watched as his left hand moved slowly and his fingers curled towards his palm.

'Oh!' She reached out and took his hand. 'Frank, I know you're in there. I know you are. We're all here rooting for you. Come back to us, please.'

He didn't react any more. She sat beside the bed holding his clenched hand until the door opened and Sally and Jenna walked in. Then she gently released his hand and let it lie on the bed.

'He made a fist.' Iona started to cry. 'He did it, Sally. I asked him to and he did it.'

Sally gulped. 'Hi, Frank,' she said. 'It's Sally. Can you hear me?'

He didn't move.

'Dad.' Jenna's words were clear and distinct. 'You need to wake up. You've been lying there far too long messing with our lives.'

Frank's head slowly moved towards the sound of Jenna's voice.

'Oh, Dad!' This time Jenna's voice was shaky. 'You can hear me. You really can.'

Sally held her breath and glanced at Iona, who was blinking away her tears.

'Can you hear me, Frank?' she said softly.

He didn't move.

'Keep talking, Jenna,' commanded Iona. 'It's your voice he's reacting to.'

Jenna looked at them anxiously and then at her father again.

'We've been doing really well while you've been asleep,' she continued. 'Mum and Iona have been keeping the company going. You'd be so proud of them.' She glanced at Sally, who smiled encouragingly at her. 'Your accountant was a shit but they found out about it. There's a new contract which will do really well. Oh, and there's stuff on your computer we want to access,' she added. 'You know, files and things. So you need to wake up to help us.' She sat back.

Frank's head moved slightly again but his eyes remained closed. His fingers, though, tightened around the blanket.

'Don't worry about anything,' said Iona. 'Just get well. We can sort out the other things afterwards.'

But there was a lot to sort out. She said as much to Sally when they went to the cafeteria a little later. Jenna had gone outside, saying that she wanted to phone Sam on her mobile.

'So what are we going to do?' she asked. 'When he wakes up?'

Sally ladled some sugar into her coffee.

'Do we still love him?' she asked thoughtfully. 'Knowing what he did? Or are we just guilty about him because he was in an accident?'

Iona said nothing.

'Jenna talks about it a lot,' said Sally. 'Whether we should throw him out. She said it'd serve him right if he had to live with you for ever.'

Iona looked startled.

'It was when she hated you,' said Sally. 'She'd downloaded the coma information and decided that he'd need long-term care and that you were the person to give it to him.'

'It's bloody difficult, isn't it?'

'I love him,' said Sally. Her hand rested on the swell of her stomach. 'He's the father of my baby. I've been with him all my life.'

'I love him too,' said Iona slowly. 'That's crazy, isn't it? He betrayed us both but we still love him. Thing is, I don't know if I can forgive him.'

'I have to forgive him,' said Sally.

'No you don't,' Iona told her. 'You can throw him out, just like Jenna says.'

'And where would he go? To you?'

Iona sighed. 'Are we arguing about him?' she asked. 'Who gets him? Is he worth it?'

'He'll need care when he gets out,' said Sally.

'And you'll have a baby to care for too,' Iona pointed out.

'So . . . we let *him* choose?' She looked at Iona despairingly. 'Why should *he* get to choose?'

'He shouldn't get to choose,' agreed Iona. 'We have to decide. We have to do what's best for us.'

'Well, then?' Sally looked at her challengingly.

'Right now?' asked Iona. 'You want to decide right now? Without thinking about it?'

'I bet we've both done nothing but think about it,' Sally told her. 'We know the pros and cons for each of us. For me, he's a father for Jenna and the baby and I've known him longer. But against is the fact that he might need help and we'll have a newborn baby to think about. For you – you're younger and better able to look after him. Against . . .' She shrugged. 'Maybe there're more pros than cons for you.'

Iona shook her head. 'You're a family,' she told Sally. 'We're just a couple.'

'You wanted a baby,' Sally reminded her.

'My head is spinning,' said Iona. 'Please, Sally, please can we talk about this another time?'

'I guess so,' said Sally after a pause. 'I guess we still have plenty of time to decide.'

❧

The following evening, since the gardai had finished with the apartment, Iona went to Dun Laoghaire to check it out. The landlord had told her to get new tenants just as soon as everything was sorted out with the gardai, so she planned to have a chat with Siobhán and ask her what was going to happen next. After she'd looked around the apartment she went upstairs and rapped on the door of Siobhán's place, but the detective didn't answer so Iona assumed that she was busy at the station.

She pressed the button for the lift to take her downstairs. The doors eased open and Enrique Martinez stepped out.

'Hello,' he said. 'How are you?'

'I'm good,' she told him. 'I had to deal with some things here.'

'So you are not here to see me?'

She smiled awkwardly.

'It's OK,' said Enrique. 'You have a complicated life, sort-of-married Iona. I understand.'

'I don't think you do really,' said Iona.

'No matter how complicated things are, they can always be helped by good friends,' said Enrique. 'And good wine. I have an exquisite bottle of Spanish white chilling in the fridge. You are welcome to join me.'

Iona thought about Frank's hand gripping tightly to the sheet on his bed. And her conversation afterwards with Sally and Jenna. It would be a betrayal of him to have a drink with Enrique. His invitation wasn't purely out of friendship.

'Also, I have some really fine olives and manchego cheese,' said Enrique persuasively. 'And strawberries.'

It sounded so appealing. It really did. Something different. And she could leave if he started to get too friendly.

'OK,' she said. 'I'd love to join you.'

'Wonderful,' said Enrique as he walked across the hall and opened the apartment door.

She followed him inside. The apartment was little changed from when she'd first shown it to him, although there was a tottering pile of books on the sideboard and a selection of financial magazines scattered around the room.

'The patio door is open,' he said. 'Make yourself comfortable outside and I will bring you some wine.'

'Thank you.'

The wooden furniture and plump cushions had come with the

apartment too. Iona relaxed on to one of the loungers and turned her face towards the evening sun.

'It's very peaceful here,' said Enrique as he handed her a glass of wine. 'I like it very much. It was a good choice.'

'I'm glad you like it.'

'Tell me about your complicated life.' Enrique sat down on one of the wooden chairs.

'Not right now,' she said.

'No problem,' he said.

He said nothing more, and Iona closed her eyes. It was quiet and peaceful on the balcony and the sun was warm but not blistering. She felt the tension in her shoulders ease. Her mind wandered on to the future and Frank's real improvement. What plan would they come up with? she wondered. It really wasn't as though they could share him. She didn't think either she or Sally wanted that. She wondered whether either of them loved him any more. That was a difficult question. Her feelings, and Sally's too, she was certain, were entirely influenced by Frank's condition. She'd already said lots of times that she'd thump him when he woke up, but of course she wouldn't. She'd be ecstatic. But after the ecstasy, then what? Who cared? she thought fuzzily. Things would happen. There was no point in always trying and trying to work them out beforehand. She sighed and her shoulders relaxed a little more.

'Omigod!' She jolted into wakefulness, suddenly realising that she had drifted off to sleep. The sun had slid behind the corner of the building and she was now in the shade.

'Ah,' said Enrique. 'You are with us again.'

She looked at her watch. She'd totally conked out. She'd been asleep for nearly three-quarters of an hour.

'I am so, so sorry,' she said hastily. 'I don't know what happened.'

'You were tired. And I was boring.' Enrique grinned at her.

'No, you weren't boring. You were just . . . It was peaceful. I'm sorry.' She felt terrible. But the sleep had been the most restful she'd had in ages. She hadn't been dreaming, for one thing, as she so often did – of being alone in the city, looking for Frank, plaintively calling his name but never seeing him. Her forty-five minutes had been dreamless and refreshing.

'You are obviously working too hard.'

'No,' she said. 'It's not that. It's just the complicated stuff is very tiring.'

'Ah.'

She looked at him.

'I have had girlfriends with complicated lives. They never last very long.'

'Were you planning on me being a girlfriend?' she asked edgily, knowing the answer already.

Enrique shrugged expressively. 'A friend, and then who knows?'

'I'm sorry.' She smiled awkwardly. 'I really like you. But it's . . . it's . . .'

'Complicated,' he said.

A noise from the balcony next door caught their attention.

'*Hola*, Siobhán!' called Enrique. 'Are you home?'

Her red curls preceded her around the dividing wall.

'Hi, Enrique – goodness, Iona! What are you doing here?' But her blue eyes twinkled.

'Sleeping,' said Iona. 'Much to Enrique's despair, I think.'

'Do you want to join us?' he asked.

'Sure. Hang on a minute.' Her head disappeared and a few seconds later Enrique let her in to the apartment.

'Hi,' she said to Iona as she walked out on to the balcony. 'How are you?'

'I came to check out the den of thieves,' Iona told her, 'and bumped into Enrique, who let me sleep on his balcony.'

Siobhán laughed. 'We're very hopeful of putting them away,' she said. 'It was a good arrest.'

'Arrest?' Enrique looked at them questioningly and Siobhán, once again, told the story of the ID scam. 'And hopefully Carl O'Connor will write a piece in his paper that reflects the fact that most of the time we do know what we're doing,' she said.

'O'Connor?'

'He's playing ball,' said Siobhán. 'Quid pro quo on this story as against . . . others.'

'Will they get bail?' Iona looked at her gratefully. 'My landlord is going demented.'

'They're being remanded in custody till tomorrow,' said Siobhán happily, 'but after that – well, I dunno, Iona. It all depends.' She leaned back in one of the loungers and wriggled her toes in the last sliver of sunshine. 'Oh, I do like a day like today.'

Iona laughed. 'I'm glad it went well for you. We had an interesting day too.'

'Oh?'

It was only after she'd spoken that she realised she didn't really want to talk about Frank in front of Enrique. She looked uncomfortably at him and then turned to Siobhán.

'Frank is responding to sounds,' she said. 'He turned his head today. He was listening to Jenna when she talked.'

'Really?' A soft gleam came into Siobhán's eyes.

'They're hopeful that he'll wake up soon,' said Iona. Enrique glanced from one to the other but said nothing.

'I need to know when he does,' said Siobhán.

'Why?'

'You know why,' said Siobhán. 'I have to talk to him.'

'Oh, come on!' Iona looked at her unhappily. 'I thought we'd agreed that there wasn't any point.'

'I can't agree that,' said Siobhán firmly. 'I'm really sorry, Iona. Once he's fit to be questioned, I do need to talk to him.'

'But we've figured it all out!' cried Iona.

'Figured all what out?' asked Siobhán.

'Not what you're obviously thinking,' said Iona sharply. 'Not that there was some malevolent motive behind it. Just that he loved us both and wasn't able to choose between us. For heaven's sake, you yourself did a whole heap of digging and didn't come up with anything.'

'I know,' said Siobhán. 'All I'm saying is that I need to talk to him. That's all.'

'I don't want my life to be a damn criminal case that lights

427

your fire!' Iona got up from the lounger and picked up her jacket. 'Just because I helped you out on the ID people doesn't mean that you can go poking around in my life now. Or Sally's. Or Jenna's. You know how that poor kid has been over the last few months! You can't mess with us now, Siobhán. You can't.'

'Iona, calm down.' Siobhán spoke gently. 'I'm not—'

'Thanks for the drink, Enrique, but I have to go.' Iona blinked away the tears that had suddenly rushed to her eyes and grabbed her bag. 'You were very nice. But now you know how complicated my life is, so there's no need to be nice any more.'

'Iona . . .' Siobhán called after her, but the other girl had already stridden through the apartment and out of the door.

Chapter 37

Every time she thought about Siobhán Farrell wanting to interview Frank, Iona felt herself get into a rage. She'd considered Siobhán to be a friend, and now it seemed the other woman was perfectly prepared to put friendship to one side to secure a conviction that could see him in jail for a couple of years at least. Siobhán had told them that the maximum term for bigamy was seven years but that she couldn't really imagine a judge sentencing Frank to seven years after all he'd been through. And, of course, he'd probably only serve about a third of whatever sentence he might get. Iona couldn't quite believe that Siobhán might arrest Frank at all as he lay in bed, but equally she couldn't see what choice the detective might have. After all, in her eyes Frank had committed a crime. She probably had a quota of arrests she was supposed to make every month, and Frank would help her meet her target.

Iona felt uneasily that she was being unfair on Siobhán, but she couldn't help herself. What on earth would they do if Frank was arrested? What would happen if he went to jail? Would they simply switch one visiting routine for another? And how would they cope with it this time? It was one thing being mature and adult and co-operative when Frank was helpless; it might be something completely different when he was awake again. Maybe it would be better if he stayed in the coma after all.

I can't want that to be the case, Iona told herself, as she drove to the hospital. If he stayed in a coma for ever I'd resent it, because I resent it now. The resentful feelings were with her because Ruth and some of the other girls from Rental Remedies were going out for dinner to a trendy new restaurant that night and she'd really wanted to go. But because of the continuing improvement in Frank's condition she didn't feel as though she could let a day go by without visiting him to help speed up his recovery.

She'd thought of asking Sally if she wanted to go to the hospital that evening instead, but she knew that the trek into the city from Bray was beginning to become a strain for Sally as her pregnancy progressed. Sally's doctor had advised her to relax and put her feet up a bit more, which, she had told Iona, was easier said than done. So because she knew that Sally was anxious about her pregnancy (even though Frank's illness had distracted her from her concerns), Iona didn't want her to feel as though she had to come to the hospital whenever there was a moment Frank might be alone. So she'd turned down the invitation to dinner. But she hadn't wanted to.

Now she strode through the familiar corridors of the hospital as she made her way to Frank's room. Perhaps today, she thought. Perhaps this will be the day when he comes back to us.

She pushed open the door. The evening sun filtered through the window and cast slatted light across the bed. Frank looked as though he were simply asleep. She pulled out the chair and sat down beside him. Then she started to talk.

⁓

The enormity of what had happened was giving him a headache. He could hear Iona's voice telling him that she was really confused about her feelings and about her life and he wanted to tell her that she didn't have to be confused, that he'd never meant to hurt anyone and that he knew he'd messed up big-time. He knew that Iona was his second wife, the one he'd chosen after Sally. He knew that he should never have married her, that it had been wrong and illegal and that – now that everyone knew about it – he'd caused nothing but trouble. He knew that to explain he'd done it because he so desperately wanted to keep her close, to have an extra family, because he was always seeking the perfect family, would make no sense to rational people. It didn't make sense to him either, when he thought about it. But it had seemed perfectly reasonable at the time.

He could hear the despair in her voice and it was like a dagger through his heart. How was it, he wondered, that when all he'd wanted was to make women happy, he'd ended up making them miserable instead?

He knew, too, that it wasn't just Iona. Sally's voice hid a tone of despair when she talked to him too. And he thought it was amazing that Sally, who hated illness so much, had spent so much time visiting him. It proved to him how much she loved him. Yet he didn't really deserve her love at all.

He had no idea how long he'd been in the hospital, but he knew it must be a long time now. The smells and the sounds were very familiar to him. The cheery voices of the nurses, the constant beeping of the monitors, the slightly antiseptic smell . . . all of those things were comforting and ordinary. There was a part of him that was happy to stay like this, surrounded by people who cared for him and not having to face the music.

'She loves you, Frank, but she's got the baby to consider,' said Iona. 'So maybe it would be better if you were with me. But you and her and Jenna and the baby – that's the most important thing. And in the end . . . I love you, but I suppose I'll get over you.'

He hated to hear her so miserable. He knew that she wasn't a miserable sort of person.

'And the detective, Frank. I think she wants to arrest you! She's been really nice to me and Sally but she's said over and over again that you've committed a crime. I mean, I know it's not like you robbed a bank or something, but Jesus Christ, Frank – maybe it would've been easier on everyone if you had!'

It was all his fault. He'd never intended for the two parts of his life to collide like this. But they had. Funny, though, he really struggled to remember how that had happened.

And then it came back to him. The pub. The sudden rumbling noise and the darkness that had enveloped him as everything had collapsed on top of him. He remembered gasping for breath and trying to open his eyes and the horrible, horrible feeling of being suffocated by the rubble pressing down on him, of struggling to get free and then of more subsidence around him and something hitting him on the head. He wanted to break free. But he couldn't.

~

Iona opened the door and called anxiously to Terri Cooper, who was in the corridor outside.

'He's getting really agitated,' she said worriedly. 'I've never seen him like this before.'

They both watched as Frank clenched and unclenched his fists and moved his head on the pillow.

'I'll contact Dr Carroll,' said Terri calmly. 'Reacting is good, but . . .'

'I'll sit with him,' said Iona. She went into the room again. Frank had quietened down but she was still concerned. She waited for a moment and then went outside to phone Sally.

~

Sally was sitting on the sofa, her legs propped up in front of her. She'd had cramps all day and a vague feeling of nausea that wouldn't go away. Six months into her pregnancy she resented feeling nauseous. She also had a slight headache which she knew was caused by knots in the muscles of her neck. But she was feeling a little better now in the silence of the house. Jenna had gone to Sam's to try to unlock the secret file on Frank's computer. Sally was pleased that she had taken such an interest in the computer and had done such a good job on the client accounts. She'd e-mailed them to Myles and now Iona's brother-in-law had a database of all Frank's contracts. He'd been in touch with the clients and Sally felt much better about things.

She wasn't as concerned as Jenna about the password-protected

432

folder. She knew that Frank loved passwords and code-keys – it was all part of his James Bond obsession. She had, briefly, wondered if the file had anything to do with another secret wife, but she was confident now that it hadn't. At least Siobhán Farrell's investigations had set her mind at rest about that, even if she was concerned about how the detective would proceed when Frank recovered. Iona had phoned her in a fury at Siobhán's reaction to the fact that he might be waking up at last. According to Iona, Siobhán was going to betray them just to have another arrest credited to her. But Sally couldn't bring herself to blame Siobhán. The girl had to do her job. She was just hoping that it wouldn't come to anything in the end.

She sighed as the phone rang and reached out for the receiver. It was Iona, telling her about Frank's agitated condition and sounding very agitated herself. Her anxiety worried Sally, who (despite the other girl's hysteria the first time they met) thought her a very level-headed person.

'Do you want me to come in?'

She hoped Iona would say no. The idea of driving into the city was very unappealing.

'Oh, Sally, I know that I'm probably getting my knickers in a twist over nothing. But he's acting really weird. Part of me thinks it's positive because he's like someone having a bad dream. But it's frightening me too.'

Sally said nothing.

'Shit, Sal, I'm sorry. I don't mean to worry you.'

'Isn't any sort of reaction good?' asked Sally.

'Yes. I think so. But . . .'

'I'll come,' said Sally.

'Thanks,' said Iona. 'I'll be here.'

Sally hung up the phone and frowned. Then she dialled Jenna's number.

'Oh, but we're really, really close to cracking this!' wailed Jenna. 'I'm not sure that I want to leave it now.'

'I'd like you to come,' said Sally. 'Sam can keep working on it.'

Jenna heard a tone of authority in Sally's voice that she never flouted. She frowned. 'OK,' she said eventually. 'I'll be there in five minutes.'

❧

He'd messed up everything. That was the bottom line of it. He'd messed it up and caused needless anxiety and he couldn't blame them for hating him. He remembered them saying that. Both of them. That they hated him. That they'd be better off without him. But they'd said that they loved him too. He could hear Iona's voice again, soothing and soft, telling him that everything was all right and that she loved him.

❧

Iona smiled in relief when she saw Sally walk in the door.

'I'm so sorry for dragging you out,' she said. 'But I thought you needed to be here.'

'What's happened?'

'He's quiet now,' said Iona. 'But he was totally agitated earlier. The doctor came in and they looked at the monitors and gave him some meds, I think. He's been calmer since. But . . .' she glanced at Jenna, who was standing near the top of the bed, 'I don't know why I suddenly felt so worried. Now that you're here, I feel better.'

'Good.' Sally pulled up a chair and sat down.

'Are you OK?' asked Iona. 'You're very pale.'

'The baby was acting up today.' Sally rubbed her stomach.

'Oh God, Sally, I really shouldn't have phoned!'

'I'm glad you did,' said Sally.

'Yes,' said Frank hoarsely. 'It's a good thing.'

Iona, Sally and Jenna looked at each other in silence. Then they stared at the man in the bed. Frank's eyes were open and he was looking at them.

'I'm really sorry,' he said, and closed his eyes again.

'Frank!' cried Iona. 'Frank, wake up!'

'Dad!' Jenna shook him by the arm. 'Dad, it's me.'

'I know it's you.' His eyes opened.

Terri Cooper walked into the room. She saw Frank and the women looking at each other. And she paged Dr Carroll.

～

'I never meant to hurt you,' said Frank croakily after Iona had given him a sip of water from the glass beside the bed. 'I never meant for any of this to happen.'

'Jesus, Frank, what did you think was going to happen?' demanded Sally, oblivious to the look of surprise from Jenna at the tone of her voice. 'You betrayed me with Iona and you ignored our marriage vows and you lied to us both every single day.'

'You should have told me,' Iona said fiercely. 'You should have told me you were married. I would've been mad at you but I could have got over it.'

'I couldn't,' said Frank. 'I – you were great. I—'

'You're a shit, Frank!' cried Sally. 'You weren't available to meet women, even great women like Iona. She has every right to be furious with you. Like I have.'

'I know. I know.' Frank coughed and Iona gave him some more water. 'But we were going through a bad patch, weren't we? And I was afraid you'd leave me.'

'Why on earth would I leave you?' demanded Sally. 'We were married. Yes, it was a bad patch, but we would've worked it through.'

'My mother left,' said Frank simply. 'And they didn't even go through a bad patch.'

Sally and Iona stared at him.

'You married me because you were afraid Sally would leave you?' said Iona incredulously. 'You didn't want to be on your own, so I was a kind of insurance policy?'

'I didn't see it like that,' protested Frank. 'I fell in love with you. I wanted to keep you. Sally too.'

'You're seriously weird, Dad.' Jenna's voice was shaky. 'You need to see a shrink.'

435

'Maybe,' said Frank. 'Maybe I should've done it before.'

'I can't believe it's all that woman's fault,' said Sally harshly. 'Bloody Christine! She was never there for him as a kid and you heard what he said. She's turned him into a complete fuck-up.'

'You can't blame her because he decided to marry two people,' protested Iona. 'Maybe she wasn't exactly a great mother, but Frank is responsible for his own actions.'

'I know,' he said faintly. 'I had a wonderful marriage. Two wonderful marriages. I was so lucky. I love you, Sally. I love you too, Jenna. You'll always be . . . my responsibility.' He closed his eyes for a moment and then opened them again. 'But Iona's going to have a baby. I could hear you talking about it when I was asleep. I have responsibilities towards that baby too.'

'You idiot!' said Iona. 'It's Sally who's having the baby. Not me.'

Frank looked at his wife in astonishment. 'But . . . but I thought you couldn't have any more babies,' he said.

'You thought wrong then,' said Sally shortly.

'My head hurts,' he said, and closed his eyes again.

'So does mine.' Sally rubbed her forehead. 'In fact . . . I don't feel very well.'

Jenna and Iona looked at her. She was as white as a sheet.

'Oh hell,' said Iona, as Sally slid from the chair and Dr Carroll walked into the room.

⁓

They put Sally on a trolley and hurried her to the maternity ward. As she was pushed through the corridors she couldn't help feeling as though she personally knew every nurse and doctor in the place by now. Her heart was racing as waves of pain hit her. She was frightened. It was far too early for the baby to come, and yet she was having an almost uncontrollable urge to push. She whimpered softly.

'Don't you worry, pet,' said the orderly who was pushing the trolley. 'We'll have you sorted out in no time.'

'My baby,' said Sally. 'Make sure my baby is all right.'

'Of course we will.'

Sally closed her eyes. Was this what it had been like for Frank, she wondered, as he'd been rushed to hospital? Frightened, worried, wondering what was going to happen to him? But he'd been unconscious, hadn't he? It couldn't have been the same. Pain stabbed her again and she cried out.

'OK, Sally, nearly there.' The voice was comforting, in the same way that the voices that spoke to Frank were comforting. Maybe they think I'm going to die, she thought. That would be just great. Frank would have to get better really quickly to look after Jenna and the baby.

'Right, Sally.' She opened her eyes. Her gynaecologist was standing beside her. 'Let's get you sorted out now. We're just going to hook you up to some equipment and insert a drip. It won't be painful.'

Why did they always say things like that? wondered Sally. Of course it was going to be painful. Everything was painful.

⌒

Iona and Jenna sat outside Frank's room. His eyes were closed again and he was perfectly still, but the doctor was in with him, monitoring him again and talking to Terri Cooper about his lucid waking moment. Jenna was chewing furiously at her bottom lip and Iona was racking her brain to think of the right thing to say to her.

'Will my mum be OK?' asked Jenna eventually.

'I'm sure she will,' replied Iona. 'I shouldn't have phoned her, Jen. If she wasn't feeling too good then she shouldn't have driven up. I'm sorry about that.'

'She would've gone mad if she wasn't there when Dad woke up.' Jenna rubbed the corners of her eyes. 'What are you going to do about him, Iona?'

'I think that if you and your mum want him home, then that's what should happen,' she said.

'He's my dad.' Jenna sniffed. 'I'm really angry with him, but . . .'

'I understand,' said Iona.

'I blamed him,' said Jenna. 'For everything. Even for the stuff that I did. But you're right, Iona. You can't blame other people when you make a mess of things yourself.'

Iona put her arm around Jenna's shoulders. 'What did you make a mess of?' she asked.

Jenna poured out the story of sleeping with Gerry and ignoring her friends in favour of Aline and Cindy and their crowd. And she confessed that Cathal Rothery had brought her home the night of the brawl outside the bar.

'Gosh,' said Iona. 'Does your mum know about that?'

Jenna shook her head. 'She doesn't know I slept with Gerry either. So please, please don't tell her.' Her face was anxious. 'We were sensible. We took precautions. I didn't get pregnant or anything. But you know, after the fight I had with Aline and Cindy he was so horrible to me. He implied that I was a cheap alley-cat kind of person.' She sighed. 'I think he was right.'

'Don't talk nonsense,' said Iona. 'You're a great person, Jenna. He was lucky to be going out with you, and Sally and Frank are very, very lucky to have you as a daughter.' Suddenly her own eyes swam with tears. 'I'd have been proud to have you as a daughter myself.'

Jenna looked at her in surprise. 'Thank you. I thought you hated me.'

Iona wiped her eyes. 'Not at all. I envy your mum and dad. I wish I had a daughter like you.'

'Crikey, I wouldn't think so!' Jenna's eyes opened wide. 'I am, apparently, nothing but trouble.'

'Oh, rubbish.' Iona smiled. 'You're seventeen. You're supposed to be trouble.'

'Did you and Dad want a kid?' asked Jenna.

Iona nodded. 'Only that won't happen now.'

'I guess not.' Jenna's gaze flickered towards her father's room.

Frank opened his eyes and stared back at them. Iona and Jenna looked at him in silence.

'I'm sorry.' They could make out the words through the window. 'I love you.'

And then the machines went crazy.

～

Sally was drifting in and out of consciousness but she knew that she felt better. She knew, too, that she could still feel the baby inside her and that everything was under control again. She felt extremely grateful for the fact that she'd been in the hospital when she'd been taken ill and that they'd been so fantastic about looking after her.

'Hi,' said Frank.

She knew that she was imagining him, but it seemed as though he was standing in front of her, looking fit and handsome as he had been before the accident.

'What are you doing here?' she asked.

'Just saying sorry,' he said. 'I messed up.'

'You more than messed up,' she told him.

'I want to blame loads of people but it's only myself,' he told her.

'It doesn't matter,' she said. 'We'll sort it out somehow.'

'Are you feeling all right?'

'Now I am,' she said. 'I was really worried for a while but they keep telling me everything's OK and I believe them.'

'I can't believe that you're having a baby. After all this time.'

'Neither can I,' said Sally.

'I'm sorry if I pressurised you about it before.'

'I pressurised myself.'

'Most of all I'm sorry about Iona.'

'You love her?'

'I love you too.'

'Oh, Frank. You really dug yourself a hole and jumped right in, didn't you?'

He smiled wryly.

'But I like her,' said Sally. 'She's been someone to lean on. I can see why you love her. In the end, you know, it would've been harder without her.'

'It's still not ideal,' said Frank.

'Oh, hell.' Sally smiled at him. 'When is life ever ideal?'

'Take care of yourself.' The image of him faded and Sally fell asleep.

～

The doctors and nurses were clustered around Frank's bed. Iona and Jenna were outside the room, arms around each other. When the alarms had gone off on the machines Dr Carroll had come out and told them that there was a problem but that they were dealing with it. Now Ashley Dalton, a student nurse, was sitting beside them. She'd given them cups of sweetened tea. Iona wondered how often nurses gave out cups of sweetened tea in the hospital.

～

Three hours later Dr Carroll stood in front of them, and although he was trying to keep his face impassive, Iona could see that he was shocked as he continued speaking.

'We were monitoring him very closely, as you know. But an aneurysm developed really quickly. We did everything we could.' He glanced at Jenna. 'I can't tell you how sorry I am.'

'You're telling us he's dead?' Jenna was shaking. 'He can't be dead. He woke up.'

They'd watched the team of professionals rush Frank back to the operating theatre and they'd drunk more sweetened tea and they'd worried about what was going on, but they hadn't believed that he could possibly die. After all, he'd spoken to them for the very first time that day. He was supposed to be getting better.

Jenna started to cry. Iona folded her into her arms and looked over the top of her head at the doctor.

'I know this is hard to accept,' said Dr Carroll. 'I know that waking up was a major event. He must have been in pain then, though.'

Iona remembered the anguished expression on Frank's face as he'd talked to them. But she'd thought that was because he realised how much trouble he was in. She tightened her hold around Jenna. 'He talked to us and we talked to him.' Her voice caught in her throat. 'Oh God, what are we going to tell Sally? She can't afford a shock like this now.'

'Sally's asleep at the moment.' Terri Cooper's voice was soft and gentle. 'We won't wake her yet.'

'He can't be dead.' Jenna was angry. 'You can't have let him die like that. Not after all this time!'

'There's a chaplain in the hospital,' said Terri. 'Would you like him to come to you?'

'No,' said Iona. 'Not just now. I want to be on my own.'

'Don't leave me!' cried Jenna. 'I can't be on my own.'

'I won't. I won't.' Iona hugged her again. 'Don't worry. I won't leave you.' She looked up at Terri. 'Can we see him?' she asked.

'Shortly,' said Terri. 'We're just doing some things for him and then you can see him.'

Jenna shivered. 'I don't want to,' she said.

'You don't have to,' said Iona quickly. 'But I do, sweetheart.'

'Will you tell my mum?'

'Yes,' said Iona. 'I'll tell your mum.'

⁓

It was after midnight when she went to the private room where Sally had been relocated. Jenna walked beside her, holding her hand tightly. Iona had gone in to see Frank. He didn't look all that different from when he'd been in the coma. Her tears had dripped on to his face and she'd wiped them away, realising already that he felt different. Lifeless. Gone from them for ever.

'I loved you, Frank.' She kissed him on the cheek. 'I know that

441

some people will say that this was for the best, but I never, ever wanted you to die.'

She looked at him, waiting – as she'd waited so often over the last weeks for a response – but she knew this time there would be nothing. So she kissed him again and left the room.

Jenna had been waiting outside with Terri Cooper and had grabbed Iona's hand as soon as she'd come out. Now Iona could feel the younger girl shivering beside her as they walked.

They went into the room and Sally opened her eyes.

'Hi,' she said.

'Hi,' said Iona.

They looked at each other and then Sally's face crumpled.

'Oh, no.'

'I'm sorry,' said Iona. 'It was an aneurysm. There was nothing they could do.'

'Oh, Mum.' Jenna finally released Iona's hand and leaned across her mother. The two of them hugged each other tightly.

Iona slipped quietly out of the room. She walked through the corridors until she could use her phone and then she called Lauren.

'I'll come,' said her sister.

'Don't,' Iona told her. 'There's no need. I just wanted you to know.'

'Io, you can't be there on your own. Sally can't help if she's hospitalised too.'

'I'm fine,' said Iona. 'I really am. Please don't worry about me. I'll call you tomorrow.'

'Iona—'

'I'll be really annoyed if you come,' said Iona. 'Besides, I might be gone by then. I don't know what I'm doing yet. There's some stuff I need to sort out.'

'OK,' said Lauren, although she didn't sound convinced. 'Call me.'

'I will.'

Iona went back up to Sally's room. Jenna was sitting on the chair beside her mother's bed, but when Iona walked in she got up and took her hand again.

'I knew,' said Sally.

'How?'

'He came to me.'

Iona said nothing.

'I know it sounds nonsense, but he did,' Sally told her. 'He said he was sorry and that he loved me.'

'Dammit, I thought everything was going to be OK.' Iona swallowed hard.

'Maybe everything can't always be OK,' said Sally. 'There isn't always a happy ending. Not that there ever would have been, given the situation we were in.'

'We would have worked something out,' said Iona. 'All of us. We've been working things out for the past few months, haven't we?'

'I know.' Sally's eyes fluttered closed.

Iona looked at Jenna, who was still white-faced and trembling. 'You need some rest too,' she told her.

'Perhaps they can give me somewhere . . .'

'You can't stay here,' said Iona. 'There's hardly enough room for patients, let alone anyone else.'

'I have to go home,' said Jenna. 'But I don't want to be there by myself.'

'You can stay with me,' said Iona. 'If Sally thinks that's all right.'

'Of course it is,' said Sally sleepily. 'It's the best place for her.'

❧

Jenna sat beside her mother while Iona made a final trip to Frank's unit and spoke briefly to Terri Cooper, who hugged her and told her that she was a strong person and that they'd grown to love both her and Sally. Iona was grateful for the other woman's sympathy and understanding. She was just about to return for Jenna when Myles strode into the corridor.

'What are you doing here?' she gasped in surprise.

'Lauren told me that you were dealing with it all yourself. She wanted to come but I didn't want her to. Maybe a few months ago you mightn't have wanted me here, Iona, but you need someone and I thought—'

'Oh, Myles!' She looked at her brother-in-law as the tears flooded into her eyes. 'Thank you. Thank you for coming. I couldn't let Lauren come, she has to look after herself.'

'I know. I know.' He put his arms around her and patted her back. 'Is there anything I can do tonight?'

'Not really,' said Iona. 'I've spoken to everyone.'

'I'm going to take you back to our house,' said Myles.

'You can't.' Iona raised her head from his shoulder. 'I said I'd look after Jenna.'

'Jenna?' Myles frowned.

'Sally's daughter.'

'I know who she is,' said Myles. 'She sent me the computer files, didn't she. I just didn't realise she was here too.'

Iona nodded. 'She's with Sally right now. But I said she could come home with me.'

'You can both come with me,' said Myles firmly. 'You'll have to share the spare room, but there's two beds.'

Suddenly Iona was too tired to argue. 'OK.'

They walked through the hospital to the maternity wing. Jenna was still sitting where Iona had left her, holding Sally's hand.

'I thought you weren't coming back,' she said anxiously. 'You were gone for ages.'

'Sorry,' said Iona. She introduced Myles and told Jenna that they'd been offered a bed at her sister's house. 'If that's OK with you,' she added.

Jenna nodded. 'It doesn't really matter where I sleep, does it?'

'No,' said Iona gently, 'it doesn't.'

Jenna kissed Sally good night and grasped Iona by the hand again. Then they walked out of the hospital together.

444

Chapter 38

It was the sound of children's laughter that woke Jenna the following morning. It had taken her a long time to fall asleep, and when she had, her dreams were complicated and unsettling. But then, at about six, when the early-morning light was poking through a chink in the heavy curtains, she'd suddenly entered a deeper state of sleep from which she hadn't wakened even when Iona got up.

Jenna blinked a couple of times as the memories of the previous night flooded back to her and hot tears scorched her eyes. It isn't fair, she muttered as she swung her legs over the side of the bed. If her dad had died straight away it would have been easier. There wouldn't have been all these weeks of coming into the hospital, trying to bring him back to consciousness. She wouldn't have spent so long feeling angry with him and her mother and Iona. It would've been over and done with. It would have hurt, but not as much as the last months had hurt. She'd begun to believe that everything could be all right, and now it wasn't and that made her feel much worse.

Someone had left a fresh fluffy towel at the end of her bed. She picked it up and walked into the en suite bathroom, where she stood under the shower and allowed the water to massage her shoulders. It felt disrespectful to be wishing that she had her favourite extra-moisturising shower soap and a change of under-wear. And it was weird to be doing a normal thing like having a shower when she'd spent the night in the house of a woman she didn't know, in the same room as the woman who'd tried to steal her father from her mother. That surely wasn't normal. She breathed out slowly through her mouth as she allowed the water to cascade over her face. All she wanted was to be ordinary. To have an ordinary life with an ordinary family and an ordinary boyfriend. She hadn't managed any of that.

She turned off the water and got out of the shower. She looked around her uncertainly and then used some of the moisturising cream from the Boots jar on the shelf before cleaning her teeth using her finger and some toothpaste. After that she got dressed, brushed her hair and made her way downstairs.

Lauren and Iona were sitting at the kitchen table, empty coffee cups in front of them.

'Hi, Jenna.' Lauren got up and hugged her, and tears welled up in Jenna's eyes again. It was hard when people were nice, it really was. 'I'm glad you finally got some sleep. Would you like some coffee? or tea?'

'Coffee, please.' Jenna sat gingerly on one of the kitchen stools. She glanced out of the window. Gavin and Charlotte were racing around the sunny garden, shrieking with enjoyment.

'Did they wake you?' Iona had noticed her look. 'They're complete terrors.'

'I heard them,' admitted Jenna. 'I didn't know where the noise was coming from.'

'They're not the worst.' Lauren placed a mug of coffee in front of her. 'Iona doesn't have the patience, that's all.'

Jenna couldn't understand why they were talking about such mundane things.

'I phoned your mum earlier,' Iona said. 'She's much better.'

'I suppose it's good that one of my parents is all right.' Jenna's voice was shaky.

'Your mum is fine,' said Iona firmly. 'Anyone who's pregnant can have a bit of a scare, and that's all it was. They're going to keep her in for a couple of days, but she's perfectly OK.'

'What about Dad?' asked Jenna anxiously. 'What's going to happen to him.'

It took Iona a moment to compose herself. 'I spoke to Sally

about him too,' she said. 'She wants to have the funeral as soon as she's able to leave the hospital.'

'He wants to be cremated,' said Jenna. 'He told me that before.'

Iona nodded. 'He told me the same.'

'But Mum never wanted that,' she said, her voice anxious. 'Mum always said it was undignified. What if she won't agree?'

Lauren glanced between Iona and Jenna.

'You need to sit down with your mum,' she said, realising that Iona was struggling to speak. 'Talk it through with her.'

'He *told* me,' insisted Jenna.

'We'll call in to see Sally shortly,' Iona promised. 'Get things sorted.'

'I need to go home and change,' said Jenna. 'These are yesterday's clothes.'

'I understand,' said Iona. 'But I have to get my car from the hospital car park first.' She grimaced. 'We keep on leaving cars there! So my suggestion is that we call a cab, go in and see your mum, then go to my house so that I can change too, and then I'll drive you home.'

⤸

Sally was sitting up when they walked into her room. Her face was pale and she had shadows under her eyes, but she smiled when she saw them. Jenna rushed over to the bed and put her arms around her and Sally held her tightly while Iona stood at the foot of the bed.

'I saw him this morning,' said Sally after Jenna had disentangled herself. 'They brought me up in a wheelchair. He looked . . . peaceful.'

Iona nodded.

'He wants to be cremated,' said Jenna quickly. 'He told me before. He's afraid of being buried alive.'

'I know,' said Sally. 'Though there's no chance of that, is there?' Her lip trembled.

447

'Well, you have to do what he said,' Jenna told her.

'I—'

'He told Iona too,' she added.

Sally looked up at Iona. 'Did he?'

Iona wasn't sure how to reply. She felt like the intruder again, the person who had no say in the lives of the Harper family. The person who wasn't really Frank's wife and who had no right to be there. So she nodded imperceptibly.

'Is that what you want?' asked Sally.

'I . . . it doesn't matter,' said Iona abruptly. 'Whatever you think is right.' She couldn't stay in the room any longer. She turned around and walked out of the door, leaving Sally and Jenna staring after her.

There was an empty bench seat in the corridor. She sat down and buried her head in her hands. Over the past few weeks she'd been part of everything, but now she was no one. Sally and Jenna would organise the funeral, and it would be their friends and family and neighbours who'd be there. And she'd be a nobody. Because they wouldn't want her to be a focus of attention. They'd want to keep up the façade of Frank being a family man. She supposed that Sally's friends knew something of his secret life now, but his funeral wasn't going to be the place to make it all public. And she wasn't going to fight about it. What was the point now? Frank was gone and none of it really mattered any more.

'Iona?' Jenna's voice was nervous. 'Are you all right?'

She wiped her eyes as she looked up. 'Yes, sure,' she said quickly. 'I'm fine.'

'Mum said that maybe you were worried about the funeral.'

'No.'

'She thought you might think we'd want to shut you out.'

'I—'

'She wants to talk to you about it,' said Jenna.

'OK,' said Iona, and went back to Sally's room.

∽

Somehow it was easier to deal with plans for Frank's funeral than it had been to deal with the hospital visits and everything to do with his coma. They agreed on the type of service and the music, and Iona said that she would meet with a priest from their parish in Bray to discuss it all since Sally would be in hospital for another day or two.

'Though I'm not sure how they'll react to it,' she said. 'I mean, he broke a whole heap of the Ten Commandments!'

Sally laughed. The three of them looked guiltily at each other, because it seemed wrong to laugh, but both Jenna and Iona then smiled too.

'Hopefully they'll consider that they're saving him from eternal damnation,' said Sally wryly. 'Iona, I really appreciate everything you've done.'

'It's OK,' said Iona. 'I'll talk to him about the readings and everything and bring all the stuff in for you to look at.'

'Thanks.'

'And the funeral will be at the weekend. You're sure you'll be out by then?'

Sally nodded.

'What about me?' asked Jenna. 'What am I going to do?'

'A reading?' suggested Sally.

'Not at the funeral,' said Jenna. 'Now. I have to go home and change but I don't want to stay there on my own.'

'Well, you can stay with me, like I said last night,' Iona told her.

'But for a few days? I can't do that,' said Jenna. 'My stuff is at home. I don't want to leave everything.'

'You can't stay there on your own,' said Sally. 'Not . . . you can't, Jen.'

'You'd be fine in my place,' Iona told her. 'Really.'

Jenna looked uncertain.

'Perhaps Iona could stay in our house,' said Sally. 'If she doesn't mind.'

'Oh, gosh, Sally – I don't know.' Iona was shocked at the suggestion.

'Please?' begged Jenna. 'I really want to be at home and I need someone with me.'

'Um . . . I suppose . . .'

'Thank you.' Jenna hugged her. 'Thank you very much.'

⌒

In the rush to the hospital the previous evening, Jenna had left her mobile phone at home. As she opened the door she could hear it beeping to signal an incoming message. She hurried through to the kitchen and picked it up, seeing that she had missed half a dozen calls and had a variety of text messages. They were all from Sam. The gist of it was that she had managed to crack open Frank's secret folder and that Jenna should get in touch with her right away.

'Where the hell were you?' demanded Sam as she took Jenna's call. 'I thought maybe you were with Aline and Cindy and that you'd frozen me out again.'

'God, no,' said Jenna quickly. She swallowed hard and told Sam about her father.

'Oh, Jen, I'm so, so sorry.' Sam was shocked. She too had got the impression that Jenna's dad was recovering. 'I'm at work today. I'll try to get off early and come around.'

'Thanks,' said Jenna. 'See you later.'

She turned to Iona, who had followed her into the kitchen and was standing in the doorway, clutching a small holdall which she'd picked up from her house before driving to Bray.

'I guess you need to see your room,' said Jenna. She made her way towards the stairs. 'I'm at the top on the right and the spare room is on the left.'

It was beautifully decorated, with luxurious pile carpet in pale pink, matching curtains and a double bed with a plump duvet with a pink and white cover. Iona wondered again how Frank could reconcile the slightly fussy decor of his house in Bray with the minimalist look of their home in the Liberties.

'There's no en suite bathroom,' Jenna told her. 'But there's one at the end of the landing.'

450

Iona nodded.

'Are you all right?'

She nodded again.

'Is it weird for you being here?'

'I was here before,' Iona admitted, 'though not upstairs.'

Jenna looked at her edgily. 'When?'

Iona told her about driving Sally home the night that Jenna had gone missing.

'She never said.' Jenna's tone was accusing.

'I don't think you and she were getting on very well at the time,' Iona reminded her. 'And you would have blown a gasket if you'd come home and found me here.'

'I guess.' Jenna sat on the bed. 'Is it all completely bonkers? You and her and Dad and me and . . . well, the way it's all turned out?'

'Slightly bonkers,' agreed Iona. 'But, well, we've got to support each other, haven't we?'

'You've been great,' said Jenna warmly. 'I hated you, of course. But . . . I can see why Dad loved you. I couldn't before. I can now.'

'Thanks.'

'Would you like more coffee?' Jenna got up from the bed. 'I have a feeling that people will start calling round soon. I guess we should be prepared.'

∽

The news of Frank's death spread quickly around the estate. Neighbours called to the house and were surprised when Jenna answered the door and thanked them for calling and told them that Sally was in hospital. And then she invited them in and introduced them to Iona, who, she said, was a close friend of her father's – and, she added, her mother's too. Iona knew that everyone who called around was in a frenzy of curiosity about exactly what was going on, but nobody wanted to cause any kind of scene in front of Jenna. They all asked about Sally, and Iona told them that she was fine and that she'd be coming home in a day or two and that she was staying with Jenna until then and that the funeral would be at the weekend. By the time most people had left (and she knew that they'd all be gossiping amongst themselves at least until Sally returned) she was exhausted.

And then Sam arrived. The two teenagers hugged each other and Sam told Jenna how sorry she was, then Jenna introduced her to Iona. Sam looked at Iona with undisguised interest and said that she was really pleased to meet her. Iona said that she was pleased to meet Sam too. And then Sam reminded Jenna about the password-protected folder.

'It wasn't that hard to crack it in the end,' she said. 'The thing is, Jen . . .'

'What?' Jenna looked at her anxiously. 'Don't tell me that there's something – someone else. Please don't. It would kill my mother.' She shot a look at Iona. 'I mean, I know we're cool about Iona now, but someone else . . .'

'No. Nothing like that,' said Sam hastily. 'I suppose I'd better show it to you.' She powered up the laptop and put it on the table in front of them. 'Here you go,' she said.

Jenna and Sam looked at the screen. The file contained scanned documents. An old photograph which had obviously been torn and put back together. A birth certificate. A death certificate. And copies of letters. Jenna's eyes narrowed as she looked at them. She zoomed in on one of them.

Dear Derek,
I really don't know what to say. I'm honoured that you would want me to be your wife, but you know how I feel about marriage. It's an outdated institution . . .
Christine

She looked at the next:

Dear Frank,
I thought I made it abundantly clear at our meeting that I had no wish to meet with you again. I do not see why the

452

birth of your daughter should change this in any way. I am returning the photograph.
Sincerely,
Christine

And the last, dated a couple of days before Frank's accident:

Dear Mr Harper,
I am writing on behalf of my client, Christine Harris. While she is aware that in the past she informed you that she had no interest in having any familial contact with you, she has asked me to let you know that she would be interested in meeting you sometime in the near future. If you are agreeable to such a meeting I would be obliged if you could contact me at this office at your earliest convenience.
Yours sincerely,
James Carlisle

'Bloody hell,' said Jenna. 'This is Dad's mum.' Her eyes darkened. 'No wonder he blames her for stuff. How could she send back my photo like that? That was horrible.'

Iona hugged her.

'I mean, everyone says I was a cute baby!' But Jenna's lip trembled.

'Well, she might not have wanted to know you as a baby, but obviously she's changed her mind.'

'Too late.' Jenna looked at Iona starkly. 'It's too late.'

Iona nodded. How awful, she thought, for it to be too late. How awful not to have spoken to someone, for whatever reason, and then to make the effort only to realise that you should have acted sooner. She wondered how Christine would deal with the news that her son had died before she had the chance to speak to him again.

'We'll talk to your mum,' said Iona. 'She can decide what to do about Christine.'

The doorbell rang again and Jenna sighed. 'Another nosy neighbour,' she muttered as she got up to answer it.

Iona hurriedly powered down the laptop as Jenna opened the living room door.

'It's Gerry,' she said, her cheeks tinged with pink. 'He heard about Dad and came to pay his respects.'

'Hello . . .' Gerry looked at Iona awkwardly.

'Iona,' she supplied.

'Hello, Iona,' he said. 'I'm sorry about what's happened.'

'So am I,' she said.

Sam looked edgily at Gerry and Jenna. 'I'd better go,' she said.

'Not yet,' said Jenna. 'I was going to make some coffee. Stay, please, Sam.'

'I'm sure you and Gerry have things to talk about,' she said. 'You won't want me around.'

'Not right now we haven't,' said Jenna. 'Maybe later.'

'Actually . . .' Gerry looked embarrassed. 'I wanted to say to Jen that I was sorry. I know that she's a good person. I bet she was provoked by those girls. And Jen, I never, ever did anything with anyone else when I was with you.'

'Oh.' Jenna blushed.

'And I won't hang around if you've got people here,' he told her. 'I just had to call and say I was sorry. I'll see you at the funeral.'

'Stay for coffee,' she said. 'You can go after that.'

So the four of them sat in the kitchen and drank yet more coffee. And every time Jenna smiled (which suddenly she was doing quite a lot), Iona could see Frank's smile. And when Jenna looked intently at Gerry or at Sam, Iona could see Frank's eyes. And she felt as though her heart was going to break.

Chapter 39

The doctor told Sally that she could go home the following day. She was sitting in the foyer of the hospital, waiting for Iona, who had promised to come and collect her, when she noticed the tall woman walking through the main doors and looking around her uncertainly.

'Siobhán.' She called out and lifted her hand and the detective turned towards her.

'Hi, Sally.' Siobhán sat on the bench beside her. 'How are you doing?' She could see dark circles under Sally's eyes, but her cheeks were tinged with pink and she looked somehow less stressed than other times when Siobhán had seen her.

'I'm OK,' she replied.

'I'm really sorry about Frank,' said Siobhán.

'How did you know?' asked Sally.

Siobhán looked uncomfortable. 'They told me,' she said.

'Who? Iona and Jenna?'

'No.' She shook her head. 'The hospital. They called to let me know.'

'Why would they let you know?' asked Sally.

'Because I'd asked them to tell me of any changes in Frank's condition,' said Siobhán.

'Oh.' Sally suddenly remembered what Iona had told her. 'You wanted to question him?'

Siobhán nodded.

'Guess this has messed it all up for you.' There was a trace of bitterness in Sally's voice.

'For sure that's what Iona thinks,' said Siobhán wryly. 'When I told her I'd have to interview Frank when he got better she wasn't happy. So she's bound to think that . . . that Frank's death is a bad career move for me.'

'She doesn't really,' said Sally. 'But she thinks . . . well, I suppose she thinks that you were really quick to remember your job and forget that we were friends for a while.'

'You're right to be sceptical about me,' Siobhán told her. 'The first thing I thought about when she told me about Frank's progress wasn't that it was good or bad for you guys, but what I had to do about it. I'm sorry. I shouldn't have thought that way. Not, to be honest with you, that I ever wanted to have to arrest Frank, but I have to follow the procedure. It doesn't matter that I like you and Iona. That's not the point.'

'I understand,' said Sally.

'But you don't like it. You don't like me for it.'

'It's not that . . .'

'Sooner or later everyone gets furious with the police,' said Siobhán resignedly. 'It's never good for anyone to have to deal with us. Doesn't matter what it's about. If your life is going well you don't need us. If it's not – well, we never do what you want. If a crime's been committed against you and we don't catch whoever did it, you think we're a shower of useless incompetents; if we do but they get off, most people will blame us. If you're the criminal you obviously hate us.'

'Gosh, Siobhán, that sounds a bit bleak.'

'Oh, don't mind me, I'll get over it,' said Siobhán. 'I didn't join the gardai to be liked.'

'Why did you?' asked Sally curiously.

'I have loads of brothers,' said Siobhán. 'It gave me the opportunity to boss them around.'

Sally laughed.

'Seriously,' said Siobhán.

They were silent for a moment, then Sally asked why Siobhán had come to the hospital.

'To see you, of course,' said Siobhán. 'I rang last night. They

456

told me you'd be leaving this afternoon. Glad I didn't miss you.' She smiled at Sally. 'You're actually looking quite well . . . you know, despite everything.'

'I'm fine,' said Sally. 'Junior's OK too. And once the funeral is over . . . well, I guess I can get back to my life again. I know I have to rebuild it without Frank, but I can do that. I've had time to think about it.'

Siobhán nodded.

'What about you?' asked Sally. 'How's your life going?'

Siobhán smiled again. It seemed wrong to be pleased with her life when things were so awful for Sally and Iona, but a lot of good things had been said about her in the aftermath of the ID scam arrests and there was talk of a promotion. Also, she'd received a tip-off about a potential armed robbery on the north side of the city and, acting on the information she'd received, the robbery had been foiled and three men arrested. On the career side of things, everything was going really well.

There was, of course, the personal complication, even if it was quite a satisfying complication. She'd gone out with Carl O'Connor the previous night. A date. A real boy-meets-girl date. They'd met in town and gone to a cheap and cheerful restaurant in Temple Bar where Carl had related anecdotes about interviews from hell and stories that had gone wrong until she'd had to wipe tears of laughter from her eyes. Afterwards he'd brought her back to her apartment building and she'd thought about asking him in for coffee, but at the last moment she'd remembered that the breakfast dishes were still piled in the sink and that she hadn't tidied up in days. And she'd told herself that, much as she didn't agree with the idea of being a perfect girlfriend with a perfect apartment, she was going to have to learn to be just a bit tidier so that she could bring attractive men home and not worry about the state of the place. That meant, she'd realised, that she was thinking of Carl O'Connor as an attractive man she'd rather like to have around the place a bit more. But, hell, she'd thought – a garda and a journalist. A terrible combination! Worse than a garda and a financier. Definitely.

'Can I guess by that self-satisfied smirk on your face that things are looking up?' asked Sally in amusement.

Siobhán blushed. She hadn't realised how easily her emotions had played across her face.

'Who?' asked Sally. 'The old boyfriend or the new one?'

Siobhán was going to ask Sally who she actually meant by the new one when both of them saw Iona and Jenna walk into the hospital.

'Mum!' Jenna hurried over to her.

'Hi, Sal,' said Iona. She looked at Siobhán. 'Hello.'

'Iona, you can't be nasty to Siobhán,' said Sally easily. 'She came here today to see me and say that she was sorry about Frank's death.'

'Sorry because she can't make an arrest,' snapped Iona.

'You know that's not true,' said Sally softly. 'Siobhán is a good person, Iona. She's done her best for us always.'

'Look – it doesn't matter what you think,' said Siobhán. 'None of it matters now anyway. I'm sure you'll be delighted to have me out of your hair from now on. So I'll head off. It was nice to see you again, Sally. I hope everything works out for you. You too, Iona.'

She turned and strode towards the exit.

Sally, Iona and Jenna looked at each other.

'Is she upset?' asked Jenna.

'Just a little, I think.' Iona looked uncomfortable. She raised her voice. 'Siobhán!'

The detective turned around and Iona walked towards her.

'I'm sorry,' she said. 'I was bothered by everything. I didn't mean to lash out at you.'

'And I was insensitive,' said Siobhán. 'I am truly sorry for how things turned out.'

'You were great to us,' Iona told her.

'Part of the job.'

'We'll keep in touch?'

Siobhán nodded. 'That'd be good.'

'Maybe I can help you organise a new apartment?'

This time Siobhán grinned. 'You never know. Different spec next time. Different circumstances. Maybe.'

'Siobhán!'

'Early days,' said Siobhán. She glanced at her watch. 'I'd better go.'

'See you,' said Iona. She watched as the other girl walked out of the building, and then returned to Sally and Jenna.

'It's cool,' she said. 'We're sorted.'

'I'm glad,' said Sally. 'I like her. She's a decent kind of girl.'

'I know,' said Iona.

'Meantime, we have other stuff to talk about, don't we?' said Jenna. 'I'll tell you on the way home, Mum. It's . . . you're not going to believe it.'

'Oh?' said Sally as she got up and followed them to the car park.

Because it was her day off, Siobhán drove back to Dun Laoghaire. She was glad that she'd bumped into Iona at the hospital. She liked her and hadn't wanted to think that there was any sort of edginess between them. She hoped that Iona and Sally would be OK in the future. She rather thought they would be. They were strong, resilient women. She smiled inwardly. Just like herself.

She parked the car and was walking up the pathway to the apartment block when a man stepped out in front of her, startling her.

'Hi,' he said.

'Carl! You scared the living daylights out of me.'

'Really? I thought you were a crack detective who brings down illegal forging cartels with a single move.'

'Get a life!' She shoved him gently. 'What are you doing here?'

'I called to say hello,' he told her.

She regarded him sceptically.

'No, really.' He shrugged. 'I was in the neighbourhood and I thought I'd drop by. I did say, last night, didn't I, that I'd keep in touch? Anyway, you told me that you had a day off today.'

'Yes, I do,' she said. 'And I have plans for it.'

'Like what?' asked Carl.

'I'm going to tidy my apartment,' she said primly.

He roared with laughter. 'Oh, Farrell, that's a good one. I can just see you in your uniform and yellow rubber gloves, squirting Fairy Liquid all around the place.'

'Crikey, crusading journo, you don't know much about cleaning,' she retorted. 'Fairy Liquid is for washing-up.'

'Also available for cleaning floors,' he told her.

They looked at each other for a moment and then she giggled. 'Possibly. I don't know.'

'Here's the thing,' he said. 'I don't know whether your super-powers of detection have made you notice this, but it's a crackingly gorgeous day. And nobody in their right mind would spend it tidying their apartment. So my plan is that we hop on the Dart to Bray and have a stroll along the seafront, and then maybe grab something to eat. And afterwards . . . we'll see how it goes.'

She could be spotted in Bray, thought Siobhán. Someone from the station could see her with Carl O'Connor and get totally the wrong impression. They'd think that she had a personal relationship with him. And maybe that would compromise her in their eyes. And then she admitted to herself that she *did* have a personal relationship with Carl. And maybe she was already compromised.

'You know, for a cop you're really not that good at disguising your feelings,' said Carl gently.

'What d'you mean?'

'Bray. Being seen with me. People asking questions . . .'

'Oh, sod off!' But she smiled a little.

'Siobhán, I won't try to find things out from you. I didn't, did I, about that bigamy thing?'

'No,' she admitted.

'I talked to JoJo and she's agreed to let it lie. I'm not trying to worm deep, dark secrets about the police force from you. I got

460

a story and it was a good one. But that's not why I want to spend time with you.'

'Why then?' she asked.

He grinned at her. 'Oh, come on! I've seen you once in a basque. I'm hoping to see it again.'

She shoved him a little less gently this time.

'I like you,' he told her. 'I have fun with you. Is that so terrible?'

'I guess not.'

'Jeez, Farrell, it's no wonder you didn't make it with your previous boyfriend. You're bloody impossible.'

'I am not,' she said defensively.

'Actually, no.' He grinned again. 'You're nothing but a softie really.'

'I don't think so!'

'No?' He put his arm around her and kissed her. And suddenly Siobhán thought that she was indeed a very big softie. And that if Carl didn't mind the fact that her apartment was a disaster area she'd be very happy to forget about it being a glorious day outside and having a wonderful time with him in Bray, but instead might just drag him to her bedroom and make love to him. Because for the first time in weeks, she wanted to make love to someone again. And he was that someone.

∽

Sally, Jenna and Iona sat at the kitchen table and looked at the open file on the laptop computer.

'I don't believe it,' said Sally as she read the letter from the solicitor again. 'I remember Frank telling me that he'd gone to see her and that she was totally dismissive of him. And then after you were born, Jen, he sent that photo. I remember that too. When she didn't contact him then he was really angry and upset. Not for himself, but he thought she might at least want to know about you.'

'Obviously not,' said Jenna. 'Cold-hearted cow. I don't know why he kept all this stuff.'

461

'You know your dad,' said Sally. 'He's a . . . he was a hoarder. It wouldn't matter if he never saw her again, he'd want to keep stuff.'

'Why did he scan everything into the computer?' asked Iona. 'Surely he has the actual copies?'

'Oh, Iona, he was forever putting things on the computer. He loved it. More of the James Bond approach, I guess. He had a safe in the attic where he kept insurance policies and things like that. The originals are probably there. Maybe he left them there so that I wouldn't see them and start asking questions about Christine. Not that I ever did, really. At the start, a bit. But he was always defensive about it whenever I tried, so I gave up.'

'He never talked to me much about her either,' said Iona. 'He told me that she could be dead as far as he knew. I didn't think he was all that upset about it, to be honest.'

'I don't think he was,' said Sally. 'At least, I suppose he always felt hurt about it, but he'd got over it.' She sighed. 'Now we have to find her and tell her.'

Iona frowned. 'D'you think she'll want to come to the funeral?'

'I hope not!' Sally looked aghast. 'I couldn't possibly face her.'

'We should contact her anyway,' said Jenna. 'Give her the choice.'

'That's providing she can get here by the day after tomorrow,' said Iona.

'Honestly,' said Sally crossly. 'He was trouble when he was alive, and he's trouble dead too.'

'Mum!' Jenna sounded shocked.

Sally bit her lip. 'I don't really mean that,' she said. 'I miss him very much.'

Jenna put her arms around Sally. The two of them remained locked together for a moment, united in their sorrow. Iona said nothing as she stared away from them, out of the window, at the apple tree in the garden.

⁓

She was glad to get back to her own house and be on her own for a while. When she got in she dumped her bag on the sofa and ran upstairs. She opened the wardrobe doors and looked at Frank's suits hanging up in a neat row, his shoes placed in the shoe tidy on the back of the door. It was hard to believe he wasn't coming back. For so many nights she'd imagined what it would be like if he did come back, if she was looking after him as a disabled person, or even just helping him to come to terms with having spent weeks in a coma, but she'd never allowed herself to think of what it would be like if he didn't come back at all.

She opened the drawer of the tall dresser where Frank kept his shirts and T-shirts. She unfolded a long white tee and slipped it over her head. She wished that it had some scent of Frank, but it didn't. It smelled of fabric conditioner.

She closed her eyes. Everyone would be telling her to rebuild her life and to move on. And she knew that one day she would have to do that. But right now she wanted to cry for Frank and the life they'd never had together.

～

Sally called Christine's solicitor in the UK and told him about Frank's death. James Carlisle was shocked but sympathetic. He said that Christine had assumed when Frank hadn't got back to them that he wasn't interested in knowing her any more. And she'd told him that she'd half expected that from her son and had been perfectly prepared to accept it. James wasn't sure how she would react to the news of his accident and death. But she was a strong woman, he told Sally. She'd cope.

Sally gave him the details of the funeral arrangements but said that she wasn't expecting to see Christine there. It was short notice and Christine really didn't have any connection with her son or her son's family. Besides, said Sally, there was an added complication.

'Oh?' James Carlisle didn't sound as though any complication would be too much for a solicitor to deal with.

When Sally told him about Iona, however, James Carlisle was stunned into silence.

'D'you think she'll come?' asked Jenna as Sally replaced the receiver.

'No,' said Sally. 'Maybe she'll send us a card.'

'I'm glad you're not like her.' Jenna shivered suddenly despite the warmth of the evening. 'I'm glad you never walked out on me. Even if sometimes I might have made you feel that way.'

Sally smiled at her. 'No you didn't,' she assured her daughter. 'You drive me mad sometimes, but that's par for the course. I love you.'

'I love you too,' said Jenna, and hugged her for about the hundredth time that day.

Chapter 40

The day of Frank's funeral was the hottest day of the year. More suited to a wedding than a funeral, Iona thought wryly, although she supposed that just as many people had to be buried on brilliant summer days as on days when the sky was cloudy and grey and chill winds blew from the north. But that day no wind was blowing at all and the air was still and warm, even in the early morning.

Iona got up and showered and then had a cup of coffee and a croissant, sitting in the morning sun on the tiny patio behind the house. In previous summers she and Frank had enjoyed many breakfasts there. She wished all memories of him weren't tainted by the fact that he shouldn't have been with her at all, but should have been in Bray with Sally and Jenna. She wanted to hate him but she couldn't. And, of course, she couldn't hate them either. Somehow Frank had brought them all close to each other and Iona felt that this wasn't exactly a bad thing. It just shouldn't have been something that had ever happened in the first place.

She'd just finished dressing when Lauren, Myles and her mother turned up. Flora and David had arrived the night before and had come back with her to the Liberties house after Frank's remains had been brought to the church for a private ceremony, attended only by Sally, Jenna, Iona and her parents and Lauren and Myles. The funeral, however, was unlikely to be as private, since they were sure that other people would be bound to show up.

Now Iona opened the door and smiled at her family. Her father wasn't coming to the church but was staying at home with Charlotte and Gavin, which was a big treat for them and, Flora had added when she told Iona, a let-off for him because he hated funerals.

Lauren kissed Iona on the cheek and then looked at her critically.

'Amazing,' she said. 'Not what I would have expected.'

Iona had elected to wear a sleeveless white linen dress which buttoned down the front and a pair of dark purple high-heeled sandals with multicoloured glass beading across the straps. Her dark hair was lightly gelled and she'd applied gloss to her rosebud lips. She looked young and pretty and as though she were about to go to a garden party rather than a funeral.

'He liked the summer,' she said. 'I didn't want to do black. And besides, I really wouldn't have felt right in it. But I wanted to look nice for him. Does that make me seem really stupid and shallow?'

'Not at all. And you look lovely.' Flora hugged her.

'Are you ready?' asked Myles.

Iona nodded.

'Let's go,' he said, and they all piled into the car.

Sally and Jenna were waiting for the car to arrive for them. Sally had been concerned that they were getting a car from the funeral directors while Iona was coming with Myles and Lauren, but Iona had told her not to be silly, that it didn't really matter and that she was happy to come with her sister and brother-in-law. Sally hoped that Iona really did think like that. She didn't want the other woman to feel sidelined in any way. Which is a weird way to think, she murmured under her breath as she looked out of the window and saw the big Daimler turn down the road. I wish I didn't like Iona. I wish that this was a private goodbye between Frank and me. And yet, she thought, it's good to know that there's someone else who cares too. Without Iona and her family there would have been very few people close to Frank to mourn him.

She looked over her shoulder to where Jenna was sitting and nodded at her.

She was surprised by the large group of people standing outside the church. Sally recognised most of her immediate neighbours, as well as teachers from her school and some of Jenna's friends – including, she noticed, Gerry Cullinan. Pete Maguire, Frank's main contractor and the man she and Iona had been dealing with in relation to the Belleza del Serene contract, was there too, along with a few other men whom Sally supposed worked with him. She also recognised the girl from Iona's office who'd been so surprised to see her a few weeks earlier. And Siobhán Farrell was there too, looking more formal than she'd ever seen her before, in a neat charcoal trouser suit, her wiry hair pulled back from her face, the young garda, Cathal Rothery, beside her.

As the car eased to a halt, the groups of people moved into the church. Sally looked around for Iona but couldn't see her. She looked at her watch. The mass was meant to start in ten minutes. She hoped that Iona would arrive in time. And that she hadn't changed her mind about coming.

Sally was very aware that Iona felt uncomfortable about the situation now. It was one thing for them to have become friendly with each other when looking after Frank, but this was completely different. This was a statement of how things were. Of who was Frank's wife. Of who was Frank's family.

'She's late,' murmured Jenna.

'I – oh, here they are.' Sally was relieved to see Myles's car pull up beside them.

'Sorry,' he said as he got out. 'I think it's the weather. Everyone was heading in this direction. They're probably all off to the beach!'

Sally smiled at him and then Iona got out of the car. The two women looked at each other for a moment and then Iona laughed. Sally, too, was wearing a white summer dress, trimmed with a navy collar. Her shoes were low navy and white slingbacks which matched her bag.

'Black maternity clothes are strictly evening wear,' she told Iona. 'And besides, it didn't seem appropriate somehow.'

'Even for me,' said Jenna. 'And most of my clothes are black.'
She was dressed in a silver-grey jacket and baggy trousers.

Flora kissed Sally on both cheeks. 'You look wonderful,' she said. 'And I'm sorry about Frank.'

'Thank you,' said Sally simply. 'I'm sorry too. For everything.'

'Are you ready?' asked Myles.

The women nodded.

'Let's go,' he said.

⤔

The church was cool and peaceful and both Sally and Iona allowed their thoughts to drift during the ceremony. At the end, Myles got up and said a few words of thanks on behalf of the family. He told the congregation that they wanted the cremation to be a private family event but that they were all grateful for everyone's support. And Iona felt tears sting her eyes when Sally reached for her and took her hand.

'We are family,' she whispered to Iona. 'He made us family even if we never intended to be.'

The drive to the crematorium took half an hour. They sat in the mortuary chapel while prayers were said for Frank and then emerged into the bright sunlight. As they left, a woman at the back of the chapel, whom neither of them had seen arrive, got up and followed them outside.

Both Sally and Iona turned to her and stared.

'She came,' breathed Sally.

Iona blinked. Then blinked again.

The woman was an older version of Frank. She had his eyes and his mouth and she was very, very beautiful. She was wearing a dark suit and a wide-brimmed hat which shaded her eyes from the relentless sun. Sally and Iona stared wordlessly at her.

'I'm Christine,' she said. 'Frank's mother. I only arrived this morning. That's why I didn't come to the church. I would've got in touch earlier but I realise that the family situation here is complicated.'

468

'We didn't see you on the way in to the chapel,' said Sally.

'I – I wasn't sure I'd be welcome.'

'Granny?' said Jenna doubtfully.

Christine pursed her lips. 'I've never been called that before.'

'I guess not,' said Sally sharply. 'I guess you've never been called Mum either.'

'Look,' said Christine, 'I know you're upset about Frank. I understand how you feel . . .'

'No,' said Iona. 'You don't. You don't understand a single thing. You left him. He was a little boy and he loved you and you left him. And I totally understand that you felt trapped and all that sort of stuff, but the least you could've done was once, just once, sent him a card or thought about him or made him feel that you gave the teeniest, tiniest shit about what happened in his life.'

'I really don't think—'

'No! You don't.' Iona couldn't contain herself. 'At least not about other people. You obviously thought about yourself and your career and what you wanted, but never once did it occur to you that Frank actually, stupidly still loved you, you callous bitch.'

'Iona.' Sally put her hand on the other girl's arm.

'Oh, for heaven's sake!' cried Iona. 'She messed up his life and she thinks it's OK to come and mess up his death too. She returned Jenna's photograph! How could she!'

'I'm sorry.' Christine's voice was tight. 'I see I'm not welcome.'

'You're welcome to be here and mourn your son,' said Sally quietly. 'But it would have been so much better if you'd bothered to come when he was alive.'

'I wrote,' said Christine. 'I sent a letter—'

'Your solicitor sent a letter,' Sally interrupted her.

'And it was too late,' added Jenna.

'Why did you bother?' asked Iona. 'After all this time?'

Christine sighed. 'I'm retired,' she said. 'I had a great life and a great career in magazine publishing and even after I retired from that I took a non-executive seat on the board. But then one day I realised that I'd given it all of my life. And that there was nothing else. I'm not saying that I regretted anything, because I didn't. I don't. But I did wonder about Frank and you, Sally. And Jenna. And I suppose I felt a tug of – of kinship.'

'You're a selfish old bat,' said Iona. 'You did what you want and now you've decided that you wanted the other stuff too. Only you can't have it because Frank is gone.'

'Iona!' Flora, who'd been listening, cautioned her daughter.

'She's right,' said Sally. 'Christine wanted everything on her own terms. But you don't always get things on your own terms, do you?'

'I don't expect you to approve of me,' said Christine. 'I didn't even expect Frank to get in touch. I suppose I just suddenly needed to know him.' She swallowed hard. 'And yes, it was all too late.'

~

Iona had been expecting to feel a little out of place back at Sally's after the cremation. It was traditional that mourners gathered after a funeral and had something to eat and drink, but this was a different situation altogether and she'd already suggested to Sally that maybe she and Jenna would like to be alone. But Sally had been adamant, insisting that Iona was part of the family, and so she'd agreed. Now there was someone else who was part of Frank's family, and this time she was a real flesh-and-blood relative. Sally (who was always so damn dignified and polite, thought Iona) had asked Christine if she wanted to come back for a cup of tea, but Christine had, unsurprisingly, declined, much to everyone's relief. Iona wasn't sure whether her own fury at Christine was because she'd abandoned Frank or because she'd finally shown up.

As they drove back towards Bray, Iona wished they were on their way home. She wanted to go to bed and not get up for weeks.

She was tired. It had come over her suddenly as they stood outside the mortuary chapel talking to Christine. The strain of the last few months had suddenly seemed to overwhelm her so that she wavered on her feet and it was only Flora's discreet grip on her arm that had stopped her from stumbling. She'd glanced at her mother, who'd returned her look with complete understanding, and suddenly Iona had been very grateful for Flora and Lauren and Myles and glad that she'd always had a family to support her no matter what.

'Stupid woman,' said Lauren as they turned on to the main road.

'Who?' asked Flora.

'Christine.'

'Sad woman,' said Flora. 'Abandoning Frank was a sad thing to do.'

'You surely don't feel sorry for her!' Iona was aghast.

'A little,' said Flora. 'I've had such great joy out of my children. She missed all that.'

'She got joy out of her magazine,' muttered Iona.

'And you know that it's a poor, poor second,' said Flora, as she put her arm around her daughter and hugged her close.

⌒

Siobhán was sitting at her desk. She and Cathal had returned to the station directly after the Harper funeral mass and now she was going through the notes of an interview she'd done with another one of the ID fraud gang. Following on from the arrests in her apartment block, they'd found links to other people involved and the whole thing had turned into a much bigger case than she'd ever anticipated. Combined with the armed robbery tip-off, her promotion prospects were improving by the second. Not that she was expecting anything immediately, but she knew that her record was now looking very good. And, of course, she'd been able to close the Harper file too, even though that was because the perpetrator had died. She knew that neither Iona nor Sally could possibly feel the same way, but she was secretly glad that Frank hadn't lived. Siobhán knew that neither of the women could have gone through the whole palaver of seeing Frank questioned and possibly arrested. They both loved him too much for that.

It's a strange thing, love, she thought as she closed the file in front of her. It turns your head to jelly and totally messes up your reasoning. And maybe that's how you know you're really in love. It's when the other person becomes more important to you than you ever thought possible.

She wondered whether she'd ever feel that way about someone. She'd thought she'd felt it about Eddie. She'd been devastated by his betrayal of her. And yet she didn't ache inside for him any more. In fact she'd hardly thought of him at all in the last couple of weeks. She thought he might be away somewhere because she hadn't even seen him when she'd called to Carl's flat. And she didn't want to see him. She was astonished at how little she cared any more. Which actually might have had something to do with the fizzy, bubbly, wonderful feeling that enveloped her whenever she thought about Carl O'Connor. A man she never thought she could possibly love.

I don't love him, she told herself sternly as she put the file away. But I'm glad I'm seeing him again tonight.

⁓

They were sitting in the garden of Sally's house. It was a pretty garden, surrounded by high-growing bushes and flowers and alive with bees which were working hard in the summer sunshine to gather pollen for the hive.

'Would you like more tea?' asked Jenna, who had taken it upon herself to hand around the sandwiches they'd ordered in the previous evening.

'No thanks, sweetheart,' said Sally. 'You've been great. You don't have to hang around if you don't want to.'

'Are you sure?' asked Jenna. 'I was thinking of calling round to Sam's for a while.'

'That's fine,' Sally assured her. 'Though what about the boyfriend?'

Jenna blushed. 'Perhaps I'll see him this evening.'

'Let me know,' said Sally.

'OK.' Jenna got up and kissed her mother on the cheek. 'See

you later.' She kissed Iona on the cheek too. 'And see you too, Iona. Thanks for everything.'

'You're welcome.' Iona kissed her in return.

Sally got up and went into the house, returning with a bottle of champagne.

'It's been in the fridge for ages,' she explained. 'Frank brought it home after a deal he'd done and we just never got around to opening it. I know I can't have any myself, but . . . I'd like to make a toast to him.'

They nodded and held out their glasses.

'To Frank,' said Sally, raising her glass of sparkling water. 'He was more messed up than I ever knew. But he wasn't a bad person.'

'And to Sally and Iona,' said Flora. 'Strong women.'

'Oh, gosh, Flora – I don't think so,' said Sally.

'Of course we are.' Iona grinned at her. 'And we'll continue to be.'

'Can I ask a question?' Myles looked enquiringly at them when they'd finished drinking.

'What?' asked Iona.

'What are you intending to do with DynaLite?'

The two women exchanged glances.

'I don't know yet,' said Sally.

'Because it seems to me,' said Myles, 'there's a really good company there with lots of potential.'

'Yes, but what can we do about it?' asked Sally. 'It's not like we know anything about lighting systems.'

'No-oo,' said Myles slowly, 'but you've both done a great job of keeping things going with the Belleza contract. Pete was asking me whether the company would be sold or wound up or what. He thinks that it should keep going. With you and Iona in charge.' Myles grinned. 'He was very impressed by both of you.'

'You're joking!' Sally laughed. 'I'm hardly a model of a businesswoman, am I?'

'You're a perfectly good businesswoman,' said Iona.

'I . . . I've been putting a few bits and pieces together,' said Myles. 'You need a sales manager who understands the business.

473

I spoke to Pete about that. There are some good guys out there. Then you need someone to run the office.'

'Frank did it all on his own,' objected Iona.

'Um, yes. But he was struggling,' said Myles. 'Not financially,' he added hastily, seeing the stricken looks on their faces. 'Just struggling to keep up with things.'

'Yeah, well, he had other things to worry about too, I guess,' said Iona ruefully.

'I know I can get the bank to put a finance package together,' Myles told her.

'So we keep the company and employ people?' Sally looked nervous. 'I'm a teacher, Myles. I've no experience.'

'Iona has,' he told her. 'You've worked on your own before, Io. You're good at office management.'

'You think I should be involved day-to-day?' She looked at him incredulously.

'Why not?'

Iona and Sally exchanged glances.

'Give us a couple of days to think it over,' said Iona.

'Sure,' said Myles easily. 'There's no rush. But Pete was telling me there's a new hotel opening in Drogheda and that lighting for their nightclub is being put out to tender.'

'Let's talk again tomorrow,' said Iona.

'Well, no,' said Sally. 'Iona, if you think this is a good idea and you're willing to be involved, then I think we should go for it. I'm already a director. We can make you a director too.'

'Oh, but Sally—'

'In fact, if you're not a director I won't employ you.'

They looked at each other. Then Iona laughed.

'OK,' she said. 'Why the hell not?'

Chapter 41

Iona was sitting at her desk in the DynaLite office when the phone rang. She liked the phone, which was slim and neat and very stylish. She liked the office too – although it was only a single room, it overlooked the sea and, because it had windows on two sides, was always drenched with warm sunlight. Iona had started work in the office a month after Frank's funeral and after the bank had come up with more money than they'd expected. This had allowed Iona and Sally to choose an office and employ a lighting expert, who was now out and about meeting existing customers and looking for new ones. He was also in negotiation with the Drogheda hotel about the lighting contract and was very hopeful of being successful. And because the spa deal had worked out so well and the building had won an award, they'd also had referrals from Anthony Brady and the order book was filling up nicely. Frank would have been pleased at that, Iona thought. He'd always been proud of his company and it was good to think that it hadn't passed into someone else's hands.

Their joint involvement in DynaLite meant that Iona and Sally continued to keep in contact with each other. It seemed to Iona now that it was almost impossible to remember a time when she didn't know Sally and Jenna. They had become part of her life and she was part of theirs. And, as a consequence, she had become more tolerant, while Sally had become – well, a good deal more adventurous, thought Iona. Because Sally, having had no apparent interest in the business at all while Frank was alive, had suddenly been the one to come up with all sorts of creative marketing plans. Not only that, but she was becoming an expert on lighting too. It was, she'd told Iona, because she had nothing else to do. The baby was due shortly and she was on maternity leave from school, and so she had plenty of time to think about LED lights and halogen lights and a hundred other different lighting options.

Iona reached out and picked up the phone.

'DynaLite,' she said. 'How can I help you.'

'Hi, Iona.' Jenna's voice was breathless. 'It's Mum. She's gone into hospital. She's having the baby.'

Iona felt her stomach tumble. Of all the things that she'd had to come to terms with over the last few months, Sally's pregnancy was still the most difficult. And she was very unsure about how she would feel when she saw Frank's child in Sally's arms. She swallowed hard.

'Is everything OK?' she asked.

'Oh, sure,' said Jenna. 'I'm here with her. But I know she'd like you to come too. And . . .' Jenna hesitated. 'And, Iona, I'd really like you to be here. It's kind of weird being back in the hospital, and I'm OK about it and everything, but . . .'

'I'll be there right away,' said Iona.

She replaced the receiver and switched on the answering machine. Then she took her bag and quilted jacket from the stand beside the door, let herself out, locked the office and hurried to her car.

It was definitely a strange experience to park in the hospital car park and walk through the entrance doors again, knowing that this time she wasn't coming to see Frank. The memories of his time there flooded back to her even as she turned towards the maternity wing and not the intensive care unit where Frank had been.

'Mrs Harper?' she asked a nurse. 'Sally? And Jenna?'

'Oh, yes.' The nurse smiled at her. 'She's just out of theatre.'

'Already?' Iona looked at her in surprise.

'Baby Harper was in a big hurry to enter the world,' said the nurse. 'Room 14. Go on in.'

Iona hurried down the corridor. The door to Room 14 was closed. She took a deep breath, tapped on it once and then opened it gently.

Sally was lying in the bed, a bundle wrapped in white in her arms. Jenna was sitting beside her. They both looked up as she walked in.

'Hi, Iona!' This time Jenna's voice was cheerful. 'Come and join the family.'

Iona walked slowly over to the bed.

'Is everything OK?' she asked Sally.

'Well, I'm knackered of course,' said Sally. 'But – it's totally worth it. Take her, Iona.'

Iona swallowed hard as she peered through the nest of wraps at the tiny baby. Her face was red and wizened and she had a tuft of jet-black hair in the centre of her head. Her eyes were scrunched closed and she held her hands in tight little fists.

'Oh my God.' Iona felt the tears well up in her eyes. 'She's gorgeous.'

'Go on then,' said Sally. 'Take her.'

'Are you sure?' asked Iona doubtfully. 'I've never seen a baby so young before. Lauren's were a day old before I got to them and they'd started to look half normal. She's so . . . so tiny.'

'You'll be fine,' said Sally reassuringly. She held the bundle towards Iona, who took her in her arms and looked at her through her tear-filled eyes.

'I don't think she looks like anyone,' said Jenna. 'But Mum thinks she has Dad's nose.'

Iona blinked the tears away and sniffed. 'It's hard to say at this point,' she said. 'But maybe.'

'And she has your hair,' added Jenna. 'All black and spiky.'

'Yes, but . . .' Iona looked up at her and saw that both Jenna and Sally were laughing. 'Well, maybe I kind of influenced her in the womb,' she said. 'Crikey, she's tiny, isn't she?'

'Well, she's a bit early,' said Sally. 'But she weighed in at seven pounds, so she's not that tiny.'

'Seven pounds.' Iona giggled. 'I remember desperately trying to lose seven pounds so that I could fit into a party dress.'

'I'm going to go on a really strict diet,' Sally said. 'So that I can regain what was left of my figure.'

The baby opened her almost black eyes and looked into Iona's face. They weren't Frank's eyes, of course they weren't, but Iona couldn't help feeling as though she was seeing a part of him again. And then the baby scrunched them closed and she was her own person once more.

'Why don't you sit down, Iona?' Jenna got up from the chair. 'I'm going to phone Sam and give her the good news. She asked me to let her know as soon as the baby was born.'

'OK, thanks.'

Iona settled into the chair. The baby nestled against her. One day, she thought. One day I'll meet someone and I'll have a baby. But even if I don't, I'll always know this baby. And I'll always love her.

She kissed the top of her head. She wasn't supposed to love her, of course. This was Frank and Sally's baby. Not hers. But she couldn't help loving her all the same.

Sally watched her as she gazed at the tiny infant. She knew what Iona was thinking. These days she nearly always knew what Iona was thinking. In fact, she realised, both of them were very good at guessing each other's thoughts. Iona looked up at her and smiled.

'She's truly lovely,' she told Sally. 'And of course I'm a little bit jealous of you, but that'll pass. I'm glad for you too.'

'I didn't want her at the start,' Sally told her. 'I was freaked out at the idea of being a mother again at my age. But I'll cope.'

'Course you will,' said Iona. 'You coped with everything else.'

'Only because you were there to help,' said Sally.

'I was part of what you had to cope with!'

'True. But you know, Iona – all of the time that Frank was in the coma and you were there . . . even when it was niggly between us and everything . . . well, it was support. And I needed it. I needed you.'

478

'You're getting soppy and sentimental because of your hormones,' Iona told her.

'Probably.' Sally grinned. 'But I'll milk it for all I can. Jenna's being so good and helpful right now, you wouldn't believe! I'm hoping she'll still be the same when the baby comes home and starts screaming in the middle of the night.'

'If you ever need a break, just give me a call,' said Iona. 'You know, if you want to go out for a couple of hours or something. I don't mind.'

'Bloody sure I'll be giving you a call,' Sally said robustly. 'You'll be her godmother, after all. At least, I hope you will.'

'Sally . . . really?'

'Nobody I'd rather have,' said Sally. 'Nobody better, in fact.'

'Thank you,' said Iona. 'I'm glad you feel that way.'

'I absolutely do.' Sally smiled. 'And for your first godmotherly duty, you can help me pick a name for her. Jenna's suggestions have been firmly rooted in gangsta rap so far. I'm looking for something a little less dramatic.'

Iona laughed. 'I haven't even thought about it,' she said. 'But I'll try.'

∽

She dropped Jenna back home later that evening. Sam was coming to stay with her and she'd already stocked up with popcorn and ice cream for the movie they planned to watch.

'What about Gerry?' asked Iona.

'We're not seeing each other any more,' Jenna told her. 'I liked him a lot, Iona. And he was really nice after Dad died. But . . . I've kind of moved on from Gerry.'

'Oh? Anyone else?'

'No. Not that at all. Just that – I don't need someone right now. He was right for me then. He took my mind off what was going on with Dad and everything. But now that I don't need my mind being taken off stuff . . .'

'Fair enough,' said Iona. 'I liked him, though.'

Jenna smiled. 'So did I.' She looked at Iona, an anxious flicker in her eyes. 'You didn't tell Mum, did you? About me sleeping with him?'

'Of course not.' Iona shook her head. 'That's between you and me.'

'Thanks,' said Jenna. 'I mean, she'll have to get used to the fact that I will sleep with guys. Or maybe only one guy. Who knows. But I don't think she needs to know about Gerry right now.'

'Like I said, she won't hear it from me.'

'You're the best.' Jenna hugged her.

'And so are you.'

'So you won't love the baby more than me?'

'Listen, that baby is the most adorable creature in the world.' Iona grinned. 'But I won't love her more. Only differently.'

'That's the thing, isn't it?' said Jenna. 'With you and Dad, and Mum and Dad. He loved you both, only differently.'

'Hmm.' Iona made a face at her. 'It's not an arrangement I'd recommend.'

'No, of course not,' said Jenna. 'But – he wasn't a shit, was he?'

'No,' said Iona firmly. 'He wasn't.'

⌒

She wasn't going to go back to the office – after all, she could collect the phone messages and check e-mails from home – but she decided to call in anyway. There were half a dozen messages, all of them confirming contracts, which made her whoop with delight, and an e-mail from Anthony saying that a magazine wanted to do a big feature on the spa and its design and that the people doing it had specifically asked about the lighting.

Iona felt as though she was walking on air as she left the office again. She was too excited about everything that had gone on that day to simply go home, so she went for a walk along the seafront instead. It was much colder now, and the wind whipped across the bay, so that she burrowed into the warmth of her jacket and thrust her hands deep into its pockets.

'Iona!'

The call came from behind her and she turned around. Siobhán Farrell, dressed in her jogging gear, was running towards her. She stopped and waited for her to catch up.

'I got your text message,' said Siobhán. 'I'm so glad about Sally and the baby. Have you been to see her? How is she?'

Iona nodded. 'Great,' she said.

'I might drop by tomorrow,' said Siobhán.

'She'd love to see you,' said Iona.

'And you?' asked Siobhán. 'How are you?'

'I'm fine.' Iona smiled at her. 'In fact, Siobhán, today I feel better than ever. It's like a weight has been lifted from my shoulders. I was so scared that I'd hate Sally when the baby was born, and hate the baby too. But I don't.'

'I'm very glad,' said Siobhán. 'How's the new business going?'

'Brilliantly.' Iona told her about the potential magazine article.

Siobhán grinned. 'I'm delighted for you. Though it's a shame you're out of the property business. I'm thinking of buying somewhere myself.'

'Really?'

Siobhán nodded. 'Joint purchase.'

'Are you serious!'

'We haven't totally decided yet,' said Siobhán. 'And I'm not rushing into getting engaged again or anything, but . . .'

'I'm so thrilled for you,' Iona told her. 'I know that on the only occasion I saw him you spent half the time under the table, but he actually seemed quite nice to me. Plus you hated him so much! It was a dead giveaway.'

'Sod off.' Siobhán shoved her amiably.

'Where is he tonight?' asked Iona.

'Interviewing someone,' replied Siobhán. 'We both spend our lives interviewing people!'

'I'm glad neither of you really got around to interviewing Frank,' said Iona.

'How about you? Anyone new in your life?' asked Siobhán.

'Give me a break,' said Iona. 'I haven't had the time. And I'm still coming to terms with the whole thing.'

'There's always Enrique.' Siobhán's eyes twinkled.

'Oh, come on. I hardly even know the man,' said Iona. 'And I haven't seen him since that day I walked out of his apartment.'

'He still asks about you,' said Siobhán. 'I don't see him that often these days but every time I do he asks about you.'

'Does he?' Iona felt her cheeks go pink.

'Absolutely. You should get in touch with him.'

'Maybe.'

'Let me know when,' said Siobhán. 'I'll sort it out for you!'

'Why is it that people with new men in their lives are always trying to sort out everyone else?' demanded Iona. 'I'm perfectly fine.'

'Yeah, right!' Siobhán chuckled. 'Anyway, I'd better get going. See you again soon.'

'See you!' Iona waved at her and walked back towards her car.

Chapter 42

The steeple was covered in a deep layer of snow and, in the gardens surrounding the church, glimpses of green from the fir trees was the only colour peeking through the covering of white. As they walked up the short driveway, their breaths hung before them in misty clouds and stray flakes settled briefly on their coats before melting.

'It's very picturesque,' said Jenna through chattering teeth. 'But couldn't we have picked a warmer day to have her christened?'

'It's your father's birthday today,' Sally reminded her. 'That's why.' She peeped in at the baby, who was completely wrapped up in warm blankets. 'Lucky thing, she can't feel the cold.'

'Well I can, and I'm bloody freezing.'

'Ah, quit moaning,' said Iona cheerfully. 'You've got to admit that this was a great idea.'

'I don't think so!' Jenna's smile was sceptical. 'I'm a city girl at heart. This is *so* the back of beyond.'

'It's where your dad was born,' said Sally.

'Yeah, well, he always did say he came from the arsehole of nowhere.'

'Jenna Harper! You're in church grounds. For heaven's sake mind your language.'

'You think God is going to send down a thunderbolt?' Jenna giggled.

'No, but I might clatter you if you're not careful,' warned her mother.

'Or I'll arrest you.' Siobhán Farrell grinned at her and Jenna grinned back. Siobhán had been pleased when both Sally and Iona had insisted on her coming to the christening with them. She'd gone out with them to celebrate a few weeks after Sally had come out of hospital and felt able to leave the baby for a few hours, and she knew that she'd always stay friends with Sally and Iona.

She shivered suddenly and Sally smiled. 'Let's get into the church,' she said. 'Jen's right. It's freezing out here.'

Theirs was the only baptism that day, and the young priest welcomed them warmly as they shuffled into the pews.

'Great to see you,' he said. 'And this is the little one? Isn't she lovely? Are you ready to start? Who's who?' He smiled at Iona. 'You're the godmother, yes?'

'And I'm the godfather,' said Myles.

'Right,' said the priest. 'Off we go. Let's welcome her into the community.'

Frank had been baptised here. Sally knew that because he'd shown her the church on one of their visits to Sligo and told her that it wasn't really surprising that Christine had left; it truly was the back of beyond. Sally thought for a moment of Christine, who had sent her a letter after the funeral telling her that she regretted how things had turned out and that she was sorry she hadn't done things differently. Perhaps, she wrote, it had been wrong to cut Frank and his family out of her life completely, even though at the time it had seemed the right thing to do. She'd asked Sally to get in touch if there was anything she needed in the future, if she could be of any help. And wished her well with her pregnancy. Too late, thought Sally again. It had always been too late for Christine. Too late to realise that she was in the wrong relationship, too late to want to meet her son. She'd send her a photograph of Jenna and the new baby. It wasn't much, but it was the best she felt able to do.

She exchanged glances with Iona, who smiled at her and gave her a thumbs-up signal as she held the baby.

'Francesca Ann,' said the priest, 'I baptise you in the name of the Father and of the Son and of the Holy Spirit.'

Francesca roared as the cool water trickled over her forehead.

The priest dabbed at it with a white cloth and Iona murmured words of comfort to her. The baby stopped crying and looked at her from her navy-blue eyes.

'Sorry,' whispered Iona.

Francesca's expression was accusing.

'Ah, get over yourself,' murmured Sally to her, and the baby looked affronted. She closed her eyes and snuggled into her blankets again.

～

It was still snowing outside. They got into the cars and drove the three miles from the church to the bay. The beach curved away from them and the green water of the sea churned at the shore. The wind was bitterly cold. Iona, Sally and Jenna got out of the cars.

'It's bleak,' said Iona.

'Yes. He didn't want to live here, but he did love the openness of it,' said Sally.

'I can understand that.' Iona looked inland. At the edge of her sight she could see the gable wall of the Harper family house. They had put it up for sale the previous week and already had an interested buyer. They had agreed to invest half of the proceeds in the business and divide the other half between them. They were, thought Iona, turning into hard-headed businesswomen after all.

'Let's make sure we get the wind behind us when we do this,' said Sally.

Jenna looked aghast. 'Mum!'

'Well, we're all wearing new clothes,' said Sally defensively as Iona chuckled.

'Are we ready?' asked Sally. Her voice shook a little.

'Ready,' said Iona.

Siobhán, Lauren and Myles watched them as Sally took the urn out of its box, lifted the lid and shook the contents into the air.

Frank's ashes were taken by the wind and carried away from

them, drifting over the damp, springy grass as they blew out towards the sea.

'Goodbye, Dad,' said Jenna.

'Be happy, Frank.' Iona lifted her hand in a half-wave.

'Goodbye,' whispered Sally.

Then Frank's family turned around and walked, arm in arm, back to the warmth of the cars.

Look out for Sheila O'Flanagan's new novel

'An exciting love story with a deliciously romantic denouement'
Sunday Express

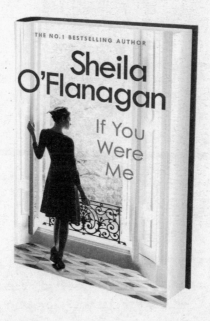

You're engaged to a great man. You're on a countdown to your wedding day.
You stopped thinking about your first love a long time ago.

But what if one unexpected, forbidden kiss were to throw your life upside down?

Carlotta O'Keefe suddenly finds herself wondering if the girl she was would
recognise the woman she has become.

She thought she was living a charmed life. What if she's got it all wrong?

What if her past is meant to be her future?

Out now in hardback, ebook and audio
Order it now at www.headline.co.uk

And don't miss...

'A really enjoyable "will they, won't they?" story that will keep you guessing right up until the end'
Heat

The things we never say:

A husband is afraid to say that selling the house his wife loves is the only option…

A son can't say how useful his ageing father's fortune will be when he's gone…

A woman hasn't said that even though they live thousands of miles apart, this man is always on her mind…

But if those things were said, the results might be surprising. As Abbey – and a whole family she knew nothing of – are about to find out in Sheila O'Flanagan's warm-hearted, thought-provoking and touching novel.

Order it now at www.headline.co.uk

Better Together

Sheridan Gray has discovered a secret. . .

When journalist Sheridan loses her dream job, she's distraught. She's forced to relocate to the countryside. Her career is over. . . until she discovers that her landlady holds the key to a big story.

But the longer Sheridan stays in Nina's home, and the closer she gets to a certain handsome man in the town, the tougher it is to expose their secrets. When it comes to love or success, will Sheridan go with her heart or her head?

All For You

Lainey Ryan has always dreamed of having a fairytale wedding.

But all of her relationships end the same way – just when she thinks she's found The One, it's all over. Will things be different with her latest boyfriend?

As her love-life hits yet another rocky patch, Lainey's estranged mother Deanna – a staunch feminist and highly critical – arrives in town. And with her visit comes the discovery of some long-hidden family secrets. Maybe Lainey's happily-ever-after isn't so impossible after all. . .

A PRIDE
OF KINGS

JUSTIN SCOTT

HARPER

Harper
An imprint of HarperCollins*Publishers*
1 London Bridge Street,
London, SE1 9GF

www.harpercollins.co.uk

This paperback edition 2017
1

First published by Granada Publishing 1984

A catalogue record for this book
is available from the British Library

ISBN: 9780008222024

Set in Sabon by Palimpsest Book Production Limited
Falkirk, Stirlingshire

Printed and bound in Great Britain

MIX
Paper from
responsible sources
FSC˙ C007454

To Gloria Hoye,
For the music that lingers . . .
my love, my beauty, my friend

PROLOGUE
Paris 1913

It started well, for a good-bye, but ended very badly.

They danced a tango for old times at a ball in the Paris embassy where Lieutenant Kenneth Ash was third naval attaché, and had their last waltz. Then a walk in the moonlight beside the Seine, both knowing it would lead to her bed at the Ritz. And finally, too soon, late supper at Maxim's, where it all went to hell.

Ash had steeled himself to accept her leaving. He had no choice. She had always called the tune. But he lost control toward the end of supper and asked her to marry him. Tamara refused.

Ash tried again, with a shaky smile. 'You know, last time I asked you said I was too young. I'm eight years older now.'

He had a faint West Virginia plantation drawl, which years of kicking around Europe and England had softened, modified and nearly erased. English was Tamara's third language. She made it mysterious with a French accent, Russian syntax, and the occasional American slang she had picked up from Ash.

'And I too am eight years older.'

'Why don't you just stop counting for a few years. Let me catch up?'

She was a sloe-eyed Russian beauty with jet hair, pale white skin and the regal bearing of a prima ballerina. Europe knew her as Tishkova and the aristocrats at the surrounding tables eyed her longingly. 'It's not just your youth, Kennet. It's *my* age. I can't dance forever. I have to protect my future.' She hushed his lips with her finger. It

9

bore the scent of their bodies mingled, but the determined coolness in her eyes reminded Ash that too was over. 'Take the sea duty you've always wanted,' she urged. 'You've got your whole life ahead of you. Find yourself a pretty girl.'

'I found her eight years ago.'

She faltered. Ash saw the shadow in her eyes, clung to it, racked his brain for some new thought to dissuade her. He looked the same as the day they had met, Tamara thought, except for the officer's moustache he had grown to please her. He was still a handsome young man with sun-streaked brown hair and a quick broad smile. His blue eyes sleepy from love making, his lean face unmarked by the few years he had spent at sea, and the fact that he had changed from his social dress uniform into ordinary evening clothes, made him look younger still. Tamara recovered, shook her head.

'I need more. Good-bye, Kennet. Don't dwell on what we had. I won't.'

Ash watched her cross the dining room. Their years in Europe were the happiest he had known. Tamara Tishkova had changed his life, altered its entire course, and turned him, willingly, into a sort of hybrid American-European, comfortable almost anywhere, rarely at home. He ran after her and caught her arm.

'Please. I love you.'

She returned a look of firm resolve. 'I may regret this often. Surely I will never forget you. But I must serve myself. I am going home to Russia. I am going to settle down, at last.'

'With the Grand Duke Valery?'

'I know you love me, but I must have more.'

'Like royal Romanov blood and lots of money,' Ash retorted bitterly, hating himself for breaking a vow not to drag it up again.

Tamara turned away, but Ash, stunned by the sheer finality of the moment, still held her arm. A tall, wire-thin

German Army officer who had been watching from the bar slipped between them.

'It would appear that the lady wishes to depart.'

'I'm quite all right,' Tamara said icily. 'If you will excuse us, monsieur?'

'Then if she is not a lady, you should conduct such business in the street.'

Ash's despair detonated a mindless, lightning punch that landed satisfyingly on target and launched the sneering German over a table and onto the floor. His first rational thought was thank God he wasn't in uniform; his second was that he had been deliberately provoked. The reason became apparent as the German climbed to his feet, helped by his fellow guards officers. Eyeing Ash with a pair of cold grey eyes, he dabbed the blood from his lip, and bowed stiffly. 'A glove is customary in Europe, but I accept your challenge . . . Are you as quick with a sabre?'

'Who the hell are you?'

'Count Philip von Basel.'

Ash heard Tamara's sharply drawn breath. Von Basel was a duellist famous for maiming his opponents. Apparently he had run out of victims in Germany. Ash had blundered into a set-up.

'As for you, Mademoiselle, I'd recommend a photograph of the gentleman's pretty face.' Von Basel strutted out of Maxim's. One of his party asked the name of Ash's second.

'You're not going to duel with von Basel,' said Tamara.

'Don't have much choice.' The fact was, putting the German aristocrat in his place just might make him feel a little better.

'Nonsense. He's a duellist. You're only a fencer.'

'I can take care of myself.'

'Romantic melodrama. Killing a man won't change my mind. Neither will dying, or being maimed or blinded.

11

You're acting like a child . . . If you duel with that madman
I'll –'

'Leave me?'

Ash's second was his friend and fencing master François
Roland. Roland tried to talk him out of it while he wrapped
silk handkerchiefs around his wrists to protect the veins
and tendons. 'It's not merely a question of being a good
fencer. You're quite good. But he's a killer. You're only a
sportsman.'

Ash glanced across the walled stable yard where von
Basel's seconds were binding *his* wrists. In the space between
the two camps, where they would fight, the doctors were
wiping the sabres with carbolic acid disinfectant. Some spectators who had seen the incident start at Maxim's had followed them here and were placing bets. It was cold. First
light had barely broken and a mist lay heavily on the ground.
Von Basel glanced back. At this distance, his bony face
looked like a skull.

'I can handle him.' Ash gave Roland a tight grin. 'I'm
better trained. Aren't I?'

Roland eyed him shrewdly. 'Did Tamara leave you?'

Ash nodded and glanced again at von Basel, who had
removed his shirt. They were about the same height. They'd
have an equal reach. Von Basel's arms and chest were corded
with wiry muscle, but Ash believed he was stronger. And he
had some weight over the German, which could come in
handy for in-fighting.

'I see,' said Roland. 'I'm sorry.' The Frenchman had seen
their break-up coming all summer. For years it had been a
brilliant affair, glittering with love and passion, the sort that
excited the people around it. But in the end Kenneth Ash
was too American to understand the complex needs of a
highly strung Russian ballerina, and too young to serve them
even if he did.

'Give me your shirt.'

Ash shrugged out of it. Cloth infected wounds.

'Wish me luck?' The air was cold on his skin. He had a round scar on his left shoulder, thick arms and a broad chest.

'Don't look at his eyes.'

Ash saw what Roland meant as he and von Basel approached each other. Wearing a mesh mask a fencer had no eye contact with his opponent. Von Basel's eyes were dead grey, composed, assured, and utterly concentrated. They locked on Ash's face and he felt von Basel willing him to stare back.

Ash looked instead at the blades, gleaming wet with disinfectant, razor sharp the length of the leading edge and half the back. A slash in either direction would open flesh to the bone. The point was lethal.

The seconds explained the rules: The duel would continue until one opponent stopped fighting; action would be interrupted to bind wounds. But was there no possibility of shaking hands and ending this before blood was shed?

'*Nein.*'

'No.'

'Begin.'

Von Basel brought his hilt to his nose, blade vertical in salute, whipped the sword down and advanced, tracking Ash with the dead-steady point. Ash retreated a few steps to see how the German moved. Then he challenged von Basel's grip with two hard beats. Von Basel returned two of his own and the stable yard came alive with the ring of steel.

Ash felt a little giddy. I suppose I should be afraid, he thought. But he really didn't give a damn, which was a hell of a way to survive a fight. And, a small voice added, a hell of a reason to tangle with a man who wanted to maim him for the fun of it.

He thrust to test von Basel's defences. Von Basel parried,

13

parried Ash's next thrust, stopped a third thrust with a vicious riposte, and suddenly jump-lunged.

It was a complete surprise so early in the fight when they were supposed still to be feeling each other out. Ash managed to get out of the way, but it was more a matter of superb reflexes than skill. Von Basel had damned near caught him flat-footed.

Buoyed by the escape, he attacked. Von Basel retreated uneasily, with weak ripostes, allowing Ash in close, lunging and thrusting. Too late, he realized that the German had suckered him.

Von Basel thrust at his cheek. Ash was too far extended to parry effectively. He saved his face, but the sabre slashed across the front of his right shoulder. He heard a gasp of pain and shock, his own. First blood. Speed had saved his face again, but not his skin. The blood poured onto his breast. The seconds stopped the action and Ash let Roland and the doctor sit him on a barrel to examine the cut.

'It's a respectable wound,' Roland said. 'You can stop.'

The doctor, an elderly naval surgeon Ash had known since Academy days, looked sick. 'You've had enough, Lieutenant.'

'Dress it, damn it. It's a scratch.'

'He's going to carve you into small pieces, Ash. Give it up.'

Ash looked at whoever had said that. 'If he can, I don't give a damn. Come on, Bones, sir. Dress it.'

While the doctor worked, Roland coached. 'You're not doing bad. But keep moving. Use your speed, and *thrust*. Don't wait. *Thrust*. Finish him quickly. The longer you take the more he'll learn about you.'

'And I'll learn about him.'

'Forgive me, my friend, but he has much less to learn about you.' Ash stood up. Roland took his arm. 'Stop this. I beg of you.'

14

'I could *order* you to stop,' the doctor said. Ash gave him a tight grin.

'Neither of us is going to believe that for a second, sir. Button up, it's cold out.' He closed the doctor's boat cloak, patted his shoulder, and reached for his newly disinfected sabre.

'*En garde!*'

Ash thrust. The sting in his shoulder acted like a goad. He felt concentrated, almost invincible. Von Basel attacked. Ash failed to break it up as he retreated. He tried to create an opening with a pair of risky feints. It didn't work.

Suddenly motor-car tyres rumbled on the cobble-stone drive and everyone, including Ash and von Basel froze. Duelling was illegal in France and the principals, the seconds, and even the doctors were liable to heavy penalties. A black car materialized out of the mist and parked silently, fifty feet away. A window slid open. Ash saw the white blur of Tamara's face. *She had come.*

'*En garde!*'

Tamara looked across the courtyard, saw the duellists caught in eerie stasis, like the figures of a tableau in the cold half-light. For a long second, Kenneth seemed to hold her stare. Then he turned back to von Basel and raised his weapon. Steel rang on steel. Von Basel stalked; he looked like a coiled spring, moments from release. They clashed. Sparks flew from their blades. Tamara eased a pistol out of her fur muff" and steadied the barrel on the door. If necessary, she told herself, she would use it.

Emboldened by Tamara's presence, Ash launched a reckless attack. He drove von Basel back toward the ring of spectators and loosed a sudden thrust at the German's wrist, intending to skewer him just above the handkerchiefs to make him drop his sabre. A clean win, finished, with no one hurt badly. His point went exactly where he had aimed.

Von Basel slipped under it with uncanny agility and

15

attacked, bearing in on Ash with frightening skill and intensity. Ash fell back. The German started going for his face. Ash retreated, frantically parrying, too busy defending himself to counter-attack through the openings in von Basel's high slashes.

The end came suddenly. As if deciding that he had to weaken Ash further before scarring his face, von Basel went again for Ash's shoulder. Feinting first at his face, he slashed across the bandage, ripping it away, and cutting, crossing the first slash. Blood gushed. Ash staggered, dropped his sabre, reached for it with his left hand. Roland and the doctor pounced on him, dragged him to the ground and pressed thick wads of gauze on the torn flesh.

Ash looked up at von Basel and felt, despite the pain and the sight of his blood that covered his torso, a sudden unearthly clarity. 'Fix me up.'

'You're hurt.'

Ash knew he wasn't. A little lightheaded and he'd lost some blood; that was all. 'Stop the bleeding before I keel over.'

'It's stopped. Just lie still 'til I finish.'

François Roland stood up and addressed von Basel. 'Enough, Monsieur. More will be murder.'

Von Basel was breathing hard, his chest heaving with excitement. 'Not yet.'

'This is France. Junker influence carries no weight here. Nor does the Kaiser. If you murder this man it will be the guillotine.'

'I won't murder him,' von Basel smiled. 'But I do intend to carve him up a bit more. After all, he bruised my lip when he struck me.'

'If you do,' François Roland answered quietly, 'I will send you home to Prussia without a face.'

'No,' Ash murmured, climbing to his feet, flexing his

stiff fingers. The new bandage was as broad as his hand. 'It's my fight.'

Von Basel looked over the Frenchman, took his measure. Roland was probably the finest fencer in Europe. Angered, he might be a formidable duellist as well. He toyed with the idea of risking it, but there was a second deterrent. Ash's doctor's cloak had slipped from his shoulders to reveal a United States Navy uniform, which cast an entirely new light on the affair.

Der Tag was coming soon. The Day. The day that Kaiserin Germany cast off the restraints of peace to take what was rightfully hers. The day Germany seized French and British colonies and took her place in the imperial sun. On *Der Tag* it could be hoped that the vigorous new American state would side with Germany. Or at least remain neutral. Reluctantly, von Basel concluded that it would be foolish to send Ash back to the US Navy with a face covered with German sabre cuts, and he lowered his weapon. For his Kaiser and *Der Tag*.

'*En garde*! said Ash, seizing his blade in his left hand.

'Your teacher has spared you further humiliation.'

'*En garde*!' Ash was weaving.

'You've already lost,' von Basel sneered. 'And you're not worth killing.'

Ash staggered after him, but von Basel never turned around. Across the drive the black car rolled into the mist. Tamara, heading for the *Gare de l'Est* and the train to Russia. She had seen it all.

BOOK I
Victoria's Children

1

Mauve curtains of lined velvet muffled the noise of the Paris street below the Frenchwoman's bedroom. Worn-out lorry engines, clattering draught horses, even the prolonged tramp of infantry on night march, sounded remote. But a deeper, richer noise penetrated the cloth; from sixty miles east of Paris came the determined rumble of German artillery barraging the French trenches.

Kenneth Ash lay awake, propped against the pillows, watching the face of the woman who had fallen asleep with her head on his chest, and listening intently to the distant assault. Across the sumptuous boudoir, among the ornate mirrors, a loose mirror rattled sympathetically in its frame. The guns had rumbled all night like the heartbeat of a stranger who had followed them here to spy on their lovemaking.

Ash had toured both sides of the battle lines. He knew what the guns meant. Between the opposing trenches cold December winds had hardened the mud in no-man's-land; the Germans would conclude the barrage with an infantry attack at dawn. It was the start of the third winter of the World War. The new year, 1917, would see Kaiser Wilhelm's armies defeat the combined forces of the English, French and Russian allies, unless the United States intervened to defeat Germany and end the slaughter.

The candles he had carried upstairs from the dining room still burned on the sconces around her bed. In the golden light her skin looked as soft as it felt, smooth as the silk-covered quilt which had spilled off their bodies and lay half on her bed and half on the carpet. She was a woman, not a

21

girl, and faint lines had gathered beside her eyes and mouth. Her elaborately coiffed hair had come undone, like a diary scrawled in the dark of what they had done. Ash kissed her hair, savouring her perfume, and reached for the champagne. Empty.

He had to leave, had to report back to the American Embassy. Duty called, such as it was. A despatch to Berlin, too important to trust to cable or letter, yet not so momentous that the ambassador himself had to make the journey. Call in the navy instead – Lieutenant Commander Kenneth Ash, special attaché to the American Embassy in London, discreet diplomatic courier, neutral observer of how the Allies and Central Powers were conducting their war, and, some might suggest, glorified mailman . . . But only one more month. Then at last a berth on a fighting ship.

She shivered; a chill had crept back into the room because the coal fire her maids had lighted while she and Ash had eaten late supper had burned low, flickers of blue flame among white ash. Ash pulled the coverlet over them, over her shoulders until only her face showed. She tightened her arms around him. Ash cupped her breast and she smiled, still half-asleep.

His gaze shifted to the room. It was a voluptuous concoction of silk and velvet, gilt carving, marble, crystal, and everywhere the gleaming, ornate mirrors. She had straddled him and they had shown her in a dozen, subtle variations. She was a *comtesse* – wealthy, arrogant and secure.

The blood-red ruby on her right hand could finance a torpedo boat, or a townhouse on Washington Square. Like most he had met of the *gratin* – the rich and titled crust of French society – she was a passionate sportswoman and an anglophile in her tastes. *Le betting au steeplechase* slipped incongruously from her tongue. They usually didn't like

Americans, but for Ash she had made a rather grand and, as it turned out, thorough exception.

At a reception this evening at the embassy she had recalled that he had skippered an American yacht in the Brenton Reef Cup cross-Channel race a year before the war, and invited him to leave with her. Nightlife was officially banned in Paris, but there were places to dance in the Montmartre section behind closed doors, doors which opened to a password, or a bribe, or a name like hers. Inside they were doing a new dance, a slow gliding version of the fox-trot called the Nurse's Shuffle.

Ash supposed that if he hadn't spent so many years in Europe he might have been appalled by the cynical response to the millions of war casualties. The English, by contrast, worried less about appearances, allowing dancing everywhere except by officers in uniform. Their new dance was the Saunter, an intricate, precision duet which borrowed from several American dances. The style was to appear nonchalant. When Ash showed her, the *comtesse* was not impressed. She had just returned from Petrograd, and the Russians, she told him, were mad for the Tango.

Her husband was a general, headquartered in Rheims, the champagne city a few miles inside the trench line, and near, judging by the sound, tonight's German artillery barrage. This house was her own, as were the servants, which was a comfort because French army officers from the country nobility were notoriously eager duellists.

'You're frowning,' she said suddenly. 'What are you thinking?'

'I was wondering what it would be like to be married to you.'

She was taken aback until Ash grinned at her. Then she laughed. 'I don't recommend it. Particularly to a naval officer.'

'I'm rarely at sea.'

'You would be with me, Commander.'

Ash laughed, stung a little by the reminder of the gulf between them. *'Touché, Comtesse.* But on occasion I've managed pretty well at sea . . .' True, years past. Last summer he had wangled a temporary command in the Philippines. Now it looked as if his luck was improving as the navy finally began building ships again. He had orders next month to become executive officer on a new cruiser and he could hardly wait, because for most of his eighteen years of navy service he had assisted staff officers and diplomats – errand boy, an officer of the line might call it. Bright young polished aide to Admiral Thayer Mahon, to President Teddy Roosevelt, to Taft, recently to Teddy's young nephew, Franklin, Assistant Secretary of the Navy; still a bright aide, still well-mannered, but not quite so young. And forty had appeared on the horizon like an unexpected landfall; or, more likely, an error of navigation.

Whichever, he had come to fear getting older, sensing that at some age there was a turning point when a man admitted aloud that lost loves, like lost duels, were lost forever.

'I've made you sad.' She smiled.

Ash kissed her; it was in his nature to fall in love, for the moment at least, with women he made love with, and at this moment he could have spent more time with the *comtesse* than he knew he would be invited to. The sound of the guns grew softer. Perhaps the wind had shifted.

'What is this?' She touched the round scar that pocked his left shoulder like a raindrop in a pond.

'A bullet.'

'From love or from war?' she smiled, entering it with her fingernail.

'An anarchist,' said Ash. She raised her brow, and he said, 'He was aiming at someone else.'

'And these?' She traced the crossed sabre scars on his right shoulder.

24

'I was run over by a freight train.'

'*Train de marchandises?* I don't understand.'

'I really don't remember much about it – that's a pretty stone you're wearing.'

The blood-red ruby glittered like an eye in the dark. She stroked his cheek, then held the ring aloft to direct a ray of reddened candle light into his eyes. Down his nose. To his mouth. She kissed where the red beam touched his mouth, moved it, and followed it with her lips. The quilt slid away again as she spiralled her body to follow the descending glow.

She knew how to tease. She lifted her head abruptly, flashed the ruby in his eyes and kissed his mouth. 'Yes, you have managed rather well. Very well.' She turned the ring toward a candle flame and gazed into it; touched the jewel to her lips.

'I smuggled it out of Petrograd. It belongs to my cousin.'

Petrograd. Would there ever come a time when the name of her city didn't evoke her name? 'Why?' he asked.

'Her husband is a Russian noble, and a member of the Duma. There will be a revolution. They're sending out all they can before the Czar falls. It's mine until she leaves Russia.'

'But if the Czar falls the eastern front will collapse.'

'Who cares?'

'*Who cares?*' Ash sat up. 'You'll care if Germany wins the war. The Kaiser will rule all of Europe, *including* Paris.'

She looked at him with cold eyes. 'Better Kaiser Wilhelm than the socialists.'

Ash's face betrayed him. The *comtesse* laughed, sprawling back on the sheets and opening her arms to him. 'Forgive me, *chéri*. I forgot you were American. You don't understand.'

'I understand pretty well that French and British soldiers are fighting a war to end autocratic militarism. They're *told* it's a war of freedom – '

'I am already free, Commander. I'd prefer a French King,

but I'd rather a German King than a French peasant republic, which is what all this freedom will bring us.' She extended her soft hand and again directed the ruby light into Ash's eyes. 'But most of all, I would prefer you. Again.'

Ash stared at her, frankly put off by what amounted to treason.

'*Chéri,*' she said, lying back and tapping the sheet impatiently, 'this is not the Chamber of Deputies. My bed is no place for debate.'

'Does your cousin in Russia prefer a German King too?'

'There is already a German cabal in the Russian court. Everybody knows that. The Czarina is German, is she not? She and the Czar are both the Kaiser's cousins – '

'And King George of England is cousin to all of them.'

'Do you think King George cares who wins the war?'

Ash actually knew George V, but the first rule of a royal friendship was discretion. One did not bandy it about, so all he said was, 'Of course he cares. He's a British patriot first, a royal second.'

'Then he's a fool. The royalty and the nobility – we are international . . . Now be quiet, or leave my bed.'

She said it with a smile, but Ash didn't doubt she meant it. He didn't exactly hate himself for staying, but he wasn't exactly proud of himself either. He might have walked out as a point of honour when he was younger, he thought, but at thirty-six a man alone developed an eye for opportunities not taken that he'd sorely miss later. And there was, after all, a peculiar grain of truth in what she had said – millions *were* dying in the name of God and three royal cousins, Czar, King, and Kaiser, who knew one another by their Christian names.

The artillery ceased rumbling abruptly. It meant dawn in the trenches. Ash could visualize the event sixty miles away. Soldiers were already climbing over the top, charging across no-man's-land into the fire of any machine-guns that had survived the night-long bombardment; and from what Ash's English friends had told him, one always seemed to.

Around the bed the candles began guttering out simultaneously.

'I have to go.'

She nodded drowsily, sleep drifting back into her eyes, dismissing him.

A kitchen maid was lighting the stove; she kept her head down as Ash strode out of the back door into the cold. He found a gate in the murky dawn light, opened it just wide enough for his body and slipped into a lane that connected stables to the street. There were no lights because of the war.

As he walked past the front of the *comtesse*'s house and looked up at the dark windows where she slept, a man stepped out of the shadows across the street.

It was Captain Wesley, senior naval attaché to the United States ambassador to Great Britain, who boomed in his quarter-deck voice, 'Thought you'd never come out, Ash.' Ash saluted and attempted to steer him away from the *comtesse*'s front door.

'How did you happen to find me, sir?'

'Somebody at the reception saw you get into her car. Here.' He hauled a thick envelope from his greatcoat. 'From Ambassador Page.'

Ash handed him a gold matchbox a woman had given him in Berlin and excitedly broke the seal. What could be so important that it had to be hand delivered by his superior officer? Wesley lit a match. Ash shielded the flame with his cloak.

Ambassador Page ordered him to break off his trip to Berlin and return immediately to England to attend a shooting party at Sandringham, the country home of King

George V. With the orders were priority travel documents – gaudily stamped and beribboned passes to get him swiftly aboard crowded trains and steamers.

Something was definitely up, Ash thought, the excitement building. Surely some kind of action. All this was very strange . . . royal invitations always allowed weeks to cancel conflicting engagements. And Ambassador Page would have wired orders and had travel documents issued by the Paris embassy unless he had a reason to keep the invitation quiet. But it was no state secret that Kenneth Ash was considered a friend by the King of England . . . Besides that, it was late in the year for shooting pheasant in Norfolk.

Wesley watched with a condescending smile. 'Action, Ash? Another princely yachting party, perhaps?'

Ambassador Page had stepped way out of regular channels to keep it quiet, so Ash folded his orders and said, 'It's not the fun it used to be, sir. The U-boats play hell with the race buoys.'

'Very amusing, Commander, seeing as how I'm off to god-damn Berlin to do your job.'

They exchanged salutes and Ash set out for La Gare du Nord, plotting the fastest route – train to Calais via Amiens because the Boulogne line was jammed with ambulance trains, thanks to another bloody British offensive against the Germans' vital railroad link to Bapaume, then the Channel ferry from Calais to Dover and with luck an express to London. Nine hours if he was lucky, a full day if he wasn't.

2

An hour after dawn a cold, wet North Sea wind sloughed through the bare woods as thirty beaters whooped, whistled, tapped the trees with sticks. The King's gamekeepers trailed on horseback, straightening their line with sharp commands. Pheasants, partridges and woodcocks retreated uneasily; ahead, the woods came to an abrupt stop at a mowed field where four guns, Ash among them, waited.

Why was he here? Ash wondered, motionless, double-barrel shotgun draped in ready position. King George was one of the finest shots in the realm, but easily half a dozen English guns could offer His Majesty top-hole competition if sport was all he wanted. So Ash's last-minute invitation suggested a charade to keep the real reason for bringing him to Sandringham private, whatever it was. And an elaborate charade at that, right down to his regular loaders crouching silently behind him with second and third guns and bags of shells; Eddison an estate gardener, Martin a mechanic in the Royal Mews, both too old to be conscripted.

The King had placed Ash fifty yards to his right for the first stand of this blustery winter morning. His Majesty also employed two loaders, indicating he planned some serious shooting. To Ash's right, at an equal distance, the King's equerry, Alex Farquhar, paced in impatient little circles as the noise of the beaters modulated with the changing wind; and another fifty yards beyond him was a man Ash hadn't met before, Lord Exeter, a giant of a man whose vast, unmoving bulk seated on a shooting stick and wrapped in enough houndstooth twill to clothe a village put Ash in mind of a deeply entrenched artillery piece puffing gun smoke each time Exeter exhaled in the cold, damp air.

When Ash had arrived from Paris yesterday evening the King had been closeted with advisers. He had gratefully requested a supper tray in his room, cleaned his guns, and gone to an early bed to sleep off the gruelling trip. The King had offered no hint at their hasty breakfast.

But in London, in the car from Charing Cross to the Royal Train at Paddington Station, Ambassador Page had explained that prior to the invitation the King's private secretary had approached him in his club and discreetly sounded him out about the courier duties Ash performed for the United States' European embassies. He had been particularly interested in confirming whether Ash continued to make regular runs to Berlin.

The beaters sounded closer. Ash grinned at the sight of Farquhar, pacing and talking to his loaders. No mistake the King had placed him where he had. The equerry was unintentionally acting as a flanker for Ash and the King. All that activity would drive more birds their way. A lone pheasant ran from the woods and took flight with a warning cry and drumming wings. She spotted the guns, veered and flew low and fast, paralleling the gun line from left to right. The King brought her down with a cross shot.

A mass of birds broke from the edge of the woods, rising swiftly in a tightly formed hard, dark cloud, climbing higher and faster than Ash had ever seen at Sandringham. The tight whirr of a hundred wings drowned out the beaters; then the loud flat popping of the guns began.

Ash fired and hit, fired again and hit, reached for his second gun without removing his eyes from the birds. Eddison took the empty Purdey and placed the loaded Holland and Holland in Ash's hands. Ash fired twice, missed once, took his third gun, the Westley Richards, and hit a fourth and fifth bird before the first fell to the ground.

'Good 'un, sir,' Eddison murmured as he exchanged the Purdey he had reloaded for the empty Westley Richards.

They were old-fashioned, handmade, hammer guns, unmatched, but reworked to be similarly balanced – an odd set that often provoked comment. Ash's favourite had been a gift from the gunmaker. There'd been nothing so crude as any suggestion that he tout the weapon, but the simple fact that Commander Ash used it lent the expensive gun a cachet wealthy sportsmen would find hard to resist. Ash shrugged away the doubt. Fact was, it was a good weapon, and, he thought ruefully, the most valuable thing he owned.

Lord Exeter and Farquhar were firing sporadically, wasting time choosing targets and coping with the thinner fly-over caused by Farquhar's earlier pacing. To Ash's left, the King banged a steady, rhythmic string of salvoes into the sky, while pheasant rained at his feet. Like Ash, the King had held onto his old hammer guns, and for the same reason; the hammers made fine sights for lining up the birds. Both men were in constant motion, shifting their feet like boxers as they took the proper stance for each shot. Years before, when they had met yacht racing and the King was still the Duke of York, he had taught Ash how to shoot. It was basically an athlete's sport, although few who shot realized it, and you had to keep moving.

The last birds flew over like ellipses at the end of a long sentence and Ash and the King turned around and brought them down. A moment's silence followed the final shots, broken by the beaters emerging from the trees and the loaders inspecting the corpse-littered ground, counting the score.

It was a modest bag by prewar standards, when a dozen guns and scores of beaters had killed thousands of birds in a single day. The beaters straggled onto the field, dressed in the traditional long blue twill smocks, and they too bore the mark of war. They were mostly old men, now, and boys.

Those few in their prime years were maimed, empty sleeves flapping or, in the case of one, struggling to keep up on crutches, their expressions less bitter than dismayed.

A game wagon drawn by an old plough horse trundled out of a distant thicket, the driver, back home on the estate, where he'd been born, coughing steadily from gas-rotted lungs. The birds were hung by the neck from the game wagon racks; a slew of rabbits flushed earlier on the walk out to the field were already trussed by the hind feet.

The King waved Ash over and they started toward the next stand. He was a small, compactly built man with a short beard and moustache, younger looking than his fifty years, vigorous, his face ruddied by the cold damp. Quiet and shy, King George was the direct opposite of the outgoing show-man and *bon vivant* his father King Edward had been. This eight thousand acres of lovingly tended game lands on the North Sea coast of Norfolk was his great joy, but Sandring-ham House itself was far less lavish than dozens of English country houses.

'I say, Ash, you did rather well for a man who hasn't shot recently.'

'Thank you, sir . . . May I ask, am I getting older or are the birds flying faster and higher?'

The King scooped a bird off the ground. Its breast was speckled red where the shot had pierced it. 'Feel this.'

Ash took the bird. It was thin.

'She's had to fend for herself,' said the King. 'I doubt a man your age has ever seen a wild-fed pheasant in England before. But we can't feed them grain any more, of course.'

The Defence of the Realm Act outlawed feeding precious grain to game birds while German U-boats were sinking Britain's food ships. The birds Ash had shot at the big shoots before the war had been raised expressly for the sport, pampered animals too fat to fly fast or very far, though still hard to hit on the wing. In fact, during those luxurious times when the rich European empires were still at peace, the beaters' job had often been to persuade the birds to take to the air rather than run out on foot.

That afternoon, as the dusk was gathering and cold rain blew in from the sea, the King said, 'We'll have a talk, Ash. After dinner.'

All Ash had ever envied the King of England was his marriage. He had been his guest often, at Sandringham for shooting, and Osborne on the Isle of Wight for sailing at Cowes, and he had come to regard the royal union as a partnership built on mutual enjoyment. Queen Mary, May of Teck, was a beautiful and intelligent woman, as shy as her husband, and considerably better educated than most European royalty.

She did Ash the honour of inviting him to sit on her right at dinner, and reminded him of their conversation of a year ago when he had recommended the poetry of Robert Service. 'He seems a little rough to me,' she said, 'though certainly a proper antidote to Mr Emerson's lives of quiet desperation. Have you read Rupert Brooke?' Ash had, and admired him, but he regretted that this was not the place to bring up the more recent war poets like Sassoon with their grimmer assessments of the carnage overtaking their generation.

The dinner guests were a mixed bag of royal household and Norfolk neighbours, landowners whose lives revolved around their shooting estates. Ash knew most of them. Other guests were conspicuous by their absence – neighbours' sons killed in France, including a boy whose death marked the end of a line that descended from the Angle kings of the eighth century.

Lord Exeter sat on Queen Mary's left, opposite Ash. Indoors, he seemed even larger, a vast mountain of a man, whose bulk seemed incongruous in the light of the nervous

33

deference he paid the King and Queen. He was in his fifties, face red and lined as if from drink, and Ash recalled now that he was rumoured to be somehow connected with the secret service.

Ash looked around the table again and realized that Exeter and his wife and he himself were the only guests outside the King's immediate circle of neighbours and household. Windsor Castle, the official country residence of the King, saw admirals and members of Parliament, European statesmen, Hungarian counts and the like purposefully gathered for political motives, but Sandringham was home. Whatever the King had in mind for Ash was private and most probably involved Exeter too.

There was no wine. George V had taken an oath of abstinence early on in hopes that his subjects would take the pledge with him to increase war production in the factories. They hadn't. The government regulated pub hours as a compromise, but the King was left dry for the duration. Ash had some brandy in his room from his travelling flask, but it was wearing off under the onslaught of apple juice and lemonade.

As usual, conversation started about the shooting but shifted quickly to the war, to the new government being formed by Prime Minister Lloyd George, to the rumours of peace. Ash listened intently and said little. This was the sort of informal conversation at the seat of power that the embassy expected him to report, not mix in. But Ambassador Page had instructed him to try to make one point clear to the King – that at least he, Page, did *not* expect the British to accept President Wilson's latest proposal of peace without victory – British sacrifices had been too great.

1916 had been a terrible year for the Allies – Britain, France and Russia. They were reeling. On the Western Front six months of murderous attacks had gained the French and British little, and as winter set in the Germans were as strongly entrenched along the Somme as they had been in the spring.

French troops had mutinied, and the previous Easter a full-scale rebellion had broken out in Dublin. The cost to Britain of putting it down with army troops had included great anger in America. And Lord Kitchener, the embodiment of the British Army, the old soldier pointing from a million recruiting posters, had drowned on a mission to Russia when his cruiser struck a German mine. So important had Kitchener been in the mind of the British public that rumours abounded that he was still alive, working on a secret plan to end the war.

At sea the great miracle weapons of the twentieth century – dreadnought battleships, the results of a treasury-draining fifteen-year arms race – had finally clashed, inconclusively. Despite great loss of life on both sides, the ferocious Battle of Jutland had not affected the balance of naval power in the slightest. Britain continued to blockade Germany with surface ships, and Germany blockaded England with submarines – a situation that naval officers the world over, Ash included, still had difficulty believing, not to mention the stalemate on land, where the unexpected defensive power of machine-guns had mired millions of infantry in trenches to the astonishment of an entire generation of military strategists.

But the Allies' predicament was most perilous on the Eastern Front, where Russian armies continued to grind themselves to death on the opposing artillery of the Central Powers. True, the Russians had won some significant victories against the Austrians, but Germany had made up for her partners' deficiencies by meting out stunning defeats from Roumania to the Baltic. And the terrible, preeminent question was – how long could the Russians last? A collapse of the Russian government, a collapse on the battlefield, a separate peace with the Central Powers, and Germany could wheel three thousand guns and a million men against the Western Front.

Lord Exeter seemed informed about Russia. The Czar's armies were 'bewildered peasants, underarmed and underfed, driven rather than led. This winter the Russian railways are on the verge of collapse, and when I left Petrograd last month food supplies were already said to be falling short in the cities.'

'Will there be a revolution?' the Queen asked.

'Ma'am, no one knows . . . least of all the Czar.'

'Poor Alix,' she murmured, so quietly that only Ash and Exeter heard her. 'Poor Nicky.' They exchanged a look. Nicholas and Alexandra, autocrats of the Imperial Russian Empire, were not remote figures to her.

'What *precisely* is the United States waiting for?' Lady Exeter asked suddenly, turning on Ash with an expression that indicated she demanded much and expected little. 'Surely you're not *still* choosing sides.'

'No, ma'am,' replied Ash, thinking to himself, *Thank you for the opening,* and presenting Ambassador Page's message with a casual glance at the King. 'In fact, I just yesterday overheard the American ambassador assure the British foreign minister that Britain deserves recompense for her struggle against – '

'We don't need recompense,' she shot back. 'We need, sir, an *ally*. Where the blazes are you?'

Lady Exeter was twenty years her husband's junior, a handsome woman with stern, chiselled features, extravagant red hair and a fiery glint in her eye. She had been, Ash recalled, a leader of the radical suffragette movement before the war. Had she gone to prison? He couldn't remember, but so many had. Probably not if she was welcome at this table, though you couldn't tell, the war had realigned so many things . . .

Ash started to explain that President Wilson, re-elected

the previous month on a promise to keep out of the World War, had to deal with a Congress that represented a peace-minded citizenry that resisted entanglement with what it considered ancient rivalries among . . . forgive him . . . corrupt and reactionary European states.

King George interrupted. 'Commander Ash does not make foreign policy for the United States. Correct, Kenneth?'

'No, sir, but I *can* say – '

'But surely, sir,' Lady Exeter said to the King, 'an officer of the United States Navy, attached to the American Embassy, has *some* inkling of his country's intentions?'

'A democracy's intentions,' Ash replied, 'are not as predictable as – '

Lady Exeter interrupted with an indignant snort and the King quickly interrupted her. 'Lady Exeter, Kenneth Ash is a fine sportsman who also happens to hold a commission in the United States Navy. Forgive me if I insist that he be allowed to be only a sportsman when he's a guest at my shoot, and *not* be pestered with questions best addressed to –'

'Your Majesty, I merely – '

The King laid the extended fingers of one hand firmly on the tablecloth. 'My dear woman, this is a shooting estate, not your London salon.'

Lord Exeter intervened before his wife could answer. 'His Majesty's right, m'dear. Ash is a first-rate helmsman and a splendid shot. Don't burden the chap with concerns he can't be expected to respond to.'

Lady Exeter bowed her handsome head to the King, then turned to Ash, her jewels flashing with the quick movement. '*Forgive* me, Commander, if I have cast a *pall* on your sport.'

Ash returned a smile he'd last offered the captain of a destroyer who'd rammed his minesweeper at a Philippine coal dock. He did not relish being considered a fool or a fop,

37

but a sportsman who happened to hold a commission in the navy came uncomfortably close to the way he too had been feeling about himself since this war began – a sort of relic of a time when a neatly cornered race buoy or the shooting maxim 'Aim high, keep the gun moving, and never check' had actually seemed important.

The King had intervened out of kindness, but he would have preferred to answer Lady Exeter himself, which he was fully prepared and able to do. But the ambassador wouldn't have tolerated it. In his own mind Ash saw Germany as the enemy already, and to hell with neutrality. German militarism had been a frightening spectre since his midshipman days at Annapolis, the Imperial German Army and the High Seas Fleet growing stronger each year, bolder, testing the older empires, challenging, attacking. They'd own the Philippines today, he thought, if a very angry, brave Admiral Dewey hadn't put the American Fleet in their way in 1898, and they had pulled similar stunts in Europe and Africa.

So the World War seemed a logical, direct macabre outcome of all the German threats and boasts. But even Ambassador Page, who so badly wanted to intervene, had to contain his utterances, and tonight Ash sympathized and wished he too could stop some of this diplomatic playacting, however good he might be at it, and swing back. He settled, instead, for a pinprick. 'It was a small pall, Lady Exeter, in the light of His Lordship's praise.'

She gave him a spirited grin and another barb. 'You're rather witty . . . for an American.' Lord Exeter, perhaps noting the glance of appreciation between them, intervened again. 'Any American who doesn't respond to an introduction with "Pleased to meet you" is all right in my book. Why do your countrymen do that, Ash? You don't.'

'May I suggest, My Lord, that the next time one says "Pleased to meet you," you inform him, "You damned well ought to be." '

Exeter laughed, as did his wife and the King, who then glanced at Queen Mary. She rose with a warm smile for Ash.

'Ladies, shall we leave the gentlemen to their cigars?'

Two thousand miles north-east in the Russian capital, Vasily Moskolenko, captain in the Czar's secret police, the Okhrana, examined a frightened prisoner with an empty gaze. Silent, she stared at the floor, but her fingers, he noticed, bunched anxiously at the hem of her apron. Perhaps she knew something; perhaps she was just afraid.

Moskolenko's office in Petrograd's Litovsky Prison looked like a cave hewed from the stone walls, and the Okhrana captain seemed both at home behind his rough wood desk and oddly out of place. His bony head, skeletal frame and emotionless grey eyes were appropriate to the notorious political prison, but there was a restless energy and swift grace to his movements which hadn't been nurtured at a desk in a gloomy cell. In striking contrast, Lieutenant Orlov, a short, heavily built man with a bald head and slug-white skin, looked as if he might have been spawned within these walls. Orlov waited at the door, his mouth working with anticipation.

'You serve in the palace of His Royal Highness the Grand Duke Valery?' Moskolenko asked the girl.

'Yes, sir.'

'You prepared tea for a gathering of officers from the Petrograd regiments?'

'Yes, sir.'

'You heard them plot against His Royal Majesty Czar Nicholas.' This time it was a statement, and she cried, 'No.'

'You heard.'

'No, sir.'

'They plotted. You served tea. How could you not hear?'

'They spoke English.'

'You're lying. The Grand Duke Valery does not allow English to be spoken in his palace. He permits only Russian. What did they say?'

'I didn't hear, sir. They spoke English whenever I came in the room.'

'Orlov! Take her.'

When Orlov brought her back about fifteen minutes later, the girl was sobbing. Her face was red and tear-streaked and she walked stiffly, but still through her tears she protested she had heard nothing. 'I'll send you back there with him if you don't tell me what the plotters said,' Moskolenko warned; and when she still admitted nothing, he nodded, 'Again.'

Two guards had to support her when Orlov returned the second time. Her face was dead white. Blearily she tried to focus on Moskolenko's expressionless, face. And when she had and her eyes registered terror, the Okhrana captain asked, 'What is the Grand Duke Valery plotting?'

'Nothing,' she whispered.

'Again.'

Ten minutes passed and Moskolenko decided to walk down the several floors to the interrogation cell. Below Petrograd's boggy ground level, the stone walls were wet. The guards opened the door on his command and shut it swiftly behind him. Lieutenant Orlov had finished with the whip and was in the act of mounting the prisoner, who was bent over and shackled naked to a table.

Her back, her wide-spread thighs and tautened buttocks were darkly wealed, and the leg irons had cut her ankles where she had struggled to pull away. Now she lay still, even as Orlov watched over his shoulder, anxiously awaiting his captain's permission to continue the next stage of the interrogation.

But Moskolenko withheld the order for a moment, moving closer to the table. Rape for either sex could be the

40

coup de pied, the final degradation that loosened a proud tongue. The combination of the shapely girl spread-eagled and helpless, and his irredeemably ugly lieutenant was amusingly grotesque. And rather erotic. He wanted to look into the victim's eyes before the straining Orlov began. But when he looked down at her face, he noticed her eyes were wide open, staring at nothing. She was dead. Moskolenko brushed past Orlov and reached for the telephone. The clumsy fool had killed her and he didn't even know it yet. Or if he did he didn't care enough to stop.

'The interrogation failed,' he told his colonel. 'Yes suicide.'

Maybe she had told the truth. Maybe she *had* known nothing of the grand ducal conspiracy to overthrow the Czar. Certainly in these troubled times servants were rarely so loyal to their masters. No matter. There were plenty more Russian peasants where she came from. Yet the key question remained unanswered, and his superiors did not like mysteries: What was the Grand Duke Valery plotting?

A butler presented a mahogany humidor to each man and a circle of blue smoke formed above the table. Conversation reverted to the shooting, and the King's neighbours, who'd sat silently through the earlier discussion, finally had something to talk about. But it was a brief respite for the rustics; Ash barely had his cigar going when the King suggested that they join the ladies. He started to snuff it out, but the King stayed him with a gesture as the others pushed back their chairs.

Farquhar ushered them out, and very quickly Ash and the King were alone in the empty dining room. A long expanse of white linen interrupted by candelabra and ashtrays lay between them. 'Move on up here, Kenneth. Bring your cigar.'

Ash moved to the head of the table and took the chair

41

Lady Exeter had occupied to the King's right. The King's invitation was a signal that complete ease would exist between them while they talked, like a ship's captain temporarily dropping formalities with a subordinate officer. The charade was drawing to a close.

'Awfully good to see you again, Kenneth. Envied you being back at sea.'

'I was hardly there before they hauled me right back here for diplomatic work.' He shrugged. 'My reward, I guess, for speaking foreign languages and knowing the difference between a knight and a baronet.'

'Oh, what I would give for a command again. If I could have my wife near me I would be the happiest man alive if the Royal Navy gave me back my minesweeper . . . So, you were sorry to give it up?'

'I've orders to join the cruiser *San Diego* next month. As executive officer. The navy promised me a destroyer in a few years. Thank God I'm finally getting back to sea. I'm damn tired of watching the race from the committee boat.'

The King smiled. 'May I give you some advice? Don't fool yourself about a naval command. You're used to a rather freer life – you're a diplomat at heart, almost a politician. You like being at the centre of things. You like Europe. Right here is the sort of action you've always enjoyed.'

'That may have been true before the war. But diplomacy has failed, Your Majesty. Somehow, if I may be frank, charm and good manners don't seem to make a great deal of difference anymore.'

'You're a man of parts, Kenneth, including a good deal more than just charming. I've seen you in action and – '

Ash shook his head.

'You're not the retiring sort, as I am,' the King insisted. 'You *feast* on Europe. London . . . Paris . . . and we know how you admire the ballet,' he added with a smile. Ash hadn't seen Tamara in three years, but people remembered. He wondered, did she?

'Look here, Kenneth . . . you know the Kaiser . . . ?'

'Yes, Your Majesty. I last saw Kaiser Wilhelm at his daughter's wedding to Duke Ernst August.' He was puzzled; the King knew perfectly well that he had met the Kaiser on several occasions, particularly that one.

'Beat him at the Cowes once, didn't you?'

'And promptly lost the next race to you, sir,' Ash replied, still puzzled. It wasn't like the King to state the obvious.

'You lost to the *Britannic*, not to me – Kenneth, I want you to do something for me.'

'Of course, Your Majesty.'

'Don't be too quick to answer. I want you to take a message to Berlin. To my cousin Willy.'

'To the *Kaiser*?'

'You should see your face,' King George said.

Ash was astonished. He had guessed that the King had a private courier mission in mind. Armed with a diplomatic *laissez-passer*, a neutral courier like himself could travel almost anywhere with a private message, cross borders without search. But it never occurred to him that the King wanted to communicate privately with Britain's mortal enemy.

'I said, my *cousin*,' the King continued. 'It's a family matter, an extremely sensitive one. I can't send an Englishman to the Kaiser, obviously, and I can't risk commercial cable or the mails. Nor can I communicate through a neutral embassy because I can't put my message in writing. If it were exposed I'd have to abdicate. And, just as important, it must be presented both privately and persuasively to Kaiser Wilhelm. I need a man not in the fight, but one whom I can trust like my most loyal subject.'

Ash said, 'I'm honoured that you'd consider me, sir.'

But his mind was tumbling through the aspects of the

King's request – pride that he'd been chosen, excitement to get in the action, worry that such a mission put him at odds with the responsibilities of his commission and his attaché duties, tricky waters at best, if not plain illegal . . . But the King had not asked an American naval officer to help him. He had asked a friend . . . a friend who just happened to hold a commission in the United States Navy . . . Ambassador Page would approve the King's mission in a flash. Anything to help Britain. The navy, however . . . but the navy – of course – was the target of the King's charade. A week's shooting at Sandringham was time enough for Commander Ash to travel secretly to Germany and return before he was due in London. And if the Kaiser tossed him into a German prison? Page and the navy could innocently disown him. So would the King. But what a chance to play the game as if it really mattered!

'I can do that, sir.'

But instead of thanking him, King George gazed into the forest of candelabra that lit the long table and said, 'There's more . . . My message to the Kaiser is only the beginning . . .'

The King's fingers trembled slightly as he raised his cigar to his lips. 'My ambassador to Petrograd and my consuls throughout Russia are convinced that my cousin Czar Nicholas's government will fall. Either to revolutionaries or palace intrigues. I'm told it's a matter of when, not if . . .' He looked closely at Ash. 'I intend to rescue my cousins Nicholas and Alexandra and their children and give them asylum in Britain.'

Ash's first and foremost excited thought was that the United States would intervene in the World War on the side of the Allies the moment the Romanov tyrant was removed from Russia. And in the process would defeat Germany and end the war . . .

'How do you intend to carry out the rescue, sir?'

'I shall send a British cruiser to Murmansk.'

Ash nodded. But Murmansk was fifteen hundred miles north of Petrograd – a long, hard run in the middle of a revolution. He asked, 'And the Kaiser, Your Majesty? What does the Kaiser have to do with your plan?'

'Protection. Another Kitchener sinking, with the Romanovs aboard, would be terrible. I want you to ask Willy to guarantee safe passage for my cruiser.'

Ash nodded slowly. To Europe's rulers, the drowning of the old general was a terrible reminder of the indifference, even the insolence of modern weapons that held no respect for rank. But he said, 'I beg your pardon, Your Majesty, but the Kaiser can't *guarantee* safe passage through mines and U-boats. Mines drift, U-boats venture beyond wireless range. You would literally need a German escort from Russia to England to guarantee the Czar's safety.'

'Exactly! An escort is precisely what you are going to ask for. You must persuade Kaiser Wilhelm to protect my cruiser.'

'That's a pretty tall order, Your Majesty. German U-boat – '

'Willy loves Nicky in a fatherly way, and loves our cousin Alix, as well he might – she's the most beautiful woman, except for my wife, that I have ever seen. Willy is not the monster he's made out to be, regardless of what the newspapers must print to encourage the nation.'

'You believe the Kaiser will put family above nation . . .'

'Do you know, Kenneth, that our grandmother Queen Victoria died in the Kaiser's arms? He cried like a baby, then tried to take over the entire funeral. That's his way . . . but he's always been kind to Nicky, if not a little too forceful in his advice on how to rule Russia. He'll see this my way. And if he does, it will help persuade Nicky to accept asylum. Nicky's stubborn, though not the fool he's

45

made out to be. With the offer of sanctuary coming from both myself and Willy, Nicky and Alix will accept . . .'

All these Willys, Nickys and Alixes made the King's remarkable scheme sound as innocuous as a house party, and Ash felt obliged to put in an objection. He couched it very carefully; King George was no fool but he was still a King and even the best of them, as this man surely was, did not easily take advice. 'Of course, I don't know who you've confided in, sir, but – '

'No one. I've told you, this is a family affair. It is to be handled privately and involve only those directly concerned. We will rescue Nicky and let our governments proceed with this damnable war . . . and we'll beat Willy, in the end, but God, what a price . . .'

'Yes, but don't you run the risk of being associated with actions that might smack of undermining your own Russian ally?'

'We have no intention of appearing to undermine anything,' the King snapped, shifting abruptly to the royal *we*. 'It is not our intention to weaken our ally, Kenneth. It is our intention to rescue our cousin – regardless of his many shortcomings, Nicky and Alix and the children will live out their lives peacefully in British sanctuary.'

'Who do you intend to send to Russia, sir?'

'Well, as you've suggested, until the Czar is replaced by an orderly Russian government, appearance *is* vital. Therefore I can't send an Englishman to the Czar, whether he be military officer or diplomat. I can't blur the lines between family and nation.'

'How about a Russian?' Ash said. 'One who knows his way around the Czar's court?'

'Not without becoming inadvertently involved in one of their intrigues.'

'Then a private citizen, like Lord Exeter? He seems to know Russia.'

The King shook his head, and Ash had an awful feeling he would never sail on the *San Diego*. 'No. Even a private agent exposed as an English subject would lead to implication with the British Crown. But I could send a neutral . . . an American . . . When does your posting to the *San Diego* take effect?'

'Next month, sir. But I don't see how I could possibly get to Russia and back before January . . .'

'I know it's a good deal to ask, Kenneth. Please feel free to decline – '

'I've been playing diplomat a long time, sir. I need action before I lose my edge.'

'Kenneth . . . I've seen you in action. Surely you haven't forgotten Berlin. I know I haven't . . .'

'I suspect if I'd had time to think I might have moved more slowly.' Ash smiled. 'I just happened to be standing in the way.'

'It's precisely what you did before you thought that distinguished your actions and saved my life.'

May, 1913; nearly four years ago, and the King was still haunted by the demented glare of the assassin's face – a look of total hatred, made even more terrifying by his expression of triumph that he had slipped past the guards. The fact that his bullets were intended for his cousin Nicky was little comfort.

All the years his father Edward had been king before him had been disrupted by periodic anarchist attacks on European royalty. They went, the King of Italy had once said, with the job. And suddenly in a Berlin palace garden, moments after a lavish wedding pageant, it was happening to him. It had been typical of anarchist attacks of the prewar era, confused – the assassin mistook him for the Czar – and especially dangerous because the man had no regard for his own life. Six inches to one side and the first

47

shot would have gone through the King's head. A foot the other way and his Queen would have died.

The King had realized later that he had noticed the man for days as he, in retrospect, stalked the wedding guests at the elaborate pageant the Kaiser had staged to marry his only daughter to Ernst August of Brunswick-Luneburg. A happy occasion in which the marriage of a plain dowdy girl cemented an ancient rift between the houses of Hohenzollern and Brunswick. It was the last time he and Nicky and Willy had all been together, and ironically the last grand pageant before the World War destroyed the myth that the European royals possessed the power to keep the peace.

The assassin had posed as an orthodox priest, and for all their Germanic efficiency the Kaiser's Imperial Guard never caught on. The final processional over at last, and the Kaiser's plain daughter finally packed off on her honeymoon, an informal party had continued in the gardens. Czar Nicholas had just walked away to address the Kaiser when the King had spotted Ash with his friend the Russian ballerina, apparently a guest of the Grand Duke Valery, her paramour – the Russians were tolerant of that sort of thing; the King had been surprised, but at least she hadn't been in the church.

The King had summoned Ash, who was part of a small American delegation from their Berlin embassy, where Ash was attached at the time. The Queen had expressed a curiosity to meet the ballerina. They were just shaking hands when the gunman rushed up in his black robes, drew his revolver, fired. People screamed and the Guard ran up. It was over in seconds, the gunman dead, May clinging to him like a child, Ash's shoulder smashed by a bullet and the dancer kneeling beside him in tears. The King would swear to his dying day that Ash had stepped in front of the gun, and Stamfordham, his private secretary, confirmed it, even though Ash steadily claimed that all he had done was throw a wild punch . . .

'Kenneth, you're the only man for the job.' The King ticked off the reasons persuasively. 'You're a first-rate officer. I can trust you to do the right thing at the right time. I can trust you to operate on your own, as you will have to. Once in Petrograd, you'll receive precious little help from me. I must remain detached for all the reasons you yourself have mentioned. In addition, you know the Kaiser and the Czar. They know I know you and would send you for this sort of thing. No need for elaborate introductions. And you *know* the Russians. Your friendship with Mademoiselle Tishkova has, I am sure, over the years given you a deeper insight into the Russian character than most, which should be quite useful in persuading the Czar and those around him.'

Ash shook his head. The hint earlier had not been idle. 'Please understand, Your Majesty, that I can't turn to Mademoiselle Tishkova for anything – '

'I was referring only to your knowledge and contacts acquired in the past – '

'It's over,' Ash said. 'Once and for all . . .'

'Of course, forgive me for bringing it up. I am so concerned that . . . I ask you to reconsider your position . . . perhaps you could find a way to have your orders postponed. Surely I could put in helpful words, indirectly?'

'Perhaps,' Ash agreed, though he knew he couldn't. Executive on a brand new cruiser was a plum a dozen officers would be waiting in line for . . . It was a lot to give up – a career even – for a friend. An awful lot. But it wasn't only a choice between friendship and career. Russia, he realized, would be a far more palatable *American* ally with Czar Nicholas out of the way. America could then intervene in Europe, help defeat Germany and end the war. And the

49

King, never mind if for his own personal reasons, had offered him the chance to help make it happen. Ash said, 'You honour me by your request. I'll give it a try.'

The King reached over and gripped his arm. 'Thank you. But I don't honour you, I believe you can do it.'

'I have one stipulation. I must clear this with my superiors.'

To Ash's surprise, the King didn't object. 'Of course. But could you confine your report to Ambassador Page?'

Ash nodded. 'I think so. It so happens that my immediate chief is in Berlin at the moment.'

'Excellent,' the King said. 'Ambassador Page will understand the situation, I'm sure . . . I wish I could give you more help. However, you may call on Lord Exeter in Petrograd for introductions and the like. He has commercial interests in Russia.'

'Exeter?' Ash asked as he stood with the sovereign. 'May I ask, is His Lordship with the Secret Service?'

'Lord Exeter is serving me in a private capacity,' the King replied, leaving Ash's question largely unanswered. It would need some investigation. Ash had no desire to act as an unknowing point man for the British Secret Service, and he wouldn't put it past that service to climb aboard the King's personal mission and steer it to the aid of a mission of their own.

The King now was saying, 'In fact, Lord Exeter is waiting to take you by motor car tonight to Yarmouth for the steamer to The Hague.'

'No – '

'No? But I thought – '

'No, Your Majesty. I'll go to Yarmouth in the normal manner, by train from London.'

'Speed is essential, Kenneth. Russia is, as they say, reeling. Let Exeter deliver you to the midnight boat. You'll be in The Hague tomorrow morning. Surely your meeting with Ambassador Page can wait until you return from Berlin.'

'It's not that, Your Majesty. But Holland is the main neutral entry point into Germany. The entire route is crawling with spies. And I would strongly prefer that German agents didn't observe me pull up to the steamer in Lord Exeter's motor car.'

3

'You're back early,' said Walter Hines Page. 'Shoot a beater?'

The American ambassador to Great Britain was a sick man and his illness, harsh and chronic, seemed to show in the dark pools beneath his enormous eyes and pinched his high-browed face. He extended Ash a bony hand and a shaky smile. He was sixty-one and looked ten years older.

Ash attributed his uncommonly informal manner to Page's long career as a newspaper and magazine writer. Woodrow Wilson had awarded him the ambassadorship to the Court of St James for his early support of his presidency, and Page had taken happily to diplomacy; he enjoyed intrigue, admired the British as perhaps only a gentleman of the Old South could, and regarded German militarism as the curse of the century.

'. . . Since Captain Wesley is in Berlin, I thought it best to report directly to you, Mr Ambassador.'

'What did the King want?' Page asked, brushing aside the chain of command with an impatient wave of his skeletal hand.

'Well, sir, it regards an extremely sensitive personal matter – '

'Spit it out, man. I've got to meet a train.'

Ash took a quick breath and tried it all in a sentence. 'King George wants to join forces with Kaiser Wilhelm to rescue their cousin the Czar from what the King fears is an impending revolution.'

'Rescue? You mean somehow get him out of Russia?'

'Yes, sir. He's offering asylum in Britain.'

'With the *Kaiser*?'

'The King will send a Royal Navy cruiser to Murmansk if the Kaiser will provide a U-boat escort for it to Britain.'

'And just who in hell is going to talk the Kaiser into conspiring with the Allies?' Page asked.

'I guess I am, sir, with your permission, of course.'

Page's eyes closed to narrow slits. 'And provided you can, who is going to present this . . . scheme . . . to the Czar?'

'With your permission, sir, it seems I'm again elected to give it a try. The King feels he must use a neutral. I'd of course need some sort of extended leave of absence from my current duties, sir, as well as from my January posting to the cruiser *San Diego*.'

'I thought you were all fired up about getting back to sea.'

'I *am*. But, sir, it's true, isn't it, that Congress would look a good deal more favourably on intervention if the Czar were gone . . . ?'

'I see . . . end autocracy in Russia *and* defeat German militarism in a single blow. Quite an achievement for a young officer, wouldn't you say, Commander?'

Ash felt a little foolish. 'I know I'm just a naval officer, sir. Actually a courier, a glorified mailman – no Admiral Dewey, for sure – but, sir, I guess what's going through my mind is what President Roosevelt used to say. He said he wanted to grab history and make the right thing happen. I'm not saying I'm the man to do it but couldn't we – '

'What makes the King think you're the man to grab the Czar?'

'I don't know that I am, sir, but . . . well, the King seems to have a somewhat overblown opinion of me . . . thinks I'm sort of a man of parts or something . . .' Ash no longer felt foolish, he felt like an ass.

'Sort of a Count of Monte Cristo?' Page asked drily. 'You'd damn well have to be to pull off something like this.'

With that, Ash was sure Page would deliver a flat no. He was almost relieved. But after a long moment a smile lifted Page's cadaverous cheeks.

'Marvellous.'

'I beg your pardon, sir?'

Page tugged his watch chain and squinted at the time. 'Get your coat, Commander. We're going for a drive.'

Hooting its chrome horns, the embassy's Pierce town car cut through the line of black ambulances that snaked into Charing Cross and onto the platforms under the glass-roofed station. Walter Hines Page felt damned proud when a policeman waved them past with a smart salute for the American flags flying from the fenders – yet another sign that United States stock was rising as the European empires battered themselves bankrupt.

'Don't get out of the car,' he warned Ash. 'I don't want anyone to see you with us.'

Ash settled back looking puzzled, and perhaps a little sorry he had confided in Page. Wait until he heard the rest of it. Page pulled down the window. The station reeked of smoke. Hundreds of men in battle dress were hurrying to the trains. Women walked with them, holding their arms; some cried, but most had assumed the mask of a stiff smile.

'Admiral Innes!' Page called hoarsely. 'Mr Banks!' The effort to make himself heard above the shuffle of hundreds of boots hurt his throat, but he barely noticed in his excitement. For too long, in his judgment, he had been President Wilson's stalking horse, drawing fire each time he urged the American people to stand with the Allies. Now intervention was in his grasp, provided he could persuade Banks and Admiral Innes to support Ash, and provided Ash was up to the job.

The portly Admiral Innes caught sight of the car. Banks,

a lanky white-haired civilian in a trenchcoat, hurried beside him. 'They're just back from inspecting French Atlantic ports,' Page told Ash. 'For troop transports if we manage to wangle our way into the war.' Ash attempted to salute sitting down as they scrambled into the car. Admiral Innes was in his late fifties, neat and rotund, a hero of the battle of Manila; in the navy he was known as a maverick. Banks, a Midwesterner, was a confidential adviser to the President; like Colonel House he spoke for the President. Holding no official title, he was in effect senior to the admiral and Page himself – the man Page had to convince. When they were seated opposite in the passenger compartment, Page introduced Ash.

Banks shook Ash's hand and displayed a politician's memory.

'Mahon's aide, weren't you, Commander?'

'Yes, sir. At The Hague.'

'Tell them what you just told me, Commander. Go ahead,' Page interrupted drily.

Ash stopped smiling. 'Sir . . . may I remind you of the conditions under which we spoke? I can't betray a confidence – '

'You can with us.'

'I'm sorry sir, I gave my word.'

Admiral Innes purpled. 'Commander, what the devil are you ranting about?'

Ambassador Page apologized. He had provoked Ash, already testing whether he had the 'sand,' as the British put it, to conduct his one-man mission into Russia.

'Gentlemen, for reasons that will become apparent, this conversation is to remain strictly confidential.'

'Does that apply to the President as well?' Banks asked.

'Until Commander Ash agrees otherwise . . .' Turning to Ash, who looked mystified and angry in equal parts, and decidedly not buffaloed by all the rank in the car, Page

55

explained, 'To help you trust us, Commander, let me say that Mr Banks, Admiral Innes and myself lead an unofficial Inner Circle created by President Wilson to expedite American entry in the war. We've been laying groundwork, even trying to provoke some incident that would tip Congress into taking action.'

'With President Wilson's knowledge?'

'I report to the President,' Banks told him. 'As does Ambassador Page. Admiral Innes is in close contact with Assistant Navy Secretary Roosevelt.'

'We've been pretty successful preparing the way for American troops to arrive in France,' Page said, 'but less so in finding a way to get the Congress off its rear. But we're trying . . .'

'In other words,' Banks said, 'the pacifists will lynch us from the Capitol dome if you tell them what Ambassador Page just told you. So you see, we're very much on the same side here.'

'I think I get your point, sir.'

'Yes, it would seem we're engaged in the same cause.'

'Yes, sir,' said Ash, and began to describe in detail the King's mission to rescue the Czar.

The car sat still, trapped in a sea of stretchers. As the driver loaded Banks's and Innes's bags, a dark ambulance train, one of a dozen that shuttled daily between London and the Channel ports, had glided ominously into the station. Nurses and orderlies carried the badly wounded to the ambulances; and a hundred and fifty 'walkers' shuffled by the car under their own steam in mud-splattered khaki and bloody bandages.

'. . . I felt,' Ash concluded, 'that with Captain Wesley in Berlin, I needed at least tacit approval from Ambassador Page.'

Page looked at Banks and Innes.

'Sounds a damned sight better than anything we've come

up with,' the Admiral said. 'No matter how you cut it, the Czar is the real sticking point with Congress. The United States doesn't want to defeat Germany only to put Bloody Nicholas in control of central Europe.'

'Hold on,' Banks said.

'What the devil for?' Admiral Innes demanded. 'If Ash can get the son of a bitch out of Russia he'll get rid of the taint of despotism from the Allies – '

'Why not have Ash here just get rid of the Czar?' Banks asked. 'Why go to all the trouble of getting him to England when . . . dispatching him would achieve the same purpose?'

Ash started to protest but Page cut in. 'Any action that threatens the stability of Russia and the Russian Army directly threatens the United States.'

'How's that?'

'Tell him, Commander.'

'Well, the Czar's sudden death . . . his violent death . . . could collapse the government and with it the Russian Army and the Eastern Front. Germany could wheel her whole eastern army – a million men and three thousand guns – west . . .'

'And just as our boys were arriving in France,' Page finished for him. 'He's right, Mr Banks. Order in Russia is vital. Assassination would be a disaster.' He turned to Ash. 'Just getting King George's royal cousin out of a pickle won't, I'm afraid, be enough. You've got to pluck Czar Nicky very damn gently out of Russia, gently as a single pickup stick.'

The car rolled out of the station and Page turned to the window. The streets were dull; he missed the chestnut men and the cornet players. London was filled with soldiers. Civilians, who seemed mostly women and old men, were shabbily dressed, shop fronts unpainted. The German U-boat success against British shipping was reflected in the

57

number of horse-drawn carriages that the petrol shortages had dragged from the stable for the first time in fifteen years. There was no question Britain was being squeezed.

'The Kaiser . . .' Banks said as they drove past a long line of people standing outside a cinema showing the documentary 'Battle of the Somme', which was drawing bigger crowds than Charlie Chaplin.

'What about the Kaiser?' Page asked. He had seen the film and had been shaken by its eloquent portrait of the hopeless, endless nature of this new kind of war; it had shown him why the men in the trenches had dubbed the mightiest British offensive of 1916 the Great Fuck-Up. Page hoped he was not just another old man scheming to send more young men to their deaths . . . He consoled himself with the thought that America would not only send new blood – new blood alone would be sponged up as swiftly as the old – but new spirit and a sense of the possible. The tanks in the Battle of the Somme, a brilliant new invention, had been wasted by the British. Too few of the trench breakers and not enough follow-up. Weary blood and dying spirit. America could change all that. And face it, he thought, the prize was worth it. Not only would democracy win out . . . the country that won this war would win preeminence in the whole world. He very much liked to think of America in that role. About time a democracy called the tune.

'Why would Kaiser Wilhelm join a scheme that would strengthen his enemies?' Banks demanded.

'Family loyalty is a powerful thing to the royals,' Ash said. 'Family and bloodlines, after all, are the source of their power. And, excuse me, but I doubt the Kaiser will see the King's plan as strengthening the Allies. Being an autocrat himself, I suspect he'll reason that removing the Czar would very much *harm* Russia.'

'Whereas,' Innes said, 'a constitutional monarch like

58

King George would conclude just the opposite – that a good government would save his ally Russia.'

'Is that the King's real motive?' Banks asked.

'I think family is the King's only motive,' Ash said. 'The Czar and Czarina are his first cousins – '

Banks raised a white eyebrow. 'No other motive, Commander?'

Ash shrugged. 'Well, I would like to know more about Lord Exeter. Is he Secret Service?'

'I've heard he is,' Page said. 'I'll find out more.'

Banks said, 'I think we can assume that the British Secret Service has its own interests in Russia. Interests that perhaps even go beyond the war . . . The British are heavily invested in Russian industry. Don't make the mistake of thinking our idea of a democratic government for Russia will be the same as theirs. They have too much at stake to worry only about the war.'

Ash said, 'I'd also like to have more information about conditions in Russia. No one I've talked to really seems to know what's going on there.'

'We'll have reports waiting when you get back from Germany,' Page said. 'Though I warn you that the American Embassy in Petrograd is, shall we say, a rudimentary affair.'

Banks said, 'We seem to have come around to approving this . . . this escapade – with one strict proviso. President Wilson must approve.'

'You can't put this in a *cable*,' Page said. 'Even in code. It's too sensitive, the risk of compromise – '

'I *know* that. That's my job – speaking privately for the President . . . Now we might as well let Commander Ash get started on his mission to the Kaiser. Good chance just to see what's going on there. And afterward he can start for Russia . . . But I'm also warning you now that if the President doesn't agree when I get back to Washington,

59

Commander Ash is going to find a cable waiting for him in Petrograd ordering him back to London.'

'Understood,' said Page. 'That way you can report to President Wilson personally and we won't waste any time here.'

'One more question, Commander,' Banks said, 'before we loose you on an unsuspecting Imperial Russian Empire . . . Why you? Why did the King choose you of all people? I mean apart from your being a man of parts.'

'Well, as I said, sir, he needs a neutral officer.'

'You can't be the only neutral the King knows.'

'He and I have shot and sailed for years and – '

'I know the British put great stock in sport, Ash, but surely he must have more reason than that for picking you for a mission so obviously important to him.'

Ash seemed reluctant to answer. 'Well . . . once in Berlin I happened to be standing in the right place at the right time and the King thinks I saved his life . . .'

'A Count of Monte Cristo, I believe Page suggested.'

Ash shrugged. What the hell could he say?

Actually Banks knew a good deal more about Ash than he had admitted. He knew that the former president Teddy Roosevelt, who had known Ash since his roughrider charge up San Juan Hill when Ash was an Academy midshipman, also considered him a man of action, as well as a first-rate officer with a talent for diplomacy. As to the obvious question, why Ash held decent rank but had no ship, T.R. had alluded to an entanglement with a Russian woman, and the navy's prejudice against diplomatic duty, and something else, less definable. Banks recalled Roosevelt's precise words. 'Ash seems to have forgotten his own strengths. Got derailed a few years ago, somehow, and he doesn't seem to be aware of what he can do anymore.'

Ash *looked,* Banks thought, like a navy recruitment poster. Fit and handsome in immaculate dress blues, sword at his side, eyes holding Banks's with a direct gaze, he was the picture of a solid officer. And yet he did not seem to understand that the King had picked him over other men because he had no doubts that Ash could deliver. All right, if not knowing his own good points was sidetracking his career, that was Ash's problem. But was Ash savvy enough to keep the US out of hot water if he went to Russia?

'Commander, can you think of any *other* reason why King George would have chosen you for this mission?'

To Banks's relief, Ash cut to the heart of his question.

'I'm aware, sir, that whatever goes wrong, the blame will fall on me, not on the King.'

'How about the United States Navy?'

'I've already asked Ambassador Page for leave.'

Page said, 'Rather than leave, I'm going to arrange a legitimate assignment to Petrograd. To make it look – if something should go wrong – as if Commander Ash took the opportunity to pursue his . . . private interests.'

'Sure you want to do this, Commander?' Banks said with a lazy smile. 'There'll be no cruisers coming to *your* rescue.'

And Banks was relieved again. Ash might not know his own strengths, but he pounced on that opportunity. 'I'd be more sure,' he said, 'if I knew my berth on my own cruiser was still waiting for me when I got back – I've got orders to join the *San Diego* in January as her exec. I've been looking forward to that for a long time. But I won't be back by January.'

'If you can manage to get the Czar out and leave Russia intact,' Page said, 'I'll personally see to it you get your own command. We can do that, can't we, Admiral Innes.'

'Would a minesweeper suit you?' Innes said.

'Make it a destroyer and you're on, sir.'

4

Kaiser Wilhelm II, Emperor of Imperial Germany, had always reminded Ash of Teddy Roosevelt – boisterous and charming when he was happy, sheer hell when he wasn't. Right now, it seemed that he wasn't.

'*Wer?*' The Kaiser's voice echoed belligerently in the gigantic reception hall he was using as an office in Schloss Bellevue, his Berlin palace. Ash knew that he hated the frigid city palace, and wished he had found him in his favourite Neue Palais several miles out in the country. The elaborately uniformed courtiers and army officers hovering around his desk looked terrified.

'Ash,' repeated the aide-de-camp, who had promised to present him because, he had confided, His Royal Majesty was unhappy and perhaps a visitor from better days would cheer him up. Unfortunately, it seemed the Kaiser had forgotten his name.

Ash had first been presented to the Kaiser at The Hague Peace Conference of 1899 when he was aide to then Captain Alfred Thayer Mahon, the American advocate of sea power. The Kaiser had shocked the newly commissioned ensign by pulling one of his famous practical jokes, squeezing Ash's hand so hard that his rings bit painfully. Ash, too young and surprised to react diplomatically, had squeezed back until the Kaiser yelped. Captain Mahon, who was the sensation of battleship-happy Europe and whom the Kaiser greatly admired, had smoothed over the fuss, and the Kaiser had invited them both aboard his yacht.

Subsequent encounters at hunts, shoots and sailing regattas hadn't changed Ash's first impression. Both Wilhelm and Teddy Roosevelt were intelligent, forceful men tuned to the restless new century and to the demands of their vigorous peoples for strong leadership. Yet both were flawed – erratic combinations of showman, bully and buffoon. The huge difference between them was the extent of their power. Shortcomings that were only irritants in President Roosevelt were deadly in the mighty German autocrat.

'*Wer?*' Screwing a monocle into his eye, the Kaiser twisted around to see where his aide-de-camp had left Ash in the charge of a pair of stone-faced palace guards. His movements were quick and jerky, and his withered left arm dragged clumsily, knocking a pen off the desk. An old general swiftly bent to pick it up. The Kaiser snatched up his sceptre, raised the jewelled staff high in the air and brought it down with a sharp whack on the general's ample, tightly stretched rump.

His astonished shout was drowned out by the Kaiser's laughter. Ash relaxed. Practical jokes were at least a sign that the Emperor was momentarily in a good mood. The Kaiser pounded his desk with his right hand and bellowed laughter while the other officers laughed nervously with him. He then aimed his monocle again where Ash waited and repeated, ' *Wer?*'

'Lieutenant Commander Kenneth Ash, United States Navy.' Ash, whose German was rudimentary, caught something to the effect of 'Admiral Mahon's young aide, Your Majesty. I felt sure you would want to see him.' Mahon's aide? The Kaiser knew perfectly well he had last seen Ash in May 1913, but the subject of the assassination attempt at his daughter's wedding was *verboten*. It had put the Kaiser in a typical quandary. On one hand he would like to have taken credit as the target, a perverse topping of his cousins King George and Czar Nicholas. But on the other hand he was embarrassed that a Russian anarchist had hoodwinked his Guard. His solution was typical as well. By unspoken Imperial edict it had not happened, and consequently Ash had not been there.

'Ash! Mahon's aide, of course.'

The Kaiser surged to his feet, tucked his withered arm to his sword haft and swaggered toward the doors. He was decked out in a cavalry officer's uniform of bright red and the sash of an order Ash couldn't identify. His boot heels clattered and his spurs jingled and he looked as if he were prepared to review horse troops today. He was a great dresser for the occasion. When Tamara had danced *Cléopâtre* for him with Diaghilev's Ballets Russes, the Kaiser had donned the uniform of a Russian colonel.

His English was as perfect as his cousin King George's. 'Ash . . . well, well, well. How did *you* get here?'

Ash saluted, bowed and even made himself bring his heels together in the Prussian manner. 'By train, Your Majesty. From The Hague.'

'I was right to leave Holland,' the Kaiser said. 'I told my army, leave neutral access to the sea. Leave the route open . . . Still would be if it weren't for the damn British blockade. They're making war on women and children, Ash. Women and children. I'd have won by now. Sea power *is* all. Too bad Mahon died too soon to know he was right.'

Ash resisted mentioning the U-boat blockade of England and said, 'Admiral Mahon certainly knew, Your Majesty.'

The Kaiser stared, wondering if he'd been contradicted, then laughed. 'Yes, I suppose he did. And how's President Roosevelt? By God, I like that man.' He didn't acknowledge President Wilson.

'Very well, sir, when I saw him last,' Ash replied, wondering if the Kaiser knew how vigorously T.R. was campaigning to declare war on Germany. Had to know.

German agents were swarming over the United States, sabotaging factories and trying to provoke the American people against England.

'What does he want?'

'I beg your pardon?'

'What does Roosevelt want? What did he send you for?'

Ash took a deep breath. The Kaiser was so mercurial, so quick to jump to conclusions. One false step and he'd be out on his ear, or in a German jail. 'I have not come from former President Roosevelt,' he said, stressing the *former*.

The Kaiser blinked, looked puzzled, then dangerous. 'Then what do you want, if Mahon's dead and Roosevelt didn't send you?'

Ash glanced around the room. The officers grouped around the Kaiser's desk were listening curiously. 'Would it be possible for you to grant me a private audience, Your Majesty?'

The Kaiser's eyes lit up. 'Wilson,' he breathed. 'Yes, yes, of course, Ash.' He turned and bellowed, '*Raus*, get out, all of you.'

He put his hands on his hips and watched them scurry off. Ash was puzzled that the military men looked extremely old; hardly the type who would be reporting from general headquarters. They were functionaries at best, ceremonial window dressing at worst, which raised a question about who was running the German army?

'Tell me,' said the Kaiser when the guards had closed the gilded doors and the two of them were alone. 'What is it? What does President Wilson say?'

'Your cousin King George sent me, Your Majesty.'

'Georgie? What the devil does *he* want?'

'It's a family matter, Your Majesty.' Before Ash left Sandringham, King George had reminded him that Wilhelm regarded himself as the older man, the fatherly relative to both George himself and the Czar. It looked as if the King was right. Concern erased the truculent bewilderment from the Kaiser's face. He took Ash's arm in his powerful right hand.

'What is it? Not May?'

May of Teck had been an Anglo-German princess before she married King George and became Queen Mary of England. It was difficult to hate the Kaiser when he turned into a worried uncle.

'No, Your Majesty. Queen Mary is well. I saw her only yesterday and she asked me to convey her warmest regards in these hard times.' That was a little more generously than she might have put it if they had discussed his mission, Ash reflected, but neither was Queen Mary alone in the Kaiser's palace in the middle of Germany.

'Thank God. Then what is the matter?' His plastic features were animated, flashing from concern to an unpleasant gloating. 'Georgie's fallen off his horse again?'

'It's Czar Nicholas – '

'That damned fool. What's the matter with Nicky – my God, he didn't get killed at the front, did he? No, of course not, I'd have known.'

'King George is afraid for the Czar's life.'

'Revolution?'

'Yes.'

'The mob.' The Kaiser nodded, assumed a sage expression that quickly changed to scorn as he spoke. 'I've told Nicky a thousand times, shoot them down. Royalty must not treat with the mob. Particularly in Russia. Let me tell you something, Ash, all the Russian peasant understands is the knout in an iron fist. The Czarina knows. But Nicky wouldn't even listen to her. He was a damn fool when they revolted in 1905 – burned some villages, hanged some peasants, which was well enough, but *then* he gave them a Duma. A council right in the middle of his capital city. I was doing my best to get rid of the Reichstag, and Nicky gives his mob a Duma.'

The Kaiser glared at Ash. 'Why am I wasting my time talking to an American. You don't understand these things. Just remember that Nicky is a weakling. They'll geld him worse than Georgie if he's not strong . . . Good God, if the old Queen ever saw what we've all fallen to.'

And Ash knew he didn't mean the World War. He thought briefly of his French *comtesse* with the ruby ring. When he was sure the Kaiser had ended his tirade he said, 'King George has a plan to save the Czar.' *No*, thought Ash, he didn't mean save the Czar's throne, he meant rescue him personally . . . 'To rescue the Czar if he's overthrown.'

'Nicky? What the hell are you talking about?'

'A plan to rescue your cousin, the Czar.'

'I know he's my cousin, for God's sake. What is all this?' He shook his head, and the dangerous glint was back in his eyes. 'Ash. Who sent you?'

'King George sent me to ask for your help, Your Majesty.'

'Georgie wants my help?'

'He *needs* your help. Without it he feels the Czar is doomed. Only you and he can save Nicholas from the mob . . .'

The Kaiser's left hand slipped from his sword, where it rested inconspicuously. His arm had been dislocated at birth. Hurriedly, he lifted it back with his right. Even in a glove it looked like a little claw. For a long moment he said nothing. At last he asked, 'Save Nicky? Is he mad? Has he forgotten we're at war? How can I help Germany's mortal enemy to save his ally?'

Ash had thought about little else on the steamer to The Hague and aboard the train across Holland and Germany. He had wondered whether a resolution of the Kaiser's conflict might lie in the past, at the turn of the century, before the naval arms race had drawn battle lines between Germany and England, when his grandmother, Queen Victoria, had died in his arms.

'King George, of course, has a similar worry, Your

Majesty. He too feels a confusion of loyalties between nation and family. But what decided him to ask the help he needs so desperately from you was another question – '

'What question?'

'What would the Old Queen have done?'

The Kaiser sighed. 'Yes. Yes, of course. But . . . poor Georgie. He simply doesn't possess a military mind.'

It was as much an opening as Ash was going to get. He charged in. 'King George proposes to Your Majesty that he dispatch a cruiser for the Czar and his family. To Murmansk. And he asks that your U-boats – '

'U-boats?'

'Yes, Your Majesty. German U-boats to escort the cruiser safely back to England.'

'England?'

'King George will offer asylum.'

'Asylum? The British public won't much like that.'

'King George feels it's not a public matter. It's a matter for family.'

The Kaiser shrugged. 'The British view of me runs the gamut. They're very fickle – which comes from being listened to.' The Kaiser turned on his heel and marched, spurs and boot heels ringing, across the room to the windows. He stared out at the square for several minutes. Ash stood where he was. At least, thank God, the Kaiser hadn't said no right off.

Then he came back, took Ash's arm and asked, 'Georgie thought of this?'

'Yes, Your Majesty.'

'*Planned* this?'

'Yes, Your Majesty.'

'No one else? No one?'

'No one. That's why he sent me, and not a British officer.' Ash waited a moment, then took a chance. 'Czar Nicholas's rescue is impossible without your help, Your Majesty.'

Still holding Ash's arm, the Kaiser spoke quietly, as if he were thinking aloud. 'Georgie's father, King Edward, was a treacherous man. He lied and schemed against me. This war is his fault. The question is, is Georgie as treacherous as his father was?'

'You must realize, sir, that King George has put his throne in your hands by sending me here. He trusts you not to betray him.'

'Why should he trust me? I'm not so sure I trust him.'

'Family, Kaiser Wilhelm. The King, I believe, has decided that in spite of the war rescuing Czar Nicholas is the duty of Victoria's children.'

The Kaiser looked at Ash, his large, dark eyes suddenly deep. 'My soldiers have died by the millions. What has George decided about their children?'

The colour rose in his cheeks and he seemed to gather his body like an animal about to charge. In an instant, the war would triumph over the past. Ash played his last card. He had been in Europe a long time before he understood how deeply monarchs believed their source of power.

'An agreement between royals, Your Majesty, is, after all, judged only by God.'

The Kaiser stared at him, intrigued but reluctant to surrender the sentimentality behind the idea of his soldiers' children. In the end royal divine right won. A slow smile spread across Kaiser Wilhelm's face. 'Yes, of course. Of *course*. Georgie is right. It's our duty to stand by Nicky. By God!'

He let go of Ash's arm and gave his shoulder a friendly slap. 'My answer is yes. I agree. I will do anything to save Nicky . . .' He paused. 'Except how shall I proceed?'

'If it pleases Your Majesty, I could approach Czar Nicholas and make the offer of asylum. When the arrangements are completed in Russia I'll ask for your U-boats.' The sight of a British cruiser maintaining half-speed to permit a pack of German U-boats to keep up in heavy northern seas would, Ash decided, be the strangest of the war. 'Is it possible for me to send you a message from Petrograd?'

'You mean do I have spies in the Russian capital?' The Kaiser laughed. 'Of course.'

'Could I approach one of your men?'

A slow smile started building on the Kaiser's face. 'What makes you think they are all men? Leave it that one of my agents will approach you when the time is right in Petrograd.'

'But, Your Majesty, can I be sure he'll know me? May I suggest we arrange – '

'When you approach the Czar, I will know.' He tapped his temple solemnly. 'You tell Georgie that I will be the *first* to know.'

Ash wanted more than a boast that the Kaiser had spies in the Russian court. 'But if I run into difficulties, Your Majesty, how can I turn to your agent for help if I don't know who he is?'

'They will watch you closely,' the Kaiser said. 'And they will approach you.'

'But how will I recognize agents I don't know, Your Majesty? How can I avoid an imposter?'

'Yes . . . I see your point . . . the Czar's police are treacherous – ' He snapped his fingers. 'I shall give you a password.'

Ash felt deflated. He had lost his manoeuvre to obtain the agents' names. 'Excellent,' was what he said.

'Now let me think . . . how right it is that we Kings band together . . . a pride of Kings. *There* is your password, Commander – a pride of Kings.'

The Kaiser shook his hand, pumped it vigorously. 'God speed, Royal Messenger.'

'Thank you, Your Majesty.' But to Ash's surprise, the

70

Kaiser, who had been ebullient an instant before, suddenly frowned; his deep, liquid eyes screwed up small and hard and his mouth tightened. What in hell had he done wrong? . . . The Kaiser's gaze fell ominously on their clasped hands. Ash kicked himself for an idiot. He had automatically tightened the hard muscle of his own hand to protect his fingers from the Kaiser's rings, but he had forgotten to pretend to wince.

He winced. The Kaiser stopped frowning, let go with a laugh and clapped him on the back.

'Your Majesty?'

'What? What is it now?' He was already propelling him toward the door, but Ash needed one more thing.

'The police delayed me at several railroad stations. May I have your *laissez-passer*?'

'Speak to my chamberlain.'

'Your Highness, King George has told no one about this . . . this family matter. No one but you, and myself.'

'And he is right. It's none of their business – ah, yes, I see what you mean . . .' He went quickly to his desk, scribbled energetically, reminding Ash of Teddy Roosevelt again, and affixed his royal seal to the letter. Ash stole a glance at it. The ploy had worked. In his haste, the Kaiser had neglected to specify the route to Holland.

'Off you go. And tell Nicky I warned him something like this would happen.'

Georgie, what are you scheming?

The Kaiser had reverted to form, and was now wondering if Cousin Georgie was trying to steal a march on him. He went to the window to watch Ash leave. Behind him he heard his courtiers returning, huddling by his desk, waiting anxiously for him to notice them; their presence eased his mind. Georgie was too simple a fellow to scheme against him. It was true he didn't possess a military mind. If he did,

71

he would never undermine England's ally by removing her Czar . . .

He watched Ash come out, cloak swirling like wings in the snow. He walked fast, snapping back the salutes offered by junior officers. The Kaiser felt a brooding gloom descend on him. He had strutted like that before the war, fast and proud like the American, when he was still the sun around which the German Empire revolved. But the war had turned into a catastrophe for him. He couldn't pinpoint the moment when he'd lost control of the army. He only knew that today, thanks to the infernal combination of machine-guns and trenches, which made war total, Ludendorff and Hindenburg made decisions at army headquarters while the Kaiser was elsewhere – isolated, and surrounded by young upstarts and old failures. For twenty-eight years, since he had taken the crown, he had inspired the military to spearhead German Imperialism, to make Germany the most powerful nation in Europe so she might take what was hers in the world. Inspired by his example, there wasn't a German boy worth his salt who didn't dream of glory in the army or the High Seas Fleet . . . But no one thanked him anymore . . . There was a time, not so long ago, when barbers made their fortune curling officers' moustaches in the exact manner he curled his. Officers copied his stance, practised his facial expressions, his very manner of talking. And there was a time before the war when his simplest request was an Imperial command. 'As Your Majesty commands,' was the instant response by generals and ministers alike. Now General Hindenburg and General Ludendorff seemed even brusque when they made their daily military report.

Ash disappeared out of the gates, but the Kaiser remained by the window staring at the snow filling the American's footsteps, alone with his gloomy thoughts. A Kaiser not fully in command was not a Kaiser, hardly better than a silly constitutional monarch like the King of England . . . He longed to regain his power.

Not for himself, of course. For Germany. Because, of course, Germany needed her Kaiser again. This abomination of a war would go on forever if Germany weren't first starved into defeat by the British blockade. Shortages had become so bad that people were actually criticizing the Kaiser himself, claiming it was extravagance to maintain his stables and Imperial train on a luxurious scale, which they didn't seem to understand was vital for morale. Germany needed her Kaiser restored to full power to win the war – or at least to stop it – and make things good the way they used to be . . . But how? . . . Strange, the way Georgie's messenger had stirred up all his thinking . . . Well, it felt good to be doing something again, even if it was only saving poor Nicky's silly neck. It had been a long time since he had been able to do anything worthwhile. He thought of Ash and resolved, impulsively, to assign his best man to help the American on his royal mission.

'Send me a guardsman!'

'Yes, Majesty.'

An officer in the uniform of the Imperial Bodyguard marched into the reception room. Up close he smelled of a combination of thoroughbred horse and French cologne.

The Kaiser liked cavalry men; a fall on the head now and then only deepened their simple loyalty. He put his arm around the man's shoulder and spoke quietly. The army hadn't yet taken *all* his power.

Poor Georgie, so weak he had to ask an American to rescue Nicky. Well, thanks to Kaiser Wilhelm, Ash would have the help of the finest German in his realm . . . And if George *was* scheming, using the American against him, what better man to stop Ash in his tracks? Dead in his tracks.

'Inform Count von Basel his Kaiser needs him.'

* * *

73

An army spy at the Kaiser's court reported the mysterious visit and the long private audience to Major Konrad Ranke, German Imperial General Staff, Gruppe IIIb – secret service. Ranke called for Gruppe IIIb files on Commander Ash, found them oddly full for an American officer, and noted that Ash often acted as a high-level courier.

Ranke promptly telephoned General Headquarters at Spa, the resort town in occupied Belgium. A superb military communication system – as well as a conviction in the German Army that the ever-volatile Kaiser bore close watching – had Ranke connected in minutes to First Quartermaster General Erich Ludendorff.

Ludendorff was in a rare reflective mood. His staff had prepared casualty lists for the year about to end so that he could calculate conscription requirements for 1917. In two great battles the German Army had held the line along the River Somme but failed to break the French fortress of Verdun. It had suffered 437,000 casualties at the Somme and had lost a third of a million men at Verdun. One might as well count grains of sand. As he listened to Ranke, he brushed a heavy hand over his closely cropped, half-bald head. He had a small black moustache, a big nose and a prissy mouth that might have gone better on a greedy shopkeeper than the second-ranking soldier in Germany. 'What,' he asked, 'do you speculate, Major Ranke?'

'The American perhaps brought the Kaiser another negotiating plan from President Wilson,' Ranke ventured.

Ludendorff glanced down at his waist. A roll of fat bulged through his tunic as if some barracks prankster had attached it the night before. Ranke was the only major he allowed to report directly to him. The Kaiser left unwatched was like a child with a box of matches, but Ranke suffered a serious lack of imagination.

'More likely the American brought the Kaiser a peace offer from King George.'

Major Ranke, in his fashion, said: 'What shall we do?'

General Ludendorff pressed the telephone receiver more tightly to his ear. Artillery at Liege the first summer of the war seemed to have had an occasional effect on his hearing. Major Ranke thought the general hadn't heard at all and repeated the question, adding, '. . . since we are not sure what was the real purpose of the visit . . .'

He *had* heard Ranke's question the first time. Gazing at the casualty lists, counting his grains of sand, he answered coldly, 'You say you are not sure, but you suspect that the American persuaded His Majesty to treat for peace behind the army's back?'

'Yes, General.'

'And you suspect that the American is at this moment returning to whomever sent him with the Kaiser's agreement about some peace scheme?'

'Agreement of *some* scheme . . .'

'And you agree that whatever they may have talked about, it is dangerous . . . because whatever else he may be the Kaiser could still persuade the German people to accept peace. Behind the army's back . . .'

'Yes, General.'

'And you still ask me what to do about the American?'

'I await your orders, General,' Ranke replied nervously.

'Major Ranke, kill him.'

5

Ash had already decided that if he were going to Russia alone he would need help. He had friends in Zurich, and friends in Paris. And some of them had friends in Russia. So Ash headed south.

The royal *laissez-passer* gave him *carte blanche* to travel anywhere in Kaiserin Germany, on any conveyance, to any border. Racing the nearly four hundred miles from Berlin to Munich, Ash brandished the letter at stationmasters in Leipzig and Plauen to force his way aboard faster trains.

He made Munich in twelve hours – good time even before the war allowed the German Army to commandeer the rails. Ahead was Switzerland, his destination. But an arm of Austria-Hungary separated Germany from Switzerland, and he worried that the Kaiser's letter would carry less weight in the German ally's territory than in Germany itself.

Major Ranke polled his agents along the rail line from Berlin to The Hague. No one had seen Ash. Supposing, Ranke speculated, Ash had gone to Vienna instead to include the Austrians in whatever scheme he and the Kaiser were hatching? He cast Gruppe IIIb's net wider. And when the telephones began ringing back, and the telegraph keys took up their busy clatter, and radio signals slithered into his Berlin headquarters, Ranke was rewarded by reports that Ash had gone south – travelling fast with the Kaiser's own *laissez-passer.*

Ranke alerted his Munich agents to cover the railroad station, and organized ambushes on the routes east to

Vienna and south across the Austrian border through Innsbruck to Switzerland.

Ash weighed his options at Munich Station. West on local lines to enter Switzerland directly at Thaingen was tempting, but those lines were often jammed by troop and munitions trains bound for the German front, where the tail end of the trenches stopped at the Swiss border. Innsbruck beckoned despite the difficulty of passing through Austria.

He noticed a man in a suit watching him while he studied the timetables; he crossed the station and bought a newspaper and the man followed, pushing roughly through a group of wounded Austrian soldiers begging for money for food.

Ash went out to the taxi queue. As his taxi pulled away from the train station the man in the suit shouldered ahead of an army lieutenant; in Germany officers were yielded seats and conveyances, but the man in the suit showed the lieutenant something in his hand, and took the cab without protest.

'Bayerischer Hof,' Ash told his driver, and when he got to the hotel the man in the suit was right behind him. Ash went inside, showed the Kaiser's letter to the manager and demanded a ranking *polizei* officer who spoke English. Being followed in wartime Germany was hardly an uncommon experience for a foreigner, but Ash wanted to arrive in Switzerland with a clean wake. He took a chair in the elegant lobby and let the manager order coffee, which arrived when the *polizei* did.

He pointed out the man in the suit, sitting across the lobby reading a book. The coffee was ersatz. The police officer returned in a few minutes.

'Could there be a mistake, Commander? The gentleman is an army officer recuperating from wounds.'

'The mistake will be yours if that man is allowed to follow me another foot while I am on the Kaiser's mission.'

The officer flushed. 'Perhaps I should detain him then.'

'I would think it's imperative,' Ash said, got up and left. Army? Why would the army be following? The police usually did the following in Germany. It made him damn uncomfortable. Getting the man arrested bought some time, but not much.

He was heading for the station again when it occurred to him that December snow had slowed infantry fighting. If artillery had taken up the slack, the German Army Transport Corps would be moving more shells than troops. Checking his Baedecker, he ordered his driver to head in a new direction.

An hour later night had fallen when Ash arrived alone at the railroad yard farthest from the centre of Munich. Heavily guarded gates told him he had guessed right, that from here the German Transport Corps sent munitions trains speeding west on cleared track. A veteran of several hunting excursions with the Kaiser's entourage before the war, and several courier trips to Berlin since, Ash felt that Wilhelmine German officials responded best to orders clearly and loudly stated, followed by arrogant silence.

'Lieutenant Commander Ash, United States Navy, on orders of Kaiser Wilhelm. Take me to the commandant.'

Whether the sergeant of the guard believed, or even understood his clumsy German, the sound of it impressed him sufficiently to send Ash, escorted by four men, to the commandant's aide-de-camp. Ash showed him the Kaiser's letter, following another of his rules – never to show papers before it was necessary. The aide asked if he could be of assistance and Ash told him firmly he could not.

The commandant's office overlooked a vast rail yard surrounded by warehouses and high walls, and lighted by lanterns and electric lamps. Switch engines were disassembling the freight trains that snaked in from the surrounding darkness and sending new trains back out as if the entire yard were a single machine and the freight cars – passing from darkness into light and back to darkness – the moving parts.

The commandant, an engineering officer, read the Kaiser's letter. He spoke English, as so many of the German officers did, but with a thick accent.

'There is passenger service from Munich to Innsbruck. There you change for Zurich.'

'I haven't time to deal with the Austrians.'

The commandant remarked with unexpectedly open scorn for his ally, 'Who does?'

'Then you see my problem, and why I require fast passage to Thaingen.'

'However,' the commandant countered, 'the fact that our Austrian allies are dunderheads does not alter the situation here. This yard, as you have evidently surmised, is a stage for munitions trains arriving from the factories with cargoes bound for the front. It is a military post barred to foreigners.'

'But the Kaiser gave me this letter of free passage to relieve just such legitimate concerns on the part of his officers. In short, the Kaiser demands that you aid me – *immediately and in any manner I ask.*'

'The Kaiser does not have responsibility for supplying our cannon with shells.'

Ash had never heard such independent talk in Germany. The commandant folded the letter and returned it. Ash said, 'The United States is a neutral. I offer no threat. I merely want to ride aboard a fast train west. And I suspect that your trains are the fastest.'

'What makes you suspect that?'

'I've seen every rail yard in Europe. I know what the good ones look like.' There was truth in that. One of the reasons Germany was winning her two-front war was that

79

she'd built a railroad system specifically designed to shuttle her armies from front to front.

The compliment softened the commandant enough to make a joke of his refusal. 'But if the United States declares war on Germany while her neutral courier is aboard my munitions train, wouldn't her neutral courier automatically become a spy?'

'Then you, sir,' Ash said with a straight face, 'will have the honour of capturing the first American prisoner.' He glanced at the blackboard behind the commandant on which were chalked the trains leaving that night and added, 'And I expect to be treated well, since you're obviously a gentleman.'

It didn't work. The commandant said, 'I can't help you, Commander. And tell your good friend the Kaiser that the *army* will beat the English and the French and the Russians, but we'd appreciate it if he'd keep the Americans out.'

Unsure of the reception he would find in Munich, Ash paid a taxi driver triple rate to drive him to a suburban station west of the city.

Ranke polled the telegraphers and telephone operators for agent reports along Ash's various possible routes. Vienna reported no sighting. Then Ranke's chief officer in Munich switched him a telephone call from the commandant of a Munich munitions depot. Ranke alerted Munich. Ash had probably left already. Search all the trains, passenger and freight.

Ash slept the night sitting up in a second-class carriage on the local to Thaingen. He woke up in the morning when the conductor shooed the other passengers out of his compartment. An army captain – a heavily built officer with close cropped hair and a face slit by a duelling scar from his eye to his jaw – entered and asked, 'Commander Ash?'

'Yes,' Ash said, rubbing the sleep out of his eyes and noting that the conductor had already backed respectfully away.

The captain told him he was under arrest.

6

'I am a United States Naval officer and diplomatic courier travelling with the Kaiser's *laissez-passer*. On your way out tell the orderly to bring coffee.'

The captain read the Kaiser's letter and tore it in half.

'Captain, if you're looking for trouble, I assure you you've found it.'

The train began to slow. The captain motioned Ash to his feet. Ash sat still. The German shifted the trenchcoat he was carrying over his arm, unsnapped his holster, drew out his Luger.

'Get up.'

'You're making a mistake, Captain.'

The captain gestured with the long-barrelled automatic pistol, and Ash rose slowly as the train pulled into a small village station and onto a siding. Passengers boarded and disembarked, but the captain marched Ash through the train to the rear car before he allowed him to step onto the platform. He held his gun close to his side, and when three country *Hausfrauen* passed near them he covered it with his coat. All very professional, Ash couldn't help thinking.

'That way.' He pointed to a stair at the back of the platform that led away from the station. A path ran parallel to the main line, which curved out of sight of the station. Two hundred yards down the line the path veered across the siding and ended at a freight depot. Ash looked back and caught a last glimpse of the back of the train, which apparently was waiting on the siding for an express to overtake it.

As they walked toward the depot the freight master came

out and hung a big canvas mailbag on the mail pickup hook beside the express track. He hailed the captain, who ordered him away. The captain kept the gun under his coat and watched until the freight master had trudged out of sight around the curve. Only then did he slide open the depot door.

A lieutenant, bearing similar duelling scars, sat at the wheel of a truck whose cargo area was shrouded by canvas. Ash felt the gun prod him in the back, pushing him toward the truck.

'Hold on,' Ash said. German officers, like British, never performed what they considered menial tasks. The long walk from the station, the concealed gun, and now an aristocrat at the steering wheel spoke more of a kidnapping than an arrest. 'Where are you taking me?'

'Headquarters.'

'What unit?'

The captain glanced at the lieutenant, which was just time enough for Ash to kick him in the stomach, draw his dress sword as the German doubled over and slash at his hand. The Solingen blade drew blood through the captain's glove. He dropped the gun. Ash kicked it across the floor and went at the lieutenant, who got tangled between the wheel and the gear shift. Seeing Ash charge, he launched himself out of the truck, gave up trying to unsnap his holster flap and fell back, drawing his own sword.

Ash kept at him. The lieutenant slashed broadly – plunging strokes in the German manner of sabre fighting – and reached across his waist for the Luger strapped to his right hip.

But despite his duelling scars, as was the case with most German swordsmen, his training had been weighted more toward the courage to receive wounds than the skill to inflict them. When his wild high slash missed and his blade had travelled too low to parry, Ash thrust as if his sabre were a foil, and managed to impale his wrist.

A murmur was the only sound that came from the German, but bravery couldn't keep his weapon from falling from his convulsing fingers. Ash glanced at the captain, who was getting uncertainly to his feet, tapped the lieutenant's holster with the point of his sword, then directed it at his face.

The lieutenant pawed it open with his left hand, his eyes on Ash's blade. Gingerly he removed the gun. The captain then made a rush for his own gun across the freight room. Ash flicked the gun from the lieutenant's hand, shoved him aside and covered the captain, who stopped short and slowly raised his hands. Ash motioned them to stand together. 'Where is headquarters?'

They looked back at him. Silent.

Ash raised the Luger and fired. The shot passed between them, close to the captain's ear. Both flinched but said nothing. Ash fired again. The express train was now closer, its engine pounding.

'Last chance.'

They looked at each other.

'You were going to kill me. Why?' And he fired again, very close. The captain grabbed at his ear. Ash aimed at the lieutenant's face. 'Why?'

'Orders,' the man said, raising his hand as if to stop the bullet.

' *Whose* orders?'

'The major.'

'To kill me?'

'Yes.'

'How?'

'We were supposed to throw you from a bridge, look as if you had fallen. Like an accident – '

'Shut up,' the captain said.

84

Ash snapped a shot past his other ear. 'Who told the major to kill me?'

The lieutenant shrugged. The captain gazed into the barrel as he said, 'I don't know. I swear it.'

Ash sighted down the barrel at a point between the man's eyes. The captain actually drew himself stiffly to attention. Ash reckoned he must be telling the truth. The express was blowing its whistle and it sounded near and moving fast, with no stop planned at this local station.

The door behind the Germans banged open, kicked in by four soldiers carrying Mauser rifles. They moved quickly, crouching, looking for the source of the gunfire. The officers threw themselves flat and shouted to fire. Ash went for the front door. Shots exploded – heavy rifle fire. Bullets cracked past his head, splintered the wooden door. Ash hit the floor rolling, slid it open, squeezed through and surged to his feet, dodging and weaving, knowing he had two or three seconds before they reached the door and got him in their sights again.

The express rounded the curve, blowing long, piercing wails. Ash scrambled toward the tracks and threw himself in front of the locomotive. He made it across, all but one boot, which the engine brushed. The impact threw him in the air in a full circle. The post office, the woods, the side of the speeding train raced across his vision. He landed hard, on gravel.

The mail pickup. The mail sack hung from a hook five feet off the ground beside the rails. Between the roaring wheels Ash saw the legs of the soldiers waiting for the train to pass, and the pale smears of their faces when they bent down to look. He headed for the mail pickup and threw his arms around the mail sack as the baggage car hurtled toward him. He caught a glimpse of a hinged hook, and the next instant the sack tried to explode out of his arm.

He saw a blur, the force broke his grip, wrenched him

sideways. He slammed into a heap of mail sacks. An ancient postal clerk holding a teacup stared.

'What's the next stop?' Ash asked.

'Thaingen,' the old man replied unhurriedly, as if all this happened every day.

Near Schaffhausen on the Swiss border. They'd search the area around the country station for a long time before they worked out what he had done. He just might make it. He sagged back on the mail sacks, breathing hard. Count of Monte Cristo? Hell, he hadn't even managed to get out of Germany yet.

He had three shots left in the Luger and the no-man's-land between Schaffhausen's German and Swiss border posts was guarded by four riflemen. It was a hundred-foot stretch of road, fenced on both sides and cleared of snow. *Polizei* watched the travellers trying to leave Germany while the customs house clerks inspected their papers and pored over official telegrams pertaining to criminals and spies. Ash knew his only hope was that the army officers who had tried to kill him were operating unofficially.

He counted the German guns and targeted the closest three. From the smallest soldier he would take a sidearm, spray the *polizei* as fast as he could pull the trigger, shoot the remaining rifleman and take off for Switzerland if he were still on his feet. A plan, anyway.

He submitted his diplomatic passport and reached inside his boatcloak for the Luger. Three shots. The customs house clerk sorted through a stack of telegrams, reading each one. Then he got up, bowed and returned Ash's passport with apologies for the delay. Five minutes later, on the far side, the Swiss attached a visa stencil to his papers and showed him aboard the train to Zurich, leaving Ash to conclude that in some way, somehow related to his visit to the Kaiser, he had aroused the considerable displeasure of some section of the German army. Or had maybe stumbled into a feud at the Kaiser's court? He also tried the notion that the Kaiser might have changed his mind and double-crossed him, except that didn't make any sense. If the Kaiser were against him, he'd be dead by now.

No answers, but at least he was alive . . .

When his Kaiser's command reached Count von Basel in enemy Russia, he set out for the front lines and crossed no-man's-land down-river from Dvinsk. The commandant of that German-occupied city put him aboard a luxurious private car attached to the Berlin Express, hoping that the spy would mention such solicitousness to the Kaiser. Von Basel bathed vigorously, scrubbing off what he thought of as the filth of Russia, then sat moodily eyeing war-devastated East Prussia. The land was German again, but little habitable remained. His mother had moved to Berlin.

She was a refined woman from a family even older than the von Basels. All through his childhood she had struggled to shield him from the simpleminded excesses of his father, a towering brute who wielded the sabre like a battle axe and made them struggle for every quiet moment.

The conflict had flowered violently when young Philip was fifteen and the Kaiser had announced he would enjoy hunting stag on the von Basel estate. His mother was thrilled, his father resentful of the expense and disruption of installing indoor toilets and running water in the thousand-year-old castle, in addition to total redecoration.

His mother had prevailed, with the firm assistance of a Kaiserin court marshal who travelled far ahead of the entourage, making sure that host estates were in proper order. Exotic foodstuffs began arriving from Berlin weeks before the hunt, accompanied by enormous bills and soon by the Kaiser's own chefs and kitchen staff lent for a price by expensive Berlin hotels. Meantime, the peasantry had to

87

be paid to paint and whitewash every farmhouse and hovel within sight of the Kaiser's carriage ride from the distant rail station, over a road which was thoroughly repaired to provide a comfortable ride.

When at last the splendid Imperial Train steamed into East Prussia, the young von Basel was already dazzled by extravagances that delighted his mother and enraged his father, and ripe for the attentions of a charming member of the Kaiser's vast entourage, a colonel of the Imperial Bodyguard who understood the boy's unrealized yearnings and ministered to them tenderly. And it was the very tenderness of a simple handshake good-bye which inflamed his father's suspicions.

When the last carriage disappeared, and quiet had descended on the estate like a blanket, Philip's father had dragged him, still in their dress uniforms, to the stable and beat him senseless with his fists. The boy came to, face down in the straw matting, vomiting. His father was sitting head in his hands, silent.

Philip dragged himself to the horse trough and plunged his head into the cold water until the dizziness passed. When he could stand he drew his sabre. His father looked up.

The sharp rap, rap of steel against the trough was an unmistakable challenge. But in case the elder von Basel did not understand, young Philip added a remark about his father's sexual demands on his mother. His father came to his feet, promising worse punishment for the fifteen-year-old.

But von Basel had made his own promise – he would never let the stronger man inside his guard. If his father wished to punish him again, first he had to divest him of the sabre he had taught him to use. And that, the father discovered, was not easily done. He had honed the boy's remarkable speed from the day he had discovered it. What

88

he had not realized was that his son's wrist had come into its own over the summer. Rage for ruining what he had shared with the colonel of the guard fuelled the killing machine the boy had become, and the father had nurtured.

Philip laid both of his father's cheeks open to the bone, took an ear and extracted a tearful apology by threatening to slice off his nose. Hours later the humiliated count shot himself, guaranteeing that his son would come into his inheritance as soon as he reached his majority, and convincing the boy that the sabre was a most satisfactory tool to redress wrong and restore order. The only thing that puzzled him at all about the affair was why his mother had grieved . . .

7

Ash remembered Zurich as a sleepy backwater before the war, but it had turned abruptly cosmopolitan when Switzerland emerged as a neutral island for bankers, diplomats, spies and political exiles. A dozen nationalities thronged the financial district's Bahnhofstrasse above Lake Zurich.

He went first to the American consulate, where he had lunch with the military attaché, an army captain he had served with in Berlin. He asked where various people they knew were staying and he asked about the Russian revolutionary exiles living in Zurich. His friend thought those in Zurich were mostly fragments of the prewar movement, but he promised to scare up the names of their leaders.

'Lunatic Bolsheviks,' the captain warned. 'The sensible ones stopped their agitating when the war began. Hunkered down to fight the Germans.'

Ash wired Ambassador Page not to expect him in London for a week as he was planning short stays in Zurich and Paris. He closed with, 'All's well,' which was not exactly the truth, considering that *some* elements of the German army were trying to kill him, but Page would know from his message that he had persuaded the Kaiser to help King George's plan, which more importantly meant that their own scheme was underway.

Having lost his bag when he was arrested on the train, he bought a dark suit. He had dinner with the president of the Bank of Rome's Zurich branch, an old friend from a Roman fencing *Salle* he'd attended the summer Tamara Tishkova left Russia for what she called 'tuning' with an Italian dance master. Albioni had given up the sword, and the lack of exercise showed in his thickening waist, though it didn't seem to bother him. Albioni's position in Zurich was a plum for a man his age, which was also Ash's age, and his mistress had come along while his wife remained at home with the family.

'All and all, my friend, not an unpleasant state of affairs. And you?'

'I'm going to Petrograd.' Until five days ago he had been telling people about his transfer to sea duty.

'Not Tishkova?' Albioni asked with a sympathetic smile.

'No. But I wonder whether you could introduce me to your counterpart in Petrograd . . . Signor de la Rocca?' It might be handy to know a banker in Petrograd, particularly one married to a Russian baroness.

He visited a brothel late that same night with an English so-called economist he had sailed with in the Fastnet Race and who had turned up at his hotel one night years before the war in Berlin with a bullet hole in his arm and a story about an irate husband that Ash hadn't believed for a minute. Rumour suggested he was in the habit of poking his yacht up various restricted German estuaries to gather naval secrets. Ash had patched him up and found papers to get him across the border. The fact that he was in Zurich meant he was probably in the spy business again; his cover story was that he was teaching economics at the University.

Taplinger – he was part German though completely English in manner – was anxious to take a Roumanian beauty upstairs, but Ash persuaded him to have a quiet brandy first.

'I need some information. I'm going to Petrograd.'

'I'd be quick off the mark, old chap. There might not be a Petrograd very soon.'

'What do you hear about the revolution?'

'It's going to happen.'

'What do the Bolsheviks want?'

91

Taplinger cast a longing eye at the Roumanian before he answered. 'You know, old son, I do believe she's got her eye on you.' Ash had already noticed, but tonight the only reason he'd come here was because Taplinger had insisted; as long as he had known Taplinger, the man had had an obsession with bordellos. This one, with its rococo drawing rooms, French Academy paintings, women of almost infinite European variety and a clientele drawn from the diplomatic corps and the banking elite illustrated one more irony of the war: lavishly appointed sin in western Europe was now most available in formerly staid Switzerland.

'What do the Bolsheviks want? Everything, I'd say. And it's for the taking. The old monarchies can't rule modern industrial nations. The Bolsheviks, of course, are as conspiratorial and ruthless as the Borgia, and they well sense the opportunity. Marxism and socialism aside, the Bolsheviks understand power as well as any emperor. They're going to be our new royals, Ash, whether we like it or not – and *now* may we pay our respects to that lady?'

'Two more questions – '

'Ash, the woman has to earn a living. Be fair.'

'Give me a rundown on the Russian parties against the Czar.'

'Briefly – dammit – Bolsheviks are sort of left-wing Social Democrats without a social or democratic bone in their bodies. Mensheviks are right-wing Social Democrats, democratic in their organization and, therefore, of course no match for the Bolsheviks. Social Revolutionaries want all power to the people and will bomb and shoot whoever stands in their way; the Social Revolutionaries are the violent lunatics. Last, and perhaps Russia's best hope, are the Kadets, the Constitutional Democratic Party. The Kadets are a powerful party in the Duma and could provide the leadership of a new government.'

'*Will* the Czar be overthrown?'

Taplinger peered owlishly across the smoky room. 'I believe she's going to come over here and rescue me.'

Ash glanced at the Roumanian woman sprawled impatiently on a chaise longue, fluttering a Chinese fan. A portly, expensively dressed Belgian was trying to speak with her, but she ignored him and smiled at Ash, or Taplinger; the room was too wide to tell for sure.

'*Will* the Czar be overthrown?'

'I'm just an economist,' Taplinger protested. 'But it's significant, perhaps, that the Czar regards the Kadets, those parliamentarian liberal democrats, as revolutionaries. With that attitude . . .'

'Who is Lenin?' The military attaché at the American consulate had mentioned a few names; Lenin was supposed to be a cut above the others.

'Vladimir Lenin. Agitator, theorist, Bolshevik leader and damned good speaker. Or used to be. Going downhill these days, people tell me. Why?'

'I want to know what's going on in Russia before I get there.'

Taplinger looked at him curiously, but said only, as if from professional courtesy, 'Talk to Lenin. He practically lives at the library. That's where you'll find him – here comes our Roumanian lady.'

She was tall and dark-haired, her skin olive where her breasts swelled above her low bodice. Swaying slightly, she fixed her eyes on Ash.

'Dammit, she wants you,' Taplinger said.

'I don't think I'm up to it . . .' The Germans kept informers in brothels like these; he purposely hadn't told Taplinger anything that mattered about the mission to rescue the Czar. Or at least so he thought.

As she approached, the Belgian came up to her again, insistent, waving his diamond-studded hands. Again she brushed him aside and headed for Ash.

'It's you she wants,' Taplinger said. 'Damn it.'

Ash returned her smile. She was, after all, extraordinarily pretty.

'Probably a German spy,' Taplinger said *sotto voce*. 'Diamonds usually do the trick in a place like this.'

'Usually,' said Ash, standing up for her. In escaping the Belgian she had turned completely around, revealing a beautiful back and swelling hips beneath her tightly cut gown. 'Good evening, *Mademoiselle*.'

'*Bon soir*, Commander. My English *très* bad. *Oui?*' She ignored Taplinger. Ash agreed to speak French. They danced to the string orchestra in the next room, and she asked his name. Ash told her. Her name was Margo. She said she was worried about her grandmother who lived in Germany. Ash said he had just come from Germany and she asked why Ash was in Zurich.

'Just passing through,' Ash told her. What else? 'What news from home?'

'Home?'

'The German invasion?'

The attack on Roumania had just begun and looked to be over in a few more days as the Germans threw the Roumanian army headlong into the Russian lines.

'I don't understand about war,' she said. 'Only about soldiers. And maybe sailors. Where do you go from here?'

Ash told her that he travelled as a diplomatic courier. Taplinger looked away angrily as Ash took her upstairs. The room was sumptuous, an original bedroom, unpartitioned for the mansion's new function. The bed was turned down with sheets of fine crisp linen. Margo came back from the bathroom in her chemise, barefoot except for stockings, and it occurred to Ash that she had very pretty feet for such a tall girl.

Smiling, apparently enjoying herself, she posed for him while he sat in an armchair beside the bed. She danced in

94

slow circles around the carpet, pulled the chemise over her head and, passing near him, laid the perfumed silk on his shoulder.

A black whalebone corset lifted her breasts, flattened her belly and thrust her buttocks out in a rich curve. She noticed his reaction and posed accordingly. She left her corset in place as she finally untied the ribbons that secured her drawers at the sides and let them fall away.

She pulled an ottoman into the middle of the room in front of Ash, straddled the low, narrow piece, laid flat, and arched her back. She looked at him over her shoulder and asked if there was something special he might enjoy, something to remember wherever he travelled.

'A fantasy,' Ash said, his mouth dry as sand, his heart pounding. He stood up and unbuckled his sword.

'What fantasy, *chéri?*' Margo asked, undulating softly side to side as she watched him.

He held the scabbard in one hand, his sword hilt in the other and stepped closer. The straps and buckles dangled in front of her eyes. She arched her back higher and ground her spread thighs against the cushion, playing the game. There were many possibilities – the straps, the buckles, the scabbard, the blade itself. She wasn't afraid. Ranking officers in uniform did not injure girls in a house like this one.

He drew the blade and she still wasn't afraid; a French colonel had flogged her once with his empty scabbard, the discomfort amply rewarded in gold francs.

'What fantasy?' she whispered.

'Pretend I'm the German officer you report to.'

He turned his wrist and the blade flicked beside her cheek.

8

Now that he had her, Ash had to deal with her. He gave her what he hoped was a murderous look, one to convince her that he would actually cut her. Somehow he kept the blade rock steady. She stared back at him, hugging the ottoman. And then she went rigid.

'His name.'

'I don't know his name. He comes here.'

She started crying. Ash steeled himself, but when goose bumps of fear prickled her flesh he had to remind himself that they had already declared war on him.

'What does he want to know about me?'

'Where you are travelling . . . please don't – ' Her eyes went to his, then back to the tip of the sword.

'What else?'

'Who you are visiting – '

'What else?'

'. . . What the Kaiser told you – '

'*What?*'

'Please – ' She sucked in her breath. Ash's hand had moved convulsively. *The Kaiser?*

Ash sheathed his sword and buckled it around his waist. She lay there crying, still straddling the ottoman, still damned provocative. Ash forced himself to the door.

'What can I tell him – '

'Tell him I told you absolutely nothing.'

'He won't believe me.'

'Tell him what I told you when we danced. And tell him I was so overwhelmed I gave you this. Here . . .' He went back to her and laid five gold sovereigns beside her face on the cushion. 'With a tip like this he'll believe I had the time of my life.'

The short, powerfully built, bald-headed man standing on the library steps was shivering in a threadbare overcoat that was no match for the unusually cold wind blowing up the Limmat River from Lake Zurich. His round peaked workman's cap did not conceal much of his baldness, and his battered shoes and cracked leather briefcase looked years beyond repair.

When he saw Ash approaching he asked anxiously in French what time it was. A moustache and a stubbly brown beard circled his obstinate mouth. Small, deep-set eyes lent a dogged look to his face, and Ash was reminded of a gambler riding out a long streak of bad luck.

'Almost ten to nine,' Ash said. 'Do they open on time?'

He seemed less comfortable in English. It took a moment before he said, 'Yes. Yes. The Swiss are good about time.'

'Are you Lenin?'

'Who are you?'

'I'm an American, a foreign correspondent. My newspaper is considering sending me to Petrograd but they want some reports from Zurich first about the exiles who live here and about the state of the revolution.' He grinned. 'In other words, my bosses want to know if it's worth sending me to Russia, or should I just stay in France to cover the fighting.'

'How do you know my name?'

'You *are* Lenin? Well, I heard your name in a café when I asked the same questions. Someone told me you might be the man to talk to. Could you spare me the time?'

'I'm very busy here.' He glanced at the library doors, which still were shut.

'I've heard you're a writer too. So you know my problem. They might even yank me home if I don't come up with a beat . . . say, how about lunch? Do you ever stop for lunch?'

97

Lenin nodded. 'I could stop for lunch.'

'I'll meet you here at noon.'

'What paper did you say?'

'Atlanta *Constitution*. Atlanta, Georgia.'

'How is Mr Grady's New South doing these days?'

The question threw Ash so completely that for a long second he just stared. Mr Grady. Who the hell was Mr Grady? It rang a bell . . . he should know . . .

Lenin looked up at him, even showing a slight smile. 'I would expect that even the stupidest reporter from America would know the name of the founding editor of his own newspaper, Henry Grady.'

Idiot, thought Ash. Henry Grady. The proselytizer of an industrial New South after the Civil War. 'He was before my time,' Ash said lamely.

The library doors at the top of the steps opened with a sharp snap of released latches, and Lenin darted up with surprising – to Ash, at least – athletic grace and vigour. At the threshold he turned back and looked down at Ash, who was watching helplessly. 'Perhaps I'll have lunch with you out of curiosity. You have three hours to dream up a better story.'

'What went wrong at Schaffhausen?' General Ludendorff demanded.

Ranke decided the question was rhetorical and kept quiet. In a few more awful minutes he would be on his way home to the relative safety of Berlin. But Ludendorff wasn't through. Belatedly, Ranke realized that his clipped tones contained a far deeper rage than he'd so far expressed. His neck turned red, flushed all the way up into his bristly hair.

'There is another matter, Major Ranke.'

'Yes sir.'

'Did you know that Count von Basel was back in Germany?'

Was that all? 'Of course, General. Von Basel reported to Gruppe IIIb last week – after, I might mention, returning unexpectedly and without orders to do so, though of course we on Staff have learned to put up with the peccadilloes of field agents – '

'Really? And where is von Basel now?'

'He departed for what he claimed was, to use his own words, a well-deserved holiday.'

'Did you know that his holiday as you call it was spent with the Kaiser?'

Ranke felt a chill.

'Are you aware that von Basel has been the Kaiser's protégé for some thirteen years?'

'Of course,' Ranke whispered.

'Did you know that the Kaiser ordered von Basel to return immediately to Russia and that he has already done so?'

'How . . . ?'

'Are you asking how do I know? Fortunately your so-called observer in the Kaiser's entourage is not my only source . . . Would you care to speculate who von Basel and the Kaiser discussed? I will tell you. A man who just happens to be on *his* way to Russia . . .' He leaped from his desk and stood nose to nose with Ranke. 'Well, Major, *would you?*'

'Ash . . .'

Ludendorff turned to his aide-de-camp. 'Inform this major that he is to report to me through regular channels from now on.'

'Dismissed,' the aide-de-camp said.

For Major Ranke it was like a death sentence.

Some instinct, Ludendorff reflected, had warned him from the start about Commander Ash and the Kaiser. And unfortunately he had been right. Count von Basel was a murderous psychopath with two passions in his life – to mutilate men with his sabre and serve his buffoon of a Kaiser. Kaiser Wilhelm loved him like a son.

Ludendorff still did not know precisely what the Kaiser was plotting, except that it clearly pointed at Russia, but the fact von Basel was summoned meant that the Kaiser regarded it as vital. It was likely that King George was also involved. President Wilson could be. Certainly Ash could serve either or both. But if Count von Basel left his post as a German agent in Russia, risking crossing enemy lines twice to deliver a report to IIIb that could have been sent by simpler means, it was clear that he had actually been summoned by the Kaiser for instructions about a plot . . . a peace plan? . . . in Russia. And peace could only bring disaster to Ludendorff and the German army.

Ludendorff paced his office. Von Basel . . . the man was a relic – an old-fashioned, out-of-date servant to royalty, one of those hidebound Junkers who still believed that the nobility existed to fight for the royalty, and utterly blind to the idiot the Kaiser had turned out to be. But for his part the Kaiser had chosen well, because von Basel was both brilliant and dangerous.

Within the closed world of the Prussian Junkers he had secured his reputation at the age of fifteen by humiliating his father, a greatly feared duellist himself, into suicide. A year later he was notorious as the Heidelberg swordsman who refused to accept a duelling scar.

The absence of 'beauties' scarring his face was due neither to squeamishness on von Basel's part nor lack of trying by his fellow students. The ancient German Student Corps demanded that first-year students be 'free as a lad' and earn manhood by fighting frequent courtesy *Mensuren*. To display bravery and obedience, the principals stood toe to toe and slashed at each other's faces until ordered to halt.

The duels were expected to yield blood on both sides so

100

that arms and bodies were padded to prevent incapacitating wounds and ears were taped to the head to minimize the risk of losing one. The resultant wounds on cheeks and brows and lips were sewn shut by medical students and doused with wine to enhance the scarring that set the elite Student Corps alumnus apart from ordinary men and coincidentally guaranteed social position through life.

Count von Basel had mocked the *Mensur* ritual and scorned the Student Corps, because, he announced on his arrival from remote Eastern Prussia, volunteering to be hacked into bloody ribbons betrayed the highest ideals of Kaiserin Germany. Where was the skill a nobleman should cultivate to serve his Kaiser on 'Der Tag'?

Muth, moral courage to accept pain, was not enough. Germany needed winners. Besides, surrender bred servility. He scorned the blunt-tipped *Schlager.* The *Sabel* – the heavy curved sabre capable of cleaving a skull in half and running a man through the heart – was a real test not only of swordsmanship but of footwork, and the courage required to face death as well as trifling flesh wounds. As an afterthought, von Basel noted that many of low rank joined the Student Corps to advance beyond their station.

Stepping on another student's dachshund's tail was sufficient to provoke an insult duel, questioning the purity of his sister equally effective. But to characterize all the members of all the Student Corps as servile, social-climbing cowards was to ensure challengers for the entire school year.

Gradually, though, it dawned on the mutilated challengers that von Basel had provoked all these incidents for the sheer pleasure of proving his own superiority in birth, courage and skill. He took great pains not to kill. A man who killed had to leave the University; he could join another, but if he killed again he was barred from all.

At last, when sufficient eyes had been put out and the use

of many hands ended forever with severed tendons, there were no more challengers and the entire *Mensur* ritual ground to a sullen halt. Remarkably, von Basel had suffered only one wound, when a Bavarian twice his weight had managed to slam through his guard and slice off a small chunk of his scalp, for which he paid with both ears. Then a dragoon officer, who was a graduate of the Student Corps and a fencing master, intervened on behalf of the noble tradition.

The new challenger was fifteen years von Basel's senior and when he entered the tavern where the insult *Mensur* was scheduled, von Basel realized by his walk alone that his opponent far outclassed any others he had faced. While the servants were wiping the blades he informed the master in a discreet whisper that, because he was not yet skilled enough to let him off with flesh wounds, he would kill him if he insisted on fighting.

The cavalry officer laughed and attacked, shredding the younger man's defences, which, as he'd suspected, were less formidable than his attacks. And when he catalogued them all, and knew for certain that all von Basel had left was his bewildering speed and the incredible strength in a seemingly tireless wrist, he loosed a series of feints to lower von Basel's guard, and when he had, he slashed. Von Basel's speed saved his skull, but the sabre still laid his brow open to the bone.

Von Basel's left cheek was next, the officer announced as the student surgeons stanched the bleeding so that he could see. Then the right cheek, and then his nose and lips, which this master informed him he could feed to his dachshund if he didn't offer a public apology.

The spectators were still laughing, when von Basel ran him through. The man was incredible . . .

Ash, Ludendorff told himself, had to be stopped before he reached Russia. Von Basel was beyond stopping. He was so secretive about his activities in Russia that even his superiors – if you could call them that – at IIIb didn't know his actual Russian identity or even how he got the information he obtained. They were reasonably sure he served in Petrograd, though it could have been Moscow. Von Basel was damn near as mysterious in Germany as in Russia.

But this Ash . . . Ash was part of the Kaiser's scheme, part of a scheme to make peace behind the army's back – indeed apparently was integral to it. The linchpin. Ash *must* be stopped before he reached Russia, somewhere along the way . . .

He called in his aide-de-camp. 'Bring me a German officer who speaks Finnish.'

'Yes, General.'

Ludendorff felt better. German agents had done a fairly good job of stirring up national feelings in the Russian Grand Duchy of Finland. Of late they had established renegade army units to disrupt the telegraph and stop trains.

Lenin bounded down the library steps at twelve on the dot. Ash joined pace beside him, and they walked to the Bahnhofstrasse, past the banks to the Carleton-Elite Hotel. Winter sun streaming in tall windows lighted the pastel dining room exquisitely.

Lenin's gaze travelled over the flowers on the tables, the pâtisserie trolley, the linen and the silver, and settled on the silent waiters padding about the lush carpets. 'I imagine it's a romantic failing on my part, but something innocuous about the Swiss makes their wealth less grating than it is in Russia.'

'I suppose there is a difference,' Ash said, 'between ostentation and tasteful comfort.'

Lenin's bleak smile suggested that his romantic failing had been indulged enough.

'Try your new story on me, Mr . . . ?'

'Ash.'

'A pseudonymous name if I've ever heard one.'

'Kenneth Ash, Lieutenant Commander, United States Navy.'

A waiter had poured mineral water when they sat down. Lenin had his halfway to his lips. He lowered the glass untouched. 'Lieutenant Commander, United States Navy? What the hell do you want?'

'Shall we order first?'

'I'm not hungry. What do you *want*?'

'I want to know what's going on in Russia.'

'You're asking the wrong man. I haven't seen a Russian newspaper in a month. I haven't received a letter from Petrograd in five weeks. The last interval between letters was six weeks. The censors.'

Ash had done some more checking on Lenin and the Bolsheviks since Taplinger had mentioned them. In the jigsaw puzzle of left-wing and revolutionary political parties – a puzzle he had paid little attention to in the past since the slightest suggestion of revolution would send Tamara into a pro-Romanov rage – the Bolsheviks, preaching class warfare and the overthrow of factory owners by factory workmen, *seemed* to fall midway between the moderate socialists, who wanted to install a democratic parliamentary government in place of the Czar, and the anarchists, who wanted to destroy all governments. But however radical and violent they had been before the War, Lenin's Bolsheviks, if indeed they were still his, had since suffered the same loss of popular support as all the European socialists.

'You're not the wrong man,' Ash said. 'From what I've heard, if anyone knows what's going on, Lenin does.'

'If I did, and I don't, I don't know why I should tell you.'

'Why not? It's possible we want the same thing.'

'I doubt it. *I* want a revolution. I want the oppressed, the proletariat installed on the oppressor's throne. I want the wealth of a few restored to the many. And I fail to see how the United States navy would want any of that.'

'I'm not speaking of the navy,' Ash said. 'The navy doesn't know I'm here. If the navy did I'd be facing a long line of officers with an even longer list of questions.'

Lenin did not smile. 'I repeat – what do you want?'

'The only way to end the war is to get America to help England, France and Russia beat Germany. But the only way to get America to help Russia is to kick out the Czar.'

After a moment Lenin said, 'You don't look young enough to believe in just wars.'

'Maybe it's because I'm American.'

'Maybe it's because you think I'm stupid enough to be entrapped in some sort of provocative scheme.'

Ash sipped his mineral water and motioned to the waiter for a wine list. 'I only know one thing for sure about you, Mr Lenin. You're not stupid. I'm talking on the square. Try to believe that. Besides, what could I possibly provoke *you* into doing?'

Ash was satisfied to see a note of interest in Lenin's eyes. He waited silently, until Lenin said, 'Go on, Mr Ash. I'm listening.'

'I'd like to get your assessment of the revolutionary situation in Petrograd, for a start. And then some advice about the Czar. What will happen in Russia in the next, say, two months?'

Lenin brought his fingers to his lips. 'My assessment, such as it is, taking into account how removed I am, is that the war has brought the socialist movement in Russia to a full stop. The moment the factory workers began producing munitions and the peasants shouldered the Czar's rifles, our cause lost its appeal. The same thing happened in Germany, and France and England. *Only* when the war is ended can we even begin to speak of revolution.'

'Our goals seem mutual,' Ash said, flipping casually through the wine list to hide his alarm. Lenin was considerably less optimistic about revolution than the supposedly learned Professor Taplinger and intelligence gatherers in the British Embassy in Petrograd. And if revolution was not a powerful threat it would be impossible to persuade the Czar and his family to leave . . .

'How is that, Mr Ash?'

'We both want to end the war, for our own reasons. I want to end it by removing the Czar. You want to end it *to* remove the Czar. We agree – '

Lenin banged the table and the silver jumped. *'No, we don't agree.* The worse the better, for me. The more killed on the battlefield, the angrier they'll be at home.'

Ash was ready to walk out of the restaurant. Lenin returned his gaze mildly. Ash shook his head. 'I thought I'd heard it all in Europe, but you are the most cynical . . .'

'Finish your sentence, Lieutenant Commander. Or do words fail you? Do you suppose that because I can sit in a fine restaurant and drink your wine that I'm a cretin who can't accept the truth of the revolution? Am I a semi-idiot who hopes that Czars and Kaisers will surrender their thrones without a fight? . . . I repeat, the worse the suffering the better the chances of the revolution. The more killed on the battlefield, the longer the war, the angrier the people.'

'But how long can *you* wait? How long can you sit around Zurich? How many years before the revolution passes you by? A whole new generation of young men and women who've never seen Lenin?'

Lenin shrugged, almost allowed himself a smile. 'Perhaps that's why I'm still talking to you . . . What advice or help do you want?'

'Tell me who I can talk to in Petrograd.'

'About what?'

'Demonstrating to the Czar that he should step down.'

'You're convinced I have a cell there, aren't you? I don't. The revolution is here in Zurich. In the library, believe it or not.'

'There must be someone I can contact in Petrograd.'

'Who do you know in Petrograd?'

'I know a few Russian diplomats and naval officers. Men I met in Portsmouth, New Hampshire, in 1905 during the Russo-Japanese peace negotiations, and again at the 1906 disarmament conference at The Hague.'

'You can be assured that the competent have long been relieved of their offices. The Imperial bureaucracy has been corrupted from the top down. Since the Czar resumed command of the army the Czarina Alexandra controls the ministries and appoints fools and thieves recommended by the monk Rasputin. Rasputin is the government now . . . Who else do you know?'

Ash hesitated. 'I have friends in the Imperial Ballet.'

'Procurers to the aristocracy,' Lenin said. 'Is that all?'

'I'm afraid so.'

'Wonderful. You're on various terms of intimacy with representatives of perhaps one per cent of the Russian people. Do you know any merchants?'

'I don't think so.'

'Intellectuals?'

'Maybe through the ballet.'

'Peasants?'

Ash thought of the drunken sledge drivers who had driven hunting parties to the bear caves in the countryside. 'Not really.'

'Workers?'

'I've toured some of your naval shipyards . . . Can you put me in contact with people who may know the state of the revolution inside Russia itself?'

'Don't be coy with me,' said Lenin. 'You want me to name a revolutionary.'

'One who will talk to me.'

Lenin looked up at the chandeliers. A waiter came running over. He waved the man away. Suddenly he smiled, as if savouring a private joke. 'Kirichenko.'

'Who's he?'

'Kirichenko is, if he's not been shot, an SR fighting squad leader.'

'Where do I find him?'

'He's underground. I imagine if you persisted in asking about him in the right places that he would find you. If he does, you have my permission to try to dissuade him from shooting you by mentioning our lunch together. Tell him I congratulate him if he's still alive. Tell him that if there is ever a revolution in Russia it will owe its rebirth to Kirichenko because Kirichenko stayed while the rest of us tucked our books under our arms and ran.'

The waiter arrived with the wine.

'Tell me,' asked Lenin, with a sly grin, 'Lieutenant Commander, have you ever *worked* for a living?'

'From the age of fifteen until I entered the Naval Academy I worked my way around the world on sailing ships.'

'Bourgeois adventuring isn't work.'

Ash put down his glass, reached across the table and laid his hand, palm up, beside Lenin's plate. 'Turn your hands over.' Lenin glanced at Ash's calloused palm and turned his own to the light. It was a strong hand, but untried. Ash said, 'You work on a ship and you don't notice politics at sea.'

'Nonsense. The sailors of the Imperial Navy have been the fiercest supporters of political revolution. Time and again they've defied their officers.'

'Maybe if they had less mutiny on their mind the Imperial Navy might have done better against the Japanese.'

Lenin flushed. 'The mutiny came *after* the defeats. Besides, they'd have beaten the Japanese if they'd been better led.'

'You sound like a patriot,' Ash remarked.

Lenin stared back, long and hard. 'If you don't understand Russian patriotism, you haven't a hope in hell of persuading anyone to leave – *including* the Czar.'

9

'Why the devil did you go to Zurich and Paris?' Admiral Innes grumbled as Ash neared the end of his report. 'I understood you were to deliver the King's message to the Kaiser and come home.'

'I had no specific orders, sir. I went where I went because I had to – '

'You almost got yourself killed – '

'Not because he didn't come straight back to London,' Ambassador Page interrupted. 'Go on, Ash.'

'I'll be operating alone and unofficially in Petrograd, sir. I've had to turn to friends and acquaintances to jury rig my own network to draw on in Russia. Now I believe I have connections with various people, including an Italian banker and his wife who's a Russian noblewoman. My friend Count Fasquelle has kindly written a letter of introduction to Sergei Gladishev, a Moscow millionaire who happens to be in the Kadet movement in the Duma – '

'What's the Kadet movement?' Admiral Innes put in.

'The Kadets are constitutional democrats. Gladishev could eventually be involved in a new government – '

'Good,' Page said.

'And as a dance correspondent for *Le Monde*,' Ash concluded his report, 'my old friend Chevalier Roland knows everyone worth knowing. He's going to Petrograd, as I figured he would be, to cover the ballet season.'

Innes's nose started twitching. 'Chevalier Roland is also foils champion of France. A very handy man in a scrap. The sort you'd want covering your back.'

'Then how come he's not in the army?'

110

'He lost his left arm at Verdun . . . '

'So you feel ready?' Page asked. Throughout their meeting, Innes had tended to challenge Ash and Page to support him.

'As ready as I will be, Mr Ambassador. I'm counting on tapping a few friends in Petrograd when I get there – if they're still around. The point is I'm not blundering into Russia all by myself. Nor will I have to depend entirely on Lord Exeter.'

'That's a blessing,' Innes agreed. He looked at Page and nodded. 'Well, you got back and that's what counts. Any idea why the Germans tried to kill you?'

'No, sir. Mostly bad guesses.'

'Well, the German army shouldn't be a problem in Russia,' the admiral said, standing up to go. 'I'm sailing to New York to report to Assistant Secretary Roosevelt. Mr Banks left last week. But Ambassador Page'll get you squared away. Good luck, Ash.'

When the admiral had gone Page handed Ash an envelope. 'King's equerry brought this for you this morning.'

Ash opened it. Written was an address in Belgravia. And the time, eight-thirty.

'Exeter?' Page asked.

'Sailing orders.'

Ash took the Luger to his gunmaker in New Bond Street. The seven-shot pistol had been developed some years earlier for the German army; the Luger was a dependable gun and, at thirty ounces, considerably lighter than the British Webley or a US Navy Colt.

When he gave his gunmaker the pistol it was eight and three-quarter inches long. When he returned that evening it was much smaller – only six inches long and less than twenty-five ounces; it could fit under his dress uniform tunic in a chamois holster in the small of his back. The chamois holster was necessary, the gunmaker explained, or his perspiration would rust the weapon.

'But you won't hit much at long range,' he warned, indicating the foreshortened barrel.

'At long range, I'll still have some options.'

He checked the mirror as he dressed that evening. The gun did not show, nor the fact that he had had his dress sabre ground to razor edges. Who was trying to kill him, or why, he didn't really know. But the next son of a bitch who tried at least was going to have his hands full.

The address in Belgravia was in a row of elegant town houses that twined the bend in a curving street with marble steps and creamy white columns lit by gas lamps. Ash knocked. The butler led him to the library. Lady Exeter put down her book.

'Good evening, Commander. I've been delegated to entertain you until my husband has finished his meeting with a rather dreary Royal Navy officer in the next room.'

Ash bowed over her hand. 'I hope it's a long meeting.'

Her extravagant red hair was piled high tonight; wisps escaping across her cheeks softened her stern face, and he thought she looked prettier than he'd remembered and more in her element in the city. She wore black silk.

'Commander,' she said with a quick smile, 'the Irish side of my family bequeathed me red hair and a fine ear for blarney.'

'I have a drop or two of French blood on my mother's side,' Ash said. 'It left me with a taste for claret and an eye for beauty.'

Lady Exeter turned to her butler. 'Graham, bring this gentleman a whisky. And please tell His Lordship that I am growing impatient.'

'Have I offended you?' Ash asked when the butler had left.

112

'I imagine you can't help yourself, but I find your propri-
etary attitude toward women not over flattering – one feels
like a candidate for a very large club with an undiscriminat-
ing membership committee.'

'I'm sorry – '

'Good God, you meant it . . . forgive me, a friend was
killed in France today. I'm in no mood to entertain. I was
against the war in the beginning and now I find myself praying for total victory . . . Where the *hell* are the Americans?'

They sat in stiff silence until the whisky came.

'I understand you were in Germany.'

Ash said nothing, but was surprised and angered that
someone had apparently told her more than he should
have.

'I have no idea why you went, but I am curious about the
Germans. Are they really starving?'

'The best hotel in Munich had no coffee.'

'What about the ordinary people?'

'They looked tired. The soldiers looked tough as nails.'

Lord Exeter came in, apologizing for being detained,
enormous in evening clothes. In his own home he was
much more direct than when Ash had met him at Sandringham. 'Hello, Ash. My dear, could you excuse us? We'll be an
hour.'

'Dinner at ten,' she said, and, turning to Ash, 'We have a
friend from Petrograd staying with us that I thought you
might enjoy meeting.'

Ash watched her go. She walked with an erect carriage,
and the billows of her black gown seemed hard put to keep
up. When he felt Exeter's eyes on him he said, 'Is it possible
that someone in your organization is a traitor?'

'I don't know what organization you're talking about,'
Exeter said, 'but if you're referring to my efforts to assist the
King in the rescue of the Czar then the answer is no. My
organization, as you call it, consists of myself, you and a

chap from the Royal Navy who happens to be distantly related to the King and has agreed to lay on the cruiser.'

'I'm referring to British Secret Service. I've had you checked out.' . . . Up to his eyeballs in espionage was how Ambassador Page had put it about Lord Exeter.

Exeter shrugged. 'So far as I am concerned I am performing a personal service for His Majesty. Just as you are.'

'The King knows I had to report to Ambassador Page. Can you – ?'

'I am not similarly bound. I report to no one. Now I want you to meet this navy man, and I can assure you he is not a traitor . . . I only brought him in this afternoon.' He looked puzzled. 'Why did you ask?'

'Somebody tried to kill me after I saw the Kaiser. Somebody knows we talked.'

'Ah. Perhaps it is the Kaiser who has a traitor.'

'Perhaps.'

'Or has changed his mind?'

Ash had thought of that. 'I'll find out in Petrograd if his agent doesn't contact me.'

'Mercurial fellow, the Kaiser . . . Were I His Majesty I might have looked for another way to protect my cruiser . . .'

Lord Exeter moved some books, opened a wall safe, pulled a slim leather slipcase from the dark inside and handed it to Ash.

Ash opened it and spread the contents on Exeter's desk, a fantasy of polished marquetry. There was a letter of credit with the Russian & English Bank.

'What limit?' Ash asked.

'None.'

Ash looked at him. 'None?'

'Merely present that code number and take what you need.'

Ash opened a thick envelope. It was filled with British pound notes and Russian roubles.

'A thousand pounds,' Exeter said as he started to count it.

Ash counted it anyway. A thousand pounds was more by some than his yearly pay as a lieutenant commander in the United States Navy. He counted the roubles; the Czar's face was on each, the Imperial double-headed eagle on the back. Another thousand pounds at the current exchange.

'I need a personal letter and *laissez-passer* from the Russian Embassy,' Ash said.

'I'll take care of it,' said Exeter. 'We don't want you stopped at the frontier.' Ash was grateful not to have to explain. Taplinger had probably told him already what he had been doing in Zurich.

Exeter said, 'The International Sleeping Car Travel Agents are empowered to book you any form of transport at any time on account. And included there is my card with my Petrograd address. I'll be along soon. I've got factories up the Neva that need attention.'

'Your own?'

'I had to leave the army to take over the family business when my brother died a number of years ago. I'm often in Russia. We produce munitions. The fuel shortages are killing us, I can assure you.'

Ash wondered if Lady Exeter travelled with him.

'At the risk of repeating the obvious, you are not under any circumstances to approach British Ambassador Buchanan. And please don't even go near the British Embassy, except when it's time for His Majesty's cruiser. Then you will contact Captain Cromwell, who would appreciate a week's notice if possible.'

Lord Exeter went to a door and returned with a tall Royal Navy captain who looked Ash over with a disapproving stare. 'Frankly I fail to see why one of our own can't conduct this mission.'

'It was His Majesty's wish that Commander Ash carry out his plan, Captain.'

'All the same . . .' He shook hands reluctantly and said, 'The cruiser will fly a plain green ensign beneath the Union Jack when she enters Murmansk. You will please instruct your German contacts that their U-boats should do the same. Any German boat not flying the green ensign will be sunk.'

'May I suggest white, sir.'

'What?'

'White. So they can see it at night.'

'All right. If you insist. White it is. They should be of sufficient dimension to be seen at a thousand yards. That's all.' He turned and headed for the door.

'Sir?' Ash called. 'Is Lieutenant Skelton still serving in the Baltic?'

'That's not the sort of information I'm likely to bandy about, Commander. Why do you ask?'

'Skelton and I played some polo at the Royal Durber in India. I recall he has a submarine based at Reval. I'll be close by. I thought maybe I'd stop in and see him if he's still there – he wasn't sunk, was he?'

Cromwell almost softened. 'He's well. I'll tell him you said hello. Good evening, Exeter.'

'Thank you for coming, Captain Cromwell.'

Exeter walked him to the door and Ash returned the money and letters to the slipcase, thinking he was lucky he had a close friend much closer to Petrograd than Murmansk, with his own submarine.

'He'll be back in Petrograd a week or so after you arrive,' Exeter said. 'Shall we join the ladies? My wife has a delicious little number visiting from Petrograd. A ballerina.'

Ash followed him apprehensively, hoping it wasn't one of Tamara's friends.

116

'Can I assume your wife knows nothing about your work?'

'Nothing,' Exeter said.

Lady Exeter was sitting by the fire in a drawing room with the ballerina. Exeter made the introductions. Her name was Vera. Vera Sedovina. Ash didn't know her; she was too young for Tamara to have introduced her, only a girl.

She was tall for a dancer, slim, and her hair was blond. She had a little bump on her nose which would keep her from being a great beauty, but there was a feeling of vulnerability and contrasting certainty about her that made Ash think she had at least the personality to be a great dancer.

Her eyes were startling ice blue. She must have Swedish or Finnish blood, but so slim, perhaps a Dane. She said hello with a light accent. A pretty voice, yet quite serious. Ash figured she was about sixteen and wondered what she was doing in London; no ballet had been performed in London since 1914.

Lady Exeter seemed to cherish the girl like a newly acquired oil painting – something exotic by the French. 'Mademoiselle Sedovina,' she said, 'has come to London to dance in the Christmas Pantomimes at Covent Garden.'

He nodded. There were small roles for balletic dancers in the children's shows that would be starting in a week. Ash asked if this was her first trip to London; she said it was.

'Commander Ash is off to Petrograd,' Exeter said. 'I've been recommending restaurants and gypsy bands.'

She looked at Exeter gravely. 'The restaurants have become very expensive since the food shortages.'

Graham came in and announced dinner.

Vera seemed awed by the Exeters' lavish dining room. They clustered at one end of a long table, and Exeter turned somewhat grandfatherly around her, inquiring if she liked

117

the wine and the first course and then, when the main dish was served, remarking, 'I'll have you know that bird on your plate met his demise at the hand of Commander Ash. His Majesty insisted I take a few home . . . Have you many friends in Petrograd, Commander?'

Ash saw where he was leading and went along. 'A few. I suspect most of them will be at the front . . . But I'll be meeting plenty of people. My embassy has asked me to survey popular sentiment in Petrograd concerning the war . . .'

'They are fed up,' Vera said forcefully. 'The war is a disaster. The people have suffered too long – '

Lady Exeter interrupted. 'I doubt the people Commander Ash intends to talk to have suffered as much.'

Ash agreed. 'I've orders to speak to military officers and people in government. Unfortunately it is always hard to find people who haven't been primed to answer in a specific way.'

'Vera,' said Exeter, 'your step-father's a *tapeur*, isn't he?'

'Yes. He plays the piano at Society balls.'

Ash noticed that she laid a disapproving stress on 'Society'.

'Could Commander Ash call on him – the *tapeurs* know everything, Ash. Everything going on at court and the city. Handy chap to know.'

'He likes Americans,' Vera said, looking Ash straight in the eye for the first time since they had been introduced.

'I'd like very much to meet him.'

'I'll give you a note to him,' she said. 'His name is Vadim Mikhailov.'

'Vadim Mikhailov.'

Then she added gravely, 'But you really ought to meet real people too. My step-father can't help you there. He's too much of a snob.'

* * *

Ash was still worried about British Secret Service meddling when he started home to his hotel at midnight, armed with Exeter's cash and letters of credit and Vera Sedovina's promise to write her father. Could the attack in Germany have been sparked by German knowledge of Exeter's role in the King's mission? Spies watched spies, after all . . . Maybe he ought to do something about it . . .

His initial suspicion reminded Ash again that the Secret Service could incorporate the King's mission into some larger plan. And were either conjecture true, or even if the attack had emanated from within the Kaiser's suite, Ash would end up the ignorant victim, rather like a courier assigned a sealed despatch pouch with a time bomb inside. He turned back and took up station in a doorway a few houses along the curve from Lord Exeter's residence. It would be interesting to see who visited Exeter after he had left. Or whether Exeter went calling at this unlikely hour.

He stood an hour, getting cold, watching the lights go out behind Exeter's curtains. At last the house was dark and no one had come. They could have telephoned, of course, but it was Ash's experience that the Exeters of the world preferred to speak face to face. He gave it another half hour, to see if His Lordship came out. Then, just as he was about to give it up, the front door opened a crack. A shadow slipped out, and the door closed.

Ash's first thought was Lady Exeter. Exeter himself couldn't have squeezed through the space. But as she passed his hiding place, Ash noticed the peculiar, almost comical waddle that dancers, particularly young ones, walk with, and realized to his surprise that it was Vera Sedovina who'd gone prowling the darkened streets of London.

Ash followed, intrigued, and a little concerned for the girl's safety. She walked swiftly, stopping only at the occasional intersection to get her bearings, then hurrying on. She walked all the way to the brightly lighted vegetable markets around Covent Garden and went directly into a busy pub open to the late-night market workers.

Ash watched her sit with a young man, a Russian seaman, perhaps, by his clothes and broad Slavic face. Her boy friend, he thought, but the way she sat apart from him seemed to negate that unlikely possibility. She talked a long time, steadily, as if imparting information. The young man listened. When at last they parted, Ash followed him to a seamen's hotel near Euston station.

Ash telephoned Ambassador Page, who dispatched a pair of State Department operatives, and by morning they knew that the seaman *was* Russian, a Bolshevik at that, and shipping out the next day to New York. Which meant, Ash had to conclude, that Vera Sedovina was very likely a Bolshevik courier. And that seemed a very handy thing to know . . . And more valuable, perhaps, than Lord Exeter's true allegiance.

Ash's final business in London was a charade for the benefit of Captain Wesley, representing the United States Navy, and Ambassador Page's chargé d'affaires. Unknown to them, both men were being set up as witnesses to prove that Ash had gone off on his own in the event something went wrong in Russia.

Ash reported to Page's office. Page, Wesley and the chargé were waiting. Page said, 'Good morning, Commander. Something very unusual has come up, but before we go into it, let me be the first to congratulate you.' He pushed himself painfully up from his desk and extended his hand. 'Cable arrived this morning. You've been promoted to full commander.'

For a moment Ash forgot why he was there. Full commander at thirty-six! Damn near unheard of. A glance at Captain Wesley told Ash that Wesley thought so too. Wesley had been forty-six when he'd made commander, fifty-three for captain. And by now Wesley must know he would never wear the broad stripe of a commodore whereas Ash's promotion made him a candidate for flag rank before he was fifty.

'Commander?' Page smiled. 'Are you all right?'

Suddenly, with such a career boost, Ash had a lot to lose, which, he reflected, was a feeling he hadn't had in a long time. 'Yes, sir,' he said honestly. 'Thank you. I'm very surprised and very pleased. In fact I feel sort of rescued.'

Captain Wesley willed himself to step forward and shake Ash's hand. 'Congratulations, Commander.' Ash admired the effort. No line officer, which Wesley had been for years, liked political pull. That was the dark side of the windfall. If Ash hadn't made any new enemies in the navy, he'd certainly made no friends among the blue-water men. Nonetheless, if he managed to pull off this mission to Russia, there'd be no stopping him, and 'Admiral Ash' had a heady ring to a man who a week ago had been a diplomatic courier with his sights set no higher than executive officer on somebody else's cruiser.

Of course Page had engineered it, and probably with the help of the President or Assistant Secretary of the Navy Franklin Roosevelt to get it so fast. And a wise notion for the sake of the mission. Europeans were extremely conscious of rank, and the Russians most of all. Commander put him on the level of an army lieutenant colonel, a rank the Russians would take seriously, the rank, by their lights, of an aristocrat.

'Sit down, both of you,' Page said, collapsing into his chair like a bundle of sticks and pausing to catch his breath. 'Ash's good fortune couldn't come at a better time, don't you agree, Captain Wesley?'

'Yes, sir. Shall I tell him, or will you?'

'Go ahead.'

Wesley turned to Ash. 'The new American ambassador

to Russia has asked that his daughter be allowed to join him in Petrograd. He's got plenty of political pull back in Ohio or some damned place so he's used to getting his own way. The girl is already in London and leaving for Petrograd this afternoon. You'll escort her.'

Ash glanced at Page. A good cover.

'Further,' Wesley continued, 'you'll be attached to the Petrograd embassy to – '

'Informally,' Page interrupted, 'you will still be attached, officially, to my embassy here in London.'

'Yes,' Captain Wesley said. 'Informally, just in case we've got to evacuate women and children from Petrograd.'

'Evacuate?' Ash asked.

'Reports from Petrograd are not good. We don't really know what's going on politically in Russia but it's our general feeling that it wouldn't hurt to have a few extra officers in Petrograd in case we have to evacuate our women and children. Now, while you're there, you can make yourself useful meeting Russian naval officers. Inspect their Baltic fleet if you can – although I'm not really sure why you'd want to – get a look before the Germans sink the rest of it, I suppose. Also, might as well look into the Russians' new torpedo boats. They've got something new and fast and we ought to know more about it . . .'

From the corner of his eye Ash noticed Page fidgeting with his papers. Apparently he had so taken in Wesley that the captain felt obliged to make sure Ash stayed very busy while away. Wesley paused, running down, and finally asked, 'Everything understood?'

'Yes, sir.'

'Steamer and train tickets will be issued. You'll have access to embassy funds at major stops along the way – Christiania, Stockholm, Haparanda.'

Page cleared his throat.

'Did you want to add anything to Ash's instructions, Mr Ambassador?'

'Yes, Captain, thank you . . . Ash, keep your eyes open in Russia. I'd like some more accurate reports on these rumours – '

'But may I interrupt, sir?' Captain Wesley said. 'Don't step on any toes in the Petrograd embassy, Ash. Whatever you do. They've got their own military attachés to gather intelligence, don't you agree, Mr Ambassador?'

'Sure, Captain Wesley. I'd imagine the American ambassador has his own operatives assessing the situation, though one might wonder from their reports – all right, listen to this, Ash. Why don't *you* send *me* the occasional private note in the embassy pouch or via the King's Messenger. The Foreign Office will forward it to me. The King's Messenger comes from Petrograd every two weeks. And if you send it to me directly instead of through navy channels to Captain Wesley there can't be any suggestion of stepping on toes . . . How does that sound to you, Captain Wesley?'

'Sounds all right, sir,' Wesley said slowly, his tone denying his words.

A knock at the door. When Wesley looked toward it, Page gave Ash a wink. It was fine cover, giving Ash complete freedom of movement, not to mention one that would allow Page to deny any connection with Ash if something went wrong.

His secretary came in. 'Miss Hazzard is here, Mr Ambassador.'

'Ambassador Hazzard's daughter,' Page explained. 'Show her in.'

Ash had to smile. She looked fifteen going on twenty-eight, and adorable. Ambassador Page introduced her and then said, 'Commander Ash will escort you to Petrograd.'

Full commander, Ash thought. Same old address, but a big jump from lieutenant commander.

Catherine looked at him again. She was fair and blonde, petite, a little shy, and seemed very serious. Her blue eyes, which were enormous, suggested strength and intelligence and Ash thought of her as a girlish version of Lord Exeter's fiery wife, though as yet perhaps unformed.

'Commander Ash is familiar with Europe. You'll find him an interesting guide, I'm sure. And *I'll* rest easier knowing he'll deliver my fellow ambassador's daughter safe and sound to Petrograd.'

Captain Wesley was frowning, perhaps recalling the night he'd waited outside the *comtesse*'s house in Paris and wondering whether this wasn't a duty better given to a married man.

Catherine asked, 'How long will the journey take, Commander Ash?'

'We have to go the long way because of the war, up the Swedish coast around the Gulf of Bothnia. Figure two days on the steamer from Newcastle to Christiania, Norway. And five to seven days on the train. If we're lucky.'

'What would delay us if we're not lucky?'

Ash, forgetting she was a kid, said, 'German U-boats in the North Sea. And Russian border guards at the Grand Duchy of Finland.'

'Don't you be frightened, Catherine,' Page interrupted.

'I'm not frightened.'

Ash saw she meant it, but Page didn't, and went on reassuringly.

'Well, you shouldn't be. The Germans don't sink Norwegian mailboats, except by accident, and besides, something tells me this is Commander Ash's lucky week. Wouldn't you say so, Kenneth? A promotion, a trip to Russia, and a pretty girl to share the ride?'

'Yes, sir. It surely is . . .'

Lucky? Maybe more than lucky. He was moving again, right into the thick of war and revolution. It wasn't sea duty,

124

no berth on a man o' war. In fact, if he pulled it off cleverly, he'd slip the Czar out before a shot was fired. But it was action nonetheless.

Lucky? Maybe the chance of a lifetime for America to stop the war. Maybe a chance to heal himself of lost duels, and lost loves. Exciting, but frightening too. Because whichever way it went, whatever happened, win or lose, would happen in Petrograd, in full view of its reigning ballerina, Tamara Tishkova. And the season was about to begin.

BOOK II
Rasputin

10

The twelve-year-old Czarevich Alexis, heir to the Imperial Russian Empire, lay screaming in a room full of expensive toys. His four sisters watched him, young girls, the eldest twenty. Alexis's mother held his hand while her hollow eyes darted between his swollen knee and the door. She glimpsed her reflection in the shiny mirror the boy used to dress in his beloved uniforms. Twelve years of dreadful anticipation had made her old.

Doom hovered capriciously; without warning a bump, a mild blow, a child's fall made a bruise which bled inside, and bled and bled. The blood collected in a nearby joint – his knee this time – and filling it, squeezed his nerves. There was no pain like it in the world, no torture so refined, and when it happened the little boy, her baby, screamed until he fainted. Unable to watch his contorted face anymore, or his poor swollen knee, and wondering would this be the time he died, the Czarina Alexandra stared at the door, waiting for her friend Father Gregory Rasputin to save him.

Czarevich Alexis's sisters, the grand duchesses Olga, Tatiana, Marie and Anastasia, felt grief tinged with guilt. It had started, they thought, with a pillow fight the night before. Alexis had egged them into it, pleading in his way for an unguarded moment of childish fun, and they had given in, playing carefully, fearfully; in terror of a nosebleed. Excited, Alexis had led a chase through their dressing room and had careened through a curtain and smacked into their silver bathtub. The bruise was dark, just above his knee. The blood inside was filling the joint, building pressure on the nerves, and starting to bend his knee into a locked, rigid angle the grand duchesses knew well from past accidents. The tighter the angle, the louder the boy's cries.

Anastasia started his train set and wound up his floating model warships, but he was too far gone to be distracted by the locomotive whistles, the miniature gate crossings, the tiny church bells or the whirr of the ship propellers. And at last, she too, turned from his suffering face, and watched the door, waiting.

Father Gregory's shadow fell across the threshold. He was immensely tall, with long black hair and a thick beard and as he paused, sweeping the room with piercing grey eyes, he filled them with hope. The grand duchesses saw in his gaze that Rasputin knew they were at fault, knew but forgave them. The Czarina thanked God he had come.

Rasputin let them stay. Whatever helped calm the child would help stop the bleeding. He knelt by the Czarevich's cot; he was so tall that kneeling he was still taller than Anastasia. The Czarina knelt beside him to pray. He let her do that for a while, best to calm her too, to calm everything in the room. Toys were clattering on the train board. He pointed a long blunt finger at it and Grand Duchess Tatiana, the great beauty of the four sisters with dark, wide-set eyes and perfect lips, stopped the toys.

Quiet smothered the room, quiet but for the boy's whimpers. His strength was failing. He would faint soon, blessed relief from the pain. But Rasputin did not want him to faint. Not yet. Relief from the pain was not enough. It would make his mother happy for the moment, but only for the moment. The boy had to be conscious for Rasputin to work his magic. If he fainted, the bleeding inside would continue. And Rasputin had to stop the bleeding first, before it killed him. *He had to stop the bleeding.*

He spoke, his voice deep, sonorous, rumbling and steady; it was a voice he brought from inside his chest, and it calmed. It did indeed. He prayed aloud for the benefit of the Czarina, who believed that God could only hear her through Rasputin. And then he spoke to the boy after motioning to Tatiana to dim the lights. She glided about the room, regal as the Empress, beautiful as the stars, achingly unattainable. For the moment.

'*Alexis . . .*'

The boy's eyes opened at the sound of Rasputin's voice and rolled feebly, searching. The monk's eyes seemed like deep pools in which he had been taught to swim. Float. Drift. Forget.

'*Alexis . . .*'

Rasputin, the monk, was enormous, shaggy like a bear, his nose enormous. Deep lines scored his face, and a boy might be afraid of him if it were not for his voice. Rich, liquid, clear as the Siberian air, rumbling like benevolent thunder from a storm that cooled a summer's day, Rasputin's voice promised thrilling stories, and peace where there was pain.

Alexis thought he smelled funny, like the kennels where the wolfhounds lived mixed up with his sisters' perfume; not quite as stinky as the wolfhounds, not quite as nice as his sisters, but somewhere in the middle like . . . like a Rasputin. But when he hurt, the awful way he hurt now, and when he was frightened that this time he would die, then Rasputin smelled wonderful, sounded even better . . .

Alexis tried to speak. He could hardly move his tongue. Rasputin leaned close and put his big hairy ear to his mouth and said, 'What?'

'Tell me a story.'

The monk's voice made wondrous vibrations in the mattress. 'That is what I came for.'

Alexis wondered through his pain which story would it be. Maybe the secret story, the one he wasn't supposed to tell, and didn't. About how while his father was so busy

131

commanding the army that Alexis himself should be made Czar and his mother regent until Alexis grew up. No, not while his mother was listening. He didn't like the story anyway. He'd rather be a soldier than a Czar . . .

Rasputin laid his big hand on the boy's chest and another on his chilly forehead and felt the little body strain, like tight guitar strings. The Czarina was staring at his hands. People thought his powers came from his eyes and hands and surely they were good, but his power, God's power, was in his voice, and the boy knew it. Felt it . . .

Rasputin spoke his name again, '*Alexis*,' and then he told him how once he had walked all the way from Siberia to Greece. Two thousand miles across Russia and into the beyond – to a monastery on Mount Athos. Alexis knew the story, had heard it again and again. But two thousand miles was a long way and anything could happen on such a long walk. Tonight Rasputin told him about a camel with gold teeth, smiling occasionally at the weeping Czarina.

A camel alone was a delight – a horse with a hump – and the boy loved to hear about camels. A camel with gold teeth, and how the beast got such teeth. It held his interest, and so kept him awake to hear the soothing, mesmerizing tones of Rasputin's voice.

Inside the little body, Rasputin sensed, the vessels that carried blood grew strong when he was calm, and weak when he was afraid. He didn't know why – and he didn't particularly care why – but fear, he was certain, made bleeding. And doctors made fear. They frightened the Czarevich almost to death. It was a joke, a very funny joke, at which only Rasputin could laugh. The more worried the doctors, the more they frightened the boy and the more they frightened the boy, the more he bled.

At last the boy began to fall asleep. Rasputin watched him closely, making sure it was not a faint but real sleep which came from well-being, and happiness and trust in his

132

saviour and friend, Rasputin. He rose wearily from the bed, made the sign of the cross for the Czarina's sake and walked quietly from the room.

They brought him a chair and gave him wine. He sipped at it, resting, letting them bask in his power. He truly was tired. There were energies he transferred from his body to the boy's in ways he himself didn't understand, but they drained him.

The Czarina came tiptoeing back from the boy's room. 'He's still sleeping,' she whispered.

'He will sleep,' Rasputin intoned. 'He will sleep. The bleeding is done.'

'Thank God.'

'God has heard our prayers.'

She sank down beside his chair and took his hand and pressed it to her cheek. The grand duchesses gathered around them, the long vigil over. He felt like their uncle; welcome in their house, this magnificent palace, trusted and loved. He said, 'I had a dream last night.'

They looked at him expectantly, and the Czarina pressed him to tell the dream.

'When the German artillery shoot at our Russian soldiers, our soldiers should run forward *under* the flight of the shells, which will explode harmlessly behind them.' With his hand he inscribed the arc of an artillery shell; he made it look like a thrown rock.

'I will tell my husband,' the Czarina said.

Rasputin looked at her. 'I also think that General Brusilov must be warned again not to advance another step. Innocent Russian lives are being wasted . . . Purishkevich attacked me again in the Duma . . .' He laughed. 'The Duma – dogs barking.'

'But their barking keeps other dogs quiet.'

Rasputin beamed. It was a phrase he had taught her years ago. He pulled some scraps of paper from his pockets on which he had written names. 'I met a good woman today. Her husband, a religious man, has waited years for a promotion. He works in the Admiralty. Do you suppose you could help him?'

'Of course, Father Gregory.'

He pressed the papers in her hand, then returned to the subject of the Duma. 'Sometimes I fear your enemies in the Duma will kill me.'

'I won't permit that,' she said. 'God would never forgive me.'

'If they do kill me,' Rasputin intoned, 'everything will be swept away . . . even the boy's throne . . .'

She heard him, and believed him.

11

Snow chased their steamer up the Christiania fjord. Inland, it looked like a blizzard and when the cab driver said there was talk of cancelling trains Ash decided to spend the night at the Grand, a modern hotel overlooking an open square up the hill from the harbour.

He counted himself fortunate to get a small suite. Christiania, the capital of the new nation of Norway, was riding a crest of war profits. The small fishing and trading town had exploded into a sort of Klondike gold rush city and the hotels were packed.

The neutral Norwegians were shipping at high wartime rates for the Allies and supplying canned meats to the German army. Consequently, Ash noticed, the dining room of the Grand Hotel was crowded with rich old gents and pretty young girls.

Catherine, so obviously American, and he in his dress blues drew a good deal of attention at dinner. A bewhiskered sea captain sent over a bottle of champagne, and several men asked Catherine to dance, bowing first to Ash for his permission.

When she came back to their table Catherine reported that the Norwegians favoured the Allies.

'What do you expect them to tell you when they've got their arms around you?' She'd been good company on the steamer and he knew by now that he had permission to tease her.

'No, it's because the Germans have torpedoed so many of their ships. And they asked me when the United States was going to enter the war.'

135

'What did you tell them?'

'I told them our position was quite similar to Norway's,' she answered seriously.

Ash gave her a smile of approval . . . Catherine's mother had become sick in Petrograd and was on her way home to Columbus, Ohio, via the Trans-Siberian Railway and the Pacific. Catherine was supposed to take her place as her father's hostess – a considerable job in a city as formal as Petrograd; still, if tonight was any example, Ambassador Hazzard's daughter would by no means embarrass him in Russia . . . Ash caught her giving him an appraising look, part girlish curiosity, part womanly speculation. He was flattered, and intrigued; of course she was very young, but she was also already a real beauty, and her rather grave manner often tended to make her seem more mature than she perhaps was. Extracting the Czar was going to be complicated enough without seduction of, or by – Ash couldn't predict which – the US ambassador's extremely lovely and precocious sixteen-year-old daughter. Quickly he short-circuited that notion by remarking how anxious he was to get to Petrograd to see his old friend Tamara Tishkova dance at the Maryinski Theatre. True. With a ticket from Chevalier Roland.

Catherine was, literally, wide-eyed. 'A ballerina? Did you meet her in Petrograd? Or in Paris?'

Ash had neglected to mention, of course, that when he'd last heard, Tamara had finally permitted the Romanov Grand Duke Valery to install her in her own mansion on the banks of the Neva River.

'Where'd you meet her?' Catherine persisted.

'Portsmouth, New Hampshire, as a matter of fact.'

'How'd you meet a Russian ballerina in New Hampshire?'

Ash stood up. 'Bedtime. Early train to Stockholm.'

'Come on, Commander, how'd you meet her?'

The dining room had begun to roar. The Norwegians looked as if they had settled in for a long night's drinking. Ash waved his thanks to the sea captain who'd sent the bottle. 'I met Tamara in nineteen hundred and five at the Russian-Japanese peace conference. I was naval aide to President Roosevelt's negotiator. Now to bed. You're falling asleep.'

'What was *she* doing in Portsmouth, New Hampshire?'

'Tamara was . . . along for the ride, you might say.'

'Well, are you still . . . are you going to marry her?'

'It seems she has her sights set a little higher than the navy.'

'How high?'

'I really am going to bed,' said Ash, suddenly very unhappy with the direction of the talk. How high? Higher, damn it, than he had ever been able to offer.

The Stockholm train pushed a rotary snowplough out of the Christiania station. They had a compartment to themselves, but the dining car was crowded and they found themselves sharing a table with a shabby-looking Russian.

He spoke good English and turned out to be quite talkative. Before the train had climbed past the first farms above Christiania, he had introduced himself and told what he did and where he was going.

His name was Protopopov – no relation to the Czar's incompetent Minister of the Interior, he hastened to assure them – and he was heading home to Moscow from a sales trip for a Russian match factory that had been built by a Scottish manufacturer on the upper Neva River above Petrograd. British investors, he said, were attracted to the location by the cheap labour and the waterpower and by the Russian government's wise investment incentives; the only difficulty was the natural laziness of the Russian worker.

Ash asked, 'How can you sell matches abroad while Russia's at war?'

'Russia needs to trade for currency to buy arms. Our factories are a disgrace. I mean, we can't produce enough arms.'

'How come you're not in the army?' Catherine asked.

Protopopov responded with an enormous, slow shrug that took Ash back to the Russia he remembered; the gesture seemed to marry European sophistication and Oriental fatalism. 'There are ways not to be drafted . . . if you know important people. But what I do is necessary – as good to pay for rifles as shoot them. Yes? The peasants at the front have no weapons. They're told to pick up the rifle when the man carrying it is shot. It is criminal. If you can believe the truth of such a story.'

'What if the Russian army just quits fighting?'

'They won't,' Protopopov answered gloomily. 'The Russian army is a peasant army and the Russian peasant knows how to suffer.'

'What does that have to do with it?'

'Suffer? There's only one way to suffer. You wait. And our peasant soldiers can wait longer than the Germans.'

'What kind of a city is Petrograd?' Catherine asked Protopopov after several earlier questions had failed to cheer him up.

'Petrograd is a pit of corruption.'

Catherine looked astonished. She turned to Ash. 'You've been there before, Commander. Do you agree?'

'Not as recently as Mr Protopopov, but I think it's the most beautiful city I've ever seen.'

Protopopov snorted disagreement. 'A swamp.'

Ash said, 'Remember Mr Protopopov told us he was born in Moscow. So asking him about Petrograd is like asking a man from Chicago what he thinks of New York.'

'You haven't seen Petrograd since Rasputin's taken power.'

Catherine nodded. 'That's the weird monk father wrote about.'

'Rasputin is a pig.' Protopopov turned red and his lips actually started quivering under his thin moustache. 'Actually, he's a monster.'

'What does he do that's so – ?'

'Rasputin controls the Czarina. She's German already and the monk corrupts – ' He paused and reconsidered and continued more calmly. 'There are rumours that she . . .' He glanced at Catherine, '. . . has been corrupted by him. Terrible stories. And some people believe them and think that she is betraying Russia to Germany. They say that Rasputin forces her to appoint ministers he selects. Corrupt incompetents and fools. And she forces the Czar to do things Rasputin tells her and the Czar goes along because he's busy leading the army, which he is incapable of doing-or so I am told.' He seemed uneasy.

'Sounds to me like the Czar's as silly as the rest of the kings who got Europe into this stupid war,' said Catherine.

'It would be better not to talk that way when you get to Russia,' Protopopov told her. 'The police are everywhere.'

'Don't worry, I'll be a good guest. But Commander, don't you find it hard as an American having to put up with royalty over here? My father says some of them couldn't get elected dog catcher back in Ohio.'

Ash was watching a pair of Swedish peasants trying to pry a sledge out of a snowdrift beside the tracks. One had his shoulder to the sledge, the other was beating a shaggy pony with a stick.

'Like it or not,' Ash said, 'royalty are the centre of social, military, political and cultural life in Europe. The Kaiser's tastes in architecture and art, his brand of patriotism are Germany's; the King of England is the pillar of the English aristocracy, who control Britain's wealth; and the Czar rules a hundred and eighty million Russian peasants who've been raised to think Nicholas II is their direct link to God.'

'That's got to change,' Protopopov blurted.

Ash looked at him sharply. That was very dangerous talk on a train to Russia. He said, 'But your royalty have a power greater than anything Miss Hazzard or I know back home. If they ever go they'll leave a huge vacuum in Europe. Who knows what would fill it.'

Catherine said, 'The United States will. Don't you agree, Commander Ash?'

Who knew what senator's vote the ambassador's daughter might someday control with her serious smile? So Ash said, 'Not without a bigger navy.' But his private thoughts were much more on the Czar, his removal without chaos and getting the US into the war on the side of the Allies.

Swedish customs officials boarded the train at the Norwegian frontier with elaborate questionnaires and strict warnings about imports. Ash presented a diplomatic *laissez-passer* Ambassador Page had procured from the Swedish Embassy, then went back to the baggage car to prevent any accidental inspection of his bachelor chest. On the way back, he noticed that the Swedes were still scrutinizing Protopo-pov's satchels. Matchboxes were spilled all over the seats.

Why, if he was selling Russian matches abroad, was he returning to Russia with matches, Swedish customs demanded to know. Could it be that he was importing Norwegian matches into Sweden?

Protopopov patiently showed them the Cyrillic Russian lettering on the matchboxes. 'I am not permitted to sell these samples. I must return the samples. I can only take orders.' He showed them his order book, pages filled with neat Cyrillic letters and Arabic numbers.

Eventually he must have convinced the customs men, for

the train started the two-hundred-mile leg across lower Sweden to Stockholm. Catherine became silent and gazed out the window at the snow, the fir trees on the gentle slopes and the frozen lakes.

In Stockholm they changed to a sleeper bound north up the coast of the Gulf of Bothnia, the northern arm of the Baltic Sea. Russian Finland lay a short boat trip across the water, but here in the Baltic the naval situation between the Allies and Germany was reversed.

The Baltic was a German sea. The Czar's navy hid in port and German squadrons controlled the surface, except for a handful of brave, even lunatic, British submariners – Ash's friend Rodney Skelton among them – who attacked German shipping from the shallow depths. The railway took the long way round.

The terrain, broken occasionally by small towns and villages, remained the same for the rest of daylight and was the same the following morning when the sun finally came up at eleven. It sloped gently to the east, down to the gulf-green fir trees, white birches, rivers and lakes flattened under snow and ice. The sun hung low on the horizon, barely clearing the treetops and lighting a spectacularly coloured dawn that kept on looking like dawn even as the afternoon approached and the train neared the Finnish border. Ash had never been so far north – fifteen degrees from the Arctic Circle, higher on the planet than most of Alaska. The train tracks ended at Haparanda on the bank of the Tornea River. Outside the customs building sleighs were waiting that carried two people each, with luggage.

The drivers cracked their whips and they started through the streets of the town – packed snow tracks between frame houses – Ash and Catherine's sleigh in the lead. The cold, the wind and pale sun were exhilarating after the hours on the train.

Suddenly the sleigh swooped down on to the frozen river.

141

The horse broke into a fast trot, heading for a windswept island in the middle a quarter mile away. '*Cold*,' Catherine said between clenched teeth, 'but isn't this beautiful?'

Ash pulled the lap robe over their legs. The sun glinted in her hair, and when the sleigh lurched she took hold of his arm; her eyes darted everywhere – the broad river, the low island, the forested slopes on the other side and the train of sleighs behind.

'Look!' A long line of freight sledges was crossing the river upstream and the sun etched their silhouettes darkly against the snow.

The horse broke into a canter, gathering momentum for the banks of the island. Catherine grabbed Ash's arm with both hands, laughed excitedly as it scrambled up the slope and dragged the bouncing sleigh to a sudden halt in front of a wooden turnstile.

A soldier wearing dirty sheepskin and a woollen hood watched them climb down from the sleigh. Beyond the gate was a loose cluster of rough wooden buildings – warehouse, barracks and customs house, all unpainted and reminding Ash of pictures of western frontier towns. The soldier put his shoulder to the gate and pointed at the customs house. Their driver threw down their luggage, whipped his horse back toward the river and left them standing alone in the snowy square on the edge of the Russian Empire.

12

A portrait of Czar Nicholas, looking fit and handsome and very much like King George, gazed paternally down on the customs desks. But a silver-framed life-size icon depicting Christ on the cross dominated the dirty, whitewashed room. Beneath it sat an old woman in black, selling candles.

The Russians among the train travellers – officers from the battalions lent to France, military attachés and a few civilians like Protopopov – crowded around the icon, bought her candles and lighted them in silver holders. By the time the Swedish sleighs had deposited the passengers and the shaggy, bearded Russian porters had dragged the luggage in from the square, the icon blazed in candle flame.

The Czar's police opened their registers, began running their fingers down endless columns of names, whispering to each other as the travellers presented their papers.

Soldiers guarded the doors, the entrances to a foulsmelling restaurant, to private offices, and the stockade, where Ash had seen forlorn faces peering through the cracks. He showed their papers, including the *laissez-passer* Ambassador Page had acquired from the Russian Embassy in London.

Catherine stayed close, awed by the grim-looking customs examiners, the conspiratorial muttering among the police and the anxious expressions worn by many of the train passengers. 'Boy, they look scared,' she whispered.

'There's Protopopov. I'd say he looks scared too.'

The Russian stood nearby, fingering his papers and casting a worried eye on his satchels, which a porter had dropped beside the examiner's desk.

The commandant of the border post burst through the private office door, welcomed by the police and soldiers with a flurry of salutes. He was a youngish-looking, cold-eyed man wearing a spotless green police uniform with a captain's insignia. He greeted Ash in precise English, then bowed over Catherine's hand. 'The daughter of the American ambassador honours our outpost.' His manner was cool, formal. 'May I have your party's papers, Commander Ash?'

Ash handed them to the commandant. 'You will excuse me, please.' He saluted, turned and disappeared.

Beside them, Protopopov's turn had come. The Russian started clasping and unclasping his hands as his satchels were opened. Nervous and it showed, thought Ash. But why? The Swedes had already let him pass.

The Czar's police noticed his fidgeting. They gathered around, ignoring the other travellers, and watched one examiner spread the matchboxes on the table while another pored over his book of names.

The customs examiner asked Protopopov a question in Russian. Protopopov answered. Another question. A second officer joined the interrogation, bringing another ledger.

The commandant came back, fired questions at Proto-popov, who continued to answer coolly and had, by visible effort, managed to get his hands under control, though his fingers kept clawing at his trouser leg.

The commandant dumped the contents of one of the satchels on the desk. Matchboxes spilled out, and the room grew quiet as the other travellers stopped their own whis-pered conversations to watch.

The officer felt inside Protopopov's bag for a false bottom. There was none, and he threw it aside in disgust. He turned his attention to the heaped matchboxes. Proto-popov spread his hands, said something in Russian. The

144

commandant ignored him. Suddenly he scooped up a single matchbox, pulled it open and scattered the matches on the table.

'What's he doing?' Catherine whispered. 'It's only matches.'

Ash watched the commandant. A bird dog sniffing the wind. At random he emptied six more matchboxes, found nothing and seemed ready to give up. Then an examiner shoved his ledger triumphantly under the commandant's nose.

'Commander *Ash* . . .'

'Captain?' Ash said coolly, reminding the Russian that beyond this outpost Ash was the ranking officer.

'Did you travel with this man?'

'We boarded the same train in Christiania.'

'And did you travel with him the entire way?'

'Yes.'

'Through Sweden?'

'I told you yes, Commandant. We were on the same train . . . the only train, Commandant, so far as I could see.'

'Did he have these satchels when he boarded your train?'

'He showed them when we crossed the Swedish frontier.'

'It is not my name,' Protopopov interrupted calmly. 'It is a mistake in the book. I am Mikhail Vladimirovitch Protopopov. You have found Mikhail *Vadimovitch* Protopopov. A man I do not know.' He spread his hands in innocence and added, 'Perhaps related to the new Minister of the Interior.'

Ash saw immediately that Protopopov had made a terrible error; the boy hadn't the experience to know that one needed to treat functionaries very seriously. The commandant flushed at the jibe; the Interior Minister's vast domain included the police.

He snapped his fingers and picked up a matchbox. He spilled the matches out as he had before, but this time he ripped the box itself apart.

145

Inside was a sheet of paper folded many times until it was as thick as a piece of cardboard. Slowly, his eyes on Protopopov, he unfolded it, spread it out on the table, then waved it triumphantly in the air. Black Cyrillic letters stood oversize on a white background, like a headline on a tabloid.

The soldiers seized Protopopov's arms and, at the commandant's orders, began to drag him away, protesting loudly. Somehow, he managed to break free and, in the instant before they grabbed him, he thrust a clenched fist into the air and shouted, '*Kill the Czar* . . .'

Catherine was shaking. Ash kept hold of her after the door slammed shut. 'What *is* it? What happened . . . ?'

The commandant turned to her. 'Not to concern you, young miss. We have detained a revolutionary.'

'What did the piece of paper say?'

The commandant picked it up disdainfully. 'Inflammatory leaflets, smuggled from Germany. He's a spy and a revolutionary. This paper incites the workers to strike and the soldiers to stop fighting.'

'What will happen to him?'

'Commander Ash,' said the commandant. 'Here are your papers. We apologize for the delay. The war . . . Your sleigh will be ready in a short while.'

But he came back in a few minutes and spoke to Ash privately. 'The prisoner has confessed something unusual. It concerns you . . . you had better hear it yourself.' He took Ash through a pair of guarded doors and into a windowless cell. Protopopov was slumped in a chair, breathing harshly through his mouth. They had broken his nose and there was blood on his face and deep cuts around his eyes. He flinched as he looked up.

Ash had finished with being diplomatic. 'Was this necessary?' he asked coldly.

'He is a revolutionary and a German spy,' the commandant replied just as coldly.

'I am not a spy.'

'Then why were you following Commander Ash?'

'What?'

Protopopov looked at Ash. 'I'm sorry. They gave me passes and train tickets if I would tell them where you were going.'

'Who?'

'Germans.'

'*What* Germans?'

'I don't know. The Germans who help the revolution.'

'The German army,' the commandant answered for him. 'The army sends spies. We catch them every time.'

'I am *not* a spy. I only did it to return to Russia – '

'What exactly did you do?' Ash asked him.

'I telephoned the German Embassy in Stockholm and told them you were still on the train and going to Petrograd. They threatened to hurt my comrades in Germany. They made me promise to telegraph if you left the train in Sweden.'

'What about in Finland? What about Petrograd?'

'No. Only in Sweden.' Then he murmured something else to Ash.

'What did you say?' the commandant broke in.

'I asked him to kiss Miss Hazzard's hand good-bye for me.'

Russian to the last, Ash thought.

And then he also thought . . . had he stepped in the middle of some powerplay between the German army and the German monarchy? But what could the German army do to him in Russia . . . ?

Halfway to the shore of Finland, Ash heard the firing squad.

Catherine started beside him. 'What was that?'

The ragged volley was wind-whipped and muffled by the

snow. Ash pointed down river at the endless line of freight sledges moving across the snow-covered ice. The caravan stretched for miles, hundreds of horse-drawn sledges in close formation. The shots could have been the snap of whips, or even the ice cracking, he told her. She nodded as if she believed him, but when Ash looked down at her a moment later, he saw tears on her cheeks. Without saying a word he slipped his arm around her shoulders and held her close to him for several long moments.

Ahead, the Finnish forest rose on gentle slopes along the river, green northern firs sprinkled with birch, similar to the forests they had seen in Sweden. But suddenly there spouted like fire from the green trees a dazzling red – the low sun blazing on a cluster of golden onion-dome church spires.

Catherine stared at the gleaming steeples, blinking and brushing her coat sleeve at her eyes. Ash gave her his hand-kerchief. His own astonished first glimpse of that quintessential mark of Russian territory nine years earlier and hundreds of miles to the south had been through tears too. But they had been tears of champagne laughter in Tamara's compartment as the majestic Imperial train glided home on cleared track, returning the Czar's delegates from the final Hague Peace Conference. All but the chief of the delegation; the Grand Duke Valery had stayed behind to represent Czar Nicholas at another meeting in Paris, and Tamara had invited Ash to escort her back to Russia. It had been the best of times. Tamara . . .

Outside the Finnish National Railroad train for Petrograd Russian soldiers and bearded porters tramped about in the snow and the strange Cyrillic letters adorned the Torneo station signs, but aboard were soft velvet, polished wood and glass, and English-speaking attendants in dapper European uniforms.

148

The third bell rang and the train moved out – a sealed capsule of Europe gliding through an alien land.

Ash was relieved when his charge went straight to bed after dinner – her compartment adjoining his. The attendants had made up his bed and he climbed in and read some Robert Service he had brought because the Queen had mentioned the author at dinner. The train was making good speed over the gentle terrain and the coach began a rhythmic swaying. Ash reached for the light switch just as there was a knock from Catherine's door.

'It's not locked. Come in.' He sat up, braced his back in the corner and pulled the blankets over his chest.

He heard her unlock her side. She was wearing a wool nightgown. Ruffles topped the high neck and ran down the front. The gown touched the toes of her slippers and covered her arms to the wrists, where more ruffles half hid her hands. He was surprised by her breasts. Unrestrained by daytime undergarments they pushed insistently against the gown. Her face was the same mask it had been since they had heard the firing squad. No . . . not quite the same; her cheeks were flushed.

'I can't sleep,' she said.

'Would you like a little brandy?'

'No. May I sit up with you a while?'

'If you want to.' He nodded at the opposite seat, which was still in the upright position. She sat there, pulled her knees up to her breasts and clasped her arms around them. She was silent. He waited. Then she said, 'Now I'm cold.'

'Go get your blanket.'

'Would you get it for me?'

'I'm not dressed.'

'Oh.' She went for it herself and returned wrapping it around her shoulders. A rag doll fell from it and landed in the doorway. She was already sitting down again on the seat and didn't notice. Ash did, and it made him smile, and tugged at his heart, at the same time.

'What did you do when your mother and father went to Russia?' he asked her.

'I made them let me try college.'

'Where?'

'Smith. Mother was scandalized. College for a girl and in the East, no less . . . but I couldn't even finish the first term. When she got sick I had to leave immediately for London . . . I feel so frightened tonight . . .'

'Mr Protopopov was fighting a war,' Ash said, picking up her meaning immediately. 'You have to understand that the people at the border thought he was their enemy. Which, in a way, he was.'

'He was so sad. And so nice. That counts for me.'

'He asked me to promise to kiss your hand good-bye for him.'

'Did he? Well, I'm waiting.'

'It was the thought.'

'You wouldn't deny a dying man's last wish . . .' She got up and extended her hand.

Ash held her small, delicate fingers in his, bowed his head and kissed her hand, wondering what Ambassador Hazzard would do to his career if he caught wind of this.

She sat down. 'Thank you, that was very nice . . .'

The blanket had fallen from his shoulder. She saw the scar. 'You were shot?'

'It's a birthmark.' He pulled the blanket up, making sure von Basel's scar was covered too.

'It is not. It's a bullet hole.'

'How would you know a bullet hole?'

'My Uncle Claude from Springfield was wounded at Gettysburg. He used to scare me with his scar, when I was little. It was just like yours. Only that's not what is scaring me now . . .'

150

'What, then?'

'. . . Do you know why I'm frightened, really? I don't know if I can take my mother's place. And my father's never even been an ambassador before.'

'He's not the first,' said Ash. 'And with all due respect to your mother, I'm sure you're going to do an even better job than she could. Besides, you won't be all alone in this. Your father has a staff ready to help. And there are other embassy wives. In fact, I seem to remember that the British ambassador's daughter is there. She's not much older than you. She and her mother will be helpful. You'll do just fine.'

'Will you be there?'

'. . . I'll be around, occasionally.'

'I'll make my father order you to come every day.'

Ash had no doubt that she could make her father shell the Winter Palace if she felt like it. 'I'd like that very much,' he said. 'Unfortunately Ambassador Page might miss me. But I will be around . . . Getting sleepy?'

'A little.' She squirmed around in the blanket, exposing an ankle, covering it. 'I hate going back in there alone tonight. I *am* upset about that man. I'd just met him and he was killed . . . Can I just stay here?'

'If you want . . . I'm going to turn the light out now. Are you sure you're warm enough?'

'If I'm not I'll just snuggle up against you.'

Ash calculated the remark to be about forty-five per cent innocence and said firmly, 'I wouldn't recommend that, young lady.'

He turned out the light and lay on his side. The light spilling from Catherine's compartment fell on the rag doll.

'Commander Ash?'

'What?'

'Who shot you?'

'A crazy anarchist.'

'Why?'

151

'He was aiming at someone else.'

'Oh . . . Commander Ash?'

'*What?*'

'Why are Europeans so . . . violent?'

'I guess maybe it's got something to do with the centuries they've had to form rivalries, hatreds, to oppress each other, their own people. It's a pretty complicated subject for bedtime discussion . . .' He closed his eyes and murmured a sleepy good-night as the train wheels clattered him to sleep . . .

Catherine woke him up, shaking his shoulder. He reached for her hand, dreaming he was elsewhere, but let go, surprised to feel such girlish fingers.

'The train stopped,' she said.

'Go to sleep.'

'There are soldiers outside.'

13

Ash peered under the blind. Car lights glared on the snow. He saw soldiers with rifles, heard them calling to each other. The train doors began banging at both ends of the carriage.

'Go to your compartment.'

'I'm afraid – '

'Then face the wall or something, I've got to get dressed.'

He threw off the blankets and got hurriedly into his blues. Heavy boots pounded down the corridor. The conductor knocked. 'Commander Ash, Commander Ash. Please open your door.'

'Go in and don't open the outside door.'

'What is it?'

'Don't know yet.' He closed her door and opened his to the conductor. 'What the hell do you want?'

Two tall soldiers were standing behind the conductor, who looked distinctly perturbed. 'The train is delayed, Commander.'

'I can see that.'

'And you are supposed to go with this officer.'

'What?' They were Finns bundled in sheepskin and hoods.

'He has papers to take you to the local barracks, Commander.'

'I'm travelling with *laissez-passer* from the Russian ambassador to Great Britain on a United States diplomatic mission. Tell him I'm not getting off this train.'

Ash started to close the door. The soldiers drew pistols

and two more appeared behind them with rifles. 'There is nothing we can do to help,' the conductor said.

'Send a wire to Petrograd to the Ministry of Foreign Affairs and another to the American Embassy.'

'The wires are cut. And the track is torn up. I'm sure the train will still be here when you get back.'

Ash wasn't at all sure. He reached for his sword to buckle it on; they gestured with their guns to leave it.

Northern Lights were flickering sporadically on the horizon as they marched Ash off the train and drove him away in a big open touring car with clanking chains to push it through the snow drifts. A machine-gun was mounted on a tripod in the back seat. Soldiers stood on the running boards and from what he could see there were several more in a car behind. Apparently not a German among them, though none spoke English. Finns and a few squat Russians. And, he realized, no officers, despite the claim of the one with the pistol.

He looked back. The train lights had disappeared. The air was bitter cold, at least twenty below. Ice froze his moustache. They had gone two or three miles when the car seemed to set out across an open field. The land fell away flat in the starlight, and when the Northern Lights flickered again he realized the road was actually a causeway over a frozen marsh. It led to an enormous dark hunting lodge set in a pine and birch forest.

The lodge was taller than the trees. Not a window shone; nor did smoke arise from the vast chimneys that spouted from the rooflike castle turrets. Ash reckoned the trees might be a place to run. The soldiers closed in on him as the car stopped.

They gestured him out and marched him to the lodge, up the main stairs, across a wooden verandah and through the front door. It was even colder inside the building than out.

One of them carried an electric lantern that cast a yellow beam across the foyer. The light landed on a second pair of doors. They pulled them open, shoved Ash in and pulled them shut.

'Hey – '

It was pitch-black. He heard the bolts shoot home, heard their footsteps fade, thought he heard the front doors slam. He took out his gold box and lit a match. He was in a room so big the light barely touched the ceiling and the far walls.

The match burned out. He walked toward what had looked like a sconce on the wall, fell over something soft, got up and lit another match. The sconce held an oil lamp. He lit the lamp, turned the wick up and looked around. He had fallen over a shrouded chair. He lit another lamp. What the hell had they put him in here for? If they were going to shoot him, why didn't they just shoot him?

The room had no windows, like a ballroom; but the massive, rough stone fireplace and the rustic design confirmed that the house had been built as a hunting lodge – probably for water fowl on the marsh. None of which explained why he was here or why every door he tried was locked.

Should he build a fire before he froze to death? Birch logs were stacked on the hearth. He was breaking up kindling when the doors opened and two tall men in greatcoats walked in. One wore the artificial wool *papaha* of the Russian army; the other, a civilian brimmed hat. They stopped just inside the door, thirty feet across the room, but before they could speak Ash said, 'I'm Commander Kenneth Ash, US Navy. I am travelling under diplomatic passport with the *laissez-passer* of the Russian ambassador to Great Britain. I demand to be returned to my train, immediately.'

The man with the brimmed hat spoke good English.

'Consider yourself a prisoner of war. I am a colonel in the

155

German army assigned behind Russian lines to recruit the Czar's Finnish troops to fight for Germany . . . they object to Russia calling their nation the Grand Duchy of Finland.'

'I don't give a damn who you are, I'm an officer of a neutral nation and – '

'This German-Finnish unit has brought you here to answer a simple question, Commander Ash . . . I have no desire to use physical means to force a brave man to talk, nor do I have any particular expertise in such unpleasantries. However, if you do not answer we will lock you in here with a canister of chlorine gas.'

He held up a gas grenade. Ash took a step backward. One part in five thousand parts of air killed. The gas was especially deadly in the trenches because it rolled before the wind and, being heavier than air, literally tumbled into the dugouts. Since the German gas attack at Ypres no soldier went to war without a gas mask.

'What's your question?'

'First raise your hands.' The man in the artificial wool cap, a Finn by the look of his long, handsome face, walked up to Ash, checked he had no gun on his hip under the cloak and patted him for a shoulder holster. When he stepped back, Ash lowered his hands slowly to his hips and asked again. 'What's your question?' He knew he should be watching the Finn, the man closest, but it was hard to keep his eyes off the gas grenade.

'What did you tell Kaiser Wilhelm?' the German asked.

Ash slipped his fingers back under his tunic and drew the cut-down Luger. The German was out of range. Ash aimed at the Finn and shouted across the room. 'Put down the grenade or I'll shoot your friend here.'

The Finn's eyes widened. *'Nein* . . . he'll kill us both . . .'

But even as he turned and ran, ignoring Ash's gun, his German partner dropped the grenade and slammed the door. The canister exploded with a loud pop, like a champagne cork poorly wrapped. The Finn screamed. A sickly yellow-green cloud enveloped him and rolled toward Ash.

14

The Finn writhed inside the yellow-green gas cloud. He clawed at his throat, tried to run and collapsed in a twitching heap. The canister hissed, spewing more gas. Ash could not see the doors through the cloud and knew where the dying Finn was only by the man's strangled cough. And the cloud kept growing, rolling.

Ash had, he calculated, thirty or forty seconds. One part in five thousand, one microscopic inhalation. He looked for windows. If there hadn't been windows earlier there wouldn't be windows now. Twenty-five seconds. A tendril of cloud reached from the mass like a finger, beckoning, choosing. The Finn was silent.

Ash backed until he hit the wall. Fifteen seconds. The canister hissed. One narrow, shrinking alley of pure air remained. Twelve feet in front of the fireplace. Twelve feet of pure air, now eleven, now ten. Ash backed into the fireplace, pressed his shoulders against the blackened fire wall and got ready to die.

The yellow-green chlorine gas hovered in front.

For one wild, joyous moment Ash thought that a draught down the chimney would hold off the gas. But when the cloud kept moving as the canister hissed in the eerie silence he realized that the cold inside the unheated lodge was so close to the temperature outside that there could be no down draught, nothing to keep the cloud from this last pure niche. Ten seconds? Should he hold his breath? Or take the poison all at once to get it over with fast?

He filled his lungs with the last pure air, filled deep.

158

The chimney.

He looked up the great flue of the enormous fireplace. The gas was heavier than air. Maybe it couldn't rise . . . Ash stood on an andiron and grabbed the rough bricks and kicked and clawed his way up the narrow shaft. The bricks blocked his shoulders. He turned himself diagonally to the opening and reached up and pulled. His fingers found iron projections planted for the chimney sweep, and he pulled on them and hauled himself higher and got his boots planted so that he was standing inside the chimney. He took a new breath, and when it didn't kill him, started climbing.

When he emerged from the chimney Ash spotted the dotted line of train lights several miles across the flat marsh. A reddish glow flickered against the trees near the house, presumably the quiescent Northern Lights. He took a bearing on the train relative to the North Star while he rested on the chimney top. Then he scanned the steep roof for a way down.

His perch was on the back side, and higher than the peak, permitting him to see the entire roof and all its chimneys. He wanted to head for a drainpipe, but it was very dark to traverse the sharply angled slate surface. The Northern Lights flared abruptly, streaming crimson across the sky, lighting the slates.

A bullet smacked into the chimney brick, inches from his hand, and a dozen shots rang out. Ash jumped some ten feet to the roof and slid down the slates. The soldiers kept pumping rifle fire at him.

He dug his heels in, slowed his descent and tried to scramble back up to the peak. The back side faced north, and the Aurora Borealis was bright enough to read by. A bullet whined past his head and caromed off the slate. He ducked behind another chimney, but they had seen him and concentrated fire around the chimney until the air was filled with ricochets.

Ash flicked his cloak tails out one side, drew their fire, and ran from the other, scrambled for the peak, flung himself over the top, out of sight of the riflemen. They had built a bonfire in front of the house beside the cars. The machine-gun raked the roof from end to end, the heavy calibre slugs ripping up the slates; high shots cracking past his head like whips. He ducked and ran, zigzagging, trying not to lose control and slide to the edge. They couldn't see him as well on this side but they had the firepower to keep at it until they scored.

Ash slid behind another chimney. They were shouting to one another from several corners, climbing the drainpipes. They'd seen him, and now trained a spotlight from the second car on the chimney. He heard the touring car's engine start. They moved it several yards to give the machine-gun a better field of fire, and again ricochets and broken slates burst all around him.

He bolted for the next chimney. They were slow with the light, and he got there first. He heard them climbing, calling back and forth. He jumped, caught the top of the chimney with his hands, hauled himself up and scrambled into the flue.

If he had come up this way, could he go down? He felt for the chimney sweep's footholds, anchored his boots, started down, fast. They'd work it out soon enough. The flue descended twenty feet of total darkness, then branched. Ash took the widest.

He heard shouting in the chimney. Were they on to him so soon? At last he tumbled with a clatter into a room lighted by the bonfire flickering through a big french window. Twenty feet below, two soldiers manned the machine-gun; a third, the light on the other car. The rest were nowhere in sight, presumably climbing to the roof and

160

covering the back. Ash found a staircase and headed down. He smelled the chlorine gas seeping through the house.

He reached the ground floor, silently opened a window and swung through onto the verandah. Thirty feet away they were training the light on the roof and firing sporadically. He ducked behind the verandah railing, edged closer, drew his Luger.

He waited until the machine-gun fired again and snapped a shot at the light. It went out, amid yells from the machine-gunners. Ash vaulted the railing and charged ahead.

The machine-gun belt-feeder spotted him first and called out. The triggerman spun the barrel toward Ash, started spinning his crank, firing as the gun bore around. Six slugs stitched through the snow. Ash hit the snow rolling, came up beside the machine-gunners, and shot them down. The soldier on the ruined searchlight pulled a pistol. Ash winged him, got himself behind the machine-gun, clumped up a few folds of the belt so he could fire alone, found the crank and raked the corner of the house as the rest of the unit streamed around it.

He hit a few, saw a few shadows disappear, sprayed the opposite corner, then directed a long stream into the bonnet of the other car. He jumped over the front seat, jammed the touring car into gear and headed for the causeway.

Rifle fire pursued him. The windshield exploded into glass shards. The tyres took several hits, but they were hard rubber and the chains kept digging through the snow. A shot whined off the windscreen post. Ash ducked, stuck his head over the low door and steered by the light of the crimson sky. At last he was out of range. He crossed the marsh, following their track in the snow, and turned toward the train.

It was where he had left it, venting steam forlornly, and he wondered who he could draft to help hold off the

161

renegade army unit if they came for him again. The machine-gun tipped the odds his way, but he needed a belt feeder. He saw a repair train had arrived from the south, and with it a unit of Russian soldiers guarding the men laying new track.

Ash knew by the relieved look on the face of the lieutenant in charge that he had already read the Russian Embassy's *laissez-passer* and had been wondering how he would explain losing an important passenger from a train passing through his sector.

Freezing, Ash brushed past the lieutenant and made a beeline for the warm train. But when he climbed up into the vestibule he recoiled from his image in the mirrors. No wonder the passengers in the corridor were staring. Black with chimney soot from head to toe and his lean cheeks sunken wearily, he looked like a coal miner dragged half-dead from a cave-in.

The Russian scrambled up after him. 'What happened?'

Ash's blue eyes seemed wild in their black sockets. His once-brown hair was pasted to his skull like a greasy black helmet. His small, even teeth shone white beneath a moustache ordinarily highlighted by glints of red and gold.

'What happened, Commander Ash?'

'Initiation rite for a Finnish fraternal order.'

Catherine came running down the corridor in her dressing gown, dodging the other passengers. 'Lord . . . are you all right?'

'Fine,' Ash said, and patted her shoulder reassuringly, leaving black prints on her gown. He turned to the officer. 'There's a renegade Finnish unit across that marsh. They can't have got far in one car.'

The Russian didn't look enamoured of the idea of night-fighting Finns on Finnish snow. He asked, 'Does that machine-gun work?'

162

'Very well.'

The train steamed south and south-east, down the Gulf of Bothnia and then diagonally across Finland's lake-pocked interior, pulling in late at the infrequent stations and leaving later. The system was collapsing.

At midnight, when they should already have arrived in Petrograd, they crossed the Finnish-Russian border at Bielostroff. Ash locked his door and went to sleep with the Luger under his pillow. It would be morning before they saw the capital.

Snow beat against the dining car window at breakfast, but at dawn an hour later, at nine-thirty, the sun climbed into a blueing sky. The clouds had blown away by the time the train reached Petrograd's northern freight yards, and Ash saw, as they crept toward the Finland Station, that the plight of Russia's railways was far more terrible than it had seemed in the Finnish province.

Whole trains stood motionless; the locomotives to move them lay abandoned on back sidings. Rail workers trudged glumly over the packed snow. Many were women, shapeless creatures in black, ragged wool. In fact Ash saw very few men at all as the train wormed through the northern Viborg slums. Children walked the railroad ties, heads down, studying the snow.

'What are they doing?' Catherine asked.

'Gleaning for coal,' Ash told her. 'From the tenders.'

Living conditions looked far worse this winter in Petrograd than any he'd seen in Berlin and Paris and London. Far worse. But this, of course, was Russia. You expected it to be worse here. He recalled Lenin's motto – the worse the better. And Protopopov's perversely proud claim that Russians excelled at suffering. If so, their time had surely come.

'What an awful looking place,' Catherine said.

163

'Just look to your right,' Ash told her. The only inspiring approach to the beautiful low-built city was from the Gulf of Finland. But even the slums offered occasional magic glimpses. Catherine pressed to the glass. 'Somewhere along here,' Ash said. 'Look between the buildings.'

'What – oh, lord, it's *beautiful* . . .'

A razor-thin gold spire soared in the distance and speared the pale sunlight.

'What is it?'

'St Peter's Cathedral in the Peter and Paul Fortress.'

'Father said the prison is there.'

'One of them,' Ash said as the train rolled into the Finland Station.

In the Litovsky Prison, Lieutenant Orlov cradled the telephone. 'Ash is at the Finland Station, Captain Moskolenko.'

Moskolenko finished reading Orlov's report on Ash's arrival in Russia. Orlov's typing was superb; each letter struck with precisely the same pressure. Equally precise were Orlov's facts. If the Okhrana lieutenant wrote that Ash had arrived at the Finland Station at four minutes past eleven – only ten minutes before he finished the report – he didn't mean three or five minutes. That precision, natural Russian doggedness and Orlov's yearning to abuse made him a brilliant police interrogator.

Moskolenko finished the report with an approving nod. 'Now listen to me. Ash is to be watched carefully. But don't overdo it at the American Embassy; our regular man is quite capable of reporting who comes and goes without blanketing Fourshtadskaya Street with half the Czar's detectives.'

'Yes, Captain Moskolenko.' Orlov scratched his bald head, hunched his thick shoulders. 'May I ask the nature of our interest in Commander Ash?'

'I think not, Orlov.'

'I only asked so that I could tell our men what to watch for.'

'I understand, Orlov, but I am not empowered to release any more information to my subordinates. Just keep track of Ash's movements and, of course, report' – Orlov brightened, sensing that the enigmatic Captain Moskolenko was going to include him in something important – 'any approach made to Ash by suspected German agents.'

Orlov ducked his shiny head. 'Yes, Captain Moskolenko. Report any approaches by suspected German agents.' This *was* important; he started happily for the door.

'Orlov.'

Orlov froze. 'Yes, sir.'

'I want to know everything about the incident in Finland.'

15

The American Embassy owned no car, except for a little Model T Ford Catherine said her father had bought for golfing, and no one met the chronically late trains anymore, anyway, so Ash hired porters and took Catherine outside to bargain fares for a fast sleigh and a carriage to follow with the bags – out of the Finland Station and into a riot.

A drunken amputee, a man with one leg, a crude wooden crutch and a military greatcoat, fell over a peddler's table of dubious looking meat pies; soldier, peddler and *piroshki* went down in a cursing tangle, and in seconds two dozen ragged children materialized from the crowds to fight for the food smeared on the cobblestones.

Ash shoved Catherine back inside; the police charged, scattering the children with boots and clubs. Catherine was white-faced, stunned by the sudden brutality. 'How could they – '

'Russia,' said Ash, taking her arm, and stepped out again into the clamour of Petrograd.

'Is it always like this?'

Ash looked around. 'The war's made it a lot worse.'

A horde of drivers came down on them, desperate men willing to bargain any fare in order to feed their animals. Ash hired a *droshki,* an iron-wheeled one-horse carriage for the bags, and a smart-looking *rissak* sleigh while Catherine gaped at the jumble of old and new, east and west that was Petrograd.

The Finland Station square was swept to dry stone, except for icy paths left for the sleighs; the work was done by old women with birch brooms dodging the brightly-

painted electric trams and shouting abuse at the station porters who tramped through the neat pyramids of snow they
piled for oxcarts to haul away.

Peddlers operated temporary stands and kiosks of old
clothes, wrinkled carrots, mouldy potatoes and greasy
piroshki. Shapeless women in black sold shoelaces and
repaired boots; all the peasant women seemed to wear black,
Ash noted. All widowed by the war. Or lost their sons. The
young men going in and out of the station were all in
uniform.

There seemed to be more foreigners too; Allies – English-
men, Italians, French, weary Roumanians with panic in their
eyes. Small boys sold the travellers city maps and daily newspapers, but the Cyrillic alphabet made a mystery of street
signs, and the Russian calendar set the date two weeks earlier than it was in Europe.

Ash had sailed from Newcastle on December thirteenth,
travelled eight days and arrived in Petrograd December
eighth – three nights before Christmas Eve in the rest of the
world. He thought, with a stab of loneliness, of Christmas at
home. Somehow ham smoked on the place and wild turkeys
shot by his hill-country uncles seemed much, much farther
from Petrograd than the six thousand miles the maps said it
was. A beggar was frightening Catherine; Ash dropped a few
kopecks in the dirty hand, concluded his deal for the sleigh
and put her aboard.

The driver whipped up his half-starved thoroughbred and
they trundled onto the Alexander Bridge, which spanned
the broad Neva. Just downstream the river split into the half-
dozen branches that separated the nineteen islands of the
delta city as it emptied into the Gulf of Finland. The result
was a flat city veined by canals and rivers and dimpled by
hundreds of low bridges. From the middle of the bridge
they got their first proper view of the Russian capital and its
elegant left bank, or South Side.

Catherine, as usual, hit the nail on the head. 'It looks impossible. How did they build it?'

'Peter the Great hired Italian architects to replicate the Dutch city of Amsterdam on a Russian scale in what was then a Swedish swamp. He wanted a window on Europe to show the Russians the modern world and show Europe that Russia was going to be the new boss of the North. He built the fortress, forced the Russian aristocracy to build palaces and levied a rock tax. There isn't a stone in the city that wasn't carried in.'

'Protopopov was wrong,' Catherine said in a voice soft with awe. 'It's beautiful.' The sun was lighting the gold spires of the Admiralty and the cathedrals and gleaming on tall windows, and Ash thought that the splendour of the South Side of the Imperial Russian capital made predictions of the Czar's downfall seem like wishful thinking.

The grand palaces that lined the Neva's left bank were painted soft pastel blues and yellows – as beautiful as they were incongruous in the pale northern light. Unexpectedly appropriate too was the extravagant Italianate architecture despite the fact that the Mediterranean inspirations – classical form wildly embellished by rococo decoration – sprawled on the granite embankments of a cold river aflood with swiftly moving ice.

Only the Winter Palace, which was painted dark, brooding red, looked out of place beside its smaller, sunny neighbours. Ash eyed it speculatively; it was the Czar's official residence, but Nicholas did not live there, preferring his isolated country palace, the Alexander, twenty miles outside the city in Tsarskoye Selo, the Czar's Village – like King George's remote Sandringham and the Kaiser's country palaces scattered across Germany far from Berlin.

Petrograd's smart set whispered gleefully that the Winter Palace's correct colour was pale turquoise, which the architect Rastrelli had chosen and Russia's rulers had enjoyed for some hundred and thirty years before the present Czar had ordered it painted red for reasons that no one could fathom – no one, the sophisticates added, with taste. Tamara, Ash recalled, had her own theory about the colour change; the shattered body of the Czar's assassinated grandfather, Alexander II, had been carried back to the Palace after the bomb attack and Czar Nicholas, still a boy, had seen the blood and torn flesh, which had left him with grim feelings for the Winter Palace. To which the sophisticates replied in even quieter whispers, because such gossip could get one exiled, that she should know since the best rumour in Petrograd said Tishkova had shared Czar Nicholas's bed. After he was married . . .

Ash looked back at the Peter and Paul Fortress. Thick granite walls thrust into the Neva, commanding the river and the city with cannon and a huge garrison. He reminded himself that it wasn't the guns within the walls but the men who aimed the guns that mattered. Mutinous troops could just as easily shell the palaces as they could repel invaders or revolutionaries.

Mansions stood near the fortress, among them, Tamara's.

The American Embassy occupied an unimposing site between two apartment buildings and shared Fourshtadskaya Street with an army barracks, some tea shops and a coal yard. Catherine eyed the shop signs – pictures of boots, thimbles, asparagus, telling an illiterate clientele what was sold inside. 'Father wrote that he's taken a lease on a much better building. We'll be moving soon.'

Ash offered her his arm as they climbed down from the car at the unimposing front door; the drab little two-storey building was only slightly enlivened by a dozen flags and a Marine guard detachment that snapped to attention when the sergeant spotted what had to be the alarming appearance of a full commander swinging down from a sleigh. Nonetheless, the Russian *dvornik* leaning on the door and a pair of porters slouching beside him robbed their arrival of whatever grandeur it might have possessed. Nor could Ash help smiling at the flickers of appreciation on the stern faces of the marines who looked alarmingly like a gang of homesick kids rejoicing at the sight of a pretty American girl.

By some invisible communication the embassy foyer filled quickly with more young men – secretaries, cipher clerks and junior officers. Catherine surveyed her new domain like a duchess coming home.

Ambassador Anthony Hazzard hurried in, apologizing for being late, and running a nervous hand through his thick grey hair. Catherine threw her arms around him and hugged him, then, as he tried to introduce her to the others, pulled him over to meet Ash, who thought Hazzard looked less like a Progressive cartoonist's image of a plutocrat than he had imagined. Hazzard kept running that hand through his hair and looked exhausted and quite bewildered. Petrograd, apparently, was proving more complex than Columbus, Ohio.

He shook Ash's hand and thanked him for delivering Catherine, then abruptly, he asked him into his office for a moment. Ash started to open his despatch pouch, but Hazzard waved it aside.

'What the hell happened on the train?'

'Finnish Nationals, as near as I could make out,' Ash replied. 'Have they hit many trains?'

'First one I heard of-course the Russians aren't big on admitting bad news – Why you, Commander? What the hell did they grab *you* for?'

Like most successful businessmen Ash knew, Hazzard thought in a straight line, and it was hard to throw him off course. He tried again. 'They might have known I was

170

carrying the Russian ambassador's *laissez-passer* and figured I was a lot more important than I am – especially travelling with your daughter.'

'My God, what if they had taken Catherine?'

Ash let that thought burn holes in the ambassador's brain before he asked, 'Does this sort of thing mean the Czar is losing control?'

'Damned if I know. I suppose that's the sort of question Ambassador Page sent you out to ask.'

'I suppose, Mr Ambassador.'

'Well... I can give you an earful, if you want one; there's no point in pretending I'm a professional diplomat – not that you have to go blabbing that to everybody.'

'Of course not, sir. I appreciate your candour.'

'Well, I don't know about the Czar and his government . . . but a walk around town will show you they're starving out there. And freezing. See this?'

He got up and led Ash to the tall french windows behind his desk. Opening them onto a narrow balcony, he pointed down the street. 'See all those shops. Those little signs say what they sell – bread, vegetables, kerosene. Now that vegetable one hasn't been open since October. The bakery opens about twice a week. At six in the morning you see the women lining up in the cold. See those women with pails? They've been waiting all morning for kerosene. So I don't know about the Czar, but I do know that if something like this ever happened in Columbus, Ohio, folks wouldn't take it lying down for very long.'

'I see – '

'I doubt you do yet, Commander.' He closed the door and sat down. 'This is a decent neighbourhood, near the best in the city. What's going on out in the factory districts? Children must be starving. Must be the reason they have so many strikes in the factories. Can you imagine that? Strikes in the middle of a war?'

'What's the attitude toward the war?' Ash asked.

'Everybody got excited when General Brusilov started beating the Austrians. He was supposedly rolling toward Berlin. But all that really happened was the Russians suckered the Roumanians into declaring war on Germany and the Germans beat the daylights out of them in two weeks. Nobody cares about the war here, anyhow – listen, this really is just between you and me and Ambassador Page. I was sent here to negotiate commercial treaties, and the State Department doesn't want to hear bad news from junior ambassadors. I'm just giving you my personal impressions, for what they're worth.'

'Thank you, that is why Ambassador Page sent me. He's concerned that if some provocative act on the part of Germany forced the United States into the war the Russian front would collapse – '

'The American people aren't going to fight for the Czar of Russia, Commander. American politics is something I do know. They'll never fight for the Czar. I don't care what Germany does.'

'I've heard rumours,' Ash said casually. 'Rumours of a coup?'

'If rumours were firewood there wouldn't be a fuel shortage. You hear about coups every day. The other night a bunch of nobles and their lady friends had a big do and the next morning everybody in town knew they'd been talking about what regiments would come over to their side.'

'What happened?'

'All it was was a lot of talk. A lot of talk in this town, Commander. Hard to tell what's hot air.' Hazzard ran his hands through his hair. 'Not *all* talk . . . one of the grand dukes is supposedly hatching something with his ballerina girl friend.'

'Which one?'

'I don't know, I just heard it.'

Tamara wasn't the only Russian dancer with a grand duke, but Ash had an awful feeling it was she, and it terrified him. Plotting against the Czar was a way to get executed. If they were caught, Valery would probably just be banished, but Tamara would be hanged.

'How is the Czar reacting to all this?'

'Seemed fine when I presented my credentials. Very pleasant, I thought. Spoke good English.'

'Will he be coming back to Petrograd for Christmas?'

'I have no idea. He used to receive the diplomatic corps on New Year's Day – their New Year's, not ours – but they say he cancelled last year and there's no word this time. Lately he's been down at the Stavka, the army headquarters at Mogilev. All my staff hears is rumours.'

'What's the latest rumour on Rasputin?'

'A real lulu. They say the monk's trying to get the Czarina to get the Czar to stop all military trains for three days.'

'What for?'

'So they can carry food and coal to the cities. The shortages are getting worse.'

'Sounds like a pretty good idea.'

'I wouldn't know. But the monk's meddling is really upsetting people. I don't know how much he actually does, but the rumours say it's a lot. But I find it hard to believe that one illiterate peasant monk could make the Czar do anything he doesn't want to do.'

Ash smiled.

'What's funny, Commander?'

'Excuse me, Mr Ambassador. I was just thinking how pleased Ambassador Page would be if I secured an audience with the Czar – you know, asked him a few questions face to face.'

'Good luck . . . the only foreigners I know who talk to him

are the British and French ambassadors and they've been here thirty years.'

'Wouldn't hurt to ask.'

'I'll put in a request through channels, but the last time anyone from this embassy got through it took six months.'

'Could you arrange a pass for me to the British sub base at Reval?'

'I suppose so. What do you want to go there for?'

The Nevsky Prospect, a two-mile-long shopping boulevard gaily decorated for the Russian Christmas, was Petrograd's Fifth Avenue. It was just coming awake in the early winter dusk. Thousands of officers in colourful uniforms thronged the sidewalks, so many that Ash wondered who was left fighting at the front. Russians, Frenchmen, Britons, Roumanians and Poles gazed in shop windows, were trailed by servants with packages and escorted elegant women in lustrous furs. Ash thought of a Leon Bakst set for a fanciful ballet, entitled, perhaps, 'City at War'.

Motor traffic, as in London and Paris, had been thinned by fuel shortages, and there were horses everywhere, drawing *likhachy* taxi carriages, and an abundance of private conveyances – two-passenger sleds for merchants' wives, fast troikas and the grand enclosed carriages of the aristocracy attended by liveried footmen and driver.

Ordinary people rode on the new electric trams, few of which had been operating when Ash was last in Petrograd. The trams went everywhere now, even, according to his new Baedecker, across the ice once the Neva froze solid in another week or two.

At the west end of the Nevsky Prospect, sprawling for hundreds of feet along the river, was the yellow and white Admiralty building, the administrative centre for the four-fleet Russian Navy. Across a huge square loomed the dark red Winter Palace. *Moujiki*, peasant workers, were shovelling snow off its flat roofs.

Ash's taxi drove past the Admiralty, which was the hub of the city, from which the Nevsky and the other main streets radiated around the domed and columned St Isaac's Cathedral and into a square stacked with firewood. Across from a small palace was Ash's hotel, the Astoria, a new five-storey building in the art nouveau style. Nearby was the abandoned German Embassy; its imposing red stone façade was scrawled with slogans and its doors and windows had been smashed by angry Russians in the summer of 1914.

As Ash climbed out of the taxi he saw two old women surreptitiously approach a woodpile. A soldier ran at them, rifle raised, and they scurried into an alley.

A sign on the front desk said NO ROOMS in five languages.

A clerk was arguing with a French officer in French, explaining there were indeed no rooms anywhere in the hotel. Another was explaining the same to an English businessman, and a third was coping with an angry Roumanian.

Ash had booked a room by cable from London. The clerks had no record of it. Ash produced the hotel's confirming cable. They apologized profusely, but they had no room.

'I intend to stay one or two months,' Ash replied, slipping the man a gold British sovereign – a fortune, but worth it. The clerk reluctantly refused the tip.

'Monsieur, I wish I could oblige – I have one tiny room under the eaves. But it is a little chilly.'

'Show me.'

The Astoria had an electric elevator, a vast affair that rose silently inside an open cage. Ash saw cots in the halls. At the top they walked up another flight. The room, a closet, really, with a single tiny window, was cold as a tomb.

'No,' Ash said. 'We'll have to do better.' Petrograd was too strict socially, too conscious of rank and precedent and wealth to take seriously a man who lived in a closet when he asked to meet the Czar.

Back at the desk an American tractor salesman was redfaced and shouting, 'That's my suite. You can't kick me out.'

'A terrible mistake, Monsieur. We are so sorry. We'll see what we can do for you tomorrow, as for now, we have a charming little room on the top floor. Only one flight up from the elevator . . .' The manager turned to Ash, smiling broadly. 'Monsieur Commander Ash, there you are. I hope we haven't kept you waiting. Your suite is ready.'

The tractor salesman purpled. 'You're giving him *my* suite.'

'Monsieur, it is *his* suite. It always was. And it will be as long as he remains in Petrograd. This way, Commander, if you please.'

'How do you do it?' the salesman demanded. 'I bribed twenty dollars for that suite.'

'Just lucky,' Ash said, straight-faced, wondering how lucky? Had Lord Exeter pulled a string to make him comfortable? Or had the arrangements been worked by a German agent? The hell with them. He had advantages on his side now. He was a neutral officer of a potential ally of Russia. He could go to the police any time he needed help. While the Germans, if there were any more Germans, had to operate undercover.

The *important* thing was the Czar.

'Any messages?'

The clerk handed him several envelopes. Ash took them across the lobby and ordered two dozen yellow roses for Tamara. The florist replied apologetically that he would have to check his stock – 'Rail disruptions, you understand, sir.' While he waited Ash opened the messages. Signor de la Rocca and the Baroness Balmont invited him to dinner the following night. Sergei Gladishev and Prince Paustovsky, his friend Fasquelle's Russian partners, each invited Ash to telephone on arrival. He assumed that some of these people could help quickly arrange an audience with the Czar.

A Vadim Mikhailov had enclosed his card and had written on the back, 'My step-daughter Vera Sedovina wrote me you would like to talk.' The piano player. *Tapeur.* He would indeed. About many things. Including when his daughter was coming back.

The last card belonged to Chevalier François Roland. The address printed was the Hotel Europa, and written on the back was the address of the Petrograd Fencing *Salle,* and the time, tomorrow morning. Here a week already, the French dance correspondent would know a lot more about the state of Petrograd society than the otherwise surprisingly well-informed Ambassador Hazzard.

'Do you like these, Monsieur?' The florist thrust the yellow roses proudly at Ash. 'Mademoiselle Tishkova will be pleased.'

Ash stared at the flowers. For years, whenever he wangled a courier mission to the city where Tamara was performing, he had announced his arrival with yellow roses. It had been one of their love rites. His roses, her card in return and a bottle of Moet chilling beside the bed. What in the hell had he been thinking?

'Don't you want them, Commander?'

'No,' he said sadly. 'They won't do . . .'

177

16

Murder, General Ludendorff thought while he waited for the Russian assassins, was the ultimate weapon in total war; blood from the right murder *behind* the lines would flow redder than from a million casualties in a pointless advance into no-man's-land. He had no patience for irony, and even less for great-man theories of history – though his own swift rise from obscure Prussian colonel to the brains behind the German army suggested that greatness did pace event – but he had seen the death of the right man at the right time affect events, which was why he was courting Russian assassins.

When Kenneth Ash died in Finland, for example, the Kaiser's plot to make peace behind the army's back died with him; in 1914 the murder of the Archduke Ferdinand had set off events which hastened *Der Tag*. Neither were great men, merely the right men at the moment.

Czar Nicholas was not a great man either, far from it; he was demonstrably the least competent leader in the world. But shockwaves from the Czar's murder and the murders of the Czarina and their monk Rasputin – the ham-handed police repression which would follow, the demoralization of already-demoralized ministers, and the ascent of the revolutionaries because Russians would see the Czar's murder as a revolutionary victory – those shockwaves would tumble the Russian government, and with it, the Russian army.

Those three murders in Petrograd would have greater effect than millions of deaths, his grains of sand, had had at the front; a perversely modern total-war version of medieval battle, and, much like chess: kill the king and the game was yours. Check and checkmate. He had planned this a year.

Telegraph keys clattered nearby like knitting needles as his orders sped from Spa to the front and the acknowledgements returned. He had just completed regular trench inspection – this time, despite the lingering trauma of the Somme and Verdun disappointments, his positions looked stronger. The trenches were remarkably clean, the men healthy despite the weather, the field kitchens and deep, well-lit bunkers as orderly as disciplined officers could make them.

As winter deepened the army lived more comfortably on the Western Front than civilians starving in the cities. The British blockade grew ever tighter, and the food shortages were making themselves known by reduced factory production – hungry workmen worked slowly.

The Eastern Front was a grimmer story. The Russians had such manpower – such a breeding ground was that vast empire – that German discipline, Krupp cannon, modern railroads and telegraphs weren't enough to dislodge their blundering army. Only a revolution would fragment their army, only a violent catastrophe to set fire to Russian cities and men against officers in the trenches.

The spark? Murder.

'They are here, Quartermaster General. Red Snow.'

Ludendorff stood up eagerly, forgetting in his excitement to smooth his tunic over the roll of fat around his waist. His murderers. They called their work assassination, but murder was what it was, and Ludendorff liked to be clear.

Two Russian officers entered.

Ludendorff was surprised by their appearance. Despite the detailed reports, he had not presumed that the leadership of a Socialist-Revolutionary terror cell called Red Snow would look like Guards officers from a noble family. But that was precisely what the brothers Vladimir and Dmitri Dan were.

Only in Russia, Ludendorff thought.

179

Their pale cheeks were clean-shaven, their dark moustaches extravagant, their black hair oiled and combed as if they had dressed for a ball. They shook hands easily, and if they were impressed by the second-ranking general of the German army – or hated him – neither Vladimir nor the younger Dmitri displayed anything but a charming smile.

Ludendorff was baffled. Where, he wondered, had such fine young men gone wrong? These were, supposedly, the flower of Russian Society. He'd seen their type fight on the Eastern Front, brave men . . . what did it to them? The answer, of course, the Russian disease – a deadly eastern combination of fatalism and immorality. A plague Germany must contain.

It shouldn't concern him for now, though. What mattered was that Vladimir and Dmitri had a far better chance of killing the Czar of Russia than any murderers the German army had sent before. Most hadn't made it across the border. But Red Snow was better organized, communicating with their cells inside Russia by coded telegrams sent through sham commercial firms to elude the censors, and possessing members of higher station like the Dan brothers who could infiltrate the Czar's own entourage.

'How will you enter Russia?' Ludendorff asked.

'As reported to your subordinate,' Vladimir answered. 'We've been stationed temporarily in France with a fusilier unit lent to the French. We will go back into France, via Switzerland, and return home in the normal manner by ship and rail. There I will take up my new commission with the Winter Palace Guard in Petrograd and Dmitri will return to his old post in the Czar's Convoy.'

'You will travel with the Czar?' Ludendorff asked.

'Not precisely with him. Usually on the second train. But close.'

'And getting closer,' Vladimir smiled, tousling Dmitri's

hair as if he and his brother were reporting home from school to a favourite uncle.

'But when the Czar is not travelling?'

'I will try to intercept him on one of his afternoon walks at the Stavka,' Dmitri said earnestly.

'And if the Czar is not at the Stavka?'

'I will be housed at Tsarskoye Selo. Close to the Alexander Palace.'

'Good.' Ludendorff turned to Vladimir. 'And how close will *you* be to the Czarina?'

'As for myself, I have made several requests to be transferred to Tsarskoye Selo, where Their Imperial Majesties live. I will use some of your gold Marks to bribe the appropriate officials.'

Ludendorff looked directly at Vladimir. 'Are you sure you can kill the Czarina?'

'Yes.'

'A woman?'

'For half a million gold Marks I could kill God.'

'And you. Are you sure you can kill the Czar when you are actually face to face with him?'

Dmitri simply said, 'Yes, I am sure,' and Ludendorff believed him, noting he had made no mention of the other half million gold Marks. Vladimir seemed more interested in the money than the revolution, Ludendorff thought. And feared killing a woman. But would.

'And who will kill the monk Rasputin?'

'We have left that to our comrades already in Petrograd. It is a matter of encouraging certain people without alerting them to our own purpose.'

'I don't understand.'

Vladimir Dan started to explain, but his brother cut him off. 'The best people to kill Rasputin will themselves be killed after the Revolution. Rightists and monarchists. Even some grand dukes.'

Ludendorff was a highly ambitious man and appreciated intrigue, but he still did not like the way they were going about killing Rasputin. He said, 'It sounds to me as if you are not trying very hard to kill the monk. Haven't we offered enough gold?'

He was convinced that assassinations would provoke police repression, which would in turn provoke street demonstrations in the Russian cities which would topple the government. Rasputin would start the ball rolling, and cheap at the price. Then when the Dan brothers killed the Czar and Czarina, Russia would explode. But he couldn't wait two or three months for the Czar's murder, not with the block-ade squeezing his own cities. It had to start sooner with Rasputin.

Vladimir Dan smiled. 'Would you care to double the price if Rasputin dies within . . . shall we say a week?'

'Of course,' Ludendorff snapped. 'Do it.'

Vladimir grinned and Ludendorff suspected he had been taken. The monk's murder was no doubt already in hand. His aide-de-camp burst into the office. Ludendorff turned on him angrily, shifting his irritation with the Russians to his own man, who ignored his order to leave and bent over his chair and whispered, 'Ash escaped.' The aide-de-camp glanced at the Russians and put his lips close to the general's ear. 'He's in Petrograd.'

'Have the officer responsible shot,' Ludendorff ordered, loud enough for the Dan brothers to hear and remember.

The aide leaned annoyingly close again, and whispered, 'Apparently Ash accomplished that in his escape.'

Ludendorff looked at the pair of officers lounging com-fortably as if they were in their club.

'Would Red Snow be interested in earning an additional hundred thousand gold Marks?'

Vladimir said it depended.

'There is an American Naval Lieutenant Commander Kenneth Ash.'

'Commander,' the aide-de-camp corrected; 'he has been promoted.'

'I suppose you also know where he's staying?'

'The Astoria Hotel in Petrograd.'

'One hundred thousand gold Marks,' Vladimir said. 'I'll do it on the way home from the train.'

'*No.*' Dmitri, white-faced, stern.

'Why not?' Vladimir asked.

'It is murder.'

Ludendorff looked at the young Russian incredulously. 'And what do you suppose killing the Czar and Czarina and Rasputin are?'

'Revolution.'

Ludendorff was silent a moment, studying the earnest Dmitri. He considered concocting a story about Ash being a counter-revolutionary, but the brothers Dan were too intelligent; and he realized he didn't understand the nuances of their lunatic hatreds. It had taken his aide-de-camp twenty minutes to explain the difference between Socialist Revolutionaries and Bolsheviks and he still wasn't sure which were which. Fortunately, Vladimir came to his rescue.

'Dmitri,' he said, putting his hands on his brother's shoulders, 'one hundred thousand gold Marks in Red Snow's Swiss treasure box will buy guns and food and medicine. It may take months to kill the Czar and Czarina. This Ash is a bird in the hand . . . Dmitri, we, Red Snow, need the money.'

'We will pay *two* hundred thousand for Ash,' Ludendorff prompted.

'Do you hear?' Vladimir said. 'Two hundred thousand.'

'I hear, my brother.' Dmitri pulled away, gazed at the maps on the wall and finally, reluctantly, agreed.

'When?' Ludendorff demanded. 'It can't wait two

months. It can't even wait until you get back to Russia. It must happen now.'

'We will wire the orders tomorrow from Switzerland. Ash will die with Rasputin. You may depend on it.'

17

Gleaming like a predatory eye, a steel point sought Ash. He retreated; it followed. He attacked; it circled, an impenetrable fan of steel, like a spinning aeroplane propeller. He feinted; it waited, mockingly still. He attacked again; the hard circle resumed.

'*Relax.*'

Ash was holding his own foil too tightly; he loosened his grip, studied his stance and relaxed his right foot, which was getting rigid, and raised his guard, which, stiffening, had begun to fall.

'Good. *Attack.*'

Ash poured across the canvas strip, his body milliseconds ahead of his mind.

'*Touché.*'

François Roland gracefully slipped his foil under the stump of his left arm, removed his mask and bowed with a smile. 'Excellent.'

Ash pulled off his own mask. The canvas rim was drenched with perspiration, as was his entire fencing suit; Roland had really given him a workout, but Ash was smiling because he had breached his master's guard.

'You've kept your speed, Kenneth, your best asset . . . And I suspect you've been practising your lunges, your weakest skill.'

'Yes. I have.'

Roland eyed him shrewdly. 'Shooting for the German count?'

'The expression is "gunning".' He hadn't hefted a sabre for over a year after von Basel had beaten him. Then suddenly he had returned to the *Salle,* practising in every city he travelled to. 'Nice of you to notice.'

'You've got to wait until the war's over to try to kill him again,' François Roland smiled. Then he added, seriously, 'But you must improve your eye. Without the most *precise* sense of distance you're a standing duck for a man as good as he.'

'Sitting duck.' They were speaking English at Roland's request, coaching in the vernacular being the only payment the Frenchman would accept from Ash for fencing lessons that ordinarily only the very rich could afford.

'You need that sense of distance to know how far you can lunge,' Roland persisted, 'how close to allow your opponent. Yes?'

'Yes. Time for another bout?'

'No. Baron Zlota's a punctual fellow, for a Russian.'

Baron Alexei Zlota's sister was a lady-in-waiting to the Grand Duchess Elizabeth, who was the sister of the Czarina Alexandra. A balletomane and an amateur dance writer – hopeless, in Roland's own words – he had agreed to meet Ash at Roland's request. Ash had already put in a request for an audience with Czar Nicholas through official channels at the American Embassy, despite Ambassador Hazzard's warning that it could take six months, and was intending to try other routes. Hazzard had promised to include him in the Embassy contingent if the Czar happened to receive the diplomatic corps on New Year's Day, but that was two weeks off, and it was doubtful it would happen in any case. An audience with the Czarina seemed more likely, and he had planned several approaches.

Roland was being very helpful; Ash hadn't told him the reason he needed royal audiences, and the Frenchman hadn't pressed, though he clearly knew this must be more than a simple inspection tour for the American ambassador to Great Britain.

Roland was a perfectionist; tall and lean, like a fine pen sketch. He respected beauty and talent and bravery and little else. About the left arm he had lost at the Battle of Verdun, he had admitted quietly to Ash in a moment of deep friendship, he was devastated by a fear of looking ugly with an empty sleeve. The loss had no effect on his phenomenal fencing – 'Unless I run afoul of a man with a dagger in his other hand,' Roland had noted with a smile. And Ash noticed as they walked along a palace-lined canal that it was still Roland's strikingly handsome face, not his sleeve, that turned the heads of women.

The only duel Roland had ever fought – skill, in his mind, being more exciting than killing – he had fought with a man foolish enough to insult the foils champion of France for being a homosexual. Once, at the end of a long night of brandy in Paris he had asked Ash straight out if it ever bothered him to be his friend, and Ash had closed the subject with the satisfactory observation that the few people lucky enough to know real passion knew that passion made its own rules.

Baron Zlota was a round little man – a roly-poly period to Roland's stern exclamation point. He greeted Roland with a dilettante's wary respect for the professional and snapped his fingers loudly when Roland introduced him to Ash.

'I remember you. Tishkova's friend.'

'Mademoiselle Tishkova did honour me with her friendship,' Ash said with self-conscious formality. Tamara. My God, why did it still hurt? Baron Zlota fingered his pince-nez, perched it daintily on his nose and glanced at Roland. Ash added hastily, 'I haven't seen her dance in some time.'

187

Zlota understood, smiled sympathetically. 'She is greater than ever. Please sit.' Waiters, old Germans in rumpled white tunics, hurried to their side.

'François tells me you wish an audience with the Czarina.'

'I've been asked to report, informally, to Ambassador Page in London about conditions in Russia. An opportunity to speak with Her Imperial Majesty would lend a real authenticity to my report.'

Zlota glanced again at François Roland, but the Frenchman's eyebrows remained noncommittally steady. 'I'm sure Chevalier Roland has explained how hundreds of people every day ask for an audience with the Czarina. Her favour can advance a social position, launch a career or a charity, attract contributions to a war hospital, such as the several she herself supports, gain a ministry post – '

Roland's brow concentrated into twin peaks. 'Unlikely that Commander Ash seeks a cabinet post.'

'Well, yes of course,' Baron Zlota said, 'but I'm merely trying to explain the difficulty. It would be so much easier if he had been presented before to Her Majesty.'

'I was presented to His Majesty the Czar at Balmoral Castle years ago and again in Berlin for the wedding of the Kaiser's daughter.'

'I see. Do you intend to seek an audience with the Czar as well?'

'I should like to, but he's at military headquarters and it might be impossible to get through to him there.'

'I see . . .' The drinks came and they toasted the coming ballet season. Roland said, 'Kenneth saw Pavlova dance in New York a couple of months ago.'

'She was great,' Ash said.

'When's she coming back is what I want to know,' Zlota grumped. 'All we've got left other than Tishkova are Karsavina and Kchessinska. There's a wonderful new one, though still young. Sedovina.'

'I met her in London,' Ash said, and Roland beamed. This was the way to reach Baron Zlota. 'She was there to dance in pantomime.'

Zlota rolled his eyes. 'Only the English would put a talent like hers in a children's show. I hope she comes back.'

'She said she would.'

The conversation drifted around dance gossip for a while, but when Ash and Roland left the club Baron Zlota promised, 'I'll speak with my sister. Of course she and Her Highness the Grand Duchess are in Moscow at Her Highness's nunnery, but I'll telegraph immediately.'

It was snowing on the street. 'Well?' Roland asked.

'Maybe . . . why's the Grand Duchess in a nunnery?'

'She founded her own religious order after her husband was assassinated.'

'Oh.'

'She's a very stylish woman. She had the habits designed by a *couturier* in Paris. Friend of mine.'

'Oh?'

'Sorry. Her Highness is not on intimate terms with her dressmaker.'

On his own Ash called on a Russian diplomat he had known on and off for years. Skobeleff, high up in the Foreign Ministry when Ash had last seen him, received him in an apartment heaped with packing cases. The diplomat was supervising the packing of his library. He had a bottle of champagne in an ice bucket on his desk and seemed just a little drunk. He offered Ash a glass.

'It is good to see you again. I heard they promoted you to full commander.'

'You hear quickly; it just happened.'

Skobeleff smiled at the compliment. But information, after all, was a diplomat's stock in trade. 'What brings you to Petrograd?'

189

'My government has asked me to observe the Conference of Allies.' It was a better lie for someone in the know like Skobeleff, and based on reality. The conference was scheduled for January.

'Unofficially, I presume?'

'Unless we declare war in the meantime.'

'Which is not likely, is it?' Skobeleff asked.

'I'm afraid not,' Ash conceded. 'I wonder if I might ask a favour of you.'

'Of course.'

'Might you be able to arrange for me to meet the Foreign Minister?'

'Unofficially?'

'Of course,' said Ash, thinking that he could persuade the Foreign Minister to present him at court. Skobeleff shook his head. 'I wish I could help you but I am afraid I am no longer in a position to request favours from the Foreign Minister.'

'I don't understand.'

'It's common knowledge. Several months ago I went to help a woman being molested in a box at a nightclub. I drove off the man with my walking stick, and the police arrested him. Unfortunately, for me, he turned out to be Rasputin. I was ordered to resign my position at the ministry.'

'But you – '

'I had to resign. The order came from the highest levels of the court. I was about to sail for London to take a new post; instead I'm retiring to my estate in the Crimea. Maybe I'll write my memoirs.'

'But you're only forty-five years old – '

'And finished . . . I'm sorry, I can't help you.'

Ash was stunned. Skobeleff was one of the best. Everyone in the diplomatic corps had assumed he would one day be Russia's Foreign Minister.

* * *

190

That evening Ash had dinner with his friend Albioni's colleague, Signor de la Rocca, and the banker's wife, the Baroness Balmont. She was from the Baltic provinces, tall and blonde, icily beautiful and a well-known huntress. Footmen wearing the purple livery of her house served twenty-five guests a meal of duck the baroness had shot on her marshes earlier in the week.

De la Rocca, cheerful and proud of his Russian wife, held forth on the subject of the war, promising his Russian guests that the Austrian army was beginning to weaken under repeated Italian onslaughts.

Few of the Russians paid much attention, chattering instead about the coming social season, the dance and Rasputin's latest depredations.

As the men rose from cigars and brandy to join the ladies de la Rocca took Ash aside. 'Albioni asked that the baroness and I help you. What is it you need?'

Ash repeated his refrain about the report from Ambassador Page, who was, after all, considerably senior to the relatively inexperienced US ambassador to Russia. At some point, higher up, closer to the Czarina, he would have to shift tactics and at least acknowledge that he carried a private message from King George, but the longer he waited the better chance of keeping the US involvement in the Czar's removal from rumour-hungry Petrograd.

An hour later, when the other guests were leaving, de la Rocca and the baroness invited him into their library. After Ash had repeated his story, she remarked on his reputation and invited him to shoot on her estates near Petrograd, which Ash declined with regret after a glance at de la Rocca told him that the Italian didn't much trust his wife alone in the country. He needed friends in court, not jealous husbands.

The baroness seemed to take his refusal with good grace and returned to the subject of an audience with the Czarina,

191

concluding, 'Not only are you a friend of my husband's friend, Signor Albioni, but the United States is a potential ally, *n'est ce pas?*'

Ash gave a careful nod.

'Well, we shall see what we can do.'

Walking home to the Astoria that night, thinking the baroness might well not help, despite her words, because he had refused her invitation, and realizing he had mistaken de la Rocca as the power in the family, Ash noticed he was being followed. He walked straight into the Europa and watched the street from the lobby. The man looked Russian. He wore a wool overcoat, a brimmed hat and galoshes, the uniform of the plain-clothes detective in Russia, at least when following a foreign officer on the Nevsky Prospect.

Ash asked the doorman for a cab and took it home. The Czar's police followed everybody at one time or another, which was fine with him this trip. They were as good as a bodyguard.

Ash breakfasted late the next morning with Prince Igor Paustovsky, business partner of his Parisian friend Fasquelle, a caviar importer. Breakfast was a meal very rarely taken by upper-crust Russians, but the prince was a gourmand of voracious proportions and seemed to relish the idea of company while pursuing his eccentric – for Petrograd – habit.

'Fasquelle cabled you were coming,' he said through a mouthful of eggs and smoked salmon, forking up more with one hand and waving for the Astoria's waiters with the other. 'Said you were inspecting something or other. Have some more of that.'

Ash kept pace, reckoning he would work it off at the *Salle*. He repeated his story, made his request for help in gaining an audience.

'Good idea. Go to the top. Horse's mouth, so to speak.

192

She's running things, you know. Making a mess of it too. Probably shouldn't tell you this, but it's all going to hell. Somebody's got to talk sense into the Czar before it's too late.'

'Can you get me an audience with Her Majesty?'

'Oh, I suspect I can. I shall work on it. Today, in fact. A matter of contacting the right people . . .'

Sergei Gladishev, the Moscow millionaire and yet another partner of Ash's Parisian friend Fasquelle, received Ash in his Petrograd mansion on the Moika Canal at eleven-thirty, pointedly too early for lunch or any other socializing beyond a brief business meeting. A butler led Ash through marble reception rooms into a large, cluttered office.

Gladishev had inherited a Moscow bakery fortune and developed it during the last decade of explosive industrial growth into an empire of flour mills and warehouses. Several years before the war, still young, he had gone into politics. He had risen quickly through the ranks of the Kadets, the Constitutional Democratic Party, and had become a powerful voice in the Duma, the quasi-parliament that theoretically advised the Czar how to govern Russia.

He was a big man with a broad chest and belly, lavishly dressed, his velvet coat flung over the back of his desk chair, gold nugget cufflinks flashing from his silk sleeves. He had thin, close-cropped hair and his high brow caused his small blue eyes to seem very bright. He was not above reminding Ash that Fasquelle and Russe-Franc-Viande were a very small part of his business.

'Fasquelle mentioned something I can't remember . . . how do you happen to know him?'

'We raced yachts.'

'Yes . . . well, the only thing you'll race here for the next months are iceboats.'

'Do you?'

193

'Iceboats? Good God, I haven't the time . . . What is it you want?'

Ash told him.

'Impossible.'

'Why?'

'The Czar and Czarina have sequestered themselves. They see few people, they listen to even fewer. There was a time I had the Czar's ear, but he hasn't talked to me since the war began. You'll find dozens like me.'

'Because of Rasputin?'

'Rasputin's just a consequence. He couldn't have happened if the Czar had had any taste for governing . . . we're an autocracy without an autocrat. And when he does do something, it's just another attempt to hold off the inevitable. That's not leadership – What do you think of this house?'

'It's magnificent.' Ash was surprised by the question. 'You should see my Moscow home. My estates. I'm one of the richest men in Russia, but because I'm a member of the Kadet Party, which demands liberal democracy, the Czar considers me a revolutionary. *Me.* I should be laughing, if it weren't tragic.'

Gladishev's open manner seemed to invite Ash's blunt question. 'How long can Russia go on like this?'

Gladishev started to answer, then seemed to change his mind. 'We'll be all right, if we make it 'til spring . . .'

'Winter just started.'

'Good day, Commander.'

Two days later, after his third fencing lesson, Ash told Roland, 'I've shot my bolt. Nobody who promised to help called back, and they won't answer my calls.'

'Not even Zlota?'

'Nobody.'

'Why do you suppose they promised in the first place?'

194

'They're embarrassed. I think Gladishev hit it on the head. Nobody can get through to the Czar any more . . .'

'Maybe you're going about this in the wrong way,' Roland said as they walked to the Nevsky for lunch.

'Judging by results, I'd say you were right.'

'The Czarina is a woman – and a very beautiful one at that.'

Ash stopped and looked at Roland. The obvious, of course, had never occurred to him.

'They tell me the Czarina loves pearls.'

'Fabergé.'

'Your mind seems to be clearing, Commander. Shall we?' They had reached the Nevsky Prospect. The jeweller's shop and workrooms were nearby, around the corner at 24 Morskaya Street.

'I'd better stop at the bank first.'

'If you would be so kind as to sign here, sir.'

The manager of the Russian & English Bank watched impassively as a senior clerk counted twenty thousand roubles onto his desk. Ash stuffed the money into his pockets. Twenty thousand roubles were worth ten thousand dollars – three times his yearly salary.

He decided the gift would be from the King – a royal bauble for his favourite – and presumably richest – female cousin, a personal gift, delivered by a friend. After he and Roland had unanimously rejected everything on the main floor, a Fabergé manager was called. He inquired about what Ash intended to spend and, on hearing the figure, said, 'I'm sure we have something. May I inquire about the recipient?'

'A very beautiful, mature woman,' Roland said. 'With expensive tastes.'

'She likes pearls,' Ash said.

They looked some more, rejecting ropes of pearls as too ordinary, and gold hearts encrusted with pearls as too romantic. 'She's a cousin,' Ash told the manager.

He produced a platinum rose with the edges of the petals

lined with pearls, which Ash rather liked, but Roland said they should look further. The manager took them to another room.

'*That*,' said Ash.

'That is the crest of the house of Romanov. I hardly think – '

'She's sort of related,' Ash said, dangling the pendant for Roland to see.

The three-inch pendant represented the top of the Russian crest – two crowned eagle heads looking to the east and west borders of the Russian Empire under a single large crown. The eagle heads' feathers were massed seed pearls, the crowns were gold, and the pennants connecting them, as well as the eagles' eyes and tongues, were cut rubies.

'What do you think?' said Ash. 'A little gaudy?'

Roland shrugged. 'Very Russian.'

'Shall we deliver it, sir?'

'I'll deliver it personally . . .' He hoped.

'How?' Roland asked on the street.

'All I have to do is get inside her palace.' That's all.

The piano player Vadim Mikhailov owned no telephone, but Ash tracked him down by messenger to a private ball he was playing at that night at the Japanese Embassy. Crashing the ball just before the late supper was a simple matter of walking in in his social dress uniform and asking the first unattached attractive woman if she would care to waltz.

She was a baroness – he seemed to be running into a lot of them lately, as if they came in threes, like big waves. She invited him to join their party for supper. Sadly, her husband was at the front, unable to get leave for the ball.

The supper tables were decorated with wicker baskets of flowers brought from the Crimea on heated trains. Ash found himself with a pair of young married couples eating

197

borsch, sturgeon and a kind of grouse. His hostess was the older sister of one of the wives.

Both men were officers. Neither had seen action. They used the English diminutives of their Russian names. Alexander was 'Sandy'. Ivan, 'Johnny'. Conversation swung from the difficulties one couple had had finishing a new summer house before the winter set in to the love poetry of Mayakovsky – '"Cloud in Pants," can you imagine his flies?' – to the documentary movie, 'The Battle of the Somme', to bear hunting, to Tishkova's jubilee at the Maryinski and back to Sandy and Betty's summer house.

Ash probed gently to see whom they knew at the Czar's court. To his surprise the baroness herself was related to a Count Dolgorouki, who was Master of the Court. It seemed he finally was getting lucky. It seemed she had already taken a shine to him. Now he looked again. She had danced well, she was quite pretty, a rather petite brunette. Cultivating her would not exactly be painful.

There was talk at the table of going to see the gypsies after the ball was over. Ash agreed to meet outside, as the baroness seemed to want to keep up appearances. He was having a cigarette by a slightly open window near the orchestra when the last dance ended and the *tapeur* rose like a stork from the forest of palms which concealed his piano.

He was surprisingly old to be Sedovina's step-father, a tall, skinny old man with a mane of white hair and a white, pencil-thin moustache. He brought out a handkerchief as Ash approached, mopped his face and gazed with satisfaction at the guests laughing and chattering on their way toward the doors.

'Monsieur Mikhailov?'

'Commander Ash? I got your message.' He pronounced it *Ahsh,* as most Russians did. 'Vera Sedovina's letter arrived the morning you did. You must have travelled together. How is she?'

198

'I met her at dinner at Lord Exeter's. She seemed like a lovely girl.'

'She is too serious.'

'She did seem that,' Ash agreed. 'She told me you know a lot of people in society here.'

The old man seemed to preen, and again Ash was reminded of a bird.

'I have played piano in Petrograd for four Czars. I have played so long that I remember when the only orchestra you ever heard at a ball was in the Winter Palace. Now they don't trust the old man to make enough noise by himself so they surround me with band instruments. Tonight was an exception. I think the Japanese are too tightfisted to hire a whole orchestra. Did you like my music?'

'Very much . . .' He had to break this off soon if he was going to catch up with the baroness. She seemed a better bet for getting his gift to the Czarina.

'I saw you sitting with the Baroness Beauharnais. A lovely woman. Her father assumed her mother's name and title to keep the family name alive. He himself was only a count, of course, but the Czar used to allow dispensation of that kind of thing.'

'I understand her uncle is Master of the Court,' Ash said, hoping to pick up a little more about her.

'Well, that's her great-uncle. His son was killed at the Battle of Tannenberg. Poor man hasn't much to live for any more.'

'But busy at court,' Ash said.

'Hah. What court? Count Dolgorouki is Master of Court at the Winter Palace. The Czar is never there. So Count Dolgorouki is Master of a Court which exists in name only. He's not part of the small entourage housed at the Alexander Palace with the Czar at Tsarskoye Selo. *That* is the court – such as it is.'

Ash looked across the emptying ballroom. The *tapeur* had

saved him days of futile manoeuvring around the otherwise attractive Baroness Beauharnais. He said, 'You seem to know a good many people . . . care to join me for a brandy?'

The old gossip beamed at the invitation. 'Thank you, sir. You are most kind.'

Ash said, 'I'd like to wait a few minutes.' Give the baroness time to leave without him.

'Of course . . . I will entertain you.' He pushed back through the potted palms and sat at the piano. Ash followed. 'I'd think you'd had enough.'

Mikhailov hunched over the piano like a question mark. Wire thin as he was, his hands were enormous and thickfingered. They poised over the keys and he looked up at Ash, a grin splitting his sunken cheeks.

'Scott Joplin?'

'Sure. Great.'

The old man played Joplin's 'New Leaf Rag' and stormed without pause into 'Euphonic Sounds'.

'What do you think?'

'I never heard it that good even down home.'

'Where do you think Americans got it from? Your Negro musicians are educated on middle-European music.' He played a complex variation of 'The Magnetic Rag'. 'That's his best one. Can we go now? I find I'm tired.'

The baroness had gone and a bitter wind was blowing off the Neva. Ash saw beggars sleeping in the lee of the embassy steps. A few taxis were left, the drivers huddling in cold cars to save fuel and eyeing hopefully the clumps of officers saying good-night.

They walked the short distance to Sedovaya Street to a nightclub that sold vodka in teacups and settled down at a table as far from the loud gypsy guitar band as Ash could bribe them.

Ash said, 'I'm trying to gain an audience with the Czarina – to flesh out a report I'm writing for my ambassador.'

'Then you're in the wrong place. Nobody in Petrograd is connected to the Court any more. The Czar's gone to hide at Tsarskoye Selo. Petrograd society goes on without them.'

The piano player echoed Gladishev, Ash thought. But he still found it hard to believe. 'He can't hide. He's leading the army and the country – '

'Of course he can hide. Russians usually detach themselves from those they rule. It's typical. Imagine any provincial family of some wealth and possessing a fine old name. The best name in the province. Who do they associate with? The merchant who buys the grain from their fields? Hardly. The lawyers who handle their business affairs? Of course not. The teachers in the town? The representative of the railway company? The actors who play in the little theatre they support? Perhaps as mistresses and lovers. The clergy? Only to dispel evil spirits and conduct services. No. This family we imagine can only associate with themselves. And if they are rich enough and live near enough they have a house in Petrograd. If not, they live alone in a sea of peasants. And that's how the Czar lives in Russia today. The head of the great house of Romanov lives a simple, empty life twenty miles from this city. It might as well be three thousand, for all the time he spends here. They are recluses. And society has learned to get on without them.'

'But there must be someone close to them.'

'A few nobody ladies-in-waiting to the Czarina. A young man or two courting their beautiful daughters – beauties like you've never seen locked away like merchant's daughters. A grand duke or two who might have the Czar's ear. His dentist, if you can imagine such a thing. He sees his generals at Mogilev army headquarters, but that isn't a court . . .' Mikhailov dragged deep on his cigarette and glanced at Ash with ancient, cynical eyes. 'All this talk of station and entourage must seem so odd to an American democrat.'

Ash nodded. He had years ago stopped explaining to

Europeans that the four hundred residents of his home town of Lewisburg, West Virginia, divided themselves into at least seven distinct social classes that separated his own family of plantation owners from railroad and coal barons, lawyers, doctors, farmers, coal miners, shopkeepers and day labourers, not to mention Negro servants and travelling salesmen.

The social lines blurred only when those who lit out for the cities returned home in better straits, and the groups mingled only in superficial and mutually agreed-on ways like at a Fourth of July picnic. The first time Ash had fallen in love was with the general store owner's nineteen-year-old daughter and because he was fifteen his father had taken him aside to explain about their different backgrounds and how their interests would diverge.

As their interests had been largely sexual, Ash had found it hard to believe his father, but the Old Man had prevailed by tempting him with a summer job on a cattle boat bound for London, which had turned out to be the first leg of his trip around the world.

'How does Rasputin fit into all this?'

'Rasputin is the sole beneficiary.' The *tapeur* peered into his brandy. 'The so-called holy man has become chamberlain, minister, major domo, privy councillor and Master of the Court all in one. Old Count Fredericks is still Chief Minister of the Imperial Court, but he's so old he forgets his own name. The Czar allows him to bumble along, so of course nothing important is accomplished except by Rasputin. The Czar autocrat rules through this single man, in effect, and will until some enraged nobleman kills Rasputin. Which many have sworn to do.'

'Can Rasputin be as bad as they say?'

Mikhailov shrugged. 'I suppose it's a matter of perception. People say he whores. Well, there isn't an interesting man or woman in Petrograd who doesn't whore. The

202

aristocracy, the liberals, the writers, the ministers, *everyone* whores in Petrograd, except the middle classes. People say Rasputin is a drunkard. Show me a man or woman not drunk in this room and I'll show you a German spy. They say he blasphemes. I don't pretend to understand zealots, but I do know that Rasputin doesn't sell religious indulgences the way the Russian Orthodox church does. They say he lies and steals, but he has no need. A rich woman gives him a bag of money for pleasing her appetites and he hands it unopened to someone who needs it. They say he stinks to high heaven. Well, so does every other Russian peasant, for that is all Rasputin is – a Russian peasant, fresh from the stable.'

'You sound almost as if you like him,' Ash said.

The *tapeur* raised bleak eyes from his glass. '*I hate him.*'

'But you've practically defended him.'

'Unless he is murdered – and they say he has predicted his own murder – Rasputin will destroy the house of Romanov. And everything beautiful in Europe will die with it . . . Did you see those people dance tonight? The beauty of the women? The joy and elegance? There is nothing like this in all Europe – not Paris, not Vienna, not that miserable bleak London. There never was, not even under the Louis and there never will be again. All because a Russian peasant who claims holy powers has hypnotized the Czarina Alexandra, who has hypnotized her husband Nicholas as only a strong, beautiful woman can. Rasputin is Czar.'

'Maybe I should ask Rasputin to help me gain an audience.'

'He wouldn't,' Mikhailov said flatly. 'He hates foreigners.'

Ash signalled the waiter for more brandy and tried to think above the nightclub racket. He was getting an idea. 'Who was that old man? . . . the one who can't remember his name?'

'Count Fredericks, Chief Minister of the Imperial Court. Or what's left of it . . .'

Ash took the pendant to the Tsarskoye Selo Railroad Station. A plainclothes police detective asked his business when he tried to buy a ticket for the thirty-minute ride to the Czar's village.

'I'm summoned by Count Fredericks.'

The detective, impressed, bowed and waved him aboard.

The train left the station on time, crossed the Obvodny Canal and slid swiftly through the factories of the Moscow District. Ash saw several works with cold, smokeless chimneys. In another, the yard of the iron mill was jammed with demonstrators; it looked like a thousand workers on strike, waving placards, cheering a man orating from a shed roof.

The train sped through a shabby suburb, passed the barracks of the First Railway Battalion and burst onto an empty, flat, snow-covered plain heading south on straight track. Railway Battalion detachments guarded bridges and grade crossings, and Ash was fascinated by the thought that this narrow line of track and telephone wire was the sole swift link between the Czar's palace and his one hundred and eighty million cold, hungry and war-weary subjects. His mission took on more and greater urgency. It was no longer merely a plan concocted from abroad. Now it impinged with an on-the-spot reality.

The elaborate court carriages waiting at Tsarskoye Selo's Imperial Station were easily distinguished by the red livery worn by their footmen. Ash eyed the Russian aristocrats and government ministers getting off the train and headed purposefully toward a carriage near the end of the line, choosing one behind an army brigadier and ahead of one entered by an imperious-looking woman whom he guessed was a royal dressmaker from one of the fine shops on the Nevsky. A detective stopped him.

'Your business, sir?'

'I am summoned by Count Fredericks.'

The detective examined Ash's diplomatic passport, entered his name in a notebook. 'Thank you, sir.' Then withdrew with a nod which threw the machinery of the Czar's Court into gear. A footman opened the carriage door, bowed low and motioned to Ash to enter. Another arranged a lap robe over his legs and shut the door, leaving Ash warm and comfortable in a plush little cabinet.

When the rest of the train passengers were seated the lead carriage turned through rococo gold-and-iron gates that led to the vast park. The broad drive, cleared of snow, was lined with aristocrats' mansions – small, elegant buildings, closely spaced. A mile into the park a blue-green palace suddenly appeared in the trees. It was long and low like the grim, red Winter Palace, but its gay colour and position alone in the country made it seem magical. A cluster of gold onion domes glittered above the near wing, the only break Ash saw in the seemingly perfect symmetry that swept across the snowy gardens. The Catherine Palace.

The carriages passed it and a quarter of a mile ahead the Alexander Palace, the actual residence of the Czar, came into view. Smaller than the Catherine, and simpler in ornamentation, the two-storey classical building still looked as if it held about a hundred rooms. Wooden boxes protected the garden statues from the weather. Icicles hung from the eaves and wind sighed in the bare trees. Crows and seagulls wheeled overhead, crying.

At the gates the tall red-uniformed Cossack Imperial Guards shared their posts with plain-clothes detectives in coats and galoshes. 'I am summoned by Count Fredericks.'

He got up the palace steps and past two lackeys in black

frock coats who opened the doors before a court official in a red cape and black patent shoes approached him with the knowing eyes of a very good restaurant maître d'hotel and asked, 'May I help you, sir?'

'I am summoned by Count Fredericks.' He sounded ridiculous to himself, with the rote answer.

'Your name, please.'

'Commander Kenneth Ash, United States Navy.'

'I've not been informed of your appointment.'

Ash said nothing.

'Could you tell me the nature of your visit with Count Fredericks.'

'Why don't you ask Count Fredericks? He summoned me.'

'Ah. The difficulty, you see, sir, is that your name was not on the morning list – '

'Then why don't you take that up with the man who makes your lists? *After* you bring me to Count Fredericks.'

'Sir . . . Please step this way.' They walked from the marble entry hall and through several state rooms, each filled with fresh flowers. The palace was heavy with their perfume – an exotic contrast with the views of the snow-covered gardens outside the tall windows.

Each doorway was attended by a pair of lavishly costumed lackeys and the rooms bustled with court officials passing quickly through them; the man questioning Ash led him to a small room off a ballroom and said, apologetically, 'Count Fredericks is getting older, you see, and occasionally forgets appointments.'

'He sounded perfectly fine to me on the telephone yesterday. Clear as a bell.'

'Please wait here.'

Fifteen minutes passed. Ash watched the guards and detectives from the windows. Finally a captain of the Imperial Guard entered. 'Commander Ash?'

'Captain.'

'Count Fredericks did not summon you to the Alexander Palace.'

'Count Fredericks,' Ash said quickly, 'does not *remember* asking me to the Alexander Palace.'

'What is your business?'

Ash glanced at the despatch case clasped under his left arm. 'I am delivering a gift to the Czarina.'

'To the Empress? May I ask from whom?'

Ash eyed him. 'I suggest you summon your colonel.'

The captain thought about it, ran his eyes up and down Ash's uniform, looked for a moment as if he would enjoy slicing Ash in half with his heavy *pallash*. 'Excuse me, sir.'

He returned in ten minutes with a grey-bearded colonel.

Ash saluted the colonel, explained that he was delivering a gift to Her Majesty from King George V and asked the colonel if he would be so kind as to inspect the contents of his despatch case before Ash entered Her Majesty's presence.

The colonel obliged. When he got to the velvet jewellery box, he weighed it tentatively in his hand.

'Please open it,' Ash said, adding, as the colonel gazed at the pendant, 'of course it should be the Czarina's decision whether to make the contents public.'

'Of course,' said the colonel, closing the box and returning it to Ash.

'I did promise King George that I would deliver it personally, along with his *personal* greetings.'

An hour later the colonel escorted him to the private wing of the palace which housed the Royal Family's apartments. He led Ash past two gigantic, colourfully garbed Ethiopians guarding the main door and turned him over to a lady-in-waiting, a plump, ordinary-looking woman, who warned him, 'You are not to tax the Empress. You will excuse yourself at the first indication that she is tired. I shall be nearby.'

The lady-in-waiting plunged into the apartments. Ash followed, clutching his despatch case. The light and airy rooms reminded him of an English country house. Chintz cushions and curtains and rugs in bright prints looked as exotic in Russia as the Crimean flowers in the midst of winter.

To his surprise, Ash was led directly into the Empress's boudoir. Mauve was the theme colour in the outer rooms, and he realized she must have chosen it because her boudoir was entirely mauve – walls, carpets, furniture. Even the purple lilacs seemed bred to be pale.

Czarina Alexandra reclined on a chaise-longue.

'Commander Ash, Your Majesty,' her lady-in-waiting said, and left Ash standing alone, at attention, three yards from certainly the most powerful woman in the world.

She was stunningly beautiful, with rich auburn hair flecked with grey and a delicate complexion. She wore a loose gown with lace at the neck and sleeves, and ropes of pearls. She regarded Ash through dark blue eyes and motioned him closer with a practised languid hand.

Ash stepped to the foot of the chaise. The walls of the boudoir were hung with icons, but three pictures dominated – a painting of the Virgin Mary, a photograph of the Czarina's grandmother Queen Victoria and, ominously, Ash thought, a portrait of Marie Antoinette.

She startled him with a voice as English as the Henley Regatta.

'*What* has Georgie done?'

'He sent me with a gift, ma'am,' Ash said, and to his relief, the Czarina looked as delighted as any regular mortal getting an unexpected present.

'Show me.'

Ash opened the despatch case, and she startled him again by patting the chaise by her feet, inviting him to sit on the edge. Ash did. She wore a lily-of-the-valley perfume. When she tried to sit up to make room for him she seemed in pain and had to brace herself with her hands. In the light shift he saw dark hollows under her eyes, and thought she looked like a woman who had suffered, and expected to suffer again. She looked, too, by the set of her jaw, determined to survive. He handed her the jewellery box.

Before she opened it she gave Ash a smile that was almost shy. 'My husband would be quite amused to see me accept a gift from a handsome young officer.'

Before Ash could think of anything remotely appropriate in reply, he felt himself blush for the first time in twenty years. She laughed and opened the box.

'How lovely.'

She gazed at it a moment, lifted the pendant from the box and held it to the light. 'You have very nice taste, Commander.'

'King George – '

'Does not shop at Fabergé.'

She picked up a little bell; the cold rage in her eyes was frightening.

'King George did send me, Your Majesty – '

'But not the gift.'

'I confess, it was a device to gain an audience.'

'A costly device.'

'I used his money, I think he would have approved.'

'Why didn't he just send me a letter?'

'He felt he could not risk that.'

She put down the bell, but left it close at hand. 'What is all this about? – wait . . . I know you . . . you're the man who saved Georgie's life in Berlin . . . ?'

'I was there,' Ash said. 'And that's one of the reasons he sent me. You would know he trusts me.'

'Would you please explain?'

Ash took a deep breath. He wished he were standing. Somehow sitting on the edge of the Czarina's chaise-longue made it harder to say, 'King George is worried about your safety, ma'am. In the event of difficulties he asks you to accept . . .' Ash hesitated. Asylum was an awful word that smacked of permanent exile. He looked at the icons and the picture of the Virgin and said, '. . . sanctuary.'

'Difficulties?'

'Political difficulties. Revolution.'

She was listening gravely now, her eyes on his face.

'King George is worried that Your Imperial Majesties might be injured in an uprising.'

'So he sent you here to tell me this?'

'Yes, he proposes sending a cruiser to Murmansk.' Some wary instinct, perhaps stimulated by the wrecked German Embassy near his hotel, made Ash hesitate to invoke the Kaiser's name in her presence.

'Georgie is kind,' she said at last. 'And I know he means well. But you must tell him it is quite impossible. We must stay and overcome the difficulties, as you call them . . . It is our duty to Russia.'

Ash reached for an answer to that one, found none. Hers had the ring of a royal edict, a manifesto, unquestionable. Might he have any more luck with her husband? Then, to his surprise, she asked him a question in conversational tones.

'How is Georgie? And May?'

'They seemed very happy two weeks ago, Your Majesty, but concerned, of course, about the war – '

'Is his leg better?'

'Yes. We shot at Sandringham and he stayed out all day.'

'Good. I miss them all. What do you think of my little

English heaven?' Another languid wave indicated the rooms he had walked through. Ash was ready to cling to anything that could extend his time with her. He said, 'I thought I was in Devon.'

'I was raised in Germany, of course, but I spent so much time in England and my mother, of course, was English . . . My husband will be touched by Georgie's kindness . . .'

'King George and Queen Mary are sick with worry, Ma'am.'

She replied forcefully, her English accent reminding Ash of Lady Exeter holding forth in her London drawing room.

'I have lived in Russia twenty-three years. I *know* what Russia needs – as does my husband.'

She waited until Ash said, 'Yes, I understand, but – '

'There are two Russias, you see. The disturbed Russia of the nobility and their snivelling politicians and conniving entrepreneurs is one. The happy Russia is the Russia of the peasants and their Czar. The first tries to come between the second. But when we strip the nobility and the politicians of their power – the Duma – the happy peasant Russia can live in harmony with the Czar. Do you understand?'

'I know very little about Russia – '

'It is quite simple. The Czar and I live in harmony with the peasants because we know what Russia wants – the whip! Russia loves to feel the whip.'

Ash felt himself stare. He tried to digest her words in the context of her background, the pleasant decor of her apartments. It wasn't easy. Nor was she speaking metaphorically. She *meant* the whip, the Cossack's lance, the gun, the hang rope.

'It is the Slavic nature,' she explained, all earnest now. 'They need a firm hand – as well as our love.'

Ash thought that in her pronouncement lay the best argument he had heard yet against autocracy – the system provided no way to correct rulers who were dull, foolish, or certifiably insane . . . But why was she going on like this? Surely she had courtiers who would listen more appreciatively than he.

'Perhaps it's too late for the whip this time, Ma'am.'

She gazed at him through her long eyelashes, and it occurred to Ash that he had not the vaguest idea of what she was thinking, never mind that he was sitting only inches away from where she lay.

'Who is to say it is too late?' she said in a barely audible voice, tinged now with a note of honest unease.

She looked hard at Ash and Ash knew he had to answer. But if she didn't understand by now what was going on in the streets of Petrograd, or in the miserable countryside, or the bloody trenches, he could hardly enlighten her. Not about Russia.

'The war, Ma'am. It's the war that has made it too late.'

She looked listlessly about the boudoir, her interest fading. Talk, Ash thought. Talk like you never talked before. He said, 'The war must consume so much of the Czar's strength . . .'

She brightened at the reference to her husband. 'Simple peasants begged us not to fight. But they didn't know what German treachery was. How could they? We had to fight Germany.'

'Of course,' Ash agreed, thankful he hadn't mentioned the Kaiser. 'And yet, the peasants were right, weren't they? The war has wounded Russia.'

'Russia has suffered,' the Czarina agreed.

'And her rulers have suffered too.'

'I cannot deny that there has been . . . conflict,' she said softly. 'Faith has been strained . . .' She extended her hand. Ash stood up and bowed over it. 'Leave me now,' she said.

Ash backed away, at a loss. But then she said, 'I will

212

consider what Georgie says. Tell him . . . thank him for his kindness. I will . . . consider his offer.'

She lay back on the chaise-longue when Ash had gone, wincing with pain from her chronically inflamed sciatic nerve, pain that sometimes made it impossible to think; yet deep pain gave her a strange bond with her son, a way of understanding what he felt when the blood swelled his joints till they threatened to explode. She heard a noise from the elevator that led to the children's rooms. Rasputin pushed back the curtain.

The holy man held her son's hand. Alexis's leg was locked in an iron brace. It was vital to keep his knee from bending any tighter; otherwise he would be crippled as the result of the last attack.

'Alexis.' She opened her arms and the boy hobbled to her and let her hold him, squirming just a little. He was recovering quickly this time. She looked up at her friend.

'You heard?' she asked in Russian.

'Yes, *Matushka*.'

Rasputin called her mother, as a peasant, reminding her that she and the Czar were respected as mother and father to every Russian peasant, beloved mother and father to one hundred and eighty million souls.

She asked, 'What do you think?'

'I think he is the devil.'

19

The mill owner's wife was waiting when a deeply troubled Rasputin got home to his Petrograd apartment the next day. She had the paper she wanted signed – some nonsense about the government paying for her husband's flour before the trains had delivered it to the city. The holy man's recommendation to the Minister of Interior was evidently worth a lot of roubles. This was her third visit and she knew by now exactly what Rasputin demanded for such a favour. As must her husband.

'I waited for you, Father Gregory.'

'Take off your clothes.'

Rasputin sat down and watched her undress; she had big breasts for such a highborn lady, but he was too worried to stay interested. The Czarina's laughter still rattled like stones in his head. Somehow, the American had shaken his hold on her.

Ordinarily she listened to him, obeyed him. She prayed with him. Recognizing his saintly powers, she entrusted to him her precious children. She defended him when enemies ran to her with tales of his sins. She praised him when the Czar occasionally slipped the noose of his thrall and questioned his own holy wisdom.

Only once before had the Czarina ignored his advice. Rasputin had warned the Czar and Czarina not to take Russia to war. He had foreseen the disaster, but they wouldn't listen, deafened by the ungodly shouts of patriotism. She knew now that he had been right, but it was too late. The cart was in the middle of the stream and the horses were drowning.

The American had frightened her with his promise of rescue. All day Rasputin had brought all his very considerable will to bear on her, but still couldn't convince her that the American was a devil. And when he had called the King of England a devil too, she had laughed out loud and said, 'My dearest friend, there are certain things even *you* can't understand.'

Which was why the Czarina's laughter still rattled like stones in his head. His power over her demanded there should be nothing he did not understand, nothing she couldn't turn to him for. Curing the little Czarevich was simply not enough to sway the Empress of all the Russias in matters outside the nursery. He could not hypnotize her like the child; she was a strong woman, as strong a person as he.

To control her, he had to cure everything. She was deeply moved by prayer, so he helped her to pray, hours sometimes, until he thought his knees were broken. And she wanted to be soothed by his eyes and the God-given healing power which vibrated from his hands, as mysterious to him as it was to her.

Drugs helped when prayer wasn't enough. Drugs the doctors feared. And some drugs the doctors didn't even know. When God's healing wasn't enough Rasputin had other resources to cure what ailed the Czar and Czarina. And thank God he did, because they turned to him with all their ills.

Cocaine in the nostrils cured a cold. Opium soothed a headache. Such use was common; Rasputin had learned about these drugs from real doctors and many people in Petrograd took them when uncomfortable. But the Tibetan herbs he had discovered in his youthful wanderings were more powerful. Some banished worry. Some made the mind wander among strange pictures. Some dissolved the will like water melted salt.

He kept them in bottles nestled behind the wine on his

dining room sideboard. He thought of using some himself, right now, but he resisted. He needed a clear head to cure the Czarina of the American.

He hadn't thought clearly at the palace. He'd been so shocked by the Czarina's sudden independence, so upset by her laughter that he'd fallen to his knees, saying, 'But you *can't* leave Russia.' He'd even kissed the hem of her dress. The bond between them was like a spider web – more intricate than strong.

'We would return,' she had answered soothingly, comforting *him*, even as she made up her mind.

'But Russia – '

She embraced him, held him to her breast, calmed him with soft words while the boy watched, eyes bright as sapphires . . . Recalling the moment, Rasputin cursed himself for his mistakes. He hadn't understood how worried she was about the children and had asked, 'But your son's throne? What will happen to your son's throne if you go to England?'

'I would never surrender my son's throne,' she replied with a smile at the boy that did not extinguish the hard fire in her eye. '*Never* . . . but I am concerned for the safety of all my children. I am considering that we might take the children to England. Then when it is time to set things right again, the Emperor and I shall return – '

'*Father Gregory.*' The mill owner's wife was waiting, standing in her pile of clothes. Rasputin's dark eyes seemed to bore through her, unseeing. He was still disturbed, frightened even . . .

There were things the Czarina didn't understand. Things only a Russian knew. The peasants would never believe in a Czar who fled. Revolutionaries would seize the throne. Or another Romanov – a grand duke from the huge squabbling family – would take the power while the Czar was in England. But neither revolutionaries nor a new Czar would give a hang for Rasputin. They would ignore him, or kill him. There were grand dukes who spoke openly of murdering him today . . .

'You will come with us,' the Czarina had assured him. But the thought of leaving Russia turned his blood cold. He was only a poor Russian peasant, a wandering preacher welcome in millions of simple huts across the endless land. This was home. He believed in God and Russia and Heaven, and he never doubted that he would pass from Russia to Heaven when his time – which loomed near – came. The great beyond – Europe, England and the seas – was as mysterious as Hell, and as unappealing. His only hope was to make the Czarina stay in Russia. He'd said, 'When the Cossacks burn a peasant's hut and the peasants move in with their relatives they are like cows and chickens in their new home – begging for every morsel.' She had answered, 'We will return, I promise you.' And then God had smiled and helped Rasputin conjure a vision which had made her doubt her decision. She had seen his eyes fill with it and had asked him, 'What do you see?'

'I see my blood on the American's hands.'

She looked genuinely alarmed, and the little Czarevich took his hand.

'He is the devil,' Rasputin repeated. 'Sent to kill us all.'

The Czarina looked at her son and at Rasputin. He knew he had at least frightened her a little this time. Enough to make her say, '. . . I must discuss this with the Czar . . .'

Rasputin had hurried back to Petrograd. Her doubts were temporary, but they bought him, he hoped, time to deal with Ash . . .

'What do you want me to *do?*' asked the woman who wanted the paper signed.

'Do you speak good English?'

'Of course.'

Her highfalutin airs were half the fun of bedding her. Of

217

course I speak English, doesn't everybody? No, madame. Real Russians do not speak English. He said, 'Get dressed.'

Her mouth dropped open. Rasputin laughed and grabbed a handful of her ample rump on the way to the sideboard that held his herbs.

Ash had not let the maids unpack. Despite the size of his luxurious suite, he preferred to live out of his bachelor chest – a commodious four-foot-high brass-and-walnut travelling box that contained drawers and compartments for his uniforms, business suit and dinner jacket, shooting clothes and the hats, shoes and boots appurtenant to them. Tamara had bought it for him the winter she'd danced in Boston.

He had lived out of it ever since, as if aboard a boat with everything in its place; but the reason he did not spread into the hotel furniture was that if he had to leave Petrograd quickly, getting his belongings back would be a simple matter of wiring the Astoria to deliver his chest to the American Embassy. Provided, of course, that revolutionaries hadn't burned both buildings to the ground.

The chest contained a shaving kit, with a false bottom for jewellery which Tamara had filled with studs and cuff links. Ash was carrying it into the marble bathroom when the telephone rang. He jumped for it. A full day had passed since he'd presented King George's offer to Czarina Alexandra. He picked up the telephone hoping to hear the dignified summons of a palace operator. 'You are called from the apartments of Her Imperial Majesty.'

But it was only the hotel desk.

'There is a lady to call on you sir. Madame Natalia Fofanova.'

'Who?'

The clerk repeated her name. It meant nothing to Ash, but he had done some lavish tipping with King George's money to cover moments like this. 'Who is she?'

The clerk lowered his voice. 'I believe she is married to Georgy Fofanov of the flour mills. A very important man, sir.'

'Send her up.' Maybe allied with the food millionaire Gladishev. But he strapped the cut-down Luger into the small of his back, in case she was not a mill owner's wife but a German agent with friends nearby.

At her knock, Ash opened his door to a rather voluptuous, dissipated-looking woman in her thirties. She had dark good looks and a sensual face, and for a moment he wondered if the desk clerk had been fooled by a prostitute. But her pearls and diamonds looked real, and she breezed into his room with all the self-assurance of a wealthy Petrograd matron. Ash gave a quick look at the hall before he closed the door.

She introduced herself in French-accented English and said, 'Father Gregory sent me.'

'Who?'

'Rasputin. He wishes you to come to his home.'

'Rasputin?'

'He wants to talk to you. He asks me to translate. His English is not good.'

'What does he want to talk about?' His luck was taking a turn up. Maybe.

'He did not say. Shall we go?'

Ash looked at her. 'I hear he hates foreigners.'

'I have no idea whether he hates you or not, Commander Ash. But he sent me to you. He wants to talk to you.'

Ash ran the possibilities. A German agent? But faking Rasputin was a crazy ploy, not credible on the face of it, given the man's well-known hostility to foreigners. So if it was Rasputin, what did the monk want? Did the Czarina – she was taking too long to get back to him. She could have telegraphed her husband in hours – Rasputin had influence over her. What the hell . . . 'Okay,' Ash said.

But outside the hotel he made her sleigh driver wait until the plain-clothes detectives who had been trailing him for several days now had started their car.

'What's wrong?' she asked.

He nodded at their ordinary-looking taximeter cab, which was hard to miss in a city bereft of motor vehicles. 'It seems the coppers are following me. I'd feel kind of lonely without them.' He watched for her reaction but all she said was, 'Yes, Father Gregory is followed too. For his protection. He's afraid someone will kill him.'

Which makes two of us, thought Ash. 'What does he want to talk about?'

'He just told me to bring you,' she said, and sat back while her well-fed horses trotted smartly up Gorokhovaya Street to the edge of the Moscow District. Ash was surprised to see that Rasputin lived in a poor neighbourhood. The streets were much darker than the Nevsky or St Isaac's Square, crowded with shop clerks and office staff walking home under the clearing sky. Bitter cold was the price of dry weather in Petrograd, and the people had the collars of their black wool coats turned up against the north wind. Yesterday, the Neva had frozen clear across.

Natalia Fofanova's sleigh stopped in front of a dimly lighted passage which led to a courtyard. At the back of the yard was an ordinary five-floor brick apartment building, as weather-worn and dirty as the others on the street. Two plainclothes detectives stopped them in the foyer.

They recognized Natalia and returned her identity papers with smirks. Ash showed his diplomatic passport. The police regarded his name and waved them to the stairs. Another detective stopped them on the third floor. The dark hall smelled of cabbage and rank cheese. Natalia knocked on a door when the detective had finished with their papers.

An old woman in a wool dress and felt slippers opened it. She stepped back without expression and let them enter a parlour crowded with massive oak furniture. There were carpets on the floor and icons and paintings on the walls and shaded electric lamps set about the room. Steam heat hissed, and Ash immediately felt too warm. Natalia spoke in Russian. The old woman tucked her scarf tighter over her head and disappeared down a hallway.

Ash smelled him first, perspiration and cheap perfume, as Rasputin stepped out of the shadowy hall, buttoning his trousers. He was huge, a head taller than Ash, but as he moved into the light, still concentrating on his fly, Ash thought he had rarely if ever seen a *dirtier* person. Rasputin's hair was black and greasy, hanging low over his ears. He had a long, matted beard, as thick as fleece. His clothes looked new, yet filthy – a brightly embroidered blouse, velvet trousers, and high, scuffed and water-stained boots.

Rasputin turned his weathered face toward Ash, and Ash thought that Mikhailov the piano player had been right – Rasputin was a Russian peasant, a countryman from a brutal grinding land who had somehow escaped from Russia's endless space. But then he fixed Ash with his deep, wide-set eyes.

It was like looking into the wrong end of binoculars – two gigantic shiny orbs descending into a fathomless beyond. They gave Ash a long, slow scrutiny, followed by the raising of his heavy, blunt-fingered hand in a gesture of blessing.

He motioned Ash into the dining room, which had the same heavy furniture, and sat down at a table under a bright chandelier. He muttered something in Russian. Natalia brought a bottle from the sideboard. She stood beside him as he poured two glasses of wine. The table was spread with cakes and nuts and jams. Water bubbled in a samovar. Rasputin took one glass for himself and pushed the other toward Ash. Ash draped his boat cloak over the back of the chair and sat in front of the wine.

Rasputin raised his glass.

Ash picked up his. It was a red wine, smelled sweet. A Madeira. He looked over his glass at the monk and toasted, '*Boje Tsaria Khranee!*' Long live the Czar.

Rasputin surprised him with a grin and a joke. '*Tsarinia.*'

He drank noisily, poured more wine into both glasses and drank again. Stuffing a handful of cakes into his mouth, he chewed reflectively. Suddenly his eyes seemed to leap at Ash.

Ash felt a shiver as the monk's gaze connected – an electric-like jolt. Remarkable. The room seemed to disappear for a second. Then Rasputin gave a lazy smile, and the feeling subsided. Ash recalled an old bare-knuckles boxer he'd met in a Manhattan bar – half-drunk and well past his prime, but still lethal. The boxer had dropped broad hints that he could still take apart any man in the place if he felt like it, then passed the threats off with a sly grin. Rasputin was toying with him the same way, flaunting his apparently hypnotic power. Ash drank the wine. It was a damned good Madeira. Finally Rasputin spoke, his eyes holding Ash's eyes while Natalia translated.

'Rasputin says he had a dream. In the dream a navy man sailed to Russia in a big boat to – ' she hesitated with the word – 'kidnap the Czar. But the navy man was killed by peasants who love the Czar . . . Rasputin says you are the navy man in his dream.'

'Tell Rasputin I smelled him behind the curtains in the Czarina's boudoir.'

Startled, Natalia translated, and it was clear from her expression that she didn't know what was going on. Rasputin, for his part, merely refilled their wine glasses. Ash found himself thinking he was glad they weren't playing poker. Hard to tell what the monk was thinking. He took a sip of wine, then put it aside. He felt like he'd had a couple too many, probably because he hadn't eaten.

Rasputin spoke. Here it came. But all Natalia said was, 'Rasputin asks would you prefer tea instead?'

'Sure.' She poured boiling water from the samovar into a waiting pot, then poured Ash a glass. Ash took it. 'Please tell Rasputin I'm waiting for an answer. I thought something smelled funny in the Czarina's boudoir. Now I know it was him. Go on, tell him that.'

She did. Rasputin answered.

'Rasputin says the Czarina has many flowers in her boudoir.' She refilled his glass. Ash tossed it back and stood up. 'Tell Rasputin she needs them with him around.'

Rasputin looked up at him. His eyes had changed. Two circles of grey marble polished like lenses. Deep, but opaque. Ash thought he could detect movement in the irises. They projected light. No, they couldn't. Ash realized he had frozen in a strange pose, half-standing, half-sitting. Rasputin's eyes flickered toward Ash's chair. Ash felt himself sinking back down to the table, onto the plush seat of his chair.

Rasputin spoke, and Natalia spoke and her full, sensual lips seemed to move at the same time as Rasputin's. The monk's sonorous, demanding voice seemed to rumble from her mouth. The monk spoke Russian and Ash heard English. Something was wrong with his sense of time. Their voices were simultaneous. Something was wrong.

'Navy man. Drink your tea.'

Ash thought, *I'm not doing anything he tells me to.* He glared defiantly into the monk's eyes. He watched his own hand pick up the hot tea glass and lift it to his lips . . . Natalia refilled the glass, and Ash drained it again. It was warm and delicious. He pushed his glass toward her for another. Rasputin shook his head. Natalia took the glass from Ash's fingers, plucked it like a flower. She looked frightened. Ash thought something odd was happening to her face. He thought, *I should be afraid,* and Rasputin said, 'No more tea, navy man. Too much might kill you.'

Ash tried to stand up. He couldn't move.

'Navy man, I am stronger than they say I am. But in some ways I am weaker. I can't hypnotize a man like you without my herbs.'

'*Herbs?*' Ash heard his own voice from a distance, clear and logical. A first-rate officer in command of the situation. *A sportsman who happens to hold a commission* . . . The monk couldn't have drugged him. 'You drank the wine too.'

'I said I am stronger. I can drink many glasses of that wine and that herb. But I didn't touch your tea. Not a drop.'

20

Ash saw Natalia's skin peel off her face.

It blistered up in thick pieces that fell away like an orange rind dug loose with fingernails. He tried to think, tried to explain.

'Be happy, navy man. Be happy.'

Almost immediately, even as he tried to think what Rasputin wanted, Ash felt a euphoric warmth spread through his body. In a remote detached way he considered that Rasputin's drugs had made him susceptible to suggestion. Strange pictures began forming in his mind, memories as yet unformed, like a slide show out of focus, and under the pictures a thought clamoured that he should not feel so happy, that Rasputin intended damage, damage to him, damage to his mission to remove the Czar of Russia . . .

The monk picked another bottle off the sideboard. Clear again, the liquid tasted like liquorice when Rasputin told Ash to drink it. Time stopped. Ash's euphoria evaporated. So did the reef of clamouring thought. In their place, fear battered his mind. His brain seemed all he could see. He clung, tried to cling, to an image of the trenches. Cold mud below, an image of the agony that he and Page's inner circle meant to stop . . .

The monk raised his hand. Ash actually cringed, afraid that Rasputin would do something terrible, afraid that when Rasputin did he couldn't stop him . . . Ambassador Page's face formed in his mind, old and tired, dying too soon to end the war. More pictures . . .

'Navy man. Can you hear me?'

'Yes.' Ash thought of his father, wished the Old Man

were here, to help him, saw his face, a big grin that faded when their eyes met. Rasputin took out a watch on a chain and swung it gently back and forth inches from Natalia's face. Ash stared. Her skin looked normal again. Her eyes followed the watch. The monk was hypnotizing her like a Viennese doctor. What the hell for? Rasputin spoke.

'You will remember nothing.'

English, Russian. Ash waited.

Rasputin hit Ash with the full power of his mesmerizing eyes. He felt physical pain, as if the monk had pierced his skull. And he felt fear as Rasputin said, 'You cannot take the Czar; you will leave Russia; you will *never* come back . . .'

'I can't leave,' Ash said. His mind screamed. *Who said that?* but the voice, his voice, went on, echoed by Natalia's translation. 'I won't leave without him.'

Rasputin spoke slowly. 'I will send you to a peasant village where all the sons are dead in war and I will tell the peasants that you are a German spy . . .'

Ash was overwhelmed by a sudden, vivid image of old men in black circling him with clubs. The drugs made it so clear. The women were behind the men, with knives, the old mothers and the young girls the dead were supposed to have married.

Ash couldn't stand even when he pressed both hands on the table and pushed down with all his might. The gun in the small of his back. He doubted he could lift it, much less pull the trigger.

'Stand up,' said Rasputin.

Ash stood up.

'Turn around.'

Ash faced the door. A minute later, or a second, or an hour, he felt his boat cloak descend over his shoulders. Rasputin stepped into view wearing a long dark coat. Beside him, Natalia, pale and eyes wide, was waiting in her sable. Rasputin's long beard, flecked with dirt and grey hair, made his face enormous, like Great-uncle Abel McCoy, Ash's mother's uncle, bearded and disreputable-looking as a bear in a rainstorm. See that squirrel, boy? More pictures. The Kentucky muzzle-loader shifted in his shaggy-backed hands and the invisible squirrel dropped from the top of a seventy-foot hickory. Stick him in the sack, boy . . .

The detective outside Rasputin's door watched them pass. Ash stared into his eyes, oriental eyes, tried to send a message. Help me. Oriental eyes. So common in Russia. Sloe eyes. Moody, dark purple. Tamara had them. Infinitely deep and beautiful. He nearly called out her name as Rasputin yanked him away from the detective; swallowed the sound. Rasputin would hurt her if he knew what it would do to Ash.

The pictures were getting worse, bright and weirdly coloured as they trooped down the stairs. Where? Ash suddenly remembered opium. Cribs of half-naked grey men in a room as dark as this stairway. The port of Shanghai. He'd been fifteen. Some of the other crew knew the ropes and he remembered sucking his first pipe and sinking into oblivion as the ship's carpenter promised, 'The stuff won't last forever if you get scared. It won't last forever if you're scared.'

But he hadn't been scared. Opium was detachment, drifting on a benign sea. Rasputin's drug was like the tentacles of a monster rocketing out of a dark ocean.

Ash thought he heard a whimper as they passed the detectives in the courtyard and the detectives saluted with claws. They had removed their winter gloves and they had claws, brown with curved talons, ivory and razor sharp. Their faces were normal, except for long teeth.

Ash looked at Natalia. Her face was dissolving in the snow. But the sky was clear – it had been earlier – it couldn't snow. Detach yourself, Ash told himself. It can't last forever. All the buildings were white. There were many people on the street. Walking fast in straight lines. Ash felt his knees buckle. Rasputin grabbed his arms. Ash hadn't noticed earlier that the monk had a steel hand. Must have lost it in the war, like Roland. Monks didn't fight. Rasputin smiled. Steel teeth. Must have chewed it off. Powerful grip. Ash tried to imagine the number of hinges you'd need to make such a hand.

Natalia screamed. The sound echoed in Ash's head, rising in pitch. The people walking kept walking. He looked at her. She hadn't screamed, but she should have. Her face had dissolved to the bone. Rasputin told her to get in her sleigh. Where is he taking me?

Rasputin started talking, his voice deep, sonorous, a comfort. They had walked some way. The buildings were still white, the people still walking in straight lines, but Rasputin was speaking. Russian, Ash understood only the odd word. The sleigh forged ahead of them, stopped. Rasputin helped him in. The driver cracked his whip. It echoed like Natalia's scream, and the sleigh lurched into fast motion.

The white buildings whizzed past, a white line. The running people kept pace, almost, walking straight, heads down, past the white buildings. *It won't last forever if you get scared.*

Rasputin emptied the second bottle of Madeira and threw the bottle in the street. He pulled another from his coat. Where had he got more? Must have a coat full of them. The monk is drunk. Ash laughed. Rasputin pressed the bottle to Ash's lips. Which was this, the drugged wine that didn't affect Rasputin, or plain Madeira? Ash swallowed.

'Listen to me,' Rasputin said through Natalia. 'This is your last chance. Tell me that you won't take the Czar.'

It was funny, Ash thought. *He can make me do anything but that. I won't tell him I won't take the Czar. He has me now, but not in the future. It won't last forever . . .*

At the river Rasputin made Natalia's driver step down and took the reins himself. Bouncing down the snow-covered stairs of a landing, he drove onto the ice. *We'll drown,* thought Ash. But the river had been frozen for days now. How long had he been in Petrograd? Six days. The river frozen for three. *We'll drown.*

'Do you swim, navy man?'

Distant, out of time, Ash heard Natalia's voice, '*No . . .*'

Rasputin made the sign of the cross, and her face turned blank as an empty page. The police, who had trailed them down the straight white streets, were gone. Natalia's coachman had disappeared. They sat alone in her sleigh, on ice, flanked by stone river walls. Above the banks, on either side of the narrow river, were dark factories. The tall smokestacks of Petrograd's electric-generating station wore rings of lights.

'Do you swim, navy man?'

Ash saw a dark hole in the ice a few feet ahead of the horses. Open water ten feet wide, wafting steam, a circle melted by the outflow from the power station's cooling pipes. The river flowed under it, moving water, black and rippled like the inside of a monster's mouth. Jagged ice on the edges were the teeth. Ash could hear the thing breathing. See its foggy breath. *It won't last forever.*

Ash looked into the mouth. He was standing on the edge of it, Rasputin behind him. He tried to remember climbing down from Natalia's sleigh. *It won't last –*

'*Swim.*'

Ash gathered his muscles to jump into the water. How could he swim in his boots and wool boat cloak? Rasputin had had all the answers all night long. Ash turned to ask him. The monk had raised his foot as if to kick him. He seemed to kick very slowly, but before Ash could stop him, the monk's heavy boot slammed into his back. He heard Natalia scream, felt violent pain in his spine and saw the electric lights disappear as cold black water closed over his head.

Ash's boots filled and he sank to the bottom. They were too tight to kick off. Thick mud sucked around his legs. The water was brutal. He felt the cold clamp his lungs, squeeze his heart. The river's current swept him off balance.

Kicking frantically, seeking something to push off, he hit some solid stone or iron from the electric power station outflow. He pushed out of the mud and kicked to the surface, only to crash into an ice ceiling. Turning instinctively against the current, he swam and dragged himself back to the open hole.

Ash tried to pull himself over the edge. He was too stiff and weak to lift the enormous weight of his sodden clothes. And the cold was sapping his will, even as it chiselled the drugs from his brain.

He felt a sudden surge of warmth, thought it was the delirious instinct of a freezing body simply to drift to sleep. But the cold returned, intense as before. In the black night above the stone wall of the river he saw the lights on the power station smokestacks. *The outflow.* The water pumped through the electric plant to cool the condensers.

Gripping the ice, he worked his way around the edge of the hole, seeking warmth. Halfway around he found it. Warmer water billowed around his body. Compared to the cold, it felt like a bath. Ash hung in it as long as he dared, absorbing the warmth, building his strength for a single push.

He reached as high as he could on the ice, then kicked,

rhythmically, trying to make his lower body float. It rose a little and when he was as horizontal as he knew he would ever get he kicked with all his strength and clawed the ice, inching his way up and forward. Forward. His tunic buttons caught on the edge, stopped his momentum. He started to sink back, felt his strength pour out of him like soupy clay that refused to harden. He'd never get the strength again.

Ash slammed his elbows against the ice and lifted his chest, lurched forward, clawed the rough surface and pulled until lights stormed in front of his eyes. He hauled his stomach onto the edge, his thighs, and then he was up, his chest heaving, his breath coming in shudders.

The cold air burned his face. He forced himself to stand, shambled toward the edge of the river, ran slipping, sliding along the wall to a landing and staggered up its snow-covered steps. His cloak and uniform and boots were sodden, chafing as they froze. He made for the lights of the power station. A car was pulling away from the front gate. A taxi. Ash bellowed as loud as he could and pulled a sodden wad of roubles from his pocket.

'Astoria,' he gasped. Shaking uncontrollably, he huddled into a ball for warmth. He wondered if he would die. But even as the car crossed the city at a maddeningly slow pace, an idea began to form in his battered mind. Rasputin thought he was dead.

Ash banged on the driver's partition and gasped through chattering teeth, 'Servants' entrance.'

It was doubtful the driver understood English, but it would have been a dull man who would have dropped a passenger in Ash's condition any place less private at the Astoria than the servants' entrance.

* * *

The back stairs were the worst. Ash spent five minutes slumped on the half-landing, growing colder. When he realized he could die there, he crawled. The hall porter saw him shambling along the corridor and unlocked his door and clucked at the muddy wet trail on the carpet.

He was vaguely aware of the telephone ringing over the roar of the water taps, but he had to get into the tub before the cold killed him. Too weak to pull off his boots, he climbed in with them on. Shivering violently, he felt like an insulated flask, his skin and flesh standing between the hot bath water and the ice in his guts.

At last the warmth penetrated. He stopped shaking. His mind drifted. Fell asleep. But wakened when the water had cooled and realized that the telephone could have been the Czarina's answer for King George.

Gathering his strength, moving slowly, he worked off his ruined boots, started a fresh bath running, wrapped himself in towels and called the hotel desk. 'This is – ' His voice cracked. He cleared his throat with difficulty and concentrated hard on saying, 'Commander Ash. Any messages?'

'None, sir.'

'Was that you called before?'

'Yes, sir. The hall porter – is everything all right?'

Why didn't she call? Contact him? What was she waiting for? He looked at the marble clock on the mantel. Two-thirty in the morning? 'I need a pot of coffee and a bottle of brandy.'

He soaked in the new tub until the hall porter knocked. Then he got into bed and drank coffee and brandy half and half until he fell asleep and dreamed of Rasputin pushing him under the ice each time he tried to climb out of the hole.

He woke at noon, stiff and bleary-eyed. He was light-headed, his back hurt. It was still hard to concentrate.

Coffee didn't help. Fragmented events of the night drifted past his mind. He was alive by the combination of a miracle and years of struggling to keep in fighting trim. He recalled moments in the water when a single ounce less of strength would have been fatal.

22

Only a few hundred yards from the Astoria, at the Yusupov Palace, in a cellar room prepared for Rasputin's murder, a Red Snow agent presented a box of forged letters and cheques to the young Prince Felix and the fiery Duma orator Purishkevich. The cellar room was well-chosen, far from the main parts of the palace and privately entered, but Narvski, the Red Snow agent, thought the killing ground looked too carefully laid out, too lovingly prepared with fine furnishings and carpets, as if Prince Felix and Purishkevich were trying to smother their fear with details. Hence the forgeries, which Red Snow hoped would goad the pair to action.

'Where did you get these?'

They knew Narvski only as an invalided soldier turned foreign currency officer for a Russian bank, a man from an ordinary family in the provinces, son of a school teacher; his mother had inherited a small textile business, and the extra money paid for a cadet education in the local military school and a commission in an artillery brigade when the war began. Wounded the first summer on the Galician Front, health forever shattered, gone to work for the bank, Viktor Narvski was as ordinary a middle-class Russian as the prince and the arch-conservative politician might meet in the capital city of Petrograd in the last week of 1916. His only secret, Red Snow.

'I discovered the cheque in the course of my work at the bank.' They were apparently written by a German agent arrested the year before, and cashed by Rasputin. 'I made inquiries. I was threatened. Then, these letters were given to me.'

'By whom?' Purishkevich asked. Young Prince Felix was dark with rage, but Purishkevich, an older, cleverer man, was not so easily led.

Narvski answered, 'I can only guess that someone who was afraid to show them to the authorities heard about my inquiries about the cheques and sent them to me hoping I would have the courage that he lacked.'

'This is disgusting,' the prince said as he sifted through them for the fourth time. The forged letters were written, purportedly, by Rasputin to the German agent. They contained secret information about Russian army movements that Rasputin could only have learned from the Czarina, if the letters had been written when Red Snow's forgers had dated them.

Would the forgeries be the last nails in Rasputin's coffin?

Prince Felix had been talking about killing the monk for a year. Red Snow agents, overhearing his boasts in nightclubs and Bohemian salons around the city, had lent subtle encouragement, steering him toward others, like Purishkevich, who might offer to help.

All had been ready for weeks now – poison, cars to bring Rasputin to the palace and take him away, a place to dump the body, alibis, a gun if needed. Red Snow's secret revelation tonight was for courage. The final 'fact' about the evil monk – ironically untrue – which would push the conspirators into action. The slender prince began pacing the vaulted room, working himself into a frenzy; Narvski had mixed feelings about Prince Felix. As heir to the richest fortune in Russia, the prince was undoubtedly the enemy of the people; yet his patriotism and love of the country he thought Rasputin was destroying were genuine, and that Narvski respected. But it was the reactionary Purishkevich, the strongest of the conspirators, that Narvski watched.

The door slammed open suddenly, startling them, and a huge man in a red coat ducked through the arch. He surveyed the three, glowering suspiciously. Behind him, two silent Cossacks stationed themselves at the door.

'Uncle Valery!' Prince Felix cried.

And Purishkevich bowed low. 'Your Imperial Highness. Thank God you have come.'

'I promised to hear you out.' The Grand Duke Valery stood six feet six inches and weighed the same hard two hundred and eighty pounds he had maintained since cadet days. He had a big, square head, pink cheeks and a walrus moustache turning grey.

He jerked a hand at Narvski. 'Is this the one?'

'Viktor Narvski, Your Highness. He's brought more evidence.'

The Grand Duke Valery glared down at him and Narvski forced himself to bow respectfully. This one would hang. Him and all his corrupt household.

'Let's see it.'

'It's disgusting,' said Prince Felix, pressing the cheques and letters into the Grand Duke's hands.

'Rasputin destroys the monarchy,' cried Purishkevich. 'He spits on the church. And now he is a traitor. For his crimes against Russia, Rasputin must die. *God save the Czar.*'

'God save the Czar,' Prince Felix echoed, with an anxious glance at Valery, who was examining each page under the light.

'Do you not agree that he must be stopped, Your Highness?'

Valery said, 'This doesn't make sense. The monk hates Germans. Besides, he doesn't need money. He has the Empress.'

'For that alone he should die.'

The grand duke ignored Purishkevich and turned to Prince Felix. 'You have married a Romanov. You bear the same responsibilities as us. We are not murderers. If you believe this "evidence" it is your duty to present it to the

237

Czar's police. We follow the rule of law. The Czar's courts will try Rasputin and if he is a traitor the Czar's executioner will hang him.'

'But Rasputin controls the throne,' Purishkevich protested.

Valery eyed him sternly. 'If Romanovs become murderers there will be no throne.'

'But Your Highness, if Revolutionaries rise because of Rasputin – '

Valery cut him off with an enigmatic stare. 'There are better ways.' He tossed the papers on the table and stalked out.

'Better ways?' Prince Felix echoed.

Purishkevich tugged a heavy revolver from the pocket it had been bulging and slammed it down on the table. 'For Rasputin, *this* is the only way. And soon!'

A relieved Viktor Narvski listened silently while the reactionary restored the young Prince's resolve. This *was* the way. Rasputin himself had predicted that if he were murdered the autocracy would fall. Red Snow believed him. And furthermore, when the monk was despatched to Hell, his American friend would be following close behind.

By evening the Czarina had still not sent a message. Two and a half days without a word. And Ash had to face the possibility, despite Rasputin's fears, that the Czarina or the Czar had decided against leaving Russia. He telephoned the Alexander Palace, but got no farther into the court than a senior telephone operator who agreed to leave word he had called with the colonel that Ash had shown the Czarina's gift to, which meant nothing . . . He had to do more, had to get through to the Czarina, somehow persuade her . . .

He had one ace. Rasputin thought he was dead. How would the monk react to a man he thought he had murdered? Could he conceivably frighten Rasputin into interceding with the Czarina, into talking her into leaving Russia? Literally scare the wits out of him.

Mulling over the idea, he had supper in his room, then put on a clean dress uniform identical to the one in which Rasputin had last seen him alive. He was still shaky, but this seemed too good a chance to let pass . . . What if he were just sitting in Rasputin's apartment when the monk came home? Waiting among his icons . . . Not so bad. Not bad at all. Scary . . .

But to break into Rasputin's apartment Ash had to elude the monk's detectives and steer clear of the police watching the Astoria as well. He put on a navy greatcoat and a Russian fur hat Tamara had given him. They hid his face and altered the familiar boat-cloak and service-cap silhouette the Czar's police had been trailing.

Then he went out through the hotel kitchen, ducked into a channel between the woodpiles and emerged on the other side of St Isaac's Square, where he hailed a sleigh that had just dropped passengers at the Maryinski Palace, and gave the driver Rasputin's address.

As they entered Rasputin's neighbourhood and Ash was wishing he had brought a flask because the night was even colder than last night, his driver suddenly hauled back on the reins with a surprised grunt. Half a block ahead, Rasputin careened into the street bellowing at the top of his lungs, trailed by three detectives hard put to keep up while they stuffed notebooks and pencils into their pockets and tried to button their coats.

Ash's driver jerked his horses into a courtyard, obviously wanting no part of the drama in the street. Rasputin ran past, shouting, laughing, his beard streaming to the sides while he hailed passersby with a Madeira bottle. His detectives dog-trotted after him, falling back half a block.

Fortunate timing, thought Ash. Why not follow Rasputin? Lie back until he found a good place to brace the monk?

He pressed a gold sovereign into his driver's hand and gestured him to follow the running figures back down Gorokhovaya Street in the direction they had just driven. The coin was worth ten roubles – before the war – for a ride which cost one or two roubles, and worth two or three times that as the rouble's value plummeted. The driver hurriedly backed his horses out of the courtyard and cracked his whip.

Rasputin ran all the way to the Ekaterinski Canal, outdistancing his detectives, who had slowed to shambling walks and seemed to be looking around for a car. At the canal he hailed a sleigh, which he rode to the Kazan Cathedral, a grand affair faced with an enormous semicircular colonnade set back from the Nevsky Prospect, where the late evening crowds turned from the glittering shop windows to stare at the not unfamiliar sight of the Czarina's holy man on a binge.

Behind the Kazan were the troikas, fast pleasure sleighs lined up for hire at great expense. The war had not changed everything, it seemed. Sporting hats adorned with peacock feathers, the drivers were proudly grooming sleek thoroughbreds while they waited for their wealthy fares. Rasputin leaped into one, pulled a fresh bottle from his enormous fur coat, and bellowed, 'Krestovsky!'

Ash made his driver hang back until Rasputin pulled away. Krestovsky was a forested delta island where the gypsies had a permanent encampment on the Nevka, a branch at the mouth of the Neva. But it was miles out of the city; Ash's sleigh would never make it, nor could it keep up with the much faster troika. He jumped aboard the next troika, handed the driver two gold coins and gestured to follow Rasputin. He pulled a lap robe over his legs for the long cold ride and wished again he had brought a flask. Rasputin apparently had a yen for gypsy music, as Russians tended to when they got drunk. No tame Sadovaya Street restaurant gypsies would do.

But before they had gone a mile down the Nevsky, Rasputin waved his arms and his troika swung onto Morskaya Street, passed Ash's hotel and parked in front of St Isaac's Cathedral. Rasputin took a drink from his bottle and ran up the cathedral steps, singing and fumbling with his clothes.

Ash motioned his driver to park in the shadows as Rasputin's detectives caught up in a smoking old crock. Rasputin began urinating in the colonnade. The detectives got out and conferred anxiously around their car. Then three orthodox priests in flapping black robes and head-dress stormed out of a brass door and charged the monk who was desecrating their cathedral. Rasputin backed away, laughing. A fourth priest emerged, swinging a long staff bearing the cross.

Ash started to jump down to help, terrified the priest would brain his best and possibly last chance with the Czarina, but the detectives clattered up the steps and disarmed the man. Another priest fell down, tangled in his robe. Rasputin yanked a third off balance by grabbing his cross by the thick chain around the man's neck, dodged the fourth and ran down the steps back to his troika, which surged out of the square while the detectives were still grappling with the priests.

Seeing a chance to get Rasputin away from his bodyguards, Ash passed his driver more of King George's gold and gestured urgently to follow. The troikas circled behind St Isaac's, ran between the Admiralty and the Winter Palace and swung onto the Dvortsov Bridge. They cut across the tip of Vassily Island – which split the Neva in two – past the Stock Exchange, and across another bridge. Passing the Peter and Paul Fortress and prison and the Arsenal, they rode through the narrow streets of a sleeping factory district for a couple of miles. A final bridge brought them to the beginning of Krestovsky Island, where, at last, the troikas came into their own. Rasputin's picked up speed. Ash's driver waited until it was a hundred yards ahead, then spoke to his horses.

The lead horse, in shafts, broke into a fast trot. But the loosely harnessed outer horses, held only by leather traces, galloped wild and free. The effect was as swift as it was improbable. And eerily silent. The Russian troika had no bells like a European sleigh. The snow muffled the horses' hooves. The loudest sounds Ash heard were the animals' breathing and runners' hiss.

The silence deepened when they left the suburban fringe of the city behind and with it its dim street lights. Even Rasputin seemed awed by the silence. From what Ash could see he had stopped throwing his arms about. Nor did his shouts carry back over the snow which glistened pale blue in the starlight. He glanced back once. The starlight glinted on a mantle of frost covering his long beard. The cold was bitter, and Ash felt his moustache turn to ice.

Ash glanced back. The police car was nowhere to be seen.

His driver drove standing, controlling his horses with the reins and a steady stream of conversation. Ash showed him another sovereign – his hands were too full of reins to hold it – and motioned to catch up. The conversation took on an urgent tone, the horses leaped ahead. They had halved the distance between them and Rasputin's troika when the monk tossed an empty bottle into the trees, where it shattered musically. Closer, and Ash heard women's laughter.

And then he spotted them, riding a slow-moving troika that Rasputin's sleigh was starting to overtake. The monk stood up, opened his trousers, and repeated his remarkable St Isaac's performance as his troika drew alongside the women's on a wide spot in the road. Shrieking laughter, they shook up a champagne bottle and sprayed him back.

'*Now,*' Ash said, standing up and removing his coat and hat, and gesturing. '*Pass them now.*'

Thirteen bottles of Madeira surely purged a man, but couldn't quiet Rasputin's fear that he had sinned in an awful way he had never sinned before. He was glad Ash couldn't take the Czarina away, but he wished he had not killed him. He had always preached that out of sin came salvation, but fornicating and drinking were not sins like murder, and for the first time in his life Rasputin doubted that God would laugh with him.

Cold champagne splashed his face as he laughed along with the women, laughed with his mouth while in his heart were tears. There were three of them – young, bejewelled and pretty in the starlight, trading ribald comments. 'Put it back before it freezes,' one called out, and they shrieked and hugged each other as the troikas careened side by side.

Suddenly, behind them, stood Ash.

Rasputin blinked. Ash in uniform. Standing in a troika on the other side of the women's sleigh. *Ash.* The starlight glittering on his medals and service ribbons. Gold cords on his shoulder. Sword at his side. *Alive?*

Rasputin felt the hairs straightening up the back of his neck, up his head, under his hat, standing up stiff as quills. He covered his eyes. Too much Madeira. He peeked out between his fingers. Ash saluted. Rasputin felt an unearthly animal howl explode in his throat. He leaped away from the apparition, backward, off the troika, and fell into a snowdrift.

The look on Rasputin's face was almost worth drowning in the Fontanka. The monk's hair had stood up on end as if he had shoved wet fingers into an electric outlet, and his howl had sounded of terror equal to Ash's own the previous night. Rasputin falling into the snowdrift was icing on the cake. Now to exploit the advantage.

243

He showed his eager driver another gold sovereign and motioned him to top speed. Behind them, both Rasputin's and the women's drivers had stopped. They were standing the monk unsteadily on his feet. There was another howl, and Rasputin leaped on his troika and gesticulated for his driver to catch up. Perfect. Ash hunched down out of sight.

The horses were breathing hard, but they were almost at the gypsy camp. Beyond the River Yacht Club, on the shore of the Srednyaya Nevka, the road veered away from the water and briefly into deep forest again. Moments later Ash's troika pulled up in a clearing lit by a bonfire. At the edge, surrounded on three sides by fir trees, was a long, low wooden building from which drifted guitar music and mournful singing.

Troikas and private sleighs were parked outside, and their drivers had grouped around the fire. Rasputin's sleigh came in moments later, the horses' coats steaming in the cold. Rasputin spotted Ash, leaped down while his troika was still moving, and ran after him, skidding on the beaten snow.

Ash ignored him and walked to the gypsies' door. Rasputin pounded up behind him, grabbed his arm and jerked him around to see his face. Ash smiled, turned away.

'Navy man?' Rasputin grabbed him again.

'Speak any English?'

'A little,' Rasputin replied, fingering Ash's coat to prove he was real.

'I have powers too.' Ash watched him. He was drunk. It was difficult to tell what the monk believed, but he certainly seemed, so to speak, spooked.

He was not, however, going to concede mystical powers in his own territory. Staunchly, even as his wide eyes swept disbelievingly over Ash, he said, 'God's will you didn't die, Navy man.'

244

Ash went for broke. 'I did die, Rasputin. God sent me back.'

'*Da?*' the monk answered dubiously.

Ash felt like a snake oil salesman trying to con a circus barker. 'God sent me to take you to England with the Czarina.'

King George might not like a holy Russian peasant roaming around the palace, but that was one small sacrifice the Royal Family would have to make to help bring the US into war. Ash took his arm and steered him toward the door. 'Drink?'

'*Da.*' Of that Rasputin was certain.

Half the single, long low room was a dancing stage and the other half a heap of pillows and blankets where the customers reclined. Twenty or thirty gypsies dressed in colourful silk, rough-cut jewels and beads, were cavorting on the stage, singing and thrumming guitars. Twice their number of revellers from Petrograd, wearing diamonds and gold, were singing, clapping time and drinking champagne on the cushions. Candles burned in sconces around the walls. Tartar waiters, tall and dark, passed around the room pouring from bottles wrapped in gold foil.

Rasputin was still staring at Ash when people started shouting his name. 'Father Gregory! Father Gregory!' Three young gypsy girls with dark eyes and thick lashes ran into his arms, laughing smiles lighting their olive faces. Rasputin scooped them up automatically but his eyes remained fixed on Ash, and a look very much like panic never left his face.

'You must persuade the Czarina to leave,' Ash said, glancing at the gypsy girls, whose expression confirmed they understood no English.

It took a moment for Rasputin to digest the language, but at last he did. Snatching a bottle from one of the Tartars he took a long pull and passed it to Ash. Champagne. Too sweet, but at least undrugged. Rasputin sank to the cushions, dragging the girls on top of him. Ash dropped beside them. 'Listen to me . . .'

The gypsy chorus was nasal sounding, almost metallic. It sang loudly, and the voices had a barbaric eastern ring. The harmonies, though, were exquisite, impossibly complex. The Russians seemed drunk on the melodies, Rasputin drunker than all the rest. He thrashed around beside Ash, alternately fondling and kissing the girls and shouting the choruses led from the stage.

And all the while Ash hammered at him.

'The revolutionaries will kill you. God saved my life to save your life . . .'

Rasputin turned away.

'If the Czar falls you fall. What will happen to all your detectives? Are you afraid? Everybody hates you. They want to kill you.'

Rasputin turned on him. 'They hate Rasputin because they hate a peasant to screw his supposed betters.'

'No matter. They hate you enough to kill you, Father Gregory. Come away until it's over. Then you can all come back.' If he believed that . . .

'I'm not afraid of mixed-blood nobles. Real Russians, the *moujiki*, will defend Rasputin – '

'Could a peasant save you if a nobleman were waiting outside with a gun right now?'

'They can't kill *me*. If they kill Rasputin they all will be lost. All Russia lost . . . I see . . .'

'What is it?' Ash prompted. It was eerie, but he could see Rasputin seeing. The monk's eyes shone almost luminously, as if he were gazing through himself beyond even the future. Ash actually felt himself drawn into their liquid depths, fathomless, warm shafts into which one could sink to the centre of the earth.

'. . . I see heaps, masses of corpses . . . hundreds of counts

246

and several grand dukes . . .' Ash wondered if he could see Tamara's Grand Duke Valery among them. Rasputin found a bottle and shoved the neck in his mouth, drank deep. '. . . And the Neva all red with blood – '

'*Save the Czarina*,' Ash intoned. 'Save the Czar, the children. *Save yourself* – '

Ash slapped the bottle out of his hand. No one noticed, they were singing the gypsy chorus.

'*Listen* to me, you son of a bitch.'

Rasputin stared at him, dumbfounded by Ash's effrontery.

'If you won't save the Czarina, then you murder her. Come with me. All of you. You *must* make the Czarina do it . . .'

Rasputin looked abruptly sleepy. A lazy grin crossed his face and he muttered, 'I can make her do anything . . . Father Czar will thank me . . .'

Ash nodded. Did he mean for taking them to England?

'The peasants will thank me, too.'

'And the Czarina,' Ash encouraged. 'She will – what's wrong?'

Rasputin's eyes had filled with tears. 'But what will I be in England?'

Sobbing loudly, he felt around for his bottle. Ash found him one half-full. It was a mistake. Rasputin sucked it dry, curled up, and fell soundly asleep.

Ash shook him. What had he meant? Would he do it? Rasputin snored. Ash stared at him, wondering where to put the bastard until he woke up. Maybe the nearby River Yacht Club. But suddenly, the monk's detectives burst in the door. Spotting Rasputin, they pushed rudely through the patrons, scooped him off the cushions, and unceremoniously carried off Ash's best hope of persuading the Czarina to leave Russia.

All the next day, Ash tried to find the monk. Late in the

afternoon, he learned Rasputin was sobering up in the baths and hurried there to confirm that Rasputin had agreed. But the monk's friends wouldn't let him in. When Ash persisted, the detectives ordered him away.

23

Ash was three-quarters through the story of the night before, describing Rasputin's face when he passed the monk's troika, and François Roland's amusement had shredded his customary reserve, when the Astoria's maître d'hotel interrupted their dinner with an envelope on a silver tray – hand-delivered and urgent.

From the Czarina, thought Ash, although it bore no crest.

Roland's eyebrows zigzagged in protest.

'No business tonight, my friend. It is New Year's Eve – in Europe, at least – and we are invited to every embassy worth visiting, including yours with that delicious child. Let it wait.'

They were dressed for the evening, Ash in social dress uniform, Roland in white tie, and were well through their second bottle of wine – a Beaujolais for the pheasant that had just arrived, following a stern Graves with the smoked and pickled meats and fishes the Russians called *zakouski*. And Roland was in doubly high spirits having confessed earlier that he was falling in love – 'or something similar', as he had put it – with an officer of the Life Guard Preob-rajenski Regiment. He had even pronounced Ash's lunge much improved at a lesson before dinner.

Ash, for his part, was celebrating just being alive, despite disappointing progress, which the envelope suggested might be about to improve. He tore it open with apologies but the letter inside was not from the Czarina. He looked at Roland. The Frenchman's eyebrows had assumed a flat, noncommittal line; Ash could tell him as little or much as he wanted to. His business.

'The son of a bitch wants me to meet him at midnight at the Yusupov Palace.'

'Rasputin? . . . Which Yusupov Palace?'

'The one on the Moika.'

'Perhaps he intends drowning you in a more fashionable canal. Shall I come with you?'

'No, thanks. I think I've scared him out of bothering me . . . He says he's visiting the Princess Irina. She's the Czar's niece, isn't she?'

'Yes. Prince Felix's wife. The Czar offered them any gift they wanted for their wedding and Felix took an imperial box at the Maryinski, which I rather admired.'

She sounded to Ash like a very good connection.

'Wonder what Rasputin wants,' Roland said, turning his fork to a lean pheasant breast.

Ash had not told Roland about Ambassador Page's Inner Circle, nor the plan to remove the Czar from Russia, nor King George's mission to rescue his cousin, a matter of discretion which his friend accepted as Ash's right to decide upon. Roland knew about Ash's visit to the Kaiser, though not the reason, and was actively involved in helping him secure audiences with the Czar and Czarina. But Ash had told him about Rasputin, minus certain details, because there was no reason not to. As to why Rasputin wanted to see him again, he could only hope that the monk had decided to intercede with the Czarina.

'I tried to get hold of the bastard all day, but his friends wouldn't let me near the baths where he was sobering up.'

He pocketed Rasputin's letter and returned his attention to dinner. The Yusupov Palace was a short walk from the Astoria and he had plenty of time until midnight . . . It could be that the monk wanted to leave Russia until things cooled down. Sounded promising . . .

* * *

All Rasputin wanted was a glass of tea. He had drunk enough Madeira to float the Baltic Fleet, but Felix kept pouring more wine. It tasted awful, as if a cow had defecated in the vat, and it made him thirsty for more tea. Something was wrong with it; usually he drank a dozen bottles. No more.

But Felix insisted, kept pouring. And if that weren't enough, the Prince demanded that Rasputin eat great batches of sweet cakes. Rasputin obliged. Ordinarily he would have kicked the young pup out of the room – and be damned whose house it was – and done what he pleased, but Felix had promised to introduce him to his wife, the beautiful Princess Irina.

At last, tonight, he would have her. He had only seen pictures and they showed her to be as beautiful as people said she was. For such beauty even the Czarina could wait. Ash could wait. The bedevilled Revolutionaries could wait. What difference could one more night make? When he fixed her with his gaze, she would be his, provided Felix's wine didn't put him to sleep first, or, worse, weaken the holy shaft.

She was upstairs, entertaining friends. Rasputin could hear the music, the same song playing over and over on the gramophone. Felix said it was an American song. It just would not stop.

'Won't she be down soon?'

'I'll go and ask her,' Felix answered. 'Have another sweet.'

Rasputin gobbled down two. They were quite pleasant, and the wine was somehow tasting a little better now. As Felix headed out the door, he was hard to see, and Rasputin wondered if he had had too much to drink after all. He thought he'd close his eyes and gain some strength for the young princess. At this rate she'd be greatly disappointed. He reached into his pants and rearranged himself. It was growing distinctly soft. What the devil was Felix feeding him? Poison? Like he fed the navy man . . . ?

It was the navy man's fault. All that talk about running away to England . . . Had God sent him? . . . After the war Russia would settle down, the peasants would be happy again. Perhaps they'd slaughter the nobility – the mixed-blood vipers – perhaps kill the merchants – the thieves – and the governors – the corrupt. Then the peasants and the Czar would live together in harmony again. Burn some estates, bring the Cossacks home to restore order. God smiled.

Rasputin grinned, thought of the dark-eyed princess upstairs and felt himself grown comfortably hard again. The music stopped, suddenly. The guests were leaving. She would be down in a minute. Some excuse to get rid of Felix, send him for something.

Rasputin looked blearily around the stone-vaulted room. A thick white bearskin rug beckoned on the floor in front of the fire. He would have her on the rug, hold her down, push her clothing up around her waist and shove into her. In the moment he'd need to recover she would get used to the idea, and when he drove into her the second time she would be ready, wetted by his juices and, if she was the right sort, some of her own. He heard the door and opened his eyes for the first look at the princess.

What he saw was Felix. Felix handed him another glass of Madeira. Rasputin drank it wearily. So tired. It was hard to remember what was happening, almost what he was waiting for . . .

'Should we go to the gypsies?'

'It's too late,' said Felix. His voice sounded far away.

Rasputin pulled himself out of the chair and wandered around the room. A little Chinese ebony chest caught his attention; it had compartments, doors, secret drawers and mirrors. It seemed like a whole perfect world he could happily live in forever if he were small enough.

He turned to Felix to tell him that. Felix had a gun.

'Say a prayer,' Rasputin heard him say. A crucifix swam before his eyes, and the gun grew larger, and suddenly roared like the devil.

Rasputin screamed – his voice as distant as Felix's – and felt himself crash to the floor. He landed on the white fur rug and his head lolled to the side. The long white hairs tickled his face, and he thought that that was how it would have felt to the princess's wide spread thighs . . .

François Roland was drinking champagne with the director of the Imperial Theatre, gossiping about the great Tishkova, who was holding court on the other side of the Italian Embassy's ballroom, when an exchange in the conversation of the next group along the bar jarred him.

'*Pardon*,' he interrupted brusquely, surprising the director and annoying the people he had intruded on. He did not waste time apologizing, yet the haughty challenges on the faces of the officers melted to ingratiating smiles when they recognized him. He was not known as a duellist, but who wanted to be the first to provoke him into changing his habits?

'Did you say the Princess Irina is not in the city?'

'Her Highness went to the Crimea to visit her parents.'

'Could she be back?' Roland demanded.

'So soon, Monsieur? It is fifteen hundred miles and the trains – '

'*Excusez-moi*.' He rushed across the dance floor, through the quadrille, pausing only to get his cloak and stick because there was a blade in it, and raced into the street, where he hired the fastest sleigh parked in front of the embassy.

'Yusupov's Moika Palace!'

He jerked out his watch as the sleigh raced toward the Nevsky Prospect. After midnight. What had Kenneth walked into?

But Ash hadn't told him . . . nor had he told his friend that the note signed by Rasputin had directed him to a side entrance of Prince Felix's private wing.

And it was there that Ash crouched in the shadows of a gatepost. When he had arrived he had heard a gramophone blasting 'Yankee Doodle Dandy', but when he had knocked on the door nearest the window the music was coming from, no one had answered. He had waited a while on the street. No Rasputin. He had decided he would wait five more minutes. Then two shots had boomed out and the music stopped and Ash had ducked behind the gatepost, out of sight of the main entrance on the canal.

Rasputin thought he was dead, but in his mind he drove into the princess, pounded while she wept and struggled, drove hard, but losing his hardness, until she rolled on top of him and ground her belly against his and shook him violently with her delicate little hands.

He opened his eyes.

Felix was shaking him. When their eyes met, Felix's face melted in horror. '*He's alive . . .*'

Rasputin grabbed Felix by the throat. The prince screamed again, pulled away, ripping cloth, and ran as if he had just seen the devil.

Rasputin struggled into a sitting position. He hurt inside and he was confused. Felix kept screaming, somewhere upstairs, 'He's alive, shoot, shoot him . . .'

Steeling his body against the pain, Rasputin tried to stand. He dragged himself to a wall, pulled up it, then worked along it to the door. Stairs. Impossible. But he remembered that they had come down the stairs immediately after he and Felix had entered the side door of the palace. If he could climb the stairs he'd escape into the street. Step by step he pulled himself up toward the outside door.

He heard their footsteps, heard Felix screaming, 'Shoot him, he's getting away . . .'

He made it to the door, fell against it and shoved it open. Cold air gave him strength. His mind was clearing. They were murderers behind him. Felix had tricked him to come here, had fed him poison, had shot him . . .

'*He's getting away* . . .'

If he could just make it across the courtyard to the   street . . . thirty feet across the courtyard, through the gate, into the street. There was a police station nearby. He would be safe . . . He saw the navy man at the gate.

'*Navy man!*' His saviour.

Ash saw Rasputin stagger across the dark courtyard. When he reached the fence he seemed lost. Then he spotted Ash at the gate.

'*Navy man* . . .'

The monk shambled along the iron fence, pulling himself on the palings. A light from the palace windows fell on his face; he was grimacing and holding his chest.

'Help me, Navy man . . .'

He started to fall. Ash hurried toward him. A man ran out the door Rasputin had come from and aimed a gun at the staggering figure. Ash pulled his own gun. 'Get *down.*'

Two more shots were fired before he could take aim, a heavy revolver that sounded like a cannon, and hit like one too. Rasputin pitched forward as the first slug smashed into his back. The second snapped his head around as if he were glancing over his shoulder, and he fell hard into the snow.

Ash fired in the direction of the blinding muzzle flashes, but the gunman had ducked back out of sight. Ash knelt beside Rasputin, tried to pull him away while he watched for the gunman to reappear.

'Father Gregory . . .'

Tugging his hand feebly, Rasputin whispered, 'Navy man . . . His eye flickered. Ash leaned lose and put his ear to Rasputin's lips. 'Save her, Navy man. Save the Czarina.'

He shuddered once, and lay still.

'If you love the Czar you'll say nothing.'

Ash looked up at the crazed face of a man he didn't know, holding a revolver and staring down at him. He looked drunk.

Two soldiers came into the courtyard.

'I've killed Rasputin,' the man said, waving his gun.

The soldiers stared at the body, crossed themselves and murmured, one after the other, 'Thank God. Thank God.'

Ash stood up carefully and backed away, holding his gun at his side. From the gate he took one last look at the corpse of his best hope of convincing Czarina Alexandra to persuade the Czar to leave Russia.

And then he ran.

François Roland came running along the canal toward him, the empty left dinner-jacket sleeve flapping as his opera cloak streamed behind him. Ash waved him away. The Frenchman obeyed, vanished into the shadows. Ash turned in the opposite direction and began a roundabout route home to the Astoria. Around a corner, less than ninety feet from the courtyard where Rasputin lay, in the darkest patch between two pools of street light, two policemen were waiting, their dark green coats black in the night.

They barred the way with their clubs. Neither spoke English, but a club pointed at his gun, still in his hand, was clear enough. Ash clicked the safety on as he handed it over. They seemed to have been hiding in the dark patch, waiting. For what? Maybe for an idiot who'd responded to a forged note from Rasputin?

A long, dark car pulled alongside the kerb. Plain clothes.

Three men got out. One frisked him and took his sword. They looked a few notches above the cops who had been tailing him around the city. Okhrana elite, he guessed. *Secret* secret police. The sort who caught assassins and revolutionaries and people dumb enough to be caught near a murder with a gun in their hand. He had a lot of talking to do.

'I am a diplomat.'

'Put him in the car.'

When all four of them were crammed into the passenger compartment and the car was rolling in the direction of the Neva, Ash repeated, 'I am a diplomat.'

The one in charge said, 'You were seen in the vicinity of the Yusupov Moika Palace.'

'I was walking home to my hotel.'

'With a gun in your hand. Did you hear anything unusual?'

'I heard a loud party as I passed the palace. I stopped. I saw a man shot in the courtyard. It was the monk Father Gregory R – '

'I've been there. There was no body. Several witnesses place you there, including two who confirm there was a dead man, briefly, in the courtyard. Where is he now?'

'Rasputin – '

'We are investigating,' the detective cut him off again. The car raced between the Admiralty and the Winter Palace and crossed the Neva on the Dvortsov Bridge. Ash considered his position. Someone had gone to a great deal of trouble to get him arrested. 'I'm a diplomat, I'm immune to arrest, I demand to be taken directly to the American Embassy – '

'My English is not so fine,' the officer said. 'I am not familiar with your phrases . . .'

The car turned from the bridge toward the dark shape of the Peter and Paul Fortress. It stopped before a huge,

257

studded gate. Soldiers checked the driver's papers and signalled for the gate to open. Ash glimpsed the palace lights across the Neva before the car drove into a dark tunnel through the fortress wall.

BOOK III
The Grand Ducal Quadrille

24

Tamara Tishkova woke up near-rigid with fear. The dark canopy loomed above her. A faint line of light showed a split in the drapes. Tentatively, she moved her hand. Her fingers slid into the icy territory beyond her warmth, and she realized she was safe, alone in her own bed. The dream, again. Her nightmare.

She suffered two nightmares. The first she had dreamed nearly all her life. It was a dream common to performers – entering the stage at the Maryinski Theatre she would discover herself without her costume. The dream thrived on detail; she saw the stalls, the glittering first ring, the Czar's box, three great tiers rising to the dome. Two thousand balletomanes applauded, seemingly unaware that she was naked. But the cheers turned to catcalls when the orchestra started playing music she had never heard before. She danced *Swan Lake* and the audience booed. She tried *Sleeping Beauty*, the same. *Cléopâtre, Giselle, Carnaval. Eros*, naked, and they laughed. The music – she dreamed the dream several times a year, and as she grew older had come to regard it philosophically almost as a familiar acquaintance. An intruder but one who left without lasting damage.

The new dream, the nightmare she had just escaped and which left her wet with perspiration, was the fire dream. It had started with the war and there was nothing familiar or friendly about it, always different, always terrifying.

Sometimes the theatre burned while she danced and danced and danced. The audience stampeded, screaming, to the doors, and the tiers came crashing down on them in great explosions of red embers. At other times she saw the city burn; flames soared from the palaces – she was watching from her house – tonight the fire had started across the river.

Tamara spread her hands and feet into the cold areas of the big bed and forced herself to stay awake until the cold pulled the last tendrils of the nightmare from her mind. It seemed she had just fallen back into a restless sleep when her maid awakened her. The Grand Duke Valery had stopped off on his way to his audience with the Czarina.

'We'll have tea in the solarium,' she ordered, shaking the night from her cloudy brain. Valery needed courage this morning. She fixed her hair, perfumed, put on a dark silk robe he liked and went downstairs to give him courage.

As she was sending him out the door Tamara rose *en pointe* and cocked his black fur hat at a jaunty angle. Valery was wearing his favourite uniform for his audience with the Czarina, that of colonel of his Life Guard Cossack regiment, and the long red coat, high fur *papaha* and heavy *pallash* cavalry sword suited a man as big as he.

Tamara could have reached his hat on ordinary tiptoe, but Valery loved the fact that she was a dancer, so she executed a playful arabesque, pleasing him in a way that pleased her. She stepped back to admire the effect, saw it had failed and rose again to return the *papaha* to its former staid position squarely on top of his head.

He looked, she thought, like what he was – good, dependable, and intensely loyal. He bent to kiss her. She turned her face and spoke in a firm voice . . . 'Tell her this is her last chance.'

'I can't threaten the Czarina like a naughty child.'

'You *know* what I mean. They will be overthrown if they don't get rid of Rasputin's ministers.'

'Why don't I just poke a sharp stick in her eye?' Valery protested. He knew the Czarina was in no condition to listen to reason, and calling on her today was not his idea.

Rasputin's body had been dragged yesterday from the river, three days after rumours had swept the city that he had been killed. The clumsy murderers had dropped one of his boots beside the hole in the ice . . . He had never believed that Felix would go through with it. Petrograd was rejoicing, but at Tsarskoye Selo the Empress mourned. And those who knew her trembled.

In her grief and rage she had already placed the Grand Duke Dmitri, one of Valery's young nephews, under house arrest, along with Prince Felix. She claimed they were implicated, as revealed by the rigorous police investigation of the crime, which was being conducted by Rasputin's own protégé, Interior Minister Protopopov.

But she had broken the law. The grand dukes – the Russian Czar's brothers, cousins, uncles and second sons when he had them – were above the law, and only the Czar himself had legal power over them. Tamara had played on Valery's anger to talk him into one last try at persuading the Czarina to appoint new ministers.

'You must say what is right. The Czar trusts you. She should too. You have served them better by far than any other grand duke.'

That was not flattery. Most of the grand dukes were quick to complain about Nicholas II, whether they were his cousin, nephew, uncle or brother, but few deigned to serve Russia the way Valery did, preferring instead to live abroad in Paris and Monte Carlo, enjoying their vast fortunes and sniping from a distance while Valery travelled constantly through Russia and Europe as the Czar's personal ambassador, negotiator and knowing observer.

'But Alexandra is the Empress,' he countered gently, reaching for Tamara again. Again she stopped him, brushing impatiently at his big hands.

'If the Czarina won't listen to you then she deserves to lose her throne.'

'Don't talk that way.'

Her sloe eyes flashed an unmistakable warning. Tamara Tishkova had inherited her Italian mother's fiery temper along with her jet black hair. And with her father's broad Russian cheekbones, pale skin and eastern slant to her eyes had come a peasant stubbornness that Valery could only marvel at. He told himself he trusted her cool judgment, which he did, but actually he was also just a little cowed by this woman he adored.

'What's wrong?' he asked. Her nose, Serov the court painter had once observed, had been fashioned by God.

'Darling,' she said, kissing his cheek but eluding his reach once again. 'If the Czarina won't change, then she and Nicholas must be replaced.'

'And what do we do with them then, may I ask? Shoot them?'

'Of course not. But for Russia they must just step down.'

'Where?'

'Darling, don't worry about that. They must be replaced. Everyone knows it. And everyone knows that *you* are the only man in Russia to do it.'

'There are many who would try,' Valery objected. 'They're coming out of the woodwork like termites.'

'But everyone knows that only you could take the throne and *hold* it. *Everyone*. Except, sometimes, you.'

'I'll do what I have to,' he said glumly.

'That's all everyone asks.'

'But first I will talk to her. Change her mind.'

'Of course you must try, darling.' She hugged him fiercely and sent him on his way, knowing full well the Czarina would never change, even with Rasputin gone. But she hoped that one more visit to Tsarskoye Selo would convince Valery what the other grand dukes and his fellow officers had been saying for months – only a real Czar could save Russia. Not weak Nicholas and his neurotic wife, but a real leader. And that leader, the royal conspirators believed, hoped, would be the Grand Duke Valery.

She stood waving good-bye from her front door as he climbed aboard his gigantic scarlet sleigh and his Cossack guard mounted their horses, admired the sight they made clattering away from her house, then returned to her solarium, which had a splendid view of the river and the Winter Palace.

Valery's sleigh headed for the bridge; the ice was still too thin to carry its monstrous weight. She watched until it vanished among the red and blue and yellow trams. On the other side the Winter Palace crouched on its embankment like a dark red lion in the snow. Tamara gazed at it, thinking about the conspirators.

Instigators was more like it. They wanted Valery to lead them and take all the risks. They reminded her of dilettante dancers – girls from rich families with fantasies of floating in the air but unwilling to embrace the punishing work such buoyancy required.

She had had mixed feelings when they first came to sound her out about Valery's reaction to a palace coup. Open mistress to an unmarried Czar would be, in many eyes, a startling achievement for the daughter of a man born a serf. The price of a failed coup, though, would be Valery's execution. And failure was likely. Already one of his servant girls had been arrested by the Okhrana. The poor, frightened thing had killed herself.

Still, she realized that the grand ducal conspirators approaching her were the best of the Romanov family and united by their fear for Russia, as well as their hatred of the revolutionaries and the German enemy. They came to her because they suspected that she could influence Valery more than they. And with that realization, Tamara Tish-kova began to experience a new dimension to her already considerable position in Petrograd.

She was a woman close to fifty years old who looked thirty and danced twenty-six, who had never married and had used the celebrity her extraordinary beauty and seemingly timeless talent had brought her to unique advantage. She knew how to get the most from a man and she had exercised strict discipline – with one aching exception – in choosing the right man. No dancers, no composers, no singers – and certainly never an impresario. They wore the same chains she did; artists were, as the system of the Imperial Theatres proved with a hundred small hurts, exotic chattels.

Even as Russia's greatest star, she had suffered a cruel reminder that no artist was above royal manipulation; and after years the memory still hurt . . . Czar Nicky, who had admired her since she was a student, had asked her to perform in private at the Alexander Palace; the new *Firebird*, no less, which had just thrilled Paris and which seemed a bold choice for such a conservative man. But His Majesty was a reader, and, well, you could never tell with a reader . . .

Tishkova rarely if ever consented to do private performances, but this was a very special exception, a considerable great honour as well as a royal command. She had submerged herself in the effort of the ballet, excited by the idea of performing for the Court and being the one to present an artist as modern as Stravinsky to an audience as venerable as the Romanov dynasty. Heady stuff, indeed, until the Czarina learned of the preparations.

Her Majesty had snapped her fingers, banned the *Firebird*. No reason given, none required. The Czar capitulated and it was over the night before dress rehearsal. Royalty had commanded a dance, royalty had changed its mind. For weeks after Tamara had felt the firebird still inside her, beating its wings with nowhere to fly . . . A mean object lesson that the right man for a dancer, including

266

Tamara, had better possess royal blood, with inherited wealth. Millionaire careerists were, it seemed, too accustomed to fighting and winning on strictly their own terms . . . while she needed and wanted a man's protection, her own life, and art, told her to stay free of consuming, uncompromising ties.

Ballerinas, of course, had been sleeping with grand dukes before the invention of toe shoes, but Valery wasn't married, which made all the difference. For years she had reigned supreme on the stage and since she had finally agreed to become exclusively Valery's, after years of putting him off, she was his consort, openly and publicly, and reigned over much of Petrograd Society as well. The aristocrats did not all accept her warmly, but when they bowed to Valery they bowed to her as well.

And now she was tasting what it might be like to be the power behind the throne, and she had to admit it was a delicious *mélange* of respect and worship she had known before only when she danced. There was a strong temptation to cultivate that power to carry her safely into the middle age she feared. A powerful temptation, and with it a fantasy. Were Valery to become Czar, might he not marry her? Make her his Czarina? Empress of all the Russias . . .

But Valery was a careful man. He was also not ambitious for power. He would not fight for the throne unless he was totally convinced that Russia would collapse without him. So Tamara gazed across the river at the Winter Palace and prayed with her eyes wide open that the Czarina would remain her imperious and foolish self when Valery arrived at the Alexander Palace this morning –

Her butler broke into her thoughts, announcing that the director of the Imperial Theatre was in the foyer. She had seen his sleigh drive up and presumed her friend had come to talk about last-minute plans for *Swan Lake,* a benefit performance she was dancing on Sunday at the Maryinski to raise money for the military hospital she sponsored for the wounded.

Her last *Swan Lake,* she had decided, privately. Her jumps were going. There were limits. One more time . . . then new roles.

'*Cancelled?*'

'By order of the Empress,' the director of the Imperial Theatre said sadly. 'Czarina Alexandra commands mourning for Rasputin.'

'Cancelled!' she repeated, her voice rising. 'Tishkova? Cancelled? My benefit. My *Swan Lake?* She can't.'

Now she realized that the director had dressed as befitted a solemn occasion. He was wearing his colonel's uniform with a tunic practically covered with overlapping ribbons and medals. They had been friends twenty-five years, and it was out of friendship he had delivered the Czarina's edict personally.

'My dear, I am so sorry.'

Tamara stood up. Such a thing could not happen to her. 'I am the greatest dancer in Russia,' she said flatly. And immediately to herself, Or at least I was.

'You are, Mademoiselle.'

'She can't do this to me.'

'Unfortunately, she can. The Empress is in mourning for the death of Rasputin. She decrees that the Imperial Theatres join her mourning and close out of respect for her murdered friend – '

'Petrograd is rejoicing. Rasputin's death is the best thing that's happened since the war began.'

The director made a motion so small that it could have been a shrug, or a nod or simply an effort to relieve the strain of his high tight collar. He said only, 'I don't hold political views. I can't afford to.'

'She's insane. Crazy as he was.'

The director rose, anxious to be away from such dangerous talk. 'The Czarina's announcement will be issued publicly on Sunday in the cathedrals.'

'She hates me because – '

He bowed and was gone. Tamara started after him calling out, 'She can't.'

The front door slammed. She ran back to the solarium, reeled about the middle of the room. Her vision seemed to turn red. The Czarina hates me because of Nicky, she wanted to scream. She picked up the nearest object at hand, the telephone, and hurled it at the distant Winter Palace. The instrument tore its wire and smashed through the double windows. Cold burst in, and the leaves nearest curled up as if the plants were wincing.

Valery! She had to call Valery. The telephone lay in the snow, the wires broken. She called for her servants, at full voice, her voice echoing in her ears. The butler came running, the footman, the coachman wielding a club to protect her, the cook, the *moujik* who tended the furnace fires, the one who fixed things. She pointed at the telephone in the snow. They scrambled for it.

The one who fixed things said he would repair the glass.

'*Nyet!*' It was the telephone she wanted.

She paced among the plants, calling for the servants to hurry. Then she remembered that Valery was en route to Tsarskoye Selo.

'Mademoiselle?' Her butler approached her tentatively.

'What is it?'

'A gentleman is here.'

'Who? I'm not expecting anyone.'

The butler squinted at the caller's card. 'Chevalier François Roland.'

'That bastard! Throw him out. No. Wait. Tell him to wait.' She had to compose herself. What did Roland want? He had accused her in a review in Paris of being too short to

269

be a truly great ballerina. All the compliments he had heaped on her since had never fully made it up to her. What in hell am I supposed to do, she had asked Kennet. Grow? Kennet had offered to shoot the critic, with a smile for which he had slept elsewhere half the night. Now she smiled, remembering how he had still been that young then and too new to her world to understand the hurt of such criticism.

When she was calm enough to think straight she called for Roland.

'Forgive me, Mademoiselle,' he said as he stepped in the door, 'but this is terribly important.'

His empty sleeve took her breath away. She had heard about his arm, of course, but he had still been too ill to attend the season last year and this was the first she had seen him since he was wounded. The pain she felt for him pushed aside the vestiges of her rage at the Czarina. The poor man; if any creature on earth should not have been maimed it was this graceful Frenchman with the strong, supple arms and legs a dancer dreamed of. And he was, she knew, so vain, like a cat discovering itself in a mirror.

Tamara looked him straight in the eye. 'You are still the most beautiful man I have ever seen.'

He looked at her for a long moment, acknowledging the bond of perfection which united them distantly, she the dancer, he the fencer. At last he bowed. '*Merci*, my friend . . . do you know that Kenneth is in Petrograd?'

'I had heard,' she said coolly.

'Did you know he was arrested?'

'*What?*'

'The Okhrana arrested him near the Yusupov Palace the night Rasputin was murdered. They took him to the Peter-Paul.'

'But why? What did he – '

'No one can tell me why. He's just been swallowed up. I

270

made inquiries through my ambassador who informed the American Embassy.'

'And?'

'Ambassador Paléologue has the impression that Kenneth's ambassador was ordered by his State Department not to interfere. It seemed he was reporting directly to the American ambassador in London.'

'They can't arrest a diplomat.'

'One would think not, but they have . . . I've exhausted my own means to help him. You're the only one I can turn to.'

What could she do without upsetting Valery? Much more than their relationship was at stake now – the entire grand ducal conspiracy. If Valery were distracted by Kennet . . . but *Kennet* . . . she was shocked by the raw intensity of her reaction to his arrest. Shocked by what she felt. God was a trickster, all right.

'I'll call my friend General Halle. He is chief of police for the Fourth District. He'll at least know the police side. Yes?'

'*Oui, Mademoiselle.*' Roland glanced at the *moujik* crouched on the tile floor repairing the telephone, and at the hole in the glass.

General Halle was delighted to hear from her. He listened gravely and promised to call back, which he did minutes later. When Tamara hung up the second time she turned to Roland with stricken eyes.

'They've moved him to the Litovsky.'

'My God. Why?'

'They say he committed a political offence. General Halle can't help . . . No one can. The Okhrana is interrogating him.'

271

25

At first when the guards took off his chains, Ash rated the new prison an improvement over the Peter-Paul where they had put on the shackles the night he had arrived. But by the time the guards came back for him – a few hours after the police had delivered him across the city in a cold, unlighted black Maria – Ash wished he was back at the Peter-Paul.

There his cell had been eerily silent, the thick walls packed with felt to prevent prisoners from tapping messages. Here screams, faint and intermittent, echoed through the corridors from some remote corner of the cold, damp prison.

Ash rose apprehensively as the guards unlocked the bars. They shackled his hands and feet again, shoved him from the cell and pushed and dragged him down flight after flight of stone steps. The walls grew wet as they descended deeper, and the screaming louder; suddenly it stopped. If it was the guards' intent to frighten him, Ash thought, they were succeeding. But fear had the side effect of honing his mind, which days of confinement had begun to soften.

The shackles had chafed his wrists raw at the Peter-Paul, and he had feared infection in his dirty cell as his mind had begun to shift from the larger concern for his mission to remove the Czar to smaller and smaller details of daily existence. The war grew more distant, the need to stop it, remote. The chains, the silence, the constant electric light and the ever-present guards watching him through a peephole took on immediate importance until Ash had begun to wonder how people like Lenin and his comrades kept their cutting edge through long periods of prison and exile. He was going mad after four days.

The Okhrana had kept Ash alone from the moment he was arrested, and the sense of isolation was so complete that he had begun to wonder if no one but the Okhrana knew he was a prisoner. François Roland had run the other way from the Yusupov Palace. So who else would have seen the police take him in their car, drive him across the Neva and through the fortress gates?

That night as they had entered the Peter-Paul Prison, which was isolated in one of the many bastions, the guards in the foyer had turned around and faced the walls of the small dark room until Ash had been marched through into a second room. 'So no one knows who is here,' the Okhrana officer had explained. Then he had ordered Ash to strip. No names. Only cell numbers.

In a room bare except for a wooden table they had confiscated his sword, billfold, passport and finally his concealed, snub-nosed Luger, which they examined with professional interest. There were hooks on the wall for his uniform, which they carried away as soon as he had hung it up, and when he was naked they gave him faded cotton pants and shirt and shackled his wrists.

Next up a flight of stone stairs, through a heavy iron door, with a guard who had glanced incuriously at yet another prisoner in shapeless garb indistinguishable from the prisoners before him or those who would follow. Down a long corridor lined with pairs of doors on the left side. Each wooden door had a small opening a few inches square crosshatched with iron straps, through which the guards watched. Between each pair of cells was the square iron fuel door of a heating stove embedded in the stone. Ash's cell had been warm, comfortable even, compared to the damp chill that permeated the new prison.

The guards had pushed a key in the door and thrown it open. Ash had caught a quick glimpse of a toilet in the corner, an iron bed and table, an electric light by the table, a straw pillow, a thin mattress, a sheet and a rug on the bed and a high, barred window; they had pushed him in and slammed the door, which had stayed shut until a few hours ago when they had moved him here to the new prison.

Now, at the bottom of the last flight of stone stairs, the guards brought him up short at a steel door and one knocked with his billy club. The signal was executed with deference, as if the jailers feared the man behind the door.

He turned out to be short, heavily built, and bald. He pointed at a wooden table in the centre of the room. The guards slammed Ash across it and swiftly fastened his manacles to the table top and his ankle irons to rings in its legs, and left him spread-eagled, bent over face down in a room silent but for his own heartbeat.

Ash tried to look around, to see behind him, but he was so tightly stretched he could barely turn his head. Something creaked. Ash craned his neck as far as he could and caught in the corner of his vision the bald-headed man, still in the cell, sitting in a wooden chair and oiling a whip.

A dozen more hung on the wall behind him in order of their length. Ash turned his head and looked over his right shoulder. He saw the door, a telephone, and the rest of the whips. The chair creaked again and the bald-headed man stood up and uncoiled six feet of black leather.

He ran the full length through his fingers, spreading the oil, then gripped the butt and cocked his arm. The lash blurred across the room and cracked like a pistol-shot beside Ash's ear. Ash jerked his head. As if that would have helped. It had fanned his face before he even heard it part the air.

The bald-headed jailer coiled it again and stepped behind Ash, out of his vision. The whip hissed suddenly through the air and cracked beside his right ear. Ash jerked his head again, this time in pain. The merest edge of the lash had touched his ear and it felt as if the bastard had grabbed him with hot pliers.

He walked around the table, trailing the whip, in and out of Ash's sight. Ash twisted his neck as far as he could. He saw the jailer's hand raise the whip and suddenly loop its wrist thong on a peg in the wall. Fighting fear, Ash watched the hand move along the rack and close on the handle of a Russian knout.

It was like the cat-o'-nine-tails the British navy had outlawed fifty years ago, but in Russia the multiple lashes were armed with wire, rendering the whip an instrument of execution as well as punishment. The bald man lifted it off its peg and shook out the trails. He planted his feet a yard and a half from the table and this time, when he glanced back to make sure he had clearance, Ash knew he meant business.

Ash felt his skin shrink in anticipation and he failed utterly in preventing a spasmodic shiver from coursing the length of his body. For the first time, the man spoke. Thickly accented high-school English. Yet clear. 'Why were you at the Yusupov Palace the night Rasputin was murdered?'

While he still had control of his wits, Ash tried to calculate what he could admit without betraying his mission to remove the Czar. What did the Okhrana already know? He'd been seen at the gypsies with the monk. And they probably knew the Czarina had granted him an audience. And that he had asked several Russians for help in securing an audience with the Czar. For that he had his cover story with the embassy. The knout cast a spidery shadow as the jailer aimed his first stroke.

'Rasputin sent me a note, asking me to join him at the Yusupov Palace.'

'Why?'

'We'd gone drinking the night before at the gypsies'. The big encampment out on Krestovsky Island. You know – '

The man with the knout raised his whip higher.

'Why?'

'He said we'd go whoring.'

'*Liar!*' The knout slashed a wide circle overhead. Ash jammed his lips against the wood to keep from yelling. Before the whip descended, the door banged open and a new voice broke in. 'I'll take it from here. We need this one alive.' It was Captain Moskolenko.

Ash couldn't see the newcomer, but disappointment leavened by respectful fear clouded Orlov's face as he returned the knout to its peg. After the lieutenant had passed from Ash's vision, Moskolenko whispered in Russian, 'Is he ready?' and Orlov nodded emphatically. The door closed.

Ash tried to collect his breath, not sure whether he was alone.

He was not. Again from the corner of his vision he saw a hand reach for the knout, heft it experimentally. He still could not see Moskolenko's face, but he recognized the same strangely accented voice as it said, mockingly, 'The man's hopeless. He'd have killed you with this before you'd confessed half. There is no subtlety with the knout. A man in your thoroughly vulnerable position is quite susceptible to less lethal persuasion. Most susceptible. Now let us see . . .'

The disembodied hand replaced the knout and perused the row of dog whips, rattan canes and riding crops, selecting, as his back came into Ash's view, but not his face, a vicious-looking riding whip about four feet long. 'We'll start with this.'

Ash suppressed a groan. It wouldn't kill him, but by the time the bastard was through, he would wish it had. His only hope was the plausibility of the whoring with Rasputin story. Somehow he had to stick to those simple facts, even when his mind screamed to give it all up.

But to defend the false story, to protect his real mission –

to trick the interrogator – Ash had to absorb all the pain the man had to give, never knowing when he would stop. He told himself he could, but a clear voice in the middle of his brain said the man with the whip was a professional, used to bravery and familiar with desperate tricks.

Moskolenko moved behind him, still out of sight. Ash heard the whip swish once or twice, teasing him, and then the voice again, as if he had read Ash's thoughts. 'A man in your position hasn't a hope of protecting a lie.'

Ash jumped. Moskolenko had touched his back with the whip. Now he traced an outline, like a carpenter scribing where to cut. The lash trailed over his shoulders, down his left flank, between his stretched legs to his knees and started up again. Ash tried to steady his breathing. But in twenty long seconds, without a single stroke, Moskolenko had completely unnerved him by demonstrating that he knew how terribly exposed Ash was, how completely in his power.

Gripped by an impotent rage Ash tore at the manacles.

'At this point,' Moskolenko mocked. 'The prisoner usually begs.'

'*Get to it you son of a bitch.*'

'Why Ash, at last you have some balls.' Captain Moskolenko rapped him lightly between the legs and stepped into sight.

'*Von Basel!*'

'Not so loud. You'll give us both away.'

'What – '

'I serve Kaiser Wilhelm.'

Ash stared at Count Philip von Basel in total disbelief. What was the German doing in an Okhrana prison? He was a spy, was the only answer, and von Basel confirmed it by saying, 'A pride of kings.'

With understanding came rage, and Ash said coldly,

'Your Kaiser has a stupid sense if humour, putting you and me in the same city, much less the same mission.'

'How could His Majesty know about you and me?' von Basel replied with a sarcastic smile. 'A duel that ended with a scratch would hardly come to the attention of the German emperor. No, Ash, a duellist must lose more convincingly to become famous in Europe.'

Ash tugged at the manacles. 'In any civilized country, von Basel, a lunatic like you would have been locked up long ago. But if you still want a duel you can have one after we get the Czar out.'

Von Basel shrugged. 'I would keep in mind, Ash, that the only reason I didn't remove your ears was my belated realization that it would be impolitic to shame an officer of a potential ally. But if you want a duel and if you think you've learned enough from that fag Roland to make it amusing, we'll arrange something. In the meantime – '

'Get me off this table. You've had your fun.'

Von Basel tapped the whip in his hand. 'Not as much as I'd like . . .' He trailed the lash over Ash's back again. 'Frankly, Ash, the pleasure of flogging you to compliant ribbons tempts me greatly, but we haven't time for you to loll about in a hospital. Russia's on the brink.' He touched Ash once more, then hung up the whip and released his arms and legs.

Ash stood up. He wanted to smash the German's face in for making him believe he would be tortured, for trying to make him grovel. Their eyes met and, though he had not grovelled, not begged, Ash knew an awful question hung unanswered between them: Would Ash have broken had von Basel used his whip?

'We'll never know, will we?' von Basel smiled. 'A shame, since humiliation worries you so.'

Ash raised his shackles. 'These too.'

'You might sound a little grateful, Commander. It took a

278

lot of doing to extricate you from the clutches of the Okhrana. There were officers who wanted you to suffer the worst sort of interrogation. Others thought you should simply disappear.' 'What for?'

'Somehow you're right in the middle of the Rasputin murder. The Empress is calling for blood. Some thought you would make a fine sacrifice. Fortunately I was able to persuade them that an American officer was an unlikely candidate.'

'How?'

'No questions. I have my own position to protect – but answer me, before we get down to business, how did you get in so much trouble?'

'I think I got framed by the German army.'

It was von Basel's turn to look confused. 'Is this a joke?' Ash shook the chains on his wrists. 'Does this look like a damned joke?'

'Explain.'

'I saw the Kaiser in Berlin.'

'I know.'

'Right after that, German army agents tried to kill me on the train from Munich. They tried again in Finland. And somebody suckered me into going to the Yusupov Palace the night Rasputin was killed.'

'Why do you think they were German army?' Von Basel led Ash through a recitation of each attack, and concluded, 'You're lucky to be alive. But then, again, you were always good at running.'

'Let me ask you something, von Basel. Is it true you got your Heidelberg duelling scar on the cheek you sit on?'

The German flushed. 'Be very careful, Ash. I could have you taken out and shot.'

'By Russians? Interesting. Tell me more about your situation . . . come on, von Basel. What are you going to do about this? I'm no good to you and your Kaiser dead.'

279

Ash had the feeling that von Basel had already known about the Finnish attack. And he found it worrisome that von Basel looked baffled and more than a little worried himself.

'I'll make inquiries. In the meantime you will avoid your hotel at least at night. I'll arrange a flat on Vassily Island – you'll be safe this evening, no one expects you to be released. Tomorrow go to the German Embassy. We'll use the wreckage as a dropping point for messages. I'll leave a key and address just inside the side doors. I will also have you watched for your protection.'

Ash took a second stab at learning how von Basel operated in Petrograd. 'Are those your boys following me around in that phony taxi?'

'I told you I won't discuss my situation here. It doesn't take huge intelligence to realize I've some police contacts. But I warn you, if you threaten my position in any way I will have you eliminated. And I can assure you I will be more successful than the German army . . . the important thing is for you to do what the Kaiser told you to do. Rescue the Czar. Where do you stand?'

'The Czarina listened to King George's offer, but since then she's refused to talk to me. I was trying to manoeuvre Rasputin into influencing her when he was murdered.'

'She's in no condition to make any sensible decisions now, I can tell you. Rasputin's death has devastated her.'

'That leaves the Czar,' Ash said.

'The Czar is on his way home from Mogilev. To comfort his wife. He will obviously stay some time at Tsarskoye Selo before returning to military headquarters. It is likely, therefore, that the Czar will receive the congratulations of the diplomatic corps on New Year's Day. I presume you can get yourself invited?'

Ash nodded.

Von Basel reached for a walking stick he had leaned

against the door. 'Understand, Commander, that Rasputin's murder completely undermines the Czarina's sanity. She holds enormous power over her husband. Her condition undermines him. Russia is collapsing. And her rulers are collapsing too. You have very little time.'

'Weeks?'

'If you're fortunate. But I would not be surprised if that telephone rang right now to inform me that a mob was marching on this prison.' He picked up the telephone, spoke rapid Russian, then said to Ash, 'You will be returned to your cell until I can make the final details for freeing you.'

Ash held out his chains. 'Would you mind taking these off?'

'They contribute to the authenticity of our pretences,' von Basel replied with a thin smile. 'As will this.' He slashed Ash across the face with his stick and kicked his shackled feet out from under him. Ash hit the floor in a red explosion of pain. Von Basel stepped on the chain holding his wrists. 'You'll need a few bruises to convince your jailers that I dealt with you severely.' He hit Ash twice more.

'Don't worry, that'll heal before the Czar's reception.'

The first year of the World War had convinced Count von Basel that he had been trained a warrior for the wrong war. Sadly, he had admitted, noblemen had no special place on the modern battlefield; there was no longer a role for the well-born, self-reliant fighting man.

The machine-gun had seen to that. The lowliest conscript from the most noisome Ruhr factory district could master a machine-gun in a week and cut down a dozen aristocratic cavalrymen before they could draw their sabres.

Seeking a nobler way to serve his country and his Kaiser than indiscriminate slaughter in the trenches – which were really nothing better than industrial slums – Count von Basel had volunteered for the secret service, Gruppe IIIb,

281

with the Kaiser's reluctant blessing, and invaded Russia by himself. As a spy.

The war, after all, would be won in Russia.

Von Basel spoke perfect Russian, learned from his half-Russian father, and practised on the von Basels' East Prussian estates; he had travelled in several disguises – a lame teacher, a consumptive newspaper reporter, a wounded army veteran – each of which had the dual advantage of allowing him to carry his sword-cane and providing an excuse for not being in the army.

He relayed reports through the Gruppe IIIb network on the rail breakdowns which affected Russian movements at the front. His reports had enabled German commanders to shift their numerically inferior troops with devastating effect on the blundering Russians; a unit completely out of ammunition would awaken to a German rifle charge; an artillery battery, laboriously assembled from the chaotic staging areas, would find itself the sole target of twenty German cannon.

Then he got lucky – although von Basel was convinced that pouncing on the luck the way he had would have been beyond ordinary men. He spent a night aboard a sidetracked train in the private compartment of a Russian policeman named Moskolenko. In the afterglow of physical contentment the policeman had talked, talked too much – he worked for Okhrana, security branch, secret police; he was travelling from Eastern Russia to Petrograd; the Petrograd police were expanding to crack down on the agitators who were slowing war production in the factories and he had been transferred; he was excited, he had never seen the fabled capital city some five thousand miles from his home.

'What about your family?' von Basel had whispered in the dark. 'Will they come too?'

'I have no family. I was an orphan. My wife and children

died of cholera.' Then he added mawkishly, 'Now I have only nights like this.'

Von Basel was not surprised. The handsome Okhrana officer had all the earmarks of an unhappy loner – too fussy for a man only thirty, a little too neatly turned out, and too querulous when small things went wrong, such as the delayed train or the poor wine in the dining car. He embraced Moskolenko again, as if to comfort him. They fitted like spoons, belly to back, von Basel behind.

He had killed before, but only with the blade. There was no chance of the blade here in the policeman's dark compartment, only his bare hands. He caressed him toward orgasm, slowly, while he built up his nerve, working his other hand up Moskolenko's chest to his neck. When he thought he could do it, he brought Moskolenko to the peak, entered him and crushed his throat just as he cried out in climax.

He stripped the body, dressed it in the clothes of his wounded veteran disguise, put on Moskolenko's clothes, threw the body out when the train began moving again and spent the rest of the journey poring over the dead man's papers.

Moskolenko's letters of introduction seemed to confirm that he had never been to Petrograd, and never met his new superiors, that he had been hired, as he had claimed, directly from his post in Siberia.

Then, when the train was on the outskirts of Petrograd, disaster. Clipped to an inside pocket was a handwritten note from an Okhrana major who promised to meet his train. It wrecked von Basel's plan to assume Moskolenko's identity. He read it again, wondering if the note held an undercurrent of an affair between Moskolenko and the major. The note ended, after all, with an invitation: 'Apartments are scarce and hotels expensive. You may stay with me until you find your own lodgings.' Fortunately the major

283

had added a postscript. 'If I am detained go straight to my apartment, 35 Bolshoy Prospect, Vassily Island. It is quite private.'

Von Basel went straight to the Bolshoy Prospect when his train arrived. And when the dejected major returned, von Basel beat his head in with a candlestick, removed his clothing and broke up the apartment to simulate a deadly lovers' quarrel.

Afterwards, not knowing whether Moskolenko had another lover waiting, he reported boldly to Okhrana headquarters. It had worked. He was allowed to take up his new post, which he had maintained for almost a year now as the cold, remote and very competent Captain Moskolenko. Better at his job than the real one, he was sure. His superiors liked his work with informers – not knowing that many were already German spies – liked how intimately he had come to know the raw underbelly of the city, and had rewarded him with this department in the Litovsky and an assistant – the demented, but nonetheless capable Lieutenant Orlov.

Von Basel's reports via the Gruppe IIIb network of mock companies in neutral countries were of the very highest calibre because they included information gathered by the single most reliable unit of the Czar's regime, his own secret police. Consequently, von Basel had discovered the strength of General Brusilov's offensive in time to alert German reinforcements to save the Austrian army. And just two months ago, when the German invasion of Roumania was poised, he had learned while interrogating a high Russian army general caught plotting against the Czar that Russia would not defend Roumanian territory.

But he served Kaiser Wilhelm first. And one fact was certain. If anyone in Gruppe IIIb or any other unit of the entire German Army thought von Basel would subvert his Kaiser's wishes for them, they were terribly wrong. And any

German agent who tried would find himself in Orlov's interrogation room wishing he were dead.

Didn't they know that the nobility had no purpose but to fight for royalty? Kaiser Wilhelm – in his wisdom, and by his divine right – had ordered Kenneth Ash to remove the Czar to England; therefore the Czar *would* be removed to England even if it took von Basel's last breath. It was a simple matter of noble obligation . . .

Ash came to in his cell, head aching. His uniform was laid out neatly beside him on the wooden bunk. The guards had removed the chains. They took him to another sealed black Maria and drove him around the city for an hour. The lieutenant escorting him returned his papers, sword and Luger.

'Who was the officer who interrogated me this afternoon?'

'Commander, you should thank God your answers satisfied him. Don't ask stupid questions.'

'I just wanted to send a little thank-you note.'

'By law a permit is required to bring your gun into Russia.'

'You want to arrest me again?'

The lieutenant pointed at the door. The police van stopped. A moment later Ash found himself standing on Sadovaya Street, half a block from the Nevsky Prospect, staring at the back of the departing vehicle, which bore no identifying marks and disappeared among the trams and carriages.

His head still ached but the cold air felt wonderful. He started walking toward the Europa. If he had the time and didn't mind wasting his meagre contacts he supposed he could track down von Basel's Russian identity. But there was no time. Nor was it worth it. Crazy as it seemed, the German count was on his side. At least he seemed to be . . .

Petrograd seemed to vibrate with colour and bright lights after five days' confinement. At the Europa he telephoned the Alexander Palace and got as far as the colonel who had approved his visit to the Czarina. 'Her Imperial Majesty will receive no one.' It sounded like von Basel was right.

Ash called Roland's room. 'Meet me in the bar.' He was on his second Scotch whisky by the time the Frenchman got downstairs.

'What happened? How did you get out?'

'Ran into an old acquaintance. Remember von Basel?'

'That contemptible – '

'Same one. Don't ask me how he got here 'cause I don't know.'

'What happened to your face?'

'I ran into a door.'

'Three of them, from the look of it. Can I presume you'll be wanting more lessons?'

'Consider it a certainty.'

'May I be the one to judge when you're ready?'

Ash nodded. 'Sure. I don't want to lose again.'

He finished his whisky and ordered a third. 'Who knows I was arrested?'

'Me. The French ambassador. The American ambassador.'

'How'd the French ambassador find out?'

'I saw them take you. So I went to him for help.'

Ash would rather he hadn't. Now that he was out. He said only, 'Do you know what the American ambassador did?'

'Nothing. My ambassador was the first to tell him, and he had the strong impression that your ambassador was ordered to stand clear.'

Relieved that he hadn't been compromised, Ash said, 'So no one else knows.'

Roland hesitated.

'Who else?' Ash demanded.

'When it seemed hopeless I went to Tamara.'

Ash's jaw tightened, sending a jolt of pain through his bruised face. He wanted to ask how she had reacted but said instead, 'I wish you hadn't done that.'

'She was my last chance.' Roland shrugged. 'Fanning an old flame seemed preferable to your rotting in jail. She called a police chief. Even he couldn't help, but he did learn you had been moved to the Litovsky.'

'The Litovsky?' All right, von Basel. A little closer.

'We gave up hope at that point. They said you were being interrogated by the Okhrana.'

'Would you please tell her I'm all right.'

'I telephoned her the moment you called.'

Ash wanted to ask more but couldn't. What had she looked like? Was she happy? . . . Was it true that her grand duke was plotting a coup? 'How'd she treat you?'

'She was kind,' said Roland, and looked at Ash, inviting another question, but Ash stared into his drink and said nothing. If she wanted to see him she could have told Roland. But she hadn't.

'Why is God so cruel?' the Czarina wailed. Her lady-in-waiting kept silent, knowing a hopeless question. The Empress had lain weeping all day on her mauve chaise-longue. Her grief had turned briefly to rage when the Grand Duke Valery visited in the morning, but now tears were all she had.

'His Majesty's train is approaching Malaya Vishera,' the lady prompted gently. 'A few more hours and he'll be home.'

No response. She tried another approach. 'Colonel Riazhin tells me that the American who brought your lovely gift from King George has telephoned again. Shall I – '

The Czarina pushed her away. Father Gregory had seen

his blood on the American's hands. If only she had listened . . . she was still crying when the Czar arrived. She went into his arms and sobbed out everything that had happened. He wore an ordinary soldier's tunic, which smelled reassuringly of cigarette smoke and oiled leather. The girls came running in in their nightdresses. They all went to Alexis's room and sat around his bed while Nicholas listened to what each of them had been doing and told them how he had missed them at the Stavka.

Later, after they had put the children back to bed, they made love. And in the night he kissed the tears from her cheeks and asked, 'Sunny? Tell me what exactly did Commander Ash say?'

26

Addressing his shaving mirror, and feeling mildly absurd, Ash practised whispering, 'I have a message from King George' without moving his lips. Over a hundred gossip-hungry Russian courtiers and foreign diplomats would be watching every moment at the Czar's New Year's reception.

Message was the problem word. Aspirations and grunts took care of *I, have, a, from, King* and *George,* but *message* demanded lip action. He changed it to *news.* 'I have news from King George.' It worked even better with a half-smile. If it worked at all.

Petrograd was nervous on New Year's Day. Rumour said strikers had mobbed the police in the Vyborg District – it was the Narva District in some versions, the Moscow in others; regiments called in to restore order had supposedly fired on the police instead; a Cossack charge had ultimately returned control to the government.

It seemed to Ash on the carriage ride from the American Embassy to the Tsarskoye Selo train station that every bakery had a long line of shivering women straggling into the street. The Russians, he had learned, called the line for bread or paraffin or sugar the *khvost* – the tail. The *khvosts* were everywhere on Vassily Island, where von Basel had rented him a flat in a slummy Maly Boulevard building inhabited by tram conductors, prostitutes and music teachers. It was twenty degrees below zero as Ash stepped down from the carriage; people were predicting the worst winter in years.

The police had roped off Zagorodny Street around the Tsarskoye Selo station and patrolled the square on horseback while eighty members of the diplomatic corps dressed in their full regalia boarded the special train to present congratulations to the Czar.

'I'm delighted, *of course,* to be of service to Ambassador Page . . .' Ambassador Hazzard said with clear annoyance, mixed with confusion, when the American delegation had settled onto the luxurious blue and silver Imperial Train. Unlike the uniformed chiefs of the Allies' embassies, he wore civilian dress, a swallowtail suit with white waistcoat, tie and gloves. And, far from delighted, he looked as if he wished Ambassador Page had sent Ash to China.

'But I don't know how to introduce you to the Czar. Too confusing to say you represent Ambassador Page.'

'Say I'm posted from London, Your Excellency.'

'I don't know,' Hazzard grumped. 'London's confusing too.'

'London would explain why you're accompanied by *two* naval attachés, sir.' Across the compartment a Captain Hamilton was eyeing Ash suspiciously, and Hazzard's military attaché, Major Sheppard, looked put out because there were two navy men and only himself from the army.

Ash wanted the word 'London' in his presentation to the Czar. Their formal introduction would last seconds only, and he needed a surefire opening. London-Scotland-King George.

'I suppose, but it's very irregular . . .'

The train started smoothly. Hazzard took a gold watch from his waistcoat. 'Two thirty-five. Right on time. Probably the only train in Russia that is. The trip back from Moscow was awful.'

The Czar's reception, which had been cancelled the previous year owing to his responsibilities as commander of the army, had caught everyone by surprise. Ambassadors had scurried back to Petrograd from Moscow and vacations in Finland. Which said, Ash thought, something for Count von Basel's sources.

Ash tried to watch the route through the ice-glazed window, fascinated as he had been the first time by the idea that this single line, in winter at least, was the only practical connection between the Czar and his capital.

Separate carriages awaited each ambassador at the Tsarskoye Selo Imperial Station. The horse blankets were covered with ice. When they had taken away the ambassadors, more carriages and sleighs appeared to take their staffs through the rococo gold-and-iron gates leading to the Imperial Park.

The British delegation climbed the palace steps first; the chief delegation, fifteen men led by the tall white-haired Buchanan. The French and Italians – the other two Allied powers – followed, then the Americans, the Spanish, the lesser European delegations and finally a Japanese chargé d'affaires.

It was warm inside. Hundreds of servants relieved the diplomats of coats and hats. Pages from the staff of the director of ceremonies led them up a staircase lined with marble vases and into the Great Hall – a gilded ballroom with an elaborate parquet floor, tall windows on the long walls overlooking the snowy gardens, and mirrors at the ends. The windows and hundreds of electric lamps cast light on the gold-and-red furniture.

The director of ceremonies positioned the ambassadors in a row, with their staffs lined up two steps behind them. Ash was at the back of the American line, behind Major Sheppard and Captain Hamilton, exactly where he wanted to be to draw the Czar back an extra step away from those who might hear. The Court worked like an exquisitely precise machine. The instant the director of ceremonies' staff had withdrawn, the doors were thrown open and thirty generals and courtiers marched in, led by the Czar.

Nicholas II wore scarlet. He strode firmly to the British Ambassador Buchanan, shook his hand and exchanged low-voiced greetings. Buchanan then proceeded to read aloud from a paper in a voice too low for the other diplomats to hear. Hazzard's counsellor and first secretary exchanged glances. Apparently the Briton had not consulted the Americans, who looked worried that Buchanan might presume to speak for the United States.

Ash thought the Czar looked thinner and quite a bit older than he had in 1913. Yet he seemed at ease and was certainly very much a royal presence in his long red coat with the *pallash* scabbarded at his lean waist. The man and the title, Czar of all the Russias, were not, in appearance at least, mismatched. His entourage, however, looked anxious. Every face seemed to reflect the strain of the war – the shortages, the defeats, the uncertainty.

At last Buchanan presented his enormous staff, and the Czar, Ash noted, took time for a word with each. He moved on and spoke briefly with the Italians. Next he went to Paléologue, the French ambassador, with whom he held a quiet conversation in French.

Nicholas was presented to the nine-man French suite, and again had a word for each. Then, still trailed by his entourage, the Czar advanced on Ambassador Hazzard and cordially shook his hand. Ash, straining to hear, heard the Czar say he recalled their last meeting three months earlier when Hazzard had presented his credentials. Hazzard replied that he had learned a lot more about Russia since then and had found much to admire.

'I'm delighted to hear that,' the Czar replied seriously.

'I have been working to promote closer relations between Russia and America,' Hazzard said. Ash winced. Closer relations could be interpreted in diplomatic circles as a

292

promise to enter the war, which Hazzard had not meant. The contrast between the naïve, earnest American and the wily old French and British ambassadors dramatized how much more seriously Europeans took diplomacy – though the fact of the current war made one wonder what difference it made.

The Czar smiled. 'Yes,' he said in his accentless English, 'I have heard of your actions in that line and think considerable progress has been made.'

Hazzard wished him Happy New Year and asked permission to present his staff. The Czar approached and shook hands with the counsellor as Hazzard introduced him by name. They moved on to the first secretary, then the second, and the third, and Ash felt his gut tightening. Close to, the Czar's resemblance to King George was uncanny, except for the eyes, which didn't bulge like the King's and were instead strangely deep, a bit dreamy. His gaze flicked over Ash for a second. Did he remember Scotland? Or Berlin?

Hazzard introduced the military attaché. The Czar shook hands. Hazzard introduced the regular naval attaché. The Czar shook his hand too. Then Hazzard said, 'Commander Kenneth Ash, recently posted from London.'

The Czar's grip was firm, his gaze ceremoniously noncommittal.

'Have you acclimatized to our Russian winter, Commander Ash?'

'I find your Russian winter stimulating, Your Majesty. Like the rain in Scotland.'

'What do the Scots call it? A soft day when it rains?'

'Exactly, Your Majesty. I don't suppose you recall, sir, but I had the honour of being presented to you some years ago in Scotland at Balmoral Castle.'

'You were a lieutenant then,' the Czar replied without hesitation. 'And almost as good a shot as King George. I doubt the winged population has recovered in that section of Scotland.'

'I have news from King George,' Ash whispered, dead-lipped with a half smile.

Czar Nicholas turned toward the next delegation. The Spanish rippled in anticipation. Ambassador Hazzard was still hovering as closely as protocol allowed, but even he could not hear the Czar's low-voiced, 'Later.'

As an officer of the Czar's Convoy, the duty fell to Dmitri Dan to escort the diplomats back to the station after lunch. He and his men saluted from horseback as the train steamed off to Petrograd. Then Dmitri took his squad to their barracks near the Catherine Palace.

Dmitri had seen Commander Ash in the American delegation – recognized him from the pictures General Ludendorff had shown them at Spa. Now he debated whether to alert his brother Vladimir. From the beginning he had had doubts about the value and the morality of Red Snow killing the American. And now, with a lot of time wasted in a too clever scheme to trick the Okhrana into killing Ash for them, Dmitri Dan wondered if the German gold was worth distracting any more comrades from the business of revolution. He and Vladimir had been gone too long from Russia, and now, back only days, did not seem the time to worry about Ash. The important jobs, now that Rasputin was dead, were killing the Czar and Czarina.

Half an hour later his squad was ordered out again to greet another special train from Petrograd. They galloped across the Imperial Park and formed up at the station just as the locomotive pulled in.

Ash got off the train. Dmitri was astonished. Ash must have boarded it in Petrograd immediately after getting off the diplomat's train. Why would a man ride from Tsarskoye Selo to Petrograd only to come straight back to

Tsarskoye Selo? A Life Guard lieutenant colonel escorted the American – *Podpolkovnik* Ivan Roskov, an officer who Dmitri knew was often entrusted with discreet arrangements.

Curious, he followed to the gate where the Alexander Palace guard would query whether he was authorized to come into the grounds, which he was not. Not yet.

A coal-black Ethiopian guard opened a final door in the royal apartments, and Ash's escort bade him good-bye. The Czar waited inside. He had changed into a plain, unadorned tunic, trousers and boots and stood, hands clasped behind his back, in the middle of a half dozen tables covered with military maps.

Billiard tables. A green-shaded lamp hung over each. Six pools of light – East Prussia taken, lost. Galicia taken, lost. Poland lost. Brusilov's offensive stopped. Roumania lost. The Baltic abandoned.

'Thank you for coming, Commander Ash,' the Czar greeted him politely in a soft voice. 'Would you be so kind as to repeat precisely what you told my wife?'

'King George begs you to accept sanctuary in England, Your Majesty.'

The Czar sighed. He seemed, Ash thought, shy, almost embarrassed.

'May I call you Kenneth?'

'Of course, Your Majesty.'

'It seems appropriate, since Georgie thinks so highly of you . . .' The Czar's voice trailed off. Ash waited, trying to be patient, while his mind raced. What did the Czar intend? He had made careful, deliberate arrangements to have Ash brought quietly back to Tsarskoye Selo. Clearly the Czarina had told him about King George's offer, and just as clearly the Czar was interested.

'Why,' Nicholas asked suddenly, 'is Georgie so worried?

Does he know something about Russia I don't? Or does he fear that my soldiers will let England down?'

He went on before Ash had a chance to answer, but his voice now turned dull and tired. 'You must tell King George that I am still determined to continue the war until victory – decisive and complete victory. Remind him that I have promised my armies we will take Constantinople.'

Ash looked away. Constantinople – the old Imperial Russian dream of a Mediterranean port. But the German army, having just seized Roumania, blocked the only conceivable route to Constantinople, and the Russians, who were still retreating, hadn't a hope in hell of dislodging them. Constantinople – and not a word of the rage crackling in his own cities.

'Is that it, Kenneth?' the Czar demanded, his voice enlivened by bitterness. 'George thinks I can't make war?'

'No, Your Majesty. Not at all. King George is deeply grateful for the sacrifices of the Russian army. The Western Front would never have held without your relentless pressure on the East . . . It is the safety of you and your family . . .'

The Czar gazed back at Ash, vague and silent. Ash wasn't sure if he had heard him, hadn't the slightest idea what he was thinking and at the moment wondered if the Czar knew himself.

'Unrest,' the Czar asked at last. 'Is it the unrest?'

'Yes, Your Majesty. Word of . . . unrest has led King George to wonder whether the actions of certain ministers have perhaps undermined the Russian people's confidence in Your Majesty – '

'It is up to the people to gain *my* confidence,' Czar Nicholas told him. 'They must display faith in me.' He walked stiffly to a billiard table with a map of Turkey and stared at it.

Ash waited. *Never say more than you have to*, his father used

296

to say. *To stop talking is the hardest thing there is.* Ash fought the temptation to answer. *Unrest?* Revolution was more like it. The talk on the delegates' train back to Petrograd had confirmed that the Cossacks *had* been called into the Narva District to disperse mutinous troops. For a few hours earlier in the week all that had stood between Petrograd and anarchy was a handful of primitive horse soldiers.

'. . . I know there is a great deal of excitement in Petrograd's smart salons,' the Czar said at last. 'But I have fifteen million men under arms and surely my own police are more familiar with real conditions than the King of England.'

He did not know what his mauled armies had come to. How, Ash wondered, could he imagine conscripts would fire on their own friends? As for his police, how many honest reports ever got past the Interior Minister? And how many von Basels had Germany slipped into their ranks?

'Don't you agree?' the Czar demanded.

Ash said, 'Your cousin is viewing events in Russia from a great distance. Perhaps his fear for your safety makes him worry a little too much, but perhaps the distance also allows him to be more objective . . .'

To Ash's relief, the Czar did not argue, almost as if he had considered that conclusion himself. He opened and closed his hands and looked around the billiard room; glanced at and over the grim maps.

'What's his plan?' he blurted out, startling Ash. My God . . . he was going to co-operate . . . ?

'A cruiser will call for you at Murmansk, Your Majesty.'

The Czar gave a vague smile, as if enjoying a private joke. 'The navy? We each have our weakness for the sea, Georgie and I . . . one's soul feels so peaceful at sea . . .' He strolled to a table in the corner. Ash followed at a discreet distance. The Czar gazed down at the map and traced with his finger the route north from Petrograd fifteen hundred miles to the coast. 'The Murman railroad is almost completed,' he said more to himself than Ash. Then his finger moved into the Barents Sea, around the North Cape and into the Norwegian Sea. Halfway to Scotland he lifted his finger and looked at Ash.

'Has Georgie forgotten German U-boats? Might I not step directly from, as you say, the frying pan into the fire? . . . and drown in the process?'

Ash took a deep breath. He feared this question more than any other, had hoped the Czar wouldn't raise it until the cruiser was at sea, because the Czarina had expressed such hatred of Imperial Germany. But now asked, it had to be answered, and Ash saw no way to avoid naming Wilhelm.

'King George asked your cousin the Kaiser for a U-boat escort to Scotland.'

'*Willy* – Oh God, what do they think of me?' He walked back to the map of Turkey and stared at Constantinople. 'Did Kaiser Wilhelm agree?'

'Immediately, Your Majesty. The Kaiser is heartsick, you know what he thinks of you, in spite of war.'

'Willy thinks I'm a dolt!' But the sudden vehemence faded quickly from his eyes, and he murmured in tones dull and lifeless as before, 'Perhaps Willy's right . . .'

Was the Czar finally losing faith in himself? Perhaps he was considering the unthinkable – abdication. Could he be pushed?

'Kaiser Wilhelm told me to tell you that this is a matter of family,' Ash said. 'Victoria's children, was how he put it, Your Majesty. An agreement – '

'I'm the last,' the Czar interrupted.

'I beg your pardon, Your Majesty?'

'I'm the last emperor. The last true autocrat. There are no others left. Willy's whole empire is an upstart. Georgie's a figurehead. Old Franz Joseph is dead. The Chinese fell years ago. The Ottoman sultans are the sick men of Europe. Who do you think will replace me, Commander?'

He's going to do it, thought Ash. *He's going to leave.*

'Who?' the Czar repeated. 'Three hundred years of Romanov succession. Who will take my place?'

'You can return,' Ash lied, moved by the man's genuine, deep sorrow despite his paramount goal of helping to end the war. 'Your family is worried about right now . . .'

The Czar looked again at his maps; Ash guessed he wished he was back at his Stavka, where the bustle of generals and aides-de-camp gave even the worst situation the hope of sudden reversal.

'Yes, of course . . . I suppose you are right . . . poor Russia, God help her . . .'

It worked. Ash could scarcely believe it. He would have the Czar out of the country in a week. The way would be cleared for the US to enter the war. And end it.

'Nicky!' The door burst open. The Czarina stumbled in. Wild-eyed, dishevelled, clumsily draped in black, she clutched Rasputin's bloodstained peasant blouse to her breast. When she saw Ash, she screamed.

27

Weaving frantically through the maze of billiard tables, the Czar extended his arms to her. 'Sunny. Darling – '

She jerked away, screaming hysterically at Ash. 'Father Gregory saw his blood on your hands.'

Her hair was tangled, loose to her waist, her skin deathly white, her eyes red from crying. The Czar reached for her again. 'Darling, calm – '

'I didn't listen. I didn't listen. Father Gregory warned me you are the devil. I should have listened.' Another outburst of tears. Nicholas held her, rocked her in his arms, murmured softly to her. Her body heaved, and she flung her hands about as if to hit Ash. The Czar looked over her head, his eyes begging Ash to leave.

'Your family sent me,' Ash said. 'I'm not the devil. Your own cousins asked me to help – '

'We will not leave Russia.'

'They want to help you and your children – '

The Czarina covered her ears. 'Make him go away!'

'*Leave us*,' the Czar commanded.

'Your Majesty, please – '

'Get *out*.' The huge black guard opened the door 'Take him out,' the Czar snapped, then turning on Ash as he backed toward the door, he said, 'It is God's will we are here and God's will we stay.'

The Ethiopian took his arm and guided him firmly out of the billiard room.

Grand Duke Valery sat alone in the gloomy smoking room of the Yacht Club, wondering if his small band of Cossacks could hold Palace Square long enough to persuade the Russian Army to accept him as the new czar. Half a dozen grand dukes, cousins and uncles, eyed him anxiously from their quinze game in the next room. Interesting, he thought, now that they had persuaded him to take action few of the conspirators would risk being seen with him – even in the most private club in Russia.

Valery snorted a laugh, and an old German waiter came running.

'Vodka.'

He supposed he was suited to be the czar . . . if anyone was. Certainly he had more Russian blood in his veins than most of the Romanov clan – poor Nicky had barely a drop, if that, when you gave Catherine the Great's mysterious antecedents a close look, as his Tamara had been fondly reminding him of late – Tamara, who had a frightening way of thrusting the world at him. He often felt like a little boy with her, but afterward he stood more the man than his limited peers. How long could he hold the throne? Longer than Nicky. Long enough to beat Germany before the troops rebelled and simply turned around and walked home.

What next? No one knew. Feeding the peasants and the workers would quiet their anger at first, but enriching the peasants always had the effect of enriching the townspeople far more. And for some damned reason the more they got the more they demanded, the louder their children complained in the universities. And most strange, the more they left the land the for festering cities.

Never mind. Winning the war was the first and immediate task. But the Russian army needed support at home – guns, food, ammunition. He remembered the awe and pride he felt in 1914 when Russia mobilized. Masses gathered at the railroad stations. More Russian men than anyone had ever imagined existed. Hordes of the Czar's subjects, thousands, millions, until the trains couldn't carry them all. Brave men who deserved more from Father Czar than Nicholas II had the power to give them.

Valery's Cossacks would fight for Palace Square to the last man. He had provided for their families on his estates since they had been assigned to protect him during the 1905 revolt. He let them recruit their replacements in their traditional way of choosing the best young man each year from their villages – a young man who would never return except in disgrace. But even the most loyal hundred fighters, he realized sadly, couldn't be more than shock troops. Unfortunately, the bold conspirators who had promised regiments were hesitating.

He surged abruptly to his feet and headed for the door. Six pairs of eyes trailed him from the card room, their owners sensing like a herd of sheep that the wolf was up to something. Who was he meeting tonight? The colonel of the Preobrajenski Regiment? A reactionary Black Hundred member of the Duma? A district police chief? What conspirator had agreed to make the first move?

Valery left them with a grim smile. He felt less the wolf than a bear lost in the forest. As for tonight, he was taking his Tamara to the French ambassador's ball.

The Czar had a friend, Lieutenant Colonel Ivan Roskov of the Imperial Convoy, who served him as a private royal courier – much the way Ash occasionally served the King of England – when Nicholas felt the need to operate with greater secrecy than his court could guarantee. He turned now to *Podpolkovnik* Roskov.

The two men had met as nineteen-year-olds nearly thirty years ago; Nicholas, then the Czarevich, had been given command of young Roskov's Horse Guard squadron. The years had treated them differently, yet their friendship had remained strong. Nicholas hardly looked older, except when he was tired or grief-stricken for his son, and the placid, dreamy light in his eyes often reminded Roskov of their youth.

Roskov, however, looked like the crusty old veteran he had become fighting Russia's wars. His hair and beard had long ago turned iron grey. A Japanese sabre cut inflicted during the Yalu River campaign creased his brow, and a German gas attack in Poland left him too short of breath to serve on the Front.

The Czar issued Roskov's orders in Russian, the language he required his officers to speak instead of the foreign French and English they often preferred. 'Bring back Commander Ash.'

Podpolkovnik Roskov arrived by train in Petrograd within the hour. Commander Ash was not at his hotel, but the staff informed him that the American had been invited to the French ambassador's ball.

The French ball was a high point in the social season – the French ambassador being a favourite of Petrograd Society. The cream of the nobility – the aristocracy, the army and the government as well as the diplomatic corps – had braved a blizzard howling off the Gulf of Finland. Ash had not been surprised by a last minute invitation. An American naval officer arrested by the Okhrana, only to show up two weeks later chatting like an old friend with the Czar at his New Year's reception, had to be of some interest to a witty gossip like the short, stout French ambassador.

His Excellency, however, was too polite, and too cagey, to launch a frontal attack, and Ash did not intend to give much away.

'You should parry so well on the strip,' Roland remarked on their way to the champagne bar.

'He was distracted. Something's bothering him.'

'He had an audience at Tsarskoye Selo this morning. I understand he was not encouraged by the Czar's grip on reality.'

No wonder. The French ambassador had only one job in Petrograd and that was to keep his Russian ally fighting their common enemy, Germany. Ash eyed the glittering throng, wondering if there was a single man or woman here capable of removing the Czar before Russia collapsed and the revolutionaries took over, ending the chance for America to enter the war on the side of the Allies.

Of all the means by which Russians traditionally flaunted their wealth, Ash thought that the most impressive was the manner in which Russian women dressed for a ball. He had grown accustomed to the great pastel palaces strung along the rivers and canals, to the perfect teams of matched thoroughbreds, to the retinues of docile servants. But nothing showed off Imperial Russia's surface glitter quite as vividly as the play of precious gems on naked female skin.

Petrograd was a city of achingly beautiful women, which the Russian upper classes spawned in infinite variety from raven-haired exotics to regal blondes. Their gowns swept low, and when they let their sables fall from their milky shoulders they revealed masses of brilliant diamonds, dazzling emeralds, rubies like blood. A quick motion to extend a shapely hand, a slow half-turn to impart a smile, and jewels shimmered wildly – emeralds, sapphires, matchless pearls – reminding one that a sixth of the earth's surface was still theirs in contiguous possession.

Suddenly, across the cream-coloured ballroom ablaze in electric chandeliers, Ash saw Lord Exeter parting the sea of gowns and uniforms; and at his side, lean as a frigate, Lady Exeter. Her gown covered her shoulders and her arms, and her only jewellery was an emerald brooch, yet in a room full of half-naked beautiful women, she still managed to look interesting.

Exeter, one of the few men not in uniform, smiled benignly when Ash bowed over Lady Exeter's hand, and exchanged inconsequentials about their arrival in Petrograd, until Lady Exeter fell into conversation with a Bohemian-looking noblewoman on the arm of an aristocratic poet; then he drew Ash aside and glanced around to see if it was safe to talk.

A lively quadrille was pounding across the ballroom; the noise of the dancers and Mikhailov's orchestra would compete with an artillery duel.

'I heard most of what happened. I presume prison was some ghastly error.'

'I'm okay.'

'Still useful?'

'Apparently. My arrest was not widely known and my embassy stayed out of it. I think I can continue as if nothing happened.'

'And nothing has happened, has it?'

'What do you mean?'

'I mean I haven't heard about any request for the cruiser yet.'

'The Czarina listened to what I had to offer,' Ash said. 'But when I got out of jail I received a strong indication that she was not interested in British asylum. I managed an audience with the Czar; I'm afraid he's not interested either.' Not after the Czarina's outburst, he added to himself.

'What are you going to do?'

'I don't know. The Rasputin killing has shaken them up pretty badly.'

'Bloody hell,' Exeter said mildly, sounding, as only the English could, neither surprised nor upset. 'Well, if they can't see the truth themselves, you'll just have to persuade them in a somewhat more forceful manner . . .'

Ash looked at the floor, as if Exeter's suggestion had

spilled on the shiny parquet like something unpleasant. British capital was a pillar of Russian industrial modernization; there wasn't a mill or a railway in Russia without British money in it, nor a town worthy of the name not served by a British consul. King George might be concerned only for his cousin – but the British Secret Service's goals might well transcend the war if the Secret Service and the foreign office feared that Russian revolutionaries might put a major trading partner out of business.

Ash's goal was simpler. Get a situation in which America could enter the war. End the war. Which meant no more Czar, and no revolution.

'Exeter, I came this close to disengaging myself from His Majesty's scheme. I waited outside your house after our dinner and I promised myself that if one person who looked remotely like one of your superiors at the Secret Service came to the door, or if you visited one, I would quit.' He would not have quit, but Exeter had to be made to understand that Kenneth Ash would not be his stalking horse.

'You're a bit of a spy yourself.'

'No. But I'm learning.'

Exeter laid a hand on his sleeve. For such a fat man he had delicate fingers, Ash thought. Ash looked at him and he removed it, saying, 'You must persuade the Czar to leave.'

'Put a gun to his head? What are you driving at?'

'You know Tishkova, the dancer?'

Podpolkovnik Ivan Roskov, the Czar's emissary, stalked into the French ball, handed the ambassador's major domo his snow-covered cloak and went looking for Ash among the several hundred guests. But just as Roskov was about to approach him, he was surprised to see the American become involved in an intense conversation with Lord Exeter.

A lifetime of watching for the Czar's safety made Roskov cautious. Puzzled that the two men should even know each other, he decided to observe from a distance before telling Ash the Czar wished to see him. As a lieutenant colonel in the Czar's Convoy, Roskov was regularly briefed by the Okhrana. He knew that Exeter worked for the British Secret Service, knew the English lord spent long evenings at the Imperial Yacht Club, surely plotting with the increasingly treacherous grand dukes. What had such a man to discuss with Kenneth Ash? . . . Whatever the subject, it appeared that Ash did not like it. He looked like a man about to draw his sword.

'Yes, I know Tishkova. What of it?'

'I hear rumblings that the Grand Duke Valery is cooking up some sort of palace revolt.'

'Exeter, what the hell are you doing in Petrograd?'

'His Majesty asked me to help you, but I'd be here anyway. I may have mentioned that my family owns munitions and cloth works up the Neva, near Lake Ladoga. Vital to the war push, but production's lagging, what with strikes and fuel shortages. I've come out to stir things up.'

'Is that all you're stirring up?'

Exeter took hold of Ash's arm again and this time he did not let go. 'Ash, my sources say that Grand Duke Valery has a damned good chance of pulling it off if he can muster enough regiments, and some more support in the Duma. Tishkova, of course, is allied with him.'

'If *you* know about it,' Ash said coldly, 'what about the Okhrana? Don't you think the police know too? It didn't take long to banish Grand Duke Dmitri and Prince Felix for shooting Rasputin.'

'This is different – '

'Damned right it's different. They'll execute them for treason.'

'No,' said Exeter. 'The Grand Duke Valery can succeed. But they need help, including, I am told, what to do with the Czar. You might get in touch – '

'*No.*'

'Why not?'

'I didn't come to Russia to overthrow the government. I came to rescue the Czar.' He had come to *remove* the Czar, but that was between him and Ambassador Page's Inner Circle.

'Well, who do you suppose is going to replace him?'

'Why don't we let the Russians worry about that? If you and the British Secret Service tip them over the brink with some damned fool scheme, the whole Eastern Front will collapse.'

'Is that your only reason?'

'It's my best reason. Any other isn't any of your damned business.'

Ash saw the Baroness Balmont, the banker de la Rocca's wife, and hurried toward her, shedding Exeter as he made his way through the crowds.

Lord Exeter watched Ash's progress in the mirrored walls. A line from Kipling's 'Recessional' ran through his mind: 'The Captains and the Kings depart.'

But who, he wondered, shall inherit what they leave behind? Neither the meek, nor the scrupulous, he was certain. Not even the cautious . . .

The tall Baltic blonde greeted Ash with a kiss on each cheek and repeated her invitation to come shooting on her estate. Her long white arms and high bosom were complimented by a dark blue gown; sapphires cascaded and glittered between her breasts. Ash inquired about her husband's health, and the Baroness Balmont replied that she had just had a channel dug so that one of her marshes opened directly into the Gulf of Finland to accommodate winter-bound yachtsmen who cared to try their hand at iceboating.

Ash admitted he was tempted. A day of shooting and

iceboating and a night in the baronial bed might be just the antidote to the catastrophe he had reaped so far. Exeter's nibbling around the edges was irritating and very likely dangerous; and his suggestion to turn to Tamara for help was downright depressing. Was *she* why the King had chosen him in the first place? That possibility was even more depressing, but whether the King had or not, Ash knew he must do *something*, and damned soon. The wood piles outside the Astoria were getting lower every day, and the blizzard howling past the French Embassy was only the first big storm of winter.

Vladimir Dan recognized Ash from photographs General Ludendorff had shown them. Only yesterday his brother Dmitri had seen Ash at Tsarskoye Selo. It seemed Ash was more than just a navy commander, which would explain partly why General Ludendorff was so anxious to buy his death.

The Red Snow leader had been disappointed when he got back to Petrograd to learn that the American was still alive; the German bounty had seemed like money in the bank. Instead, Vladimir's brother Dmitri was complaining it wasn't worth the effort. Vladimir had gone hunting anyway, only to discover that Ash never slept in his hotel. Spotting Ash at the ball tonight was a piece of luck.

'Who are you looking at?' asked his fiancée, a pretty girl from a rich family who knew nothing about Red Snow but was a necessary accoutrement to his carefully maintained existence as a loyal young officer to the Czar. Her only drawback was a habit of uncommon jealousy, and while he was looking at Ash, speculating how to kill him tonight, Elena thought he was making eyes at the very handsome Baroness Balmont. Fortunately her Italian husband came along and took her away.

But when he said, 'I'm sorry I have to take you home after midnight supper,' Elena pouted and accused him of planning to meet the Baroness Balmont at the gypsies'.

'I don't know where you get these ideas,' Vladimir Dan protested. He rarely considered the personal effect the revolution would have on his life when it was won. He had a vague idea of continuing much as he did now, with an army career and a proper wife, a house in Petrograd and a country estate and, if her dowry was as ample as suggested, a month or so a year in Paris. None of this, of course, would be at the expense of the peasants, as such luxuries now were. A competent government run by the people would eliminate the bottlenecks of production and the rapacious middlemen who were ruining the Russian economy. There was no reason why a decent man couldn't live comfortably as long as Russia was run on modern, efficient lines, like England or even America.

His brother Dmitri envisioned a rather more spartan revolutionary aftermath, but then, Dmitri had always been the stern ascetic. With such a future in mind – and it wasn't a future he dwelled upon, just occasionally thought of – it occurred to him that Elena could be a hellish wife. Particularly when it came time to take a mistress . . . 'I'm as faithful as any man in Petrograd. I'm terribly sorry, but my colonel has ordered me back to barracks early – '

'Why you?'

'The officer of the day asked to be relieved early. He hasn't fully recovered from his wounds . . .' Half-truths, because he would not put it past her to have one of her many brothers trail him around the city, and he did have to go to his barracks to get a gun and maybe a hand grenade.

The quadrille grew louder. Two hundred dancers followed the lead of a couple in the middle who offered intricate steps which the rest followed as precisely as a ballet corps. The man leading, a tall cavalry officer in a light blue uniform, called out instructions for each new figure and the ballroom resounded with laughter as the steps picked up speed. Ash had led one once with Tamara. There was nothing like it; make one wrong move and you'd send two hundred people careening into the mirrors.

'Ash!'

A short sandy-haired Royal Navy lieutenant parted the onlookers and came to rest in front of Ash, springing up and down on the balls of his feet like an aggressive terrier. Rodney Skelton, whom Ash had been intending to visit at the British submarine base at Reval. An odd coincidence? Or a good omen? Ash's emergency escape route if the cruiser failed. At least that had been his plan before the Czar said no.

Skelton noticed his promotion and tossed a mocking salute. 'Commander? The American navy seems bound to become all chiefs and no Indians.' There was an edge in Skelton's voice; they had had a set-to in India and neither had fully recovered from it. They had beaten the local Rajah's polo team in a remote province and the Rajah, in a rage, had ordered his entire team's horses put to death. Knowing nothing about it, Ash and Skelton had taken their gin-and-quinines for a walk in the Rajah's gardens and had stumbled on the slaughter. The stable yards reeked of blood, and Skelton, in the finest British tradition, had ordered the Indians to desist. Ash had seen things differently – some thirty angry men with knives intent on finishing what they had started – and had forcibly marched Skelton back to the British compound. Skelton had called him a coward; Ash had called Skelton a damned fool, and though they had continued to play polo together it had rankled through the long Coronation Durbar summer.

311

'What are you doing in Petrograd?' Ash asked as they shook hands. 'I was planning to visit you down in Reval.'

'I'm a Russian hero.' Skelton grinned. 'Making speeches for war bonds.' He had received 'permission to stop shaving', as the Royal Navy put it, and had grown a luxurious yellow beard, and Ash reflected that all in all Rodney Skelton looked the epitome of the British sportsman turned warrior for king and country.

'I sank three ore ships trying to carry iron from Sweden to Germany. Ought to put a crimp in Krupp. What are you doing?'

Ash could not hide his envy, though a close look at his old teammate revealed that two years' action in enemy waters had had a price; behind the open boasts Skelton was strung tight as a wire stay – but a command . . . command of a man o' war!

There were acquaintances you had to brag to, and before he could stop himself Ash was spouting his fondest hopes . . . 'I might get a destroyer soon.'

'When?'

When? When I rescue the Czar for your king. The same Czar who just tossed me out of his palace. 'Late spring, I hope – listen I really do want to come down and see your base.' Somehow, dammit, he was going to get the Czar out, but the tougher it got the more he might need an emergency escape route.

'Delighted to have you,' Skelton replied with the toothy grin that usually preceded a dig. 'Better wire ahead in case I have to sink a battleship that morning – or a couple of destroyers – ah, there's one of my hostesses. Good to see you, sport. Don't lose your despatch case.'

Ash traded nods with the food exporter Prince Paustovsky, who had never called back after promising an audience with the Czarina, and who now turned quickly away. Moments later he was snubbed by Sergei Gladishev, the Moscow millionaire and Kadet Party leader. He was wishing he hadn't come when he was hailed again, this time by Catherine Hazzard, whom he had not seen since they had arrived in Petrograd.

'Commander?'

She was on her father's arm. Her golden hair fell straight to her shoulders. She looked a little awed by the splendour and glad to see a familiar face. Her impossibly blue eyes sought Ash's. It no doubt was her first Petrograd ball. Ash bowed over her hand.

'You look lovely, Catherine. Good evening, Mr Ambassador.'

Hazzard pulled an envelope from his evening jacket and passed it to Ash. 'From Ambassador Page. King's Messenger brought it in.'

Ash slipped it in his own pocket. It was thick, and he was itching to read it but had to spend a decent interval with the ambassador and his daughter to convince Hazzard, who still looked resentful over his arrest, that he expected such communications to be routine.

He felt Catherine's gaze and turned to her. 'The ball is wonderful, isn't it?'

'I can't believe I'm here. The music is so beautiful and the colours . . .'

Ash looked around the room as if seeing it for the first time, and indeed the electric bulbs blazing in the chandeliers highlighted an incredible variety of red, blue, green and white uniforms, all dripping gold braid and ribbons; and on the arm of each officer a beautiful woman in a bright gown and shimmering jewels.

Suddenly the dancers stopped and turned expectantly toward the rococo doors from where a hush spread across the ball like a silent ocean breaker.

'Some bigwig's coming in,' Ambassador Hazzard whispered.

'Oh look!' Catherine's hand closed on Ash's arm. 'Oh look at them.'

Ash felt a dark pit open inside his heart.

28

'Who is that, Ash?' Ambassador Hazzard asked. 'Looks kind of familiar.'

'The Grand Duke Valery, cousin to the Czar, Your Excellency . . . I imagine he'll be representing His Majesty tonight.'

Valery wore a red uniform crossed by a blue silk sash. The decorations of a lifetime serving the Czar glittered on his chest. Ash thought he looked even more arrogant and self-possessed than he had twelve years ago at the New Hampshire peace talks, but he had to admit the grand duke still stood well. Half-bald, with a greying monk's fuzz around his ears, he had a high forehead . . . like Lenin's. Ironic.

'Is that his wife?' Catherine asked.

'No . . . no, he's not married. That's Tamara Tishkova, *prima ballerina assoluta* of the Imperial Russian Theatre.'

Ash had never seen her more beautiful.

The Black Swan. Her gown was black silk, her lustrous black hair coiffed high on her shapely head and banded with pearls. She promenaded on the grand duke's arm, jewels flashing on her deep décolletage, long drop diamond earrings caressing her white shoulders. Valery's gifts, for flaunting her as his consort. Her sensual mouth formed the elegant half-smile she always wore in the spotlight, a smile Ash had loved to watch grow broad with laughter, full and hungry in bed.

'Isn't she the woman you told us about?' Catherine asked.

'Would you excuse me, Catherine? Mr Ambassador?'

315

And Ash was gone, his chest hammering, before either could reply.

Tamara was proud of their entrance because no one at the ball could guess their turmoil, not even the frightened conspirators deserting Valery. The same men, she raged inwardly behind her steady smile, who had urged him to lead a palace coup but lost their courage the instant the grand duke had returned from his visit to the Czarina announcing that she was out of her mind and had to be removed to save Russia.

There was Sirotkin strutting about in the green uniform of the Preobrajenski Guard, units of which he had promised would seize the Winter Palace but which were suddenly 'too loyal' to commit *before* Valery's coup was successful. And there, Kamenev, sweet-talking Princess Paley; the men of his Jaegerski regiment were just as suddenly 'conscripts too fresh to trust.' And splendid in the blue of his Semonovski regiment, Captain Sokolov leading the quadrille – all he would lead, it had turned out, another noble Life Guard officer who preferred to talk while Valery fought.

Poor Valery. Czarina Alexandra had received him draped in black mourning, weeping, railing against the dark forces that attacked her friend Rasputin. And when Valery had tried to persuade her to release Grand Duke Dmitri, because only the Czar could legally arrest a grand duke, the Czarina had lost all control and thrown Valery out, screaming that *she* was the Czar. Hurrying back to Petrograd, determined to overthrow her and Nicky, Valery had been astonished to discover that while his brother grand dukes and officers still swore they would support Valery *after* the Czar was deposed, no one wanted to be first.

It was a classic case of belling the cat. Every duke offered to help form a new government, and every soldier among the conspirators promised his regiment would restore order. But first, Valery had said to no avail, raging until Tamara thought he would shatter the windows of her solarium with his voice, *some* regiment had to seize the Czar. Another take the Winter Palace. And a third besiege the police. And still a *fourth* escort agreeable members to the Duma from their Turide Palace to the Winter Palace to express public support.

Risks and details. What the army called logistics. The work a dancer did to free dreams from gravity. They were lazy cowards and their desertions were gnawing at Valery's resolve. He too was on the verge of losing stomach for it. He was saying, 'Perhaps if we just get through the winter . . .'

Tamara knew he was also worried about the Czar. What *exactly*, he wanted to know, would happen to Nicky? What shall we do with him? Troublesome Czarinas were traditionally bundled off to a nunnery. But the historical record on overthrown Czars was grimmer, Fyodor Godunov and Paul I both murdered. And Valery had already said he would take part in no palace coup that threatened to end in Nicky's death. He had demanded arrangements for the Czar's safety before he made a move.

Such cool-headedness was one of the several qualities Tamara admired in her very good if somewhat dull grand duke. But the question of Nicky's fate was becoming vital as one by one, day by day, Valery's allies turned cowards.

Was it perhaps for the best, she wondered, as they continued promenading about the ballroom. Who knew where poor Russia was going? Who really knew what should be done?

Tamara inclined her head, granting the merest nod to Sergei Gladishev. What a shame Valery hated the Moscow millionaire on principle. As a dancer she was accustomed to moving freely among court, Life Guard, Bohemian, artistic and even some merchant circles. A man like Gladishev, with his powerful allies in the Duma, could add such impetus to a coup, bring many powerful men along with him in support of a new czar. But staunchly conservative grand dukes like Valery and flashy industrialists like Gladishev distrusted each other on every issue Russia faced.

Yet Gladishev nodded back. Shrewd man. He understood.

And how had she become mixed up in all this? Why would a woman who reigned on two stages risk them both? Ironically, Valery himself had put it best when finally he had agreed to lead the palace coup. 'If not us, the revolutionaries. Or worse, the Germans . . .' Survival.

Ambassador Page's message was short, to the point, impatient: 'What the hell is going on? Please report.' In the same envelope, which had been carried to Russia by the King's Messenger, was a second message, an unsigned query which by its content had to be from George V: 'We are anxious to hear whether matters are in hand.' Same message. Different backgrounds.

Ash disposed of both in the men's room. He'd report when he had something to report, dammit. Back in the ballroom he circled the floor, careful to stay out of Tamara's way, yet unable to resist watching her at Valery's side. On or off a grand duke's arm, in a room full of beautiful women, she turned heads, like a runaway freight train.

Tamara stumbled. She was indulging Valery in a waltz when suddenly she saw Kennet. He was one uniform in a sea of uniforms, but she always knew him by his walk. She had seen him the first time walking in the sun –

'My ballerina trips?' Valery teased.

'The difference between me and an oxcart is that the ox

leads.' She practically gaped at Kennet as Valery steered her around the floor, stunned by what the sight of him still did to her.

She had seen him walking in the sun that first time in New Hampshire near the sea. She had climbed into a little boat tied at the end of a pier in a blue bay beside the Wentworth Hotel. A breeze was blowing from the Atlantic Ocean. The Wentworth sprawled along the shore, five white clapboard storeys, big as a city, all by itself on a spit of sand and trees a few miles down the New Hampshire coast from the Portsmouth Naval Station.

She lay in the boat, looking at the Wentworth's flags and turrets, trailing her fingers in the water, thinking about Nicky and the new dance she was doing in New York, and Valery, who even then was earnestly pressing her to be his alone. The summer of 1905, eleven and a half very long years ago – magnificent years, until the war ruined them.

And then Ash had walked onto the pier. Tamara had watched him through half-shut, sleepy eyes, watched his quick walk. By the time she had awakened to the probability that she was in his boat, it was too late to move and then, suddenly, she was lost.

All thoughts of Nicky and Valery and even the dance left her mind. She saw only a young man in white shirt and trousers, his skin bronzed by summer, his unruly hair sun-streaked with gold. His footsteps shook the pier, shook the boat where it touched the pier. His gaze was focused on the bay, examining the water the way she examined a new set. He did not see her until he knelt to untie the rope.

'Have I taken your boat?' Tamara smiled up at him.

His eyes filled with her. 'It's not mine. I borrowed it.'

Tamara lay still, moving only to lift her fingers slowly from the water. 'Then I am in your way?'

She knew her effect on him, was confirmed in it as he had answered quickly, 'Not if you want to come for a sail.'

319

She watched him prepare the boat, fascinated by his young, lean body – a fencer's body, perhaps, or a dancer's, but too big in the arms and shoulders for either. His hands were big too, and calloused from sailing. But not rough, oddly. Not rough when he touched her. No . . .

Valery squeezed her arm. 'Are you enjoying yourself, my dear?'

Ash was in no mood for midnight supper, and the French ambassador's announcement that 'the bold, British submariners' would make speeches during the meal clinched his feeling. When the guests began their exodus to the next room where the tables were laid, he had a smoke with Mikhailov while the piano player took a break. The old gossip told Ash a fantastic rumour. It was claimed by the *moujik* peasant workers that the Czar's daughter, the beautiful Grand Duchess Tatiana, had disguised herself as a lieutenant of the Horse Guard to watch the murder of Rasputin.

'She ordered the dying monk castrated because he once attempted to violate her. After that Rasputin was thrown in the river still living.'

'Do you believe that?' Ash asked, knowing damned well he had seen Rasputin shot dead before his eyes.

Mikhailov shrugged. 'The peasants believe in vengeance. And they know that a man drowned can never be made a saint . . .'

'In other words the Okhrana started the rumour to discredit the monk.'

'Perhaps . . .'

'When is your step-daughter coming home?'

'She's on her way. She'll be dancing Effie in *La Sylphide* next Sunday. She'd better make it soon.'

'She looked more the Sylphide.'

'She's made too many enemies at the theatre with her political ideas to get the best parts.'

Ash was not surprised, considering he had watched her meet a Bolshevik seaman in the middle of the night in Covent Garden. Did the old boy know? 'You must be happy.'

Mikhailov ground out his cigarette and brought his eyes to bear on Ash. 'I'm worried. I didn't want her to come back. If there's a revolution she'll be right in the middle of it.'

'Maybe there won't be a revolution.'

'And maybe my piano will walk to Moscow.'

Ash went back in after the dancing resumed, but it looked as though Tamara had left early. He was planning to call it a night when Lord Exeter saw him at the french doors. 'Ash, be a good chap. I must go up river. There's trouble at one of my factories. Could you see Lady Exeter home?'

He looked badly agitated, so Ash, who really wanted nothing more than to be alone, agreed and Exeter hurried off, his voluminous dinner jacket flapping like the wings of a condor.

Ash got Lady Exeter's coat and waited in a corner of the foyer watching the Russians retrieve their furs. He noticed a Horse Guard lieutenant colonel who seemed to be watching him; he looked like the Czar's officer who had escorted him to the Alexander Palace. Then Lady Exeter swept grandly out of the ballroom, talking with a poet and an artistic-looking woman with short black hair, and the officer turned away.

Podpolkovnik Roskov, the Czar's emissary, had lost sight of Ash when the dancing stopped for supper. He sat with a pair of ladies he had enjoyed affairs with over the years, suffered through some interminable speeches by some insufferable British submarine commanders, who seemed to have conveniently forgotten that the last time the Royal

Navy had operated in the Gulf of Finland, many years ago, it had been attacking Russia and was soundly stopped by the fortress at Kronstadt. The English had ambitious dreams and short memories.

He decided, while dining, to run Ash down at his hotel. Through the long evening the American had spoken with many people, but Exeter was the only suspicious one among them; so Roskov decided it was safe to bring him to the palace.

As luck would have it, he spotted Ash in the foyer, waiting with a woman's coat on his arm, but when the woman appeared, it was Lady Exeter, Lord Exeter's wife . . . Roskov veered away, deciding that he had better inform the Czar of Ash's strange companions.

'Commander, you look like a little boy about to cry.'

'It must be the smoke, Lady Exeter. May I?' He helped her into her sable. She said, 'My husband apologizes, but he had to take the carriage. I thought we might walk, if you don't mind the snow, and then the carriage can take you home when it gets back from the station. I've got boots.' She raised her gown to show him, and he realized she had her pumps in her hand with her bag.

'I hope your husband's trouble isn't too serious.'

'It is. Another strike, apparently. The last one shut the factory down for three weeks.'

'What do they make?'

'Artillery shells . . . precisely what the Russian army is most short of.'

Tamara huddled under Valery's fur-covered arm; he had insisted on using his favourite open red sleigh, even though it was snowing so hard she could barely see the Cossack outriders. They had taken a passenger, Sirotkin of the Preobrajenski Guard, to whom Valery was explaining once again the necessity of immobilizing the Czar *before* he announced a new government. Sirotkin still seemed determined to waltz into the Winter Palace on Valery's coattails.

She watched the bridge lights shine on the Cossacks' lances, and thought of Kennet. God was a trickster. He had given her so much – her talent, the will to use it, her beauty and the power to manage those, like Valery, who wanted to possess her. All those gifts which made her Tishkova.

Then, He laid before her a young man, far too young, poor, a sailor, and an American democrat. That was God's joke on her, to have everything she wanted, except . . . She had almost given it all up to be alone with Kennet, to be just a dancer with her beautiful young lover, but an injury had saved her from such madness, an injured metatarsus that had been an excruciating reminder that a dancer's body had a future as uncertain as a spider's web in a doorway.

The snow was falling hard, driven across the Neva by a north wind. They walked with heads bowed from the French Embassy on the embankment to her apartment in the Admiralty district. It was less than a mile but slow going.

'At least the wind is at our back,' Lady Exeter remarked halfway.

'Shall I find a cab?' Ash stopped and faced her under a street lamp. 'No, I'm fine, if you are.' Her coat had a hood and the rim of dark fur around her face softened her rather angular features and highlighted her pretty eyes. Snowflakes had gathered on the wisps of red hair that escaped the hood.

The apartment building was beside the Ekaterine Canal and overlooked the Alexander Museum gardens, now deep in snow.

'Would you like to come up for a brandy?'

323

Ash hesitated. He had thought he wanted to be alone, but it had been pleasant walking together and he felt better than he had all night.

'Our carriage will be back from the station later. You'll have no trouble getting back to your hotel.'

To be safe he had to go out to Vassily Island, but he could always hire a sleigh at the Europa or a troika behind the Kazan.

The Exeters' building was typical of the wealthy neighbourhoods – luxurious apartments on the first two floors and rooms for servants and coachmen, drivers and grooms above.

Lady Exeter sent the butler to bed and poured the brandy herself. They sat by a fire in the library. 'Feeling better?' she asked.

'Much,' said Ash, 'but Bonaparte is going to be annoyed when he finds out where his personal keg of brandy went.'

'My husband has the most unusual sources for *everything*. Once when we were in Peking we were supplied ducks by the same farmer who raised them for the Chinese emperor.'

Ash wondered if she knew Exeter was in the Secret Service. Wondered if she knew that the King had asked him to 'rescue' Czar Nicholas and had asked her husband to help.

The thought flashed through his mind that Exeter might have told her to work on him to agree to team up with the Grand Duke Valery. But that seemed a little farfetched. Not that it wouldn't be interesting, he thought with a smile. She was a lovely woman.

'May I ask what was troubling you?' she asked, refilling their glasses.

Ash pushed his feet closer to the fire. The brandy was delicious, beginning to buzz in his head; he hadn't felt so comfortable for a long time; and suddenly he wanted to talk.

'I saw an old friend, it was . . . it sort of upset me.'

'Who?' asked Lady Exeter. Ash looked at her. An inquiring smile lighted her stern face; she seemed interested rather than curious, interested in listening if he wanted to talk. 'It was hardly a secret. I was involved with Tamara Tishkova for several years. Coming back to Petrograd has stirred up a lot of old feelings.'

'Involved?'

He told her how they had met and spent their years in Europe; how he would wangle postings city to city when she toured; how she had filled the years he might ordinarily have been expected to marry; how he loved her . . . At last, after Lady Exeter had refilled their snifters and Ash had put another log on the fire, she asked, 'And now it's over?'

'Since the end of 1913. Tamara decided she had to settle down.'

'That's three years, Commander. A long time to hold on to a memory.'

Ash shrugged. 'Maybe memories hang on longer than people.'

'Surely you have not remained . . . shall I say *faithful* . . . to Tishkova's memory all this time?'

'Well, I haven't tomcatted around like I used to before we met.'

Lady Exeter smiled. 'What a horrible expression. American?'

'Down home.'

'Perhaps you're just older, *n'est ce pas?*'

'Or choosier.'

Lady Exeter stood up, smoothing her gown, went to the window and parted the drapes. 'There's a Russian officer standing in the snow . . . just standing there, staring at the building . . . probably waiting for his mistress's husband to go to bed. They're so insanely romantic here, don't you think?'

Ash joined her at the window. Snow was blowing through the streetlight. The officer stood just beyond the chief light spill from the three-globe lamp, his eyes fixed on the apartment building. He wore the *papaha* of one of the Life Guard regiments.

Lady Exeter said, 'They say the reason the aristocracy dislikes the Czarina so much is that she was such a prude about their affairs.' She laughed. 'She actually cut transgressors from the palace invitation list, but before she knew it there was no one left.' She closed the drapes and faced Ash with an easy smile, betrayed by a tiny vein throbbing in her temple, and an intent glitter in her eyes.

'It's still snowing. Would you care to spend the night?'

Ash was a little surprised. She did not seem the type of woman who could carry something beyond a mild flirtation. 'The French have a saying, Lady Exeter: to love another man's wife is civilized. To love a friend's wife is anarchy. I am very flattered, and while I hardly think of your husband as a friend, I did meet you together at the home of a friend, and have enjoyed your hospitality – '

'Are you stalling, Commander?'

'I suppose I am. I'm a little confused tonight, as I've told you.'

'I'm not confused. I haven't slept with my husband for years.'

'Do you love him?' Ash felt stupid, not sure what he wanted. He liked her. Making love with her could create a bond, her marriage be damned. A friendship and a real affair. And Ash didn't know if he was ready, particularly after seeing Tamara tonight.

Lady Exeter was studying him with a smile, watching him think.

'Do you love him?' he repeated, still stalling.

'He rescued me. My dearest friend in the women's rights

movement threw herself under the racehorses in the Derby. When she died a lot of the fight went out of me. My husband has tried very hard to make me whole again. I'm not there yet but I'm gaining strength and when this damned war is over I'll be back in the fight . . . Do you believe in women's rights, Commander?'

'All of them, Your Ladyship.'

'Including my right to suggest you make love to me . . .'

'No,' Ash said, 'I'll ask. You've flattered me too much already.' He kissed her just beneath her ear, savoured her with his lips. Trembling slightly, she pulled back and eyed him. 'I'll forget my husband for the night. Will you forget your dancer?'

Ash kissed her again, decided to try once and for all to bury the past. 'Who?' It tore at him as he said it. But it was best this way. End it. Tamara had, three years ago. How the hell long would it take to get the idea through to his own heart? End it now with a special woman like Lady Exeter. He kissed her mouth, hard, trying to seal his decision. Too hard, he frightened her; she pulled back, like a young girl afraid. Ash kissed her again, very gently.

'You're kind,' she said, taking his hand. 'Come.'

The doorbell rang.

'Damn – the telephones lines are probably down again. Probably a message for my husband. I'll be right back.'

Ash looked at his hands; they were shaking. He went to the window, opened the drape. The officer under the streetlight was gone . . . He picked up the telephone. The line buzzed, the operator answered. He ran after Lady Exeter and caught up in the foyer as she started to open the door.

'The telephone's working.'

'Then it's our coachman. I'll send him home.'

Before he could stop her she opened the door.

'Where is the doorman?' she asked sharply.

And then she fell back, and the officer they had seen beneath the window pushed into the foyer. Ash reached for his gun. He was too late.

29

Vladimir Dan cursed his own impudence. Red Snow deserved better. Of course the English woman was still in the apartment. It was probably hers. He should have waited for Ash even if it took all night. But the blizzard was so cold, the snow had seemed to draw blood from his face. Now he had to kill two people.

With his gun he gestured their hands into the air.

An English woman and an American murdered in the exclusive Admiralty district? The police would go crazy. Such a killing would provoke them into the sort of pains-taking detective work they were best at – not hunting the revolutionary he was but a common criminal. People must have seen him outside, heard him in the hall. Maybe the doorman he had eluded heard him barge through her door. What an irony it would be – caught as a criminal while committing an act of revolution, caught, like Raskolnikov, by 'trifles'.

A lucrative act of revolution, he reminded himself, worth two hundred thousand German marks in a Swiss bank in an account held by a Red Snow company, the treasurer of which happened to be Vladimir Dan. They were watching him closely, he saw the speculation in their eyes – each wondering could he be taken. He could tell them the answer was no.

'Back,' he told them, his mind whirling. He had a brilliant idea. Make it look as if her husband had surprised them in bed. Make the murder look like a crime of passion. 'Back. Into the bedroom.'

The American tried to comfort the English woman with a

glance. Their fingers strayed together a moment before Vladimir ordered them apart. So? His scenario wasn't so far-fetched. He grinned nervously at the thought that it would apply to half the highborn women in Petrograd and no one would question the conclusions. Except the husband, but the police would expect him to deny it.

'Bedroom,' Vladimir repeated. The hand grenade he had taken from his barracks tugged at his belt under his cloak, but this plan was better with the gun. Required the gun. After all, what husband, even the most suspicious, entered his wife's boudoir with a hand grenade?

They backed slowly into the drawing room. Rich, thought Vladimir. Repins and Serovs on the walls. And ancient icon paintings worth a fortune. And here and there some avant-garde painters. Chagall, Goncharova, Kandinsky.

'Bedroom. Not here.'

Lady Exeter spoke for the first time since she had demanded the whereabouts of the doorman. 'Which bedroom?'

'Yours, Madam.'

Ash said, 'Look, Lieutenant. You and I can settle this outside – '

'Your room, Madam. Quickly.' He cocked his revolver, a British Webley-Fosbery he had picked up in France for its incredible hitting power and which, being an English weapon, would strengthen the case against her husband, dropping it on the way out . . .

Lady Exeter lurched against Ash and murmured, 'Keep away from the bed.'

'Stand apart.'

Ash stopped moving, to distract him. 'Leave her out of this. You're after me, I know you are and there's no reason to – '

330

'*Move.*'

Ash moved. The Russian was too tensed up to push any further. *Stay away from the bed.* What did she have in mind? He was waiting for the man to look the other way for a moment so he could get to his back holster.

Lady Exeter stopped at the first door in the hall, asked coolly, 'Will this do?'

Vladimir glanced into the little bedroom, obviously a guest room with its two single beds. 'No. Your room.'

She paused at the next door, pointed again. 'This is mine.'

Vladimir almost laughed. It was prim as a schoolgirl's, with a narrow bed and a night table covered with books. He could just imagine a grizzled Petrograd homicide detective finding their bodies here and grunting, 'Absurd.'

'Your husband's room.'

He would shoot Ash first and undress the body after he killed the woman. No. There'd be bullet holes in Ash's tunic. And it would take too long after the noise of the shots to get his clothes off anyway. *Dmitri, if only you were here.* Dmitri would not have rushed it. Dmitri would have waited until Ash came out even if the snow drifted ten feet over his head.

'Here,' Lady Exeter announced at the end of the long hall. Ash crowded next to her as she pointed. Vladimir ordered them in and had a look. Good. Dimly lighted by a single lamp on a table beside the enormous bed, it was a symphony of dark wood and leather. A rich man's room. It was not hard to guess their relationship, but the bed was just right. She would have taken Ash here if he hadn't interrupted.

'Inside.' He gestured, pushing her and stepping out of Ash's reach. He felt much better now, with the killing ground chosen. He pretended he was Dmitri, got control of himself to make a simple plan.

'Take off your boots, Commander.'

'Hold on.'

Vladimir whirled toward the woman and aimed the gun at her head. She backed toward the bed. 'Do as I say. *Now.*'

Ash went to the chair in the corner. Vladimir followed him with the gun. Ash was stalling. 'Hurry up.'

'You don't have to kill us both.'

'Shut up.'

'Whoever you are, for God's sake leave her alone.' Vladimir felt the blood rushing to his face. He was working himself up to pulling the trigger. But not before the clothes . . .

'Take your boots off'

Ash sat down slowly and started to tug at one of his boots.

Vladimir heard a sharp click to his left. Lady Exeter was standing where he had left her beside the bed. The nighttable drawer was open. In her hands was another Webley. Her husband's gun.

Vladimir turned to fire at her. It seemed to take forever, and by the time he had her in his sights two immense blows flung him backward, slammed him to the door frame and dropped him in a heap. At last, he heard the shots.

Ash was moving across the room, tugging the Luger from his back when Lady Exeter's shots struck home and it occurred to him as he stepped on the Russian's wrist and wrenched the gun out of his hand that Lady Exeter *did* know what her husband did for British Secret Service and very probably did it with him.

'Is he dead?'

'Breathing.'

'Towels, quickly.' She brushed past Ash, knelt by the Russian and tore open his tunic.

'Careful,' Ash said.

'Hurry. He's alive.'

332

Vladimir's face had gone white, he gritted his teeth. She had placed the slugs little more than an inch apart high in the chest. It was remarkable that he was still breathing. His hands convulsed at his waist, and Ash now realized, too late, that he was grimacing with effort as much as pain . . . the effort it took a dying man to pull the pin from a hand grenade.

It thumped out of his hands onto the carpet, the pin ring looped around his finger. It rolled. Ash managed to push the Russian's body onto the grenade just as it exploded. The muffled boom tossed him against the bed. Shrapnel shattered a mirror, peppered a chest of drawers, but the Russian's body had absorbed most of the force of the explosion. The room was shrouded in smoke.

'Kenneth!' Her voice was small, a note of pleading. He saw her through the smoke, trying to stand but unable to as a crimson stain spread across the front of her white dress. Redder, darker than her hair. She reached for him, and Ash caught her in his arms and moved her gently onto the bed.

'I'll get a doctor.'

'Don't leave me.'

'Let me see.' He reached for the buttons at her neck. She stopped him with her hand. 'Just hold me.'

'Let me help you.'

'I'm all apart inside . . . I can feel it . . .'

'Oh, God, I'm so sorry – '

'Listen to me . . . I don't know all you're doing with my husband . . . but you can't be found here with all this. Get away . . .'

'They'll think you – '

She took a deep breath, trying to gather strength, managed a smile. 'I suspect where I'm going there'll be ample time to reconstruct my reputation . . . if you get the opportunity some time tell my husband what I told you about what he did for me . . .' And she said something else, which Ash couldn't hear. He had her propped in his arms and put his ear to her mouth. 'What did you say?'

'I said, Commander, I wish you and I had had another hour.'

The Czar let *Podpolkovnik* Roskov out one of the secret doors in the maze of private passageways that connected the royal apartments. Roskov had reported an hour after he had seen Ash with Lady Exeter in the foyer of the French Embassy. The Czar was drowsily sipping a glass of hot milk and examining the latest maps from the *Stavka*. Such was the sovereign's devotion to duty, Roskov noted approvingly that the maps were revised daily and sped by train from Mogilev.

The Czar had been very disturbed when he had returned without Ash.

Roskov had explained his fears. The Czar listened attentively and nodded agreement. 'You were right, of course, to be cautious.' He became silent. Roskov waited. He had no idea what the Czar wanted to talk to Ash about, but it seemed important . . . he seemed so worried.

And the Czar thought . . . Whom could he trust?

Not Ash. Nor, he realized sadly, King George. It had been his cousin's idea to send Ash with an offer of sanctuary. Georgie could have planned the whole scheme to get him off the throne and put his own choice in his place. Somebody Georgie thought would do a better job of fighting the war.

Maybe it was all a British Secret Service trick using Georgie's name. Willy always said Georgie hadn't a military mind . . . but he would never know.

And Willy? Arrogant, bullying, bad-mannered Willy didn't know a thing about the asylum scheme. Georgie or Lord Exeter or even Ash had made that up to gain his confidence. He felt ashamed that they would even think him vulnerable to such a trick.

Poor Father Gregory had seen clearer than he would ever know. There *was* blood on Ash's hands. All around him the Czar saw treachery and deceit. Members of his own family had murdered Rasputin, Romanovs who were common criminals. And betrayal extended, he now believed, even to his royal cousin Georgie.

But he was not alone. He still had a family that mattered – his beloved wife, suffering in her grief, his beautiful girls and baby Alexis. They needed him, he needed them. Together, the seven of them would stay in Russia until whatever God, in His wisdom, might choose for them.

In the Admiralty district they had what looked like a double suicide – another of the bizarre death pacts which had become common among the city's wealthy Bohemian classes whose salons Lady Exeter was known to frequent.

Did his brother Vladimir mingle with such people, the police asked sympathetically. Dmitri Dan succeeded in making his rage seem like grief. Ash had killed his brother, and had ruined his own best chance to kill the Czar, because now he had to go underground. The homicide police might be fooled, but the Okhrana would guess something closer to the truth about Red Snow and the plot to murder the Czar. So for the sake of the Revolution he dishonoured his brother's name and said, yes, Vladimir knew such people, Vladimir talked of suicide. And yes, he knew an Englishwoman. And the police went away, for a while at least, and Dmitri Dan disappeared so that he might survive to attack again.

'You must call upon Tishkova.'

Lord Exeter had chosen a cemetery on Vassily Island less than a mile across a lightly wooded field from the frozen Gulf of Finland. They drove out in sleighs from an Anglican church on the Nevsky. The gravediggers built fires to thaw the ground. The smoke had blackened the snow around the hole. Steam billowed as the *moujiks* lowered Lady Exeter's coffin.

'The Grand Duke Valery is our only chance to remove the Czar alive.'

Ash angrily wished he hadn't come. It was wrong to talk in her last minutes. But if he hadn't come Exeter would be all alone. A group of Russian painters and writers watched forlornly from the side. Her friends. It was as bleak a day as Petrograd could conjure, damp and cold and grey as lead. And he was the cause of their being here.

'We are on the edge of chaos,' Exeter murmured while the *moujiks* worked. 'You don't understand the Russians, Ash. Don't imagine that Russia is the most eastward bastion of western civilization, as they say. Russia is really the most westward tentacle of the East. Fatalistic, corrupt, they're like children, and like children they love destruction. They are destructive people, Ash, like Celts.'

Ash stared at the hole in the ground.

Exeter said, 'The Grand Duke Valery is the best of a bad lot. By far the best. He – '

'Then why don't *you* help him?'

'He doesn't trust me.'

'I wonder why.'

'These people don't like us. They don't like any foreigners. They'll take our investments and hire our engineers, but they don't like us and they don't trust us.'

Ash looked at Lord Exeter, and realized that the bitterness in his voice might be directed as much at his own terrible loss as at the Russians. The Englishman was stoic, his grief buried, but not so deep. Exeter sensed Ash looking at him and turned from the grave. 'Good of you to come today, Ash. She would have been pleased.'

'My Lord, do you want to know how she died?'

'I know she didn't die the way the Russian police say.'

'No, she didn't.' Ash described what had happened, leaving out only her invitation and his half-hearted acceptance, and finished with, 'She saved my life. And then she even tried to save Vladimir Dan's.'

'You did well to get away. You'd have been finished for the King if the police had found you there.'

'Thank you for saying that, sir . . . She was a lovely woman.'

The *moujiks* started heaping earth on the coffin. They worked quickly, glancing at a steely snow line blowing in from the Gulf.

Exeter said, 'Now I will tell you something you don't know.'

Ash wondered if he had guessed what had happened between him and Lady Exeter.

'This so-called Bohemian Russian served with a fusilier unit lent to France.'

'Yes, I heard that.'

'But you didn't hear that shortly before Vladimir Dan returned to Russia he crossed into Switzerland and from there to Germany.'

'Are you sure?'

'I believe a friend of yours is named Taplinger? Taplinger

keeps a close eye on movements through Switzerland . . . So what was Vladimir Dan up to?'

'A Russian revolutionary working with the Germans.'

'My conclusions as well. Do you know the group Red Snow?'

'Never heard of them.'

'Nihilistic Social Revolutionaries. We know nothing about them except that they exist and specialize in assassinations and attract a broad spectrum of Russian zealots, from factory malcontents to someone like Dmitri Dan.'

'Who's Dmitri Dan?'

'Vladimir's brother. He's in the Czar's Convoy. Or was . . . he disappeared the day after his brother killed my wife. I think it's fairly obvious that he was employed by the Germans to assassinate the Czar, don't you?'

'Who did he see in Germany?'

'We've traced him and his brother as far as Spa. Who he saw at German Headquarters we don't know.'

'Ludendorff is at Spa.'

'Yes, he is. And he has a penchant for Russian revolutionaries.'

The snow hit hard and fast. The *moujiki* put their backs to the thick, wet, windblown flakes and shovelled a mound over the grave. Exeter stared at it, blinking, and continued talking in the same insistent tone. 'I think the Czar's life is in danger. You must act, act fast, Commander. And your best hope is the Grand Duke Valery.'

Ash said nothing. Had he imagined the German army, having twice failed to kill him, would just give up? If he had only thought it out, only kept his eyes open, Lady Exeter would be alive. And now Exeter was pushing him at Tamara. And her Grand Duke.

'He needs you as much as you need him.'

Ash wondered if he had known from the moment the King asked him to rescue the Czar that it would lead to her.

No good could come of it; he'd get hurt as bad as last time, like walking into an aeroplane propeller. A small personal price perhaps to remove the Czar and end the war – but now, if he lent impetus to the Grand Duke Valery's faltering cause, wouldn't he be putting Tamara right back into danger? Get her killed, just like he'd got Lady Exeter killed? The Czar of Russia and the Okhrana did not deal gently with revolt. No matter how noble its instigators, nor how beautiful.

'I heard you discussing poetry with Her Majesty at Sandringham,' Exeter said. 'Do you by any chance recall Lowell's "Present Crisis"?'

Ash did. For a West Virginian the Civil War had a particular impact.

'Once to every man and a nation comes the moment to decide,
In the strife of Truth with Falsehood, for the good or evil side.'

Tremendous gusts blew sheets of snow; in moments the mound over Lady Exeter's grave was covered white. Exeter bowed his head. When he raised it again he said, 'The evil side is Germany, Ash. Grand Duke Valery is the best hope for us. But his supporters have lost their nerve. He needs help. And you certainly need help, if you are to carry out your promise to rescue the Czar. It seems to me your course is clear.'

Ash left a note inside the wrecked German Embassy, in a hole where an electric sconce had been torn from the wall, as von Basel had instructed, and a message arrived at the Vassily Island flat the next morning. 'In front of the Stock Exchange. Five o'clock.'

It was a safe place with escape possible in four directions. The Stock Exchange overlooked the eastern spit of Vassily Island, the leading edge of the wedge-shaped island that split the wide Neva. Trams crossed the spit from a bridge to the north and from the busy streets of Vassily Island to the west. South, the Dvortsov Bridge spanned the river to the palaces. East, a fleeing man could run into the dark on the frozen river.

It was snowing. The temperature had plummeted so that fresh flakes sparkled like diamonds in the streetlights. Ash turned his back to the Stock Exchange and looked east up the dark river. Palace lights shone to the right, the Peter and Paul Fortress loomed to the left.

He turned around and looked at the Stock Exchange. It was shutting down for the night, and hundreds of clerks in shabby overcoats poured down the steps, collars turned up against the snow. Suddenly von Basel materialized from the midst of a group of them queued up for a tram, dressed as they were in a dark coat and a cheap wool hat.

The German tucked his walking stick under his left arm and shook Ash's hand as if they were old friends meeting by chance. An act for onlookers. There was nothing friendly about his cadaverous face and wary grey eyes.

'Rasputin,' he sneered. 'And now Lady Exeter. Who else do you intend to befriend in Petrograd?'

'If your men saw me with her why didn't they help? Why'd they let that – '

'They lost you in the snow. They didn't expect you to walk. By the time they worked it out, it was too late.' Now he smirked. 'The autopsy showed she hadn't had intercourse. You were a little slow on the draw, Ash.'

Ash had a fist up before he realized how stupid that would be. He lowered it and asked, 'Do you know Red Snow?'

'Only by name. Highly secret, highly organized fanatics. If they're caught they kill themselves.'

'That's all you know?'

'There are three million people in this city, Ash. And only six thousand police. Why do you ask?'

'I think that General Ludendorff hired them to kill the Czar.'

340

Von Basel leaned on the granite railing and looked at the Neva. Snow sticking to his coat and hat made him look almost ghostly. 'It seems to me you'd better get the Czar out of Russia fast. Do you have a plan?'

'What support can you give me?'

'What did you have in mind?'

'Can you immobilize a police station?'

'Possibly.'

'Arrest certain very important people?'

'Such as?'

'Guards officers. Railroad officials. Ministers.'

'For a while. Anything else?'

'Do you know any revolutionaries?'

'A few.'

'Can you introduce me to Kirichenko?'

Von Basel stared. 'If I knew where to find Kirichenko the Czar would make me head of the Okhrana and give me one of his daughters. Where did you hear about Kirichenko?'

'From a man named Lenin in Zurich.'

'I'm afraid you'll have to settle for a lesser revolutionary than Kirichenko.'

'Do you know one who can blow up trains?'

'Trains? More than one?'

'Several. At once. Miles apart.'

'No, I don't.'

'Could Kirichenko?'

'Possibly. But first you have to find him.'

'I can't if you don't call off your detectives. They're following me everywhere again.'

'For your own protection.'

'Would they be protection against Kirichenko?'

Von Basel considered that. 'I'll call them off.'

'Start now. And try to find out where Kirichenko operates. I'll meet you here tomorrow night.'

Ash headed for the tram queue. Von Basel grabbed his arm. His fingers felt like wire cable. 'Where are you going?'

Ash shook him off. 'Where I have to.'

Jostling aboard a crowded tram, he watched the lean figure of von Basel fade in the snow. He rode a mile down river and got off after the tram crossed the river on the Nicholas Bridge. There, in the lower part of the Admiralty district, he waited for the green-and-yellow lamps of the Number Eight tram to the Finland Station. He let several pass, eyeing the homeward bound crowds until he was sure he had not been followed.

His heart started pounding before he laid a glove on her front gate. He pushed through the geometrically patterned wrought iron into the snow-covered entrance garden. Up her front steps to the massive carved doors. Mansions like this were laid out casually, unlike the classical palaces of Petrograd, wings and turrets set whimsically.

Ash knocked, straightened his cloak and hat, waited. Last time he had seen her in Petrograd she had lived in an apartment in the fashionable Liteinaya Quarter, not far from the British Embassy. She earned a fortune dancing, but she sure as hell hadn't bought this place on what the Imperial Theatre paid her. Of course she could have tucked away her earnings from her last European tour; she had, after all, danced solo to packed music halls in Paris and London. But she hadn't toured since 1912, and Ash had never known her to save a penny in her life.

He knocked again, wishing he had sent a note first.

She had been his life and he was a damned fool for not . . . for not what? For not being born a Russian nobleman? If Teddy Roosevelt and Admiral Mahon had thrust Ash into the parade of Edwardian Europe, Tamara Tishkova had played the music. Music that roused him to every new moment and sweetened every day. Music that lingered.

An old butler opened the door, glowering suspiciously at a strange face. Ash squared his shoulders. 'Please ask Tamara Nikolayevna if she will receive Kennet Karlovich.'

The butler ushered him into the foyer. Their Christian names and patronymics, pronounced in the Russian manner, indicated that Kenneth, son of Charles, had come to call on his friend Tamara, daughter of Nikolay.

The butler returned to lead him to a solarium off the marble ballroom. Ash stopped in the ballroom to admire the Serov portrait of Tamara as Odile, the seductive Black Swan. The former court painter – he had quit after the Cossacks had massacred workers in the Palace Square in 1905 – had chosen an informal setting, her dressing table. Serov had captured Tamara's pride and beauty, which was, Ash thought, a fairly straightforward matter of painting with his eyes open. But his genius showed in her laughing smile, as if he knew intuitively how Tamara preferred to go against the grain.

Or used to . . . This was quite a house, filled with imported French furniture. The solarium housed an enormous jungle and had a breathtaking view of the palace lights across the frozen river. The floor was an elaborate tile mosaic, probably laid by Italian artisans . . .

A domestic Tamara was a little hard to imagine, though he supposed that on her it would probably wear very well, like everything else. Then he noted with relief that the house was a little untidy, as all her homes were. He walked, his heels clicking loudly, he thought, to the windows that faced the Winter Palace. Snow swirls raced down the river.

In a house like this she could have received him in a sitting room off her boudoir, but she had chosen this less intimate place. A reminder that their intimacy had ended three years ago? Ash picked up a carved ivory elephant. A gift from her father. She took it everywhere. Then this was a special room . . .

She came in with the swift exuberant rush . . . the way she always took a stage. Perfume, Coty's *Violette,* and the airy folds of her tea gown trailed her. Ash stared. He had not come within fifty feet of her at the French ball. Here, in her own home as he put down the ivory elephant and walked toward her on unsteady legs, he saw her so vibrant, still so young that it was impossible to believe that she had reigned triumphant on Russia's stages for nearly thirty years. I made my debut early, she used to say.

Her dark eyes flashed when she saw him, and Ash felt his heart stop. He knew her so well, knew in the particular movement of light in her eyes that she was excited to see him. And she called him Kennet, as she had from the first. But her greeting was stiff.

'Hello, Kennet.'

'Forgive my dropping in like this, I thought at this hour it might be all right . . .' Petrograd was such a late city that at six in the evening a lady would not have begun to dress, whether she was going out or dining at home.

'I saw you at the ball the other night,' she said. 'You looked the same . . . But here I think I see a shadow in your eyes.'

'I saw you too. You looked more beautiful than ever.'

'Thank you.'

Tamara extended her hand. Ash kissed it. He felt a little electric jolt. Had she shivered? Or had he?

'Kennet, why have you come here?'

'To ask your help.'

'Only my help?'

'Of course not.'

She looked around the solarium as if she had never seen it before. 'I'm not free to . . . be with you, you know.'

'I'm sorry. I guess I hoped it wasn't still true.'

'It's true – oh, don't look at me that way. You know about Valery.'

'Should I congratulate you?'

'A woman my age to be loved by a man like him? To be cherished? Yes, you should congratulate me.'

'You've done very well. Congratulations.'

'I can't dance forever, you know. And you have no right to look at me that way, or be critical of my house, as your eyes tell me you are. How dare a child like you judge.'

'How long will I stay a child to you?'

'Always.'

'The difference in years between us shrinks as we get older – '

'As I get older.'

'We can't be back to that again. We've just started.'

'We've *not* started anything, Kennet. It is over . . . no matter how wonderful it was.' She stared at him defiantly . . .

Two years after New Hampshire they played a French bedroom farce in The Hague. And when the grand duke had had to go to Paris, Ash had wangled a courier mission to Russia and Tamara, who was fiercely independent, then, had invited him aboard the Imperial Train, which was steaming back to Russia with the Peace Conference delegates and their wives and mistresses.

In the summers after – when the grand duke went off on army manoeuvres or toured the Russian continent for the Czar – Ash and Tamara had joined in England, in the south of France, Italy and once even in Russia – long blissful months alone and free. And Ash still thought that the only thing the matter with their relationship was that it had ended.

Ash heard his own voice blurting now, like a hurt kid. 'It's not fair.' He tried to smile. They were standing face to

345

face, six feet apart. But all he could manage was, 'I love you and I always have.'

Tamara flushed and spewed a torrent of angry Russian, her nostrils flaring, her breasts straining the tea gown.

'Stop,' said Ash, 'stop, I can't keep up. I don't remember all those words – '

'The only words you ever learned were bed words.'

'I've forgotten them too. I need practice.'

'What I *said* was, it's you who is not fair. You haven't a line. You haven't even a grey hair.'

'I've grown a few on my temple just for you . . . or on account of you.'

'That is not funny, Kennet,' she said, her voice quiet now. 'You're like a mirror. I see my face getting older in yours.'

'And you are like a . . . a kaleidoscope. Every turn's more beautiful than the one before.'

Tamara stepped back, a smile filling her voluptuous mouth. 'Kennet Karlovich, did you mean that?'

'The Grand Duke Valery is the luckiest damned man in Russia.'

'Show me that grey hair.'

Ash turned his head. 'It's in here, someplace.'

'Bend down . . . may I?'

'Of course – *ow.*'

She held up a grey hair, kissed the spot it came from and danced lightly away. 'So you've come for help?'

'I've come to take you to bed,' Ash said, reaching for her. 'Well, you can't. So how else can I help you?'

Tamara pulled a bell cord and spoke to the servant in Russian.

They had tea by the fire. She rarely drank alcohol, and then only champagne. Ash felt the old electric tension still between them, undiminished. And he enjoyed, too, their

346

easy companionship while they talked about what each had been doing since they parted.

He sometimes thought that the worst loss, the real waste, was the loss of their friendship. And he began to fancy that maybe he really was older. Mid-thirties was a much different time from the twenties. Maybe he was closer now to her feelings of age. Could it work again? He was dreaming.

'What is the help you want?' she asked finally, reminding him why he had come, what he had to do before the palaces across the river turned to flames.

'It involves Valery . . .'

'*Kennet?* You *are* a child. Do you expect me to ask Valery to help *you?*'

'Why not? You've made it quite clear that I'm no threat to him.'

'What man knows that, Kennet? Valery's as jealous of you as . . . all Valery knows is that when he first wanted me I was not available.' Ash looked at her, but she would add nothing to that. She knew all his secrets – except this new one to remove the Czar. And he knew hers – except the truth behind Petrograd society's gossip that linked her with Czar Nicholas. 'And when Valery finally thought I was available,' she went on, 'suddenly an American naval officer seemed always to be around. So you see it is too complicated. I do have my own position to consider. I would not be happy to lose Valery.'

'You don't need Valery. If he left you tonight ten thousand men in this city would rejoice.'

'Perhaps, Kennet. But how many would be grand dukes?'

Ash shook his head. Arguing with Tamara had always been like duelling with twelve-inch guns – direct hits and damned few ricochets.

'Do you realize,' he said, 'that Valery and I have never met?'

347

'A mystery maintained with some difficulty, I can tell you . . . No, dear, I cannot ask the grand duke to help you.'

'But I can help him.'

'I beg your pardon?'

'I know about your plans.'

Tamara set her face in a mask. 'I don't know what you are talking about, Kennet . . . I do think, though, that you better leave.'

She stood up and crossed her arms under her breasts. Ash sat where he was and looked her in the eye. 'I'm talking about a palace coup.'

Tamara held her rigid pose. 'You are frightening me, Kennet. What are you trying to do to me?'

Ash got to his feet. 'I'm not trying to frighten you. I'm on your side.'

'How is that . . . ?'

'I've come to take the Czar to England. King George has offered asylum.'

'But . . . that's wonderful . . .'

'He won't go. I heard about Valery. And dammit, Tamara, I can tell you that too many already know about you.'

She nodded. 'That is the risk of asking people to help. They don't all say yes and they don't all keep quiet. But somebody has to do it. Russia begs for a firm hand, like the old days.'

'I see that Ivan the Terrible still has your vote. How did you get mixed up in this? Just for Valery?'

'I've told you before. Art demands order. For me to dance there must be a theatre building, musicians, artists, training schools for the corps *and* audiences able to afford tickets. All that demands order.'

'Was a coup your idea or his?'

'I support him.'

'Can you ever support yourself?' Dammit. He realized too late he wasn't talking about the coup.

'What is that supposed to mean?'

'You were already the greatest dancer in Russia. What did you have to fasten onto Valery for?'

'And leave you?'

'Yes.'

'What could you do for me, Kennet?'

'Whatever I did I did for eight years. I thought I did it fairly well.'

'You did. Yes . . . but it wasn't enough. *Stop* this. I won't talk about it. It's the past. What is happening now is more important. Russia. And Valery.' She sat there, silent, angry, abstracted.

Ash got hold of himself. Something else she had said bothered him. He hadn't come to Russia to weaken the Allies. Just the opposite.

'What,' he asked carefully, 'does Valery propose to do about the war?'

'Win it.'

'How?'

'He plans to start with the railroads. Our greatest strength is in our numbers. We can still field huge armies, but we can't move them or supply them. Surely you are aware of this.'

'I am. I didn't know you were.'

'Valery understands all this. He teaches me. He is a good man, Kennet.'

'So how can I help him?'

Tamara sighed, walked to the windows and gazed at the palace lights that shone softly through the blowing snow. 'My God, Kennet, you are complicating things.'

'I knew that when I came here. But I think we need each other.'

'Valery's worried about what to do with Nicky.'

'Well, that works out fine. I'm here to take him away.'

She turned to him again. 'Kennet, the whole scheme is falling apart. Valery's supporters are cowards. I'm afraid it won't work.'

'I heard that too . . . let me talk to him.'

Tamara shook her head. 'Oh, God . . . yes I believe you must.'

The butler knocked and announced a telephone call for Mademoiselle Tishkova. She was gone a long while. When she came back, she was smiling almost coquettishly. 'That was Valery.'

'What does he say?'

'Oh, I couldn't tell him tonight. The telephone is not safe . . . would you care to have dinner with me?'

'An understatement.'

'Poor Valery. He is out at Tsarskoye Selo and the Czar wants him to stay the night. Poor thing, stuck in that dreary household.'

'What a shame.'

'Don't you get the wrong idea.'

'May I at least sit with you while you dress for dinner?'

Tamara smiled. 'Of course – but no more talk of the coup. Wait for Valery.'

It was an old habit of theirs. She dressed and did her hair behind a floral Chinese silk screen while he sat in a nearby armchair and talked with her. He told her a little about the trip from London. She had not travelled since the war. And he described Paris and London and Berlin as he had last seen them. She asked about fashions, and he told her what he had noticed and how women were working at all kinds of jobs. He told her about the new ballroom dances in Paris and London, the Nurse's Shuffle and the Saunter.

'I'll show you.'

'No,' she said firmly. 'You stay right where you are . . .

tell me about the dance.' She meant the ballet. Ash said, 'I saw Anna in New York. They loved her.'

'Yes, she wrote me she saw you. Was she good?'

'Very.'

'Good.' Tamara liked Pavlova, they were friends. She was one of the few ballerinas Tamara had open, unreserved admiration for.

'And there's no more Ballets Russes in Paris, as you know. Nothing in London. Not a single ballet in London except for *divertissements* in the Christmas pantomimes.'

'Stupid war. Well, for the dance, at least, it's a good time to be in Petrograd. It's a brilliant season.'

'And Tishkova its star?'

'Of course.' She snaked her hand over the top of the screen. Her arm was bare – creamy white and rippling with long, shapely muscle. 'In fact I may dance my Jubilee . . . at last.'

Ash laughed. It was traditional to celebrate a jubilee twenty years after a début, a tradition Tamara had steadfastly ignored.

'What will you dance?'

'I haven't decided. Everyone's doing fantasies this season. Benefits for military hospitals and war bonds. Even lovely Kchessinska had a grand triumph last week – though I am told that the theatre carpenters worked half the night to repair the stage.'

Ash grinned at the screen. He personally thought Kchessinska a fine dancer and a good-looking woman besides, but saw little profit in convincing Tamara. Kchessinska too had a grand duke wrapped around her finger, but she had had a child by hers and Ash suspected that rankled, though Tamara, in her inimitable way, insisted that children should be kept in dark places to mature like wine.

She popped her head over the screen. Her hair was a

wild tangle of black curls, her eyebrows high in inquiry. She had removed her dressing gown. Her shoulders were bare.

'Would you like champagne? It's next door.'

Next door was her bedroom. The champagne stood in an ice bucket beside her vast canopied bed. Ash opened it, filled their glasses, carried them back to her dressing room and stepped behind the screen.

Her hands went to her breasts. 'Don't look at me.'

But Ash was already looking, gazing in open admiration. She was seated naked on an upholstered stool before a mirror. Full-bodied, toned like an athlete, she was at once hard and voluptuous, at once a finely sculpted machine and as sexual as a courtesan.

'Please don't look at me.'

'Why not? You look so beautiful.'

'My breasts are sagging.'

'They're not. They're as lovely as ever.'

'Liar.'

'And if they ever did sag do you think I'd give a damn?'

'Liar . . . why do you say that? That you wouldn't care?'

'Because they're yours.'

'Liar . . .' She kept her hands crossed over her breasts, but she watched his eyes flicker over the rest of her body. Slowly, she crossed her legs and arched her back. 'Tell me about your women, since me.'

'Don't twist me in circles.'

'Why do you let me?' she asked.

'Your hands are different.'

'My *hands*?' She thrust them under the light. 'What do you –'

Ash knelt swiftly and kissed her breast.

'. . . You tricked me.'

Ash held the champagne glasses behind her back and nuzzled her with his lips. 'Whatever you are, I love it. And I love you.'

'Kennet. This is dangerous.'

'Shhh.'

Her hands closed behind his head. 'Kennet?'

'What?'

'Kennet, you know me. I won't leave a grand duke for an American lieutenant commander. Valery's of the blood royal, Kennet. I won't give it up. I warn you . . .'

Ash drew her nipple between his lips and mumbled, 'Commander.'

'What? What did you say? Oh, don't stop . . .'

'Full commander. They promoted me. I could make commodore by fifty.' He showed her the three broad stripes on his sleeve.

Tamara threw back her head and laughed. She looked at him and her eyes turned liquid soft. 'Shall I congratulate you?' she whispered. 'Just this once?'

31

A gramophone on a marble pedestal near Tamara's bed provided Chopin between their lovemaking. They drank champagne and spooned grey caviar into each other's mouths while the music played. An old Russian woman brought the caviar, tsking angrily at Ash, refusing to acknowledge him even though they'd first met when she was Tamara's maid on the trip to New Hampshire.

'Don't worry, she's safe,' Tamara said as she got up to change a record. She could feel his eyes track her.

'I love to watch you wind that thing,' Ash said. Tamara gave him a wicked smile over her shoulder. Her breasts brushed the flared sound horn and her bottom wiggled as she turned the crank that wound the mechanism. She loved it when he admired her, but she said, 'You, you just say those things. You don't mean them.'

'Come back here.'

He lifted the quilt. She covered her breasts with her hands again as she slid back beside him. 'How is it you make me feel so naked?' It was a mystery. She actually felt herself blush.

Tamara let a cry escape when she opened to him. She drew him in and he kissed her lips, crushed her mouth with his and fought for more of her.

His eyes burned into hers. She felt him fighting to keep her, knew he was trying to force his taste and scent and touch into her memory. She felt herself drowning again, as she always had with him, as he drowned in her. She allowed it. Here the years between them didn't anger her, here he didn't mirror her age, here he was black glass, mysterious, promising. In their sex they were both without age, new, unhampered by time, at once precocious and knowing, and yet always astonished.

He filled her. With his eyes he begged, then demanded she be with him and share her spirit as she shared her body. And when she did, when she took his mouth as insistently as he took hers, begged back with her eyes, the hard lens of desperation melted from his look.

He exploded and set off a barrage in her which left her gasping, clinging and suddenly laughing as she hadn't laughed since she couldn't remember. He spoke gently and stayed inside her, kissing her face until he grew hard again and began to move. She pulled down his shoulders, clasped his legs, and felt the fire . . .

Now *she* was desperate, thrusting under him, lifting him with hard muscle, proud of the strength she had for him, demanding strength back. More. She had made him whole, told him what he was, so he was able to smile into her eyes and play, tease her the ways she had taught him . . . ways they had learned together . . .

'No . . .' She was too late. He retreated slowly, farther and farther. 'No.' Farther until only a kiss of flesh seemed to remain to bind them, so small that it could break at the least unwary motion. But he was moving, and he stroked her with his fingers, making her move too, making her shudder with joy.

She gasped, afraid that their flesh would part. Her body betrayed her, leaping for him. 'No.' The bond would break, they would part. 'No.' But though her body ached and heaved he kept them connected. And suddenly he had entered her again. Slid deep, but he was all gentle now, no longer desperate, easy and sure in those few minutes and hours, and filled her with a promise that he was hers to keep forever.

* * *

355

In the night they woke up and made love sleepily. Then again with deep longing that erupted into a fierceness. Shuddering in each other's arms, wide awake afterward, they whispered in the dark.

'Why wasn't it enough?'

'Love is more than sex and companionship and affection.' For a long moment she was silent. Then she said, 'Even more than seeing the world through double eyes.'

'So why are you crying?'

'I am not crying.'

'Something's making my chest wet.'

She erupted into a half-giggle, half-sob and felt his chest, then traced her fingers to his lips. Brushed his cheeks. 'The same reason you are, I suppose . . .'

'We were, as they say, made for each other, Tamara.'

'But I'm old. My jumps are going.'

'You said your jumps were going in 1908. Three years later, 1911 for Christ's sake, François Roland wrote that "Tishkova employs an unfair advantage over ordinary ballerinas in that the rules of gravity do not apply to her." '

'But they will go, someday too soon, and when they do so will my young lover.'

'The rules of gravity may not apply to you,' Ash said exasperatedly, 'but the rules of time apply to me. I'm not the kid you met in Portsmouth. That was nearly twelve years ago. I'm older, changed. But still in love with you – I don't give a damn if you dance – '

'You don't.' She was shocked, hurt.

'Not true. I do care. I admire your work. I'm overwhelmed by it. But I don't love you for your work.'

'Why do you love me?'

'Why? Why is your hair jet? Why is your skin pearl white? Why are your eyes darker than black, your mouth – '

'My hair is jet because my mother was Italian. My skin white because my father was a Russian and like most

Russians has Viking blood from some thousand-year-old rape. My eyes are dark because another ancient rape put Tartar blood in my veins as well. And my mouth . . . what did you say my mouth was?'

'I didn't get a chance, and I don't have the words. All I know is that I want it.'

'I don't deserve you.' She sighed.

'Probably not, but you've got me anyway so why –'

'What do you mean, probably not?' She climbed on top of him and grabbed his hands, and their talk dissolved into teasing and play and it was not until he was inside her again that she admitted to herself the fear that lay beneath all her decisions, the fear to take the final chance – risk everything without a man to support her – the fear that bastard Roland had intuitively guessed, in that same review, when she danced *Schéhérazade* with Vaslav Nijinski and Roland shrewdly surmised she could have done more. But Roland was the only critic who had. Not another soul knew that she could have danced Zobeide with even greater abandon than she had, but had been afraid. It wasn't really age. Everyone feared age. For all her brave talk of never marrying, it was fear one day of having no one but herself. A nightmare. Alone in the burning streets. Her audiences dead. Her lovers fleeing.

Sunlight was streaming into Tamara's bedroom. Ash's arms were filled with her warm sleepy flesh when the maid burst in. 'Mademoiselle, mademoiselle!'

Ash couldn't catch all the Russian, but the way Tamara leaped out of bed told him that the Grand Duke Valery had returned from his business with the Czar.

32

Tamara pushed him toward a little dressing room down the hall. Her maid had hung up his scattered uniform as if she had planned for a quick escape. His boots were polished, his scabbard cleaned. Ash heard a commotion outside. He pulled on his trousers and glanced out the window.

A gigantic red sleigh, big as a house and drawn by eight Arabian bays, was swinging off the road from the bridge. Cossack outriders formed a protective cordon around it with long lances. The sleek horses were as fine a matched team as Ash had seen, their harness like the sleigh itself inlaid with gold. A footman in red livery leapt down to the snow, flung open the door and bowed.

The Grand Duke Valery stepped down and looked up at the mansion. He wore a long red Cossack coat and a high fur hat. Ash moved away from the window. Something in Valery's stance had told him that the grand duke didn't actually live here, merely had visiting privileges. It made Ash feel a little better that Tamara was at least still that independent. Not yet *totally* committed.

She hurried in, drawing an apricot robe over a silk nightgown. Her nipples stood darkly through the silk. 'Give me a couple of hours to get used to the idea. Come back for lunch. We'll see what the three of us can work out . . . You better shave.' She smiled.

'Quite an arrival down there.'

'Valery's a damned fool riding around Petrograd like a target. I keep telling him he'll get killed by revolutionaries but he loves that sleigh . . . do I look like I had a good night's sleep?'

'You look like you had a good night.'

She leaned against him, warm, pressed her forehead to his chest. 'I did. My darling, thank you for coming to me.'

The door knocker boomed through the house.

'Go on now,' she said, closing her robe, covering her breasts. 'Olga will show you the way.'

The back door, again. He crushed her against him, then Olga, the old woman, led him down back stairs and through a maze of kitchen gardens and stable yards. Wet snow had started to fall. The air was chilly, damp seeped out of the ground. He startled a *moujik* shovelling horse manure. 'Good morning!'

He boarded a tram at the Finland Station, got off at the Nevsky and walked up the boulevard, which was deserted so early in the morning except for servants and shopkeepers. He went into the Europa, shaved in François Roland's room, after which they walked to the fencing *Salle* for another lesson. They had lunch. Ash was starving. By one o'clock he was back at Tamara's mansion. Trying to control a foolish grin that kept grabbing his face.

Valery's Cossacks stopped him at the door. Tamara's butler identified him. She and the grand duke were waiting in the solarium. Tamara had changed into black silk. As she stepped forward and let Ash bow over her hand, she allowed herself, and him, a secret smile for their night.

'Your Highness,' Tamara said formally, 'may I present Commander Ash?'

Ash bowed. Valery thrust out his big hand. 'You ought to know from the start that I have agreed to talk because Mademoiselle Tishkova vouches for you. She has relayed everything you told her.'

Not everything, thought Ash. But the grand duke seemed willing to let that other level of their entanglement hang unspoken between them. 'Nonetheless,' he continued, 'I have questions.'

'As I do, Your Highness.' He had to establish a partnership to make this work.

'Does the American government know that you've come to Russia to rescue Czar Nicholas for the English king?'

'My superiors hope that removing Czar Nicholas will make it possible for the United States to join the Allies' war against Germany.'

'How is that?'

'Bluntly put, Your Highness, most Americans think of Czar Nicholas as a bloody tyrant.'

'If they think Nicholas II is bloody, what did they think of Peter the Great? Did you inform King George of your government's interest?'

'No.'

'You seem to serve two masters, Commander.'

'No, Your Highness. I am an officer in the United States Navy. My mission to remove the Czar without knocking Russia out of the war *coincides* with King George's concern for his cousin – but now that the Czar refuses to leave of his own accord, perhaps *your* goals coincide with ours.'

'Perhaps. At the start, anyway . . . but tell me, Commander, why did you come to me? Why not the Vladimirs?'

'Idiots,' Tamara murmured. The Vladimirs – the wife and sons of the Czar's uncle Vladimir – had figured prominently in the rumours Ash had heard about palace coups.

'They don't understand how to take control of Russia.'

'And a United States navy officer does?'

'You don't have to *seize* the Czar, Your Highness. You merely have to isolate him.'

Grand Duke Valery went to the windows and stared across the Neva at the Winter Palace. The snow had stopped. Sunlight flickered here and there, pale yellow on the ice.

'He's twenty miles from Petrograd,' Ash prompted. 'And it's winter. The roads – '

'Yes, Commander, you needn't draw the picture for me. I agree. Isolate the Czar. You're not the first man to dream up blowing the rail line between Petrograd and Tsarskoe Selo. I presume you have a larger plan.'

'I have some notions, and I think I can recruit some supporters you might not have thought of . . .'

The grand duke faced the window again, clenching and unclasping his hands behind his back. Tamara looked at Ash. Abruptly she came to a decision. 'Valery, I'm going to the school to rehearse. Would you two drive me over, please?'

Valery's footmen sprang to the red sleigh's doors as they came out of the house. The Cossacks mounted, and a kitchen *moujik* ran up and poured fresh embers into the foot-warming brazier. The coachman bellowed. The footmen jumped onto their platform at the back and the sleigh slid into motion as eight horses dragged it off the road across a field toward the river embankment.

They sat shoulder to shoulder, the grand duke in the middle with Tamara's small hand curled in his huge fist. Surrounded behind and on the sides by the high seat, they were protected from the wind and the sight of the curious. Ahead was the circular bulk of the coachman and the heads of the straining horses. Above the sky.

The sleigh rode as heavy as a freight train, and Ash shivered as it crashed down landing stairs onto a path on the ice which was lined with pine trees stuck in the snow piles. Counting horses, the sleigh must weigh six or eight tons. The coachman alone looked good for four hundred pounds, the grand duke another three, while beneath the ice the Neva ran swift and deep.

'The Czar has already isolated himself at Tsarskoye Selo.' Ash broke the silence which had hung heavily while

361

they waited for Tamara to dress. 'He might as well be in England right now if it weren't for the railroad, and the telephone and telegraph. All we have to do is block the railroad tracks – north to cut him off from Petrograd and south to block him from contacting the Stavka at Mogilev. And cut the telephone and telegraph lines, of course. And they run right beside the tracks.'

'I repeat,' Valery said, speaking only after Tamara nudged him. 'Do you think you're the first man who's thought of blowing that line? Even if you could find the men to do it, the First Railway Battalion would mobilize ten thousand troops in an hour. In two hours twenty thousand, *and* an armoured train. In three they'd hang the survivors from the telegraph poles.'

The horses scrambled up the landing steps of the French Embankment – embassy row upstream from the palaces – and broke into a smart trot alongside the Field of Mars. Artillery men and horse soldiers drilling among the stacked firewood saluted as the red sleigh passed.

'I think Kennet has more to say,' Tamara said. Her prompting kept them talking.

'I do,' Ash said. 'The First Railway Battalion's officers will think twice if they receive new orders from the Winter Palace, where you will be in attendance with key members of the Duma.'

'You don't understand the timing,' Valery said. 'The Czar will march on the city the instant the line is repaired.'

'I'll guarantee they won't repair it in three hours.'

'How?'

'A little trick the Filipino Insurgents taught the US Marines the hard way. There's more than one way to stop a railroad. Even the Czar's railroad.'

When the sleigh turned left off Sadovaya Street onto the broad Nevsky Prospect, traffic police in high boots and white gloves halted trams and carriages to let the grand

362

duke pass. Trotting up the boulevard they drew stares from the early afternoon shoppers, salutes from the guards officers and an occasional cheer for the grand duke, who leaned forward to show himself and nodded sternly left and right and raised his huge hand in a gesture that looked half salute and half wave.

'One must be visible,' he told Ash. 'One cannot rule an empire from one's country house.'

'One is going to get a revolutionary's bomb tossed into one's lap one of these days,' Tamara muttered. Ash, for his part, sat back, glad of the high seat. After a coup it wouldn't do for an American naval officer to have been seen too much in the company of the man who had plotted to become the new czar. A column of horseguards halted right in the middle of the boulevard, left-faced and saluted as the grand duke passed.

Ash glanced at Tamara; she was loving every minute of it even as she berated Valery for making himself a target. As indeed he was. Not everyone was saluting. A yellow tram had stopped to let them turn off the Nevsky Prospect into Catherine Square. It was packed with factory workers – on strike if they were off this early, Ash presumed – and each window contained an angry face.

Valery sat back and took her hand. 'We must be visible. Since the Czar-liberator Alexander was assassinated in his carriage, we Romanovs have become invisible, afraid of anarchists, afraid of revolutionaries. In a sense the assassin killed us all. What are the people supposed to believe in when they cannot ever see us?'

The sleigh passed through Catherine Square, around the columned Alexander Theatre and into Theatre Street, the eight horses smartly navigating the tight turns. They stopped in front of the Imperial Theatrical School. Tamara stood up. 'They can't see God either.'

Valery gave her an indulgent smile as the footman helped

her down. He called after her, 'God doesn't have the responsibility for collecting taxes.'

'Pick me up in two hours. We'll have *zakouski* – the three of us – and you'll tell me what you've decided.'

Ash watched her disappear in the doors. He turned to see Valery's eyes on him. 'Do you see that window?'

Ash looked where he was pointing. The ledge was twenty feet above the street. 'Yes.'

'Many years ago His Majesty was suddenly taken with a beautiful young girl, a dancer. The Czar was already married, and an uncommonly faithful man in the vows – he does truly love that woman – but he was enchanted, bewitched, as only Tamara can bewitch. He could not call on the girl himself, of course, so he sent me to fetch her to a little picnic. She sat on that ledge, and her hair was even longer then, black on her skin that was so white. She had her legs curled under her. She smiled down at me in my carriage. Romantic nonsense, some might say, but I fell in love with her at that moment. I was also obliged to tell her for whom I had come . . . You may think me an old fool to let her treat me the way she does. I certainly think that sometimes. My country is on the brink, but often when I sit with the men of the Duma, humouring liberals and Kadets and the Black Hundred reactionaries who want their serfs back, or with the generals at Mogilev and the munitions manufacturers and the railway managers, trying to get our house in order, her face forms in my mind and I hear her laughing and I see her dance . . .'

Ash thought of the first time he had seen her too, a beautiful woman in white, when he had known only girls, smiling up at him from the stern of a pretty sailboat. And he thought what a gentle soul lay inside this giant in a Cossack uniform.

'If you value your life, Commander Ash, you'll not see her again.'

The Cossacks had stayed on their horses, watching the street and the buildings, but Theatre Street, insulated from the nearby Nevsky Prospect by the Alexander Theatre and the twin classical buildings flanking it, was silent except for the horses' hard breathing. It was so quiet Ash could hear the riders' lances creaking in their black leather gloves.

'They'll skewer you like shish kebab on my command, but I'd prefer to do it with my own hands.'

The sudden shift had caught Ash by surprise. Was that all this talk was about? He met Valery's hard look with one of his own. 'What's stopping you, other than the fact your country's falling apart and you with my help seem at the moment to be its only hope?'

A *injal,* the long Cossack dagger, hung from Valery's belt beside his *pallash.* His hand closed on the hilt.

'Go on, try it,' Ash taunted him, feeling the years of frustration. 'You think I enjoy watching you hold her hand in front of me?'

Two Cossacks edged into lance range. They did not know English, but they recognized a fighting stance, a threat to their master.

Valery sighed. 'What's stopping me is that she would never talk to me again if I so much as bruised your pretty face.'

Ash fought his anger. 'Your Highness, I think we owe Russia a truce.'

'I agree. What terms?'

'Neither of us touches her until you're the czar. Then she decides.'

'*Da.*'

They shook hands, and Valery said, 'You've made a good deal in the short term, but you will lose in the long term.'

Ash shrugged. Anything not to watch him touch her.

Now at least he could concentrate. Though Tamara, if he knew her, might have something to say about their divvying her up.

At five o'clock Ash met Count von Basel again on the spit of Vassily Island. The German spy wore the shabby hat and overcoat of a stock exchange clerk once more, and though he moved quickly down the steps, Ash noted, he took care to lean on his walking stick as though he really needed it.

'I'm in business. Right in the middle of a palace coup.'

'You made a good choice. Just the other day a police agent overheard the French ambassador suggest undiplomatically that Russia needs a Napoleon. Maybe you've found him. What do you want from me?'

What an unlikely alliance, Ash thought. Constrained to remove the Czar without knocking Russia out of the war, Ash felt like the middle horse inside the shafts of a troika. On one side a jealous grand duke galloped fitfully, and on his other a German spy he hated. A funny thought surprised him; he didn't really hate von Basel. He just wanted to beat him.

'Before the grand duke can take the government, we have to block the rail lines in and out of Tsarskoye Selo, as well as telegraph and telephone. We have to draw troops hostile to the coup away from the Winter Palace, quietly. And we have to gag public figures who might denounce the coup.'

'There won't be any of those,' von Basel remarked drily. 'Except of course for provocateurs taking advantage of temporary chaos. I will arrest them.'

'Have you found Kirichenko?'

'Try the Moscow District. He's in there someplace.'

'I'll need you to provoke an incident to draw off troops barracked near the Winter Palace that the grand duke can't persuade to his side.'

366

'Whatever you ask,' von Basel replied with a mocking smile. 'As the Kaiser's servant, I am your servant.'

A Napoleon? Ash mused after he left von Basel. The Grand Duke Valery was no Bonaparte, but he just might be able to hold the whole mess together until something like one came along. Or at least until the US got enough troops into France to make a difference. What, he wondered, did von Basel think of that? Or did he just do exactly what his beloved Kaiser asked and the hell with the consequences?

Kirichenko was his main problem, and best hope.

Valery had insisted on knowing exactly how Ash would blow the line. Ash had explained as best he could while they rode around the city waiting for Tamara.

'It's a trick the Filipino insurgents taught the US marines. They blew a little hole in the main line from Manila to Cabanahuan. Just enough to knock out both tracks but too small to have been set by anybody other than hit-and-run amateurs. So the marines rode out on a couple of repair trains, one from each direction. Both hit mines. Now they had to clear *two* trains, repair three holes and search every inch of the line for more explosives. That's what we got for fighting in the other guy's backyard . . . It will slow them down considerably. The Czar is certainly not going to ride an armoured train to Petrograd until they've checked the entire line. By that time you'll be greeting your fellow grand dukes and key members of the Duma in the Winter Palace. And I will take him to England.'

'Who precisely will dynamite the lines?'

'I have contacts among revolutionary elements,' Ash replied, which was stretching it. 'People you will be able to deal with – and control – when you have restored order.'

'There can't be so many that they would threaten me, I suppose.'

'And a good government will defuse its enemies.'

'And you think I will make a good government?'

'I doubt that you can make one worse than this one.'

The grand duke nodded. No Napoleon, but a lot better than Nicholas II.

'But what about Nicholas? How exactly will you remove him to England?'

'The Czar's safety has to be my responsibility,' Ash said firmly.

'But how?'

'For reasons of safety, security, I won't share my plans with anyone not directly involved . . . but I can assure you that His Majesty's safety is guaranteed.'

And security aside, Ash could not mention the Kaiser to the grand duke. He knew by now that Valery would cut off his own arm before he would shake hands with the likes of Kaiser Wilhelm.

33

'They've stolen my army.'

The Imperial Guardsman keeping Kaiser Wilhelm company shook his head sympathetically, but the dullness that lurked like a sleepy animal in the man's vacant eyes provoked the Kaiser to emphasize the depth of his loss with the postscript, 'And they didn't even have the decency to tell me themselves.'

Down in the courtyard the major who had delivered Hindenburg and Ludendorff's curt message glanced up at the window as he climbed into his staff car. No salute. How quickly pawns ceased pretending respect. From this day on, it seemed, the Kaiser's two top generals were too busy to report daily in person. His Majesty was invited to call at general headquarters whenever he cared. But that meant living in Berlin in the awful Schloss Bellevue. Even Georgie was treated better.

He watched his reflection harden in the window as night crept from the forest up the palace walls and the servants scurried silently behind him lighting the lamps. His eyes, deepset, looked enormous and deep and liquid, almost like Nicky's, but not, thank God, with Nicky's rather vacuous stare. *His* glittered with intelligence, he assured himself.

The thought cheered him. He had been so depressed for so long, thanks to the war chipping away at his power and his crown, that he was surprised that at this moment, though he tried to mourn, he couldn't. Ludendorff and von Hindenburg had aroused something inside him. His upstart generals had thrown down the gauntlet. Well, by God he would pick it up. They had the army, but he was still Kaiser Wilhelm II, Emperor of Imperial Germany.

Victoria's blood flowed in his veins and his tough old grandmother's spirits coursed beside the power that had been Frederick the Great's. He would put that upstart Colonel Ludendorff – colonel was his rank before the war – and doddering old von Hindenburg in their place. He had done it nearly thirty years ago to Bismarck, he would do it today.

. . . But how?

Inspiration struck. Yes. Like a great Krupp cannon – the war was his downfall but suddenly he knew how to win the war and take back his crown. He clenched his fist, pounded the windowledge. His crown and all the majesty, all the power. How? Simplicity itself.

He, Kaiser Wilhelm, would give Czar Nicholas asylum. *Not* Georgie.

He would parade the fallen Czar through Berlin. *His* prisoner of war. Leaderless Russia would collapse in days. Her armies would disintegrate. He would command his eastern army to force a quick surrender, then order those million men and three thousand guns to wheel west and smash England and France before the United States could intervene.

His subjects would thank him for defeating the Allies by capturing the Czar. They would demand that Kaiser Wilhelm II take the helm of Germany once again. Germany would see him as the conquering general it had known before the war. He patted his left hand, securely perched on his sword hilt, and considered that if he took the initiative immediately upon winning the war, he could even abolish the Reichstag.

Poor simple Georgie, he thought, a smile appearing on his lips, and his reflection smiled back. 'So kind and cousinly of him to try to save Nicky. I will save Nicky, whether he wants it or not. He will trust in cousin Willy . . .

'Guardsman.' The Kaiser motioned him near and threw his arm around the man's shoulder. 'Bring Count von Basel.'

'Sedovina?' Tamara's eyebrows rose as if Ash had asked whether she wanted to assist her cook in the marketing.

'She's dancing Effie next Sunday. What do you think of her?'

'A talented girl, despite her unruly yellow hair and rather – how do you say it – gangling stance.'

'I've heard her compared to you.'

'Darling, that merely means she's caught their fancy for a season. She's actually quite good, but quite good doesn't mean she has the staying power. Ask me again in a few years.'

'What do you know about her?'

'She runs with an unsavoury crowd.'

'That's what I really want to know. I don't care about her dancing.'

'Darling, this is all making you very tense.'

Ash looked at her smiling at him across a lunch table at Berrin's, a sweets shop on Morskaya Street. They had walked here from the school after her morning rehearsal. The truce with Valery was working brilliantly; he was able to spend a good deal of time with Tamara between trying to put together the elements of the coup; it was like courting her, an old-fashioned life they had never had. But he was no closer to Kirichenko, the fighting squad leader, and von Basel, who ought to have been more help, had disappeared. Three notes at the wrecked German Embassy lay in the sconce hole, untouched.

'What crowd?' he pressed her.

'Revolutionaries. It's a miracle she hasn't been dismissed.'

'Tamara, there was a time when you thought failure to say God Save the Czar aloud indicated revolutionary tendencies. What do you really mean?'

'I mean *revolutionary,* dammit, Kennet.' Her small fist hit the table for emphasis, and their hot chocolate cups bounded in their saucers. 'One more false step and the Imperial Theatre will dismiss Sedovina. Her lover – '

'Lover? She's sixteen.'

'*Lover,* and she's twenty. Dear heart, one learns early to conceal one's age. Anyway, her *lover* was exiled to Siberia for agitation. Shot trying to escape . . . What is your interest in her, may I ask?'

'What? Oh . . . her friends . . .'

A Russian armoured car rumbled up to a trench a hundred and fifty yards from the German line firing its heavy machine-guns. The infantrymen in the trench, which was a shallow morass of marshland, pleaded with their countrymen inside the slab-sided vehicle to take it elsewhere. A perfectly normal afternoon of exchanging sniper fire was turning to hell as evening lowered because the armoured car was drawing terrible fire.

The Germans were trying to disable it by the unlikely method of shooting at the armoured radiator grill and the laborious task of shooting the hard rubber tyres to pieces. Soon it seemed as if all the enemy for two miles was flinging small arms fire at the car, which replied with murderously active machine-guns and the sullen boom of a two-pounder. The Russians in the trenches hunkered down for the inevitable artillery barrage.

Count von Basel watched the iron beast with amusement. It was there at his orders, to provide distraction. A German shell suddenly screamed across no-man's-land and burst twenty yards from the armoured car, throwing Russians in the air like toys. A second shell landed closer. Shrapnel rattled off its sides.

Suddenly the car stopped moving. There was a lull in the firing for a moment or two, and von Basel realized that its engine had stalled. Sure enough, a crewman popped out and ran around to the front to turn the starter crank. The Germans opened up and the Russian mechanic took hit after hit, doggedly cranking the engine. Von Basel did not wait to see what happened. He moved out of the Russian trench and started across no-man's-land, while every eye was on the stricken car and the artillery shells cratering around it.

Von Basel found the Kaiser, half-moved into the cold, drafty Schloss Bellevue, bellowing at his ragtag band of courtiers. Saddened by the sovereign's worn-out look, von Basel put on a bright face to try to cheer him up. But the Kaiser surprised him. No sooner had he dragged him off to a private room than he erupted excitedly into his plan for the Czar.

Von Basel was delighted. Blood always prevailed. The Emperor, battered by the war and his generals' treachery, was fighting back. Could von Basel do it, the Kaiser asked. Could he somehow get the Czar out of Russia? Von Basel said he could.

The Kaiser wanted to award him the Iron Cross, First Class, on the spot, but von Basel respectfully refused. It was an honour to serve – *poor* Ash . . .

He made an obligatory report to Gruppe IIIb by telephone so they wouldn't detain him, then stopped to see his mother in the Berlin apartment she had moved to when the Russians overran their East Prussian estates at the beginning of the war.

She looked as beautiful as ever – she begged him now to

stay a few days, but he was depressed by the way the food shortages affected even their class in Berlin – as opposed to Russia, where the only indication of shortage was higher prices that the rich could afford. Besides, he was anxious to get back across the lines. The Kaiser had asked what he would do about Ash. Von Basel smiled at the thought. He had told His Majesty about Ash's plan to support the Grand Duke Valery's palace coup.

'I think I will let Commander Ash do exactly what he intends to. I'll even help him. It would be more difficult to seize the Czar from his own Guard, or from a revolutionary government, than to take him away from a single American naval officer.'

The Kaiser had clapped him on his back, then ordered a private car from his own Imperial Train to be attached to the express to occupied Riga so that Count von Basel might return to the front in a style befitting a German nobleman in service to his emperor.

Von Basel tried to luxuriate as the train thundered east, but he was too impatient to enjoy, too anxious to get back to Petrograd where he could keep an eye on how Ash was progressing.

34

Sedovina danced. A hush fell over the Maryinski Theatre. Ash sat in the stalls, shoulder-to-shoulder with Russian army officers. When she finished her first solo the men surged, roaring, to their feet. Overhead applause thundered from the tiers of boxes and came down from the high gallery.

Ash had held her in his opera glasses. The great Karsavina performed the Sylphide, but Petrograd waited for Sedovina's solos and roared its approval again and again.

Sedovina danced with the icy precision the Russians demanded, the price of entry to their hearts. Without perfect form they would hiss her off the stage. To the precision she brought grace, also expected. Her style was youthful, an image as yet unformed, but her presence, in spite of her age, was irresistible.

The great blue curtain descended for the *entr'acte* and the officers broke into excited discussion about the new sensation as they made for the stairs to the first box tier. Ash headed that way himself, hunting Sergei Gladishev. He squeezed past three ancient captains of the Jaegerski Life Guard, resplendent in their bemedalled dark green uniforms and arguing the merits of the performance. Choreography, they agreed, had fallen on hard times, but Sedovina . . . she was a *ballerina*. When would the Imperial Theatres award her a principal role worthy of her talents? But hadn't he heard? Sokolova, the great dancer of the eighties, was preparing her for *Giselle*.

In the first tier the ladies had thrown open their doors and were gathered in the anterooms at the rear of their boxes, smoking and talking with men visiting from the stalls. In the next tier pinkly shaven merchants were hurrying back to their boxes with chocolates for their wives, while down the stairs from the gallery streamed the 'Gods', student dancers, laughing and chattering as the girls pretended not to ogle the officers in their bright uniforms.

Ash found Gladishev on the second tier drinking champagne with some grave-looking men he presumed were Duma members. To his relief, when Gladishev saw him hovering, the Kadet Party millionaire excused himself and motioned him to the champagne, where he bought Ash a glass. 'I understand you've telephoned, Commander,' he said.

'Five times this week. And I stopped twice at your mansion.' He tilted his glass in silent toast and said, 'This is the first time since I got to Petrograd that you haven't snubbed me. What's up?'

Gladishev had a big, round face and an almost perpetual grin, which was either good-humoured or brusque depending on the squint of his eyes. They narrowed now and the grin turned hard, amused, but not mirthful. 'That's because I saw you on the Nevsky the other day with Tishkova,' he said. Ash had called the second time at Gladishev's mansion *with* Tamara. Apparently the ploy had worked.

'We're old friends.'

'I admire her very much.'

'So does the Grand Duke Valery.'

'I always thought his tastes were much more advanced than the rest of his clan.'

There was the opening Ash had been waiting for. So Gladishev had heard, or guessed, something about the grand ducal conspiracy to overthrow Czar Nicholas, and had surmised Ash was part of it. He said, 'Mademoiselle

376

Tishkova and I will lunch at Berrin's on Wednesday after-noon. Three o'clock.'

Ash returned to the stalls. The lights dimmed, the blue and gold hall grew quiet and he heard one of the old Jaegerski Guards whisper happily, 'And next month Tishkova's jubilee!' . . .

Provided, thought Ash, Petrograd wasn't in flames next month. He had seen his first street demonstration earlier in the week. Factory workers marching up the centre of Sedo-vaya Street had borne signs draped between long poles and chanted, *Duma! Duma! Duma!'* – an angry demand to make the elected body more than a debating chamber.

More of an immediate threat to Russian stability was another cry, a thin echo of single voices in the marching throng, *'Khleba . . .'* Bread.

The police had wasted no time pouncing on several dozen whom they clubbed into paddy wagons. In ten minutes the busy street was back to normal, but to Ash, who had been moved by the stolid courage on the faces in the front lines of the demonstration, it looked as if the police had won only the first of what promised to be many battles . . .

A canal looped around the back of the Maryinski theatre, iced and deep in snow. Carriages and motor cars lined up at the stage door. At intervals it opened on a cloaked figure that would scamper across the swept snow, revealing a glimpse of shiny hair or a pretty nose. A hand extended from the coach and the dancer slipped inside as it clattered away.

Other girls came out in groups, arm in arm, squealing at the cold, laughing excitedly, growing quiet when a group of young officers approached. But after a while the last carriage pulled away, leaving only Ash and a few Russian officers. Had he missed her? Five minutes passed. No one came out.

One of the Russians knocked on the stage door. An old woman told him to go away. 'Sedovina?' he asked; she nodded and he returned to his group. Ash looked over the competition – fresh-faced subalterns wearing the double-headed eagle and imperial red of the Cavalier Guard regiment. Aristocrats, newly commissioned. And younger than ever as the Russians accelerated their cadet classes to make up for the slaughter.

It was hardly a contest. He had waited outside a hundred stage doors for Tamara Tishkova, courting and recourting her over the years, and he knew the ropes. He let them go first.

She came out, wrapped in a wool cloak that completely hooded her head except for a gleam of golden hair and her nose with the little bump. The officers crowded up to her, shouldering each other aside to try to kiss her hand. Ash watched her eyes flicker over them. She seemed neither frightened by the onslaught, nor pleased. He was surprised to see a moment of disdain on her face. It passed, and she smiled noncommittally and turned away. Ash stood in her path.

'I saw Pavlova last November in New York City – I didn't know until tonight why she left Russia.'

Big eyes met his – blue and young and startled, and still aglitter from the excitement of performing. Ash tried to hold them with a smile, but something was wrong. Either she didn't remember meeting him at the Exeters', or she hadn't liked what he had just said.

Sternly she replied, 'Thank you for saying that. I know you mean it as a compliment, but artists are not competitors.'

'Yours will be relieved to hear it,' Ash said. 'Do you recall, Mademoiselle, we met in London?'

378

She looked at him. 'Commander Ash. Poor Lady Exeter. What a strange death. I was so sad, she was awfully kind to me. I stayed at their home even after they left for Russia . . .'

'Would you have supper with me? . . . there's something I'd like to ask you.'

'I don't usually . . . I like to sort of think about things after a performance. What went right and wrong . . .' She glanced around. The Russian Guards officers were still waiting. Ash let his cloak fall away from his uniform. 'Good *night*, gentlemen.'

He received an obedient salute, some dejected good nights, and off they trooped.

'What did Pavlova dance?'

'*Giselle*. I heard tonight that Sokolova is preparing you for it. She coached Pavlova in the part too, didn't she?'

'How does an American know so much about the dance?'

'Tishkova is an old friend.'

She looked disdainful again, the way she had reacted to the Guards officers, and Ash was puzzled by an undercurrent of anger. Sedovina said, 'She and her entourage of grand dukes. They think the ballet is their toy.'

'Shall we go?' Ash said. He had learned long ago to steer clear of the likes and dislikes that sprang up at the *barre* and flourished in the wings. 'Will you join me for supper?'

'The ballet should be for everyone, not just the aristocracy. Tishkova encourages that exclusivity.'

'Shall we go?'

'First tell me what it is you want to ask me.'

'I want to meet a man named Kirichenko.'

'Who?' she asked, but she looked frightened.

'Kirichenko. He's a Social Revolutionary squad leader, allied with the Bolsheviks. Lenin knows him.'

'We have nothing to talk about.' She whirled away from

379

the stage door and hurried toward the big square in front of the theatre. Ash caught up. 'Please. Have supper with me. We'll just talk – '

'I will scream for police if you don't go away.'

'I'll swear to the police we were talking about *Giselle* – '

'I *will* scream.' She looked around. A tram was coming.

Ash said, 'Or should I tell the police we were talking about the Bolshevik sailor you met in Covent Garden?'

She grabbed his arm. Her eyes were now very large.

'I won't hurt you,' Ash promised. 'I won't tell anyone but I must meet Kirichenko.'

'Who else knows?'

'No one. I followed you from the Exeters'. We're on the same side.' Not really true again, but close enough. 'I need your help.'

'I don't know him.'

'Think about it.'

She looked around. Theatre Square was deserted now, except for old women sweeping the snow. Her gaze lingered on each.

'Let's walk.'

Relieved, Ash let her steer him into one of the several streets that converged in the square. 'This runs beside a canal,' she said in a tight voice. 'There's a bridge . . .'

It was suspended across the narrow canal by a pair of black chains anchored in the mouths of exquisitely sculpted black-and-gold lions. Sedovina touched one of their heads. 'My friends, when I first came to the Maryinski . . . this was the long way to my home but I preferred to see my friends . . .'

She looked down the canal, a graceful trough of snow that caught the light from the surrounding buildings and the regularly spaced street lamps. 'I haven't come this way in a while.'

They walked quickly along the canal until it veered away

and shortly came to a narrow boulevard, one of the principal streets that radiated from the Admiralty.

She began walking faster, and Ash had trouble keeping up with her on the slippery snow. The wind chewed at their backs, tossing their cloaks and cutting to the skin. Away from the canal the street lights were fewer, and they trudged for intervals in the dark.

When Ash did get a look at her face under one of the intermittent lights he was shocked to see a profound weariness. Or despair?

'What is it?'

'I am wondering what happens if the police break me.'

'What?'

'I don't know that much, but it all matters . . . I should probably kill myself.'

'What are you talking about? I'm not threatening Kirichenko. I just want to *meet* him. Why would I want to hurt Kirichenko?'

No answer. She had subsided into another of her long silences, one she had not broken by the time they reached St Isaac's Square. The domed cathedral loomed darkly on the far side, but the Astoria and the graceful Maryinski Palace spilled golden light onto the firewood piled in the square from nearly every window. Music from both drifted thinly on the wind.

Sedovina was walking with her head down and didn't see the sudden rush toward them from the shadows. An old woman darted out of a woodpile and ran straight at them, clutching a stick of firewood. There was a shout as she scrambled past them, and a soldier came after her, raising his rifle like a club.

Ash acted without thinking, stepped inside the swing and doubled the soldier up with a fist to his middle. The soldier's gun clattered to the ice and he sprawled, moaning, as the old woman ran into an alley.

A second soldier came running down the narrow corridor between the piles, saw his companion on the ground and pointed his rifle at Ash. Sedovina whispered, 'Give him money.'

Ash let his cloak open, as he had done before. The soldier noted his uniform. Ash slowly reached into his pocket and extracted his billfold, pulled roubles from it and held them up. The soldier glanced once at his companion, who was starting to sit up, lowered his gun, took the money. Ash took Sedovina's arm and hurried toward the Astoria.

'You were kind,' Sedovina said. 'They would have beaten her. They don't realize that she's the widow and mother of ones like themselves.'

'Thanks, but I didn't think . . .'

'Well, we're both lucky they weren't drunk. They'd have shot us if they were.'

Ash thought they were also lucky that she'd had the quick wit to suggest a bribe. He glanced at her. She seemed curiously unaffected by the incident, seemed to have already put it from her mind. He reminded himself, as he often had to when he first got to know Tamara, that Russians were different, more emotional and more romantic than Europeans but at the same time so enormously fatalistic as to freeze all emotion with an icy dose of acceptance. She had meant it earlier when she said she would kill herself. No doubt about it.

He looked around the front of the Astoria. It looked clear. Red Snow, by now, would have given up on the hotel. It was as good a place as any for late supper. He invited her in.

'No, I want to go home.'

Ash signalled for a sleigh from the line at the kerb. Sedovina settled back and gave the driver her address. A mile up the Nevsky Prospect he turned off and pulled up beside the mighty columns of the Alexander Theatre. 'I live down that lane.'

The opening was too narrow for the sleigh, an almost invisible slit between two buildings. Inside, the houses were wooden with pointed gables leaning toward each other. Sedovina headed toward an alley covered by a first-floor passage between two houses. There was a window in the passage and a lighted lamp in the window.

'My room,' she said. 'Isn't it wonderful the way it floats in the air?'

She passed under the room and worked a key into a wooden door that opened on a small, shabby parlour. The light from upstairs cast dark shadows on the wallpaper. She started to close the door.

'Kirichenko?' Ash asked.

Sedovina nodded. 'Tomorrow at five. Can you meet me at the ballet school on Theatre Street?'

Sedovina collapsed against her door, listening to his footsteps fade. She crossed her arms and pressed her hands to her breasts. She tried to make her mind go blank, to shed her panic. Who was he? Why had he followed her? What had she said? Would he come back with the Okhrana?

She had kept looking for detectives on the long walk from the theatre, kept waiting for the sudden swoop of a police car; she could almost feel their rough hands clamping hold of her arms, dragging her inside.

Kirichenko. She calmed her mind with thoughts of him. Usually he frightened her – the few times they had met – but not now. She would tell him what Ash wanted. Let Kirichenko decide if Ash was dangerous. Kirichenko would know what to do with the American.

After turning out the light she opened the door, ran down the alley and roused a youth who slept in a flat off the courtyard. He came back with her, listened to her message and ran off, chewing one of the apples she kept by the door for delivery boys.

Somewhat calmed by action, and reassuring herself that if Ash were dangerous Kirichenko would kill him, she got ready for bed. Her body ached from the fear and tension.

She and her step-father were almost out of paraffin, which meant hours tomorrow morning on the *khvost* in hopes of buying more. How, she wondered, as she often did, did ordinary people survive? They were poor, but both had steady incomes and there were no children to feed . . .

She was still awake when Mikhailov came home, a little drunk but exhilarated by the night's playing. He knocked on her door and sat on the edge of her bed. 'Where did you play?' she asked.

'The Paley ball. They came in raving about your Effie.'

'I was terrible tonight.'

'They didn't notice,' Mikhailov smiled.

'They never do.'

Her step-father worked the stiffness out of his big, blunt fingers. 'You're too harsh, Vera.'

She said nothing. The discipline she had embraced as a child, a student, and the discipline that made her a dancer had found new strength in the Revolution. She took comfort in the conviction that the cruel inequities of Russian life could only be relieved by total dedication on the part of those who could see the need to change. It *required* a cold eye.

Coryphées spilled down the stairs of the Imperial Theatrical School into the quiet trough of Theatre Street. Laughing and calling, the young dancers dispersed toward the Nevsky in little groups, arms linked, heads bobbing for secrets. Cold snow fell hard, and a thin mist rose from the ground and haloed the street lights. By the time they reached the Alexander Theatre Ash could barely see the girls.

Children burst next from the school, ducklings herding Sedovina in their midst, she like a swan bent over deep in conversation with a little ten-year-old. Ash hung back until she kissed the child and came toward him. She slipped her arm through his, affectionately, except that her body was stiff and the affection was quite obviously an act for anyone watching from the school. She steered him in the opposite direction from the Alexander Theatre and the Nevsky. Her face was ghostly white, her mouth an anxious line.

Left at the end of Theatre Street, through a tiny square, she stopped on a bridge that humped over the Fontanka River. 'Listen to me. I am walking into the Moscow District. You are to follow twenty yards behind. If I stop, you stop. Do not approach me.'

'Are you taking me to Kirichenko?'

'Comrade Kirichenko wants a good look at you first.'

She continued across the bridge, her shoulders stiff. Ash waited twenty yards and went after her. She was easy to identify by her long blond hair cascading from her hat, her height and the blur of milk-white skin when she turned her face to look back. Walking beside the river for a block, she turned left on Gorokhovaya Street, past the building where Rasputin had lived. Within another block the factory neighbourhood, which was wedged between the last vestiges of gentility east of the Fontanka and the railroad tracks of the Moscow line, had deteriorated from shabby to impoverished.

Sedovina hesitated. The narrow streets ahead teemed with factory workers and *moujiki,* street vendors and shoppers lugging pails for milk and paraffin. Long lines spilled from the shops and market stalls. A legless beggar slithered up and tugged at her skirt.

Sedovina recoiled, then caught herself and dropped a coin in his hand. She forged ahead. Ash followed, forcing himself not to look for whoever was watching him. The streets narrowed on the crowds. Lights were few. They *were* watching. He felt it.

The street narrowed again, squeezed into a *pereulki,* a lane deep in slush and half-frozen mud, and Ash worried that his clothes stood out in the shabby crowds and might draw the attention of the police. His boat cloak covered his sword. His boots had got as muddy as everyone's, but the polished black visor and gold eagle on his service cap still made him look out of place.

He took it off, but a bare head stood out even more. No Russian would dare go hatless in the dangerous cold. In seconds it seeped through his thick hair and set a chill travelling down his spine. He spotted an immensely tall, swarthy Tartar selling old clothes from a filthy sack, waved a couple of roubles at him and bought a used fur hat that had seen better days.

Down another lane past low glass-fronted factory buildings with arched roofs . . . through the dirty windows Ash could see men and women hunched over machinery. Sedovina stopped. A pair of drunken soldiers lurched at her from a doorway. She sidestepped them just as Ash moved to help. Before he reached her one of the grey-uniformed policemen patrolling the streets kicked the drunks away. Sedovina whirled and ran. The *gorodovoi* ordered her to stop, but she disappeared in the crowds. The cop shrugged and kicked the drunks again. Ash circled around them, scanned the street quickly and saw no one who seemed to be watching. Sedovina?

He spotted the bright gold of her hair as she crossed a little square where half a dozen lanes joined A wagon heaped with firewood and trailed by a mob of anxious shoppers blocked Ash's way. When it and the people had passed, Sedovina was gone.

He pushed into the square. Gone. He ran to each lane, looked down several alleys and ventured into courtyards surrounded by decrepit tenements. He had lost her. He went back to the square and looked there. A beggar tugged his cuff . . . '*Khrista rady*,' a copper for Christ's sake. Ash gave him a few, looked farther. The beggar tugged his cuff again.

'*Nyet. Nyet.* You already got me – '

But the filthy hand which Ash had filled with kopecks now held a stubby revolver.

35

His long, ragged coat sleeve hid the weapon. Only Ash could see – though throngs of people were brushing past – and all he saw was the enormous circle of the muzzle. The beggar stood up. He had been perched on a box. He held Ash's cloak with his free hand and backed him into a doorway.

Two men marched him up three dark flights of wooden stairs to a room with an oil lamp and a single window that overlooked the square. They gestured for him to lean against the wall, pulled off his cloak, and patted him down for weapons. They left, but the beggar had followed them up the stairs, his gun still out.

Ash slowly lowered his hands and turned around. The beggar did not object until he tried to move away from the wall; Ash leaned back, waited. The square below the window was filling up with people. On the side that Ash could see, a couple of men were stringing electric light bulbs between a pole and a tenement.

The two men came back, accompanying a third. Kirichenko? Definitely the boss. He planted himself in front of Ash, feet wide apart, looked him up and down.

Ash ran his own inspection. What he saw was a short, medium-built, clean-shaven Russian dressed like the others in a factory worker's short leather jacket and forage cap whose peak sloped close to his brow. Dark hair fluffed out from the back of his cap. He had a full mouth and long nose and kept his face turned slightly to the side, which gave him a wary look. His jacket hung open. Two guns were stuffed in his waistband.

'Who sent you?' His accent was heavy but he pronounced each word clearly as if he had learned English in school.

'Are you Kirichenko?'

'Who sent you?' He was surprisingly young, but his darting eyes and tough expression made it easy to believe that he had survived underground since the war began and the police had decimated the revolutionary apparatus.

'I come for myself. But Lenin told me about you.'

'Lenin?'

'In Zurich.'

'Lenin is a coward. He is a bully. A backstabber. If he walked into this room this minute I would blow his head off.'

'He expressed a good deal more admiration for you.'

'Maudlin claptrap. You probably surprised him at a moment when he was feeling guilt for abandoning the Revolution . . . Have you any better reasons why I should trust you?'

'Your men missed my pistol. It's hidden in the small of my back.'

'No, they didn't miss it, but we were curious how you would react.'

'Did I pass the test?'

'No. The test hasn't started yet. In fact we haven't decided whether we'll even administer the test – what do you want with me?'

'I want you to blow up a railroad.'

'Only a lunatic would come here and joke. What railroad? Why?'

'The Tsarskoye Selo line.'

'Why?'

Ash looked at him.

'You should be able to guess why.'

'I have not survived three years of Okhrana pursuit

guessing.' He pulled a revolver from his waistband and pressed the muzzle to Ash's forehead. 'Why?'

Ash knew he was dead unless Kirichenko thought he was of use. 'It's necessary to isolate the Czar to bring off a palace coup – '

'*Whose* coup?'

'I didn't tell them your name and I won't tell you theirs.'

'They perhaps didn't hold a gun to your head.'

'They trust me.'

'I trust this gun. Whose coup?'

'You'd never trust me if I told you.'

'You expect me to blow up a railroad for someone I don't know?'

'I need to know more about you before I . . .'

One of the men looked out the window and spoke to Kirichenko. Kirichenko lowered his gun. 'We'll talk about it and how I should help you, and particularly *why*, later. After your test. Take out your gun.'

'Now?'

'In your hand, you damned fool, in case you need it. Come on.'

Kirichenko took Ash to a dark room on the first floor. The window was wide open. They crouched by the sill, a few feet above the hundreds of people who had crowded into the square. Suddenly the lights Ash had watched strung were turned on. The crowd surged around the bright circle cast on the muddy snow.

'What's going on?'

'Do you like the theatre?'

'What are you talking about?'

Six men laid beams on the ground and covered them with heavy planks, taking care that they lay smoothly. A stage? The audience stamped their cold feet and murmured in anticipation.

Kirichenko made a gesture. Ash followed the direction. A

man with a rifle stood on a roof across the square. Ash scanned the surrounding buildings. Three more rifles. Kirichenko held a pistol and slipped his other hand in his pocket. Ash held his gun at his side, hardly believing that he had been bamboozled into standing guard for Russian revolutionaries. His test.

'Theatre?'

'We're the ushers. In case the *pharon* come. The cops, you call them.'

They put a table on the wooden stage. For a moment it sat alone in the lights, then six men walked into the light carrying a coffin on their shoulders. They walked solemnly around the table, circled the edges of the light and finally laid the coffin on the table. A hush fell over the crowd. All attention was on the coffin. Suddenly, there was a loud bang, the sides fell open.

Rasputin lay dead. The crowd murmured. Rasputin sat up and made broad comic signs of blessing with his arms. The crowd laughed, and the man dressed and made up to look like Rasputin lay down again, dead as before. A play had begun.

A horn sounded a fanfare. Now actors representing Czar Nicholas II and Czarina Alexandra marched into the circle of light in tawdry regalia. The resemblance of the actors to the portraits all over Russia indeed seemed extraordinary. The Czar looked exactly like the Czar, from his pointed beard to his dreamy eyes, and the Czarina looked as imperious as she had the first time Ash had seen her in her mauve boudoir.

The horn blew again, and four young girls with the red sashes worn by grand duchesses skipped onto the stage followed by a boy in a uniform. The Czar's children. They filed past the coffin, and as each girl bent in prayer over the dead Rasputin, the monk's hand lifted her skirt and gave her bottom a pat. The crowd laughed. The boy pantomimed jealousy, putting his hands on his hips and pouting and the girls picked him up and carried him away as the audience laughed even louder. Again the crowd rippled with anticipation. Now only the Czar and Czarina and Rasputin were on the stage.

Ash noticed young men in leather jackets posted as lookouts at each lane. He glanced up at the riflemen on the roofs. This was one part of Petrograd where the Revolution seemed to be going along nicely, thank you. Ash looked at his own gun and hoped to hell the cops agreed –

The horn. The Czar raised his arms and yawned with elaborate gestures, lay down behind Rasputin, yawned again and shut his eyes. The Czarina stepped up to the table and put a hand on Rasputin's chest. She gazed out at the audience and chanted in Russian what sounded to Ash like a prayer.

The crowd began laughing again. A mouldy carrot began to rise from between Rasputin's legs. When it was pointing skyward, the Czarina trailed her hand down his chest over his belly and clasped the carrot. The audience began shouting, encouraging her. It was the first joviality Ash had seen on ordinary people's faces since he had arrived in Russia.

The Czarina bantered back, asking what they wanted, and they shouted and catcalled, urging her on. The Czarina clasped the carrot in both hands and bent over it. The Czar commenced loud snoring, and she gave him a look of scorn, delighting the old women in the square. The Czarina raised her enormously painted eyebrows and her whole face seemed to ask the audience, What should I do? They answered by chanting encouragement and at last, with a gigantic shrug and another scornful glance at the snoring Czar, she bit down on the carrot.

Ash noticed that the older people laughed considerably more than the younger, many of whom looked away, embarrassed. But suddenly all laughter ceased in a single gasp, as Vera Sedovina burst into the lights. She wore white, a flowing white gown, a white peasant's headband around her golden hair and even a white mask that covered her eyes but not the little bump on her nose. She commenced a slow, stately arabesque, pirouetted and leaped into a deep and graceful bow. The musicians then began a haunting country melody on their guitars, and Vera Sedovina, ballerina in His Majesty's Imperial Theatre, danced for the people . . .

A child watched near Ash from its father's shoulders, its face awestruck. The boards beneath Sedovina's slippers were like a polished stage, the string of naked light bulbs, stars. Even the shabby costumes on the Czar and Czarina seemed to glow. There was, though, nothing ethereal about Sedovina's performance. She knew her audience, danced as broadly as the actors had played, portraying peasant work with great swoops of her body – tilling soil, hammering machinery, carrying – a divine figure in the flowing white robe, representing, *being* Russia herself. Now she glided up to the table where Rasputin lay in his coffin beside the snoring Czar and delivered a tremendous kick in the rump to the Czarina. The Czarina straightened up with a shriek, the carrot still in her teeth, reeled comically about the stage and fell backward over the Czar.

When the laughter subsided Sedovina reached for Rasputin. The audience gasped as the dead monk sprang to life and landed lightly beside her. Their *pas de deux* revealed that *he* was no renegade from the Imperial Theatre, no *danseur noble,* yet a decent enough *porteur* and the audience shouted delight at Sedovina's leaps.

She dispensed with the earlier broad strokes, but again the point was clear – Russia and Rasputin were one. The evil monk in the eyes of the few was a fellow peasant to the many. Holding hands, they bowed to the audience, shared a chaste kiss and danced arm-in-arm as the guitars took up a peasant dance. Behind them the Czar crept off the table and pulled a long black gun from his scarlet tunic. The audience shouting warnings, but the Rasputin and Russia danced on. The Czar stalked, leering cruelly as a vaudeville villain.

Ash looked at Kirichenko, who ceased inspecting the conjunction of streets and alleys long enough to sneer. 'A ham from the provinces.'

'But a brave man.'

'Valentinov would sell his own mother to play in Petrograd.'

Valentinov, the actor playing the Czar, levelled his gun. Children screamed. The dancers, oblivious, broke into a lively mazurka. Valentinov flashed a final gap-toothed leer and pulled the trigger. At the loud bang of a blank cartridge Rasputin clutched his back and fell on the table. The Czar fired again.

Sedovina pirouetted a silent scream so real that the hairs rose on Ash's neck, staggered to the table and collapsed slowly across Rasputin until she and the dead monk lay still and silent like the arms of the Cross.

'Children,' Kirichenko said. 'Playing at revolution.'

'Then what are you doing here?'

Kirichenko scanned the applauding audience. 'Patience, Commander . . .'

Sedovina and her partner got up from the table and bowed to the square. Peasants, workmen, maimed veterans beat their ragged mittens together, and though it was obvious they were shouting for her, Sedovina made her *porteur* take every bow with her. Here and there parents bent down to explain to bewildered children how the beautiful woman in white had come back to life.

The other players emerged from the alley that served as backstage. The audience greeted them with angry shouts and shaken fists and Ash was astonished by the gusts of raw hatred sweeping the square.

'They'll enjoy His Majesty's trial,' Kirichenko remarked with satisfaction.

'What do you mean?'

'The Czar's trial, after the Revolution. His guilt must be exposed publicly before he dies.'

'Why bother? Why not just send him into exile?'

Kirichenko looked at him sharply. 'Your little friend Sedovina just brought the news back from *our* exiles. The Bolsheviks in Zurich, London and New York all agree. Imprisonment, trial, execution.'

'Won't you have your hands full just holding the country together?' Ash was thinking that if the Grand Duke's coup failed and the Bolsheviks led a popular revolt instead he would somehow have to fight his way out with the Czar. It didn't seem likely. 'Won't you have more important problems, like fighting off the Germans?'

'We'll deal with the Germans when we have to,' Kirichenko told him, his quick eyes sweeping the rooftops. 'But the Czar is our real enemy. We can't let him form a government in exile and rally a counter-revolution. The party has decided and we Social Revolutionaries agree – the Czar stays in Russia, and dies in Russia.'

'What about the trial?'

'His trial will be conducted publicly, immediately prior to his execution.'

'Hardly seems worth the trouble – '

'Russia deserves a trial.'

On stage the Czar and Czarina continued to grimace before the wrought-up crowd. Finally, when it appeared that the more frenzied in the front rows would attack, the actress playing the Czarina lifted up her wig, revealing a rather ordinary-looking Russian woman with a long face and aristocratic nose similar to the Czarina's. Valentinov waited until interest in her had passed before tugging off his beard, which he waved in the lights. He was a small, lithe, middle-aged actor – obviously the troupe's director and impresario, but when he stuck the Van Dyck beard to his chin again, his resemblance to the Czar was uncanny. Ash thought he looked more like Nicholas than King George did.

Reluctantly Valentinov acknowledged the audience's shouts and brought Sedovina, still masked, forward for another bow. Her gaze travelled over the audience to the alleys.

'*Pharons,*' Kirichenko snapped.

Shouts echoed from one of the alleys entering the square, and the crowd dimpled there as people tried to move away. A phalanx of Kirichenko's young men in leather jackets tried to form a defence line as the police stormed in swinging clubs.

Now they poured in a second alley, clubbing screaming people to the snow. More police burst in a third alley, tall men in long coats, attacking in disciplined formation. The audience stampeded toward the stage.

The actors tried to run. Ash caught a glimpse of Sedovina, saw her golden hair, but lost her as the screaming mob swept her away. Valentinov herded the girls through a tenement door and then Ash lost sight of him too.

'Do something,' Ash called to Kirichenko.

'Wait.'

'*For what?*'

Quickly the square was divided. The police formed a battle line on one side, trampling on the injured, while forty or fifty young workers tried to hold them off until the audience could escape down the streets and alleys. A police officer shouted at them, and the workers responded with jeers and a barrage of snowballs. The catcalls, though, died on their lips when two dozen police reinforcements swarmed into the square.

396

'Come on.' Kirichenko hurried out of the dark room. Ash followed, his gun at his side. Outside, the police were backing the workers toward the alleys. A hard-packed snowball knocked an officer to the ground. On orders, they drew guns and started firing in the air.

Snowballs arced through the glare from the stage. Kirichenko trotted into the no-man's-land, his gun pressed out of view against his leg. Ash had only a moment to decide to join him or melt into the crowd, escape from the square. The police were forty feet away, firing in the air and advancing into the snowball barrage.

'You're in it now,' Kirichenko muttered with a mirthless grin. 'Get ready to run.'

An officer blew a whistle and the police line tightened up in preparation to charge. Kirichenko walked calmly to the front of the worker line, where he reached into his leather jacket, pulled a snowball out of his pocket, lobbed it at the cop with the whistle.

The officer swatted it contemptuously with his club. Ash heard a loud *clang*. The club fell at the officer's feet and Kirichenko's 'snowball' rolled among the police, freezing them, and then the white bomb exploded red.

36

The square echoed with blunt thunder. Before the smoke had cleared Kirichenko tossed a second bomb. Five police had fallen around the smoking crater. Four lay still. The fifth, the officer, clawed at a shattered leg. Kirichenko's second bomb landed beside him.

A rifle sounded from the roof, driving the police back into the alley, from where they directed steady fire at the rooftops. Kirichenko extracted a third bomb from his pocket and threw it into the alley. A dud. The police answered with a burst of pistol fire. A bullet smashed one of the stage lights, extinguishing the whole string and plunging most of the square into darkness.

Ash followed Kirichenko into the night . . .

'Why should I help replace the Czar with a grand duke? Another Czar?'

'Same reason you threw that bomb.'

They sat in the back of a tearoom that sold vodka. The owner had come in moments after they arrived, taken one look at Kirichenko and replaced the standard unlabelled bottle without a word. The first had tasted watered. This was like fire.

'You didn't need the bomb.'

'And what would you have done?' Kirichenko said, seemingly unconcerned by their narrow escape. He had led Ash down an alley, with a police searchlight flicking at their heels, into a tenement basement, through a long wet corridor and into an underground room that contained a printing press. A second tunnel had exited a hundred yards away in a well in a courtyard, where a lieutenant reported that the actors had made good their escape.

'I wouldn't have made the situation worse by throwing bombs. How many people were shot? – good God, Kirichenko, the only reason you stood guard was for the trouble. You knew the police would come.'

Kirichenko shrugged. 'Perhaps I informed them. Did you think of that, Commander?'

'That's why you'll help me help a grand duke replace the Czar.'

'Why?'

'You and Lenin both – the worse the better.'

Kirichenko poured more vodka. He tossed the glass back in a single gulp and looked at the drunks sleeping at the other tables. The room was thick with smoke from the few men sober enough to hold a cigarette. Two of Kirichenko's comrades sat at the door. Five more waited in the narrow street.

'The worse the better? Is that what you tell your grand duke? What Romanov would destroy to build?'

Ash said nothing. He was trying to play both ends against the middle. The only question was how far each side would go in its hopes of winning out in the end.

'You are betraying him. Or me. Or both of us.'

'This isn't my fight,' Ash said. 'My government wants the Czar removed so the United States can enter the war against Germany. That's my *only* interest. As soon as the Czar falls, I'm going home.' *But I'm also taking him with me, you son of a bitch . . .*

'Your grand duke will have the same fate as the Czar.'

'That's between you and him.'

'No, Commander, I'm not interested in your schemes. There are easier, better ways to use the worse to get the better than to risk my men blowing up the Czar's railroad for your convenience.' He stood up; his men flanked the door.

399

'How much money would make it worth the risk?'

Kirinchenko shrugged. 'What good is money when I can't use it to buy what I need? . . .'

'You have a point . . . maybe I have an answer . . .'

'Ash, I hope to God you know what you're doing.'

'The revolutionaries want high explosives, Lord Exeter. Your factory has plenty of high explosives. We're going to trade dynamite for their support.'

'A full lorry load to blow up two rail lines?'

'Could you lend a hand here, My Lord?'

The drive up the rutted roads beside the Neva had taken most of the day. Now, while Exeter's chauffeur waited in the limousine outside the factory gates, Ash and Exeter were loading wooden crates of high explosive into the back of a truck.

Independently they had both decided to dress in shooting tweeds, and it was apparent that while the enormous Englishman was powerful enough, he was hardly accustomed to ordinary manual labour. Nor did he seem, Ash thought, likely to develop a taste for it.

They packed the boxes in straw. The place was empty, though army guards were outside the fence because it was still on strike.

'I say, Ash, this is a lot more explosive than they need. I know this business. They could level the Winter Palace with this lorry.'

'May I remind you, My Lord, that it was you who persuaded me to join up with the grand duke.'

'And you were right to.'

'Well, the grand duke needs the railroad blown up and the saboteur needs explosives.'

'But I told you – '

'It's the only payment he'll accept.'

'I really thought we were driving up here to get four

crates. This is rather much. What else is he blowing up?'

'I don't know. But he's not blowing up anything until after he does the railroad.'

He brought Kirichenko to an empty cowshed on an abandoned farm beside the Gulf of Finland and showed him the truck inside. Kirichenko opened the canvas. 'Excellent.'

'There are thirty-five crates,' said Ash. 'You can use four for the railroad. Leave the rest.'

'Why?'

'If you remove five, the whole thing will detonate.'

Kirichenko flushed. 'You've sabotaged the truck?'

'I've marked these four crates which you can remove safely.'

'You renege?'

'No. Ten days after you have blown the Tsarskoye Selo lines I'll show you how to disarm the detonator.' . . . If Valery didn't have total control in ten days he never would, Ash had decided.

'I have men who can disarm it.'

'They'll land in Zurich if they try. And you'll be without the whole truckload. You haven't seen this much dynamite in your whole life . . . just take your four crates and wait for the rest.'

'You son of a bitch.'

At Berrin's *confiserie,* tall elegant French waitresses served sponge cakes, ices and hot chocolate to well-dressed children in the company of grandmothers and nannies.

'Will you look at them eat.' Tamara shuddered.

Ash was watching the foyer in the mirrored wall, watching for Sergei Gladishev. 'I already offered to take you to a bar.'

'A bar? Then champagne. Moments later you're booking a room at the Europa – '

401

'Don't start.'

She smiled at Ash and brushed the back of his hand with her fingernails. 'Fun. Yes?'

'Yes.' Fact was, Ash thought, they were having fun, despite the feeling she probably would never leave Valery for him, and despite Ash's promise to the grand duke which sat between them like a constant chaperon. Each was enjoying rediscovering the other, courting chastely. Enjoying it to a point. There were moments, like this afternoon, when the sexual tension flickered like heat lightning and Ash would not have been surprised if one of those children waving a metal spoon were suddenly singed.

'There's Gladishev.'

Tamara checked her face in the mirror, touched a lock of hair and assumed her best professional smile. If the Moscow millionaire weren't eating out of her hand in half an hour, Ash thought, he'd be a man of strange tastes; the real problem, of course, would be to get Gladishev to eat from *Valery's* hand before the increasingly difficult grand duke bit his head off.

Gladishev, fortunately, looked anything but difficult. His round face grew radiant as he inhaled the aroma of chocolate and he beamed at the gobbling children like a Santa Claus. He wore a grey suit, a red carnation in the button hole, a dark waistcoat with a gold chain, spats and a cheerful polka dot silk tie. Greeting Ash civilly, he bowed over Tamara's hand when Ash introduced them, then sat down.

'I love this shop,' Gladishev bubbled as he enveloped one of the tiny chairs. 'But, mademoiselle, how do *you* eat here and keep your figure – '

'Glad you came,' Ash interrupted. That was not a subject to endear him to Tamara.

'I have long admired Mademoiselle Tishkova on the stage. How could I resist coming?'

'There is an expression in Kennet's country,' Tamara said. 'Politics make strange bedfellows.'

Gladishev acquired an interested gleam in his eye which Tamara, having got his full attention, coolly extinguished. 'His Imperial Highness, the Grand Duke Valery, and you, Monsieur Gladishev, have more in common than many bed-fellows, however. In fact, I suspect that were he to see you in an objective light, His Highness would admire you.'

'On what basis, may I ask?' Gladishev replied, wary once he realized how swiftly she meant to get to the point of their meeting.

Tamara surprised Ash by rattling off three occasions on which Gladishev had triumphed in the Duma by a speech or adroit backroom manoeuvring. She had been surprising Ash a lot lately, since he had joined forces with her to encourage the grand duke. Over the years with Valery she had picked up a fair knowledge of the inner workings of Russian politics.

Gladishev looked impressed. 'You are well-informed, Mademoiselle Tishkova. And you flatter me.'

'With a purpose.' Tamara smiled. 'I am going to ask a favour.'

Ash sat quietly. She was starting this meeting between Gladishev and the grand duke better than he could, employ-ing a bold strategy of softening up Gladishev, whose temper-ament was an unknown factor, instead of concentrating on her own Valery.

Gladishev said, 'If it is in my power, Mademoiselle.'

'I'm going to ask you to be accommodating.'

'I think I've had some experience in the art of compro-mise – '

'But I am asking you to compromise your pride . . .

'I'm not sure I understand.'

'The grand duke is a very proud man. Very stubborn. He might seem narrow-minded, at first. He is also *blunt*, partic-ularly with people not of his class – '

'I've had some experience with the nobility and aristocracy.' Gladishev smiled.

'Well, you'll need it all this afternoon.'

'Can you be more specific?'

Tamara gave him a look that said don't be coy. 'I can think
of only one subject we would have to discuss. *Oui?*'

Gladishev looked around as if belatedly concerned that
the nearest nannies wiping chocolate off their charges'
mouths might be Okhrana spies, and whispered back, '*Oui.*'

Tamara sat back, her job done. 'Kennet, I'm starving.'

Ash waved for a waiter. For days they had prepared Valery
for this vital meeting with Gladishev; in the next hour they
would find out if they had succeeded in making an alliance
between a rather hidebound royal and a liberal industrialist,
or if the gap between old and new, autocracy and parliamen-
tarianism was too wide to bridge.

Gap, hell, it was a chasm a century wide, with Gladishev
embracing twentieth-century progress – with the glaring
exception of labour unions – and the grand duke defending
the eighteenth century – pre-Enlightenment eighteenth . . .

Suddenly the children scrambled from their tables and
pressed to the glass as the Grand Duke Valery's great scarlet
sleigh filled the shop window, and the Arabian bays and the
Cossack escort's dark horses clattered to a halt on Morskaya
Street. A footman entered the shop.

Ash paid, over Gladishev's protests. Outside the footman
helped Tamara into the sled. Gladishev looked up from the
sidewalk and eyed it dubiously.

'Get in,' Ash said.

The millionaire politician glanced up and down the narrow curved street. 'Ought I to be seen riding in the open like
this, with . . . him?'

At that, the Grand Duke Valery poked his big, square
head over the side. He was wearing a formidable bearskin
papaha that made every hat on Morskaya Street seem

somehow inadequate. His voice matched the annoyance on his face. 'I've never skulked around Petrograd in my life and I won't start now. Get aboard or step aside.'

Gladishev's big round face flushed angry red, but Ash already had his elbow, and the footmen helped lever his bulk onto the sleigh. Ash jumped on as it lumbered into motion. The vehicle was so large that all four could share the wide seat with the high back and wraparound sides. Tamara had arranged it so she and Ash had the opposite corners, which put Gladishev and the grand duke in the middle, side-by-side. Warm air wafted up from the brazier at their feet.

Gladishev, Ash noticed, relaxed a little when he saw that few could see them from the street. 'Mademoiselle Tishkova said we should talk,' Grand Duke Valery said bluntly. 'What do you have to say?'

Gladishev looked at Tamara, who smiled back encouragement.

'Your Highness,' he said, 'the situation is desperate this winter. My warehouses are bulging with grain but I have no way to transport the grain to the cities because the Czar has let the railroads collapse. Starving people accuse my companies of holding back grain to raise the price . . . the Czar is responsible for this . . .' He glanced past Valery's stone-cold expression to Tamara, apparently gathering courage. 'The Czar must pay, Your Highness. The war is an abomination. Russia and Germany have been too long related to destroy each other now.'

Ash groaned inwardly. The notion of peace without victory was hardly the way to Valery's heart.

'How does a millionaire become a conspirator against his government?' the grand duke asked.

'We need change.'

'But the kind of change the Duma discusses might well be more than a millionaire bargains for.'

405

'Not if I'm in on it,' Gladishev replied with a hard smile, moving happily into his own element. 'There will be give and take, just as in business. All Russia will be better for it. You can't conduct modern business in a medieval state ruled by one man.'

Valery looked at Gladishev. 'I warn you, I have utterly no intentions of forming a parliamentary government.'

'What about the Duma? Surely – '

'*If* I overthrow His Majesty the Czar and form a government, the Duma may sit and advise. *I* will act.'

The sleigh followed the gracefully curving Morskaya Street under a gigantic arch that connected the two wings of the General Staff Building and at Valery's command pulled up beside the huge Alexander Column in Palace Square. Ash looked at Tamara. This was the square, site of the Bloody Sunday massacre, that Valery's supporters would have to hold while he formed a government in the Winter Palace. The grand duke looked about sombrely, taking in Gladishev last.

Gladishev eyed the grand duke. 'I am willing to compromise.'

'What?'

'You have a responsibility to lead a coup, Your Highness.'

'You dare to tell me my responsibility?'

'I dare to help.'

Valery blinked, and Ash and Tamara began to hope again.

'Then help, support me, bring your Duma colleagues to the Winter Palace. Instruct them to – '

'It's not that simple, Your Highness. There are pockets of democracy already in Russia and one is in the Duma. I cannot *instruct* fellow members to do anything. I can only try to persuade.'

'Then persuade them.'

406

'Give me some ammunition.'

'What kind of ammunition?'

'Good ministers. The men you appoint will either save Russia, or lose her forever. We have no more time for fools.'

'I will appoint good men.'

Gladishev wet his lips and glanced at Tamara. 'Your Highness, could you mention one or two names?'

'Valery . . . go on, darling, you've made good decisions.'

Valery sat up straighter. 'The Grand Duke Nicholas will take command of the army again. Brusilov second in command.'

Gladishev nodded. 'The troops seem to like the grand duke and Brusilov wins battles.'

'Skobeleff will be foreign minister.'

Skobeleff had been Ash's idea – the young career diplomat had been a vociferous supporter of the Allies before Rasputin exiled him – and Valery had bought the idea. 'Excellent,' Gladishev said. 'But have you considered who will take the vital Interior post?'

'Rodzyanko.' Valery named the current president of the Duma.

Gladishev laughed in genuine admiration. 'You'll silence your worst critic by placing him in your own government. It's a wonderful idea if he accepts the post . . . have you thought of a ministry for Kerensky?'

'A *post* for Kerensky?'

'As leader of the Trudovik Labour Party, Kerensky is one of the most powerful members of the Duma, perhaps a bit radical – '

'A *bit* radical? The scaffold will be a perfect post for Kerensky.'

Gladishev's good-humoured mouth tightened. 'Kerensky is a good man. Many people will rally to him. You can't go about hanging elected representatives as if the year were seventeen hundred and you were Peter the Great.'

The grand duke said nothing.

Gladishev pressed on. 'In order to manage a shift of power without undermining the stability of the government you are obliged to make your revolt as nonviolent as possible. You can't hang your opponents, you must follow the rule of law – '

'You sound like Commander Ash, here. All for stability. But stability and power go hand in hand. I will leave Kerensky be – if he stays out of trouble.'

Gladishev looked out at the Winter Palace. Here and there the dark red paint was scaling away, revealing not stone but weathered plaster of paris crumbling from the damp. Valery waited, his silence daring Gladishev to find fault with his plans for Kerensky. He was feeling pleasantly in charge.

Dmitri Dan timed how long it took a shovelful of snow to fall from the top of the arch, which connected the two wings of the General Staff Building, to the square below. The assassin had perched himself among the galloping bronze horses of the triumphal chariot on top of the arch, nearly eighty feet above the ground. Grand Duke Valery's red sleigh was clearly visible in the lights that spilled from the thousands of windows in the walls around the square. In the sleigh sat four people, the grand duke, beside him a large man in a civilian coat, a woman Dmitri assumed was Tamara Tishkova and Commander Ash.

Dmitri had been stalking the American at the nearby Preobrajenski Barracks, where Red Snow observers had seen Ash several days running. He had already disguised himself as a *moujik*, a faceless peasant with a snow shovel and a lunchpail looped over the handle. But instead of a poor man's pound of mouldy bread – a day's sustenance, if he were careful – Dmitri had stuffed his pail with rusty nails and fulminate of mercury, a highly unstable, powerful explosive ordinarily used to detonate dynamite because it went off on contact.

The Red Snow leader had been surprised to see the grand duke's sleigh trundle into Palace Square and stop in the middle beside the Alexander Column. Dmitri Dan had stared so hard that he almost gave himself away. *Moujiks* did not stare. *Moujiks* slumped in exhaustion or they worked. Dmitri had bent to his shovel. Ash *and* a Romanov. Two birds with one stone.

But the Cossack outriders were the usual deterrent. A skilled horseman wielding a ten-foot lance tipped by a razor-sharp twenty-inch blade commanded a dangerously large area. Dmitri Dan was afraid of very little, but when one looked at the grand duke's escort with a practical eye one saw oneself slipping and sliding over acres of snow-and-ice-covered cobblestones chased by riders who had galloped bareback on the steppes before they had learned to walk.

Shooting several in an attempt to get close enough with the bomb was futile while the others were at large. As well as lances, each had a carbine slung over his shoulder. The grand duke turned out to be less vulnerable than he appeared, when one tried to kill him.

But then, when the sleigh hadn't moved after several minutes, it occurred to Dmitri that the normally cautious grand duke had made a bad mistake. It was getting dark, and if the Romanov kept to his usual habits, when he did move he would go directly to the Imperial Yacht Club for his evening cocktail. If he did there was only one logical route – back to Morskaya Street under the arch between the wings of the General Staff Building.

Dmitri had hurried into a service entrance of the General Staff Building, waved his shovel at the guards and shuffled to a back staircase, up which he raced to the roof. Seeing the sleigh still in place, he began shovelling snow over the edge, as other *moujiks* were doing on the palace and barracks roofs, timing the drop, calculating by how much to lead the sleigh when it moved within range of his bomb.

When Gladishev spoke again he had apparently decided to drop the subject of how the grand duke would handle Duma member and Labour Party leader Kerensky.

'If I were to support you I would need your word that autocracy would not last forever – a solemn promise that you will bring Russia's government more into line with modern practices – '

'I've made it clear to Commander Ash that my government will appear more benign than the present government so that his nation may be persuaded to enter the war. But I will tell you, Monsieur Duma Member, that my autocracy, as you call it, will last as long as Russia needs it.'

'The people who support your coup will reserve the right to review that need – '

'*Russia* is my concern, and Russia has always fared best under a strong Czar. Peter, Catherine, the Alexanders Two and Three. Strong Czars made the power you see here.' His big hand swept the circle of buildings that ringed Palace Square. The great semicircle of the General Staff Building – divided by the arch – the Imperial Archives and the barracks of the Preobrajenski Regiment loomed on the south and east sides. The gigantic yellow Admiralty blocked the west. North, the dark red Winter Palace hid all but a sliver of the snow-covered Neva, darkened to mauve as the sun settled earthward through a thickening scrim of cirrus cloud.

'Power forged by strong Czars, the power to build all this from nothing in a cold, stinking swamp – '

'Illusion, a hollow shell,' Gladishev broke in.

'*Illusion?* A thousand rooms in that palace alone are packed with Russia's wealth and her prizes of war. We are not like ordinary nations that have to scramble around the

410

world establishing distant, undefendable empires. We have multiplied our empire. In only a hundred years the Black Sea steppes, the Polish provinces, the Ukraine, the Crimea, Transcaucasia, Bessarabia, Finland, Amur . . . the list is endless.'

'What we see here, this is not true power,' Gladishev insisted. 'This is only, forgive me, the cream skimmed from an enormous vat of milk.'

'Then where is the power?'

Gladishev pointed east. 'Out there. The power in Russia is numbers. The peasants in their numbers have power, there are too many Russian peasants for one man to feed and clothe and control. All those victories? Too many borders to defend. We've won everything, you say, but we can't *hold* it, administer it without a modern government.'

Valery pointed at the Preobrajenski Barracks. 'The autocrat is not alone, just because he doesn't have a so-called modern government. The Czar-autocrat's army protects his borders. The Life Guards protect the Czar. His Cossacks maintain order among the peasants. And the Czar's police control the cities – '

'Not anymore.' Gladishev shook his head. 'And we've lost two armies to the Germans. When will the third walk home? As for your Life Guards? Conscripts and officers dragged up from the lower ranks. The old aristocratic corps died in nineteen fourteen. Even the Cossacks have fallen before the Germans.'

'But a strong Czar can repair the damage,' Valery protested.

Gladishev shook his head. 'Look at those windows.'

Thousands upon thousands of windows were beginning to glow yellow as the dusk deepened, to shine in the endless sweep of the General Staff Building, the Archives and the Admiralty. 'Behind each window a dozen clerks – little men in shabby coats who write reports all day long about places they'll never see, people they'll never know, ships they'll never sail.'

'You agreed my selection of ministers was progressive,' Valery said.

'It requires more than a few talented ministers. One-man rule has smothered the natural growth of *efficient* bureaucracy, which must be nurtured by good ministers *and* representatives elected by the very people who will be administered.'

He pointed east again. 'No one knows what's going on out there. What is Russia doing? What does Russia need? The first the Czar knew that Russia hadn't a modern navy was when the Japanese sent his Imperial Fleet to the bottom of the Tsushima Straits. The first the Czar knows that the peasants in some region are displeased is when they burn our estates. The first the Czar-autocrat knew his army had no rifles was when the Germans slaughtered us in Poland. The first the Czar knew our railroads were decrepit was when we tried to feed our soldiers and cities at the same time. You remember, Your Highness, before the war when a clerk lost a single salary voucher and schoolteachers in some eastern province nobody had ever heard of starved to death?'

Valery shouted angrily at the coachman and the sleigh lurched into motion, swung in a broad circle and headed back toward the arch in the General Staff Building. Ash elbowed Gladishev. Last chance. Gladishev didn't need much encouraging. He tapped the grand duke's sleeve, ignored Valery's glare and said, 'Look at that window. It could be any of a hundred. If God came down to the province that civil servant administers and turned every man, woman and child to pillars of salt, the first the Czar's Imperial Bureaucracy would know would be when the price of salt fell in neighbouring provinces. *One man can't rule Russia.*'

Valery shook him off. 'One man will try.'

'He'll try alone. Stop the sleigh, damn you.'

'Wait,' Ash said.

Gladishev jumped down, caught his balance and stalked off.

'Stop the sleigh,' Tamara said. *'Stop* it.'

Ash jumped after Gladishev. 'Wait. Monsieur Gladishev . . .' He looked back. Tamara had persuaded Valery to stop just short of the General Building arch. He caught up with Gladishev.

'The war is killing Russia. Help me get the Czar out and America in and we'll end the damned thing in a year. The grand duke is man enough to be beholden to you. Make your peace now. Work out the details later.'

'Details? He wants to be Czar of all the Russias, just like the one we've got.'

In disgust, Ash looked skyward . . . and caught motion from the corner of his eye, focused on it and saw a figure lean out from the bronze horses on top of the arch. A man gripping one of the bronze hoofs and swinging something from his free hand, eighty feet above the sleigh where the grand duke sat arguing with Tamara –

'Oh, my God . . .'

413

37

Ash reached under his boat cloak. But the distance was too much for the short-barrelled Luger. Almost in despair he snapped two shots over the ears of the white Arabians . . .

'Valery you are being imposs – '

The sleigh jerked forward, hurling her back against the seat. She heard two sharp cracks, a heavy boom, something rattled against the back of the sleigh. A horse screamed. She jumped up to look about. A Cossack was down and his screaming animal lay kicking on its side, disembowelled by shrapnel. The other horsemen were shooting their rifles up at the arch. She saw Ash running, so remarkably small and vulnerable on foot. Valery yanked her to the seat and threw his body over hers. More shots. The sleigh stopped inside the archway. The horse's screaming echoed on the walls, and the rage she felt for the kind of human being who could do that to a horse was directed at Gladishev . . . how could he believe that a Duma could stop the mindless violence in the Russian soul? Horseshoes rang on the cobblestones. From underneath Valery she caught a glimpse of the Cossacks blocking the ends of the archway. The shooting died down. A final sharp pistol crack and the horse stopped screaming.

Valery got up cautiously.

Ash dragged Gladishev into the passage and helped him up to the sleigh. He had a gun in his hand. His eyes met Tamara's.

'Are you all right?' she asked, choking off the word *darling*.

414

'Yes . . . you?' His eyes went to the mouth of the passage as the lieutenant of the guard clattered in; his men stayed in the square, aiming their rifles at the arch, seeking out the bombers.

'How is the rider?' Valery asked.

'The man is wounded, the horse dead, Your Highness.'

The Cossack lieutenant, Valery and Ash quickly agreed to make a run for the Yacht Club across Nevsky Prospect on Morskaya Street while the outriders covered the top of the arch with their rifles. Several raced through the passage to take up position in front of the sleigh. The coachman called out and the Arabians burst from the passage. Tamara looked up, spine tingling in anticipation of the next attack.

They made it safely to the Nevsky, where they picked up a police escort. Gladishev gripped Valery's arm. 'This *proves* things have gone too far, Your Highness. I will support you . . . for stability . . .'

Valery took his hand. 'For Russia.'

Tamara looked at Valery's determined face and believed that Czarism could still work, with a *real* Czar.

Ash decided not to spoil the new friendship by suggesting that the bomb was probably Red Snow's, and meant for him. Ironic, that an attempt on his life had apparently ended in making an alliance . . . never mind how temporary . . . between the two forces he so badly needed to bring off his mission . . .

Okhrana detectives slipped into the office in the Litovsky Prison to report to the cold-eyed security officer they knew only as Captain Moskolenko.

'Commander Ash was seen entering the home of the ballerina Tishkova. A short time later His Royal Highness the Grand Duke Valery arrived, having crossed the ice in his sleigh. In ten minutes, the Grand Duke Valery Romanov and Commander Ash came out together and rode across the river. They entered the Imperial Yacht Club at five o'clock and stayed for many hours.' . . . 'Heinrich Ballin, a waiter at the Imperial Yacht Club, was questioned. Ballin reported that Commander Ash and the Grand Duke Valery sat by a fire talking for hours and drinking little.' . . . 'It is reported by the assistant to the Imperial Yacht Club secretary that Commander Ash has been given a temporary membership in the club at the request of the Grand Duke Valery.' . . . 'Commander Ash was observed entering the British Embassy at noon. He reappeared half an hour later and lunched . . .'

Von Basel received their reports with brusque ill humour; the Kaiser's new plan to seize the Czar himself put the scheme to rescue Nicholas II in an entirely new light, and von Basel himself in a much more demanding role. It put him in the difficult position of having to keep track of what Ash was doing, partly to make sure he did not pull off any peculiar moves, and partly to keep him from blundering into trouble. This was, after all, and despite its many problems, still Russia, and Russia's rulers had never taken kindly to revolt, nor, if one looked at history, had they been all that susceptible to it.

So it was a very anxious von Basel who received the detectives' reports.

'Commander Ash was seen entering the American Embassy. He left the premises some time later with the American ambassador's daughter, Catherine Hazzard, and took her by hired carriage to Berrin's in Morsakaya Street, where she ate sponge cake and ice cream and Commander Ash smoked cigarettes and drank coffee. His cup was obtained in the kitchen. The contents revealed no spirits added, but the ashtray contained many cigarette butts and it was the opinion of the observer that Commander Ash was anxious.' . . . 'Our man inside the American Embassy reports that shortly after Ash was there the British King's

Messenger arrived with messages for Ambassador Hazzard and took messages for London in return. Ash had entered with a small despatch case which he was not in possession of when he left with the ambassador's daughter.' . . . 'Commander Ash and Captain Putilov of the Ismailovsky Guard went ice yachting at the River Yacht Club on Krestovsky Island. Police Detective Borisov, who was captain of the Third District ice-yachting team before the war, commandeered a second yacht to follow Ash and Putilov. Commander Ash proved elusive and eventually drew the pursuing boat into a lead – '

'A lead?'

'A break in the pack ice, Captain Moskolenko, in this case a very narrow one between high walls of pack ice into which Police Detective Borisov crashed his commandeered yacht. The steward of the River Yacht Club expressed – '

'Dismissed.'

'. . . Captain Sirotkin of the Preobrajenski Guard, the Grand Duke and Commander Ash went shooting on the estate of Baroness Balmont. When it snowed they inspected a new ice yacht on the neighbouring estate of Baron Leskinen and – No, Captain Moskolenko, the Italian was in Moscow.' . . . 'Heinrich Ballin, employed as a waiter at the Imperial Yacht Club, reports that Ash and the Grand Duke Valery held a long discussion with Captain Putilov of the Ismailovsky Guard Regiment – '

'Bring this Heinrich Ballin.' . . .

Von Basel proceeded to extract from the frightened old man everything he had overheard between Ash, the grand duke, Captain Putilov, Captain Sirotkin of the Preobrajenski Guard and several other grand dukes with whom Valery was known to be close. It wasn't much, but every bit helped in trying to keep even with what Ash was up to.

Then there was a report that Ash had hidden a truckload

of dynamite outside the city, which the Okhrana explosive expert von Basel had sent to investigate reported was set to explode if disturbed. Von Basel had the truck under observation.

Then more reports. A bombing . . . 'Ash and Mademoiselle Tishkova were joined by Duma member Sergei Gladishev at three o'clock at Berrin's . . .' *Gladishev*. Ash was getting close. The American and the grand duke were making the right contacts, building an alliance with the Duma, the Life Guards, the police through himself, and maybe Kirichenko. Soon, now . . . then suddenly a worri-some mystery. A very nervous detective who covered the railway stations reported. Von Basel could tell from his fear alone that it was bad news . . .

'Commander Ash was observed embarking from the Baltic Station. He previously purchased a train ticket for Reval. This information was sent by telegraph to Reval. When the train arrived, however, detectives waiting for Commander Ash apparently lost sight of him in the crowds of passengers – '

'For how long?'

'That was last night.' The detective squirmed. 'Unfortunately, Captain Moskolenko, sir, Commander Ash has not been resighted as yet.'

'Get *out.*'

'The detectives in Reval are being severely reprimanded.'

'Out.' Von Basel was so angry he almost said *raus*.

Why did Ash go to Reval? *Apparently lost sight of him?* Ash allowed himself to be watched. Why did he suddenly change his mind in Reval? What was in Reval?

But before he had time to put more thought to the problem, an immediate and potentially deadly conundrum took its place. As a precaution, to protect the grand ducal conspiracy, von Basel had put surveillance on the growing number of conspirators themselves, among them Lord

Exeter, the Grand Duke Valery, Tishkova, Captain Sirotkin and Captain Putilov. This last, the captain in the Ismailovsky Life Guard Regiment, was suddenly in serious trouble, trouble which threatened the entire conspiracy.

Another branch of the Okhrana which specialized in army loyalty had learned that Captain Putilov was persuading his officers to join in an as yet unnamed grand ducal palace coup. The Okhrana was debating whether to keep listening for more specific information concerning the identity of the grand duke in question or to arrest Captain Putilov and wring it out of him by interrogation. General Globatachev, chief of the Okhrana, was himself taking charge of the inquiry, which meant, von Basel feared, that Captain Putilov would be spilling his guts in damned short order, naming the Grand Duke Valery and Commander Kenneth Ash.

38

The ancient Baltic harbour of Reval, a town of narrow cobblestone streets and medieval houses, had been an important Russian port before the German navy sealed the Gulf of Finland. It was two hundred miles west of Petrograd, near the mouth of the gulf. The journey across Estonia had taken Ash thirteen hours crammed into a freezing train compartment with half a dozen officers of the Czar's Motor Division who were trying to get back to the front's volatile northern sector.

On arrival Ash had shaken off von Basel's detectives and hid the rest of the night on a cot in the hall of a second-class hotel. In the morning he set out for the harbour, where he located the Royal Navy submarine base – and the depot ship *Dwina,* moored to a guarded, fenced pier.

Half a dozen smallish E-class British submarines nuzzled around the depot ship, which housed fuel, crew quarters, supplies and repair facilities. Thick coats of glistening ice softened the harsh, spiky lines of hulls and conning towers. The crews were making repairs in the sunshine – welding and beating steel with hammers. The clanging echoed to the foot of the pier, where the guards stopped Ash and made him wait until Rodney Skelton was located. He came jauntily into the guardhouse half an hour later.

'Yes, that's him, sergeant. He's harmless. How are you, Kenneth?'

'Hope I'm not interrupting anything,' Ash said, indicating Skelton's greasy jumper and trousers.

'Just a major overhaul.'

They walked out on the pier and Skelton proudly pointed out his boat. 'Nasty little brute, isn't she?'

The submarine had a massive dent in its conning tower, as if something enormous and angry had punched it.

'What'd you do, surface under the *Dwina?*'

'Very amusing, Commander. I understand it's hell in Petrograd since the Czar banned the tango.'

'Rodney, what would you say if I told you you owed me your life for that time in India?'

To Ash's surprise, Skelton didn't bridle. To the contrary . . . he suddenly looked exhausted. 'This bloody war . . . I feel different about a lot of things. Just between you and me, I guess the Indians would have slit our throats along with those poor horses . . . you were right.' He looked up at Ash, openly for a second, before his feisty grin ended the confession. 'Should I thank you?'

'No . . . but I do want a favour . . .'

Back in Petrograd, Ash telephoned Captain Putilov from the Baltic Railroad Station and walked across the Obvodny Canal to the Life Guard Ismailovsky barracks on Ismailovsky Prospect. Petrograd tram drivers had called a one-day strike, so the sidewalks were jammed with pedestrians.

Putilov was waiting, as planned, outside the barrack walls. Ash liked him. Putilov affected the lazy, bored air of a typical aristocrat officer, but it was a sham, which the record and his character bore out. Wounded in Poland, and again the previous summer taking Stanislau during Brusilov's offensive, Putilov had refused medical retirement and, against his will, took his present post in Petrograd to recuperate sufficiently to be allowed back at the Front.

Unlike others Ash and the grand duke had tried to recruit, who were afraid to take the risk, Putilov's reservations had derived from his oath of fealty to the Czar. He recognized the need to act to save Russia, but breaking his word was for him a deadly serious matter of honour.

Once he had finally come around, however, he had totally embraced the Grand Duke Valery's cause. Valery, who was unnervingly straightforward himself, had warned Putilov twice to be more discreet, and had finally confessed to Ash that he couldn't risk meeting Putilov anymore. Ash had agreed to make the next contact to assess what support they could expect from the units under Putilov's command.

He waited now outside the main gates of the Ismailovsky barracks looking for all the world like a czar's officer preparing to review troops in full sight of the entire general staff.

Ash steered him quickly into the crowds, scanning faces as he did. Almost immediately he was glad he had taken the precaution of putting on the fur hat and greatcoat he had worn in Reval to elude von Basel's men. The US Navy service cap and boat cloak were too damned distinctive.

'You're quiet this afternoon, Commander,' Putilov remarked after they had gone several blocks.

'We're being followed. Don't – '

But the Russian aristocrat was already looking around like a tourist from Moscow. Among the throngs of pedestrians Ash had spotted the long raincoat and galoshes that usually marked the Okhrana detectives. What worried him was that the man didn't seem to be making much of an effort to stay out of sight. He spotted a second and then a third, strolling purposefully after them. They looked less like they were following than pursuing. As if preparing to make an arrest.

Ash and Putilov were walking north, heading in the direction of the Astoria Hotel about a mile ahead. Ash looked for a place to hide. Immediately ahead was the Fontanka River. A block to the right, the Technological Institute.

'Closed today because of the strike,' Putilov replied calmly when Ash suggested it. He was a compact man in his forties, with an open, innocent face; his wounds had left him pale, with a tremor in his cheek which his smile tended to obscure. 'Are you sure we're being followed?'

'Damned sure,' Ash said. 'And they're closing up.' He glanced over his shoulder. Half a block back the detectives were moving swiftly through the crowds, shoving people out of their way. Suddenly a long black automobile shot from behind a line of wagons, screeched in a tight turn over the tram tracks and slid against the kerb beside Ash and Captain Putilov.

'Don't run,' Ash said. 'It'll only make them ask why.'

'I won't,' Putilov replied, squaring his shoulders.

But instead of police officers boiling out of the town car to arrest them, the window opened in the driver's compartment and Count Philip von Basel snapped, 'Get in, they're on to you.'

Ash yanked open the rear door, shoved a confused Putilov inside and jumped in after him. The car roared from the kerb followed by the Okhrana men on foot, pushing people out of their way until one pulled a gun, fired it in the air, which cleared a path as people dived for cover, then fired at the car.

Von Basel wrenched the large vehicle onto the narrow street beside the Fontanka, raced along it for several blocks, turned north, skidding and screeching the tyres, shot over an Obvodny Canal bridge and started past the Baltic Station. The car hit an ice slick in the station square, slid out of control, spun in a full circle and slammed sideways into a tram-wire pole. The engine shuddered, coughed. Von Basel tried to coax it back to life as uniformed police officers

423

came running from the station. It abruptly revved up again and he drove through them, past the station and deep into the Narva District.

'Who is this man?' Captain Putilov demanded.

'A friend, with police connections. It seems the Okhrana had a spy in your barracks.'

The car went down lanes barely wider than it was, scattering peddlers and women lined up outside bakeries and paraffin shops.

Von Basel turned abruptly into a noisome alley and got out. 'Quickly, before the district police find it.'

They hurried down the grimmest streets Ash had seen in Petrograd, or in any other city for that matter. Drunks filled the gutters and vacant-eyed children huddled together for warmth. The sky appeared a dirty slit of grey between the leaning tenements.

Von Basel stopped now in a doorway, motioned them both through, checked the street and bolted the door. He hurried down a half flight of stairs, and they emerged in a cavelike cellar with a heavy, vaulted ceiling blackened by smoke and mottled where pieces of plaster had broken off. Thin partitions formed cubbyholes with plank beds. There was one square window, high up in the wall, covered with ice.

'What is this?' asked Putilov.

'Home for the *boysaki*,' von Basel told him. 'The barefoot. Dock workers, when the port isn't iced in. The dregs.'

'What – '

'This is for you,' von Basel interrupted, handing Captain Putilov a sheet of paper he pulled from his coat. Puzzled, Ash watched an equally puzzled Putilov move closer to the smoking oil lamp. He read a few lines. 'What is this about Grand Duke Dmitri Pav – '

Von Basel had followed. A dagger appeared in his left hand. He slid it quickly in and out of Putilov's back.

'*What?*' Ash couldn't believe his eyes as the Russian's knees folded and his body drifted quietly to the floor.

'Don't touch that paper.'

The paper was clutched in Putilov's stiffening fingers. Ash reached for it. Von Basel whipped his sword out of his stick and touched the point to Ash's neck. 'Don't,' he repeated. 'The Okhrana was going to pick him up. When they made him talk it would have ruined everything for us.' Von Basel sheathed the thin sliver of whippy steel. 'You must protect yourself. Go immediately to the Astoria. Go to the bar and have drinks with people. Stay in view. If the police question you, insist you walked from the Baltic Station to the Astoria and talked to no one. Get rid of that coat and hat, and stick by your story. They can't be sure what they saw in the crowds. If they're stubborn, go to your embassy.'

'What's on that paper?'

'I had a forger construct a simple note from Captain Putilov to the Grand Duke Dmitri Pavlovitch informing His Royal Highness that he has changed his mind about supporting Grand Duke Dmitri's coup.'

'*Whose* coup?'

'Some of the Grand Duke Dmitri Pavlovitch's cousins tried to persuade him to lead a coup. They've gone so far as to approach regiment commanders, as you have. The grand duke, I understand, has refused to lay hands on the Czar – perhaps because he hasn't my help and yours,' von Basel added with a thin smile, 'to remove His Majesty – but the Okhrana is already onto the plot. You would do well to pray that this little charade convinces the investigators that Putilov was recruiting conspirators for Grand Duke Dmitri and not your Valery. Let the police presume he wasn't trusted.'

'You didn't have to kill the man – '

'It was him or you, Ash. And I need you alive. They

425

would have forced a confession, he'd have named you . . . as well as the Grand Duke Valery. *And* your friend Tishkova.'

Ash stared at Putilov's body. He had no answer to that last.

Von Basel wiped his dagger on the dead captain's trousers and slipped it back into his coat. He tapped Ash's arm with his walking stick. 'Get to the Astoria.' When Ash didn't move quickly enough for him, he added, 'Do you think the Okhrana would treat her any more kindly in their cells just because she happens to be a beautiful woman?'

Ash started for the stairs.

'By the way, Commander Ash . . .'

As Ash turned, von Basel thought how seriously Ash took death. It put the American at a disadvantage . . .

'What did you do in Reval?'

'The grand duke wanted me to meet a general from the Northern Sector. Reval was a convenient halfway point . . .'

What Ash had hoped would sound like a plausible reason, masking his real purpose in Reval, was to give von Basel considerable pause about Grand Duke Valery. At first he puzzled over Ash's reply; the American had answered a little too quickly for a man as upset as he had appeared, and the stated reason for going to Reval had a somewhat glib ring . . . *but* if it were true, von Basel began to worry as he negotiated the dark streets of the Narva District, were it true that the Grand Duke Valery was including Russia's line commanders in his conspiracy, it pointed up a serious flaw in the Kaiser's scheme to win the war and take back control of Germany.

Grand Duke Valery would make a good Czar. Too good a Czar.

Von Basel had already hinted at the possibility in Berlin. Might the grand duke not rally Russia to a new war effort? The Kaiser had considered it unlikely that a usurper could replace a rightful heir without disrupting the already

426

faltering nation. Perhaps, von Basel had agreed reluctantly
. . . but at the moment Valery Romanov seemed to be conducting the grand ducal conspiracy in a step-by-step manner
that was a little frightening in its purposefulness. Valery was
becoming a threat . . .

Clinging to the snow in a thin wood a quarter of a mile from
the Tsarskoye Selo line, Ash hid with the SR fighting squad
leader Kirichenko from a mounted detachment of the First
Railway Battalion that trotted slowly by, patrolling the tracks.
The rails rode an embankment several feet higher than the
snow-covered flatlands between Petrograd and the Czar's
village, silhouetting horse soldiers like paper cutouts in a
shadow box.

Kirichenko confirmed the time of their passage on a tin
pocket watch. 'Snow,' he said, 'is our friend and our enemy.
When it falls it covers our mines. When it stops falling, we
leave tracks.'

Ash had already seen his men retreat from the embankment when the patrol was due, sweeping out their footprints
with birch branches. He looked at the sky, lowering for
night. 'Snow in the morning?'

Tomorrow the Grand Duke Valery was to seize the Winter
Palace. Kirichenko's lieutenants had a second group of sab-
oteurs working ten miles south of Tsarskoye Selo, mining
tracks and telegraph wires just as they were doing here. 'Do
you think it will snow?' Ash repeated. Not that they could
postpone for the weather. Czar Nicholas was leaving in two
days for Mogilev.

Kirichenko shrugged, but one of his constant bodyguards
who understood a little English and was apparently a countryman nodded. 'Yes, snow.'

At the *Stavka*, the Czar would be inviolable. It was now or
never.

'Make it a blizzard,' Kirichenko said grimly.

427

The bodyguard looked north in the direction of the Gulf of Finland, from where the heaviest snow came. 'Maybe.'

'It will still be fairly dark at nine when you set the charges,' Ash pointed out. Slightly longer days hinted at spring, which was due by the calendar in little more than a month, though unheralded by either rising temperatures or lessening snow. All Ash could see from their hiding place in the wood was snow, ice and more snow broken only by the stubby telegraph poles, their almost invisible strands of black wire and a fence beside the rails.

Kirichenko shook his head. 'But I can't arm the mines until daybreak. We don't want an early train setting off mines before your grand duke is sufficiently awake to receive his friends in the Winter Palace.'

'He's not quite as dull as you think, Kirichenko.'

Kirichenko smiled, obviously not convinced.

He was wrong, thought Ash. Only this afternoon Valery had warned him that they ought to guard Petrograd's main telegraph offices in case revolutionaries considered taking advantage of temporary chaos to send their own messages across Russia and Europe.

'How will you know if my explosions are successful tomorrow morning?' Kirichenko asked when Ash prepared to return to the city.

'I'll know the minute you've cut the line,' Ash told him, though he would not know at the moment Valery headed for the palace whether the secondary explosions had the hoped-for effect of holding off the Czar's regiments long enough for Valery to seize control.

Aivazovsky's *The Ninth Wave,* a gigantic seascape portraying the most convincing shipwreck Ash had ever seen on canvas, loomed ominously over the smoking room in the palatial Imperial Yacht Club where several hours later Ash met to confirm final details with the Grand Duke Valery

428

and the captains of the Guards' regiments they had rallied to the support of Valery's palace coup; all the painting showed of the sinking vessel were its mastheads disappearing into an angry sea and a single boat of survivors about to capsize on a broken spar.

Ash and the grand duke sat in armchairs beneath the painting. Facing them was a third chair, and in the centre, a low table with vodka and caviar on a gold tray. It was as close, Ash thought, as he at least would ever come to holding court, and it was a heady few hours. In the next room a covey of grand dukes, not in the plot, glared over the tops of their cards as their rounds of quinze went on and on. Through another door Ash could glimpse Ambassadors Buchanan and Paléologue hunched together like a pair of owls, pretending interest in their own talk while, it was obvious from their expressions, they would cheerfully have sold their own children to Afghan slavers to hear what passed between Ash and Valery and the men who one by one joined them in the smoking room, shared a vodka and left.

In fact, had they been able, they would have heard little more than a series of toasts. '*Boje Tsaria Khranee,*' Captain Sirotkin said to Valery as he raised his glass, and Valery repeated, 'God save the Czar.' In Sirotkin's case it meant his Preobrajenski units were ready to seize Palace Square and storm the main gates if the light palace guard proved troublesome.

An artillery officer, Kustodiev, came next. '*Boje Tsaria Khranee.*' He had charge of the main guns in the Peter and Paul, which commanded the palace across the river, and had pledged to keep them silent in the event that the Czar got a message past the blown lines to fire on the Winter Palace.

'*Boje Tsaria Khranee!*' Sergei Gladishev said, his face wreathed in nervous smiles. Forty men of the Duma, mostly

Kadets, had agreed to follow him into the palace provided the square was in Valery's control. Another twenty reactionaries had given Valery himself their pledge.

Captain Sokolov of the Semonovsky Regiment, whose men would surround several police stations after von Basel had manoeuvred most of the detectives away from the area; half a dozen grand dukes who had promised to stand by Valery when he announced his new government; the Guard Cossacks lieutenant who would protect the main telegraph offices . . . all filed casually into the club, had their drink with Valery and wandered back into the night. The only ones missing were von Basel, who would be entirely at home here if Germany and Russia weren't at war, and Kirichenko, whose appearance might raise a few grand ducal eyebrows even if they didn't realize his line of work.

Ash kept deliberately moving his glass out of reach; nervous and keyed up, he had to stop himself from tossing back the vodka out of need for something to do with his hands. One of the grand dukes who had promised to stand beside Valery when he announced the coup jarred Ash by replying to Valery's *'Boje Tsana Khranee'* with *'Bye Jidoff.'*

Beat the Jews, the traditional Russian reply to the old drinking salute, God Save the Czar. People said it automatically, but in 'Beat the Jews' festered the canker of middle-European anti-Semitism, a virulent bigotry that made a lie of Europe's grandeur and history and culture. If this ancient civilization were so grand, so rich and refined, why did otherwise normal people sink to the level of hating the Jews?

Ash's father had fought in the Civil War against slavery. And Ash's mentor, Admiral Mahon, had reduced anti-Semitism to its ultimate Christian absurdity – 'That Jesus Christ was a Jew covers the issue of His race for me.' So how had Kenneth Ash ended up on the edge of it, politely lifting his glass as Valery and his troglodyte cousins traded

'Bye Jidoffs' the night before they seized the throne of Imperial Russia?

Relieved when the last conspirator had paid his respects and Valery nodded to say they had stayed long enough, Ash reminded himself that removing the Czar to end the war was *still* the most important goal . . . Yet it was strange how he could never seem to escape from the shadow smiles of diplomatic compromise.

A waiter approached with a message. A lady in the foyer insisted on speaking to Ash. Ash and the Grand Duke exchanged glances. Sedovina, he thought. Some hitch in Kirichenko's attack on the railroad. 'I'll meet you at Tamara's, Your Highness.'

He strolled casually from the smoking room, but broke into a run when he was beyond sight of the curious ambassadors and grand ducal quinze players. It was not Sedovina in the foyer, however, but a frightened Catherine Hazzard.

'Catherine. Are you all right?'

Her father had bought her a Russian fur. The dark hood framed her blond hair and blue eyes like a cameo and it occurred fleetingly to Ash that if Ambassador Hazzard stayed much longer at his post he'd likely end up with a Petrograd aristocrat for a son-in-law.

'I'm so glad I found you.'

'What's wrong?'

'A man named Harold Banks arrived from Washington.'

Ash felt his heart skip. 'I don't understand,' he said carefully.

'He got very angry when my father couldn't find you. You weren't at your hotel and Chevalier Roland said he hadn't seen you in days. Mr Banks ordered Captain Hamilton's marines to search the city. I'm afraid they'll hurt you.'

'Why?'

431

'Because he told them to bring you in no matter what.'

'But do you know why?'

To Ash's surprise, Catherine said, 'Yes. Mr Banks cabled Washington as soon as he arrived, to confirm his orders. President Wilson told him to make you stop what you're doing.'

39

'How'd you know to find me here?'

'Remember when you took me to lunch at Berrin's. You told me the Grand Duke Valery had put you up for temporary membership, but not to tell my father because he might feel bad he wasn't invited.'

Ash nodded vaguely, his mind in turmoil. 'How do you know that President Wilson cabled Mr Banks to stop me?'

'I know all the boys in the cipher room,' she replied with a hint of a smile.

Ash laughed in spite of everything. 'I'll bet you do.'

'I *knew* Mr Banks was coming about you. I just *knew*. What are you doing, Commander? My poor father hasn't a clue.'

'Is Banks at the embassy?'

'No. He went to the Europa.'

'Come on.' Ash hurried the short distance to the Europa, with Catherine on his arm. She was good cover; they dodged a marine patrol on the crowded Nevsky Prospect.

Harold Banks was in his room, in shirtsleeves, having a drink. Relief and annoyance crossed his face when he saw Ash. He asked Catherine, 'What are you doing here, little lady?'

'She found me for you,' Ash said, glad that Banks was alone.

'Just in time, Commander. Five more minutes and I was going to blow the whistle on you.'

'I think we'd better talk, sir.'

Banks glanced at Catherine. She had already seated herself on the bed and had fixed her big eyes on the troubled men like a lively cat. 'Miss Hazzard, please tell your father that we have located Commander Ash and Captain Hamilton's marines can return to the embassy.'

Catherine reached for the telephone.

Banks glanced at Ash. Ash said, 'Maybe you'd better report personally, Catherine?' She got up reluctantly and asked Ash to take her down to the lobby. As he helped her into a *rissak* sleigh, she asked, 'Did I do right?'

'As far as I'm concerned you did.' He bent to kiss her cheek; she turned her mouth to his, then informed him archly that his moustache tickled.

Upstairs, Harold Banks said, 'The boss wants a democracy.'

'A democracy? In Russia?'

'We know what you're up to and he wants a democracy. How the hell you got yourself mixed up with another autocrat – '

'But that's crazy. I'm getting the Czar out, like I was told to; and I'm leaving behind a stable government that'll keep on fighting the Germans.'

'The President wants a democratic ally to convince Congress to declare war. He won't support another autocrat.'

Ash shook his head in frustration. 'What he'll get is Russia collapsing – and with her the whole damned Eastern Front – just in time to strand the first hundred-thousand American troops in France. Green recruits against reinforced, battle-hardened Germans. It'll be a massacre.'

Banks stood up, unfolding his lanky frame and running a hand through his white hair. 'Admiral Innes said to remind you of the difference between an order and a command. This is a command, Ash. No discretion. Just obey it.'

In the silence that followed, Ash asked quietly, 'May I ask, sir, how the President caught wind of all this?'

Banks shrugged. 'Not that it matters, but a British agent who was trying to get President Wilson to go along with one of their anti-German propaganda schemes softened him up with some inside information.'

Details, Ash thought angrily, likely supplied to British Secret Service by Lord Exeter. He knew he shouldn't –

'Now listen to me,' Banks said firmly. 'You've got two hours to convince the Grand Duke to pledge a democratic government or I blow the whistle on your coup.'

'But, sir –'

'It's a command, Ash. Get that pledge. Or stop him.'

'I absolutely refuse,' Valery was saying before Ash could get the new terms out of his mouth.

'*Kennet*,' Tamara put in, 'you are out of your mind?'

'Well, damn it, my government tells me that it will be impossible for the United States to recognize a new government that isn't at least pledged to a democratic government. What the hell more can I say . . .?'

Valery and Tamara were sitting side by side in Tamara's solarium; snow hissed against the windows, yet between gusts of the hard, frozen pellets the lights of the Winter Palace could be seen across the Neva.

The grand duke stretched to his full height and glared down at Ash. 'Do you really think that I would sacrifice my family's three-hundred-year dynasty as the Czars of all the Russias for recognition by *America?*' He pointed across the river. 'Catherine the Great sat six thousand nobles for dinner in that palace when you people were still living in log huts.'

Tamara stood beside him and took his enormous arm in her tiny hands. 'Kennet, what can you be thinking; you must be mistaken . . .'

What Ash was thinking was that all his compromises and small evasions were coming home to roost. Banks had knocked the props out from under him, and as he fell everything he'd done looked to be crashing down . . . 'Both ends against the middle' had been a plausible-sounding phrase to mask the implausibility of joining the radical Kirichenko with the reactionary Grand Duke Valery in an effort which Ash alone, it seemed now, thought would serve democracy, his country . . . but it *would,* damn it, if only temporarily . . .

'Kennet Karlovich?'

Ash looked at Valery. The grand duke had never addressed him by his patronymic before. Only as 'Commander.'

'You people of the west do not understand us. You think Russians are barbarians. Incapable of your high accomplishments in government and economics. We are not as highly developed in some skills as you, but we are not barbarians. We are, actually, rather simple people, with deep faith and much bravery.'

'That's absolutely true – '

'Kennet Karlovich, I ask you, could England and France have stood this long were it not for Russian bravery?'

'No, Germany would have taken Paris long ago.'

'And pushed the British Expeditionary Army into the sea . . . Kennet Karlovich, this is my promise to you – Russia will fight until Germany surrenders.'

Ash looked away.

'And the bomb throwers?' Valery asked. 'The assassins? No, Kennet. The Social Revolutionaries and the Bolsheviks would slice through a democratic parliament like my *pallash* through flesh. They are already organized. The labour unions would seize the railroads and the cities. Soviets, workers' councils, would strangle your democracy. Kennet, I don't want to fight you, but I will.'

'*Why?*' Tamara asked.

'He's been ordered to stop us. Can't you see it in his face?'

Tamara looked at Ash. 'No. No, Kennet, you wouldn't . . . Valery, would you leave us a moment?'

The grand duke walked out of the solarium. Ash stared at the Winter Palace. For a while he and Tamara just stood there in silence. Then he said to her, 'Look . . .'

Valery's Cossacks were spreading out in front of the house. Ash nodded at the side window. The lancers were surrounding the house. 'He doesn't trust me, it seems.'

'Should he?' she asked coldly.

Ash walked to the side window and stretched to see toward the back of the house. The flaw in the Cossacks' cordon was the kitchen yard . . . the riders who guarded the back door, which led into the maze of kitchen gardens from a number of mansions, would be forced to dismount in the confined space. From there it was less than ten minutes on foot to the Finland Station, where he could stop the grand duke with a single telephone call.

'*Should* he?'

Admiral Innes's order, actually a command, had activated a sense of the whole of Ash's eighteen-year naval career. The Academy had trained men o' war's men by enlarging their capacity for judgment *and* obedience. To obey and decide were an officer's skills. But to ensure that under fire an officer would act instantly, not wasting time weighing alternatives, well, certain mottoes were issued as ironclad articles of faith –

'Should Valery trust you?' Tamara demanded again. 'Kennet, don't go against us. Please. What do you care what happens in Russia? It is Valery who will fight the war. You will get what you want. Tell me we can trust you.'

Be fearless in the face of duty . . . Seared in the mind of an eighteen-year-old midshipman was an image of standing firm while enemy shell splinters screeched across the bridge. But who was the enemy? They didn't teach that one, not under circumstances like these.

Trust yourself . . . he *knew* the grand duke was the best hope of saving Russia's army . . . President Wilson and Admiral Innes were six thousand miles across the world in Washington, DC. But *Trust the Navy* and *Bye Jidoff* kept ringing in his head . . .

'Then do this for me. *Please*, Kennet.'

'So you can be the empress?' A cheap shot, he knew as he said it, confirmed when she reached up and deliberately slapped his face.

'I don't want to be anything over your dead body . . . don't you understand? Valery will kill you if you try to stop him. It is in his grasp. He will shoot you down like one of your pheasants.'

'I can take care of myself,' and immediately winced at the sound of the empty boast.

'Do you think I would choose the *victor?*' She sounded insulted.

Ash turned back to the windows and again inspected Valery's grim picket line. 'This isn't about us,' he said quietly. 'We're just pieces in a – '

'But you *know* what is right. You've made this happen. Valery couldn't have done it alone. Why did you help?'

'I thought it was the best chance to get rid of the Czar and end the war.'

'And now? Because some fool thousands of miles away thinks Russia should bow to an upstart who . . . who doesn't *know* . . . Kennet, Valery will kill you tonight. And then he'll proceed with the plan. And if something goes wrong along the way you won't be there to help him. Or me . . .'

Or her . . . Ash had a sudden vision of a dark car at the door of her house, plainclothes Okhrana detectives emerging to arrest her . . .

'Get Valery.'

She slipped her arms under his, squeezed him tight and

438

ran from the room. Ash turned the other way and headed for the back door.

Off their horses, and without their lances, whips and carbines, the tall, blue-eyed Cossacks looked somewhat more like ordinary men. Ash knocked down the first at the kitchen door with a right uppercut. The second Cossack went for his *kinjal*. Ash feinted a jab as the dagger flashed out of the sheath and hooked him with a left. By the time the yelling started he was three houses away, bleakly confident that no one in the pursuit had quite the experience he did in leaving ladies' lodgings by the back door.

It was three in the morning, but thirty women had already lined up outside a shuttered bakery. Others hurried toward the line, yawning and rubbing sleep from their pinched faces. In the Finland Station Square thousands of soldiers milled about in the cold. Ash asked an officer what was going on; it looked like an insurrection.

It was not. Two regiments of Caucasian Rifles were stranded on their way to the front. 'No locomotives,' the officer explained. 'The boilers burst from the cold when they ran out of fuel.'

In the dark window of every shop was the same sign. *Nyet.* No bread, no oil, no fuel, no potatoes, no carrots, and of course no meat. Ash pushed into the station and found the telephones. *Trust yourself, but trust the Navy.* Outside they were chanting, '*Khleeeeee-ba.*'

When his call was answered, he gave his telephone number and said, 'A Pride of Kings.' Then he hung up and waited, intently watching the station for Okhrana detectives. The telephone rang, shortly.

'A Pride of Kings.'

'What's wrong?' asked von Basel. He had set up this emergency contact for the coup, and he sounded like he expected trouble.

439

'Plenty,' Ash replied. 'A very important American named Harold Banks is at the Europa. Do you suppose he could be mistakenly arrested and held for the night?'

'No problem,' said von Basel. 'They all say it's a mistake.'

'May I ask why you changed your mind, Kennet Karlovich?' a relieved-looking Grand Duke Valery asked.

'Just don't be surprised if I apply for a commission in the Imperial Navy.'

Tamara waited until they were alone for a moment. 'I hope you didn't come back just for me,' she said with the suggestion of a smile that said she hoped he had.

'I came back for a lot of reasons. But you're the only one I'm sure of.'

A dark car that might have belonged to the Okhrana slowed noticeably as it passed Tamara Tishkova's mansion. It distracted the Grand Duke Valery's Cossack guards, allowing Count von Basel to slip unnoticed up to the window of the coachman's room, half-underground in the mansion's cellar.

Von Basel could see a fire flickering in the grate, a vaulted ceiling, hooks in the stone walls for cloaks and hats, and, in a couple of huge wooden chairs draped with furs, two enormous coachmen. They were drinking vodka in front of the fire. They had their boots propped up on a sled brazier, which would be filled with hot embers when the grand duke's sled was ready to go.

The bigger man, wearing red livery, was the grand duke's driver. Tishkova's, the host, made several trips to the vodka cabinet while von Basel watched. Finally, as grey light appeared in the east, the grand duke's coachman stood up, belched mightily, jammed a tall hat on his head and rumbled out into the dawn. Soon, von Basel heard a team being harnessed. Tishkova's coachman, meanwhile, stretched out on a bunk in the corner, where he broke into thunderous snores.

Von Basel waited until the sun touched the tip of the gold spire of the Peter-Paul. Then he went in, straight to the brazier on the hearth. He opened the top and put inside a dozen sticks of dynamite attached to a blasting cap and fuse, which were both heavily wrapped with lead. He sprinkled ash from the fire over the package, concealing it. When a *moujik* filled the brazier with hot embers, to warm the grand duke's feet, the coals would slowly melt the lead, ignite the fuse, detonating the blasting cap and exploding the dynamite. A crude, but effective, time-bomb.

The coachman awakened suddenly, sat up, and peered blearily around the room. His bloodshot eyes fell upon von Basel, just shutting the lid of the brazier, and he stood up and reached a huge hand for the German.

But the cessation of snoring had alerted von Basel and he whirled around and hit the coachman with the fire shovel. Two more blows in quick succession drove the giant to the floor. Von Basel replaced the shovel and dragged the unconscious driver back to his bunk, where he laid him out and covered him with furs for the benefit of the *moujik* who would come for the brazier.

40

Ash watched the sun light the golden tip of the Admiralty spire as Tamara Tishkova picked up the telephone in her solarium and asked the operator to connect her with the Alexander Palace at Tsarskoye Selo. So much for Kirichenko's bodyguard's snow; the damned stuff had stopped before dawn, and it was anybody's guess whether the First Railway Battalion patrols had uncovered the track mines.

When the palace operator answered, Tamara identified herself as Madame Egersky – one of the longest-lived of the legion of mistresses entertained by Count Vladimir Fredericks – and asked to speak with the ancient chief minister of the Imperial Court. Count Fredericks was the same old man whose name Ash had used to bluff his way into the Alexander Palace with his gift for the Czarina. He saw no reason not to use him again, since at the Czar's New Year's reception he had observed a pair of red-cloaked equerries ease the old nobleman gently into a chair when he dozed off in the middle of a conversation with the Italian ambassador.

The Grand Duke Valery betrayed some anxiety by repeating aloud what they all already knew: 'The poor old man's so dotty it will take them a quarter hour just to find him.'

Ash nodded. Fifteen minutes was plenty of time for the line to go dead. If Kirichenko hadn't blown the telegraph poles by then it would be because he was already hanging from one. Ash was nervous too, but it made him silent. He leaned close to Tamara and listened to the telephone popping and hissing. Her perfume was heady. What a time for such a reaction. She wore a quilted silk robe, black, black slippers, and her hair coiled around her neck. Before the telephone call she had been sipping dark French coffee from a Limoges cup. Now she stared through the solarium's windows at the frozen Neva and the dull red Winter Palace, its north face in cold shadow. She felt him watching her, met his gaze with large eyes. Two hours from now it would all be over, one way or the other.

The palace operator came on the line again. 'We apologize, madame, for the delay in locating His Excellency Count Fredericks.'

'*Merci.*'

Outside her mansion Valery's red sleigh faced the river. The eight white Arabians were groomed as if for a dress parade; a triple guard of Cossacks waited on their mounts; two more sleighs carried armed men from Valery's own household. They had a Maxim 'Sokolov' machine-gun under canvas in the back seat of the rearmost sleigh. As Ash watched, and Tamara waited on the line, a *moujik* in a dirty sheepskin and bright red blouse appeared from behind the house and hoisted a brazier of fresh coals into Valery's sleigh.

Tamara started. 'They found him,' she whispered. 'He's coming. Kennet, what happened to the line? It still *works*'

Valery's lips tightened. The key men of the Duma who had pledged to support him were breakfasting at this unlikely hour at the Astoria and the Europa, less than five minutes from the Winter Palace, waiting to install him on the throne of Imperial Russia. He looked at Ash. Why wasn't the line blown?

'*Bonjour,* Your Excellency,' Tamara said in a choked voice, her eyes wild with panic as she turned to Ash. 'What should I do?'

Ash thought of Banks, held at the Litovsky prison, living proof that he had virtually committed treason in a cause that had just collapsed. Kirichenko? Had the revolutionary double-crossed him? Or were the horsemen of the First Railway Battalion at this moment trampling his men into the snow?

'*Je suis . . . allo? allo* . . . It's *broken*,' she said.

Ash grabbed it, hit the plunger one, two, three times, then cradled the telephone and looked at the grand duke, and then at Tamara. 'The railroad line is blown. Your Highness . . . good luck.'

Grand Duke Valery took a deep breath. The colour returned to his face. He put his hand on Tamara's shoulder and she touched his fingers with hers. He kissed her black hair, put on his fur hat and took Ash's hand. When their eyes met he impulsively clasped Ash's hand in both of his.

'I wish you could ride with me.'

'So do I.' They had already decided there was no place for the US Navy in Grand Duke Valery's sleigh this morning.

'I have one more favour to ask you, Kennet Karlovich. If something happens . . . take care of her – '

'Nothing's going to happen,' Tamara interrupted with annoyance. 'And please remember that I can take care of myself.'

Valery bowed over Tamara's hand and walked out to his sleigh. He stood up and waved once as it started moving, trailed by the horseguard and the two sleighs that were flanked by more Cossacks. Standing beside Tamara in the window, Ash wondered how they would appear from across the river on the Palace embankment. The convoy grouping was unusual. Yet the Cossacks always carried their rifles slung over their backs, and lances. And grand dukes often travelled with bodyguards. The Maxim gun was under wraps . . . and the Winter Palace was empty except for servants and a small guard . . .

444

The sleigh plunged down the bank and on to the Neva and headed southwest, diagonally across the river on a course that would take it straight to the landing on the quay in front of the Winter Palace. The sun had risen high enough now so that its rays splashed the ice a pale yellow. The Arabians broke into a fast trot, pulling ahead of the sleds of armed men. The Cossacks, red figures on dark animals, stayed close –

A maid screamed and Tamara's coachman staggered into the solarium, shouting. His face was bloody. Tamara cried, 'He says a man hid something in Valery's sleigh. Kennet – '

Ash was already hurtling himself toward the door. The sudden contrast of temperature between the solarium and the snow outside nearly stopped him dead in his tracks. His chest heaved, he stumbled for a second, then his breathing returned and he was running for the bank, where two old Cossacks stood holding their horses and watching the grand duke's column cross the ice. Scarcely checking his stride, Ash leaped into the saddle of the nearest horse and kicked it out on to the river. The rest of the house guard streamed after him. It could only be a bomb. Someone had betrayed them.

Making twice the speed of the heavily-laden sleighs, he closed rapidly. He called out, but the wind tore the words. He pulled his Luger to fire a warning shot. The sleighs were halfway across and he was near. Valery's coachman stood up and turned around.

Fire spouted under the scarlet sleigh, mushroomed, and the horses seemed to be crossing burning ice. Shattered ice flew like shrapnel. It scythed down the outriders. A chunk hit Ash in the face, threw him off his horse. Thunder pealed across the river. The blast lifted sleigh and horses above an enormous black hole in the ice. The animals kept running, galloping on flame.

445

But where the ice had been was only the Neva, dark and swift, and into it vanished the grand duke, his sleigh, and his horses.

BOOK IV
The Czar

41

The silver button on François Roland's foil swam in front of Ash's eyes. He blinked, and it seemed to shatter.

'Get your guard up.'

'I can't . . . I think – '

Roland slipped his foil under the stump of his left arm, caught Ash with his right hand and helped him off the strip. 'Too much too soon, my friend. What do you expect?'

Fencers crowded around as Roland eased Ash, dizzy and nauseous, to the floor of the *Salle*. The Frenchman banished them with an annoyed look.

It was two weeks since the Grand Duke Valery had been killed. Ash had been delirious when he woke up in a hospital. As he slowly recovered his memory, he tried to figure out who had bombed Valery's sleigh, and why. The timing pointed to von Basel, but the German's motivation was less clear – von Basel was, after all, his partner in the scheme to remove Czar Nicholas – which opened the possibility that Kirichenko had betrayed them in the best, or worst, revolutionary tradition. Or did von Basel have some other irons heating?

Then two days ago Roland had burst into his hospital room with the news Ash had most worried about, and he suddenly stopped caring about von Basel, Kirichenko, Czar Nicholas or even the war. Okhrana detectives had just arrested Tamara Tishkova for plotting to overthrow the Czar. It was a secret arrest; the censors allowed nothing in the papers, though this, like most Russian secrets, had not escaped the French ambassador. Ash knew it meant Tamara was held beyond the law. They could do anything to her . . .

He brushed Roland's hand away and tried to sit. 'Gotta get limbered up . . . François, help me. I *have* to.'

Roland sighed and pulled Ash slowly to his feet. 'You've had severe concussion. You are not fully recovered. You are lucky you're not dead.'

Ash picked up his foil. 'I'm just *stiff*, dammit. Come on, *en garde.*'

Roland looked hard at him. 'Am I to assume that you intend to rescue mademoiselle by fighting your way into the Peter-Paul Fortress with a sword?'

'I have to do something, what else *can* I do?'

Ash had gone everywhere, begged everyone he knew who had influence. No one could help. Sergei Gladishev was a trembling wreck at the Duma, waiting at any moment for his own arrest. Tamara's old friend, the director of the Imperial Theatres, was devastated but helpless. Her friend the police chief of the Fourth District blustered, then admitted he could do nothing. And Ambassador Hazzard's counsellor had already warned the ambassador that the United States had neither business nor interest in the legal difficulties of Russian citizens.

When he went to Lord Exeter the Englishman had said, 'I'm very sorry, Ash, but I'm afraid the real issue still is . . . what are you going to do about the Czar?'

'I just got out of the hospital, Tamara – '

'I'd get cracking, my friend. You must put personal considerations aside. There isn't time to spare. The railways have collapsed. The food is gone. The police expect bread riots within days. What they've been told of the grand ducal conspiracy has frightened the Czar and Czarina. He's gone back to the Stavka, she's consulting mystics.'

Ash had stared at the Englishman without seeing him, his mind chewing the grim thought that, if he hadn't come to Russia with his mission to remove the Czar, then the Grand Duke Valery's conspiracy would simply have dissolved into talk, like all the other schemes festering in Petrograd's salons. Tamara would not be locked in the Okhrana's prison.

Lord Exeter demanded he put aside personal considerations, as *he* had when his wife was killed. But if Ash hadn't come to Russia, Lady Exeter would still be alive. Two women, one he admired and one he loved, had paid for his failures. And Ash couldn't help thinking that it would have been better for all if von Basel had killed him in Paris. Tamara –

'*Mystics!*' Lord Exeter shouted. 'And now the Czar has left the woman in charge of Petrograd, while he runs back to his army.'

'I know.'

'Meanwhile no one's found this Red Snow assassin, Dmitri Dan. Can you imagine the chaos if the Czar were murdered now? You've got to get him out. Quickly.'

'Yes, I know . . .'

'And there's something else you ought to know. Kirichenko got impatient. His men tried to defuse my lorry. What the hell did you do to it?'

'Just attached a detonator to the springs. Take off too much weight and – '

'Well, they did. Kirichenko had already lost men blowing the Tsarskoye Selo lines. He of course blames you for everything. I'd say you've made a rather dangerous enemy . . . whose stock can only rise as the Czar's sinks.'

Ash reckoned that Exeter was exaggerating the situation to jolt his mind off Tamara, but when he telephoned the Alexander Palace to plead for her, he discovered that Exeter wasn't far off the mark. He at first ran smack into the same impenetrable wall of the Court that he had had to vault to present King George's offer of asylum. He got no farther than a remote-sounding Colonel Riazhin. 'Russia's peasants have an old saying, Commander. "Father Czar would save us from this unhappiness, if he only knew."'

'*Tell* him.'

'It would be the end of my career to even mention Tishkova's name in the Czarina's palace.'

'The woman's life is at stake. God knows what they're doing to her.'

'As for the Czar,' the colonel went on coldly, 'His Imperial Majesty has more on his mind at the *Stavka* than interceding on behalf of a woman accused of turning the Grand Duke Valery against him.'

'That's malicious rumour – '

'Perhaps, but I can tell you another rumour . . . if His Imperial Majesty's government were not reluctant to trouble a potential ally in his war against Germany, there is a certain American naval officer whom the Okhrana would have hanging by his thumbs in the Peter-Paul beside the great Tishkova.'

This was not news. The Okhrana had apparently satisfied itself with several interrogations in the hospital. But the cruelty about Tamara was unforgivable, and Ash let the pretence of courtesy drop from his voice.

'May I ask how His Majesty could leave when Petrograd is about to explode?'

To his surprise Colonel Riazhin answered him seriously, which Ash took as an indication of how frightened the Court must be. 'Minister Protopopov promises quiet in Petrograd. Hooligans who won't work and exaggerate bread shortages are not such a threat that the Czar of all the Russias can't lead his armies in the field. And I am told,' the colonel continued in confidential tones, 'that a lady-in-waiting to Her Majesty returned from a week in the city and saw no serious disturbance. Nothing the police can't put down.'

452

What makes you think my spies in the Russian Court are all men? the Kaiser had boasted. Why not a lady-in-waiting? . . .

'*En garde,* then,' Roland said. 'If you insist.'

But Ash lowered his foil and walked off the strip.

'Where are you going?'

'Von Basel.'

'Are you insane?'

No, thought Ash, but I'd deal with the devil to save her. He left a note in the sconce hole at the German Embassy, and the Kaiser's spy agreed to a meeting in front of the Stock Exchange on the spit of Vassily Island. Ash waited an hour. Von Basel did not show. He went back to the wrecked embassy. No message. But on his desk at the Astoria was a typed note.

'You're still being followed by Okhrana detectives investigating the explosion. Try Grisha's on the Bolshoi Prospect. Alone.'

Ash took it as a warning he was coming unhinged by worry over Tamara. He went out, spotted the detectives, lost them on the Nevsky Prospect and took several trams to Vassily Island. Grisha's was a middle-class restaurant. He sat for an hour, drinking glasses of tea. There was not much left on the menu. Von Basel sat down and ordered herring, which he ignored. Ash marvelled at the attention he paid to details. He leaned on the walking stick as if he needed it, and buttered a piece of bread in the careful, reverent Russian manner by which bread was buttered in middle-class restaurants. When the full slice was smoothly covered from crust to crust, he brought his cold eyes to bear on Ash's anxious face. 'I've made arrangements for a special train on the Murman line.'

'Why did you bomb the grand duke's sleigh?'

'I did not. And why would you think I did?'

453

'All I can figure is you thought he'd make too good a Czar.'

'And defeat Germany?' von Basel smiled. 'Not very likely.'

'Then Kirichenko?'

Von Basel shrugged. 'It makes no difference now. But *our* problem remains unsolved. Do you have a plan to get the Czar to the cruiser at Murmansk?'

'Not until I get Tishkova out of the Peter-Paul.'

'Tishkova?' Von Basel sat up, suddenly alert now. Ash cursed himself. He had assumed that with his police contacts at the Litovsky Prison von Basel knew Tamara had been arrested. He *hadn't.* And the interest in his eyes made Ash wish he could erase his slip.

'Can you help me get her out?'

'No. It's beyond my power.'

'Can you see her for me?'

'And have Tishkova start screaming that's Count von Basel, the German duellist?'

Ash slumped back. Von Basel was right.

'Your first and overriding objective . . . which we share . . . is to remove the Czar from Russia. But I wouldn't worry so. If the revolution is as imminent as my sources indicate, Mademoiselle Tishkova will be free quite soon . . .

Clinging to those words like a drowning man Ash followed von Basel out to the street, where the German spy added '. . . provided, of course, that the revolutionaries don't hold her monarchistic tendencies against the lady . . . Tell me when you're ready for the U-boats, and any help you need with the Czar. I emphasize that time is running out, Ash. It is fifteen hundred miles to Murmansk. Once the Revolution is underway, there will be many people trying to stop you.'

Are you one of them? Ash suddenly found himself wondering. Von Basel barely concealed his pleasure in

Ash's misery about Tamara. A highly tenuous, makeshift at best, link, this thing of getting the Czar out of Russia . . . for two men who otherwise were enemies. Had it broken, without actual declaration or acknowledgement? Were they now, as they parted in front of Grisha's restaurant, backing away from each other, each at least privately acknowledging to himself that the other was, after all, an enemy?

What was all that talk about Murmansk? The Murman run certainly seemed to be important in von Basel's mind . . . 'Keep in touch,' von Basel said, and limped toward the tram stop.

Volatile fellow, the Kaiser, Lord Exeter had warned . . . Could it be that the Kaiser might have broken the link among a pride of kings, had maybe changed his mind about rescuing his cousin? If so, wouldn't the German U-boat escort suddenly become a killer and torpedo the cruiser? . . . Possible . . . but not likely . . . the Kaiser had enough troubles with Ludendorff, why get involved in a dangerous plot to kill his own cousin? Even the Czar had said that Ludendorff had all but taken over the real power in the German Empire. Trouble enough for the Kaiser, more than enough to keep his mind on that overriding problem, any threat to him . . .

Ash stopped walking abruptly and two old women lugging an oilcan bumped into him. His logic about the Kaiser began to weaken . . . had von Basel killed the Grand Duke Valery not only because he feared Valery would be too good a Czar, and so make Russia a stronger enemy, but also because it would be more difficult to seize the Czar when Valery was firmly in control of the situation? Had the Kaiser decided to use the Czar as a pawn in his own power struggle with Ludendorff and the army? That, dammit, made sense, too much sense for Ash's comfort . . . explained why von Basel was his enemy even in the plot, and why the royal link had likely been broken. Kidnap the Czar . . .

455

though the Kaiser, of course, would call Nicholas a prisoner of war – an enemy captive to refloat the Kaiser's sinking fortunes. Power-lust was thicker than blood . . . It made sense, too much sense . . . well, at least Ash could be glad he'd clinched backup arrangements for a sub with Rodney Skelton at Reval. Von Basel probably had his suspicions about that. Had to. But one thing was damn sure – there was no way von Basel could persuade Ash to let him help transport the Czar, much less get within a hundred miles of the Czar . . . In refusing to help with Tamara, the *way* he had refused, von Basel had betrayed his hand, made too clear that they were enemies again, in *everything* . . .

She was cold for the first time she could remember since the Yusupovs had plucked her from her father's circus. She thought longingly of her solarium – so warm that tropical plants Valery brought her from the Crimea stretched to the sunny windows even as the snow scurried past, and big enough to dance in if she liked. Strange how a whole house in memory became a single cherished room, a whole life a single moment – Valery marching a giant clerodendrum into her solarium, bellowing at his Cossacks to shield it from the snow. All dead, now. His entire guard had perished with him as the weakened ice gave way.

Her cell was tiny, silent and cold despite the stoves she had seen buried in the passage wall. Part of her mind, which thankfully had detached as if to protect her sanity, suspected that soon something would happen to make her afraid. So far, confinement itself was the horror – the inactivity, the cold. The jailers, rough and coarse, she barely noticed; but when the commandant had come personally to greet her in her cell, she had granted him a hint of civility in her response, acutely aware that with Valery dead this man had power over her.

The warder had ordered the guards to remove the chains

from her wrists. She caught herself debating whether a smile might suffice to free her legs.

Vera Sedovina was standing in the *khvost* when the Czar's police found her. This particular tail was attached to a bakery just around the corner from the Alexander Theatre. But the line of shivering women seemed ten thousand miles from the columned portico where lavish court carriages lined up each night to whisk the rich from their entertainment to their dinners in the expensive restaurants that somehow still had food.

On the way home from rehearsal she had seen an enormous *khvost* stretching from the Railway Ticket Bureau up Mikhail Street all the way to the Nevsky. Her stepfather had told her that people who could were leaving Petrograd, fleeing south to the Crimea or north to Finland over to Sweden, and even east on the luxurious Trans-Siberian Express to Vladivostok and America across the Pacific Ocean. Those who couldn't get out were burning rowboats and cemetery crosses for firewood.

She was talking with two women – a housewife with a cruel cough and a cook for a middle-class family. Were it not for the bitter cold and the need to rest her legs after a full day's rehearsal, she would almost enjoy the *khvost*. They were wonderful places to talk. There was nothing else to do, so people ignored social barriers that before the war would have prevented the work-worn housewife from speaking to a cook, and the cook, who fancied herself superior because her employer was rich, from talking to the housewife.

The newspapers had been proved liars too often to believe, so it was in the *khvost* that the people of Petrograd learned something of the truth about the war, the shortages, the treason in high places, and as the *khvosty* lengthened the police withdrew, knowing the anger they would provoke. And so people spoke more freely than usual. The *khvosty*

457

were also perfect places for revolutionaries to spread the word.

The explosions two weeks ago were still high on the list of favoured rumours this snowy afternoon, second only to the story that six trains of grain and cooking oil had been diverted from Petrograd on Sunday and sold to the Austrians. Sedovina dutifully repeated the diverted food story, as her comrades were doing on every *khvost* they stood at, then listened politely to yet another retelling of the explosions.

The cook claimed her master had seen it with his own eyes from his desk in the Stock Exchange on the spit of Vassily Island, which had a clear view up the Neva. A sleigh had fallen into the river. Sometimes the story said two. This man had seen three. They were said to belong to a grand duke. Scarlet, it was said . . . and Sedovina wondered was it coincidence that last week haughty Tishkova was seen weeping in the theatre?

Sedovina had looked from the Palace Embankment the day after, but if there had been a hole in the ice the deep cold had frozen the river again. Now a piano teacher she knew slightly from their neighbourhood interrupted the housewife.

'Not one explosion, three.' She held up her mitten as if to show three fingers and the others laughed. 'Three,' she repeated.

'On the river?'

'No, silly, the train to Tsarskoye Selo.'

'Three explosions on a train? Was it the engine?'

'No,' Sedovina said. She had heard this rumour several times. 'They say the tracks were blown up. And then when trains came to repair it they were blown up too.'

'Who did it?'

'Revolutionaries.'

'German spies,' the cook said, and the housewife and the

piano teacher nodded grave agreement, which provoked a conversation about *izmena* – treason – and traitors. The housewife looked around carefully and said, 'The German woman,' and the others nodded, knowing she meant the German-born Czarina Alexandra.

Sedovina had heard that the police had swept through the factory districts after the explosion, breaking down doors in the Vyborg District, Narva, Vassily Island, Alexander Nevsky and particularly the Moscow District, where she had performed with Valentinov's revolutionary troupe. Hundreds were arrested. She hadn't seen Valentinov since the night Kirichenko had rescued them – partly from fear, largely from the intense preparation she was putting into her *Giselle*.

'They say she would betray her own husband the Czar.'

'Perhaps the Czar agrees with her,' Sedovina said softly.

The others looked at each other, suddenly alarmed, and she knew she had gone too far. Confused, frightened, cold and hungry, ordinary people like these could only accept so much uncertainty. The housewife and the piano teacher and the cook might question the competence of the Czar's government, but they weren't ready to turn against him, yet. She smoothed it over by saying, 'They say he loves her deeply, it's hard for a man to resist a woman he loves,' and the cook and the housewife and the piano teacher smiled tentatively and switched to how poorly the city government was removing the snow this winter.

It was then that two police officers in black uniform led by an officer in grey stepped out of the swirling snow and took hold of her from either side.

'Vera Vadimovna Sedovina?'

'Yes,' she said, hearing her voice tremble and sensing the other women back away.

'I place you under arrest for crimes against the Czar.'

* * *

An old lawyer with a white beard came to Vera's cell. He looked appalled by the wet stone walls, as if he had never seen a prison before. Vadim Mikhailov had somehow persuaded him to help. He had vague connections at court that garnered him a small amount of respect from the prison guards, but they still wouldn't allow him in the cell with her alone.

Speaking slowly, with a shaky voice, he explained what he knew about her situation. 'A conspiracy to overthrow the Czar has been detected. The police have arrested hundreds of suspected revolutionaries. Among them, the members of a theatrical group that had been performing seditious plays in clandestine theatres. Under questioning a member of the troup, a child – '

'A *child?*'

'They interrogated the child,' the lawyer continued, 'and the child revealed your name. I certainly don't believe that you would be involved with such people, and neither does my friend Vadim Mikhailov, but the police were obliged to act.'

'What's going to happen to me?'

He couldn't face her. Her stomach clutched, her mind raced so that she couldn't think. The lawyer tried to make her sit down on the filthy cot. 'Can you help me?' she asked.

'The offence is considered very serious, but I will do what I can.'

'In other words, you can't help me.'

'Do you suppose that the Imperial Theatre might help you?' he asked, and she knew then that she was lost . . . not only wouldn't the Imperial Theatre help, but at the slightest hint of political scandal she would be dismissed.

'No, I suppose they won't.' He answered his own question. 'I will do my best . . . Mikhailov sent you this warm cloak.' He draped it over her shoulders, after the guard inspected it for contraband.

Sedovina twisted it around her trembling hands. Had her boyfriend Anton been so frightened when they arrested him? She glanced at the guard leaning against the cell door. He stared back with a lewd smile. How long would her modest fame protect her from people like him?

The lawyer started to go, and suddenly she thought of a last desperate straw . . . 'Tell Vadim – ' The guard was listening.

'Yes, my dear,' prompted the lawyer, grateful to perform any small service.

'Tell my father to speak to his friend from America.'

The commandant of the prison in the Moscow District looked surprised to see him. 'What are you doing here, Moskolenko?'

Von Basel indicated his short, round assistant. 'I've brought Lieutenant Orlov to interrogate a prisoner. Have you a room we can use?'

The commandant barely concealed his distaste for Orlov.

'Which prisoner?'

'Vera Vadimovna Sedovina.'

'The dancer?'

'Yes.'

'Sorry, you missed her.'

'I thought the charges were too serious for bond.'

'No bond, Moskolenko. Not likely. They've moved her to the Peter-Paul.' And then because he didn't like Moskolenko either, the commandant added what von Basel already knew, 'You'll have a hard time prying her out of the Peter-Paul. They do their own interrogating.'

Von Basel brooded in the car on the way back to the Litovsky Prison. In one real sense he regretted having to separate from Ash because to abandon Ash he would also have to abandon 'Captain Moskolenko', and with him all the information that 'Moskolenko' was able to gather for

461

Germany. But it looked as if Ash might already have abandoned him.

Reval was the question. The more he thought about why Ash had gone to the Baltic port, the more likely it seemed Ash had gone to the British Navy submarine base. What else could possibly have drawn Ash? Ash claimed he had met with a Russian general from Riga . . . but what Russian general would travel to Reval when he could make Ash come to Riga?

A British submarine? A submarine, instead of a cruiser with German escorts to take off the Czar. It would be a long, dangerous voyage to England. But if Ash no longer trusted him, might Ash not risk it? If that was Ash's plan, then von Basel would have to kidnap the Czar himself, not wait for Ash to do the job for him. Yes . . . it would mean the end of Captain Moskolenko, and worth that *only* if he had no other choice. He had to find out without question what Ash had done in Reval. He couldn't risk his whole carefully built cover on the basis of speculation . . . no matter how plausible it might be. Too much was at stake.

'I retained a very famous lawyer,' Vadim Mikhailov assured Ash.

'What's he done for you?'

'He used his influence to see Vera.'

Better than I've done for Tamara, Ash thought.

'Also, he learned what the charges are.'

'What are they?'

The old *tapeur* looked on the verge of tears. 'They are charging Vera with acting in seditious plays.'

'Why did you let her?'

'How could I stop her?'

'You're her step-father – '

'Ever since her mother died I've tried to protect her, but

462

she's always been so . . . angry. You must help me, Commander Ash. Please . . .'

'I wish I could, but how?'

'She asked for you,' Mikhailov said quietly.

Ash walked to his window and looked down at St Isaac's Square; a sledge was pulling away from the Maryinski Palace heaped high with furniture. The firewood was nearly gone and the Astoria Hotel felt cold. He glanced at François Roland, who met his look, thinking what Ash was thinking.

'My own very dear friend Tamara Tishkova has been imprisoned three days. I've tried everything just to see her. They won't let me.'

'Tishkova? A performer so famous and once the Czar's friend?'

'Even a fling with the Czar doesn't seem to make a woman immune from the Okhrana,' Ash said bitterly. 'You're lucky, Vadim, at least they admit they're holding Vera. She'll have some legal protection.' Even this old gossip hadn't heard . . . they could do anything to Tamara.

Vadim sat on the edge of a love seat wringing his hands. A tear drifted down his cheek, dried in the wrinkles.

'Where are they holding her?' Ash asked.

'They moved her to the Peter-Paul.'

Ash looked at Roland again. God, if he could somehow get permission to see Sedovina then he might see – but that was impossible. He'd been locked in the Peter-Paul himself. Each cell was isolated, each prisoner chained alone, buried inside an impregnable prison hidden in an equally impregnable fortress.

'The lawyer couldn't do a thing,' Vadim admitted. He clenched both fists and got to his feet. Grief and fear had made him look even thinner. He turned to Ash, his eyes intense. 'Do you still want to see the Czarina?'

'I beg your pardon?'

'Do you still have business with the Czar?'

463

'What are you saying?' Damned right he had business with the Czar. Pressing business, if it weren't already too late. Ambassador Hazzard had related news from America – President Wilson was making some headway in his efforts to convince Congress to declare war on Germany. Popular resistance was still fierce and would remain fierce, in the opinion of Harold Banks – who, released with apologies by the Okhrana, had sent a cryptic message congratulating Ash, as if Ash had bombed the grand duke's sleigh, for God's sake – until the Czar-autocrat was removed. But Germany had resumed unrestricted submarine warfare.

U-boat attacks on American ships might provoke American sentiment toward intervention, which lent a new, and dangerous, wrinkle to the Russian situation; if the Czar hung on so long as to set off a cataclysmic revolt, American soldiers might land in France to find their most important ally collapsed. So Ash's 'business with the Czar', the need to remove the autocrat, was doubly pressing – triply, considering the havoc if Dmitri Dan and his Red Snow nihilists managed to assassinate the Czar.

'Yes, Vadim, I believe I still have business with the Czar – what are you getting at?'

'If you help my daughter, I will bring you to the Czarina.'

François Roland saw that Ash was about to explode and intervened. 'Monsieur Mikhailov, if you could take Commander Ash to the Empress, then you yourself could ask Her Majesty to help your daughter.'

'And while you're at it, see what you can do for Tamara Tishkova.'

'I can send you to her, but that's all.'

Ash went to the window. Roland took the old man's arm. 'It would be best if you left now, Monsieur.'

'You don't understand – '

'I do understand,' Roland told him, steering him toward

464

the door. 'Your daughter is a lovely child and a beautiful dancer and I'm sure *you* can understand that Commander Ash is as upset as you are. *Bonjour, Monsieur.*'

Vadim Mikhailov clamped one of his big hands on Roland's wrist and tore loose. 'I didn't say *I* have influence with Her Majesty. I said I could get Commander Ash to her. Commander, I can get you a private audience with Her Majesty.'

Ash turned from the window. He was nauseous and another headache had started. He felt perspiration suddenly cool on his temples. 'How come you never offered this to me before? You knew I was trying to get an audience.'

'I couldn't before. But now I have an old friend who suddenly has access to Her Majesty's chambers – '

'Suddenly, Vadim? Just like that?'

'Yes.'

'Vadim, I wish I could help you but I can't. Don't claim you can help me unless – '

'It's *true*. My friend has become her friend, I mean since Rasputin.'

'What?'

'He . . .' Vadim hesitated. 'Her Majesty grieves . . . my friend . . .' He trailed off as if reluctant to tell or as if he didn't believe it himself.

'Can't your friend speak for Vera? A word from Her Majesty and Vera would be released.'

'I begged him. He can't. His position is not that secure . . . But he could bring you with him.'

'Why would he?'

'You'd see why if you talked to him.'

'Who is he?'

Vadim crossed his long arms. 'I won't tell you until you help Vera.'

Ash and Roland shared a sceptical glance. Was he lying or just exaggerating? Would the Czarina see him, again, even if the old man were telling the truth? Roland shrugged. In the end, Tamara tipped it. Ash was desperate. Vera Sedovina was held in the Peter-Paul. So was Tamara. If their cells were at opposite ends of the prison, separated by a hundred walls, he would still be closer to Tamara than sitting in his suite in the Astoria Hotel.

The Okhrana captain who had questioned him in the hospital inquired about his condition when Ash telephoned. He said he was much better.

'And your memory?'

'Clear . . . I wonder if I might ask a difficult favour.'

'Commander, I can tell you right now that if this favour concerns a certain woman – whom I shall not name – I can do nothing more for you than repeat my earlier advice that you disassociate yourself from her completely.'

Ash tried to stay calm; he could hear in the police captain's voice that the Czar's government was terrified that news of the grand ducal conspiracy might reach the Russian people.

'I understand what you're saying. I'm not referring to that woman. But this is very delicate, nonetheless. Very delicate.'

'Let me judge that, Commander.'

'The daughter of a friend, a young girl, has been arrested. Her father is beside himself. I would like to see her.'

'Who is the girl?'

'Unfortunately, Captain, it is a political matter about which she was arrested.'

Ash waited. The police officer was silent. 'And she's being held in the Peter-Paul Fortress.'

'That is very difficult – '

'I wondered if you could direct me to the proper authorities who might get me permission to see her.'

'Her name?'

466

'Sedovina.'

'*Another* dancer?'

'Purely coincidental, sir.'

Silence. Then: 'It would be extremely difficult . . .' Again silence. Then: 'Perhaps you might tell me something . . .?'

'If I can.'

'When we spoke last your injuries had affected your memory . . .'

'I'm almost fully recovered.'

'Good. We now have evidence that the third sleigh in the Grand Duke Valery's entourage carried a machine-gun. Do you know anything about it?'

'Of course.'

'Of *course?*'

'It was a Maxim "Sokolov" seven-six-two millimetres, 1910 model.'

'Do you happen to remember why it was aboard the sleigh?'

'Well, it's my understanding that His Royal Highness had requisitioned several machine-guns to test at his estate. He had been informed that the manufacturer had been skimping on certain specifications . . . the feed blocks were jamming . . . in fact, now that we speak' – Ash embroidered the lie – 'it was my impression that His Highness was preparing charges against certain officials in the Ministry of Interior.'

'Interior? Surely you mean the army – '

'No. His Highness indicated the culprits were in the Ministry of Interior.' *Figure out who, you son of a bitch.*

When Ash finally hung up the telephone, Vadim's eyes were on him. 'Yes?'

'Yes, Vadim. A visit.' Ash stood up. The blood rushed from his head. He steadied himself on the chair.

'A visit?'

467

'I think I have permission to see Vera.' And maybe, God willing, the girl might know something about Tamara.

'How will you get her out?'

'Out?'

'Out,' Vadim Mikhailov shouted. 'Free. You must *free* her.'

'Vadim, I'm just – '

'I won't help you get to the Czarina through my friend until you free Vera from the Peter-Paul . . . *and* take her to America.' . . .

'Out?' Roland echoed, when Vadim had gone. 'Is he crazy?'

Ash shook his head as he watched the old man scurry down the hall. 'He's crazy terrified. Just like me.'

'There wasn't enough time to make her talk,' Lieutenant Orlov was saying. 'These revolutionaries take time and patience, Captain Moskolenko. Particularly the women. But the commandant wouldn't let me have her long enough – I think he has his own ideas – all I could do was soften her up a little.'

Orlov's pudgy face wrinkled up with sincerity. 'I know I would do much better in my own work space, Captain Moskolenko. Can't we bring her here to the Litovsky?'

Von Basel slowly nodded. He had begun thinking along slightly similar lines. Since the Peter-Paul commandant wouldn't turn them over, why not kidnap the women? Let Captain Moskolenko maintain the deception at least for a while longer . . . and give him a considerable hold over Ash by having Tamara Tishkova.

He really needed Ash . . . the Czar was impregnable at both the Stavka and the Alexander Palace, where Tsarskoye Selo's mansions screened an armed camp; only aboard the Imperial Train was the Czar even slightly vulnerable to a seizure, but von Basel couldn't wait for the Imperial

Train to move at the Czar's pleasure. Nor did he have to with Ash doing what he told him.

Kidnap the women from the Peter-Paul. Hold Ash's beloved Tishkova hostage. For ransom. A trade. Czar Nicholas II for Tishkova.

Ash would persuade the Czar to leave for England, then Ash would hand the Czar to von Basel, and von Basel would take the Czar to Germany. Orlov could have Sedovina and, thus occupied, the Okhrana lieutenant would hardly challenge von Basel's claim that Tishkova had somehow escaped, disappeared . . . Two hours later von Basel had every forger loyal to him preparing papers to show the Peter-Paul prison commandant, while von Basel himself paid a call on the man to determine the proper bribe.

The commandant of the prison in the Peter and Paul Fortress was an immense, jowly man, a muscular blond who had gone to fat. He looked as if he enjoyed his work.

Whistling cheerfully, he led Ash from his office in a low building that housed barracks and offices out to the snowy yards of the sprawling fortress. The gold spire and the onion dome atop the Cathedral of St Peter and St Paul flashed red in the afternoon sunset. The fortress walls hid the river and the city so that the yards and drilling fields could have been anywhere in Russia, thousands of miles off in the country, a bucolic impression enhanced by the lines of horse sleds delivering firewood.

The commandant turned into an alley between two long structures, one of stone, the other the more common Petrograd stucco painted yellow. He entered a heavy door at the end and gave a shout in Russian so that as Ash entered the small, dark room the guards turned and faced the stone wall, just as they had the night Ash had been arrested.

He followed the commandant into a second room, bare except for a wooden table and hooks on the wall – the search room where they had taken his clothing – then up a flight of stone steps through a guarded iron door and into the long corridor lined with pairs of wooden doors. It was colder than Ash remembered.

The commandant gestured to raise his hands. Ash did, and the Russian searched him thoroughly. He took his sword and leaned it in a corner, patted down his arms and legs and felt for a shoulder holster and belly gun. Then the neck, the back. His grin froze when he hit the hard lump of the chamois holster.

He snapped his fingers. A guard came instantly, pointed a pistol at Ash. The commandant gestured him to open his tunic. Ash undid the buttons and raised it. The commandant reached behind him and removed the contents of the holster.

Ash held his breath. The commandant closed his huge hand and ordered the guard away. When they were alone again in the corridor of wooden doors with iron mesh peepholes the commandant opened his hand. His grin had returned, wary, speculative, interested.

The gold clinked dully as he opened the leather sack. British sovereigns, heavy and gleaming. Ten of them. What kind of fortune were they worth on the black market? He stared at the gold, hungering to take it, and finally shrugged with an almost sheepish expression. It wasn't worth his life.

Only in fantasy had Ash imagined he could buy a prisoner out of the Czar's chief political prison. But could he buy a moment alone with Tishkova? He said her name.

'Tishkova?' A complex expression replaced the sheepish disappointment on the commandant's face. She was here, all right, but the commandant was wondering how Ash knew. Ash had asked Vadim for the Russian word for 'visit'. He tried it now, massacring the pronunciation, tried it again.

The commandant's eyes widened. All that gold for a *visit*? That might be possible.

Ash indicated the money was his for that.

The jailer weighed the coins in his hand, then poured them back into the pouch and jammed the pouch in his pocket. He led Ash to a door, pushed a key in the slot, threw it open. Ash stepped in, the door clanged behind him. The cell was like the one he'd been in. There was a high barred window and, turning from it, a frightened Sedovina. Hope flared in her eyes; Ash put down his disappointment and tried to smile. Maybe the commandant would take him to Tamara afterward . . . maybe . . .

She stayed by the window, cut near the vaulted ceiling. She had been holding the bars and staring out at the red sky. They had put her in a shapeless muslin dress and felt slippers, but at least her long golden hair still looked attractive. The cell was chilly. She had chains on her wrists and on her ankles. *Chains, for God's sake.*

Ash looked at her and imagined Tamara. 'How are you?' His voice was, unaccountably, a whisper.

Sedovina said, 'No one can hear you. They put felt in the walls so we can't talk to each other between cells. I was so frightened, you were the only person I could think of . . .'

The electric light switched on from somewhere in the prison, and Ash could see her a bit more clearly than by the fading daylight from the window. He was shocked.

'My God . . . what happened to your face?'

'They hit me.'

He felt sick. An ugly welt cut across her cheek from her lip to her ear.

'Who did that?'

'They asked me questions.' She faced him, but still held the bars with one hand, her body extended as if she were dancing. 'When I had nothing to tell them they hit me and they told me it was to remember . . . that they would come again for me.'

Ash crossed the few steps of the cell and took her face gently in his hands and turned her cheek to the light. 'What did they ask you?' he said, feeling ridiculously helpless, his eyes riveted to her cheek while his mind traced the welt on Tamara's face.

'They told me tomorrow.' She started to cry. 'They said they're coming back tomorrow, at sunset. They said to watch the sun and when it was gone they would come and get me – '

'They are just trying to frighten you . . . but don't do anything foolish . . . Valentinov has been arrested with all of his actors.' The police, her father's lawyer had discovered, had made a clean sweep of the revolutionary troupe – Czar, Czarina, Rasputin and the five children. 'You can't protect them, Vera. They've all been caught. Just answer their questions.' But what are they asking *you*, Tamara?

Sedovina pulled away. 'They didn't ask about Valentinov . . .'

'Kirichenko? Don't worry about him. Nobody's caught him yet. You don't know a thing that would hurt him. Just answer their questions.'

'They asked about you.'

'Me?' That was crazy. He'd been flat on his back in the hospital for ten days. He'd been there for the plucking anytime they'd wanted. The grand duke was dead, his conspiracy died with him. What could they ask her they couldn't have asked him?

'What did they ask?'

'They said they wanted to know what you did in Reval . . .'

Von Basel.

Her blue eyes filled with tears again. 'I didn't even know you had gone to Reval. How could I? I told them. They said I was lying.'

'Is that why you asked Vadim to come to me?'

'No, I didn't know. It was at the first prison. I just thought you could help somehow . . . I didn't know anyone else. Then they asked me about you . . . I don't really understand.'

Ash put his arms around her. She had nothing under the thin muslin, and she felt soft and surprisingly slim for

473

such a powerful dancer. Fright shook her body. 'What can I tell him when they question me tomorrow?'

Ash took a deep breath. Von Basel had access to the prison, access to the prisoners . . . 'Tell them I went to Reval to meet a Russian general from the Northern Sector.' Swiftly he sketched in details to make it seem plausible. 'I did it for the Grand Duke Valery. He was asking for the general's support.' Sedovina looked puzzled. 'It was an attempted coup, a palace coup, Vera. The duke was going to make himself Czar.'

'Were you part of the coup?'

Ash took another breath. This attempt to save her more agony was getting out of hand, but he saw a chance to help Tamara. 'Some might think so . . . they're confused . . . arrested Tishkova instead, and she had nothing to do with it.'

'They arrested Tishkova?' She seemed incredulous that such a symbol of the establishment could have been scooped up in the same net as she.

'She's in the Peter-Paul too. Have you seen her?'

'There's a woman in the next cell, I think. They keep us alone, I've only seen guards and the commandant. But when they opened the food slots I heard a woman crying.'

Ash looked at the wall. A foot of plaster, stone and felt . . . he touched the wall. 'Are you sure?'

'No. And there are many cells, Commander. And many prisoners.' She put a hand on his arm. The chains dragged on his sleeve, but his own misery seemed to calm her. Finally Ash pulled himself together to ask, 'Who questioned you about me?'

'The guards who held me called him Orlov . . . Lieutenant Orlov.'

The name meant nothing to Ash. Just a name von Basel could have used . . .

Ash stared at the wall. 'Was he Russian?'

474

'Of course.'

'What did he look like?'

'Short and fat and he had no hair on his head.'

Not von Basel . . . the assistant. The one with the knout. Ash felt sick. 'Who was with him?'

'Guards.'

'What did *they* look like?'

'Just guards.'

'Was there one about my height, very thin and a bony face?'

'No.'

'Did the commandant come with Orlov?'

'Just to my cell, he didn't come outside.'

'Outside? What do you mean outside?'

'They took me to another building.'

'Where?'

'I'm not sure . . . in the fortress. They seemed rushed, in a hurry to bring me back here.'

'Did you go outside the same way you were first brought in?'

'I think so; it was dark the first time but we walked between those two buildings before we crossed a yard.'

Her hand suddenly went to her face, her eyes grew large. 'My God, Tishkova . . .'

'What?'

'He was frightening me and I started to cry and he said I'd have company tomorrow and they'd make us dance . . . that's what he meant . . .'

Ash sagged to the bunk. Orlov was von Basel's man, all right. The German couldn't risk Tamara exposing his true identity, so he'd sent Orlov to question Vera first and then Tamara.

And then a terrible realization . . . Tamara didn't know the real reason he had gone to Reval either. He had to give her more than the lie he'd given Sedovina. He'd put the girl

475

in real danger, even though he'd tried to protect her. Besides his mission was still paramount . . . except when it came to Tamara, who was more important than anything . . .

The door burst open. The commandant motioned him out. When Ash hesitated the man stepped in, grabbed his arm and pulled him into the corridor while two guards slammed the cell door shut. Sedovina was left there, watching in her chains.

'Tishkova?' Ash said to the commandant.

The man let go Ash's arm, hitched up his pants so Ash could hear the gold coin clink, and grinned. '*Nyet.*'

Ash slammed him aside and threw himself at the door beside Sedovina's. 'Tamara.' He called out the name as loudly as he could, clawing open the peephole. 'Tell them I went – '

Two guards hit him from behind, wrestled him to the floor and carried him out of the prison, the face of a stranger locked in his memory – young and frightened, with bruises to imagine a hundredfold on Tamara's face.

He left notes for von Basel in their drop in the wrecked German Embassy and slipped into the shambles several times in the night and hourly the next morning.

Von Basel made no reply. The sun faded as the day wore on, and by early afternoon the snow had begun falling. Laden clouds promised another Gulf blizzard. As for Lieutenant Orlov's taunt about sunset, today its moment could only be guessed at by Sedovina and Tamara as they watched the sky from their barred windows.

43

The peasant woman's son had come home from the war with one leg and a rusty German pistol. God provided, in His fashion; the boy guarded her sledloads of green birch logs from the thieves and deserters roaming the country-side. Green or dry, the fortress bought firewood and paid cash. They paid no more than before the war when every-thing else had cost a quarter of what it did now, but at least they paid. Her son said she was a fool, that she could get three times as much from the palaces across the river, but she had never crossed the Neva and did not intend to start now, not a widow with a crippled son.

He sat grumbling, driving the horse. She stood on one of the wooden wings that stuck out a yard each side to stop the sled turning over. Ten *versts* from the fortress, still on a sparsely travelled lane, a strange vehicle bore down on them. It looked like a motorcar, but the front wheels were attached to skis and it had no wheels at all at the back, instead a wide, ribbed belt spun underneath and made the motorcar go by clawing the snow like the hundred feet of a caterpillar.

Her son cursed and forced the pony to the side while she shouted at him to look out for the ditch. Imagine her and him with his one leg trying to free the sled. The caterpillar belt stopped turning and the vehicle skidded to a halt, block-ing the road.

Three men got out. Her son reached for his rusty pistol, but she stopped him. These were not the type to rob wood. The eldest was lean as a stork, grey-skinned and bony and even older than she was. He wore a long tailored coat, what

477

country people called a *diplomat,* though this one was frayed. The young ones wore the cloaks of aristocrat soldiers. One had an officer's moustache, the other had lost an arm. God provided – if her son had lost only an arm instead of a leg he would have gone to the city and left her alone.

The old stork reached into his *diplomat* and pulled from the coat pocket thick wads of roubles. She had never seen so much money in her life but she could count and it looked like enough to buy a horse and a cow and roubles left over for potatoes to last until summer. The old stork said she could have the money if the gentleman with the moustache could ride into the Peter-Paul Fortress under her heap of wood.

She asked how he would get out again. She said when she took manure from the fortress stables in her empty sled the guards stuck bayonets into it as she left.

How he would get out was not her concern, the old stork answered sharply. All he wanted was to get in. Her son shrugged. A crazy man with money was no concern of theirs. They drove the sled into a copse, out of sight of the road, and hid the wood they removed to make room for the man. The snowcar followed; her son was bewitched by it . . . he said it made a railroad track out of the snow. She told him to shut his mouth; the aristocrats were speaking. Her son knew some French words but he shook his head. They were speaking English.

'This is less a plan than a hope,' Roland chided as Ash prepared to climb into the sled.

'It's also my only hope.'

'I wish you would reconsider, let me come in with you – '

'I need you outside. I want that snowcar warmed up and raring to go in case I come out with a posse after me.'

'"Posse"? What is "posse"?'

'*Gendarmerie,* is what it is. The sheriff and a whole bunch of deputies.' Ash lay down in the sled, and Roland mo-

478

tioned the peasants to cover him with the logs. 'Like the cops?' Roland asked, and Ash said, 'Yes, except on horses.'

Roland touched his shoulder. *'Bonne chance, ami.'*

When they had buried the one with the moustache to the satisfaction of his companions, the old stork and the one-armed aristocrat did a strange thing. The stork held the money in both hands for her to see. The one-armed man pulled a silvery blade from his walking stick and sliced the roubles in half. His blade cut the thick wad like butter. He gave her one half and kept the other. The stork said she could have it when their friend got out safely.

She protested how could she be blamed if he didn't get out of the fortress, they were taking advantage of a widow, but the old stork fixed her with his beady stare and she knew in her heart that he knew that she had had every intention of telling the guards and demanding a reward . . . because the money for a horse and milk cow was not enough. Before she could buy them she had to pay the *koulak* to whom she owed her debts, and then the tax collector who would demand his share for the horse and cow.

Ash ducked down as a squad of conscripts, fresh from the farm by the look of them, marched past the woodpile where he had crouched for the hour he'd been watching the prison entrance. The drill sergeant bellowed, and the unit right-flanked away from the firewood.

The fortress, which housed some twenty-five thousand troops within its walls, was busy as a city this evening; in spite of the steadily thickening snow the lamplit yards between the low barracks and storehouses echoed tramping feet and the rattle of rifle bolts. When the sled had first left him in the woodpile, which covered nearly a quarter acre, Ash had worried that the soldiers would still be drilling when von Basel's men came for Tamara and Sedovina.

479

After a while he began to wonder if he'd somehow missed them.

Ash edged out of the shadow a little. It was dark now, later than Lieutenant Orlov's sunset taunt, but the soldiers continued to drill by the light spilling from the windows.

At last a cannon boomed six o'clock. The soldiers fell out, and minutes later the yards were deserted except for some black-robed priests walking slowly toward the cathedral. Ash stood up and walked boldly toward the passage that led to the prison. Two men in civilian clothes were approaching the passage from the direction of the main Neva Gates. Ash veered close enough to get a look at them, then headed for the cathedral. Neither was von Basel, but one looked fairly short and squat. Sidelong, he watched them turn into the passage beside the prison.

He went up the cathedral steps now, and when he looked back again he could barely see the two-storey yellow building through the snow. He went inside and knelt by a tomb near the door. The priests had gathered before a huge altar at the far end; there were no pews but many tombs.

Ash timed the progress of the two men in his mind, following them into the prison while his eyes played over the surprising sight of Roman letters. He was praying at Peter the Great's tomb, the Czar who had built the city, this fortress and cathedral and the prison . . . visualizing now . . . up the passage, in the main door, the foyer and the search room, then presenting some passes of some sort and waiting, perhaps, while the guards went up the stone steps, through a door down to the end of the first corridor, turn right and to the end of the second corridor, halfway down the third to Sedovina's door. Key in the lock, throw the door back, take the frightened girl with Tamara nearby. Key in the lock, throw the door back, take Tamara. Throw blankets over their shoulders, walk them out the door, down the corridor, left turn, down the corridor, left turn down the

480

corridor, through the door, down the steps and hand them to the two men, who take them from either side, through the search room and the foyer and into the snow. Ash got up and hurried out of the cathedral, loosening his sabre.

The yard was still deserted, the snow thick. No one came from the passage. Ash looked both ways. No one. He ran to find their tracks before fresh snow covered them – and just then they stepped out of the passage. They had taken the extra minutes to remove the ankle chains.

Tamara. She was holding herself erect, stiff, as if angry. Ash prayed that angry meant she wasn't hurt. The short one was holding Sedovina's arm, the other Tamara's. Ash drew closer. The short one was speaking to Sedovina in Russian, his voice insinuating, threatening. He became silent when he saw Ash approaching, confirming that this removal was clandestine and that at best the prison commandant had been paid off to look the other way.

Sedovina looked terrified. Ten feet from them now, and Tamara saw Ash. Her face lit up for a moment, then went blank. She drew back, momentarily distracting the man holding her. Ash took the opportunity, pulled his sabre like a boarding cutlass and smashed him with the hilt. For once it worked like they'd promised at the Academy. Surprise and slippery footing helped. The man went down hard as Ash whipped the point to Orlov's throat.

He pulled his Luger and held it under his cloak. Orlov's eyes went from Ash's blade to the gun and back to the blade pricking his throat.

'I remember you,' said Ash. 'I'll kill you if you don't get us out of here.'

'You can't use my papers, they know me at the gate – '

'Take us with you.'

'They won't let me.'

Ash slid the sabre back into his scabbard and aimed the gun at Orlov's eyes. 'Try.'

481

Orlov's companion stirred on the ground. Ash yanked the man to his feet, snapped his arm into a hammerlock, held the pistol on Orlov again. 'We're walking across the yard to those woodpiles. Tamara, stay close. Hold Sedovina.'

'Go on.' He jerked the man he was holding and shoved the pistol in Orlov's back. They crossed the yard, passed dangerously close to some of the lamps, finally made the woodpiles. Ash looked back. Had they been spotted from any of the windows?

He let go the hammerlock and hit the Russian in the back of his neck. Orlov started to move again. Ash covered him, ordered him to kneel. He looked down at Orlov. 'Where were you taking them?'

Orlov hesitated, then: 'The same as yesterday. A barracks room. I was only going to question – '

'Shut up and listen to me . . . I'll kill you the first hint I get that we can't escape from here. You're taking us out of here . . . your life is in your own hands. Now get up and get us out.'

Orlov did and turned toward the Peter Gates.

'No.' Ash stopped him. 'The river gates. Take us to the river, damn you.'

Count von Basel found the lingering aroma of his police chauffeur who'd gone to relieve himself sufficient to impel him to pull down his window, ignoring the cold snow the wind was blowing up the river. He was parked on the ice a hundred yards from the fortress, which was a dark, barely visible presence, looming in the night. A faint light marked the river gates, where Orlov would soon emerge, if there was still a God in heaven, with Vera Sedovina and Ash's Tamara Tishkova.

Von Basel and the commandant had reached a fair bargain after von Basel provided a blizzard of official

482

memoranda to make the commandant appear properly innocent. And Lieutenant Orlov, completely unaware of what was going on, his primitive mind slavering over the young ballerina, was armed with the finest papers signed by the most important officials money could buy. There were moments, von Basel thought with a smile, when one could really learn to love Russia.

The needle tip of a sabre touched his throat. Carefully, slowly, he looked to see, framed in the car window, hat and cloak covered with snow, Chevalier François Roland. For a moment the silence was so complete he thought he could hear the river rushing under the thick ice.

'Step out of your car, Count von Basel.'

In all these years in Russia von Basel had never been caught by surprise. And now, by of all people . . . it was almost worse than if Ash had done it himself.

'You goddamned French queer.'

Roland's eyebrows dropped. 'If that is a proposition, my dear, I must confess I never couple with leprous Arabs, syphilitic dogs or German counts. Put your hands where I can see them, and get out.'

Von Basel saw the returning driver moving up in a crouch behind Roland. The man straightened up, raised his pistol like a club. Perhaps instinct warned Roland, von Basel thought, perhaps the abrupt cessation of snow on his back when the police chauffeur blocked the wind with his body . . . whatever, once warned, the Frenchman was impressive in his speed and accuracy. He whirled, slashed – and not, von Basel noted as he made his way across the seat and out the opposite door, not just anywhere. Right to the throat, so that the man died silently.

Von Basel rested a gun on the roof of the car and aimed at Roland. Roland allowed himself a smile. 'Put it away . . . you can't use a noisy gun any more than I can. If you could you wouldn't be lurking out here.' He walked around the car. Von Basel pulled his sword out of his walking stick and opened the hilt bars.

Roland shook his head. 'Surely your psychotic tendencies do not include the suicidal. Keep in mind that my training was somewhat more rigorous than yours, which I gather consisted of butchering impetuous, untutored university students.'

Von Basel ignored the taunt. 'I'm a duellist – ' he raised his sabre – 'you're only a fencer.'

'I think I saw enough killing at Verdun to last me a lifetime, but I can and I will kill you if you don't surrender that weapon – '

'I also have a second advantage,' von Basel said, no smile on his face. 'Two arms.' He pulled out a long dagger, rapped it twice against his sabre.

'*En garde.*'

'Drop back,' Ash said. 'Let them out first.' Ahead, officers leaving for the night on passes were converging on the brightly lighted river gate from various paths. They stopped under a tree, one of many lining the path which contributed at this point to the feeling of an urban park.

'Vera, take his other arm, and Tamara you take mine. Hold her, Orlov. She's supposed to be your prisoner. Show your chains, Vera.' Her wrists were still shackled, Tamara's weren't. As they neared the gate Ash held Tamara's arm conspicuously and nudged Orlov with the gun through his cloak.

The gate was a pass through the wall, about fifty feet long with a vaulted ceiling. Iron grills barred it inside and out, and soldiers guarded the grills, which were kept closed until they opened them to allow someone through. Ash reflected that while they were crossing the fifty feet between the two grills the guards had time to change their minds.

Orlov slapped his papers in the guard's hand and

answered insolently in Russian when the soldier asked him something. Ash looked at Tamara, who nodded it was all right. The guard opened the gate grill and they passed through, Orlov starting to hang back.

'Keep moving.'

They reached the second, outer, grill, and Ash again watched Tamara's reaction as Orlov spoke to the head of the guard. The conversation was longer this time, but at last the grill swung open. Ash nudged Orlov. He pushed Sedovina through and Ash followed with Tamara. Shouts echoed through the stone pass. The guards looked toward them.

Ash saw a commotion at the first grill, saw the man he had left at the woodpile shouting and pointing. Sedovina called out a warning. Orlov pulled a gun from his coat.

'Raise your hands, Commander.'

44

Ash shot through his cloak and caught Orlov's gun as the Russian detective fell. The startled guards had no idea where the shot had come from. Their officer, however, pulled a revolver from his flap holster. Ash knocked him down with Orlov's gun, but the officer kicked Ash's feet from under him. Ash was put on his back with a bonejarring crash.

The guards lunged at him. Tamara scooped up the revolver the officer had dropped and shot the nearest guard. Ash got to his feet, ordered the other guard to put his hands on the wall. Tamara waved her gun and translated. The guard did as he was told, and the officer buried his face in the snow.

'Run.' Ash pushed Tamara toward the river. She caught Sedovina's shackled wrist, and they ran together across the stone terrace, down the landing stairs. Backing after them, Ash fired shots down the vaulted gateway, scattering soldiers now running through it. He made for the landing and caught up on the ice. Sedovina had fallen and Tamara was pulling her to her feet.

Ash searched the dark. 'Where's Roland?'

Muzzle flashes showed beneath the black cliff of the fortress. The crack of pistols was joined by the deeper sound of rifles. The cutting wind carried snow so thick that the lights of the Winter Palace had vanished only half a mile across the river. Ash took Tamara's hand, she held Sedovina, they ran.

'Roland . . .'

The muzzle flashes homed in on his voice. They dived to

the ice, crawled from the gunfire. Ash spotted the dark shape of a car, got up, stumbled over a snow-covered body. Roland? He turned him over. A stranger, his throat slashed. And it wasn't the snowcar. He heard another motor, and the snowcar loomed out of the dark, Roland at the wheel. Rifle fire again, bullets snapping past their heads, caroming off the car.

Roland turned it clumsily. Ash pushed Tamara and Sedovina in the back, jumped in beside Roland as the rifle fire concentrated once again. Roland reached for the gear stick, groaned, slumped against the steering wheel. His face was a white blur in the dark. He managed to get out . . . 'Von Basel . . . poniard . . .'

Ash pulled Roland from the wheel. The weapon was stuck in his chest . . . von Basel had stabbed Roland with a heavy dagger while Roland had tried to fend off von Basel's sabre with his single arm . . . God, how in hell had Roland cranked the car? How long could he last?

The fortress searchlights flung white beams into the night. Ash eased his friend into the passenger seat, climbed over him, found the clutch and gear stick and skidded into a tight turn – a circle of light came swiftly over the ice and caught the car.

'*Down*,' Ash instructed. 'Heads down.'

Tamara stretched over the front seat and cradled Roland in her arms while bullets slashed the canvas top and ricocheted off the metal.

'He beat me . . .' Roland whispered.

'He had a poniard, friend, not exactly an even fight . . .' Ash found second gear.

The Frenchman tugged his sleeve. 'He's better than we thought . . .'

Ash felt the caterpillar track bite deep, but the searchlight blinded him and he skidded back toward the fortress.

'Kennet – '

He veered too late, a second light caught the car – a pair of hugely wide-set eyes. Ash tried to steer away. Cat's eyes, gauging when to pounce. Ash slewed a hundred and eighty degrees, put the lights behind the car, headed for darkness. 'Got to find a hospital – '

Roland was silent. A machine-gun opened up with a grinding noise that overwhelmed the rifles and the labouring engine. Bullets chewed up the ice, seeking the car in bursts; Ash turned hard left, hard right, repeated the manoeuvre, zigzagging to confuse the gunner, but the man was too skilful and the heavy slugs continued to crack past their heads, ricochet off the car. The left ski shattered. The car lurched, sagged to the ice but kept moving.

A third searchlight closed in. Ash risked a glance back. The fortress looked on fire with white lights and the flickers of rifle shots and the steady red tracing of a machine-gun high up on top of the bastion.

Sedovina shook Ash's shoulder. 'The tram. The tram on the ice. It's downstream, you can't drive over it.'

Ash nodded, started to put the crippled car into a gentle turn upstream with the blazing fortress on his left when he heard a dull boom and the petrol tank erupted in flame.

'*Out.*' The snowcar skidded to a halt. Ash ran around the car and grabbed at Roland. A second explosion ripped the front of the car, rocking it and hurling Ash against Tamara.

'Leave him – '

'I can't –'

'He's *dead*, Kennet. Please . . .'

They found Sedovina and ran together downstream as more searchlights found the car. Ash looked back. Roland's arm was stretched toward the lights, his head was thrown back against the seat . . . almost, it occurred bizarrely to Ash, as if he were acknowledging applause from the fortress.

The car was engulfed by fire and as they ran into the night and the swirling snow, and the noise of the rifle and machine-gun fire died away, they heard a new sound – hoofbeats – the rumble of Cossack lancers coming after them . . .

They ran from the lancers, from the searchlights, from the glare of the burning car. The ice was rough, and the new coating of snow made it difficult to see the variations in it. Sedovina stumbled, she had lost one of the felt slippers. Ash managed to retrace their steps, found the slipper and brought it to her. Tamara knelt and put it on. The girl seemed in shock.

'I can't keep up . . . go ahead and – '

Tamara and Ash took Sedovina's hands in case she got any more crazy ideas about stopping. Suddenly ahead was another searchlight. Ash was about to dive into the snow when he saw it was moving rapidly. Tamara saw it too and guessed what it was. 'The *tram*. Come on . . .'

Behind them horses sounded closer; the riders were calling to each other, their voices moving apart as they spread across the ice. Ash spotted the slight ridge of the tramline and then the headlight illuminating the power wire over-head and the line of poles that held it, and finally the gleam of the steel rails.

Behind the headlight shone the windows of a two-car tram. People were wiping at the iced glass, peering out at the flashes of gunfire and the burning car. Tamara went onto the track and proceeded to hail the speeding tram like a taxi.

Sedovina scrambled after her. The tram screeched, locked wheels scattered sparks. Ash pulled Tamara over the embankment as the tram slid past and banged to a halt. Ash didn't know which way to go . . . the Cossacks would reach the line in seconds. Downstream was the icy empty waste of the river . . . and the embankments were too far to run to . . .

But Sedovina suddenly came to life, took control. She went aboard the tram and raged at the occupants in Russian. Some backed away from her. Others glanced in the direction of the Cossacks. Some started shouting at the driver, who crossed his arms and shook his head.

'What'd she say?'

'She's asking, *telling* them to help us,' Tamara said.

'Come,' Sedovina called out. 'Hurry.'

Ash looked at Tamara. They could hear the Cossacks. 'We'll be trapped,' she told Ash.

A group of men who had been shaking their fists at the driver surged into the aisle, ran to the front and pushed him away from the controls. Moments later the tram jerked forward.

'*Come,*' Sedovina repeated. '*Hurry . . .*'

Ash looked at Tamara. They ran for the rear step as the car picked up speed, swung aboard the hot stuffy car to the cheers of the passengers. They increased speed, but suddenly the lancers galloped into the light that spilled from the windows, came alongside and kept pace while their officer shouted for the men driving the tram to stop.

Ahead, Ash saw the light pick up the distant Palace Embankment through the blowing snow. The officer drew his heavy sabre and slashed at the window in the driver's compartment. The passengers driving the tram ducked from the shower of broken glass, but one grabbed the stick used to raise the electric contact, leaned half out the broken window and swung back at the startled officer, who pulled his horse up and gave a command.

The Cossacks whipped their rifles off their backs.

'Get *down*,' Ash called out.

But instead of doing what Ash told them, the passengers climbed to their feet and stood in the windows.

'Tell them to get down, they'll be killed – '

'They won't get down,' Sedovina said. 'Not again.'

The officer slashed and shouted again. Tamara pulled at Ash's arm. 'He's telling them to shoot.'

The passengers stood firm. A few horsemen halfheartedly raised their guns, but none fired even as the tram picked up speed and the track began rising to the Palace Embankment. One by one the lancers stopped their horses. Ash watched until they were lost in the dark. The last he saw of them was the officer turning his horse and riding slowly back to the fortress.

The passengers cheered and, as the tram slowed and they prepared to run before the police came, two workmen hurriedly opened a sack of tools and chiselled the manacles off Sedovina's wrists. One, a worn-looking man in his forties, knelt, whispered something to Tamara, kissed her hand and hurried back to the tram . . .

They crossed the Nevsky Prospect and hurried by back streets the short distance to the troika-stand behind the Kazan Cathedral.

When the racing sleigh had finally left the city behind and was breaking into the woods of Krestovsky Island, Ash, who was sitting between Tamara and Sedovina with an arm around each, saw that Tamara had tears in her eyes. 'Is it something the man from the tram said to you?'

She shook her head. 'I was thinking of Roland . . . '

Sedovina, huddled against Ash, said, 'He told Tishkova that when he was a young man, before he had a family to feed, he had waited two nights in the snow to buy a ticket in the highest seat of the gallery to see Tishkova dance. He said it was the most magnificent moment of his life and in twenty years he'd never forgotten.'

Vadim Mikhailov sat alone in a crowd of drunken Russians singing to gypsy guitars. Wondering if any were police spies, Ash hurried through the revellers and sank down on the cushions beside the old piano player. 'They're okay, at the River Yacht Club.'

'Thank God.'

'Have you found a place to hide? They can't stay there.'

'Can I see her?'

'What about your friend, Vadim . . . you promised – '

'He's coming any minute, he will come and help you, and hide the ladies.'

Ash wasn't sure whether he believed Mikhailov. He was exhausted, and heartsick over François Roland. The gypsy songs were a grating din and there seemed more cigarette smoke than air . . . He'd willingly risked his whole mission to save Tamara, but really never thought Roland would be the price . . . 'Dammit, where the hell is your friend?'

Vadim Mikhailov fidgeted, poured tea from a nearby samovar and looked anxiously at the door each time the candles blew. Suddenly he turned to Ash. 'You said yesterday that Tishkova had an affair with the Czar.'

'Years ago,' Ash said bleakly. 'What's that got to do with – ?'

'It troubles you – '

'Dammit, Vadim, it's none of your business.'

'Well, it's not true. They were friends, briefly, when she was a girl and more recently again. He was taken with her – so beautiful, such a splendid dancer, but I believe no affair. I know people who were commanded to perform in the *Firebird* at the Alexander Palace – '

'The ballet?' Ash asked, aware how good it felt to believe she hadn't slept with Nicholas.

Mikhailov, relieved to have been able to distract Ash, nodded, vigorously. 'Right after it was performed in Paris the Czar invited Tishkova to dance *Firebird* for the Court at the Alexander Palace. A great honour. The sets and costumes were shipped from the Paris production – the Czarina cancelled it.'

'Why?'

'Jealous, perhaps . . . or perhaps she just did not like Stravinsky . . . anyway, as a result the sets and costumes lie in the cellars of the Alexander Palace, and the great *Firebird* has never been danced in Russia.'

Ash looked at the door. '*Where* is your friend, they're not that safe at the club.' . . . Nor, judging by the mood of that crowd on the tram, Ash thought, did the Czar have much more time.

Tamara refused to stop moving. If she did she would think, and if she thought, she would remember . . . the running and shooting, the explosions, and Roland dying in her arms, and the thunder of the Cossacks. And if she let herself remember that, she would be as frightened as Sedovina.

Kennet had done well indeed . . . a warm room, a huge bath, clothing, boots, even a wig to cover her all too famous jet black hair. She bathed quickly, though she ached so from tension in every muscle she felt it would take a year to rid her body of the strain and the stench of the prison. She vacated the tub for Sedovina and left her to soak while she made up, arranged the auburn wig and chose her clothing.

She got Sedovina out of the bath, got her dried off and into one of her dresses, which was a bit short in the hem and full in the bosom. She sat her in front of a mirror and began pinning up her beautiful golden hair, envying its thickness.

'I couldn't believe such things would happen in Russia . . . the guards were despicable, look at your face. No wonder people are angry – '

'The guards are brutalized by the established order,' Sedovina murmured. 'That's how the Czar rules.'

'They're brutes,' Tamara agreed, stuffing the girl's hair under one of her sable hats.

'No . . . the guards are Russian too. The Czar has ruled by making us hate each other. Peasants, Cossacks, artists, soldiers – *we* are Russia. We don't have to fight each other –'

'Good,' said Tamara, 'at least you seem to be snapping out of it.' She looked closely at Sedovina. God she was beautiful, bump on the nose and all. What did Kennet think of her?

'I was terribly afraid,' Sedovina said, on the edge of tears. 'I wanted to be brave but the noise – '

'You were very brave when you had to be, when it counted. You saved us on the tram . . . Well, we have to cover that mark on your face.'

Wielding her softest powder brushes, Tamara worked pale rouge over the welt. Sedovina winced. Tamara made her laugh by saying, 'Haven't you heard it hurts to be beautiful?'

When she was done she draped one of her coats over the girl's shoulders. Sedovina said it was too fine, her father had left her own coat.

Tamara insisted. 'The police aren't so likely to be hunting escaped prisoners in sable.'

'There!'

An old man shuffled in. He was ancient, haggard-looking, thinner, if that were possible, than even Mikhailov. He had the aloof stare of an aristocrat.

'My friend,' Vadim said proudly. 'His Royal Highness Prince Kurakin.'

Ash was not impressed. Russia was littered with impoverished nobles, and this one's cape looked a hundred years old. 'How is he going to get me to the Czarina?'

'Prince Kurakin is a necromancer. He holds seances. He has raised the ghost of Rasputin – '

'Mikhailov, I warn you – '

'Yes, yes, it's true. He has raised the ghost. Interior Minister Protopopov himself attends his seances – asking the ghost for advice.'

Ash groaned. Why had he even for a second believed Vadim –

'He is summoned by the Empress. He's been to Tsar-skoye Selo every night this week. He'll bring you with him, now.'

Ash held back and considered . . . Lord Exeter had claimed that the Czarina was consulting mystics. He looked at the prince. 'Sounds like a faker who got lucky. Why would he help me?'

'Faker or not, I won't judge, but Prince Kurakin has con-cluded that the Czar must leave.' Ash looked at Vadim. 'How come he's friends with a piano player?' To hell with being diplomatic at this point.

'His Highness is poor, very poor. He permits me to buy him drinks . . . Whatever you think, at least pretend to take him seriously.'

Ash glanced again at Prince Kurakin. 'All right, let's hear what he's selling.'

Ash caught the prince's eye and indicated with a nod that he should join them. Kurakin looked away and stared at the gypsy dancers. Mikhailov said, 'He is a nobleman, Com-mander. We must go to him.' Ash bit his tongue and they did. Prince Kurakin invited them to sit. He spoke in a qua-vering voice with a funereal tone that struck Ash as intended to promise intimacy with the supernatural. But instead of the hocus-pocus Ash feared, he got to the point matter-of-factly.

'Rasputin has repeatedly warned me that revolution is imminent. Last night he informed me that His Imperial Maj-esty the Czar is the cause of the people's anger. He told me to tell the ministers to form a new government.'

Ash refrained from remarking that Rasputin seemed to have assumed the attitude of an anxious nobleman.

'Mikhailov tells me I can help you . . . Your Highness.'

Kurakin raised a spidery hand. His eyes were bright, no doubt with a mystic light. It wasn't hard to imagine him holding a seance in thrall. But again he spoke like a

495

nobleman who had suddenly come to realize that the mob was about to pull Petrograd down around his ears.

'The Czar must be removed. But not harmed. Rasputin was adamant. Their Imperial Majesties must not be harmed.'

Wondering if his last hope of reaching the Czar lay with two deluded old men, Ash said, 'Your Highness, may I ask your interest in this? What do you want from me?'

'I am a Russian,' Prince Kurakin said. 'I see visions of the future, and that future is red with blood . . . still, I have hope Rasputin might be our saviour. By removing the Czar, as Rasputin directs, maybe we can stave off the slaughter.'

Ash nodded. Whether Kurakin meant it or not didn't matter a hell of a lot if he could help him get the Czar off his throne and thereby keep Russia stable enough to go on fighting Germany . . . and make Russia a palatable ally for the US. Strange how it all came back to Rasputin . . . almost as though it had been preordained or something . . . dammit, Ash thought, I'm thinking like a Russian . . .

The police stopped their troikas at the palace bridge. Ash and the prince were in the lead, on their way to the Tsarskoye Selo Railroad Station. He tried to signal Tamara, Sedovina and Mikhailov in the second troika but it was too late. Mikhailov was taking them to the prince's apartment near the Moscow Railroad Station – as unexpected and therefore safe a hiding place as they could find in the city. Ash hadn't expected a roadblock at the palace bridge so many hours after their escape.

The women were dressed like a pair of wealthy Petrograd matrons out for a big night, their faces almost hidden in fur . . . Still, if the police launched a full search . . . but it turned out the police had their hands full diverting traffic from the palace area because thousands of demonstrators were marching down the Nevsky Prospect. The windblown snow carried thunder – *Khleba. Khleba. Khleba . . .*

They could still hear the chanting at the station. Prince Kurakin was recognized and ushered aboard a waiting train with elaborate courtesy. He remained silent for the thirty-minute ride through the night. There was no sign in the dark, or on the smooth Tsarskoye Selo roadbed, of Kirichenko's explosions. Where, Ash wondered, had the fighting squad leader gone to? Probably to the middle of Petrograd, tonight . . .

Kurakin was equally silent in the court carriage that took them past the aristocracy's mansions and the Catherine Palace, but he suddenly rapped his stick on the roof of the carriage. It stopped, bowing footmen opened the door and Kurakin climbed out in the snow. The lights of the Alexander Palace were still far ahead, but Kurakin's attention was drawn to a cluster of flaming torches some distance off the drive. Wrapping his black cape around his shoulders, he motioned Ash to join him.

'Where are you going?'

'Rasputin's tomb.'

Through the snow Ash could just make out a small structure, and as they drew nearer he saw it was a chapel, still under construction. Prince Kurakin followed a path of wooden planks. 'He won't be here long,' he said in his most dirgelike tones.

A carriage was parked outside. Ash waited for an explanation.

'Rasputin predicted that his ashes would be cast to the wind – his body returned to God.'

Footmen attended the carriage. An equerry who looked like he hadn't been outside in years shivered at the entrance to the chapel in patent leather shoes and the red cape embroidered with the double-headed Imperial Eagle of his office. He bowed to Prince Kurakin, who said, 'Inform the Empress that her friend appeared at my seance tonight.'

The equerry took this information as routine and retreated into the chapel. Kurakin turned to a sceptical Ash. 'I don't make things up.'

'Of course . . . Your Highness.'

Kurakin glowered and drew his threadbare cape closer around his scrawny throat. The equerry returned. 'Her Imperial Majesty requests that you pray with her.' He led them into the chapel, which smelled of freshly sawn wood and hot wax. There, praying before a candlelit icon on a flower-spread altar, knelt Czarina Alexandra.

Her head was bowed and her eyes were closed and she made no sign as the equerry cleared flowers on either side of her to make space for Ash and Prince Kurakin. Ash knelt and watched sidelong. She looked remarkably well, Ash thought, far better than the rumours had led him to expect, her face smooth, her expression calm, almost placid; erase, as did the flickering candles, the hollows of pain and suffering normally under her eyes, and a girl of exquisite beauty shone through.

She opened her eyes, looked past Prince Kurakin to Ash. Her eyes became wide, and for a second Ash expected her to scream as she'd done when she'd seen him in the Czar's billiard room. 'You again push yourself into my life, Commander.'

Ash said nothing, tried to meet her steady gaze while hoping for the prince to interrupt. The prince kept silent. Ash waited . . . 'When I was informed that you had accompanied Prince Kurakin, I wondered whether you would have the nerve to desecrate this holy place. What sort of monster are you?'

Ash knew this was his last chance to persuade the royal family to leave. The Romanovs were finished and Russia was finished with them, but a disintegrated Russian army was too high a price to maintain this one family in splendid isolation twenty miles from the capital, even one extra day.

'Begging your pardon, ma'am, but you're acting like a damned fool,' Ash heard himself say, and rushed on before he lost his nerve. 'If you want to save Russia, not to mention the lives of your children, and if you want to beat Germany, you'll accept King George's generous offer right now. For God's sake, they'll burn the city down and then come out here and burn your palace down around you.'

'*Get out . . .*'

Ash thought of Tamara, hunted like a felon in her own city, and of François Roland, dead on the Neva, and of the Grand Duke Valery, under the ice, Lady Exeter in a marshy grave . . . 'You stupid, selfish bitch.' He stood up, stalked to the door.

'*Wait.*' Her voice was like a whipcrack.

Ash stopped at the door. 'Does it occur to you that's just about your last imperial command?'

'*Wait . . .*' And then, quietly she added a distinctly nonimperial 'please.'

She got up from her knees and beckoned him. There were, he saw as he came closer, tears in her dark, violet-blue eyes.

'Don't leave me,' she said in what could only be described as a frightened voice . . . She reached for his hand, spoke to Ash as if they were alone and Prince Kurakin had disappeared to join Rasputin's ghost.

'I came here tonight because my children are sick, they have measles. Whenever they were sick Father Gregory comforted them. My son, my little boy, suffers from a blood disorder which causes him the most excruciating pain, pain such as neither you nor I have ever known. Before he faints from it, while he can still cry, he says the only words a little boy can say. He says, "Mummy, it hurts. Please make it stop." . . . Do you have any children, Commander Ash?'

Ash shook his head.

'Even if you did, you couldn't understand, because a child doesn't turn in its last resort to its father, it turns to its mother. Did you not turn to your mother when you were a child?'

'I was very young when my mother died . . . I suppose I did, though . . .'

'My baby begged me to stop the pain, screamed for it to stop but I could do nothing but sit beside him until he fainted, wait through the night to see if he died. Then Father Gregory came. Because of Rasputin my son lives, and because of Rasputin, when my baby screamed to please make it stop, mummy, I could make it stop . . . until they murdered him . . . My own family killed my only friend. Now, alone, I must support my husband. The Czar needs me. I am his and our love is the only sun in his life . . . But with Rasputin gone, I have little to offer him but love . . . Father Gregory had the power to divine the loyal from the disloyal around us, to help me choose who should serve my husband. Without Rasputin, we are lost.'

Well, thought Ash, here we go. He glanced at Prince Kurakin, who obviously was overwhelmed by his Czarina's presence. Ash stood up, aimed a meaningful look at the old prince.

It seemed to work. Clutching at his cape, screwing up his courage, he said in a quavering, sepulchral voice, 'Rasputin knows, Your Majesty. Rasputin said you should leave this place of turmoil . . .'

The Empress smiled faintly at Kurakin. 'You are his messenger.' She turned to Ash. 'And you are his instrument.'

'Can the children travel?' Ash asked her.

'Yes.'

'Then we must go, before it is too late.'

'Just for a while . . . to England, just for a while . . .'

'Of course, until matters settle down.' Their voices echoed in the chamber, though both had begun to whisper. Kurakin seemed to realize his work was done and, bowing, backed out the door. Ash said, 'How soon can the Czar return here?'

'He's on his way.'

'His Majesty has left Mogilev?' Ash asked with sudden alarm.

'Sometime after midnight. What is wrong, Commander?'

Von Basel was what was wrong. The Czar's person was inviolable at the Stavka, just as it was in Tsarskoye Selo, protected by an enormous Imperial Guard, Convoy Guard and bodyguard, but not aboard the Imperial Train. In spite of the Convoy Guard and the railway battalions the route between Mogilev and Petrograd passed through enormous empty stretches of Russian countryside – thirty and forty miles between towns. And what was more predictable than the route of a train confined to its lonely rails?

45

'A German spy will try to kidnap your husband from the Imperial Train, Your Majesty.'

Her forehead wrinkled as if she were reassessing her opinion of an officer who had dared to make an absurd statement.

'It's true . . . he has already infiltrated sections of the Okhrana. He had an office in the Litovsky Prison, and a Russian assistant named Lieutenant Orlov – that's all I know, but it's the absolute truth. You must believe – '

'Help me walk,' the Czarina snapped, and limped on Ash's arm from Rasputin's chapel. The carriage took them quickly across the Imperial Park. In moments she had the head of the Okhrana on the telephone, and an answer minutes later. 'He used the name Captain Moskolenko. He has disappeared. The Okhrana assures me they will have him soon, *and* that he presents no threat to my husband.'

The same Okhrana, Ash thought, that von Basel had infiltrated; the same Okhrana that, the French ambassador had informed François Roland, routinely forged letters of respectful appreciation to the Czarina purportedly from loyal subjects. Ash said, 'May I have your *laissez-passer*, Your Majesty? I need to meet your husband's train.'

She wrote it out in a swift, broad hand and said she would telegraph the Czar that Ash was coming.

'Ma'am, I suggest you not – '

'Don't worry, Commander, we telegraph in code.' When Ash still looked dubious, she added, 'We give people our own names . . . including you. Nimrod – the hunter – we called you when we discussed your visits.'

Ash took the document, and asked for an aeroplane.

The airfield was north of Petrograd. By the Czarina's order a special train returned Ash to the city and a police convoy escorted him through the night. But though the lights of the hangars were on and a pilot stood beside a warmed up British B.E. 2C, the snow was hopeless.

The sky was lightening in the east, but dawn promised nothing except more snow. Ash watched the sky; the B.E. 2C was as stable a plane as there was, but he also knew that a thousand feet off the ground the pilot wouldn't be able to distinguish up from down.

The police drove him back to the city to put him aboard the morning express at the Warsaw Station. But what greeted them in Petrograd was ten thousand men and women marching up the Liteiny Prospect under the red flag, ignoring both the snow and the police. They seemed in a gay mood, bantering with the soldiers and Cossacks who hemmed them in on both sides.

Ash jumped from the car and headed for the Warsaw Station. The Nevsky Prospect writhed black in the grey morning light as thousands of workers marched down the broad boulevard shoulder to shoulder and from sidewalk to sidewalk. They were pouring off the Liteiny Prospect, coming from the Alexander Bridge, which meant they had probably marched on the centre of the city from the Vyborg Factory District across the Neva, beyond Tamara's mansion. There seemed to be more women than men.

Khleba. Khleba. Khleba.

The railroad terminal was mobbed. Ticket lines spilled into Ismailovsky Prospect. Ash pushed through them, found the stationmaster's officer and presented his pass. An empty private compartment was found on a train heading south. Lunch was promised aboard, despite whatever rumours the 'honourable commander' might have heard to

503

the contrary. There were no difficulties on the trains outside the corrupt and pestilent city of Petrograd, he was promised.

But when the stationmaster had gone his young assistant refused a tip and looked Ash in the eye. 'I'd be careful who I showed that particular travel pass to, Commander. If the wrong person sees it you're carrying your own death warrant.'

Ash showed his pass to the chief conductor, requested a map of the railroads between Petrograd and Mogilev. 'This and everything else I say to you is to be kept in the strictest confidence. You're to keep me informed of the whereabouts of the Imperial Train.'

'The Imperial Train has left the main line, Commander.'

'What?'

'His Majesty often shunts to secondary lines so as not to interfere with military trains.'

Secondary lines passed through even more isolated countryside, desolate and remote. Ash had the conductor point out likely routes on the map.

'At each station,' Ash told him, 'you're to confirm by telegraph the exact location of the Imperial Train.'

The conductor said he of course would . . . Ash stared gloomily at the birch trees – ghostly white shadows on the snow. It wasn't hard to imagine von Basel in a similar conversation with a railroad official, in spite of the Okhrana's claims, and von Basel was miles ahead of him. Ash pored over his map, shaking off sleep, and tried to figure out where the German would strike.

The express was making speed at last, after a slow start, travelling, Ash presumed, between supply trains fore and aft. They roared through local stations and ignored express stops, halting only for coal and water and to disgorge bewildered passengers. Ash dozed between stops, where he checked the telegraph. Then at noon, at Dno – crossroads between the Petrograd-Mogilev line and the west-east track between Pskov and Bologoye – word came over the wire that the Imperial Train had reached Smolensk.

The Czar was shunting onto the Moscow-Petrograd line. Ash saw by the map that the northbound Imperial Train and his southbound Mogilev express would steam past each other on separate lines fifty miles apart.

Ash got off at Dno, telegraphed his intention to the Czarina and boarded a train heading east so as to intercept the Czar at Bologoye. But a hundred miles down the line – just sixty from Bologoye – his new train stopped outside the town of Dolmatova. A palpable shiver passed through the first class carriages; rebellious troops were reported blocking the tracks.

The conductor decided to hold his train until troops arrived from Dno. When none came and dusk began to fall he decided to go back to Dno. Ash climbed down. The train backed away. Its headlight receded to a pinprick, and then he was alone on the rails, in the snow, where flat, frozen marshes met a line of hills. He began walking toward the hills and came soon on the lights of Dolmatova. The town looked peaceful enough except for a big bonfire near the station. Some soldiers were drinking and singing around the fire and watched Ash curiously; deserters, it seemed, but not bothering anybody and certainly not blocking the tracks, though the telegraph had somehow been cut.

Ash showed the stationmaster the Czarina's pass and asked for a train to Bologoye, thinking that if he were von Basel he would telegraph false reports and then cut the lines to confuse the railroad situation and perhaps force the Czar's train to change routes. Which direction? West, toward the front, closer to German territory . . .

The stationmaster scared up an ancient yard engine with driver and fireman and Ash resumed steaming toward Bologoye. Thirty miles short of the junction town they were shunted, permanently, onto a siding to let pass an endless stream of battered food and munitions trains struggling west to the front beyond Pskov. The engine crew began loudly debating what they should do.

Ash borrowed cleats and a key and scrambled up a telegraph pole. He was just tying into the line when a snort from the yard engine told him the crew had reached a consensus. The engine backed off the siding onto the main line and disappeared back in the direction from which they had come.

The snow quickly swallowed its headlight. Ash discovered the telegraph was still dead. He slid down the pole and tried to read his map by the light of windblown matches. The terrain was hilly, the roads grim, but by angling north overland he might intercept the Czar thirty miles up the main line from Bologoye. The alternative was to flag down an eastbound train that might never come.

Six o'clock. Ash's last report on the Czar's train had indicated a speed to bring it to Bologoye by nine and Likhoslavl by ten. Likhoslavl was twenty miles overland.

He dog-trotted up the tracks, looking for the lights of a village, spotted a handful of crude houses that serviced the siding. Snow lay thick everywhere. Smoke trickled from the chimneys, and smelled like they were burning dung. Ash decided if he'd come to the end of the road, this was an appropriate place . . . and aroma . . . for it.

None of the cottages even remotely resembled a tavern or any sort of public building; he was going to have to knock at one of the windows in which candlelight flickered dimly. Which window? He doubted anyone in the whole village knew a single word of English; the closest he'd ever come to such a place was bear hunting one winter years before the war with Skobeleff . . . which at least gave him an idea . . .

He already had a map and the name of the town he wanted to go to – Likhoslavl. What he needed was a fast

506

ride overland through snow that was beginning to look very much like another blizzard. So instead of knocking at any window Ash started down the street peering behind stable gates at the people's sleds. There were a few light ones and a half-covered one in front of the largest cottage. But even the smallest hovel had a *rozvalny*, and it was those crude sledges made of two long runners connected by a frame of rope and lath that Ash inspected closely. Commonly used in the country to haul hay and firewood, the *rozvalny* had neither back nor seat and the driver knelt on his load. But at the twelfth house Ash found one with a sturdy board seat big enough for two drivers. He knocked at the window. It was a bear-finder's sled, designed to run all night deep into the forest to remote caves where the hunters took wealthy sportsmen. Their fee, Ash recalled, was calculated by the weight of the bear.

An old man in a high wool hat opened the door; beside him stood a hefty son. Ash greeted them in Russian, said, 'Likhoslavl' several times and held up the map and a wad of roubles. They motioned him inside, and it wasn't until they had taken him through a cold dark passage into a room with an enormous brick-and-plaster stove that Ash realized how terribly cold he was. An entire family was grouped around the stove drinking tea, and staring at him. In the light of the candles around the icon Ash showed the old man the map and the money. He took the money and spoke to his son, who put on a sheepskin he'd been drying by the stove and went out to hitch a team. A woman poured Ash a glass of tea and indicated the communal sugar bowl from which Ash gratefully took a lump of sugar, put it between his teeth the way Tamara had once laughingly taught him and drank while the family, including children tucked into shelves above the warm stove, watched closely. Thanking them, Ash pulled out his watch and showed it to the old man, pointing to nine.

Father and son sat on the front plank. Ash lay full length on a bed of straw in the sling between the runners and covered his face with his cloak. Two ponies proceeded to pull the sledge into the forest. The runners hissed, the fresh snow muffled the horses' hooves, the drivers murmured to each other, sharing a bottle and occasionally talking to the horses. Ash dozed, abruptly awakened sensing danger. The *rozvalny* was crossing open ground and the snow was drifting. He could hear the worry in the drivers' voices as they searched for *veshky*, bushes that had been planted in the snow as roadmarks . . . then the track returned to forest and they were again sheltered from the wind.

Ash dozed off, awakened again.

The snow stopped and gradually a mantle of stars spread through the feathery tops of the birch trees.

The lights of Likhoslavl were few and dull by comparison to the long, orderly string of lighted train windows pulling swiftly from the station.

'*Faster,*' Ash called to the drivers. 'Faster, dammit.'

They whipped up the horses and the *rozvalny* careened down a hill into the little town. But they were too late. The locomotive was pounding a steady beat. The train was up to twenty miles per hour and pulling steadily into the night.

Ash wanted to kill somebody.

'*Sir, sir . . .*' The boy was pointing. A second train appeared from behind the station.

'*Da,*' Ash yelled. 'Go.' He remembered that the conductor had told him a special always preceded the Imperial Train. 'Faster . . .'

The *rozvalny* hit the first street of the town, went through startled spectators who had gathered to salute the Czar as he passed through their station; the majestic beat-beat of the steam engine was accelerating, and when they swung around the last building the train was already moving at a

508

fast clip. Ash leaped from the *rozvalny* and ran, clawing the Czarina's pass from his tunic. He caught up to the last car, waved the paper at a soldier who guarded the doorway with a rifle and managed to swing aboard.

He was instantly surrounded. Two men held bayonets to his chest while an officer took over. When he'd read the pass he welcomed Ash aboard. At least, Ash decided, von Basel would find a direct assault similarly impossible without an invitation. Direct, yes. Indirect . . . ? 'What's the news from Petrograd?'

'Not good, sir. Not good at all.'

Ash nodded, asked them to take him to the Czar.

The city burned.

Prince Kurakin's shabby apartment was on a barely reputable block near the Moscow Railroad Station at the upper end of the Nevsky Prospect; the drawing room was entirely black, the site of Kurakin's seances, though through the day that Tamara Tishkova and Vera Sedovina hid there, whatever spiritual mood the gloomy rooms evoked was thoroughly dispelled by the chanting demonstrators below in the street, the sudden bursts of gunfire, the screams and then the songs resuming – songs of triumph.

Sedovina wanted to go into the street and join the parades, but Tamara had persuaded her to stay. When the fires broke out after dark it was Tamara who left first. Sedovina could go into the streets if she insisted . . . but Tamara was too concerned about the safety of her house to sit still anymore.

Tamara threw one of the prince's black cloaks over her own sable, which Kennet had left at the River Yacht Club, and walked out, clutching the gun she had picked up outside the Peter-Paul Fortress. It was a mile along the Liteiny Prospect. The mob had broken into the Liteiny Arsenal, so now they were armed. She made it to the

Alexander Bridge, across the Neva to her home. From her solarium, she watched the fires turn the night sky red . . . her fire dream at last. *Kennet, where in God's name are you . . . ?*

The Law Courts burned. So did the arsenal on the Liteiny and the Litovsky Prison, which she prayed von Basel was still in. Dotted across the darker districts of the city where the poor lived were red balls of flame, each marking one of the Czar's police stations.

But as the fires spread Tamara realized that the mob was indeed breaking into homes as well. She could actually see the people surging along the embankments, because now the flames reflecting on the snow made whole sections of Petrograd as bright as day . . . Earlier Prince Kurakin had reported after one of his timid excursions out to the Nevsky that something that called itself the Petrograd Soviet was meeting alongside the Duma in the Turide Palace. Sedovina had been delighted at the news . . . Fascinated and shocked by the sheer numbers of people parading through the city and crossing the river on the ice when the police blocked the bridges, Tamara watched for hours. Until she saw a mob crossing the ice merge with another surging off the Alexander Bridge, overrunning the police and heading straight for the necklace of mansions on the embankment – of which Tishkova's was the jewel.

She rang again for her maid.

'Bring me red ink and a large sheet of paper. *Quickly.*'

Vera Sedovina had run into the street from the prince's home when she saw a crowd of workers carrying the red flag up the Liteiny join hands with a unit of a Guards regiment marching down the Nevsky Prospect. Not a shot was fired by the soldiers, not a stone thrown by the people. Soldier and worker, conscript and peasant walked together through her city. The police had vanished. There was no one to arrest her. No prisons to hold her. She thought of Anton, dead in Siberia two years too soon to see his dreams. She joined the march, linked arms with an old man on one side who told her he'd been in jail since the 1905 rebellion, and with a woman who said she had been a servant and was going to go back to her village where she believed her family would at last have a piece of land. They sang the *Marseillaise* and the *Internationale* and surged down the Nevsky Prospect.

The Admiralty, though, was still in Czarist hands. Revolutionary soldiers laid siege to it with rifles and machine-guns. Just then Vera saw a palace burning on the Moika, and she suddenly was afraid for the beautiful Maryinski Theatre. She ran when the march ended at the besieged Admiralty, ran past Kennet Ash's hotel and St Isaac's, straining to see smoke and flame . . .

Theatre Square was deserted except for an empty tram stalled at a broken wire. The Maryinski was intact. She went to the stage door and knocked. The old woman who guarded it opened and let her in. She heard loud voices from the stage and slipped into the wings.

Valentinov was declaiming from centre stage, gesturing wildly as he bellowed Chekhov at an empty auditorium. His wife sat in the front row while their children gaped at the glorious gold-and-blue proscenium.

Sedovina walked on stage.

Valentinov gave a glad shout. 'We're free; they burned the prison to the ground.'

He tried to throw his arms around her. Sedovina backed away. Valentinov gestured at the theatre. 'Now this is for everyone; now people like me can perform here – '

Sedovina slapped his face. Valentinov had no business here. He was a terrible actor.

A general wearing the staff pin N-2, one of several officers clustered about maps spread on the long dining table while stewards watched from the galley, was explaining that Ash could not possibly see the Czar before morning. He was interrupted when Czar Nicholas himself appeared, looking for Ash. He wore a plain tunic with colonel's shoulder straps and A-3, in gold, for Alexander III, his dead father and commanding officer.

The generals snapped to attention. The Czar appeared to be the calmest man on the train.

'Good evening, Kenneth,' he said as the general propelled Ash forward like a prize of war.

The Czar insisted on holding doors as he led Ash onto the platform between the dining car and his carriage, through a vestibule and into a wood-panelled study. In the absence of noise, draughts or vibration it was hard to remember that the Imperial Train was hurtling through a bitter cold night at fifty miles per hour.

The Czar's study was furnished with a map table, some comfortable-looking leather armchairs and a desk. Photographs on the walls showed him at the helm of a racing yacht, on a bicycle, on horseback and posed in front of Balmachan House in the Scottish Highlands with a Westley Richards draped over his arm, a Russian fur hat on his head and wearing a Savile Row shooting jacket especially tailored with long deep pleats for easy movement and big pockets for extra shells.

He went to the table and stared down at the map.

'Our destinies seem connected, Commander . . . the Czarina telegraphed about this German spy and added a strong suggestion I listen to you . . . you've come with another offer from King George?'

'The same offer, Your Majesty.'

The Czar shrugged. 'We won't concern ourselves over a single German . . . what does he want?'

'He wants to kidnap you and take you to Kaiser Wilhelm as a prisoner of war.'

512

'Willy . . . ?' He shook his head. 'I always thought my end would be sudden. A bomb, like my grandfather the Czar-Liberator. I thought I would die in blood. Instead I'm dying of slow disease, like my father, but mine is not of the body. It is of my people. Insurrection, Commander. Spread by the vermin of deceit, treachery, cowardice.' He glanced vaguely at the maps again, and when he raised his hand to rub his eyes Ash saw a man deeply tired, weary unto death . . .

The map depicted the railroad triangle Ash had travelled trying to intercept the Imperial Train ahead of von Basel – Petrograd and Tsarskoye Selo in the north, Pskov and the front west, and the Moscow-Petrograd line on which the Imperial Train was currently steaming in the east.

'I'm chased by rumours,' the Czar said abruptly. With a red pencil he circled the town of Tosno near Tsarskoye Selo, Bologoye to the rear, and Pskov in the west. 'Rumours that some monstrosity calling itself a Provisional Government will stop my train at one of these towns.'

'Where are we now, Your Majesty?'

The Czar gave another shrug. 'About ten miles south of Malaya Vishera – it looks bad but there is still hope. The Czarina has telegraphed that the situation is improved in Petrograd, and the troubles do appear to be confined to Petrograd.' He crossed himself.

'That's excellent news, Sir.'

'I have loyal troops headed there at this very moment.'

The train jolted and slowed rapidly. There was a knock at the door, and when the Czar gave permission to enter, a general walked in and saluted. 'We're coming into Malaya Vishera, Your Majesty.'

'We were closer than I thought. Is the station signalling a telegram?'

'No, Your Majesty.'

'Then why have we stopped?'

513

'The special has stopped, Your Majesty.'

'Why?'

'The special has received a report that rebel battalions have blocked the tracks with machine-guns, Your Majesty.'

46

Von Basel, Ash thought as the Czar's staff circled the map-strewn dining table and debated what to do. The rebel units were supposedly at Lyuban, the next station up the line, but to Ash a report of machine-guns on the tracks, which no one had actually seen, sounded like Dolmatova all over again – a minor disturbance cooked up by von Basel's German agents to provoke an exaggerated response from the jittery train crews and the panicked imperial entourage. A trick to steer the Czar nearer the front. And it seemed to be working.

None of the Czar's staff had the stomach to run a machine-gun gauntlet, even with the special train leading them; some wanted to retreat all the way back to Mogilev, though the majority pressed to reroute the Imperial Train west to Pskov. Pskov, they argued, was nearer to loyal troops at the front. Ash knew he was powerless to interrupt, and it was obvious that Czar Nicholas, facing the disintegration of his entire empire, had now forgotten entirely about von Basel. Aides ran in and out of the dining carriage with telegraph messages.

The Czar stared at his maps while his staff went on debating.

'What is the news of Petrograd?' he asked.

'Apparently an isolated situation, Your Majesty.'

'Moscow?'

'Reports are inconclusive – '

'Is there any news of the army?'

'No, Your Majesty.'

'And these insurrectionists?' he asked, pointing at the railroad map.

515

'Apparently they hold Lyuban and perhaps Tosno, Your Majesty.'

'Are we sure?' He raised his eyes to his staff, all of whom began talking at once. Beneath the hubbub Ash heard Nicholas murmur, 'I want to go home.'

'Your Majesty,' Ash ventured. *Home* was just where Ash wanted him – away from von Basel and close to the Gulf of Finland.

Czar Nicholas turned to Ash, who had remained just behind him since the staff had filled the carriage. 'Yes, Commander, what do you think of all this?'

The generals and noblemen turned to him, worried what the stranger would say.

'Might it not be better to first join your family, Sir?' Ash needed to try to keep him from the generals long enough to consider the danger of being separated from the Czarina and the difficulty of escaping to England if they weren't together.

'Yes, I suppose,' Nicholas said, but it was clear he wasn't yet ready to surrender, not yet prepared fully to acknowledge the danger.

'Your armies,' the generals repeated. 'You must contact your armies, Your Majesty. What are a few traitors in Petrograd compared to the fifteen million Russian soldiers under Your Majesty's command?'

'Yes, of course.'

And another general put in, 'We must communicate with loyal units, Your Majesty.'

'*Yes*, of course,' and then he asked, peering at the map, 'Where is the nearest Hughes terminal?' He was referring, Ash knew, to the American-designed Hughes keyboard telegraph printer which the Russian army used for internal communication.

'Pskov, Your Majesty,' his entourage said almost together – and Ash knew von Basel had won.

The Czar touched the map. 'To Pskov then, before this matter is ended.'

The Imperial Train backed into the Bologoye Station at nine in the morning and sat there half the day, bombarded by rumours that the Duma was preparing a plan for a constitutional monarchy. But in the afternoon no delegates had arrived from the Duma and the blue-and-silver train steamed west.

In the last carriage, an additional barracks coupled on for extra guards, a young officer of His Imperial Majesty's Own Convoy struggled to take off his boots in the cramped cubby hole where he slept. He felt older than God. Not a single man of his cadet classes who had gone into the line regiments was still alive. He was wondering if the dead were the lucky ones now, gone in a burst of glory for Czar and Russia while a few like him waited to be overwhelmed by a new world of strangers' making. The steward knocked at the door and brought in tea.

'Put it there.'

The steward closed the door and leaned against it; there was hardly room for two in the compartment. The officer looked up, gasped. '*Dmitri?* What are you – ' He leaped up, even before he completed the thought . . . *Dmitri Dan* . . . Dmitri had a knife . . .

When it was done and he had shoved his old friend's body out the window, Dmitri Dan put on the Convoy officer's uniform over the servant's costume he'd worn to board the Imperial Train, cleaned his dagger and lay down to wait. He was calm. His mind was empty of all but the thought that he, and the Revolution, were only two carriages behind the Czar's private quarters.

Ash sought out some Convoy officers and got himself invited to share tea. They were jumpy, knowing that there was little they could do if the tracks were mined or the rebels managed to obtain artillery.

The rumours resumed that Duma delegates were coming by train from Petrograd. As the Czar had not invited Ash back to his own car again Ash was as in the dark as the rest of the entourage. The Convoy officers admitted they were watching for a German spy, but none of them seemed to take von Basel's threat very seriously, not compared to the fate of the Imperial Russian Empire. Ash, however, was not surprised when the train headed west again and the new rumour promised that the Czar would meet the Duma delegates at Pskov.

He got his cloak and went forward. Armed soldiers stopped him at the barracks car behind the locomotive. Ash claimed he wanted a breath of air and persuaded them to let him stand in an open vestibule. Outside, alone in the biting cold, he climbed onto the roof.

The train was doing close to forty, and the wind was fierce. Sheltering himself behind a ventilator, Ash watched the flat, empty white landscape for signs of von Basel.

The endless open fence flowed beside the rails beneath an equally endless row of telegraph poles. Snow-covered fields disappeared toward an horizon of trees. The vast sky was clear and starry except for a dense cloud line in the north that marked another Gulf of Finland blizzard over Petrograd, a hundred and fifty miles away. Some five miles ahead of the locomotive's smoke spume he could see the red lights on the back of the special that preceded the Imperial Train.

The lights of a town shone ahead. Porkov. The special passed through the lights and stopped, followed by the Imperial Train, which slackened its pace and glided to a stop in the station. A trainman jumped down and questioned the officials lined up in dress uniforms on the platform, as similar ones had manned every platform the train had passed through today. Petrograd might be burning but here in the countryside the passage of the Imperial Train was still an occasion for respectful salute.

The trainman got aboard and they started rolling, which meant, Ash presumed, no new telegraph messages from Petrograd. Ahead lay fifteen miles of desolate field, marsh, birch forest and the occasional dark village. Ash glanced back. The town officers and railroad officials were still at attention. The graceful onion domes of their church floated in starlight above the station.

The next town on the map was Podsyevi and beyond it, thirty empty miles to Pskov. It was in that last long stretch that Ash expected von Basel to strike. The trains would be alone for nearly an hour, more than enough time to stop them with a barricade and a few machine-guns, plus maybe some armoured cars. It was so simple – stop the train, a show of force, remove the Czar and drive away. But a hundred and fifty miles overland was still a long run.

Ash scanned the sky. He thought he heard music, pressed his ear to the roof and heard it louder and remembered the officers in the lounge car had a gramophone. Then another sound intruded on the rumble of the wheels and the rushing wind and the beat of the locomotive, a steady hum from behind that grew swiftly to a drone. An aeroplane swooped over the train and flitted through the upper glow of the locomotive headlight like some great bat. In the instant Ash saw it flash ahead of the train he thought it looked like a two-seater British-built DeHavilland bomber.

Von Basel's men had probably commandeered the aeroplane from the Russian Imperial Air Service, and Ash hurriedly repainted the picture in his mind of how the German would seize the Czar – a fire on the tracks, or the special would be mined, anything to stop the Czar's train midway between Podsyevi and Pskov. Then half a dozen armoured cars on either side, courtesy of turncoat army units recruited by von Basel's German agents, headlights and machine-guns and artillery pointed at the Imperial Train . . . the Czar hustled to the aeroplane waiting on the frozen snow, strapped into the rear-gunner's seat. In two hours Nicholas II would be in German territory. And twelve hours later von Basel would present his prisoner of war to the Kaiser . . .

The lights of Podsyevi appeared dead ahead. The special slowed and passed through the town, by which time Ash could see the silhouettes of the onion domes. Most of the town lights seemed to be on the railroad platform. Four officials waited, coming to attention as the Czar's train neared. They had a telegraph. What did they think when they heard the news from Petrograd – the elderly station-master bent from the long years of his life for the Czar, the freight manager who had watched his rolling stock disintegrate before his eyes, the telegrapher whose key must have clattered relentlessly all day, the wounded war veteran leaning hard on his cane? What did they think . . . if they dared think at all?

47

Count von Basel had positioned himself some distance from the civilians, as befitted a veteran in the service of the Czar, and none had presumed to question his presence on the platform. A gleaming black locomotive glided past, and von Basel raised his hand to his service cap in reverent salute. He was close enough to the blue-and-silver train carriages to touch the double-headed Imperial Eagles on their sides.

A trainman leaped down while it was still rolling, shouting – were there telegrams? The telegrapher stepped forward, holding his salute, and pressed sheaves of paper into his glove. The trainman disappeared inside as the train ground to a stop.

Von Basel followed the telegrams' passage. They appeared next in the hand of a Guard subaltern who walked them through two carriages and turned them over to a captain in the dining car in front of the Czar's own carriage. A group of generals pored through them.

Next the Czar himself appeared from his carriage, third from the end of the train, just ahead of his servants' lodgings and the Guards' car at the end. He looked worried but calm. The Czar took the telegrams and passed on to the dining car.

Von Basel knew the contents of every one of those telegrams, except, of course, the private wires from the Czarina, who'd been bombarding the Czar with unfathomable references to Nimrod, the hunter; he'd had an agent on top of a telegraph pole tap into the line a mile from here since dark. Conditions had got so bad in Petrograd that he no longer had to plug his own electric forgeries into the line;

his last false message had been eighteen hours ago, warning the Czar of nonexistent rebel troops at Tosno and blocked tracks at Malaya Vishera.

The Imperial Train had turned back, just hours from the Czar's Palace, and since then the Russian populace and the madmen of the Duma, already fighting among themselves, had kept the Czar on the run. But once the train had left Bologoye its route was absolutely predictable. Pskov. The Czar was escaping to his army. Too late, Your Majesty, too late . . . Von Basel slipped into the shadows, and when the train whistle blew, he was already crouched in the snow on the dark side of the train.

Ash had seen too much indecision bordering on paralysis aboard the Imperial Train to attempt to convince either the Czar or his Guard that a German agent was going to stop the train fifteen miles down the line. Simpler to stop it first, explain later. As the train started from the station he ran forward over the roof. He'd show the locomotive engineer his snub-nosed Luger and let him draw his own conclusions.

From the vantage point of the stalled engine, Ash would be in a much more practical position to persuade the Convoy Guard to wait for reinforcements to clear the line. Preparing the jump the slot between two cars, he glanced back at the station to make sure he wasn't seen . . . they'd shoot him down if they saw a shadow heading for the locomotive. No guards. The three railroad officials were still saluting like statues, but the old soldier had gone. He faced the wind, jumped the first slot and ran forward.

He was creeping silently over the final car just before the tender – it was a Guards' barracks car – when he glanced back . . . something nagged. He noted that Podsyevi station appeared as a single bright light. As in the previous town, and the towns before, the silhouettes of the onion-dome church steeples were the last shapes seen from the desolate plain, standing as patient a watch as the last men loyal to the Czar had stood on each railroad platform . . . Why had the soldier left, where had he gone . . .?

Von Basel.

No armoured cars. No machine-guns.

Ash ran for the back of the train, cursing his stupidity, fighting the wind at his back that filled his boat cloak like a sail.

Of course . . . von Basel intended to kidnap the Czar alone, force him to leap from the moving train, take his chances on the snow, then aboard the two-seater bomber, with a knife in the ribs for the pilot.

Ash jumped the gap between two cars and raced toward the rear of the train, crossing the two cars of officer accommodation, the roof of the lounge car and the dining car to the Czar's. He was about to drop to the front vestibule when he saw that the last two coaches, that carried the Czar's personal servants and the additional rear guard, were separated from the rest of the train. Already a hundred feet back, they were disappearing into the dark.

Von Basel . . . he'd disconnected them and was lying in wait. Ash crossed the Czar's car, treading lightly as possible, and lowered himself to the vestibule. The door was slightly ajar. He opened it, slipped in and let it shut. He drew the Luger from the small of his back and moved silently across the vestibule. He opened the inner door. The car was swaying, having lost the stabilizing tail of rear cars.

Ash reviewed the layout of the Czar's car. It had a huge bedroom and bath and two sitting rooms, one in mauve and grey, which must have been the Czarina's before the war, and the Czar's at the front, his study.

Gun in hand, Ash stepped into the rear room, found it

empty, moved into the bedroom. A servant was sprawled on the bed, unconscious and bleeding from a bruise on his temple.

Ash opened the last door.

Von Basel rushed him. The German had been waiting at the forward vestibule door at the front end of the Czar's study. He had his sword cane in one hand, a gold pocket-watch in the other. He needed to time the ten minutes until the train reached the aeroplane. The Czar had not returned from the dining car, where he customarily conferred with his generals and aides when telegrams arrived.

Von Basel had shed the bemedalled Russian army greatcoat he had worn on the station platform and now wore a black leather flying jacket and service hat. In a single, smooth motion he clicked the watch stem and went at Ash, raising the cane in a tight arc that twisted into a long thrust. He covered half the study's twenty-foot length before Ash got his cloak off his arm and let him have a look at his gun. Von Basel appeared to stop short, but stole four more feet doing it. He came to rest, lightly balanced, countering the sway of the train, two yards from Ash.

Ash gestured with the Luger.

'I wasn't aware we had agreed to new weapons,' von Basel said, trying to give the impression that he'd given more ground than he had.

'Some other time. Drop that damned cane.'

Von Basel lifted his hands, the watch dangling in his left, the cane in his right.

'*Drop it.*'

Von Basel's grey eyes seemed to glint at his watch. The cane dropped from his other hand. For an instant everything was in motion – the cane, the watch, his eyes, both hands. He caught the cane, it flashed like a dark snake and bit the small bones in the back of Ash's hand.

Before Ash made a sound or his Luger had thudded to

the carpet, von Basel drew steel from a hardwood scabbard. Roland had warned him about the man, that he was better than they'd thought. He'd obviously meant the German's speed.

Ash wanted to go for the gun but von Basel was too close. He feinted a lunge at the floor. Von Basel replied with a wide slash an inch over the gun butt, but at least Ash was able to use the time to draw his dress sword.

'Much better,' von Basel said. He pocketed his watch, gripped the cane in his left hand and advanced.

Ash knew he needed more room. He backed through the door into the big bedroom, which was nearly thirty feet long. Russian trains were wide, and the room approximated a fencing strip with the exception of the bed intruding into the middle and the ceiling, which would have the good effect of limiting the high slashes Ash expected from von Basel. The servant was still unconscious on the bed; it appeared that von Basel had clipped him with the cane, which he held in his left hand in case Ash tried to in-fight. Was there also a dagger in his jacket, like the poniard he'd put in Roland's chest?

Von Basel followed, his sabre steady, the point tracking Ash like a finger. The blade, Ash thought, looked lighter than his, consequently more flexible. An ingeniously designed set of prongs had folded out of the hilt, forming a protective bell for von Basel's hand, which was already protected by a heavy leather glove.

Despite himself, Ash's gaze fixed on the whippy steel. The razor edges cast mesmerizing ribbons of light. Much as he had hoped, and hard as he had trained to fight him again, Ash had to admit that this German aristocrat, lean and flexible as his blade, was probably the most dangerous swordsman in Europe. Hadn't he already beaten Ash? And, astonishingly, François Roland, too? Ash's own master? *Poniard* or no, von Basel had still had to breach

Roland's awesome guard to get close enough to use the dagger. Ash had promised Roland to ask when he was ready to fight von Basel, but Roland was dead.

Von Basel advanced. Ash retreated. He had ten feet to his back, then the bed to climb over or squeeze past, two yards more a narrow door, fifteen feet of the Czarina's sitting room, the tiny vestibule – and then nothing but tracks roaring under the train at forty miles per hour.

Von Basel seemed to read his thoughts . . . 'The Czar's servant was waiting to help him dress for dinner, which means he'll come in alone. So you see, merely *occupying* me will not serve your purpose. If you warn the Czar you must warn him *before* he enters this carriage. But for that you'll need to get me first . . . which is to say, a clever defence will not suffice. Though I suppose you could simply turn tail and throw yourself off the back. The snow will break your fall . . . No? All right, you've got ten minutes. Then I shall be obliged to end this. After all, I've promised to take His Majesty flying . . .' He kicked Ash's gun under a leather armchair, and advanced. Ash watched him come, fascinated by the eerie stillness of the point of his sword. It floated as if it had a life and powerful will of its own.

All right, Ash lectured himself, a little less respect and more action. This man intends to kill you . . . He proceeded to test von Basel's grip. Von Basel replied. The car rang with the sound of steel on steel. Ash tried a thrust. Von Basel parried, thrust and lunged. A pleased smile. Ash had escaped the thrust, but he'd also, in so doing, retreated.

Already von Basel was past the bedroom door. The German lunged again. Ash went back as he parried, but von Basel's lunge had been a feint that bought him space to kick the door shut behind him so that now when the Czar entered his carriage he'd see nothing wrong in his study.

Von Basel, Ash realized, had manipulated him like a damn novice. He sensed the bed behind him. Von Basel thrust again. Ash riposted, and von Basel retreated to the door until his left heel was touching it. Ash pressed his attack. Von Basel drew back even closer to the door until it appeared he had no more room to retreat.

Recalling how von Basel had lured him too close last time, Ash attacked cautiously, feeling him out. Thrusting, parrying – striking at von Basel and shielding himself from his opponent's thrusts – Ash hunted for a weakness. He discovered, instead, a frightening strength.

Von Basel's sense of distance was so accurate that it allowed him to parry late – wait until Ash's point was an inch from its target – then riposte with remarkable speed at the very moment Ash was too extended, too stretched into his thrust to counter-parry effectively. That was how he had got him the first time.

And again, it was with a late parry-riposte that von Basel drew first blood.

It flew scarlet from Ash's right sleeve. His forearm felt as if it had been pierced by a hypodermic needle. But this time, they weren't stopping to bind wounds; before Ash fully realized he'd been hit, von Basel jump-lunged like an express train.

Anger and a hot dose of fear goaded Ash to swift recovery, parry and counter-thrust. Von Basel parried late again and repeated the riposte. Again it caught Ash off balance and too far extended to parry, but then Ash did something that wasn't in the fencing rules and whipped his boat cloak around von Basel's sabre with his left hand. He pressed his sudden advantage, and von Basel let him close enough to lash his head with the hardwood scabbard. Ash fell back on the bed, seeing stars and the point of von Basel's sabre corkscrewing toward his eye. He tried to roll away, got tangled in his cloak and collided with the unconscious servant. Von Basel thrust again. Ash flipped backward, kicked blindly at the blade, dived over the servant and hit the floor.

Von Basel was winning, and he knew it. Ash squeezed his tunic sleeve to soak up the blood so that it would not drain into his hand and ruin his grip. He was ten feet farther from warning the Czar than he had been before the exchange. But *was* the son of a bitch really that good? Was he perfect? Ash had to find a flaw. Maybe von Basel was overconfident. Well, Ash thought, he had every reason to be at this point. But did his famous refusal to have his face scarred derive from fear? The man's grey eyes showed nothing. Maybe his broad style, the wide slashes, indicated too much sabre training and not enough in the exacting foil. Clutching at straws, Commander. *He's better than we thought,* Roland had said, and he'd been right.

Never mind now. The options were gone. Ash attacked.

Von Basel was rather impressed. He admired Ash's timing, his speed, his point control and his sense of distance. The precision of his hand was superior – almost up to Chevalier Roland – what one might expect of an Italian professional of the sort von Basel had secretly trained with when his mother had bundled him off to the Jewish doctors in Vienna after his father killed himself. Ash also possessed a considerable ability to recover from disaster – a flexibility that came, he knew, from the power to relax. The American had control of himself and his skills. He also detected in Ash a gift for combat – the ability to restart after each phase. Then why, he asked himself as Ash came gliding around the bed and opened a new attack with a hard beat, couldn't the American launch a convincing attack? He shrugged him off with a spanking parry. Ash's brilliant defence seemed all he had. He couldn't attack. And in the long run a brilliant defence was a map to the cemetery . . .

Here he came now, dead-steady point, marvellous control, a lightning thrust. Short. Another. Short again. Von Basel parried and countered. Ash parried masterfully, thrust. Short. Had he lost his sense of distance? Von Basel thrust. Ash parried at the last instant and riposted. Short again.

Von Basel established a series of parries while he retreated into his mind to puzzle it out. Ash had begun to imitate his own late parries – the mark of a great fighter was the ability to learn in action – and he cut it very fine, showing his distance was perfect. But his ripostes still fell short. What was wrong with the man? He had never really believed Ash was a coward, but he was fighting like a man afraid. Of what? It was a question von Basel had to answer before he risked his final, killing attack.

He couldn't wait much longer, though. The Czar would walk in at any moment – a fact that von Basel realized was affecting his own concentration, since he had to keep himself ready to throw the Czar off his feet while he finished Ash. And the aeroplane was waiting several miles up the line. Five minutes. No more.

Von Basel attacked, spanked Ash's blade aside and jump-lunged, slashing wildly to unnerve the American . . .

The blades clashed, kissed, sparked in the dim electric light, seemed to whip around each other in impossible embrace. Ash felt his grip tightening, which made his wrist rigid and reduced his point control. *Relax*, Roland demanded. Relax. In Paris he had put Ash in the on-guard position and left him there for five minutes while he strutted about his *Salle d'armes* instructing his other students. If Ash's grip had tightened when Roland came back he was told, 'You'll never be a fencer,' and banished for the rest of the day. *Relax*.

Ash eased his grip and retreated, waiting for von Basel to make a mistake, searching for openings in the wide slashes, watching for signs of overconfidence. The last, he thought

529

uneasily, seemed the best bet. He had made his own mistake in his training. Characteristically blaming himself for the humiliation in Paris, he had concentrated exclusively on his own skills, forgetting to consider von Basel's. He knew now, possibly too late, that he should have expended more effort figuring out what made his opponent tick. Instead, he was fighting a stranger, for the second time.

Chimes began to play the Brahms Lullaby.

Von Basel extracted his watch from his pocket with the hand holding his scabbard. The watch was playing the melody. Von Basel showed it to Ash and put it back in his pocket again. It happened so quickly Ash hadn't been able to react. Von Basel said, 'Your time is up, Commander. You've done quite well, for a sportsman . . . better than last time.'

And von Basel attacked. He had his man now, knew what ailed Ash. It was Chevalier Roland. Ash thought von Basel had beaten his master. So how could he be expected to beat von Basel?

What neither Roland nor Ash understood was that duelling was more than skill. Roland, for all his reputation, had turned out to be a gentle soul, a brilliant technician but even in a death fight more interested in technique than killing . . . His death had killed Ash's belief in his own strengths. Ash's thrusts and lunges, perhaps always his weakest skills in any case, fell far short because he no longer *believed* he could launch a successful attack. And now it was too late, because now von Basel knew everything he needed to know to kill him.

Von Basel also had the ability to adjust to an opponent and a situation. When Ash's parries and the relatively confining walls and ceilings of the Imperial Train proved too much for his broad sabre cuts he began to thrust as if his sabre were a foil.

530

Surprised, Ash retreated rapidly while he adjusted. And when Ash had adjusted, at the cost of being driven back around the bed and halfway to the door of the rear compartment, von Basel feinted with the sword and smashed his face with the cane.

Ash fought back any sound to give away his pain, and in spite of himself, it occurred to von Basel that, if he had ever felt the need for a friend beside his sovereign, the Kaiser, it might have been a man like this – and then he cauterized the thought. The brain tended to play tricks in combat.

Ash launched an angry attack energized by pain. Von Basel tried to capitalize on the American's show of temper, but it served to drive Ash, not unsettle him . . . anger helping to make up for low confidence. Von Basel realized that Ash might, after all, succeed in making a forceful attack. He retreated, seeking to regain initiative.

Ash broke his defence, slashed at his scabbard, sliced it in half. By the time von Basel realized it was only a feint, Ash's sabre whipped up from the downstroke. The razor edge jumped at his cheek. With an astonishing twist of his entire body, von Basel wrenched his face out of the path of Ash's blade, which left him far off-centre – his body in one plane, his weapon in another. He threw himself backward onto the bed, collecting space and time to regain his equilibrium. He landed hard on the servant he had earlier knocked unconscious, who groaned and rolled over as von Basel levered himself off him and landed on his feet on the opposite side of the bed in the *en garde* position.

Ash felt the fight go out of him. Von Basel had made a shambles of his best attack. The servant groaned and tried to move again, and in doing so revealed a long knife that had been lying under him. While Ash was still trying to work out where it had come from, von Basel, closer, grabbed it up and started toward Ash with a blade in either hand.

Ash ended his silence. 'I'm flattered. You needed two for Roland, too.'

'Don't flatter yourself. Roland slipped on the ice. He was not properly balanced with one arm – '

Smug bastard – Ash hurtled at von Basel, onto the bed, across it, slashing down at von Basel like a horseguard. Von Basel allowed him close, then thrust the servant's dagger. Ash was ready . . . a darting thrust, and his sabre skewered von Basel's left wrist, slid between the bones, in and out like ice.

The ice left a trail of fire. Von Basel dropped the dagger. Ash slashed at his face. Von Basel parried, his own blood spraying in droplets from Ash's blade. Ash went at him, drove ahead, *around* . . . and suddenly von Basel realized that Ash was done fighting, was forcing his way past him to get to his gun in the study and warn the Czar . . .

Exhilarated that he had finally bloodied von Basel, sinking his point exactly where he'd aimed it, Ash now slashed and thrust, tried a couple more late parries. He had manoeuvred von Basel half out of his way and was preparing to break for the door to the Czar's study when the German caught on to his intent.

'*Nein.* Fight. For this.' He snapped his left arm and the blood flew. '*Fight.*'

And von Basel exploded into a new attack, driving a startled Ash against the wall and leaping back to his old position between Ash and the door to the Czar's study. He drove Ash backward with cold skill, to the bed, around it, and past. His thrusts were long and rapid, his parries like Roland's spinning steel shield, the shield Roland would raise when he wanted to remind Ash who was master and who was student.

Ash tried to break up the attack. He riposted with a stop-thrust and paid for it. Von Basel let loose a slash that tore through Ash's cloak and stung his shoulder. Warm blood spread onto his chest. Von Basel kept attacking.

Ash retreated, hoping von Basel would exhaust himself. It was clear now that he intended to drive him through the rear sitting room and out to the vestibule and off the back of the speeding train. Ash retreated because the alternative would be to be slashed again, run through.

Von Basel was fighting at his peak. Ash knew he had lost the earlier initiative. He backed through the door into the sitting room and retreated suddenly as he slammed the door on von Basel's sword. Von Basel was ready for that, moving forward and kicking the door open so that it threw Ash backward.

The rear door opened out against a hydraulic spring. Von Basel worked Ash through it with thrusts like jets of flame. The spring kept Ash from slamming the door on his blade. Von Basel held it open with his boot and came through. Trapped in the narrow vestibule, Ash backed through the last doorway.

Cold air blasted into the vestibule. Ash tried, and failed, to hold his position. Von Basel's thrusts were too accurate to parry with his back pinned to the door. Ash retreated to a last stand on the open platform. The wind tore at his cloak; the rear wheels thundered on the worn roadbed.

Von Basel seemed to get tangled up in the door. Ash thought he saw his chance. He leaped up the ladder on the back of the car and climbed for the roof, to run forward and warn the Czar.

Von Basel slashed up at his leg, his sabre slicing through Ash's cloak, his heavy boot and wool trousers. Ash felt a narrow tug of pain on the back of his calf, inches above his Achilles tendon. Von Basel slashed again, lower, hunting the tendon.

Afraid of a crippling cut, Ash dropped down to the platform with a last-ditch off-balance parry. He was wide open when von Basel riposted, and took the thrust in his upper arm.

His fingers opened convulsively. His sabre began to slip from his glove. Ash clamped his left hand over his right, held his fingers on the hilt and just managed to parry von Basel's next slash while he manoeuvred for a little more space on the platform. He was running out of room . . . von Basel had driven him the length of the Czar's car from the study in front, through the big bedroom, through the rear sitting room, through the vestibule and now outside on the open rear platform. Ash tried to hold one side while von Basel thrust and slashed to drive him the remaining six feet to the back and over the edge to the tracks racing away below . . .

Czar Nicholas pushed open the door, and peered outside, into the dark where the servants' car had been. He called, squinting to adjust his eyes to the change of light. Von Basel shot out his left hand, grabbed hold of the Czar's tunic and yanked him out onto the platform while he tried to spank the blade from Ash's stiff fingers.

Ash held on, parried von Basel and pushed the Czar back to the door. He lunged at von Basel. The German's stop-thrust slid the length of Ash's blade. They slammed hilt-to-hilt, and a scream whirled them both around with the same thought – while fighting for him had they somehow run the Czar through?

The Czar's back was to the door, but the scream had turned his head too.

Dmitri Dan surfaced to consciousness. The last he remembered, he had been waiting in the Czar's bedroom, where Bloody Nicholas was sure to come along to dress for dinner. Then he heard a loud noise and the car began swaying as if it were the last. He started back to investigate when a man

534

with a cane suddenly appeared from the sitting room behind the bedroom.

Dmitri had quickly bowed, playing his servant role, and the cane, preceded by a heavy *swish*, had crashed into his head. It knocked him onto the bed, and blanketed him in darkness . . .

He felt something warm on his face, touched it, spread it to his lips. Salty, blood. His own? He opened his eyes. Someone had shaken him.

It was Czar Nicholas. Incredible.

The Czar was already turning away from the bed, hurrying toward the back sitting room that led to the rear of the train. Dmitri felt for his knife It was gone. It had been under him, he remembered. The Czar disappeared through the door to the sitting room. Dmitri groped for the knife. It wasn't on the bed. He stood up slowly, reeling a bit. The blade shone in the lamplight, on the rug at his feet, with drops of someone's blood already on it.

Dmitri reached for it. His own blood rushed to his head and he fell. He managed to grab hold of the knife, willed himself to stand up and make for the rear door, after the Czar.

Nicholas had already crossed the rear sitting room and was pushing through the vestibule door at the back, calling for his servants. Dmitri lunged after him, gaining strength with each step, eyes fixed on the Czar's back. From the vestibule door he could see the Czar leaning out the last door, peering into the night, where the last two carriages of the train had been.

Beyond the Czar, outside on the rear platform, Dmitri saw the man who had hit him with his cane, and he saw Kenneth Ash. They were fighting with sabres, and the sight clearly had all the Czar's attention. Running into the vestibule, Dmitri Dan felt a scream . . . an explosion of triumph well out of his chest – a scream, by his lights, for every Russian ever starved and tortured, a scream for his brother and their comrades, especially a scream for the last Romanov – he lifted his knife high and plunged it toward Czar Nicholas's back, just as the tyrant was turning his head to look at death.

48

'Nein' and 'no' came simultaneously from von Basel and Ash. The object of both their affections was about to be dispatched and both their missions violently aborted. They disengaged their sabres and almost as one thrust at Dmitri. The Czar was bracketed by their blades. Ash tore the assassin's knife arm, von Basel pierced his left shoulder. Dmitri Dan crashed into the Czar and slid down his back to the platform where, twice wounded, he grabbed his fallen knife with his left hand and made to slash up at the Czar.

Ash kicked the knife. Dmitri surged to his feet, screaming, and lunged for the Czar with his bare hands. Ash knocked him aside. Von Basel, exposed as he loosed a slash at Ash's head, caught the assassin's shoulder hard in his stomach. The blow doubled him up. He tumbled against the low railing at the edge of the platform, fell over it and rolled down the embankment, flailing at the snow.

Ash caught a glimpse of the aeroplane, a black silhouette, like a crow sunning itself in starlight. His vision was blurred by increasing distance, but he could swear he saw von Basel staggering toward it . . .

'The German spy?' Czar Nicholas asked with rather impressive calm.

'Yes.'

'And this one?' The Czar looked down at Dmitri Dan writhing at their feet. Ash kicked the knife further from his fingers.

'Russian.' Ash heard his voice moving into the distance . . . still pursuing von Basel . . .? Their fight wasn't finished.

'You've been hurt,' the Czar said.

'I'm all right, Your Majesty,' Ash replied, and collapsed on top of Dmitri Dan.

He awakened with a yell, which the Czar cut short by clamping a hand that smelled of expensive soap over Ash's mouth. A second man, a doctor by his plain frock coat, was dribbling iodine into the puncture in his upper arm, and with the pain came memories of the same hideous burning.

The Czar ordered silence with a finger over his lips. Ash gritted his teeth and tried to look around. Daylight was evident behind drawn shades. The train had stopped moving. He was propped up on a heap of blankets and pillows in the Czar's personal car. The doctor untied a bandage around his forearm, revealing a long wide slash already liberally oranged with iodine and crusting on the edges.

The Czar tightened his grip on Ash and the doctor poured iodine the length of his forearm; the pain arched his back, tears popped out of his eyes.

Ash hung on to the thought that somewhere, if he had survived the fall in the snow, von Basel might be going through the same thing. The doctor rebandaged his forearm while Ash tentatively flexed his fingers. Not so bad.

Another dose of liquid fire on his leg and the doctor was through. He washed his hands in the sink, cautiously opened the door and disappeared through it. The Czar sat down and spoke in a remarkably sad tone of voice, as though it were almost too much for him to speak.

'No one knows about the German but you and me. Only the doctor and the officers who removed the assassin secretly to the Pskov hospital know about the assassin. I told them that you received your wounds defending me from him.'

'But why?'

'I've not been able to contact the Czarina. I want nothing

to prevent you from going to Tsarskoye Selo to tell her what has happened here . . . When we arrived in Pskov last night Petrograd was in flames. Police stations were destroyed, my ministers arrested, regiments ordered to put down the insurrection had gone over to the insurrectionists. I dined with my generals aboard the train and telegraphed others. It was the opinion of my generals that I must grant a full constitution – grant full power of government to the Duma – otherwise Russia would plunge into anarchy and my armies collapse.'

Good, Ash thought. The American people would accept a *constitutional* monarchy as an ally against the Kaiser's Germany. The Czar stared at the tiles above Ash's head. What about Tamara, Ash wondered . . . he had to get back to Petrograd, *then* to the Czarina at Tsarskoye Selo . . .

'But this morning,' the Czar went on, 'I learned that the political situation was far worse. Particularly inside the Duma itself, which is divided. There are two factions . . . the majority have formed a Provisional Government to lead Russia in these difficult times, but they are opposed by the Social Revolutionary Party and the members of workers' committees – the soviets, that are opposed to my having *any* part in the government. So the ministers of the Duma are helpless, the workers' soviets already control Petrograd and the railroads and the telegraph.' He nodded at the little window. 'And so here we are in Pskov . . . while my wife is alone at Tsarskoye Selo.'

They've isolated him, thought Ash, just like Valery and I tried to do.

'A strong government must be formed to resist these soviets, restore order and continue the fight against Germany. It is imperative that you carry this message to the Alexander Palace. Tell the Czarina to stand fast, tell her it is God's will that I defend my throne – '

'May I ask you how, Your Majesty?'

'How? I will command our loyal troops to march on Petrograd. I have fifteen million men under arms, they can't *all* be disloyal – '

'Sir, what can the Czarina do when I tell her this?'

'Provide an example, encourage the garrison – '

'Has the Tsarskoye Selo garrison remained loyal?'

The Czar hesitated . . . 'I don't know . . . we are cut off here on the train . . .'

'Sir, I know this sounds presumptuous of me, but I ask you to reconsider what you are saying. If the soviets threaten the very existence of the Provisional Government, aren't they likely to resist you as well? Even you . . .' And added to himself, Especially you . . .

'I will crush them with Cossacks, Brusilov's soldiers, cavalry.'

Ash realized there was nothing more to be gained in debating with the Czar. His father used to say there was a time to tell the truth and a time to tell a man what he has to hear.

'Of course you have loyal regiments, Your Majesty . . .'

'Then you will make your way through the lines to Tsarskoye Selo, to my wife . . . we must not give in to fear.'

But he hardly sounded convinced by his own words. Lenin had cautioned Ash in Zurich not to misunderstand Russian patriotism, nor underestimate it. He looked the Czar in the eye. 'But what will happen to Russia, sir, if your capital is destroyed . . .?' For a moment Ash thought the Czar might hit him . . . His fists clenched. He looked away. He was still wearing his grey Cossack uniform. Ash decided to press one last time, *this* time to say to Nicholas what he knew was the truth but could not say to himself. 'I believe there's a saying, Your Majesty . . . that there are many tests of a soldier's courage . . .'

* * *

540

It had happened. The Czar, with Ash's prodding, had made a soldier's decision. Late that night Ash watched the Imperial Train steam south toward Mogilev, where the Czar had received permission – God, Ash thought, what *that* must have done to him . . . received *permission* – from the Provisional Government to say good-bye to his army. He hoped to rendezvous with his mother there to explain to the Dowager Empress why he had abdicated, as he had put it, 'my father's throne'.

He had asked Ash to report to the Czarina, to tell her he was safe, that he would be with her soon.

'May I tell Her Majesty that you will go to England?'

The Czar had only shrugged. His thoughts of the future were his own. He had precious little else left.

At the Pskov station a machine-gun covered the empty platform as the Czar's train steamed into the dark. When the train lights had disappeared Ash closed his boat cloak, straightened up his service cap and walked slowly to the ticket office. On to Petrograd to find Tamara.

A ragtag gang of soldiers stopped him; their battle-scarred sergeant wore the grey face of the trenches and an officer's coat with its epaulets ripped off. He read Ash's pass and sent a man running. Ash was trying to explain that he was an American citizen when the runner returned with the Social Revolutionary fighting squad leader Kirichenko.

Kirichenko received a nervous salute from the sergeant and one look told Ash that the soviets had dispatched their most ruthless agent to Pskov to seize the power slipping from the Czar. He looked the same as when Ash had last seen him, preparing to blow the Tsarskoye Selo line. He wore the same leather jacket, open as usual as if he didn't feel the cold, a peaked forage cap over his eyes and a pair of guns in his waistband. His heavy lips and long nose seemed more prominent in a face drawn with fatigue. Somewhere, he had picked up an incongruous-looking pair of spats. He regarded Ash with little interest, as if meeting him were a minor event in an otherwise important day.

'What are you doing in Pskov, Commander Ash?'

'On my way to Petrograd.'

'But why are you here?'

'I'm passing through on American government business; that safe-conduct pass was issued by the Provisional Government – '

'Ah? The *Provisional* Government.' Kirichenko held the pass to the light and carefully read the signature, then tore the paper into small pieces which drifted to the railroad platform. 'You need passes from the Railroad Workers' Soviet, and, of course, the Petrograd Soviet . . . But there's no need, in your case. I'm sending you to Petrograd anyhow. Your train will leave in the morning. And your room will be waiting for you in the Peter-Paul.'

'You're arresting me?'

'Certainly.'

'On what charge?'

Kirichenko lifted the peak of his hat enough for Ash to get a good look at his eyes. 'Suspicion of counterrevolutionary activities. Your monarchist associations are well known. And there's also the matter of the death of several of our comrades murdered in an explosion you arranged – '

'You have no authority to arrest me – '

'I have the authority of the Railroad Workers' Soviet throughout Russia. And the authority of the Petrograd Soviet in Petrograd.' He nodded at the sergeant and two soldiers grabbed Ash's arms; he stifled a yell when one inadvertently squeezed the puncture in his right. Kirichenko noticed, but a second group of soldiers came running out on the platform, carrying a stretcher and shouting, '*Tovarishch* Kirichenko.'

They had found Dmitri Dan. The Red Snow leader was wrapped in hospital sheets and heavy blankets. He looked weak, but when he recognized Ash he managed to lift his head as surprise turned to rage. He then started shouting at Kirichenko, introducing himself, it seemed. Ash recognized a few of the words he kept repeating: *Krasnyi*, which meant both red and beautiful; *sneg*, one of many Russian words for snow; *vozhd*, leader; and again and again, *tovarishch*, comrade.

Kirichenko listened until he was done, then pulled one of the pistols from his waistband and shot Dmitri Dan through the head. The bullet passed through Dmitri's skull and through the stretcher and ricocheted on the cement platform; the report echoed in the train shed. The soldiers holding his stretcher gaped white-faced at what they were carrying. The ones holding Ash let go, stunned.

Kirichenko addressed them briefly. They looked at each other, looked at Kirichenko still holding his gun, and tentatively saluted. Kirichenko returned their salute and turned to Ash. 'He said you prevented him from killing the Czar.'

Ash looked at his gun. 'Am I next?'

'Oh, no. The soviets are grateful. The Czar must stand trial, be made an example of. There will be no summary execution for the Czar.'

'Why did you shoot him?'

'We have no place in the Social Revolutionary-Bolshevik Revolution for fanatics.' Kirichenko slipped his pistol back into his waistband, and with a look at the soldiers added, 'Or for dissenters.'

Ash knew then, here in Pskov, that even the Czar's abdication wouldn't change Russia's course. Hours old, the Revolution was hurtling toward chaos, and the soviets

543

intended to use the Czar to justify it, to provide it with legit-imacy. That above all must be avoided if the US were to get involved, and if Russia were to continue as an ally against the Germans. More than ever it was necessary for Ash to get the Czar *and* his family to England.

BOOK V
The Death of Kings

49

Ash was among the first new prisoners in the Peter-Paul Fortress. Many more joined him in the next few days – bloodied ex-ministers, actually grateful the Red Guards had saved them from the mob; frightened aristocrats, their clothing ripped and smeared, or wearing hastily put on and transparent disguises; Life Guard officers, scabbards empty, insignia cut away; and even bewildered citizens who were once functionaries in the Czar's bureaucracy. They were all herded into large communal cells.

Ash tried to get disinfectant and bandages to patch up the new arrivals, pumping them, as he did, for the latest information. Two governments, it seemed, were running Russia – the Provisional Government, which represented the establishment, minus the Czar, who was rumoured to be under arrest; and the soviets, who represented the workers. The Provisionals spoke for the nation, the soviets controlled the major cities and communication between them, and it was the soviets, Ash heard over and over, who demanded that the Czar be arrested and tried. A single name emerged from the chaos and seemed to promise stability: the Duma member Sergei Gladishev had so strongly defended – Alexander Kerensky. Appointed Minister of Justice by the Provisional Government, Kerensky was taking charge, bridging the gap between the old establishment and the soviets. Kerensky promised to continue fighting Germany.

But a crippling debate raged over the Czar. Ash got hold of an English-language newspaper a new prisoner had held to a wound in his chest and read around the blood. It was filled with lurid accounts of supposed eye-witness reports of sex between Czarina Alexandra and Rasputin, as well as stories about religious desecration and the Czarina's connections with German spies.

Summing up the debate were two opposing columns under a single heading: WHAT TO DO WITH THE CZAR?

A minister of the Provisional Government suggested that after a 'suitable investigation of alleged wrongdoing' the Czar should either retire or be exiled. How convenient. The catch, of course, was the 'suitable investigation'. The second article was by a radical member of the Petrograd Soviet and he echoed Kirichenko. Bloody Nicholas must pay. He added that a former Czar abroad in exile would become a rallying figure for counter-revolutionaries.

The Czar was the focus. The whole country could blow up on account of him. Ash had to get him out . . . but he couldn't get himself out.

Four days later they brought in Lord Exeter. Ash watched the Englishman fight hard for his dignity. He had been struck repeatedly about the face; he was bloody and bruised. When Exeter's lungs finally stopped wheezing Ash asked him, 'How'd they get you?'

'Had my name on a list . . . My embassy's trying to get me deported.'

'We've got to get the Czar out before he sets off total civil war – '

'The soviets are dead set against him leaving.'

'We need to make it seem that the King has withdrawn the offer of sanctuary, make the soviets think the Czar couldn't go if he wanted to. And then we must secretly get him out.'

'You seem to forget you're in prison, Ash.'

'Get word to Gladishev to get me out of here. He's Kerensky's friend.'

'Kerensky's hanging on by his fingernails.'

They were eating a vile thin soup when the guards came for both of them and locked them in a small cell. After a few hours they appeared again, with an attaché from the British Embassy. 'Deported,' Exeter said. 'I'll give your *regards* to our friends in England.'

The guards left and came back once more. Ash was expecting to be shot. They took him down to the courtyard. Ambassador Hazzard was waiting in a hired car.

'Don't thank me, Commander. Thank the USA. The Petrograd Soviet wanted to throw away the key but the Provisionals said it was more important to be friends with the United States. You've certainly made some bad enemies, Ash.'

'Do you think we'll declare war on Germany soon?'

'President Wilson is addressing a joint session of Congress on April second. We're getting closer. If this whole damn country doesn't blow up first.'

'Mr Ambassador, I'm going to need passports to get out of Russia . . . ten of them.'

'*Ten?* What the hell for?'

Ash took Ambassador Hazzard's arm. The movement caused a dull twinge in his own arm in both the places von Basel had scored.

'Please cable Ambassador Page, sir. In code, and don't use my name. Ambassador Page will know what you mean.'

'I'll bet he will . . . Ash, what the hell are you up to?'

'See what Ambassador Page says, Your Excellency – '

'Lay off the "excellency" stuff, Ash. You're not talking to one of your European bluebloods . . . Ten?'

Ten, thought Ash. The Czar, Czarina, four grand duchesses, the boy, Sedovina, as he had promised Vadim and who could be very useful if he could persuade her to leave . . . that was eight. He was nine. And Tamara, somehow, was ten.

'Well, one thing's for sure,' Hazzard broke the silence as the car drove onto the Palace Bridge. 'If and when we get into this war, we're going to end it damned soon.'

'Not without Russia,' Ash said.

'Of course not without Russia. God . . . what a mess if they pulled out. Shall I drop you at your hotel, Ash?'

'The Winter Palace.'

Ash was taken through halls and chambers so huge and extravagant as to reduce the palaces of Europe and England to pallid imitations of royal display. Their classic proportions were perfect decisions of height and breadth, embellished with rococo ornamentation, gilded and fantastic.

'There are a thousand rooms like this one,' Sergei Gladishev said, greeting him. He was standing over a billiard table in a room with lapis walls. 'What is it you want, Commander?'

While Ash explained, Gladishev puttered about the table with his cue, missing shots and flicking the balls with the back of his hand.

'Everything is set,' Ash said when he had concluded telling the Duma member what he had told Exeter. 'I've got a route out. The Czar will go. King George's offer still holds, regardless of what you might hear. I'm ready to go.'

'Except that the Petrograd Soviet won't let him leave the Alexander Palace. Kerensky himself is interrogating the family – '

'What *for*? The Provisional Government doesn't want to put him on trial, does it?'

'No. I believe Kerensky is hoping to persuade the soviets that the Czar should not stand trial. Let him go into exile.'

'They won't,' Ash said. 'The Bolsheviks won't let him go –'

Gladishev shrugged. 'The situation is volatile. Give Kerensky time, we'll help you if it becomes necessary, but attempting to get the Czar out of Russia at this moment would be dangerous for us all . . . wait.'

'There isn't time, you're not going to make the Bolsheviks change their minds. And meanwhile things are getting worse, more dangerous – '

'Wait.'

For your own funeral, Ash thought.

General Ludendorff had requisitioned an hourglass. His aide-de-camp delegated a secretary to fill out the forms, and in due course an hourglass appeared on the desk of the quartermaster general. He took to turning it regularly, often before the hour was up. The sand fascinated him. His grains of sand, his casualties on the East and West, had kept mounting through the cold winter, and with spring approaching would accelerate.

There were boys in the line now, children stunted by nearly three years of short rations. And there were old men, hungry too, and cautious. Ludendorff laid the hourglass on its side; the sand settled into two imprisoned heaps, one larger, one small. He stared at it a while, then turned the large heap eastward. Russia. The small pile of grains on the other side, Germany.

His aide-de-camp knocked, sparing him from his increasingly morbid imagination. 'You asked to see me, General?'

'Can the Provisional Government win?'

'It might. An appeal to patriotism over politics. They say the Russian soldier believes in God, the Czar and Russia. And he's still got God and Russia.'

'That's what worries me,' Ludendorff said. 'There are too

551

many, and they are too brave. We've got to undermine them . . . what do you think of this von Basel situation?'

His aide-de-camp hesitated. It was not an idle change of subject.

Ludendorff said, 'All right, this is how I see von Basel. Number one, he has decided the Kaiser is hopeless. Hence the renewed reports to Gruppe IIIb . . . Number two, whatever his demented condition, he is a German patriot. Number three, though he was forced to go underground when the Czar abdicated, he is still a potent force inside Russia. Do you agree?'

'Yes, General. His reports indicate he is still working for Germany under difficult conditions.'

'And Count von Basel's advice?'

'Divide Russia by creating conflict between the soviets and the Provisionals.'

'My feelings exactly,' Ludendorff replied. 'I think it's time to gather up those scum in Zurich and swing the balance of power.'

'The Bolsheviks, sir?'

'Yes. Bolsheviks, SRs, Red Snow, Mensheviks, every damned one you can find. Offer them passage to Russia.' He upended the hourglass and the large heap began trickling into the smaller. 'Be sure not to let them off the train in Germany even to stretch their legs. They'll infect our people . . . and order von Basel to give them all the help he can.'

An ecstatic Lenin received the news that the Germans would send him home while he was writing a letter about the revolutionary role of the soviets. News from Russia was still sketchy, but the Bolsheviks who had always looked to him for leadership were anxious for 'the Old Man's' thoughts upon the great fires raging. Events were unfolding too quickly to know exactly what was transpiring, but of one thing Lenin was positive – the future of the Revolution lay in the hands of the soviets.

So this was the message he wrote to his faithful followers. Already the workers' councils were a powerfully organized outpouring of the people's will. If they were armed, the soviets could appropriate the Revolution by seizing control from the Provisionals. And when that happened, Lenin's Bolsheviks would appropriate the soviets.

Red flags flew from the Admiralty and the Peter-Paul. Anarchists dressed in black roamed the streets of Petrograd carrying machine-guns. Ash tried to call Tamara from the Winter Palace, but the telephones were out. On her embankment across the river he could make out black holes where houses had recently stood. He couldn't see hers. There were no cars for hire. He caught a tram part way and ran on foot the rest of the distance to her mansion. But as he neared the embankment, he slowed . . . Up close the burned-out hulks looked as if they had been shelled. Here a wall stood free, there a chimney, and beside it a garden filled with bits of furniture, too big for the looters to carry or damaged beyond saving. He rounded a final bend – and there was Tamara's, still standing, with its windows dark.

A sign on the door told why:

PROPERTY OF THE PETROGRAD SOVIET
TRESPASSERS WILL BE SHOT

Ash pushed open the gate, walked up the unshovelled path and banged the door knocker. Maybe the bastards knew where she'd gone . . . been taken . . . But no one came to the door. He thought he heard movement inside, knocked again. A curtain slid from a side window, a face peered out. The door opened wide.

'*Kennet.*'

As she threw her arms around him, Ash caught a

glimpse of her black boots, black fur, black hat, cheeks pale and hair so very beautiful. 'Inside, quickly.'

It was bitter cold in the house. Ash embraced her. 'God, I thought they'd done something to you – '

'Not yet,' she said, pulling away with a steely note in her voice Ash had heard only in her rehearsals. 'Are you all right? You disappeared.'

'What's that sign about?'

A quick smile. 'I wrote it myself. No one's bothered me.'

'You can't stay here.'

'I don't intend to. I'm going to Paris.'

'Paris? How?'

She looked away. 'I've made arrangements.'

'Tamara. You can't go across town without a pass from the revolutionaries.'

'I've got one.'

'You?'

'Now, listen. There's someone I want you to meet and I would appreciate it if you would behave yourself.'

'Who?'

She hurried without a word toward the solarium. Ash followed. All the plants were dead. Across the river many of the buildings flew red flags.

The balletomane Baron Zlota stood rubbing his hands before a small fire made from a smashed chair. He wore the hat and coat of a Russian Guards officer, with a big red cockade on the hat, and on his shoulder where the Czar's insignia had adorned his epaulets was a red ribbon. He cast avid eyes on Tamara.

'Baron Zlota, may I present Commander Ash?'

'We've met,' said Ash.

'Hello there, Ash. We worried when we heard your knock.'

'Baron Zlota has a travel pass to the Crimea. He is taking me to Paris.'

'I am honoured to perform that service.'

'Would you excuse us?' Ash said coldly.

'I beg your pardon?'

'Tamara,' he said quietly. 'Get him out of here or – '

'André, be a dear. Kennet and I must discuss something of a private nature.'

Baron Zlota stood up, smiling expansively. 'I'll be right outside. Don't forget, we're leaving very soon.'

Tamara closed the door and turned on Ash. 'How dare you – You know damned well what the Revolutionaries will do to me when they discover I'm here. They've burned all my neighbours' houses already. Sedovina warned me to get out; she knows I'm in danger. I'm a monarchist. I'm rich – in poor eyes at any rate – and I was the Grand Duke Valery's mistress.'

'Do you have to do it like this? Running off with that little – '

'Don't judge me! – *You* have your American diplomatic passport. How the hell am *I* supposed to get out of the country with the Czar abdicated and these damned Provisionals and soviets and God knows what taking over?'

'Get out on your own, for Christ's sake. What can that idiot – ?'

'He's a liberal. The revolutionaries need him.'

'For the moment. And what does he need you for?'

'He's a gentleman. He'll respect my grief for Valery.'

'Like hell he will, Tamara. Do it yourself. For once. You don't need that sort.'

'Are *you* going to help me?'

'Don't you realize you're better than a courtesan?'

'*Are you going to help me?*'

Ash hesitated. 'Yes, but we can't leave right away. It's going to be a little while. A week or two.'

555

'A week or two? Kennet. Don't you see what's going on here? I'll be back in prison in a week or two. Or worse . . . You can't give me what I need,' she said bitterly. 'As usual.'

'You know for the first time I don't feel any need to apologize. You've got yourself, which is more than anyone else can give you. Use yourself.'

'How? I've lost everything but my jewels and Baron Zlota may even need them for bribes.'

'*Your* jewels. You've picked a real beaut.'

'He's got *a. pass*. For *two*. And I don't have to wait, while some damned soviet decides to arrest me because of Valery.' She looked at Ash, at last, and defiance softened to a plea. 'What can I do, Kennet? I'm just a dancer.'

Ash felt his anger dissolve in a terrible wave of sadness. 'For the first time in our lives you disappoint me.'

Tamara's angry retort was choked off by tears. The Czar's police had locked her up like an animal. The Revolutionaries hated her. Kennet opened his arms to comfort her but he held her body like a stranger. She pulled back and looked up at him; his eyes were kind and sad and a little empty. And for the first time since she had known him, she feared he did not adore her.

'I'm frightened,' she explained. 'Sedovina warned me – I think she's defended me, but she's just one girl. I'm afraid.'

'I know. I know. I'm sorry.'

She pressed against him. He was there, but he wasn't there. She whispered against his chest. 'Sedovina is organizing benefit performances for the troops.'

'Really?'

'Many artists are contributing; they're afraid not to.'

'Is she dancing?'

'She says she's too busy presenting the benefits.'

Tamara stole a glance at Ash and hurried along, trying to kindle his interest before he let her go. She laughed, 'Show me a performer who joins management and I'll show you a performer who's lost her faith in performance. You – '

'Why don't *you* dance?'

'Me?'

'Do a benefit.'

'Why?'

'Dance for a pass.'

'A pass? No. Tishkova does not – '

'Why the hell not? Dance for a pass. Your *own* pass. You don't need that clown.'

'Dance for a mob of revolutionaries?' Tamara shuddered.

'They're just men, Tamara. You've never had much trouble handling the breed before.'

Tamara looked up at him. She moved closer, thinking. '. . . But darling they've never seen ballet.'

'Neither has anyone else who hasn't seen you dance.'

'Thank you, darling. But this is – ' Was he holding her more tightly? A little. 'You know,' she reflected, 'I keep thinking about that worker on the tram who saw me dance . . . Sedovina's artists have performed at some of the smaller theatres . . . I heard Kschessinska flounced around the Conservatoire.' She shook her head. 'It must have taken courage . . .'

'Tishkova could dance her jubilee.'

'Kennet, that's not very nice.'

'I'm serious. Go out in style.'

The thought raced through her that she didn't want to go out; she wanted things to return to the way they had been; she wanted to reign over Petrograd Society; she wanted to enter balls on the arm of the Grand Duke Valery; she wanted to be *prima ballerina assoluta* of His Majesty's Imperial Theatres forever.

'You can do it,' said Kennet.

Tamara stared out of the window. Across the Neva a silken red flag flew over the Winter Palace; it stood straight out, blown by a hard spring gale off the Gulf. Snow swirls raced up the frozen river. She had no choice. She was going, whether she wanted to or not. But how grandly she went was still her choice. Wasn't that what Kennet was pleading, begging her to be what he admired? What he loved.

'If I were to dance, I would perform at the Maryinski . . . What am I saying? Good God, Kennet. Two thousand revolutionaries . . . I wonder what I would dance? . . . *Swan Lake,* I suppose. I've rehearsed it already. It's pretty. And it's simple enough for them to understand . . . What do you think?'

Kennet was looking at her strangely. 'What about *Firebird?*'

50

Increasingly anxious to rid the Provisional Government of the Czar's divisive presence, yet at the same time not up to challenging the soviets who were hell-bent to put the Czar on trial – a forum from which they could attack the aristocratic and bourgeois elements of the Provisional Government as well as the Czar himself – Sergei Gladishev and Justice Minister Kerensky allowed Ash to persuade them to take what seemed a good way out of their dilemma. Kerensky ordered the captain of the guard holding the Czar to help Ash hide Nicholas and his family in the stage sets of the *Firebird* ballet, which had been stored for some time now in shipping crates at the Alexander Palace.

After that, Ash would be on his own. The crated sets would be sent to the Maryinski Theatre, where Tamara Tishkova would perform *Firebird* to honour the Revolution. From the theatre it was up to Ash to smuggle the family, disguised and carrying American and British passports, to the Finland Station, then by train across the Finnish-Swedish border.

But it was the first twenty miles of the escape that was certain to be most difficult. The Tsarskoye Selo village soviet, the Railroad Workers' Soviet and the Petrograd Soviet had an iron grip on the route between the Alexander Palace and the Maryinski Theatre. And the revolutionary guards that served them were more than likely to inspect any crates that passed through their territory . . .

Vera Sedovina was Ash's only friendly contact among

559

the soviets – Kirichenko had been less than pleased when the Provisional Government had released Ash from the Peter-Paul – Sedovina's bravery, her courier missions for the Bolsheviks and her dancing in the slums were widely known, as were her efforts since the Revolution to bring dance, music and theatre to 'the masses'.

Ash found her in a bitter-cold rehearsal hall near the Maryinski, overseeing acts to be presented to revolutionary soldiers. Valentinov, the provincial actor whom Ash had seen play the Czar when Sedovina danced in the Moscow District, was badgering her for a role.

'It is *ballet*,' she told him firmly.

Valentinov gave an enormous shrug. 'You are a hard woman, Vera.' At the door he slipped his Czarlike beard around his chin and called out, 'I, Nicholas the Deposed, *command* that Valentinov play Petrograd. What do you say to *that*, Vera Sedovina?'

'I say *out*.'

'Is he that bad?' Ash said after the man had gone.

'He would take advantage,' she said bluntly. 'It's wrong.'

Ash looked at her. Her blond hair was crushed into a tight bun. She wore wire-frame reading glasses and a heavy wool sweater over her rehearsal clothes. Dancers were working out at the barre, their breath steaming in the frigid air. Vera sat at a desk covered with neatly stacked papers. And Ash thought she did not look very happy.

'You seem upset. What's wrong?'

'I'm just tired, there's so much to do, so much confusion . . .'

'I'd have thought you'd be happier, I mean with the Revolution here – '

'Yes, of course . . .' Except she didn't sound very convincing.

'Vera . . . would you have lunch with me? I need to talk to you about something.'

She started to refuse, changed her mind, gave some instructions to a few people and got her coat. They walked along the Ekaterine Canal. 'First of all,' Ash said, 'you convinced Tamara. She'll dance the *Firebird* at the Maryinski for whatever audience you invite.'

'Tishkova?' Her eyes lighted with pleasure.

'She'll want a travel pass. She wants to go to Paris . . .'

'Yes, I guess I can understand that. Things must seem strange now to a woman of her position . . . well, if she dances I think the soviets will give her permission . . . Why *Firebird?*'

At that moment a huge limousine roared by, diverting her from waiting for his answer. Armed soldiers lay on the running boards and poked guns and red flags from the windows. They saw Sedovina and gave out admiring catcalls. Sedovina moved closer to Ash. He slipped her hand through his arm.

'They're patrolling for counter-revolutionaries – '

'They're joyriding,' Ash said. 'When they run out of gas they'll steal another car. Except they'll call it appropriating. It's getting out of hand, Vera. The whole city's going to blow up again.'

Sedovina's voice sounded very tired. 'Those men in the car are still the poor, the Provisionals are still the rich . . .'

'Whatever, but you've got a civil war coming if you keep thinking that way. Is this the Russia you imagined?' He looked at her and saw tears in her eyes. Her guard had come down. For a moment the frightened young girl had reappeared. 'Your step-father asked me to take you to America – '

'*No.* This is my country. We just somehow have to move ahead – '

'Russia's not likely to be moving any place as long as the soviets try to destroy the Provisional Government.'

'But I'm a Bolshevik, Commander . . . the soviets *should* destroy the Provisional Government – '

'I saw Kirichenko murder a man in cold blood because he happened to belong to another political party.'

'The fanatic Dmitri Dan? I heard.'

'Doesn't that bother you?'

'Yes . . . of course . . . but as the peasants say, when you chop wood, chips fly – '

'Well, those chips are going to catch fire, Vera. How much more chaos can Russia stand? Do you want a civil war? My father fought in one. A million men died. And we were a very small country at the time. At least the Provisional Government stands between you and anarchy. Sure . . . let the Bolsheviks take over in time, but let it happen slowly, Vera. Let the soviets take power peacefully; if they really represent the people, let them do it without fighting.'

Sedovina shook her head. 'I'm confused, I don't like what I see. I know it's wrong to feel this way, but it's almost as if we've discovered a new oppression, our own stupidity – I don't want to talk about it anymore . . . Why did Tishkova choose *Firebird,* of all things? You never answered me.'

'Because I asked her to.'

'You? Why?'

He took a deep breath, and explained. Then he asked her to help.

'Have you told Tishkova?'

'She's going to have enough, dancing her Jubilee for two thousand revolutionaries without worrying about a Czar hidden in the cellar . . .'

'You really trust me, don't you?'

'Vera, there are three people in Russia I trust. You, Tamara Tishkova and myself.'

Tears filled her eyes again. 'I guess that's why I'm crying,' she murmured. 'My list is no bigger. Everyone seems to have lost their way . . .'

51

The cavernous stage was bare from wing to wing, empty from the proscenium arch to the back wall. Tamara looked more sad than angry, but her eyes flashed as she paced a tight circle. 'I am performing in thirty-six hours and still there is no set? No scenery. No drops. No scrim.' She clutched a fistful of her thick practice sweater. 'And *this* is not a costume, for the information of gentlemen who keep promising miracles.'

Her friend, the former director of the defunct Imperial Theatres, glanced imploringly at Ash, who had his own considerable reasons to be concerned about the delayed sets. Ash said, 'I'm sure everything will arrive in time for the carpenters to fly the sets tonight.'

'*You're* sure.'

'Sedovina persuaded Kirichenko to issue new passes for her crew. She'll get through to the palace this time, I'm sure.'

Tamara ran both hands through her thick black hair. 'Why did I let you talk me into *Firebird*? I could have done *Swan Lake*. Every theatre in the city has sets for *Swan Lake*. Damn it, why didn't you let me go to Paris with Baron Zlota?'

Ash massaged her shoulders. 'You're tense. You've rehearsed yourself to death. Everyone thinks you're wonderful – '

'Absolutely,' said the director.

'*Tense?* How would you feel if they sent you to sea without a ship?'

Which was just about how Ash did feel. Yesterday and

564

the day before the soviets had turned the Maryinski's haulage men back from Tsarskoye Selo in spite of Vera Sedovina's reputation and credentials. The reasons were less political than bureaucratic ... with responsibility so divided among Petrograd city soviets, railroad soviets and Tsarskoye Selo soviets, chaos reigned. There always seemed to be one more official demanding a pass than Sedovina had passes.

'Tonight,' Ash promised.

'Where are *you* going?'

'The embassy,' Ash lied.

'You can't leave me today.'

'Tamara, I do work for the United States government and its ambassador has told me to show up . . . good luck at rehearsal.'

'You are an out and out bastard.'

Ash reached for her and she dodged; she relented on his third try and let him hold her. 'It's all going to be over soon.'

'Try to get back early. I'm going to be a wreck tonight. Seriously, Kennet, I'm going to need you very badly.'

He saw no way to tell her he was heading out to the Alexander Palace; Tamara was getting her pass by dancing, which was a far surer way of getting out alive than knowing about his scheme to rescue the Czar . . .

Tamara was not the only one with nerves on edge. Sergei Gladishev greeted Ash with a strident warning. 'Last time, Commander. If you don't get them out today it's over. Two times I have taken you to the Alexander Palace pretending to interrogate the Czar for Justice Minister Kerensky. My colleagues wonder how many more times I can ask why he appointed bad ministers. Two times we put the Czar and his family in packing crates, and two times no theatre crew collects the crates.'

'Last chance,' Ash agreed. 'Tomorrow's the performance.'

They were, as usual, stopped twice on the way to Tsarskoye Selo, and on one occasion Gladishev's bodyguards exchanged fire with gunmen hidden in the trees.

Slovenly guards admitted them to the palace grounds. The captain of the Provisional Government's guard, a taciturn front-line officer, conducted them to the cellar; only he and a few loyal officers and ladies of the household were aware of the plan.

The family was waiting. It was nearly a month to the day that the Czar had abdicated his throne and the right of his son to inherit; time and events had affected him and the Czarina differently. The Czar looked like an old man; deeply scored wrinkles had added twenty years to his face, yet he was calm and if Ash had to guess at his emotions he would have thought sorrow was the dominant one. Czarina Alexandra, on the other hand, had blossomed. Indeed she looked quite beautiful, in charge of the situation. She greeted Ash cordially when he bowed over her hand . . . a considerable change from previous encounters. Perhaps it was that the ghost of Rasputin's injunction for the Czar to resign had been carried out, and her husband and family were about to fulfil her mentor's prescribed destiny.

'Better luck this time, Commander?' She was almost cheerful.

'To be sure, Ma'am. An audience of two thousand revolutionaries must lend weight to the idea that the show must go on.'

Her children were strangers to Ash. Four girls aged from sixteen to twenty. Olga, the eldest, quite pretty and rather serious looking; Tatiana, as regal a beauty as her mother; Marie, a pretty girl about Catherine Hazzard's age; and Anastasia, a happy-looking child. The Czarevich, or ex-Czarevich, Ash reminded himself, stuck close to Czar

Nicholas as if most sensitive to his father's grief. He shook hands with Ash gravely, as did his father. Both greeted Sergei Gladishev as 'Mr Duma Member.'

The captain of the Provisional Government's guard reappeared shortly. 'It looks as if they're getting through. The Tsarskoye Selo Soviet has allowed them to enter the Imperial Park. They're less than a mile from the gates.'

The Czarina hugged each of her children, and kissed the Czar.

The flats, backdrops and scrims had been broken down in Paris seven years earlier to fit railroad cars. There were a dozen crates eight feet high and eight to fifteen feet long in addition to costume and prop boxes. All but the boy and the Czarina entered them singly. Alexandra feared the boy would be hurt if he were alone; and she was unable to stand for a long time on account of her sciatica, so in the centre of a huge prop box they had constructed a bed of blankets on which she would lie down holding the boy.

There was no one to say good-bye. Closest friends had already been sent away from the palace. Those few who remained were upstairs in the royal apartments maintaining the fiction that the family were in their rooms.

Ash and the captain of the guard nailed each crate shut. Ash saved the Czarina's for last. She thanked him when he wished her luck. He was pounding in the last nail when the cellar's huge outer doors banged open and a gang of roustabouts trooped down the ramp, Sedovina in the lead.

As a leader of the newly organized Theatre Workers' Soviet, she had put together a crew from various theatres, men not known to each other, and who therefore took little notice of Ash, who like them was dressed in sheepskin, forage cap and *valenki*, oiled felt knee-high peasant boots. He joined the crew hoisting the crates onto dollies and wheeling them out the cellar and up the ramp to freight sledges waiting on the frozen snow. Nor did they notice when one of the haulers – the actor Valentinov – stayed behind in the cellar, until the captain of the guard escorted the actor upstairs to the royal apartments . . .

Outside the Alexander Palace, Provisional troops stood around a fire roasting one of the tame deer shot in the park. When the sledges were loaded, the horses started for the gates that led to the Imperial Park, and the theatre crew hopped on wherever they could find space. The Provisional troops waved them through the great grill gate. The troops of the Tsarskoye Selo Soviet promptly stopped them on the other side.

Ash sat on the prop box housing the Czarina and Alexis and tried to look as unconcerned as the theatre workmen. Red Guards swaggered around the sledges while Vera Sedovina presented papers to their officer.

Sedovina was having a hard time keeping her temper. 'We passed this way an hour ago,' she reminded the officer.

'Quite right, comrade, but now you have cargo.'

'Which you and I discussed an hour ago, comrade, when I showed you these permits and informed you that you yourself will be a guest at the people's ballet tomorrow night, provided these sets and costumes arrive there on time.'

'I would be derelict in my duties to the Tsarskoye Selo Soviet if I did not inspect the contents – '

'*I* would be derelict in my duties to the comrades of the Petrograd Theatres' Soviet not to inform *you* that two thousand Russian soldiers, Red Guards, sailors of Red Kronstadt, SRs, Bolsheviks and the workers' soviets are invited to the Maryinski Theatre to see a performance by Comrade Tishkova using these sets.'

'I am responsible – '

'Then get *on* with it.' She pointed to a crate. 'Open that one.'

'Why that one?'

'Because, comrade, that is the only crate I did not have time to inspect myself.' She nodded and her crew levered it open with crowbars.

'Careful,' Sedovina shouted as a soldier reached inside. 'Do it yourself, comrade,' she told the officer. 'That is part of a scrim, very fragile.' He poked around, then noticed another crate on another sledge while the workman nailed the first crate shut again.

'Comrade, please,' Sedovina asked with a smile. 'We're really late.'

He glanced at the papers. 'This is signed by Comrade Kirichenko?'

'Comrade Kirichenko told me that he is very curious to see why the great Tishkova was the Czar's favourite. You understand?'

'Proceed.'

Flying red flags, a small black locomotive wheezed onto the Tsarskoye Selo freight siding with a boxcar. Sedovina's crew slid open the doors and started hoisting the crates up from the sledges. A delegation of the Railroad Workers' Soviet bustled officiously among the horses, crates and sledges, shouting, waving papers and generally getting in the way. The Maryinski roustabouts indicated Sedovina was boss. The ballerina reached for her own papers but the chief of the railroad workers' delegation recognized her, tugged off his leather cap and tried to kiss her hand. 'Little Mother', he called her, an almost mystical phrase of peasant respect. He told her he had seen her dance in the Moscow District with Valentinov, and that she had given him courage so that instead of running from the police he had fought back. He then ordered his delegation to help load the crates.

They rode in the boxcar with the crates. Ash again

stationed himself on the box holding the Czarina and her son as the locomotive moved slowly toward Petrograd. The man on the next box tried to make conversation and, when that failed, passed a bottle. Ash drank as little as possible without raising suspicions so that he was still reasonably sober when the train reached the city.

Things, it seemed, were finally looking up, Ash thought as he backed onto the platform holding a corner of the Czarina's prop box and muttered as much to Sedovina as she brushed close by.

Then he saw Kirichenko.

The SR fighting squad leader and representative of the combined railroad soviets was striding down the freight platform trailed by bodyguards. Ash ducked his head and tried to turn his back; the prop box was enormously heavy and he could not let go his corner without provoking dismayed shouts from the men holding the other three.

Sedovina froze. She could bully and cajole the workmen; she could receive homage from those who considered her a young female revolutionary hero. Not with Kirichenko. She looked at Ash for help. Kirichenko was only twenty feet away. Ash had to keep carrying the prop box.

'He likes you,' Ash muttered. 'Use it.'

Sedovina couldn't believe it . . . Kirichenko?

Ash shuffled past with the box, trying to keep his head down. 'Imagine you're Tamara, do *something* to distract him . . .'

'*Tovarishch* Kirichenko,' she called gaily. He looked surprised. No wonder . . . not a word of scandal had ever been connected to his name, not a hint of a mistress. Kirichenko personified the dour, puritanical side of the Revolution. His eye went to the box that Ash and others were struggling with – the box that secreted the Czarina and the Czarevich – and Vera Sedovina moved quickly into territory she had up to now only seen from a distance . . . she slipped her arm

570

through Kirichenko's, smiled and sickened herself by saying, 'We never would have made it with these sets without your name on the passes.'

Kirichenko looked at her as if she were out of her mind. She waved her hand at the other crates, and turned him away from Ash. 'There's confusion among even the soviets,' she said. 'Your name cut through it. The people's ballet will be danced at the Maryinski, thanks to you, *Tovarishch* Kirichenko.' She even squeezed his arm. Kirichenko scarcely reacted. Sedovina was reminded of a caged wolf. Fighting squad leader Kirichenko was sweet on no one, clearly not very susceptible to her reluctant wiles. Still, the distraction had apparently worked; Ash had disappeared in the direction of the trucks carrying the crates across Petrograd to the theatre. She let go of Kirichenko's arm. 'I hope you enjoy the ballet,' she said, more coolly.

'I'll be there, I've never seen you dance indoors.'

So he was human. 'I'm only dancing the princess. *Firebird* will be Tishkova's night.'

Was that a flicker of humour animating Kirichenko's sharp features? He had been looking around the train platform, at the broken crate wrapped in ropes. Now he turned back to Sedovina, who pushed a wisp of blond hair back under her hat.

'I'm sure it will be interesting to experience the pleasures of the Czars – but I for one am grateful for the opportunity to see you dance without having to watch that ham Valentinov. There were nights I thought of turning him into the Okhrana as a public service . . .' He took a final look around and nodded to his bodyguards. 'Well done, Comrade Sedovina. And good luck tomorrow night.'

There remained getting the Czar and his family out of the scenery crates without being noticed by the theatre carpenters who, urged on by a near-frantic stage manager, were

571

eager to fly the flats. Ash went ahead of the trucks to the theatre, changed into his uniform in Tamara's dressing room and sat in the front row of the darkened house until Tamara and her Prince Ivan rehearsing their *pas de deux* took a break.

She came out of the lights with a towel around her neck and smiled down at him. 'Thank you for coming so soon.'

'I had to lock the ambassador in the closet . . . You look marvellous.'

'Getting there . . . I'm told the sets are on the way.'

'Sedovina thinks it would be a nice gesture to address the stage carpenters before they start. They'll be working all night.'

'You tell Sedovina I grew up in the circus and I've never slighted a single member of any company in my life – even *before* I had to call them comrade.'

'She's young – '

'And then tell her that when I was her age in the Czar's Imperial Theatre, dancers who cut rehearsal the day before a performance ended up dancing in Turkestan.'

Count von Basel sat in the dark, watching. As soon as the posters announcing the great Tishkova's Jubilee were pasted up beside the strident revolutionary broadsheets that covered every blank wall in the city von Basel suspected that at the Maryinski he was likely to find Ash, and what Ash was up to.

Now why had Ash stayed in Petrograd? A week ago the United States had formally declared war on Germany, as was expected once the Czar was overthrown. He had to smile about that. Yes, the Czar had abdicated and the United States could now feel easier about being Russia's ally . . . Some ally . . . Still, he wondered why Ash hadn't been immediately recalled for sea duty. The United States was badly unprepared for war. It would take a year to

572

mobilize a major army in France. Wouldn't they call home every experienced officer?

It was a puzzle that worried von Basel, a concern more important even than his fury at Ash for frustrating his attempt to capture the Czar for Kaiser Wilhelm, almost as important as the debt of honour Ash owed for their unfinished duel –

Ash and Tishkova had stopped talking. Von Basel leaned over the gallery balustrade and looked down. The entire theatre was dark except for low lights on the stage. Tishkova was sprawled face down on a blanket. Ash had climbed on the stage and was kneeling beside her, massaging her shoulders.

Von Basel's bony head made him look like a wary hawk. Ash's government, he decided, hadn't recalled him because Ash was still involved in some intrigue in Russia . . . which could only mean trouble for his Kaiser and Germany.

He tried to flex the fingers of his left hand as he gazed down at the figures on the stage. Ash had severed tendons with his lucky thrust. Two of his fingers had curled up almost like the Kaiser's . . . Still enemies, Ash and himself. More than ever.

Thirty years earlier, deep in the cellars of the Maryinski, a squirrel of a stage manager had stored the gas lights when the theatre was electrified. There was no reason for anyone to enter the storeroom, and so it was there, among discarded foot and border lights, coils of copper tubing, an old gas valve switchboard table and ancient limelights that Ash had hidden Czar Nicholas and his family.

They were chilled from the long ride in the crates, and because the theatre backed directly on to a canal the walls were wet, the room cold. They huddled in blankets. Ash spirited a hot samovar out of the stagehands' workshop. They made and drank tea while Ash displayed the clothing

573

he and Sedovina had assembled to go with their various passports.

'Nuns?' the Czar said with a smile for his three eldest daughters.

'A good way to hide a pretty face. Olga, Tatiana and Marie have British passports listing them as nursing sisters with the Anglo-Russian hospital.'

'And my wife's pretty face?'

'Grey hair, for Her Majesty. Alexis and Anastasia will be your grandchildren.'

'And who am I?'

'An American secretary of the Young Men's Christian Association. The YMCA. You've been visiting the *Mayak*, the Lighthouse brother organization here in Russia. Her Majesty's passport is British, to explain her accent. Yours is flatter and can pass for American.'

The Czar took him aside afterward.

'We are grateful, of course, Commander, but are you still convinced we can – ?'

'Can I guarantee to get you aboard a train and across the Swedish border? No, though I'll promise you a damned good try . . . Can you guarantee your family's lives in Russia?'

'Not without the Provisional Government's protection.'

'Well, I wouldn't bet on them too long . . . tomorrow night every revolutionary leader worth his salt is going to be sitting upstairs watching Tishkova dance.'

'She *is* distracting.' The Czar smiled.

'She is more than distracting to me,' Ash told him, a chill in his voice.

'I did not mean disrespect, Commander, merely admiration . . .'

Ash broke the brief silence that followed. 'I'm afraid you're also going to have to say good-bye to your beard.'

* * *

574

The next afternoon, while Tamara Tishkova and her friend, the former director of the Imperial Theatre, drove their company through dress rehearsal, two corporals of the Automobile Unit of the Engineer Corps concocted what they decided was a brilliant idea as they roared up and down the Nevsky Prospect in a commandeered armoured car.

The Bolshevik leader Vladimir Ilyich Lenin was due to arrive from Zurich late that night. Why not go out to Tsarskoye Selo, arrest the Czar in the name of all the soviets and to hell with the Provisionals, and then present their prisoner to Lenin when he got off the train at the Finland Station? A magnificent welcome-home gift.

They were sharing a bottle, and the one who had had the least cautioned that the Provisional Government troops might resist a single armoured car. So they drove out to the Smolny Institute, rounded up three more cars with like-minded crews and headed out to Tsarskoye Selo in convoy. One car crashed on the way, but the rest made it in an hour, a remarkable time considering the ice and frozen ruts.

Smashing through the front gates, scattering the sentries, they skidded to a noisy halt at the main entrance, levelled their cannon and machine-guns and announced from their steel turrets that they had come to arrest the Czar in the name of the Petrograd Soviet. A hard-bitten Provisional captain came down the stairs and threatened to arrest them.

It was the first resistance they had met, and while they could have shot him, he was no imperial dandy but a soldier more like themselves. In that moment of reflection some began to wonder whether the Provisionals might be readying an artillery piece. Someone offered a compromise . . . 'Let us see the Czar so that we can tell the soviet the prisoner is in your custody.'

The captain did not like that idea at all, but there were

three cars and among them two cannon and at least six heavy machine-guns. 'You may come in . . . the prisoner Nicholas Romanov will be brought to you.'

'We want to see the royal apartments.'

'The children are ill – '

'We want to see the heir.'

'You can't,' the captain said. He had regained some control of the situation and led them into the palace and lined them up at one end of the central reception hall. He then went up to the royal apartments, after mustering a ragtag Provisional guard to keep an eye on the armoured car soldiers.

The actor Valentinov had never entered a stage tentatively, and he did not propose to do so now. The captain of the Provisional Guard had tried to soothe him by promising his guard would stand between him and the soviet soldiers who demanded to see the Czar, but that, he was certain, wasn't necessary . . . he was, after all, wearing the Czar's own clothes, and the soldiers had seen only pictures of Nicholas II. Now here he was in person, dazzling in scarlet and dripping gold braid, medals and a silken sash. He even had a sword, which the captain took away, explaining that as a prisoner he would not logically be allowed to keep it. And the captain reminded him again that the servants weren't to be trusted, since many had been enlisted as spies for the soviets.

'Act like a prisoner,' the captain had told him. 'Not Caesar.'

Valentinov had promised but when he entered the reception hall and saw the soldiers waiting, he lost control. Instead of parading back and forth at a distance to make clear that he was in custody, he marched straight at the soldiers and offered to shake their hands.

Astounded, several did. Others just gaped in disbelief.

Finally the captain of the guard clamped Valentinov's arm in a grip of iron and marched him away.

'How did I do?' Valentinov asked on the stairs.

'They will tell their grandsons that they shook the hand of Bloody Nicholas, Czar of all the Russias.'

'Thank you, sir.'

The captain eyed him. 'Valentinov, have you no idea of the danger you will be in if the real Czar is caught?'

'No more than you.'

'I am a soldier. And when he's gone the Provisional Government will thank me. The soviets will kill you if they learn what you're doing today . . .'

'For three years before you were a comrade, Comrade Captain, my acting troupe played under the noses of the Okhrana.'

'But now you have your revolution. Why risk – ?'

'I agree with Comrade Sedovina. Now that we have our revolution, we have to risk our necks to save it.'

'Well, with luck you'll be back in Petrograd tomorrow.'

With luck, or a miracle? Valentinov wondered. Impersonating the Czar was going to be the performance of his life.

52

Tamara Tishkova watched strangers invade the Maryinski. Gone were the colourful uniforms of the Life Guards. Gone too old friends gathering for Society's entertainment. No laughter trilling from the first ring as the ladies of Petrograd inspected the officers parading in the stalls.

Ordinarily, with the dance settled in her mind, she would be relaxing these few minutes between dress and performance, staring into space, jumping up to prowl her dressing room, adjusting to the elaborate headdress, but tonight she was irresistibly drawn to the stage manager's peephole at the side of the curtain to watch the people trooping into her theatre.

The soldiers wore frontline khaki, the revolutionaries shabby suits if they were moderates or black leather jackets if they were radicals like Kirichenko, who was taking a seat of honour in the Imperial Box – *the Czar's own box* – flanking an anxious Justice Minister Kerensky with an equally nervous-looking Duma member, Sergei Gladishev.

The soldiers and revolutionaries made an oddly quiet audience as they gaped at the dancing figures painted on the great domed ceiling, the gold decorations, the crystal chandeliers and the plush blue seats. Many seemed awed by the splendour, but as many looked angry.

Tamara turned away from the peephole. Backstage was chaos such as she had rarely seen. Monsters, demons and goblins huddled in the wings; the dancers were terrified of crashing into each other, almost unable to see out of the grotesque masks which had arrived only the previous night from the Alexander Palace. Because Igor Stravinsky's music was so unusual they were afraid they might not hear their entrances. And if the late sets and costumes, the at least partially hostile audience, the panicked stagehands and murky cues were not enough to unsettle the company, everyone, including the golden princesses perched on the stairs of Kostchei's enchanted castle, knew that Pavlova herself had turned down the part of the Firebird in Paris on the grounds that the music was incomprehensible.

Tamara looked out the peephole again, and suddenly knew she had been fooling herself this whole season. She was too old. A young girl like Sedovina could charm men like those in the audience. Not Tishkova. Not any more. She hadn't worked enough this year. Hadn't rehearsed. Hadn't practised beyond her normal daily workout. Valery's coup had taken so much. And then Kennet had come . . . yes, she knew the tricks of experience that allowed a dancer to accomplish movement with less effort, but they were limited by ageing bone, sinew and muscle. How could she ever drag herself out there and – ?

'Five minutes.'

She brushed past the stage manager and ran to her dressing room. Of course it was filled with mirrors. She closed her eyes and felt her way to an easy chair, sank into it and listened to the blood rushing through her brain.

Someone started knocking on her door.

'Go *away*.'

'Five minutes, Mademoiselle.'

'I'm not a horse you drive from the stable. Go away.'

Silence.

She felt with closed eyes for the ivory elephant her father had given her when the Yusupovs took her from the circus. When she had it firmly in both hands she slowly gathered her strength to open her eyes . . . The mirror. Tamara looked back in wonder. The Firebird was a most beautiful costume – a crown of gold and bright feathers, a scarlet bodice shimmering with sequins, gold dust sparkling on her bare shoulders. Slowly she stood up. The sparest *tunique.* She leaned to the mirror. Not a hair was out of place. Not a line showed through her makeup. She turned. Her legs, at least, were still Tishkova.

Tamara touched her lips to the little ivory elephant and put him down. She was as ready as she would ever be. She gave the Firebird a rueful smile. What was a dancer without a mirror to remind her who she was and what she could do? What indeed . . .

Hurrying out to the stage, she ran into her partner, a boy with just the air of simplicity to play the Prince Ivan she was supposed to enchant. He looked terrified. Tamara kissed him, and reminded him that Diaghilev's original presentation of *Firebird,* in Paris had also gone on with only one rehearsal. And when he still looked doubtful Tamara added that today's dress rehearsal had convinced her that she was extremely fortunate to be paired with him. He melted.

She commenced a brisk walk around the stage, stretching her arms and legs. Under ordinary circumstances the stage manager would have ordered her shot for such behaviour only moments before curtain, but this was no ordinary night. Ordinarily the Grand Duke Valery would be sitting in the Czar's box, his enormous hands pounding out adoration she could distinguish from all the rest of Petrograd's applause.

Her purpose now was to calm the company as well as herself. She paused often as she circled the stage to smile and nod at the monsters, goblins and demons. She curtsied to the terrified princesses on the castle and coaxed them to curtsy back. She hugged Vera Sedovina, the first princess, and told her her Russian dance had been spectacular in dress rehearsal. Sedovina was either frozen with nerves or possessed of a remarkable *sang froid* as she straightened one of her feathers and told Tamara she was beautiful.

'Two minutes,' said the stage manager, nodding approval as Tamara returned to the peephole by his desk and again looked out at the audience.

Kennet was taking his seat in a box with the American ambassador and his pretty little daughter. They were among the few non-revolutionaries in the theatre, but the Americans were heroes to many since they had recognized the new government so quickly. Looking at Kennet, Tamara remembered her shock an hour ago in her dressing room when he had told her that he had been suddenly recalled to London. His train would leave tonight. His last sight of her would be on the stage. He had held her and told her he loved her. They promised to meet in Paris. She recalled her thought that these were frightening times to be making promises . . .

Abrupt movement now drew her eye to the Czar's box in the centre of the first ring. Kirichenko, ignoring Gladishev's attempt to make conversation, was leaning forward to see across into Kennet's box.

Kennet looked at his watch.

The musicians began tuning again. Tamara took a final look at the expectant throng and retreated to the wing as the houselights dimmed.

The music began with cellos and bass throbbing in the lowest registers, like an insistent, quick-timed *Dies Irae*. Sullen horns mounted the strings, threatening. To Tamara it was ancient Russia, vibrating with medieval, pre-Peter-the-Great eastern rhythms one either felt in one's bones or didn't feel at all. Russian music for a Russian fairy tale. An enchanted half-woman, half-bird – a Firebird – tried to free a handsome prince and a beautiful princess from a terrible ogre. But first she had to free herself.

The curtain rose on a dense forest and Tamara felt her

audience shimmer with recognition. Had they not fought the worst battle of the war in the gloomy Pripet marshes? Hidden from the police in evil slums? She started counting. The tempo increased. Flight. An amber spot circled the stage, heralded the Firebird, and Tamara swept into the light on a chain of swift leaps and poses. She heard a single gasp from the audience, seized it, wove their wonder into the music and took wing . . .

She moved, Ash thought, like a light in a mirror, crossing the stage with enormous *grand jetés*. She returned, weaving *tours en l'air* among the jumps. A ricochet, leaping, turning, back and forth in constant motion, flaming through the dark forest as beautiful as a bird, as free.

The lights flashed on her scarlet costume, her crown of gold, but Tamara's dark eyes shone even brighter. Ash decided that Stravinsky might have written it with her in mind. He expected her to continue the showy jumps through her long solo, but she suddenly shifted to the great strength that distinguished her from every other dancer alive. The Firebird was beautiful and the Firebird was free, but the Firebird was also a woman, and to Tamara Tishkova, dance and sex were inseparable.

Her timing was perfect. Ash could feel the audience release into fantasy . . .

Some deep instinct had said *now*. She danced as if each man of the two thousand were finally coming home after three years of war. She danced to welcome, imagining a room full of children and grandparents. She danced to entice, imagining their room when the others had gone to sleep. She danced until they were utterly silent, until they knew she had given all she had to give.

And when she cast off every restraint she had ever clung to, she exploded again into the exuberant apparition she had first introduced. *Grand jetés* – a sudden focus stage centre where she whipped through *fouetté* turns – and more *grand jetés* into which she wove her airborne turns. And then she tripled them, astonishing even herself – three full turns in the air before touching the stage to rise again.

Tishkova reminded revolutionaries they were Russians. They came roaring to their feet.

The music kept going. She could not stop for applause. Stravinsky had written no pauses in his score for the conductor to stop and let her take a bow. The soldiers clapped and stamped their feet even as the orchestra kept hurtling her through her solo. Prince Ivan was waiting to come on knowing full well that they would probably tear him limb from limb. She was very happy, but couldn't work out what to do as she launched into the high-speed spin that would climax the solo when Ivan seized her. Finally the conductor realized her predicament and the music stopped, quieting for a moment the screaming audience.

Tamara opened her climactic spin into a deep curtsy. Again she felt the applause thunder out of the house. She took bow after bow, exhilarated and proud, and finally raised her head to blow Kennet a kiss.

He was gone.

Old Vadim Mikhailov, Sedovina's step-father, was in Kennet's seat next to the American ambassador, as if, she realized through her disappointment, the old *tapeur* had filled the seat to make it look as if Kennet hadn't left . . .

Kirichenko was leaning forward again, as he clapped, obviously trying to see into the shadows of Kennet's box, and Tamara now felt a sudden chill . . . Kennet was up to something . . . and Kirichenko suspected . . . The conductor's baton rose tentatively and the soldiers settled into their seats as the orchestra found a place to resume the music.

Kirichenko half stood now, craning his head. Tamara counted into the music, rose *en pointe* and played the rest of her solo toward the Imperial Box, where she had directed many a performance over the years with, she was pleased to see, similar results as Kirichenko slowly resumed his seat.

Perhaps, she thought, her performance was buying time for Kennet . . . in whatever he was up to . . . as it was buying her passage to Paris. Where, if they were lucky, they would meet again one day . . .

53

A brass band started playing as they entered the Finland Station and the Czar stiffened automatically to attention before he remembered the music was no longer for him. He shared a wan smile with his son and took the boy's hand. Half-bald and beardless, having shaved his widow's peak as well as his Van Dyck, his face lined by his ordeal and wearing an inexpensive suit Ash had filched from the United States Embassy, the man whose portrait had hung in every public room in the Russian Empire was virtually unrecognizable.

Nicholas II looked instead exactly like what his passport suggested, a tired, old underpaid American YMCA official heading home in second class, accompanied by his grey-haired wife – a woman who walked with a limp but had, if one bothered to look, remarkably serene and beautiful eyes – and their two grandchildren, who seemed subdued and no doubt a little frightened by the huge, enthusiastic crowds gathering in and around the station to greet another exile – this one coming home and not in disguise.

Outside, searchlights from the Peter-Paul Fortress split the sky above the station square where the crowd waved red and gold banners. An armoured car was parked outside the Czar's reception-room entrance, defying the Provisional Government's futile ban on such vehicles in the city streets. As Ash had helped the Czar and his family off the tram they had taken from the Maryinski Theatre, he had seen a couple of hundred Bolsheviks march into the square in smart formation from their headquarters in Kschessinska's appropriated house.

Draped in the nuns' habits of the Anglo-Russian field hospital nursing order, the Czar's daughters led the way across the station. Many in the throng bowed and pushed other people out of their way. As Sedovina had predicted, the field nurses were about the only unassailable heroes left in the war. Even the Red Guards at the train platform gates treated them with respect, glancing at the papers and waving them through. Ash went next. An unshaven English-speaking functionary in a dirty uniform read his diplomatic passport and told him to board the train. He then thrust out his hand, demanding the Czar's papers.

Nicholas looked momentarily confused. The Czarina pressed forward and spoke for them in imperious tones that she was either unable to curb or oblivious to. 'We are returning home to America,' she announced sternly. 'If you will kindly expedite our passage.'

Ironically, her tone had the desired effect. The functionary waved them toward the train and even inclined his head in the semblance of a respectful bow. But there was a second blockade at the platform just the other side of the gate. Red Guards had set up an impromptu customs inspection and were searching luggage. They had already let the grand duchesses in their habits pass, and the Czar's daughters were walking out on the platform toward the waiting train. A line of Russian sailors were standing at attention on the next platform, an honour guard awaiting the next arrivals. Ash caught a glimpse of a locomotive headlight far off in the yards, heading for the station.

The Red Guards pointed at his valise. Ash showed them his diplomatic papers, which made his valise inviolate. They told him to put it on their table and called someone over who could speak English.

'You travel light, Commander.'

'This is a diplomatic pouch, you can't open it.' But a brief exchange convinced him he had no choice if he

586

wanted to get on the train. The Czar, the Czarina and the boy and Anastasia were still stuck behind him. He opened the case. They pawed through his clothing, pulled out a heavy wooden box and opened it.

'What is this?'

'A sextant.'

'For what?'

'For determining a ship's location by the stars or the sun.'

'But you are travelling by train.'

If I'm lucky, thought Ash. If not, it will be damned hard finding Rodney Skelton's submarine without a sextant. 'It's a gift for my commanding officer.'

The Russian turned it over in his hands, noting the mirror and lenses. 'But this is made in Leipzig, in Germany . . .'

'I *bought* it on the Nevsky Prospect. Yesterday. The receipt is there.'

'It is German-made. A store here selling German products?'

Ash put his hand on the box. 'Russia and the United States are allies now, *Tovarishch*. We've recognized the new government. The Czar has abdicated. I'd like my sextant back . . . who knows, maybe it will help my commanding officer sink a German submarine.'

The Russian grinned, nodded and passed him through. And then he turned to the Czar.

Ash made a show of rearranging his bag so he could stay near, and was relieved to see that they ignored Nicholas and the children. But their attention fixed on the Czarina, who went pale when they ordered her to open her valise.

Ash's heart sank. The expression on her face told him she had disobeyed his order not to smuggle her jewels. The Red Guards ordered her to open the bag. She had packed a second travelling suit, several pairs of sensible looking low-heel shoes and a collection of modest embroidered linen underwear.

The Czar's face reddened as they went through his wife's clothing. Was there, Ash wondered, a bulge in the bag's lining, or had he heard a dull clink as the Red Guard pushed a garment aside, disturbing a necklace sewn inside a hem?

Ash repeated rearranging the contents of his bag. Their train was less than a hundred feet away, but to him it might as well have been on the other side of Europe. The Red Guard probed deeper. He tapped the bottom of the Czarina's valise. It sounded hollow . . .

The floor trembled as the arriving train trundled into the station and came to rest beside Ash's. The naval guard sprang to attention, and a moment later a mob ran past the gates, past both guard points and raced cheering onto the platform.

'Lenin . . . Lenin . . .'

Hundreds surged onto the platform as the cry rose through the Finland Station and echoed back from the square beyond. Ash, the Red Guards, the Czar and Czarina and the two children were buffeted from both sides. The crowd started pouring back, bearing the stocky, bald figure of Lenin on their shoulders and calling for him to speak. The naval guard saluted and a travel-weary, happy-looking and somewhat surprised Lenin saluted back.

Someone jumped up and pressed a bouquet of red roses into his hands. The crowd kept chanting for a speech.

'May I go now?' the Czarina took the opportunity to ask.

The Red Guards, held by Lenin's first words, waved her along . . . 'Yes, yes, tell the world what is happening here . . .'

The Czar helped her close the bag. As they started toward the train, he asked, 'Who is that?'

'A Bolshevik named Lenin,' said Ash. 'One of their leaders.'

The Czar stopped, in spite of his wife's imploring, and stared across the empty track at the gesticulating figure delivering a speech from the shoulders of his comrades. Did Lenin notice his stare? When the mob interrupted him with applause, Lenin looked back across them in the direction of the Czar some forty feet away – at Ash, and puzzled recognition showed on Lenin's face.

The Czar shook his head. 'He told them there will be worldwide revolution. Isn't Russia enough for him?'

'Be grateful he came when he did,' Ash said, taking his arm. 'He just saved our lives. Please come along, before they change their minds.' And before, he added to himself, Lenin gets curious about where he saw me first and what I'm doing now.

The Czarina took the Czar's other arm and said under her breath to Ash, 'I am sorry, Commander, about the jewels . . . I just couldn't bear to leave them. One must keep something . . .'

Lenin now did remember the worried-looking officer urging the old man toward the train on the next platform, but he couldn't fit Ash's face to his boat cloak and naval service cap. Nor could he recall where they had met, though it had been recently, and the man had not been in uniform . . . Well, events were swift and wonderful. He had wondered if the Provisional Government would put him into the Peter-Paul. Instead a naval honour guard from Red Kronstadt was drawn up on the train platform as if for a Czar; people stuffed his hands with flowers, lifted him on their shoulders like a conquering hero and demanded a speech. Over their heads he saw a cadre of

Bolshevik men and women march into the station in strict formation. Discipline. Perhaps Russia was ready for a *real* revolution . . .

The old man was staring at him. The officer held one of his arms and a grey-haired woman the other, apparently urging him to board their train. And suddenly Lenin remembered another train, another station . . . Zurich . . . a United States Navy officer . . . *Ash* was his name . . . off to Russia to rescue the Czar . . . too late . . . But why was this American officer still in Petrograd? Was it his imagination that the man seemed worried, anxious? He didn't think so . . . The welcome dinned around him, distracting . . . And then Lenin thought he saw why the officer had seemed anxious. A woman, hooded by a fur cape, her face hidden behind a dark veil, slipped through the mob and ran toward Ash. Everything about her seemed delicate and precise, from the small valise she carried in her black glove to her shapely high-heeled boots. When she threw back the veil and drew the officer's head down to kiss his mouth, Ash's face transformed. Worry and anxiety seemed to melt into astonishment, which in turn became intense pleasure. Lenin turned away, uneasy at having looked on so intimate a moment in another man's life.

'It is *my* pass. I can travel anywhere I want. And I *want* to travel with you.'

'But I'm – Tamara, I can't let you.' They weren't even on the train yet. The whole scheme could blow up any second.

'I suddenly knew I would never see you again if I didn't go with you – '

'Tamara, believe me, it's impossible, too dangerous.'

'That's what I mean . . . Kennet, I don't know what you're doing, but I must stay with you . . .' She touched a black glove to his mouth. 'I'm coming with you. The subject is *closed*.'

And now she saw Vera Sedovina hurrying toward them. 'Why is she here? Is there something I should know about Vera?'

Ash glanced at the train. The Czar and Czarina were boarding. Lenin was disappearing on his supporters' shoulders toward the station. Red Guards were everywhere. Maybe there was a chance to protect Tamara. He glanced at Sedovina, who was wearing a cloth coat and a babushka that hid her hair and much of her face.

Tamara reached into her handbag. 'I think I will kill her,' she said, pulling the revolver she had taken from the guard at the Peter-Paul.

'Put that away, for God's sake, you'll get us all arrested – '

'Is Vera travelling with you?'

'Only to the Swedish border, she's got some comrades in the train crew . . . Tamara, meet me in Paris; go out alone, it's much safer – '

'Believe me, Kennet, one of us won't live if we go alone. I know, I can feel it.' She took his arm and steered him toward the train. Sedovina caught up, passed them and whispered, 'Kirichenko's spy at the Alexander Palace spotted Valentinov. Hide in the luggage store-room at the far end of the platform. Comrades will take you to the baggage car. Go with him, Tamara, if Kirichenko sees you . . .'

It was a dimly-lit room lined with trunks in storage racks bisected by a tall heap of packages wrapped in brown paper and string. Ash checked the other side, but Sedovina's friends had not come yet.

'Kennet?' Tamara was calling from the door.

591

'They're not here, yet – '

'Kennet.'

Ash rounded the heap in the middle of the room, and stopped dead.

Tamara was pressed against the door, the point of Count von Basel's sabre at her throat.

54

'First, the gun you carry in the small of your back, Commander . . . Now, yours, Mademoiselle, from your purse . . . Now, Mademoiselle, you will bolt the door . . . Thank you, and now you will come here – oh, I've cut you, I am very sorry. Perhaps you should move with the blade, as if it were your partner – '

Ash lunged for him, stopped abruptly when von Basel moved his sabre's needle point from her throat, slid it under her veil and laid the razor edge alongside her cheek.

'Commander, you've crippled me.' He held up his left hand. Two fingers were curled like barbed wire. 'Draw your sword.'

'Half the Red Guard is out there – ' Ash began.

'It will give me pleasure as a German soldier to inform them that you are attempting to take the Czar. His trial by the Bolsheviks will tear Russia apart, which is good for Germany. But I am going to finish you first, Commander. Once and for all. *En garde* – stay there, Mademoiselle. Tell her, Ash, if she moves I'll slice off her lips.'

Ash pulled his sabre. Von Basel backed her into a corner, one eye on Ash. Through the veil Ash saw a dark trickle on Tamara's neck where von Basel's sabre point had broken her skin.

Ash shook the cloak off his sword arm, feinted with a single beat and thrust at von Basel's face.

Von Basel parried. 'It seems love makes you aggressive, Commander.'

God, Ash hated his posturing, goddamn Teutonic smugness . . . Ash tried a high slash, again at the face, repeated two more, and thrust. Von Basel easily stopped all three slashes and nearly got Ash's hand late-parrying the thrust. But now a slightly wary look moved into his eyes . . . he was too experienced a fighter not to know that Ash was up to something . . .

Ash had learned two important lessons in their last encounter. The fact they weren't wearing fencing masks had held him back again. He was unaccustomed to such vivid eye contact and it had intimidated him, as Roland had warned him it would in Paris. More important, he had concluded that von Basel's chief concern was protecting his face, his chief desire to mutilate before he killed.

Ash now slashed repeatedly at his face, high, broad swings, risking each time he raised his sabre that von Basel would breech his guard and thrust into his exposed belly. They fought as if they had picked up exactly where they had left off on the Czar's train. Neither was wasting time feeling the other out.

Suddenly von Basel went on the attack. Ash retreated, concentrating on frustrating the German, relying on his own speed and eye to parry and occasionally unsettle von Basel by imitating one of his own late parries. The inevitable price was a touch. But even as the pain lanced through his forearm, Ash knew von Basel was a captive of his own deep-grained cruelty. He always went for the extremities, it was predictable . . .

Von Basel's sabre leaped again like a snake. Just missing Ash's forehead, it knocked his hat off, slicing the visor and reminding him that knowing von Basel's weakness and exploiting it were two different matters.

'Get *back*,' Ash called out as from the corner of his eye he saw Tamara break for the door. She froze at the urgency in his voice, and he was grateful that for once she did as she was told.

Ash broke up von Basel's next attack with a stop-thrust

and another slash at his face. The German retreated, winding up as he gathered for his next attack. Ash tried to use his point control and sense of distance to slash closer and closer to von Basel's face without sacrificing his own.

'That's a dangerous game, Ash. No one has ever marked me. Not even your precious Roland.'

Ash cocked his arm to raise his sabre up high. Von Basel's blade leaped to protect his face and counter-thrust – but Ash dropped his arm and jump-lunged a long, low thrust into von Basel's belly . . .

'*Nein,*' von Basel said. His voice was a deathly whisper. His grey eyes opened very wide. He stared, first into Ash's eyes, then down at the hilt pressed to his belly. His own sabre fell from his fingers. He pushed at Ash's hand, trying to push the steel out of his body. Ash backed away. His blade seemed to slide forever.

Von Basel fought to keep his feet but his knees collapsed underneath him. He looked up at Ash, eyes clouding. 'You did not mark my face . . .'

'No . . . but Roland would have . . . That's why you murdered him with your poniard.'

Tamara was twisting handkerchiefs around his cut forearm when the knock came at the door. Outside a pair of frightened-looking railroad workers had a baggage cart ready with a narrow slot between trunks and mailbags for Ash and Tamara. Tamara translated, 'Sedovina has everyone aboard.'

Inside the slot, which the railroad workers covered with more bags, Ash felt his knees begin to go. The iron-wheeled cart ground along the platform to the train. He heard the locomotive blow its whistle. Bells answered.

'Are you all right?' Tamara whispered.

'I felt him die through my blade.'

She pressed against him, 'Oh God, this can't be happening. We weren't supposed to end our lives like this.'

'It's been happening since 1914,' Ash managed to get out as the cart bumped aboard the train and the train started moving.

Von Basel was not dead yet. The floor shook as the Finland train rumbled out of the station, shaking him back to consciousness. He felt no pain, only a massive numbness from his waist down. He found his sword, found the walking stick, sheathed the blade. When he tried to crawl to the door he felt an unknown, profound weariness. He forced himself to keep going, reached the door, somehow got it open and crawled onto the platform. Overhead was the train shed roof; in the distance, the station.

Halfway there, he looked back. The lights showed a long, dark trail of blood, as if some ghastly, wounded insect had slithered up from the rails. Von Basel gathered himself, planted the walking stick on the platform, pulled himself erect.

Leaning heavily on the stick, he made himself walk to the station. It took tremendous concentration to move his legs. Each step demanded purpose. The few people left in the station stared at him.

Then the Red Guards came . . .

Moments later the SR fighting squad leader Kirichenko was leaning over his stretcher. 'Who are you?'

Von Basel found he had trouble talking.

Kirichenko leaned close, put his ear to von Basel's mouth.

'The train . . .' von Basel got out. 'He's on the train.'

'Who?'

And von Basel suddenly knew his last words on earth.

'The Czar.'

* * *

Ash and Tamara had just located the Czar's family crammed into a steamy compartment two cars ahead of the baggage car when Sedovina ran down the corridor from the front of the train. 'My comrade in the crew says the soviet has signalled the train to stop at the next station.'

'Kirichenko?'

'Probably. They'll search the train.'

Ash went into the Czar's compartment. The family looked at him with a mixture of gratitude and misery. 'They're stopping the train, I'm afraid we have to jump off.'

'Now?' the Czar asked.

'Now,' the Czarina said. 'Children!'

The grand duchesses pulled their valises down from the luggage racks.

'But you can't jump,' the Czar protested. 'The girls can, but not you and Alexis – '

'I can jump if Commander Ash says I must. It's Alexis I'm worried about.'

'I can jump,' the boy insisted.

'I'll go off with him,' Ash said.

'No. You'll hurt him if you fall on him. Better a scrape we can control. The snow will cushion our fall.'

Ash led them to the vestibule at the back of the car. Sedovina guarded the front. The moon on the snow showed a steep embankment ending in forest. It could not have been worse, even though the broken-down engine was doing less than thirty miles per hour.

Suddenly the trees stopped at an open field. Ash heaved the bags. The Czar went first, followed by his daughters. The Czarina saw them slide across the snow, across a frozen crust.

Tamara took the boy's hand. 'He will jump with me.' And to the boy she said, 'I was in the circus, no one can jump like me. We're going to jump and run. Can you do it?'

Alexis murmured he didn't know as he eyed the ground racing away beneath him. 'Jump,' Ash told the Czarina.

And she did, over the side onto the snow.

'Hold tight,' he told the boy. 'Ready, Tamara – *go*.'

Ash watched them, black figures against the white snow. They hit the crust running hard to keep their balance, down the embankment and onto the field, still running, nearly a hundred feet before Tamara broke through the crust and fell hard. The boy sprawled a moment later.

Ash signalled Sedovina and jumped. He slid down the steep bank and crashed through the crust, tucking his shoulder and rolling to his feet only to fall over his sword. Sedovina skidded on top of him. The train rumbled past, trailing silence.

For a moment she was soft in his arms, and he asked her why she had come.

'You are more convincing, Commander, than you apparently know. You, and they, are not out yet. I want to see that you are.'

He let it go at that . . .

They found Tamara, rubbing her ankle and watching anxiously as Alexis's sisters grouped around him. Tatiana held snow to his face.

'A nosebleed,' Tamara whispered, and when Sedovina looked puzzled because no one in all Russia but the immediate family knew, she added, 'He's a bleeder.' Valery had told her, and even he didn't know all the details.

It was, Ash thought, one of the ruling family's worst mistakes to keep it secret and short-circuit their subjects' sympathy. 'We can't stay here,' he told them. 'Everyone, let's go, find the bags and move – '

'Where?'

'Down to the Gulf, onto the ice, break our trail and find a place to hide.'

598

'Then what?' asked Olga. She was the oldest, twenty.

'Help your mother,' Ash told her. 'We'll take the boy. Alexis, on my back.' . . . And then what, he thought, was a damned good question.

Alexis, obviously an experienced patient, threw his head back and pinched his nostrils. 'What if I faint?' he asked.

'I'll be right next to you,' Tamara said. 'I'll hold your nose if you faint. It's not far.'

She looked at Ash and together they surveyed the long moonlit slope. Half a mile to the treeline and another mile through the trees. And below the trees, the barren ice of the Gulf of Finland.

Aggravated by the fall from the train, the Czarina's sciatica made each step agony. They stopped in the trees, and Ash hacked off some pine boughs that he and the Czar bound with strips of clothing into a crude litter. They laid Alexandra on it, let her examine the boy, whose bleeding had not stopped, and then started down again through the soft, deep snow of the forest. The girls, the Czar and Sedovina spelled each other, dragging the litter in pairs. Ash carried Alexis while Tamara pressed snow to his nostrils. 'What circus?' he asked suddenly. His voice was weak, as if he were growing sleepy. Tamara thought he had fainted.

'My father's. I was younger than you are now,' she told him.

'Your *father's*. You're lucky . . . Father Gregory told me about two humped horses.'

'Oh, we had lots of them,' Tamara said, replacing the snow, as she struggled to keep up with Ash.

Suddenly the boy said, 'I hear a wolf.'

'Just saying good night to us,' Ash said, wishing it were a wolf, instead of a train whistle. The first search party.

* * *

The forest stopped at a frozen marsh – one of the northern extremities of the Neva delta. Ash had them cross in single file in case a spring flood had weakened the ice. When they reached the Gulf of Finland it was three o'clock and the moon was inclining toward the west. Surface thaws and freezes and an afternoon rain several days ago followed by two days of hard freeze had left the ice flat and smooth. A hard wind blew from the north. The trees had blocked it, but here in the open it stung badly.

'Bring me Alexis,' the Czarina called from the litter. Ash sank to the ice beside her and caught his breath while she examined the boy and the Czar and their daughters crowded around. Tamara and Sedovina watched the slope for moving lights.

'The bleeding is better,' the Czarina said, 'but we can't go on dragging him around. He must lie still.'

Ash pointed up the slope. A train moved slowly along the line, probing the snow with searchlights. 'They'll find our tracks at first light. We have to move.'

The Czar looked at his wife. 'Then we must surrender. I will not kill my son for my freedom.'

'Nor will I,' the Czarina said. 'How long could we hide anyway?'

'Do you know this area, Your Majesty?'

'We have sailed the Gulf every summer of our marriage.'

Ash opened his valise, removed the sextant from its wooden box and found the Gulf of Finland charts he had hidden under the navigational instrument. The charts did not cover this far east . . . he'd had no intention of being here, but he had a land map that showed the coast of the Petrograd Bay where they were at the head of the Gulf. The wind nearly tore the map from his hands. 'Exactly where are we?'

The Czar turned a slow circle, examining landmarks and skyline. Ash held the map to the moonlight and the Czar pointed. 'Here. There are dachas, all along the shore.' Ash looked at the slope. Forest and field alternated. The occasional light showed in the clearings. Ash turned his back on the slope and faced the endless expanse of flat ice.

The Gulf of Finland extended three hundred miles west to the Baltic Sea. Ash imagined he could see the entire distance, the moon and stars were so bright, the ice so empty. Somewhere out there was Rodney Skelton's submarine . . .

'Your Majesty, how far do you think the Gulf is frozen?'

The Czar looked up from where he had crouched beside Alexis and the Czarina. 'Ice? Middle of April? Still some two hundred miles.'

Ash held up the map to him. 'Isn't the Balmont dacha near here?'

'A few miles north,' the Czar told him, tracing the coastline with his finger. 'If you are referring to the Baroness's shooting marsh.'

'That's the one. Let's go – '

Tamara broke in. 'Kennet, just because you went shooting there doesn't mean she'll hide us.'

'There are,' the Czar added, 'closer places to hide. Estates all along the shore, though of course they will search them.'

'We're not hiding,' Ash said. 'Wait until you see her neighbour's iceboat.'

'Iceboat?'

It had snowed one afternoon, too heavily to shoot or sail, so they had piled into troikas and visited the next estate, which was owned by a tall, elderly Finnish nobleman who had two passions in life – his neighbour the Baroness, and sailing.

'A monster, Your Majesty. Six hundred square feet of canvas.'

'Have you ever sailed an iceboat, Commander?'

601

'Not one that big.'

'But you do know it's not like sailing on water.'

'Hardly . . .'

It was slow going into the relentless north wind. The footing was treacherous, the litter heavy with the Czarina and Alexis. They hugged the shore, to avoid being silhouetted against the moonlit ice. Another train probed the night on the slope, and above the tracks along a road truck lights scoured the snow.

They had gone two miles when Ash spotted a break in the shoreline, the channel the Baroness Balmont had dug through her marsh into the Gulf. It was another mile to her lover's estate.

Kirichenko cruised the rail line in the cab of a locomotive festooned with searchlights and hauling a dozen flatcars. Red Guards jumped off every few hundred yards to patrol on foot. Telegraphers were perched each mile on telegraph poles. And half a mile up the slope motor and cavalry squadrons were searching house to house.

'Comrade Kirichenko.' The engineer pointed ahead and quickly eased off his quadrant and throttle. A telegrapher was scrambling down a pole, gesturing for the train to stop.

'A trail in the snow, Comrade Kirichenko. Down to the ice.'

55

Smooth ice stretched like a tongue into the dark mouth of the boathouse, which looked like a big barn with the front wall gone. Behind it, quarter of a mile up the slope, the main estate mansion loomed darkly. Smoke plumed white in the moonlight from the servants' cottages that circled it, but the boathouse and the lower fields were uninhabited.

The slim frame of the boat – a cross with steel runners on either arm and a rudder in the back – was painted white. The enamel gleamed ghostly in the moonlight reflected from the ice. Ash kicked the runners to unstick them and pushed her outside with the help of the Czar's daughters.

Thirty-five feet long and twenty wide, the iceboat was light and glided easily; the two parts of the frame – the long, narrow hull and the thin runner arm that crossed it – were virtually the entire boat. Hull and crosspiece were braced with wire cable, but neither cables nor the small flat cockpit at the back added any significant weight.

'We need the mast,' Ash said. 'Stays, mainsail, jib, lines and running gear.'

The Czar spoke and his daughters hurried into the boathouse, and reappeared almost immediately dragging the mast. Nicholas and Alexandra exchanged a quick glance, and the Czar said to Ash, 'We did not raise helpless young ladies.'

The mast was a brute, pear-shaped to reduce wind resistance but much heavier than a yacht mast so as to stand the extraordinary strains of an iceboat. It took Ash, the Czar, the four grand duchesses and Tamara and

603

Sedovina to step it up into its hole, where the hull and runner arm intersected, after Ash had run the sail halyards through the top. He fastened stays fore and aft and rigging on either side and tightened them with turnbuckles.

The rig was modern, a triangular Bermuda sail. The much smaller jib had its own boom and was rigged to be self-tending, which Ash knew would be a blessing on a crowded cockpit, as would the roller reefing.

'There's not enough room for all of us,' the Czar said. The boat looked designed for a crew of five . . . they were ten. Ash extended the cockpit with the spare jib, stretching the canvas between the iceboat's frame and the wire cables that braced the arms of the cross. The Czar rigged safety lines to hold onto. Ice axes, chisels, files to sharpen the runners, spare runners and heel spikes were already aboard in the lockers built into the long, narrow hull. The Czar lashed their valises to the deck in front of the mast, checking clearance for the jib boom. The deposed sovereign would be a help.

Anastasia laughed. 'We'll look like gypsies, Papa – '

'I see lights at the main house,' Tamara called out.

It looked like two trucks or cars. Ash heard doors slamming, shouts. More lights flared in the cottage and the mansion.

'Tamara, get them on board. Leave room aft for the Czar and me – '

'Aft?'

'The *back*. By the tiller.' Ash and Nicholas fitted the boom to the mast and started attaching the sail while the grand duchesses helped their mother stretch out on the canvas cockpit with Alexis in her arms, still holding a compress to his nose.

'They're lighting torches,' Sedovina called. 'They're coming down.'

Ash's fingers were numbing from cold as he forced the

604

last of the mainsail's parrel balls into their groove in the mast. He glanced up the slope. Soldiers were racing down with flaming torches.

'Hoist the main, I'll rig the jib.' Ash didn't have time to feel awkward at ordering a recent Czar as though he were a midshipman.

The Czar and his daughters heaved the iceboat around until it was facing dead into the north wind, raised the big sail which glowed in the moonlight and crackled like rifle shots. Ash finished clipping on the jib, hauled it up and tied off its sheet. He'd try to figure how to set it once they got moving.

'All aboard, tend the main.'

'Perhaps I should take the tiller; I know the coast,' the Czar said.

'Beg your pardon, sir, but we've got one skipper and I'm afraid I'm it. Tamara . . .'

She came running around the boathouse . . . 'Soldiers.'

'Get on. Sedovina, sit by the Czar. Do what he tells you. Ready on that sheet, sir. Let's kick her around.' He grabbed the tiller and swung his leg over the side, dug his heel spike into the ice. The Czar, Tamara and Sedovina did the same, but the boat wouldn't budge. The runners had frozen to the ice while they were sitting.

Two soldiers waving torches and rifles careened off the slope.

'*Push*,' Ash ordered.

The soldiers sprawled on the ice. A third planted himself in the snow, started firing a pistol. Sedovina and Tamara jumped off, ran to the right runner and pushed hard against the arm. The runner broke loose and the boat lurched to right angles with the wind, which filled the mainsail.

'*Get aboard*.' Ash hauled in the tiller, and the iceboat started to move. Sedovina sprawled onto the cockpit and

605

reached for Tamara. The iceboat picked up speed. Rifle shots sounded behind them. Tamara slipped from Sedovina's hand. Ash lunged for her, missed. She grabbed the lifeline, and the boat pulled her off her feet just as she tried to get her legs onto the cockpit. Still holding the tiller, Ash tried again, caught her other hand, pushed the tiller to head the boat into the wind to slow it, and managed to drag her aboard.

Now a truck had made it down from the main house, crashing onto the ice and skidding after the iceboat. It caught them in its lights, and the men in it started firing.

'Down,' Ash ordered. 'Haul in, sir.'

The Czar pulled the sheet, the sail tightened. The boat picked up speed . . . but the truck still gained.

'Sedovina, pull that line, *pull* it!'

It was the jib sheet and the effect of her action was immediate. The iceboat seemed to leap forward, the truck fell back. Bullets still spewed in their wake, but moments later they were alone on the Gulf of Finland, heading across a moonlit, wasteland at sixty miles per hour.

Half an hour later Ash and the Czar were still experimenting with the sails when the Kronstadt Fortress came into view. Some twelve hundred pounds of passenger weight slowed the boat markedly whenever the wind dropped, which it did with disturbing frequency since they were still in the narrow head of the Gulf. They were down to fifteen or twenty miles per hour, and Ash was looking anxiously for the point where the Gulf broadened to its true hundred-mile width when the searchlights of the island fortress's gunbattery split the night.

Kronstadt was Petrograd's main sea defence, and the huge beams were capable of sweeping the ice for miles. Twice they caught the boat, but the operators apparently couldn't distinguish the white sail from the surrounding ice. The third time they focused better and the gun battery opened up with a flash.

Roaring like a freight train, a shell passed overhead and a moment later detonated a mile away.

'Twelve-inch gun?' Ash asked the Czar incredulously.

'Of course,' and Ash thought he looked proud of it in the glare of the searchlight. A second shell rumbled through the sky, so close they all ducked. It exploded a quarter mile away, and Ash could feel the heat on his face. A third shell landed just ahead of the boat, blowing a huge hole in the ice. The water was black, and Ash decided the gunners were trying a new strategy – drowning them would be just as effective as a direct hit.

He swung around the hole and headed straight for the battery, five or six miles to the south. Dead ahead the cannon flashed.

'Where are you going?'

'I'm betting he's got that gun depressed as far as she'll go.'

He steered into the glare of the searchlights, directly at the orange cannon flashes. Shells roared past, exploded in numbing eruptions of sound and fire. The boat lost speed. 'Easy with the main, Your Majesty, she doesn't like running downwind . . .' He steered another mile straight into the teeth of the Kronstadt guns. '. . . All right, back on reach; we're heading west again.' Two shells rumbled high overhead . . . apparently the frustrated gunners had stopped aiming –

And slowly they passed out of the searchlights' range. Another hour, with the wind freshening, and they moved out of the narrow Petrograd Bay into the main Gulf. The boat built up speed, and the rigging began a metallic whine.

Kirichenko pursued Ash on a train manned by soviets – a special train that sped west running parallel to the coast on track cleared straight to Helsinki. Coal and water were waiting along the way, and telegraphers listened at open keys for news of Ash's iceboat. At Vyborg Kirichenko learned that Ash had somehow managed to escape the guns of Kronstadt. At the next coaling stop he telegraphed the bad news to the naval soviet in Helsinki.

Dawn lighted the tips of the high-pressure ridges a translucent red. Here at sea, fifty miles from the nearest coast, the ice had been forced up in wild, angular eruptions thirty feet high. The wind was blowing a near gale, and the boat was carving a beautiful mist of shaved ice. Ash was getting tired. As he tried to gybe between two of the pressure ridges, trading the wind from one side to the other, he misjudged the tiller. The sails smacked over, and the force spun the boat in a complete circle.

Tamara, Sedovina and two of the girls were thrown to the ice as the boat crashed into the nearest pressure ridge. The Czar had gone to his wife the instant he felt the boat gather the speed that led to the spin, holding her and Alexis.

'We'll have to lash them down,' Ash told him. The women got back to the boat as Ash inspected the runners for damage. They had survived, and when the Czar had tied his wife and son in place Ash got underway again, veering north toward the Finnish coast to escape the pressure ridges.

He shot the sun when it rose higher, and checked the chart. 'That smoke's Helsinki. We've got a way to go.'

The smudge on the horizon grew darker as they neared, developed a hard core. It puzzled Ash . . . It looked like a steamer but there were surely no steamers out here on the ice. But by the time he made out what looked like a domed cathedral in the city and a lighthouse, he realized that it definitely was a ship, and that it was moving.

An icebreaker, pouring black coal smoke from a huge stack and blasting a narrow channel from the port to a pressure-ridge icepack several miles off shore.

'Why is he doing that?' the Czar asked. 'The ships can't get out yet.'

He's after us. Hang on everybody, we're gybing about . . .'

But as he looked back, Ash saw horsemen galloping onto the ice from a promontory east of the Helsinki Peninsula. The wind was gusting this close to the shore, and he knew he couldn't outrace the cavalry back to the clear ice. He had to pass the icebreaker before she cut the ice all the way to the ridged pack.

He played the sails for speed, steering a weaving course around rough ice and angling for the best wind. A mile from the labouring icebreaker he began to hope he would make it. 'Get your heads down, they probably have something to shoot . . .'

They did . . . a slow-firing one-inch cannon, nearly useless as the vessel plunged up and down while it charged the ice, backed off and charged again. They were nearly in front of the icebreaker. It had backed into the path it had opened and was charging forward again, bellowing smoke. It hit the ice and was again thrown back, but the heavy bow had done its work. A crack twenty feet wide zigzagged from the icebreaker the two hundred yards to the pack ice.

Ash ordered the Czar to haul in the main and Sedovina to tighten the jib as he steered a little closer to the wind for speed, which also put him on a collision course with the iceboat pushing triumphantly into the open water it had prised through the ice. Ash veered away at the last moment and shot at the black water. The grand duchesses, in front, screamed. The ice-yacht became airborne, skimmed the water, and crashed onto the ice on the other side.

*   *   *

Kirichenko ordered three boxcars filled with cavalry when he had his special train shunted onto the coastal line that served small towns west of Helsinki. A few of the Finns were reluctant to bow to his every wish, and one in particular demanded, 'Just who is aboard that ice-yacht?'

Kirichenko put a gun in his face. 'None of your business.' And it damned well wasn't, Kirichenko thought. All Russia did not have to know that an American named Ash was trying to escape with its Czar. The last reports still had him heading west along the Finnish coast. Exactly how Ash had managed up to now Kirichenko didn't know . . . but one thing was certain – he was running out of ice.

Ash shot the sun from the moving boat, calculated their position. 'Steer south-west, sir.'

'I think I see open water – '

'It's just a lead, I'll tell you when to stop.'

Fifteen minutes later he shot the sun again. As he did he felt the iceboat move strangely, rise and fall like a ship. He looked at the others. They had felt it too. They were near the open sea, and ground swells were rocking the ice as if it were a great white rubber sheet.

Tamara said, 'How far are we from land?'

Ash was taking a bearing with his hand-held compass on the point of a peninsula. 'About five miles . . . All right, sir, turn her into the wind.'

The Czar brought her around, and the iceboat stopped, facing the north wind – and the Finnish coast. It was nearly noon. The high sun had melted the surface, making a skim of slush and water.

Ash took an ice axe from the locker and started chopping. The Czar followed his lead. The ice was over a foot thick. 'I hear horses,' Alexis said. Ash looked at him. He had been so quiet in his mother's arms. Now he raised his head, moving tentatively, not wanting to start his nose bleeding again. 'I *hear* them.'

'I don't,' Anastasia said.

Ash scanned the coast with the binoculars he'd found in the locker. A tight pack of black dots was moving toward them. He dropped to his knees and hacked at the ice.

'What is it?' the Czar asked.

'Cavalry. Alexis is right.'

Seawater welled up in the hole. Ash widened the edges, submerging his hand in the bitter-cold water. He ran to his valise, pulled out the wooden sextant box and smashed it to pieces with the ice axe. A pair of hand grenades rolled out of their hiding place: signals for Skelton's submarine.

'Make way.' They stepped back from the hole. Ash released the safety pin, dropped a grenade in the hole and ran. Nothing. And then seawater fountained out of the hole, and the ice shook with a dull, muffled bang. No answer to the relentless drumming of the oncoming horses.

He looked at the coast. They were closer, distinguishable through the glasses as men on horseback flying red flags on their lances. He waited two minutes, counted forty, fifty riders in the glasses, and dropped his second grenade. Again the water geysered. Nothing more. Where the hell was he?

The Czar and Czarina looked forlornly at the advancing cavalry. Their children moved instinctively closer.

'Get your things off the boat,' Ash said.

'Is there really any point?' the Czar was saying, and Ash knew he had no good answer.

Rodney Skelton's submarine crashed out of the ice a hundred feet away.

It still had the big dent in the conning tower. What wasn't dented was rusted and it was still absurdly small, but Ash thought it was beautiful.

611

Hatches popped open, and Skelton himself was first out.

'You can't bring that, friend,' he said, pointing at the ice-boat. He cut the forced levity when he saw the cavalry, and started issuing orders. Seamen laid a plank gangway from the sub to the ice and stood by on their end to help all aboard while a gun crew unlimbered a heavy machine-gun.

Ash guided Tamara and the Czar's family onto the gangway.

'Take it sort of easy with that gun,' Ash called out. 'They're still allies, more or less . . .'

'Always the diplomat, Ash. But I don't think they see it your way at the moment; – all right, men, at least give them something over their heads to think about.'

The gun cut loose with a clatter as Skelton turned to salute the Czar and Czarina coming aboard. His sailors helped them through the gun hatch. Tamara stepped aboard, then paused in the hatch, for a last look east toward Russia . . .

The gun fired again. The horsemen spread out, still charging.

'Come on Ash, we don't have all day – now where the hell is *she* going?' Sedovina was walking across the ice toward the cavalry.

Ash ran after her, caught her arm. 'What are you doing?'

'I'm going home, Kennet. I have to. You were right in what you have done. I am glad I could help. But I belong – '

'Kirichenko will kill you. Is your life worth a revolution that's going to hell?'

She removed Ash's hand from her arm, touched his glove to her cheek, and suddenly kissed his mouth. 'It's just starting. I have to believe that . . .'

612

56

The American Embassy reception for General Blackjack Pershing and the one-millionth United States Army soldier to land in France, by coincidence the son of a prominent midwestern senator, was typical of the afternoon parties taking over Paris during the summer of 1918. It was only July, but the pattern was set; an energetic cosmopolitan crowd was too happy feasting on itself to mind the heat.

US Staff officers outnumbered their British and French colleagues. American businessmen ran a close second. Most of the women were French, which never hurt a party, though there was the usual contingent of wealthy American ladies who had come to Paris to nurse at the more fashionable hospitals or raise hell in what the enormous American Expeditionary Force was making the hottest city in the world. Painters, scientists and aerial aces wandered in and out, and a wall of war correspondents blocked the bar talking about their novels. Sprinkled about the guests like diamonds on a veil were Russian *émigrés* whose dazzling manners and easy laughter camouflaged from all but each other who they might have been before the Revolution, and whether they felt sadly uprooted or merely transported to a smaller Petrograd-on-the-Seine. Ash arrived late and got onto the tail end of the reception line. He thought General Pershing looked like William S. Hart would have looked if he had spent his life chasing Pancho Villa around Mexico instead of making movies. Resolute looking with a hard broad mouth, military moustache, squint lines around the eyes and a long, solid nose. Lafayette, we are here. Indeed.

'Sailing that transport desk late again, Commander?'

'I had to convince a French harbour master that we like our gunners and their artillery to arrive at the front together. Good to see you, sir. Congratulations on your million troops, sir.'

'Are they ever going to give you a ship, Commander?'

'Same old story, sir. They're convinced I talk better than I sail because I supposedly know the Europeans, so I'm stuck coordinating transport . . . Now they're promising a ship at Christmas – '

'The war's going to be over by Christmas.'

For the first time since 1914 that seemed true. The Russian Provisional Government had held out until November, when the Bolsheviks finally gained enough control of the soviets to take power, and it wasn't until March that Russia made a separate peace with Germany. By then American soldiers were pouring into France.

The music stopped, and the American ambassador climbed the podium. 'Ladies and gentlemen. *Messieurs, mesdames.* May I have your attention, please. News has come over the Reuters wire . . .'

The party went silent.

'From Russia we have word that the Czar, the Czarina and all their children have been murdered by Bolsheviks in the city of Yekaterinburg in the Ural Mountains.'

Kaiser Wilhelm received the news in his bathrobe. Though it was late afternoon there were many days since Count von Basel's death in Russia that he did not really care to put on a full dress uniform and make grand entrances into empty rooms. With that noble German's death had died his last dreams of somehow stopping General Ludendorff and probably winning the war.

Ludendorff had won Germany, but Georgie's American

allies were almost surely going to win the war. And now Alix and Nicky, murdered by revolutionaries. How could the world have gone so wrong?

He prowled his empty rooms until he found a goldframed photograph of Nicholas and Alexandra at their wedding. God Himself could not have made a more royal union. 'I tried to save you,' the Kaiser told their picture. 'We tried . . . if only you had listened, Nicky . . . I told you something like this would happen.'

General Pershing looked stunned when the ambassador had finished. 'Why in hell did they have to kill the whole family?'

'Russia's a grim place, sir. And getting grimmer.'

'You knew the Czar, didn't you, Ash?'

'Yes, sir, I did . . .'

Lord Exeter came toward him as soon as Ash was alone. There still seemed to be an empty space at his arm where the lean figure of Lady Exeter had maintained escort.

'Tragic news about the Czar.'

'Tragic,' Ash agreed, 'though I doubt they'll find any bodies.'

Exeter glanced around before adding, 'Not unless they kill those poor actors . . . Have you read the latest news of the charade?'

Ash nodded. 'I read the interviews, and that article by the boy's tutor. I'm glad they finally got around to ending it before somebody realized it was all phony.'

'Well, it's over, and the water is good and muddy – by the way, the King asked me to remind you he's looking forward to shooting whenever you can get to England. And I promised to give you this.'

It was a thick, heavy brown envelope.

Ash went out on a terrace for privacy. An American

battalion was marching down the boulevard like occupation troops. In the envelope were two small boxes, one long and one square, a packet of newspaper clippings and a letter written on stationery that smelled of Penhaligon's lily of the valley.

Ash looked at the clippings first. They were articles about the Czar in captivity, and being moved from Tsarskoye Selo to the Siberian town of Tobolsk and finally to Yekaterinburg. Witnesses who had met the Czar before the Revolution reported on brief meetings overseen by his jailers. There were even photographs.

A haggard-looking Valentinov sitting on a tree stump. Ash had to smile to himself. The symbolism was so heavy that Valentinov must have come up with the pose himself and directed the Bolshevik photographer. Other photographs showed Valentinov's 'family' in costume portraying the imprisoned Romanovs gardening or sitting together under the watchful eye of revolutionary guards.

Kirichenko had made the best of a bad deal, and afterward Ash had expected him to rise high in the new government, but just two weeks ago he had been shot in a purge of some fifteen hundred leftist Social Revolutionaries who were too radical even for the Bolsheviks. A mistake, Ash thought . . . he would have been an asset, he was flexible . . .

Vera Sedovina, as it turned out, had actually arrived in England ahead of the submarine, dispatched by Kirichenko with a deal for King George. If the King would keep the Czar forever under wraps, hide him and never allow Nicholas to reveal that he had escaped, Kirichenko promised that Russia's revolutionaries would not hunt the Czar to his death.

'He can live in fear, and be murdered. Or he can live peacefully in seclusion.' What the soviets, the Social Revolutionaries and the Bolsheviks asked in return was that they be allowed to keep the Czar in legend. That he and his family be forever acknowledged as dead at the hands of the Russian people. A dead Czar Nicholas could never lead a counter-revolution . . . And a troupe of terrified actors, including their 'Czar' Valentinov, was not likely to reveal their role in the deal.

King George had ordered all aboard Rodney Skelton's submarine taken secretly to Balmoral when it arrived at Scapa Flow. He had urged the Czar to accept the offer. George V had no desire for Britian to be a staging place for a counter-revolution; nor did he want the Czar murdered on British territory, for there was no doubt that the revolutionaries could carry out their threat, even if it took years. Nicholas, encouraged by his wife, had agreed . . .

Ash next took up the letter, which was from the Czarina. It was, of course, unsigned, and without a post-mark, for not even Ash knew any more of their whereabouts than that they were in some secluded spot in the Empire, but she had written to Ash several times, and by now he knew her quick style and recognized her brisk dashes and ellipses.

My dear Commander,

We have settled comfortably in our cottage and even have a vegetable garden in. The girls are adjusting, though I know that T. more than the others chafes to enter society, which sort, of course, we can't fathom . . . A. is extremely well and it is beginning to look as if the doctor's predictions that he might have a normal life if he survives to adulthood might come true . . . He's taller, filling out and talks about going home some day. I tried to tell him he can't and suddenly realized he meant it – in some manner he might . . .

My husband is – I hesitate to say happy – perhaps peaceful is more correct. I astonish myself how happy I am here – my grandmother's simplicity seems to flow in my veins, more than I ever imagined. But of course it is easier for me than my husband. I started out as only a little princess while he was – well, you know what he was – and I know what he hoped to be . . .

We have always thought ourselves to be the most fortunate people because of what we are to each other. The worst moments were those apart when he had to be at the *Sta* – there, I've almost used a forbidden word. You must burn this – but my husband and I still have each other and our children. It is they, of course, who have lost the most – we have already had our life. But they, being young, can best adjust. And will have to . . . Forgive this chattiness, but we did share a long, long ride, didn't we, during which we almost settled some of our earlier arguments . . . The small package is from my husband. He is aware that recent events diminish the cachet of an ennobling honour, but he wants you to know it comes from his heart. From mine too.

Ash opened the box and gave a silent whistle of amazement. It was the star of the Imperial Order of St Andrew.

'As the collar and badge are rather a cumbersome affair,' the Czarina wrote, 'we sent them to your shooting friend who will hold them for you.'

Cumbersome? If he remembered correctly the collar was made of seventeen gold medallions studded with diamonds.

'. . . The longer box I'm sure you recognize. It was a lovely gift, but I shan't be wearing that sort of thing. Perhaps your lady . . .'

Tamara Tishkova was surrounded by an admiring covey of US Air Service aces when she noticed Ash alone on the terrace. Detaching herself from the fighter pilots with a smile that left each man convinced life back in the States would never seem the same, she started toward Ash only to be intercepted by Ambassador Walter Hines Page. The trip from London had obviously exhausted the poor man, but nothing, not even the sickness which would surely kill him within the year, could conceal Page's delight with events.

His manners were a blend of graciousness and informality which lent certain Americans she had met an easy elegance she once associated only with fellow artists. Kennet would grow older this way . . .

Page kissed her hand and said how much he had enjoyed meeting her at Balmoral. He nodded toward Ash, alone on the terrace. 'He used to call himself a glorified mailman when he was my courier. Now he says he's a glorified traffic cop, directing troop transport. I hope he isn't too miserable. He once said he wanted to grab history, make it instead of observe it . . .' Page looked around the reception, grinned at the sight of General Pershing marching out with his staff, heading back to the front. 'Well, I'd say he's done all right – excuse me, he seems headed this way and I don't think that gleam in his eye is for an old man . . . '

Ash turned her toward a mirror and draped the pendant over her head by the chain. She reached back and touched his hand as the pearl-crusted, double-headed eagle settled between her breasts.

'From an old friend, to me, to you.'

'It's beautiful. My God, I could open a dancing school with this.'

'Maybe you won't have to,' said Ash. 'I got one too.'

He showed her the eight-pointed star on his chest.

'*Kennet.*'

'Haven't you ever seen a nobleman?'

'Good lord, Kennet. The Order of St Andrew is the highest honour in Russia.'

'Was . . . but I have a feeling it could still come in handy.' He glanced around the still-crowded reception. 'I love you, I have always loved you and you know it. I also think you are the most beautiful woman in the world. Hell, I know it. Tell me, if you won't marry a lowly American sailor, how about a Russian noble?'

Tamara, forever the performer even in love, raised an eyebrow, touched the star of St Andrew, and raised her dark eyes to Ash. 'But of course, Your Excellency.'